EMMA BLAIR OMNIBUS

The Blackbird's Tale

Flower of Scotland

Also by Emma Blair

WHERE NO MAN CRIES
NELLIE WILDCHILD
HESTER DARK
THIS SIDE OF HEAVEN
JESSIE GRAY
THE PRINCESS OF POOR STREET
STREET SONG
WHEN DREAMS COME TRUE
A MOST DETERMINED WOMAN
MAGGIE JORDAN
SCARLET RIBBONS
THE WATER MEADOWS
THE SWEETEST THING
THE DAFFODIL SEA
PASSIONATE TIMES
HALF HIDDEN
AN APPLE FROM EDEN
GOODNIGHT, SWEET PRINCE
WILD STRAWBERRIES
FORGET-ME-NOT
MOONLIT EYES
FINDING HAPPINESS
TWILIGHT TIME
LITTLE WHITE LIES

EMMA BLAIR OMNIBUS

The Blackbird's Tale
Flower of Scotland

EMMA BLAIR

timewarner
paperbacks

A *Time Warner* Paperback

This omnibus edition first published in Great Britain by
Time Warner Paperbacks in December 2005
Emma Blair Omnibus Copyright © Emma Blair 2005

Previously published separately:
The Blackbird's Tale first published in Great Britain by
Michael Joseph Ltd 1989
Published by Sphere Books Ltd in 1990
Reprinted 1990 (twice), 1991, 1992
Reprinted by Warner Books 1992
Reprinted 1993 (twice), 1995, 1996 (twice), 1998, 2000, 2001
Copyright © 1989 Emma Blair

The extracts on pages 384 and 385 are from the poem 'Burnt Norton' in
Four Quartets by T.S. Eliot. The extract on page 392 is from the poem
'Vampire' in *The Hawk in the Rain* by Ted Hughes. All three extracts are
reproduced by permission of Faber and Faber Ltd.

Flower of Scotland first published in Great Britain in 1997 by
Little, Brown and Company
Published by Warner Books in 1998
Reprinted 1998 (twice), 1999, 2001
Reprinted by Time Warner Paperbacks in 2002
Copyright © 1997 Emma Blair

The moral right of the author has been asserted.

A CIP catalogue record for this book is available from the British Library.

ISBN 0 7515 3778 0

Printed and bound in Great Britain by Clays Ltd, St Ives plc

Time Warner Paperbacks
An imprint of
Time Warner Book Group UK
Brettenham House
Lancaster Place
London WC2E 7EN

www.twbg.co.uk

The Blackbird's Tale

PART 1

The Day Before Yesterday

Chapter 1

'Will you marry me?'

The suddenness of the question, coming as it did right out of the blue, brought a lump to Cathy's throat, and made her heart swell within her.

Bobby glanced away, his face now filled with the flush of embarrassment. 'I do love you you know,' he added in a low, husky voice.

It was the first time he'd told her that, though she'd known it for some while. But then Glasgow men rarely confessed to strong emotions, believing any such utterances to be signs of weakness, to be avoided at all costs.

Cathy sucked in a deep breath. How she loved and adored Bobby McCracken, so much so it almost hurt. She would have walked over broken glass for the bugger.

'I was beginning to think you'd never ask,' she replied.

'You knew I would then?' he queried gruffly.

How silly men could be, she thought. 'Of course I did. What I didn't know was when. And now you have, you've succeeded in catching me completely off-guard. Since picking me up at home you haven't given the slightest indication that today was the day you were going to pop the question.'

His face brightened to hear that and, unconsciously, he puffed out his chest. 'Aye well, there you are then.'

She didn't quite know what he meant by that, but he was clearly chuffed he had caught her by surprise.

She looked up at the sky, bright beyond the grey pall of chimney smoke that hung lowering over the city, and made a mental note of the date, Sunday the 6th of July, 1913, the day Bobby McCracken had finally proposed to her. Her heart swelled again while her stomach seemed to dissolve into a mass of gooey, squidgy jelly.

While Cathy was looking at the sky Bobby was looking at her,

3

drinking her in. He remembered the night they'd met and how he'd been bowled over by her. She was a bit thin with hardly a brilliant figure it was true, but there was something about her, her personality if you like, that was just right for him, that clicked. Her best feature was her eyes, a hazelnut colour that he found totally beguiling. If she would have let him he would have sat for hours gazing into them, quite content to do that and that alone.

'Well?' he prompted. 'What's your answer?'

'Yes, of course. What else did you imagine it would be?'

His expression became sheepish. 'I didn't know. I mean, I wasn't sure.'

'You're a daftie!' she chided gently, and reaching out took his hand in hers: a hand that was hard and calloused from his work as a coalman delivering bags of coal round the streets of Partick where they both lived. He worked from the same horse and cart as his father, who was also a coalman.

Cathy's eyes flicked to the left, then the right. Turning her head she glanced behind her. 'Why don't you kiss me?' she said to Bobby.

The sheepish expression changed to one of alarm. 'What! Where folk can see?'

'We're all alone. Look for yourself.'

He did, and she was right. There were bound to be other people in Thornwood Park but wherever they were, there weren't any at that moment round about them.

She pulled him to her till his face was only inches away. 'It's not every day a lassie gets engaged,' she smiled.

The scent of her was strong in his nostrils now, and had the same effect on him as it always had. It was as if his strength drained right out of him.

'Oh, Cathy!' he croaked.

She waited with eyes closed, refusing to kiss him, insisting he kiss her. His lips pressed against hers, hesitantly to begin with, then with force and passion. His tongue crept into her mouth to twine round hers. With a grunt at the back of his throat he pulled her tightly to him.

They continued kissing, the seconds turning into a minute, the minute into two. Finally she pushed him from her.

'I'll say this for you Bobby McCracken, you're a smashing kisser. I have no complaints in that department.'

4

'Oh! Is there a department you do have complaints in?'

Using the tip of her finger she traced an imaginary line down his cheek. 'Not one.'

'That's good then.'

'Nor do I imagine I ever will have a complaint. If you take my meaning.' She was referring to the fact they'd never been to bed together. It would never have entered her mind to get married other than what she was, a virgin. As indeed was Bobby. Kissing was as far as she'd allowed him to go. He'd attempted to touch her once, and got his face slapped as a result. She wasn't 'that sort of lassie' she'd rebuked him, and if it was 'that sort of lassie' he was looking for then he'd better look elsewhere. He'd apologised, secretly pleased that she'd rebuffed his advance as she had, for she would have gone down in his estimation if she hadn't – at the same time thinking a chap had to have a go, it was only manly after all! – and that had been that.

Another couple strolled into view, they too dressed in their Sunday best as were Cathy and Bobby, and Cathy, on spying them, immediately pulled herself away from Bobby and straightened her hat which had become slightly skew-whiff. While she was doing this, Bobby, without realising he was doing so, straightened his red tie which didn't need straightening.

Engaged, Cathy thought, and went prickly all over. She couldn't wait to tell . . . 'What about the engagement ring?' she queried.

'I thought we might go into Sauchiehall Street next Saturday and buy it then,' he replied.

She nodded her approval. The best jewellers' shops were in the town, and there were four in Sauchiehall Street, Glasgow's best known and arguably most popular street. 'Right, that's what we'll do. But listen Bobby, I want us to keep our engagement secret for the now, until we get that ring, that is. We'll only let on to our immediate families.'

'Aye, sure. If that's what you want, Cathy.'

She could see he was puzzled. 'Och, I don't want to be saying I'm engaged with no ring to swank as proof. When I tell the girls at work and others, I want to show them the ring as evidence.' She laughed. 'That might not make sense to you but it does to me.'

It did make sense to him, now that she'd explained. Wee matters like that were important to women.

5

She grasped his hand again. 'I'm so happy I could burst, Bobby.'

'So am I.'

Realising she hadn't repeated to him what he'd said to her, she whispered, 'And I love you. I think I've loved you right from the very beginning.'

He swallowed hard, his Adam's apple slowly going up and down.

'You know something,' she went on, this time in her normal voice, 'I'm so excited I can hardly think. Whose parents shall we tell first, yours or mine?'

'Yours, they live closest.'

'Then mine it is.' Letting go of his hand she jumped to her feet and quickly smoothed down the front of her dress. When he stood up she linked an arm through his, as he crooked his arm to accommodate hers.

Mrs McCracken, she thought as they made for the park gates, *Mrs* Bobby McCracken. What a lovely sound that had to it. A lovely sound indeed!

Tears burst from Winnie Ford's eyes as she took in the news that Cathy had just announced. Her elder daughter could do a lot worse than Bobby McCracken, an awful lot worse. He was a good man, and a kind one. He'd make a grand husband and father.

John Ford swept Cathy into his arms and squeezed her close. Just for the moment, he couldn't trust himself to speak.

Lily, Cathy's young sister, stood a little apart beaming broadly. This had certainly livened up a dreary Sunday afternoon and no mistake.

Letting Cathy go John turned to an embarrassed Bobby and stuck out his hand. 'Congratulations son,' he said in a tight voice as the two men shook.

Cathy quickly explained about them wanting to keep their engagement secret, except from their immediate families, until they'd bought the ring. 'So you just mind and keep your mouth shut!' she warned Lily.

'No need to worry, sis. If your secret does get out during the coming week it won't be from me. I promise.'

'I wish we had some bevy in the house to celebrate with, but there's not a drop I'm afraid,' John apologised to Bobby and Cathy. There had been nearly a full half-bottle in the press but he'd drunk that the night before as his Saturday night tipple.

'That's all right, Mr Ford,' Bobby replied.

'I think it had better be John from here on in, don't you?'

Bobby gave a swift sideways glance at a smiling Cathy, then brought his attention back to her father. 'Right you are then . . . John.'

'That's the ticket.'

'And you had better call me Winnie,' Winnie said.

'Fine then . . . Winnie.'

'Engaged to get married, eh!' John muttered, shaking his head. And thinking, not before time. Cathy was twenty-two after all: most lassies her age had been wed a year or two by then. He'd been beginning to get worried she was destined to be left on the shelf. Not that she'd lacked for boyfriends, she'd never that. It had been her keeping them that had been the problem. She was such a strong willed lassie which, combined with a terrible stubborn streak, had contrived to put the lads off. Except for Bobby McCracken, that was, it didn't seem to bother him. But then Bobby was deceptive. On the surface he appeared quiet and shy, and so he was, but underneath there was an enormous amount of mental strength and self-confidence. Bobby was able to handle Cathy all right, which was just what she needed.

Winnie stopped dabbing her face with the end of her pinny and, with a sniff, rose from the old settee where she'd been sitting. Going to Cathy, it was now her turn to take Cathy into her arms. In her mind she was seeing Cathy as a baby, changing the wean's nappies. That and a thousand other memories that made her choke inside.

'You'll be happy the pair of you, I know you will,' Winnie said.

'We're that already, Ma.'

Winnie kissed Cathy on the forehead. 'I'll tell you what, how about I put the kettle on and we celebrate with a nice cup of tea?'

'That would be the very dab, Ma.'

Releasing Cathy, Winnie grasped hold of Bobby and pecked his cheek which caused his face to flame.

'Here, what about me! Don't I get to kiss my brother-in-law to be?' Lily declared loudly, coming over to stand beside Winnie.

7

'Watch it, you!' Cathy said, wagging a finger at Lily. But it was good natured fun between them; they were the best of pals.

'Scared of the competition, eh?' Lily retorted with a salacious wink.

'That'll be the day!'

Lily stared Bobby up and down. 'He is very . . . Hmmh!' And with that she sort of waggled her hips. If Bobby's face had been red before it was positively scarlet now.

'Don't worry, I won't eat you.' Lily teased him, and with that grabbed his head and planted a big smacker full on his lips.

'Cheeky monkey!' John exclaimed, laughing, he too aware that this was only a bit of fun on Lily's part. His younger daughter – there were six years between her and Cathy – could be a right case when she took the notion.

'That's enough now!' Cathy said, tapping Lily on the shoulder.

Bobby looked at Cathy and made funny poached egg eyes which made Cathy laugh. Then, with a stiffened finger, he jabbed Lily in the ribs which caused her to break off the kiss with a yelp.

'Much more of that and I'd have died of suffocation,' he joked.

'I'll bet you don't say that to Cathy.'

'He'd better not let on what he does say to me, That's strictly private,' Cathy said. This time they all laughed together.

'All the best, sis. You know I mean that,' Lily said quietly to Cathy when the laughter had died away.

'I know,' Cathy acknowledged. The sisters embraced, a sheen creeping over Lily's eyes as they did.

Winnie filled the kettle and placed it on the black-leaded range. Luckily she'd made some griddle scones earlier which she'd serve with a pot of last year's Victoria plum jam. They would go down a treat with the tea.

'So when is the wedding going to be?' John queried.

'And I hope I'm going to be a bridesmaid?' Lily added.

'*Chief* bridesmaid. I'll be relying on you,' Cathy answered her sister with a smile. Then to John she replied, 'We haven't discussed a date yet.'

'No, I'm afraid we haven't,' Bobby confirmed.

John was thinking how much the wedding was going to cost him – a fair old packet if it was going to be done properly. And

8

done properly it would be, from hired cars to champagne at the reception. There would be no stinting on his Cathy's big day. Fortunately he had a good whack put by in the bank which should cover most, if not all, of the expense. And just to be on the safe side he'd start putting in some overtime, of which there was a lot going begging at Thompson's Yard (Tommy's the men called it) where he was employed as a patternmaker.

John glanced over at Lily. Once Cathy's wedding was out of the way he'd have to begin putting away for her. A couple of years yet before that though, he reassured himself.

'So many things to think of from here on in,' Winnie said from where she was laying out scones on a plate. 'So many things.'

'When we've had our tea we must away over and tell Mr and Mrs McCracken,' Cathy said.

'Aye, you must,' John agreed.

'Well I hope you get married as soon as possible,' Lily declared with a twinkle in her eye.

'Why's that?' Cathy inquired, falling right into the trap that Lily had set for her.

'Because the sooner you do the sooner I can have our bed to myself,' Lily retorted quickly. She and Cathy shared a double bed, which they'd done since Lily had grown too big for a cot.

Cathy laughed. 'Oh, see you!' she said.

'And see you too!'

It was a Glasgow expression, indefinable to anyone not of the city.

For the second time they all laughed together.

Cathy and Bobby came to a stop outside her front door, he having escorted her home from his house where they'd broken the news to a delighted Rob and Ina McCracken.

Darkness had fallen about an hour previously which meant that the close gas mantles were lit, the flickering yellow flame from the one situated at the centre of the landing where they were standing casting weird and wonderful shapes on the walls around them. The gas jet itself hissed and occasionally sputtered; a comforting sound Cathy had always thought.

'I still feel as if I'm walking on a cloud,' Cathy said in a low voice.

'I know what you mean.'

She laid her head on his shoulder, and put her arms round him. Her Bobby, she thought. Her Bobby for ever from here on in. Closing her eyes, she sighed.

He stroked the top of her arm, grimacing slightly when his hard calloused hand snagged the material of her dress. He stopped stroking to just hold her arm.

'Bobby?'

'Hmm?'

'Don't you think we should set a date now? I mean, is there any reason we shouldn't?' Having said that she lifted her head to stare into his eyes.

'None at all. When do you fancy?'

'I don't want one of those long engagements. I just don't see the point in being engaged for years and years, do you?'

'No,' he whispered.

That was what she'd been hoping he'd say. 'So when?'

'Let me see.' His brow furrowed in thought. 'It's July now. How about towards the end of the year? Or at the latest the beginning of next?'

'Oh aye, that would be just fine.'

'That would give everyone a decent chance to get organised. For don't forget we've a house to get and furniture to buy.'

'Are you . . . are you all right for money? I mean, have you enough saved for furniture and that sort of thing?'

He grinned at her, suddenly feeling playful. 'You being a working lassie I thought you'd buy the furniture, and maybe pay the rent as well when we get the house.'

Realising she was being teased she pretended outrage. 'Are you serious Robert McCracken?'

'Oh, dead serious,' he replied, his lips twitching with suppressed laughter. He went on. 'And what about you? Do you have anything saved?'

'A few quid.'

'How few?'

'That's my business.'

'If I'm to be your husband there will be no secrets from me. I'll have to know everything.'

'Oh aye, and who made that rule?'

He screwed his face up into a mock glower. 'Are you saying you'd defy me, woman!'

'I am.'

'Then . . . ' he paused dramatically, 'there would be nothing else for it but . . . ' again he paused, 'the strap.'

'The strap!'

'Like we used to have at school. Though this time it wouldn't be across the palms but across the bare . . .'

'Bobby!'

She was genuinely shocked, which amused him. 'Yes?'

'You'd never do that, would you?' For the space of a few seconds his acting had been so good it had taken her in.

He didn't reply.

'Of course you wouldn't?'

He couldn't sustain it, the twitch came back to his lips. 'I might.'

'Och, away with you. You're pulling my leg.'

'It's a lovely leg. I wouldn't mind pulling it in the least.'

She hit his gently with her fist. 'Now don't talk dirty.'

'It's hardly that.'

'Yes it is.' She paused, her mind going back on their conversation before he'd started on about straps and bare . . . 'I've got a good bottom drawer. I've been buying bits and pieces for years now. Sheets, pillowcases, towels and the like. Enough to get us started.'

'And I've got thirty-four pounds, fifteen shillings saved.'

She gasped. 'As much as that!'

'I've never been one to waste money. I'm not mean, you understand; it's just that I can't bide waste.'

He was certainly not mean, quite the contrary. She'd found him to be most generous. Then again, maybe that was just because it was her; a thought she found very flattering indeed. 'I've only got £7 in the savings bank, but then I only earn a lassie's wage.'

He took the hand from her arm and put it round her neck. 'Once we're married you can stop work if you want to.' Some women did, others carried on till a family was on the way.

'Let's wait until I'm . . . ' She blushed, a rare occurrence with her though a common one with Bobby.

'In the pudding club?'

'Bobby!' she scolded. 'That's a horrible expression.'

'All right then. How about till you've got a bun in the oven?'

11

She punched him again, this time harder. 'Idiot!'

He started to laugh, but the laugh died in his throat as he stared at this woman he loved so much. Something twisted inside him as he bent and placed his lips on hers. Their mouths seemed to be filled with exploding fire as they kissed, a kiss that was long and deep and left them both with heaving chests.

'I'd better away in,' she whispered.

'Cathy?'

She looked into his face.

'Let's say the first Saturday in October. That all right with you?'

She nodded.

'Then that's the date.'

'Right,' she agreed. 'That's the date.'

'Will I see you Tuesday night as usual? We could go for a walk or to the café and make plans.'

'Tuesday night as usual,' she confirmed.

'And Cathy?'

'Yes?'

'I do love you.'

Twice in one day, she thought. Wonders would never cease. 'And I love you.'

Her hand was shaking as she put her key in the lock.

On Saturday morning Bobby collected Cathy and they took a tramcar into Sauchiehall Street, alighting at Charing Cross. It was raining, but that didn't bother Cathy. She wasn't going to let a wee bit of rain spoil what lay ahead of her.

When they reached the first jeweller's shop they stood and stared at the display in the front window. Then they moved round to the side window and had a look in that.

'What do you think?' Bobby asked eventually. 'Shall we go in here?'

'Let's see what the others have to offer first, eh?'

It was going to be a long morning, Bobby decided. And he was right. They looked at all four jeweller's shops in Sauchiehall Street *twice* before Cathy chose the one she'd go into, which transpired to be the jewellers' shop they'd looked at to begin with at the Charing Cross end of the street.

The assistant was a middle-aged man with a pseudo Kelvinside plum in his mouth, who couldn't have been more helpful despite his pompous phoney accent.

Tray after tray of rings were laid before Cathy and Bobby for them to peruse, all below the top figure Bobby had stated when the assistant had inquired, 'What price range did sir have in mind?'

The minutes ticked by but Cathy wasn't going to be hurried and, to give the assistant his due, nor did he try to hurry her.

'Take your time,' the assistant purred. 'Madam must find the ring that is just right for her.'

Smooth as syrup, Cathy thought. But nonetheless, genuine with it.

Bobby was amazed at the assistant's tightly crimped hair. He'd never seen hair like that on a man before. It fascinated him. (Done with curling tongs like the lassies used, he wondered?)

Another customer came into the shop. 'Excuse me,' the assistant murmured, and moved off.

'How about this one?' Cathy asked. The central diamond was surrounded by a cluster of chips.

'Lovely,' Bobby replied.

'Or this one?' she demanded, replacing the diamond and cluster with another, this also a diamond and cluster but in a rectangular arrangement as opposed to a circular.

'Lovely,' Bobby nodded.

That ring was replaced in its velvet slit after which she selected a ring that was a diamond flanked by two tiny sapphires.

'This is a bit different, don't you think?'

'Lovely,' Bobby answered.

'Or this green one?' The ring she pointed to was a small emerald encircled by diamond chips.

'Lovely.'

She glared at him. 'Is that all you can say?'

'What do you mean?'

'*Lovely*. You keep repeating yourself like some bloody parrot.

He grinned. 'Does it matter what I say?'

'Of course it does!'

'But I think they're all lovely. You haven't put on one yet that doesn't suit.'

'That's not the point!' she exclaimed softly, vexed.

A clock chimed, followed by others, all chiming the hour.

13

Bobby glanced over at the other customer, a posh-looking woman whom the assistant was showing a silver cigarette case.

'What about this one?' Cathy queried.

'Smashing.'

And a few seconds later. 'This one?'

'Smashing.'

She glared at him again. 'I hope you're not going to be like this when we choose the flowers.'

'What flowers?'

'For the wedding.'

'I'm not choosing any flowers! I don't know one flower from another. A rose from an aspidistra.'

'And what if I insist you participate?'

'Oh *participate*, is it!' he jibed mockingly. 'My, that's an awful long word that. Did you read it in a book or something?' He knew Cathy loved books and forever had her nose in one.

'I'm only surprised you know what the word means,' she jibed back.

'I may be working class, a Glasgow keelie, but I'm no' higgerent,' he retorted quickly, which made her laugh.

'Are you not?'

'No, I'm not.'

'You should know about flowers then?'

He thought about that for a brief second, then replied. 'Well we all have gaps in our education, and flowers is a gap in mine.'

She regarded him steadily. 'What if I ask you to come along to the florist's as a support?'

He regarded her steadily back. 'We could do without flowers at the wedding, you know.'

Her eyebrows flew up in surprise. 'Do without flowers! We'll do no such thing! A wedding without flowers would be like . . .' She thought furiously.

'Chips without vinegar?' he offered.

She laughed again. 'Aye, you could put it that way.'

'Well if you want the flowers you'll have to arrange them yourself. Without my help.'

He was quite determined about this, she could see that. She might be stubborn herself, but Bobby could be just as stubborn. More so even.

'Tell you what,' she said.

14

'What?'

'When we leave here you can buy me a drink and we'll talk about this further.'

'I'll certainly buy you a drink. I rather fancy a pint myself. And you can talk all you want, till the cows come home, but it won't do you any good. Not the slightest.'

She smiled at him. 'I'll twist you round my little finger using my female wiles.'

He returned her smile. 'No you won't.'

He was gorgeous, she thought. Absolutely splendiforously gorgeous.

The ring they finally settled on was a diamond set in a bed of tiny garnets. It was one of three Cathy had swithered over, the deciding factor being this particular ring fitted perfectly which meant she could wear it straight away.

'If I may say so, madam has made an excellent and tasteful choice,' the assistant enthused, ladling on the syrup. 'And now sir . . .'

Bobby reached for his wallet, having been to the bank in Partick before they'd got on the tram.

When they emerged from the shop they were pleased to discover it had stopped raining. 'Look!' Cathy cried excitedly, pointing skyward, 'A good omen.'

Bobby followed the direction of her indicating finger to see a shining rainbow. A good omen indeed, if you believed in that sort of thing. He wasn't sure whether he did nor not.

Cathy turned round at the sound of quarrelsome voices. There were two young men coming towards her and Bobby, the pair of them arguing the toss. The taller poked the shorter in the chest, and the shorter immediately, somewhat viciously, poked back.

The young man who'd first poked swung angrily away from the other, clearly intending to cross the road and leave the shorter chap behind. The second young man promptly did an about-wheel and started off back the way they'd come.

'Are neither of you going to say hello then?' Cathy called out.

'Who are they?' Bobby queried quietly.

'My cousins. I'll introduce you.'

The taller of the young men who was just about to step off

the pavement halted at the sound of her words and glanced towards her, as did the other young man.

'Hello Cathy!' they both responded in unison.

When they'd joined her and Bobby, Cathy said, 'Bobby these are my cousins Craig and Ronnie McIntosh. But they just get Big Toss and Wee Tosh.'

'I'm Big Tosh,' said Craig, sticking out his hand, which Bobby shook.

'And I'm Wee Tosh.' Bobby then shook hands with Ronnie.

'I'm Bobby McCracken.'

'My *fiancé*,' Cathy stated with heavy emphasis, and waggled her engagement ring under Big Tosh and Wee Tosh's noses. 'What do you think of that then? We've just bought it, right this very minute.'

'Congratulations!' declared Big Tosh, and bent over to peer at the ring.

'Aye, congratulations,' echoed Wee Tosh, and also had a closer gander at the ring.

'You're the first to know outside the immediate family,' Cathy went on.

'But we *are* immediate family,' Wee Tosh said.

Cathy pulled a face. 'You know what I mean!'

Wee Tosh shook his head. 'No, I don't. We're full cousins. Your mother is my mother's sister, therefore immediate family.'

Cathy sighed. 'Either of these two would start an argument amongst a choir of angels,' she said to Bobby.

'He might, but I wouldn't,' Big Tosh sniffed.

'Yes you would!' Wee Tosh challenged.

'Och away and raffle that turnip you call your heid!'

'You away and raffle yours!' Wee Tosh retorted fiercely.

'I've just about had enough of you and your lip for one day, so I have,' Big Tosh spat out.

'Is that a fact? Maybe you want to do something about it?'

Although Big Tosh was eighteen months older than his brother and considerably taller, Wee Tosh had the advantage in weight and build.

'Will you two stop it at once!' Cathy exclaimed crossly.

'Blame him, not me,' Wee Tosh muttered.

'Blame you, you mean!' Big Tosh accused.

'Shut up!' Cathy exploded in what was almost a shout.

16

What a pair, Bobby thought.

There was a few seconds' hiatus, then Big Tosh said apologetically, 'It's a very nice ring, Cathy. I wish you and Bobby here all the best.'

'Me too,' Wee Tosh added.

'Thank you, lads,' Cathy smiled.

'Do we get an invite to the wedding?' Big Tosh asked.

'Of course you do,' Cathy replied.

'Then we'll look forward to it. Won't we Ronnie?'

'We will that.'

'Make sure you invite lots of unattached lassies, now,' Big Tosh said, giving Bobby a wink.

'They'll have to be blind ones if you're to get off with them,' Wee Tosh quipped.

'Now look, I told you . . . .!'

'Only a joke! Only a joke!' Wee Tosh said quickly, holding his hands fearfully in front of him as though he was afraid of his older brother, which was the last thing he was.

'You've got a mouth large enough to drive a tram into,' Big Tosh said.

'Well at least that's something we've got in common,' Wee Tosh riposted, quick as a flash.

Bobby laughed.

The foursome chatted for a while longer, then Cathy and Bobby made their excuses and left her cousins, who continued along Sauchiehall Street together.

'Are they always like that?' Bobby inquired when the brothers were out of earshot.

'Always. Since they were bairns. They're the original cat and dog. Did you notice Big Tosh's left pinky?'

Bobby shook his head. 'No, I didn't.'

'That's because he hasn't got one. Or only the stubb of one. Wee Tosh bit it off during a fist fight when they were young.'

'Good God!' said Bobby. 'Bit it completely off? Right through the bone and everything?'

'Right through the bone and everything,' she confirmed.

'How horrible.'

Bobby then got Cathy to talk at length about her cousins and the rest of her family, which she did throughout their visit to the pub and the tram ride home.

17

The subject of flowers was totally forgotten, as Bobby intended it to be.

Cathy was taking her coat off when there was a sudden shriek from Kate Binnie, one of the girls she worked alongside at Mavor & Coulson's, an engineering firm.

'She's got an engagement ring on!' Kate squealed, stabbing a finger at Cathy.

'Who has?' Lorna McQueen demanded.

'She has. Cathy.'

Instantly Cathy was surrounded by girls, all pushing and shoving in their eagerness to see.

'Come on, let's have a dekko!' Christine Drysdale demanded.

'Wait a minute! Just hang on, will you lot!' Cathy pleaded, thoroughly enjoying this. She hung up her coat before holding out her left hand for the ring to be admired.

'Oh, it's rare! A real brammer!' Pat Smith cooed.

'When did it happen? When, eh?' Kate asked eagerly.

'I take it it is to Bobby McCracken?' Christine queried.

'Well he's who I've been going out with these past six months,' Cathy replied.

'Just making sure, getting the facts straight. Are those garnets?'

'They are,' Cathy confirmed. 'Bobby said they complemented my eyes.' Bobby had said no such thing. It was something she'd thought herself.

'How romantic!' Eileen Niven burbled, thinking her Sammy never said anything nice like that to her. If he ever did she'd probably die of shock.

Cathy related how she and Bobby had become engaged the Sunday before yesterday – it now being Monday morning – and how they'd decided to keep it a secret until they bought the ring, which they had in Sauchiehall Street that Saturday morning.

'How much was it?' Peggy Malone asked.

'Mind your own business,' Cathy replied frostily.

'Aye, that's not a question to ask,' Christine admonished, though it was a question she'd have loved to know the answer to herself.

'You can see it's an expensive one,' Babs Tait said.

'Oh aye!' 'No doubt about that!' Those and various other affirmations were chorused.

18

Cathy manipulated the ring so that the diamond sent out flashes of light.

'That's beautiful so it is,' murmured cross-eyed Mary Hastie who was so plain she'd never had a boyfriend, even though she was now nearing thirty years old, and had got to the stage where she didn't believe anymore that she ever would.

'Well, you said Bobby McCracken was the one, and you weren't wrong.' Kate smiled at Cathy.

'No, I wasn't,' Cathy agreed.

'That'll be cakes on you at afternoon teatime,' Babs said. It was the custom that whenever one of the girls got engaged she bought cakes all round, the cakes being purchased from a nearby branch of the very popular City Bakeries.

Cathy nodded, having come prepared with enough money to pay for the treat.

'A chocolate éclair for me,' Pat Smith said, her eyes bright in anticipation.

Just then Curley, their foreman, appeared, pocket watch in hand. 'Come along, ladies. You're being paid to work, not stand here gassing!' They all liked Curley, looking on him as a father figure.

'Cathy Ford has got engaged!' Mary Hastie blurted out.

'Oh, has she indeed!'

'Show him the ring Cathy,' Christine prompted.

'My, my!' murmured Curley, studying the ring and nodding his approval. 'So it's cakes this afternoon is it?' He was always bought a cake too.

'Yes, Mr Curley,' Cathy said.

'Then mark me down for a slice of fruitcake. Now come along yous yins, if you're not at your tables within thirty seconds I'll be in line for getting my jotters.'

The girls scampered away, hurrying to their tables where they sat during their work-day, binding conductors with tape. The last thing they wanted was Curley to get the sack which he could easily have done if they were late starting, his superior Mr Lind being a holy terror who would just as soon fire you as look at you.

All through that day Cathy kept glancing at the ring winking and sparkling on her left hand, and every time she did a smile lit up her face.

★

That Friday night Cathy was putting on her make-up prior to going out with Bobby when there was a rap on the outside door.

'I'll get it,' said John, glancing at the clock on the mantelpiece above the range. That would be the factor who called every Friday night for the rent. The factor was the owner's agent, in this case a Mr Tressell. The owner was called Nicholson and he owned twenty-five closes in the street. As there were three houses, or apartments on each stairway, and each close consisted of five flights, that meant Nicholson owned a grand total of three-hundred-and-seventy-five apartments, ranging from single ends (one-room apartments) to three room and kitchens (four-room apartments). Nicholson was considered to be a small owner amongst the Glasgow landlords, who were a powerful and organised cartel. There were many far bigger.

Cathy powdered her face from a brass compact that had been a birthday present from her parents several years previously. She only wore make-up when going out in the evening and never during the day as some of the girls did. She thought that wearing it during the day ruined the complexion, of which she had a particularly good one.

She and Bobby were going to the pictures that night, though they hadn't yet decided what they would see. They might go locally, or then again they might go into the town.

Cathy paused in what she was doing when she heard her father's voice raised in anger. Looking over at Winnie sitting darning by the side of the range she saw that Winnie had paused also.

'It's the week for the gas rates,' Winnie said softly.

Cathy nodded; that explained it. There was always a slanging match between John and the factor when the gas rates were collected.

The general rates John had to pay for their house consisted of the water and police rates, the poor rate – collected once a year – and the big bogey, the gas rates for stairhead lighting. The latter was a bone of contention because the factor collected it along with the rent, the two combined for the week of collection. The gas rates were paid four times a year – with the gas rates variable; the person paying the rent and rates having to take the rate factor's word for it that that was what was owed.

Everyone knew the factors were on the fiddle, not only from

the house renters but also at the other end with the municipality who were charged twenty per cent for the alleged difficulties of collection.

Many complaints had been made to the owners in the past but as nothing had ever been done about the complaints it could only be assumed that the owners were in on the fiddle, receiving a portion of whatever their factor, or factors, 'creamed off'.

The outside door slammed with a 'bang!' and a fuming John came back in and threw himself into his chair.

'It's a liberty! A diabolical liberty!' he said through gritted teeth.

'How much this time?' Winnie queried.

'I'm only guessing mind – I can't really say – but I think the bugger's done us for about a bob. Maybe even a couple of coppers more.'

Winnie's lips thinned in anger. You could buy a lot for a shilling. More for one and two.

'Fair makes my blood boil,' John muttered.

'And there's nothing we can do about it,' Winnie stated.

John shook his head. 'Not a damned thing.'

'The whole system is corrupt, rotten through and through,' Cathy said.

John glanced at his elder daughter. He couldn't have agreed more.

'What's all this commotion about?' Lily demanded, coming through from the other room where she'd been busy sorting out her tallboy.

'It's gas rates night,' Winnie replied.

'Oh!' No more needed to be said.

With a final flourish Cathy finished her make-up. 'Is it the dancing later?' she asked Lily.

'No, I'm going to stay in.'

That surprised Cathy. 'What's the matter, are you ill or something?'

'No, I just prefer to stay in.'

'Her pal's winching, so she's got no one to go out with,' Winnie explained. Winching meant courting.

Cathy thought for a few seconds, then said. 'You can come with Bobby and me if you like. It's only the pictures you understand, but you're welcome to come along.'

21

'Not on your Nellie Duff, thank you very much!' Lily retorted. 'How do you think I'd feel with you two sitting there kissing and cuddling?'

'Well, we wouldn't if you were with us.'

'I couldn't bear to deprive you. But thanks for the offer anyway.' She was touched by what Cathy had done.

A quarter of an hour later Bobby arrived and away he and Cathy went. After discussing it they decided to go local, the main feature at the cinema they chose being *The Goddess of Sagebrush Gulch*, a Biograph production starring Dorothy Bernard and Charles West.

Minutes after the big picture had started Bobby put his arm round her shoulders, and she laid her head sideways into the crook of his neck. Closing her eyes she thought how ecstatically happy she was: she couldn't have been happier.

Wasn't life grand? Wasn't it just!

Once a month the girls in Cathy's clique at Mavor & Coulson had a night out together. Usually this merely consisted of having a drink and a good old gossip, but that month Christine Drysdale had said she was going to arrange something different, and subsequently instructed the clique to come to her house where the 'something different' would take place.

Mary Hastie was the last to arrive at Christine's. Two members of the clique hadn't been able to make it: Sonja Moscrop because she was at home in bed with a bad dose of flu, and Effie Robertson (known as the quiet one) because her boyfriend had arrived in from a long voyage that afternoon.

A bottle of whisky, lemonade and some sherry had been purchased, the girls having chipped in the day before, and now they all sat sipping their various drinks, waiting expectantly to see what Christine was about to spring on them.

'Come on Christine!' Lorna McQueen urged. 'We're all agog.'

'Aye, what is it? What have you lined up?' Peggy Malone quizzed.

'She's not here yet, you'll just have to wait,' Christine replied mysteriously.

'Who?' Cathy probed, thinking this was exciting.

'Just wait and see.'

22

The girls looked at one another, while Mrs Drysdale, Christine's mother who was in on the secret, grinned at them. Mr Drysdale had been told to go out for the night and so had taken himself along to the Labour Club.

Clang!

'That'll be her now,' said Christine, jumping to her feet, for the clang had been the door bell.

'I wonder who it is?' Kate Binnie whispered to Cathy.

'Search me. Your guess is as good as mine.' She was as intrigued, as clearly was everyone else.

'At least it's a bit different from the dreary old Clansmens' Arms,' Eileen Niven said to the pair of them – the Clansmens' Arms being the pub they usually went to on their nights out.

Cathy and Kate both nodded, neither of them would have disagreed with that.

The elderly woman Christine ushered into the kitchen had a weatherbeaten face with a mouth that had shrunk in on itself through a combination of age and missing teeth. Her white hair was lank and greasy, pulled back and tied at the nape of her neck. Her clothes were extremely old and, like the woman herself, could have done with a right good wash. She was carrying a much battered and scarred Gladstone bag.

'This is Mrs Gan,' Christine announced. 'A spaewife.'

Immediately a buzz went round the kitchen, a spaewife being a fortune teller who, often as not, was also a witch.

Mrs Gan had the look of Ireland about her, Cathy thought. And from her dress and the general demeanour was probably a travelling tinker of whom there were quite a number in Scotland.

'Good evening,' Mrs Gan said in a voice that was heavily accented, though the accent not particularly Irish or Scots, and made a mystical sign with her right hand.

'Nobody is forced to go in and see Mrs Gan, only those who wish to,' Christine said, doubting if there was anyone present who wouldn't want her fortune told, which transpired to be right.

Christine then took Mrs Gan out of the kitchen and into the bedroom where a small table and two chairs had been set up for the spaewife and her clients.

'I'll explain to them what the arrangements are then send them through to you one after the other when you're ready.'

23

'Thank you, dear.'

'Could you take a dram before you begin?'

'That would be very nice, and most hospitable of you. Neat if you don't mind.'

Christine went off to get the dram, and when she returned she found Mrs Gan sitting at the table with a crystal ball on a black plinth set before her. These had come from the Gladstone bag, as had the garish cloth covered in suns, moons, planets and various signs, and which had been placed over the table.

Christine laid the hefty dram to the side of Mrs Gan. 'Just tell me . . .'

'Five minutes,' Mrs Gan interjected. 'Give me five minutes to collect myself and prepare myself mentally, then send the first one through.'

'Right. Fine.'

Mrs Gan made a vaguely dismissive gesture, and Christine left the room. As soon as Christine was gone Mrs Gan had a swallow of the whisky. Good stuff, she thought. A lot better than the poteen she was used to drinking. But then that only cost a fraction of what this did.

In the kitchen it had already been decided that Babs Tait would be first, followed by Pat Smith and Peggy Malone. Lorna McQueen was fighting back a fit of the giggles thinking all this a right hoot!

Christine went round collecting the per capita fee which was a very modest amount. The spaewife would be given the money at the end of the session.

'Another drink?' Kate asked Cathy.

Cathy shook her head. She would in a wee while, but not for now. When it came to drinking she liked to pace herself.

When the five minutes was up Christine took a suddenly nervous Babs through to the bedroom where Mrs Gan, who'd drawn the curtains and lit the two gas mantles in the meantime, was waiting for her. Christine left them, snicking the door closed behind herself.

Several of the girls had consulted spaewives before, stories of which they now related while the others listened avidly. Eileen Niven was telling about one she'd visited in Dunoon when Babs returned.

'How was she?' Christine asked eagerly in a whisper.

'Fabulous.'

'What did she say?' Kate demanded.

'Before we hear I have to send Pat through,' Christine said.

'Here we go then,' said Pat, rising.

'Good luck!' Lorna whispered.

When Pat was gone Babs launched into her story.

It was almost an hour later when Cathy's turn came. 'On you go then,' Christine said, giving her the nod.

Cathy found her palms were sweating while her breathing was shorter and sharper than it had been. Don't be daft! she told herself. The door to the bedroom was closed. Knock or just enter? she wondered. She went in without knocking.

Mrs Gan looked up, and into Cathy's eyes. Her own blue ones were piercing in the extreme, something Cathy hadn't noticed when the spaewife was in the kitchen.

'Sit down,' Mrs Gan instructed.

Cathy sat facing the spaewife across the table, and folded her hands in her lap.

'Your name is?'

'Cathy. Cathy Ford.'

Mrs Gan took a deep breath, and closed her eyes. She made a pass over the top of the crystal ball, then another. She could murder a second dram, she was thinking. She'd have this Cathy Ford relay the message on to the Drysdale lassie that she would appreciate her glass being refilled.

She muttered a gypsy incantation, then repeated it, this time injecting a slight tremor into her voice. The girl was wearing an engagement ring she'd noted, she'd start with that. The rest would be a concoction regarding the subjects all young girls wanted to hear about, with a few warnings here and there to spice up the tale.

'It's a true love match between you and your fiancé,' Mrs Gan said, staring deeply into the crystal ball. 'He worships the ground you walk on . . .'

Cathy also gazed into the crystal ball, and was it her imagination but did there seem to be things moving around inside? Nothing she could actually identify, just shapes swirling this way and that.

Mrs Gan wasn't an out and out charlatan, there were occasions when she actually did have the 'sight'. But those occasions had

25

become fewer and fewer during recent years, and in the mean-time she did have a living to make.

Mrs Gan went cold all over, icy prickles racing up and down her spine. She forgot all about the patter she'd been about to give Cathy, and continued to stare deeply into the crystal where pictures were beginning to form for her.

Her throat constricted at what she saw. What horrors were these? What terrible, terrible horrors?

Fire, fury, bloody slaughter. Death, agony, unbelievable privations. Men, countless men, lines and lines of them all walking, marching, into the very maw of hell itself.

Screams rent the air, and singing. And what sound was that? Tch! Tch! Tch! Tch! Tch! She couldn't place it. There it was again, now dominating all other sounds. Tch! Tch! Tch! Tch! Tch!

Bullets, it dawned on her. That's what those were, machine-gun bullets.

'Ahh!' Mrs Gan said suddenly, sitting right back in her chair. Her face had gone a pasty white, while her eyes were round and popping. What she had overseen had scared her almost witless.

'What was it? What did you see?' Cathy asked anxiously.

Mrs Gan laid a gnarled hand across her forehead and eyes, her heart was going nineteen to the dozen. What *had* she seen? Whatever, she wished she hadn't.

The atmosphere in the room had gone chill, Cathy realised. Chill and clammy. It made her feel quite uneasy.

'What did you see?' she asked the spaewife again.

To tell or not? No, Mrs Gan decided. She'd keep those horrors to herself and spare the girl. But she shuddered to think what lay ahead for Cathy Ford, and not only Cathy, but for multitudinous others.

'Are you all right?' Cathy demanded, for the spaewife looked decidedly unwell.

'Nothing to do with the crystal ball,' Mrs Gan replied, removing her hand from her forehead and eyes, and smiling. 'Just a slight funny turn. I get them from time to time.'

Cathy wasn't at all convinced. 'Are you sure about that?'

'Certainly I'm sure. What I did see was all good. You and your fiancé have a shining future ahead of you. With three children.'

'Three!' Cathy exclaimed, delighted.

'Aye, three. I couldn't exactly make out whether it was two boys and a girl, or the other way round. Let's have another look shall we?'

Mrs Gan had to steel herself to gaze again into the crystal ball, but this time there was nothing there. Only emptiness.

'Two boys and a lassie,' she said firmly after a while. 'Two handsome boys and a bonny lassie.'

She didn't forget to ask Cathy to have a dram sent through to her. If she'd needed one before, she needed one an awful lot more now. She still felt sick with fear at what she'd overseen. She hoped she never saw anything like it ever again.

Purdon Street was off Dumbarton Road, which was the main artery running through Partick, and not all that far from where Cathy now lived with her parents and sister. The empty house she and Bobby were in had a room and kitchen on the third floor.

'All it needs is a bit of distemper,' Bobby said, gazing round.

It wasn't a bad house at all, Cathy thought. The previous owners had looked after it. 'But do we need a room and kitchen? Why not just a single end? There's only the pair of us after all, and a single end would be cheaper.'

'I can well afford a room and kitchen,' he replied, 'so why not have the extra space? And I hope it's not too long before the first of those children the spaewife predicted for us arrives.'

Cathy laughed. Truth was, so did she. 'There's a couple in our street brought up six weans in a single end. Talk about being crowded!'

'I've heard of worse than that,' Bobby said – overcrowding being endemic in the Glasgow tenements.

'It's only a pity this doesn't have an inside cludgie,' Cathy murmured wistfully. She would have given her eye-teeth for that, but there were few tenements in Partick that did boast inside toilets.

'Aye well, you can't have everything. But come here and look at this.' And with that he took her by the hand and drew her to the kitchen window.

'The coalyard I work out of,' he said, pointing to the left.

Cathy immediately recognised the coalyard which she'd only ever seen from ground level before. There were the stables

27

where the horses were kept, and to the rear a great mound of loose coal waiting to be bagged.

He went on. 'Couldn't be more convenient, eh. Downstairs, round the corner and that's me there. And when you are at home with the family you'll be able to wave me away on my cart in the morning. I'll look up every time we go through the gates and give you a wave at the window.'

What a lovely idea, Cathy thought. It would give her great pleasure, and satisfaction, to be able to wave him off in his horse and cart every morning.

'That settles it then,' she declared. 'We'll take the house.'

'I knew you'd like it.'

She gazed down at the yard, picturing him coming out of the gates on his horse and cart and her standing on that very spot waving to him, and him waving back, The image conjured up in her mind brought a warm glow to her insides.

'Let's get back to the factor and tell him we're taking the house,' she said.

'A kiss first,' he smiled, catching her in his arms.

She pretended to try and push him away. 'Och there's no time for that!'

'There had better be always time for a kiss.'

'You'll get tired of the kissing after we've been married a while,' she teased.

He shook his head. 'Never.'

'I'm telling you . . .' Her words were smothered when his lips pressed against hers. Oh, but he was a smashing kisser her Bobby. His kissing made your toes fair curl up. And lots more. Aye, a lot, lot more.

Never. She hoped he was right.

As she hurried along, Cathy was going over in her head the prices the printer had quoted her. The wee firm of Dickson & MacKay had come highly recommended, nor had she been disappointed in the samples shown her, or the prices quoted.

At one point she had been tempted to have her wedding invitations embossed the way posh folk had their invitations done, but in the end had decided against that as a self-indulgent extravagance, and quite unnecessary expense.

Although adjacent to Partick, Hillhead and Kelvingrove

weren't areas she knew very well. A lot of university students lived hereabouts, and middle-class professional people.

She paused for a moment to take her bearings, and that was when she spotted it. A bookshop.

It was like iron to a magnet, she just had to go over and have a look in the bookshop window. She'd adored books since learning to read, and nearly always had one on the go. She'd been on first name terms with the librarians at the local library for years.

She gazed into this Aladdin's cave (which could have done with a bit of dusting she noted) staring at the treasures within.

And then the idea came to her. She'd been searching the shops in Partick and the town trying to find something special to give Bobby on their wedding night, a wedding present from her to him.

So far she hadn't been able to find anything that had struck her as right. She'd considered cufflinks, and a wallet, but neither these or anything else had been 'special' enough. If she could find the right book, one that he would like, that could be the answer.

She would go inside, she decided. Knowing full well she would have gone in anyway without the idea. She wouldn't have been able to stop herself from doing so.

The door tinged as she opened it, and immediately the delightful smell of books, old and new, assailed her nostrils. A smell similar to that at the printer's, yet different somehow.

The man at the desk was sitting hunched over, reading a book open before him. His eyes flicked up to regard her steadily from behind the gold-rimmed glasses he was wearing, then the eyes dropped again to the book.

Somewhere in the shop a clock was ticking, the only sound to be heard. Tick-tock! Tick-tock!

She didn't know why, for they both contained books and had that bookish ambience, but bookshops were better than libraries. Perhaps, and this was a new thought to her, that was because you kept those books you purchased from a bookshop (broadly speaking that is), whereas you had to return those you borrowed from a library. Yes, she thought, that could well be it. Or, to put that another way, bookshops were personal, libraries a mere service.

KIPPS by H.G. Wells. Her hand closed over the red-bound

book, published, she saw glancing at its spine, by Collins, a good Glasgow firm.

BOOK 1, she read, THE MAKING OF KIPPS. CHAPTER 1. THE LITTLE SHOP AT NEW ROMNEY.

She knew the story, having read the book several times in the past. Would Bobby like it though? she wondered. She wasn't at all sure he would.

She read the introduction by Edward Shanks, then looked back to where she'd taken the book from to see if *Love and Mr Lewisham* was also there, which she hadn't read, But it wasn't.

Not *Kipps*, she decided. Not for Bobby. She moved slowly down the bookshelves (all needing a bit of a dusting like the window display), her eyes sliding from title to title, a half-smile having settled on her face.

'Are you looking for anything in particular?' a male voice inquired.

The inquiry startled her, she having been completely lost amongst this world of books; in a dwam, as Glaswegians say.

Not at all the usual kind of female I get in here, David Katzav was thinking to himself. Definitely working class; with those clothes she was wearing she couldn't have been anything else.

Cathy turned round to discover the man who'd addressed her was the same one who'd been at the desk. He was taller standing up than he'd appeared sitting down. He had a kind face, but his eyes behind the gold-rimmed glasses, though keen and intelligent, had a tinge of sadness about them.

'Nothing in particular,' she replied. 'I've been trying to find a special present for my fiancé and thought I might find it here.'

'Ah! Your fiancé likes books, then?'

Her expression became sheepish. 'Not all that much, I have to admit. I'm the one who does that. I think they're magic.'

'Magic,' David Katzav repeated. What a marvellous word to describe books. He couldn't think of a better. Magic, that's precisely what books were. He regarded Cathy with new interest.

'You've read extensively, then?' he probed.

'As much as I've been able to, and as widely as possible.'

'And what is your favourite type of book?'

'The novel, no doubt about it. And preferably one with a romantic theme. I could read books like that morning, noon and night.'

'So, you're a romantic then?' he teased gently.

'Aren't most women, at heart? Unless it's been knocked out of them.'

'Knocked out? How?'

'By life. The hardness of life.'

This girl, this young lady, was beginning to intrigue him. 'There is certainly plenty of that in Glasgow,' he answered.

If David Katzav was intrigued by Cathy, she was fascinated by him. His physical appearance was totally unlike what she was used to in men. The shape of his head for example, and sallowness of his skin. She'd never come across a Scot or Irishman with skin like it. He had a great beak of a nose, like a bird of prey she thought. And yet he exuded gentleness. His fingers were long and slim with nails that gleamed whitely at their tips. He was just so completely different, so . . . alien!

It was terribly forward of her she knew, impertinent some might have said but she didn't think he'd take offence. 'You're not Glaswegian are you? Or Scots?'

'I'm a Jew.' he admitted. 'From Lithuania.'

'Lithuania!' How exotic that sounded.

'Do you know where Lithuania is?'

She had to cudgel her memory, recalling her geography. 'Isn't it north of Poland? North of Poland and facing Sweden across the Baltic Sea?'

He clapped his hands in glee. 'Very good! Very good indeed!' He was most impressed.

'I enjoyed geography at school. And history. But most of all I enjoyed writing compositions. That was great.'

She might be working class, but then so too was Robert Burns, he reminded himself. 'You're a writer yourself then, maybe?'

'No!' she laughed. 'Compositions were my limit. I work for Mavor & Coulson, an engineering firm.'

He nodded his head in acknowledgement. 'I've heard of them. A big firm.'

Cathy laughed again, tickled at the idea of him thinking her a writer. 'I haven't met them but I know we've got some Jews in Partick. They seem to be well liked from what I've heard.'

'If only that was the case the world over,' David Katzav sighed, remembering the dark days in Lithuania before his

31

family had fled the country. Dark days and darker deeds that would haunt him for the rest of his life.

'Do you own this shop?' Cathy asked.

'I do.'

She glanced around. 'It must be marvellous to own a bookshop. Working here mustn't be like working at all. More like a permanent holiday.'

'Most pleasant. I agree. Though not very lucrative I'm afraid to say. However, I get by and that's the main thing.'

Cathy reached over to pick out a copy of *The Old Curiosity Shop* by Charles Dickens. The copy was an extremely old one, the pages inside brown and mottled. This was also published by Collins of Glasgow.

'Do you like Dickens?' David Katzav inquired.

'He's all right. But I much prefer Robert Louis Stevenson. My favourite of all his novels is *Catriona*.'

'You know I've never read that. I must get round to it,' David Katzav said.

'Oh you must!'

His lips twitched. 'It's a love story, is it not?'

'Very much so. But like all good love stories there's a lot more to it than just the love interest. There's adventure, and intrigue, high drama and . . .' She stopped in mid-sentence as the thought struck her. 'You wouldn't have a copy of *Kidnapped* in stock, would you?' *Catriona* was the sequel to *Kidnapped*, the latter a man's book if ever there was. Bobby would be certain to enjoy it.

David Katzav's brow furrowed. 'Yes. I believe I do,' he said after a few seconds. 'Come with me.'

He led her to another part of the shop where he used a small set of steps to get to the top shelf which was about three feet above his head when he was standing at floor level.

He came back down off the steps. 'Not there. Perhaps along a little?' he apologised, and nudged the steps along to his left. Swiftly he mounted the steps again. 'Ah!' he exclaimed almost at once. 'Got it. And *Catriona* too.'

The books he handed Cathy were bound in leather with the name of the novel and author in large gold lettering on the front. The paper inside was crisp, the printing bold and clear. Each contained half a dozen excellent illustrations.

32

'How much are they?' Cathy queried.

'Look at the end of each book. There should be a slip there with a price pencilled on it.'

They weren't expensive at all, Cathy thought when she found the slips. Not when you considered they were bound in leather and in such pristine condition. 'I'll take both,' she said. '*Kidnapped* for my fiancé, and *Catriona* for myself. We'll keep them side by side; a pair.'

She was most definitely a romantic, David Katzav thought to himself. 'Side by side, like you and your fiancé, heh?' he smiled.

She smiled back at him. 'That was it precisely.'

'I'll wrap them for you,' David Katzav said, thinking that this young lady had brightened up what until then had been a very dull and boring day. Side by side; a pair. He liked that.

He wrapped them in tissue paper, presenting them to her after she'd paid him and he'd given her change from the ornate brass till that stood to one side of his desk.

'I'm glad you found that special present here,' he said.

So was she. 'Thank you for everything.'

'Thank *you*. 'Come again.'

'I will. Now that I've found your shop you can be assured I will.'

Outside she stopped to take her bearings again, then crossed the road to continue on her way home to Partick. There she halted once more, and turned to look back at the shop she'd just left.

The Blackbird Bookshop, she now saw it was called. And there, on a narrow ledge above the fascia, a large stone carving of a blackbird in the process of launching itself into flight, from which clearly the bookshop derived its name.

How unusual, she thought. You didn't come across many stone carvings on buildings in Glasgow, and those you did were almost always gargoyles. At least that was so in her experience.

The Blackbird Bookshop, she thought. What a lovely place and equally lovely man. She would indeed be back.

'Your turn to get the bevy in, china,' Gordon Manson said to Bill Coltraine, who was sitting beside him. It was Bobby's stag night and he was out with his pals from the coalyard, plus several other close friends including his brother Gavin who at nineteen was four years younger than him.

'Aye, right. Pints and drams all round again is it?' said Bill, coming to his feet.

'Of course!' cried out Jack Smart. He was already half cut, and having a whale of a time.

Bill lurched off.

'This time tomorrow you'll be a married man,' Tim Murchison teased Bobby.

'Aye,' Bobby acknowledged.

'And getting a bit of . . .' Gordon Manson made a rude gesture with his arm, 'before the night is over. Eh?'

Bobby blushed bright scarlet.

'Nookie.' Jack said, and laughed raucously.

Gavin grinned at his brother who was squirming. He wasn't prone to blushing as Bobby was. Their wee brother Mathie was a blusher as well.

'It's a night you'll not forget in a hurry,' Colin Baker said, giving Bobby a lewd wink. He'd got married the year before to a lassie from Whiteinch.

'Do you mean you haven't tried that bed you've bought yet?' Greg Wylie asked, and sniggered. He knew fine well that Bobby hadn't.

'No, I have not!'

'What's wrong with you, man? You're no' scared are you?'

Bobby knew it was all good-humoured teasing, and the usual for a stag night, but he was right embarrassed nonetheless. 'No I'm not,' he mumbled in reply, wishing Gavin wasn't there, which made the whole thing all the worse.

'I remember the first time I saw a woman naked,' Tim Murchison said, a faraway gleam in his eyes. 'I swear to God I thought my heart was going to stop at the sight of her. I tell you true, yon was the most beautiful sight in the world.'

'What woman was this then?' Bobby queried, for Tim wasn't married.

Tim tapped his nose. 'That's for me to know and you to wonder about. I'll just say this though, she was a married woman whose hubby was, and still is as far as I know, in the army.'

'Look at that, would you!' Gavin exclaimed, and gave a soft whistle.

The female in question had come swaggering into the pub in the company of another, and not as pretty, female.

'A couple of tarts,' Sandy House said.

'Let me put it this way,' Gavin replied quickly. 'Tart or not I wouldn't crawl over her to get to you.'

They all laughed.

'Here's to Cathy Ford! You've got yourself a good one there! One of the best!' Colin Baker toasted, gesturing with his glass at Bobby.

'One of the best!' others repeated.

'Although what she sees in him, I don't know,' Gavin said cheekily in an aside.

'Watch it, you!' Bobby retorted.

There was a bit more banter, then Bill was back carrying a large tray sagging with drink. 'Here we are, lads,' he cried, setting the tray before them, others having quickly made space for it.

'Should we try and get those two over? I wonder how much they charge?' Tim Murchison said, referring to the tarts.

'Do you think they really are on the game?' Gordon Manson queried, not at all convinced that they were.

'Of course they are. Look at them for crying out loud! If they're not whores I'm the Sultan of Punjab.'

'Hey!' exclaimed Sandy House, clicking his fingers. 'How about we all chip in and give Bobby a stag night to really remember. A wee bit practice you might say, before tomorrow night.'

'A dry run you mean?' laughed Colin Baker.

'I hope the hell not *dry*!' Sandy House quipped back, which produced a huge roar of laughter.

The only one not laughing was Bobby who was alarmed in the extreme at what was being suggested. 'No, no, no,' he declared firmly, shaking his head. 'You can forget anything like that for me. I'm not on.'

'I'm sure you'd enjoy it,' Kenny Tamm said, knowing damn well *he* certainly would.

'I don't wish to know about any tarts, and that's final,' said Bobby.

'Be that as it may,' Tim Murchison chipped in, reluctant to let this go, 'let's get them over anyway. I'm sure they'd be amenable to us buying them a drink.'

'Aye, let's do that,' agreed Bill, and burped. He liked this idea.

'I'll speak to them,' said Gavin, rising.

'No. I don't think . . .' Bobby began to protest, but Gavin had already left the table.

'Cheers!' toasted Bill, raising his whisky.

'Cheers!' the others responded.

'In a one-er now. In a one-er!' And with that he threw his whisky down his throat, his companions feeling obliged to follow suit. It was a celebration after all.

'He's got them. Your brother's got them!' Gordon Manson exclaimed excitedly to Bobby.

Gavin had, Bobby saw now. And he was bringing the two tarts over.

After introductions had been made – the prettier of the two was called Josie, the other Agnes – Gavin insisted they sit beside Bobby, one on either side.

'So you're getting married tomorrow,' Josie purred to Bobby, curling long fingers round his upper arm. 'How very interesting.'

'I'll get another round in,' Gavin grinned.

The long fingers dropped from Bobby's upper arm to come to rest lightly on his thigh.

Bobby shot his brother a murderous look that only made Gavin grin all the wider.

Cathy glanced at the clock on the mantelpiece above the range. Only seventeen hours to go and she'd be Mrs Bobby McCracken.

'Nervous?' Winnie asked. She and Cathy were alone in the kitchen, John and Lily being out.

Cathy shook her head.

'It would be quite natural if you were. I remember I was shaking like a leaf the night before I married your father.'

'Honestly Ma, I'm not.'

'Everything will be hunky-dory, I promise you.'

If anyone was nervous it was her mother, Cathy told herself. 'I'm sure it will.'

'When your da organises something you can bet your boots it's well organised,' Winnie went on.

'That's true enough.'

'And when you get back to Purdon Street a week on Sunday

night you won't have to worry, I'll have a fire waiting for you and all the necessary in for you to make yourselves a meal.' Cathy and Bobby had booked themselves into a wee hotel at Largs where they'd be honeymooning for a week.

'It's only a pity we're getting married at this time of year, but there we are,' Cathy said.

Winnie nearly replied flippantly that even if it was freezing out, the pair of them would be able to keep one another warm, but bit that back. Her hands flew, making her needles go clack clack clack.

'Is there . . . Is there *anything* you want to ask me? Anything I might be able to advise you on?' Winnie said softly, staring hard at her knitting. There! She'd finally come out with it. Something she'd been trying to do for weeks now.

Cathy realised immediately what her mother was driving at, and was completely taken aback. Apart from how to deal with menstruation, and what that was about, her mother had never before offered to discuss anything that might be considered intimate with her. She'd learned about the facts of life on the street and at school like everyone else she knew. Not one of her friends and acquaintances had been told the facts of life by his or her parents. They were just something you picked up as you went along.

There *were* a number of practical details Cathy would have loved to ask about, but now the opportunity had presented itself she couldn't bring herself to do so. Not in a million years. It would be just far too embarrassing. 'No, nothing,' she muttered in reply.

Winnie heaved a sigh of undisguised relief. Thank goodness for that! She felt as though a huge weight had been lifted from her shoulders. 'That's fine then . . .', she said, laying her knitting aside. 'Now how about a nice cup of tea?'

'I'll put the kettle on.'

'No, you sit where you are and let me.'

Winnie started to hum as she filled the kettle at the sink. It hadn't hurt her on her wedding night, and she was sure it would be the same with Cathy. And once that was over with, everything else was plain sailing.

Nothing at all to worry about.

*

'Listen!' said Rob McCracken, laying the newspaper he'd been reading on his lap.

His wife Ina cocked an ear. 'Somebody singing. In the closemouth it sounds like.'

They both listened to the ragged, discordant bellow that was now booming up the close. Ina caught the words to one line of the song being sung, and clapped a hand over her mouth.

'They can't sing that in the close!' she exclaimed, taking the hand away from her mouth. 'It's filthy!'

It most certainly was, Rob thought to himself. It was a dirty song he hadn't heard in years. 'I think the boys are home from the stag night,' he said.

'Our Gavin and Bobby singing a song like that! I don't believe it!'

Rob shot her a sideways glance that was filled with amusement. Did she think they were still wee tykes kicking a ball round the back courts? They were both grown-up men.

'What will the neighbours say?' Ina whispered.

'Nothing at all. They all know it's Bobby's stag night. And don't try and tell me our neighbours haven't heard songs like that before now. They'd be liars if they said they hadn't.'

Another line of song rang clearly out, the words making Ina wince.

'I'd better let them in. If they're as drunk as they sound it'll probably take them an hour to get a key in the lock,' Rob said, getting up out his chair.

Ina also rose intending to accompany him to the front door.

'What a state!' Rob laughed when he and Ina were out on the front landing. Bobby, Gavin, Sandy House and Tim Murchison were on the landing below, Bobby being supported by Gavin and Sandy, who each had an arm round his waist with his arms draped over their shoulders.

Bobby looked up and squinted, trying to focus. He hiccuped and hiccuped again.

'Wheest, you lot!' said Ina anxiously, gesturing the singers, Gavin, Sandy and Tim, to be quiet.

'Shhh!' said Tim, taking this up, and placing a finger over his lips.

Gavin and Sandy finished on a rousing note; it was the end of the song anyway.

'You appear to have had quite a time of it,' Rob smiled, thinking that was an understatement if ever there was one.

'Smashing time. Absolutely smashing!' Bobby hiccuped.

'Pished as farts.' Sandy House said.

'We're helping Bobby home,' Tim Murchison explained quite unnecessarily, and fell back against the wall.

A foolish expression lit up Bobby's face. 'Hello Ma! Hella Da!'

'I'll give you a hand,' said Rob, coming down the stairs to the landing below.

Bobby partially disentangled himself from Gavin and Sandy, to lean on Rob.

'You know something, Da?' he slurred.

'What son?'

'They couldn't get me. They tried their damnest but couldn't get me.'

'Who couldn't?'

'The two whores.' He hiccuped again, then glanced at Ina who was looking aghast.

'Couldn't get me, and you know why?'

'Why son?' Rob asked.

'Because I love Cathy that's why. Because I love my Cathy.' And having made that declaration he passed out.

'Cathy,' he mumbled as they dragged him upstairs. 'Oh, Cathy!'

The gas popped as Cathy lit it, and pale yellow light flooded the kitchen. She then lit the mantle at the other end of the range, and the light grew brighter.

It had been just after eleven pm when she'd slipped out of the house to come to her own in Purdon Street. She wasn't at all tired, and knew it would be hours yet before she was able to go to sleep. As she'd told Winnie, she wasn't nervous but she was certainly becoming excited. Excitement that was rapidly growing within her like a flower opening to the day.

She and Bobby had done so well, she thought. All their relatives, friends and neighbours had been so tremendously generous in their wedding presents. The show of presents she'd had the previous week was certainly the best she'd ever seen.

39

The house still smelled of distemper and paint, she thought. Bobby and his brother Gavin had done a grand job of redecorating, and had done the house throughout.

The curtains that hung at the window she'd made herself, as she had the ones in the bedroom, That had been a big job, but hadn't taken her too long once she'd got stuck in.

She ran a hand slowly over the top of the mantelpiece, then slowly back along the gleaming brass rail that hung below it.

Besides the distemper and paint she could also smell the new linoleum that had been laid. A very comforting smell, she thought. A homey one.

Taking her time, she went through the house, looking, touching, thoroughly enjoying herself.

She was still there when the wag-at-the-wa' clock – a present from the girls at Mavor & Coulson – chimed the hour, ushering in the new day.

Her wedding day.

'How do you feel?' John asked Cathy as their hired motorcar approached the church.

'How do you?'

'A bit keyed up shall we say. I'll be glad when the church business is all over and we can get down to the wheeching and dancing.'

She laughed. 'I'm looking forward to the wheeching and dancing too, but not as much as the service.'

He understood that. 'No,' he said, nodding his head. 'You wouldn't be.'

Reaching over he took her hand in his and gently squeezed it. Suddenly he had a lump in his throat that seemed the size of an ostrich egg.

Bobby felt terrible, but not nearly as bad as he had when he'd woken that morning. Thank God for the Worcestershire Sauce concoction his father had made him, and insisted he swallow every last drop of.

He was sweating again, he realised. He didn't know whether that was as a result of the heat in the church or the amount of booze he'd swallowed the night before. (Talk about having a good bucket, that had been a bucket and a half!) Probably the

40

latter he decided, giving his forehead a quick mop with his hanky.

He glanced at Gavin who was acting as his best man, and hoped Cathy wasn't going to be much longer. This waiting, particularly feeling as he did, was awful.

'Here Comes The Bride' . . . The organist went crashing into the tune, announcing Cathy's arrival at the top of the central aisle. Behind Cathy and John, whose arm she was holding, were the bridesmaids, Lily, Kate Binnie, and Sandra McCracken, Bobby's wee three-year-old sister.

The minister rose from where he'd been sitting close to the bottom of the pulpit, and so too did Bobby and Gavin, taking up their places in front of the spot where the minister now positioned himself.

Bobby turned to look at Cathy, and the sight of her nearly took his breath away. Every girl should look beautiful on her wedding day, and Cathy was most certainly that. She was a shimmering ivory-coloured confection out of which two gorgeously beguiling hazelnut eyes sought and fixed on his own.

He smiled at her, and she smiled back. He was the luckiest man alive, he told himself. The luckiest man alive.

When she joined him the ceremony began.

The moment Cathy and Bobby appeared out of the church they were showered in confetti from wellwishers.

The various motorcars that had been hired were lined up, waiting to transport the immediate family on both sides to the reception which was being held in a Co-operative hall – but first photographs had to be taken.

'Smile!' called out the photographer when the wedding party was assembled and that was followed by a flash. A number of photographs were taken, the final one of Cathy and Bobby alone, and then that was over and they could escape to the cars with Cathy and Bobby to go off in the lead car.

A great many children from the surrounding streets had foregathered, eager for the 'scramble' that traditionally took place on these occasions.

'Hard up! Hard up!' the children cried, milling round the car door, jockeying for position after Cathy and Bobby had got in.

'Watch none of you get run over!' a woman shouted from outside the throng of heaving children.

'Hard up! Hard up!' They would only stop their chant when money was thrown.

Bobby had a pocketful of change, brought along for this very purpose. He now scooped it into his hand and threw it over the heads of the nearest children. As the car moved off they left the children scrambling on the pavement for the cash.

Every car in the line was subjected to the same treatment of 'hard up! hard up!' and every car had money thrown from it. When the last car had gone the children pronounced their verdict amongst themselves. It had been a 'rare' scramble. The families involved hadn't been meanies.

Aye, good luck to the bride and groom!

'May I have the pleasure?' asked Big Tosh of Cathy, who was standing talking to relatives of Bobby. Bobby himself was up dancing with an ancient aunt of his, Aunt Bet from Coatbridge. Big Tosh's face was flushed and there was a slight glaze to his eyes.

'Of course,' Cathy replied, pleased to dance with her cousin. Cathy excused herself, then they walked over to where the dancing was taking place and immediately joind in. The dance was a waltz.

'You look as though you're enjoying yourself,' she smiled.

'I am that. Your father has been very generous with the bevy. Hasn't stinted in the slightest.'

'Have you had some of the food?'

'A large plate of tatties and boiled ham, thank you. And right tasty the ham was too.'

Wee Tosh went swirling past, dancing with Christine Drysdale, all Cathy's pals from Mavor & Coulson having been invited. As he went by he called out, 'Save a dance for me, Cathy!'

'Hmmh!' sniffed Big Tosh, and swung Cathy round so that her back was to his brother.

'Have you two had another barney?' she demanded.

'We're not speaking if that's what you mean,' Big Tosh replied huffily.

She wanted to laugh, but didn't. 'What's happened now?'

'I don't wish to talk about it if you don't mind. He isn't worth talking about.'

'That serious eh?'

'He's contemptible, my brother. Absolutely contemptible.

Big Tosh wouldn't be drawn any further on the subject, and was chatting in general about the reception when the waltz ended. They were both applauding the band when Winnie appeared at Cathy's side.

'Time to get changed and go Cathy,' she said quietly. She, with Lily and Kate Binnie helping, had already laid out the clothes Cathy would be changing into in an ante-room.

Cathy caught sight of Bobby, who had Gavin speaking to him. He would be being told it was time to go as well.

'Right then, Ma.'

She turned again to Big Tosh but before she could speak he said, 'You run along now. Just remember, everyone wishes you all the happiness there is. But I'm sure you know that.'

She kissed him on the cheek. 'Make certain you come and see me away.'

'I will.'

She and Winnie left the dancefloor while Big Tosh went off in a different direction, heading for the bar.

Cathy burst out laughing to see what they'd done to the motorcar. Old boots, shoes, tin cans and even a corset had been tied to the rear bumper. A square of cardboard with the words JUST MARRIED had been fixed to the spare wheel.

'I might have guessed,' Bobby said to Gavin, who'd been behind this.

'I had help you know. We all wanted to see you off properly, in style.'

'Well, an old corset is certainly style,' Cathy chipped in, still laughing.

'All aboard that's going aboard!' Tim Murchison said, opening the car door and bowing low.

'Goodbye Ma, goodbye Da,' Cathy said to her parents, and swiftly gave them each a hug and kiss. After them there was the same for Lily, Kate Binnie and wee Sandra, Bobby's little sister, who'd been the third bridesmaid.

Winnie started to cry, huge tears welling from her eyes to go running down her cheeks. John put an arm round her, and pulled her close.

There was more hugging, kissing and shaking of hands – with a few ribald pieces of advice being shouted out – then Cathy was in the car and seated, and Bobby beside her.

The driver engaged gear, and they moved off, the car getting a loud 'hooray!' when it backfired, en route to the Central Station to catch their train.

Cathy and Bobby continued waving until the car turned a corner, and those they'd been waving to were lost to view.

'That's that then,' she smiled.

'Aye, that's that.'

It gave Cathy the thrill of her life when they got out at the station and the driver called her Mrs McCracken, the very first person to do so.

She made Bobby give him an extra large tip because of it.

Bobby lay in bed awaiting Cathy's return from the corridor toilet. He'd raked up the fire before getting into bed so that it was burning brightly, turned off the gas but left on the oil lamp that was standing on the table by his bedside, Also on the table were a bottle of whisky and two glasses, one of the glasses, his, with a large dram in it.

Taking up his glass he had a sip, then another. He didn't taste a thing. Cathy had got undressed and into her nightie and dressing gown while he was at the toilet, he'd got undressed and into the brand new pyjamas he'd bought for the occasion while she was there.

The door opened, and she was back, a funny strained smile on her face. 'Shall I lock the door?' she asked.

'I suppose you'd better.'

The small brass bolt sliding home sounded ten times louder than it normally would have done.

'I raked up the fire,' he said, a husk having come into his voice.

'Good.'

She glanced at her side of the bed, then at him, where Lily would normally have been.

'Would you like some whisky?' he asked.

Dutch courage, she thought. 'Yes, that would be nice, but only a small drop.'

He poured it for her, then turned to stare at her as she took off her dressing gown and draped it over a chair. Her nightie was snow white with tiny flowers sewn on the collar, and not nearly as long as the ones she normally wore.

'Like it?' she queried.

He nodded.

Her next move was into bed, she told herself. Not that she wasn't eager for what lay ahead, she was. It was just . . . 'Can I make a confession Bobby?'

'Of course.'

'Last night Ma kept asking me if I was nervous and I kept assuring her I wasn't. Nor was I earlier, before the ceremony, during it or after. But I am now.'

'You know something?'

'What?'

'So am I. Bloody terrified.'

His words were like a cork being taken from a bottle, and she immediately felt her nervousness begin to drain away. He was only her Bobby after all, her Bobby whom she so desperately loved. Why should they be nervous or embarrassed with one another? There was no need, none whatever.

'Do you want me to take this off before getting in?' she asked, touching her nightie.

'Only if you want to.'

'It would be easier.'

He nodded.

With her lower lip caught firmly between her teeth she slid the nightie up and over her head, then allowed it to whisper to the floor.

Bobby stared at her, thinking Tim Murchison had been right the night previously. It was the most beautiful sight in the world. Naked Cathy wasn't as thin as she appeared with her clothes on, her breasts larger and fuller than he would have expected, her hips more round.

'What about you?' she said levelly

If she could do what she just had, then so too could he. Where she had led, he would follow. That didn't stop his hand shaking as he laid her drink on the bedside table. He then got out of bed and moments later he too was naked.

'I'll have that whisky now,' Cathy said, getting into her side of the bed while Bobby climbed back into his.

Their hands touched when he gave her the glass, and it was as if a zzzzttt! of electricity passed between them.

Later, Cathy lay in the darkness filled with wonder, amazement, and feelings she'd never before experienced. She also felt for the first time in her life truly a woman.

'Bobby?'

'Uh-huh?'

'I have no complaints. None whatever.'

For a few seconds he was puzzled by her saying that, then he recalled the conversation they'd had the day he'd proposed. 'Me neither,' he replied, laughing.

When they finally fell asleep, the muted glow from the now dying fire like a small red sun at the far end of the bedroom, they were holding hands.

And both were smiling.

Chapter 2

As soon as Cathy stepped from her close into Purdon Street she sensed the change of atmosphere from what it normally was. Something was different. Something was *wrong*!

She glanced about her, and felt her skin prickle with goosebumps. Everything seemed as it should be on a working morning, or appeared to be anyway. Perhaps it was just her imagination playing tricks on her, she told herself as she hurried to her tramstop.

Bobby left for the coalyard a full hour before she did for Mavor & Coulson, his being a particularly early start. He always made his own breakfast, saying it would be daft for her to get up with him when she didn't need to. He was quite capable of making tea and toast after all; culinary skill was hardly required for either operation. And there was always a fresh cup of tea for her in bed just before he went out the door, that a real treat.

WAR! GREAT BRITAIN DECLARES WAR AGAINST GERMANY! WAR!

Her heart seemed to leap right up from her chest and into her mouth to hear the newsboy's words. War! It had been threatening mind, but she'd never believed that the crunch would actually come and Great Britain get involved.

'War! Great Britain Declares War Against Germany! War!' the newsboy cried out again.

She hurried over and bought a paper. 'Going like hotcakes today. Hardly surprising, eh?' the newsboy grinned cheekily. She could have slapped him.

The *Morning Post* carried the news in screaming headlines of heavy black type, the largest and most dramatic headlines Cathy had ever seen. War had been declared at eleven pm the previous night: Britain's answer to the invasion of tiny Belgium.

She looked up when she heard the clank of a tram, and saw it was hers. Continuing on her way she joined the grim-faced queue at the stop.

The faces on board the tram were just as grim, most of them peering into newspapers with every so often the occasional head being shaken in disbelief.

War! All she could think of was her Bobby and how this might affect him. Oh please God, he wouldn't have to get directly involved. Please God!

She began reading a long statement made by Prime Minister Asquith.

When Cathy arrived at Mavor & Coulson she found Lorna McQueen crying, with Mary Hastie and Sonja Moscrop trying to comfort her. Cathy remembered then that Lorna had two older brothers who were both in the army.

'I can't help it, I've been like this ever since I heard,' Lorna sobbed.

'They're bound to be in the thick of it right from the word go,' Sonja said to Cathy.

Cathy pulled a face. What a stupid thing to say in front of Lorna. It was obvious that would be so, but there was no need to spell it all out.

Kate Binnie, Babs Tait and Eileen Niven arrived together. 'It's odd outside on the streets, have you felt it?' Kate asked Cathy.

Cathy nodded. 'It hit me the moment I stepped out of my close.'

Kate shivered. 'It gives me the willies.'

'What's wrong with Lorna?' Eileen Niven whispered to Cathy, who also replied in a whisper, reminding Eileen about Lorna's two brothers being in the Queen's Own Cameron Highlanders.

'Oh!' Eileen exclaimed softly. 'Aye, right enough.'

'I'm sorry. I really am,' Lorna bubbled.

'Don't you mind, hen. You're amongst friends here,' Babs Tait said gently.

Effie Robertson, the quiet one, arrived looking completely distraught. Her boyfriend was in the merchant navy, and currently at sea. 'I don't know how I made it in this morning

48

neither I do,' Effie said in a voice crackling with emotion. Then she saw Lorna, and tears immediately sprang into her own eyes.

Christine Drysdale appeared, with Pat Smith and Peggy Malone turning up directly behind her.

'We'll beat the hell out the buggers!' Christine declared loudly, her face filled with determination and defiance.

'Knock them for six!' Pat Smith agreed.

'Our navy will blow theirs to smithereens,' Christine went on; she had a cousin aboard the cruiser Cressy.

'Shut up!' said Effie Robertson in her usual soft tone, but her voice somehow stabbing home like a stiletto.

Christine Drysdale blinked; it was unknown for Effie to speak like that. Effie who wouldn't say boo! to a goose.

'I'm sorry,' Christine mumbled, instantly contrite. 'I didn't mean to offend.'

'It's only . . .' Effie took a deep breath, and then she too broke down. Her shoulders hunched forward, and she clasped her hands over her face.

Christine was the first to reach her, and put an arm around her. Now there were also tears in Christine's eyes. 'I'm sorry Effie. You must be worried sick about Colin. I just wasn't thinking.'

'What's all this then?' a male voice demanded. It was Curley, their foreman, looking as if he'd been up all night, which indeed he had. He'd been at a Masonic 'do' that had carried on until the early hours, and on the way home had learned the awful news. There had been no sleep for him after that. He had a son just turned eighteen.

'Some of the girls are a bit upset by what's happened,' Cathy explained to him.

'Aye.' He didn't really know how to answer that. He was upset himself.

'My damned hanky's sodden through,' Lorna McQueen complained through her tears.

'Here, take mine. It's an extra large one. I like them that size,' Curley said. Producing the hanky he gave it to Lorna who accepted it with a weak smile of gratitude.

Curley glanced at his pocket watch. It was a full minute past the time when the girls should have started. If Mr Lind . . . Oh sod Lind! he thought. The man would just have to make allowances. War had just been declared for Christ sake!

49

War! Every time he thought, spoke or heard the word the bottom of his stomach seemed to fall away.

Eventually the girls got to work, but the number of conductors bound that day was far short of what it normally was. The strangest thing was that although Mr Lind was aware of the fall off in output nothing was said about it, and no one was threatened with the sack far less sacked.

Perhaps the man was human after all!

Cathy jumped out of her chair the instant she heard Bobby's key in the front lock. Going to the range she lifted the pan of water that was boiling there, and was carrying that to the sink when he entered the room.

She poured the boiling water into the enamel basin already in the sink, then, still holding the now empty pan, turned to look at Bobby.

His face was filthy as it always was when he came home from work, his hands and lower arms solidly black all the way up to his elbows. While he washed she usually put out the tea. Then, when he was finished and the tea dished up, they'd sit down together.

'Evening love,' he said. 'I'm absolutely starving.'

'It's toad in the hole. That all right?'

'As the saying goes, I could eat a scabby heided wean, I'm so hungry.'

Revolting expression, Cathy thought, as she thought every time she heard it.

Bobby had already hung up his jacket on the peg in the hall; he now began stripping down to his waist for his wash.

Cathy put the pan away. 'You've heard the news?'

'Oh aye! People have been talking about nothing else all day long.'

When he was stripped he went to the sink and ran some cold water into the hot, turning off the tap again when the temperature was to his liking. Taking up the bar of soap he started on his face, after which he'd do his arms and torso.

When she saw he was almost finished Cathy took the toad in the hole from the oven that was part of the range and placed the dish on the table. Using a serving spoon she scooped a portion onto his plate, then another onto hers, his portion being by far the bigger. There were also boiled tats and a green vegetable to go with it.

'Grand,' said Bobby, sitting down, having already put his shirt back on.

She sat facing him, and proceeded to push her food round her plate. She wasn't hungry in the slightest. If anything she felt vaguely sick.

'Bobby?'

'Hmmh?' he queried, his mouth full.

'They won't expect you to get involved, will they?' she asked in a tumble of words.

He regarded her steadily while he continued chewing. After he'd swallowed he said, 'This won't come to anything as drastic as that. There's the regular army for a start, and already youngsters are queuing up in their thousands to join. That'll be more than enough to take care of the Germans. For don't forget, it's not only us fighting them but the French as well. And they have a terrific army.' Bobby shook his head. 'The lads and I were talking about it at the coalyard before we left, and you know what we think will happen?'

'What?'

'There will be one huge Godalmighty battle which we'll win, and that will be the finish of it. Germany will withdraw back within its own national boundaries, and that will be the end of the whole sad, sorry affair.'

He laughed. 'Good grief, they not only have Great Britain and France against them but Russia as well. What chance have they against a line-up like that? None at all. I'm telling you, one big battle, maybe two, though I doubt it, and goodbye Fritz.'

Relief surged through Cathy. If that was true she had nothing to worry about, Bobby would be safe.

'Anyway,' he added as an afterthought, 'even if I did want to be a hero and join up – which I most certainly do not as I'm no hero – they wouldn't have me because I'm a married man, see.'

'An old married man of *ten months*,' she said, which made them both laugh.

'Seems like ten years,' he muttered, teasing her.

'You don't mean that!' she exclaimed, pretending outrage.

'Ten minutes more like,' he smiled. And her heart seemed to melt within her.

She went on to tell him about how upset Lorna McQueen and Effie Robertson had been at work that morning, and how the whole work-day had been affected by the news.

After a while Bobby changed the subject and, for the rest of that evening anyway, the war was forgotten.

Cathy came awake suddenly, and realised almost instantly that it was far too early for Bobby to get up. It wasn't even dawn yet she saw, glancing at the drawn bedroom curtains. If it had been there would have been a chink of light where they met.

What had woken her up? She didn't know. She didn't think she'd been dreaming. If it had been a dream, or nightmare, that had wakened her, surely she would remember something of that dream or nightmare? Which she didn't.

Reaching across under the bedclothes she touched Bobby. How warm he was. And how comforting it was to touch him.

He took in an extra deep breath, held it as the seconds ticked by, then exhaled in a long sputter. When they'd first been married it had half frightened her to death when he'd done that, it seeming as if he wasn't going to breathe again. But he always, eventually, did. In the past she'd known him hold his breath for almost a full minute before the sputtering exhalation.

He grunted, then mumbled something. Talking in his sleep. He mumbled again, but she couldn't make out what he was saying.

Ten months married, she'd wisecracked at teatime. It might be only that but it seemed to her that she'd been married to Bobby McCracken forever. She just couldn't imagine life without him. He was as part of her as her arms and legs. More so.

She felt so secure lying here beside Bobby, she thought. Secure and . . . all of a piece. Before Bobby there had been something missing, together they made up a whole.

How lucky she was to have found her man in a million, her 'true fate' as the Glasgow lassies called it. There had been those years prior to her meeting him during which she'd begun to think she might have to compromise and marry someone she wasn't head over heels in love with, and then, just when she was about to give up hope, along had come Bobby McCracken and that had been that.

How she loved him. He was the sun, moon and stars all rolled into one for her.

She was still telling herself how lucky she was when she again drifted off to sleep.

Bobby's face was set hard as granite as he read the latest from France in the *Weekly Review*. In August there had been Mons, in September the Marne, and now they were battling at a place called Ypres.

A glint of wetness crept into his eyes as he read the account of how the depleted British Expeditionary Force had been pushed back and back till finally outside Ypres it had stopped and turned once more to face the enemy.

At Nonne Bosscher – Nun's Wood – a wedge of thicket on the breast of a gentle rise in the ground, the British had waited for the final onslaught, and prayed for reinforcements.

Prussian Guards, fresh and untried, but trained to razor-sharp precision, had been moved in to further strengthen the poised German line.

And then, almost at the last moment, the British reinforcements arrived. Hastily formed platoons, a raggle-taggle bunch of cooks, spud bashers, dishwashers and orderly room clerks; sanitary orderlies and waiters from the officers' mess; storemen and quarter-masters, wagonmasters and messengers, all non-combatants who'd never expected to face the business end of a rifle, sent to face the best that Kaiser Bill could send against them: the very cream of the German Army.

Bobby read on, fiery Celtic anger swelling within him. The raggle-taggle platoons had gone into battle armed with picks, shovels, entrenching tools, anything they could find because there hadn't been rifles available to arm them with. And so they had fought, discarding whatever they had brought with them when they were able to snatch up rifles from the killed and wounded. Rifles they had then used at point blank range.

They should have been quickly overrun, annihilated. But they hadn't been. They'd stood their ground, and continued to stand it till in the end the German advance had not only been stopped but thrown back. From the very jaws of defeat victory had been denied the Germans.

Bobby's chest was heaving. Picks, shovels and entrenching tools against Prussian Guardsmen! Jesus Christ! And to not only stop such troops but throw them back! Here was a miracle, a saga of superhuman courage and effort.

The end of the story, and why it had been allowed to be printed in such detail, was an appeal for more volunteers. Many of the original volunteers had now completed their training and were en route for France – Kitchener's Army they were being called – but more volunteers were desperately needed.

The Empire was beginning to rally round. A large contingent of Canadians had set sail for France, as had a reputedly tough fighting regiment of Indians from Bombay. As for the French (a poor showing on their part) they were bringing in troops from their colonies in Algeria and Morocco.

Bobby laid the *Weekly Review* aside. It made him feel positively ill to think how wrong he'd been about the Germans. One big battle, two at the most, and they'd be sent packing back across their national boundaries. How wrong he'd been! Germany was proving a far stronger and more resilient adversary than he, and many like him, had anticipated. Stronger, more resilient *and* more resourceful.

He'd thought the war would be over in a few short weeks. Well, those weeks had become months, and who would now dare prophesy how many of those there would be? Certainly not he.

But who could have foreseen, amongst other things, this new business of digging in and staying put that had begun at Aisne? Trench warfare it was being called. The men on both sides were digging in, in some places only yards apart, and fighting from there. No doubt, providing the British continued to hang on, it would be the same before long at this . . . Bobby had to search out the name again, it was so hard to remember some of these French and Belgian names! This Ypres.

Bobby brushed the wetness from his eyes, not wanting Cathy to see him so moved. He was fully composed once more when she came into the kitchen from the bedroom where she'd been changing the bed in preparation for her weekly visit to the 'steamie', which she made every Thursday night. The 'steamie' was a public laundry where you paid for use of its facilities.

'A cup of tea?'

'I wouldn't say no.'

'I'll put the kettle on, then.'

Bobby glanced at the *Weekly Review* which he'd dropped to

the floor beside his chair. Picks, shovels and entrenching tools! He shook his head in amazement, and not a little awe.

'Now, who's that?' Cathy exclaimed when there was a knock on the outside door.

Bobby made to rise, but Cathy was already on her way out the kitchen. When she returned she had her father, John, with her, carrying a brown paper bag.

'I brought a couple of screwtops,' John said to Bobby.

'I was about to have some tea, but beer's a lot better. I'll get glasses.'

'You sit here Da,' Cathy instructed, ushering John to what was normally her chair.

'I don't want to put you out!' he protested, knowing it was hers.

'You're doing nothing of the kind. Now sit there or I'll be upset.'

'Always likes to get her own way,' John smiled at Bobby, at the same time giving his son-in-law a fly wink.

'So do children,' Bobby jibed back, which caused John to give a hoot of laughter, and smack his thigh.

'Watch it, you!' Cathy warned Bobby, wagging a finger at him. But it was a good humoured threat, one she didn't mean.

'Ah!' said John when he was handed a glass of beer. He had a large swallow, then another. 'That's rare!'

'It is that!' Bobby agreed, having also had a taste.

John looked over to where Cathy was getting the teapot ready (she preferring tea to beer). 'I dropped by because I thought you'd like to hear what's happened.'

She shot him a sideways glance. 'And what's that?'

'Craig and Ronnie have joined up.'

'You mean Big Tosh and Wee Tosh.'

'Aye,' said John, nodding. 'They leave for training Monday morning.'

'Have they gone into the same regiment?' Bobby asked slowly, thinking these were the first men he actually knew to join up.

'The Royal Scots Fusiliers.'

'Good regiment,' Bobby acknowledged, though he favoured the Highland Light Infantry himself. The H.L.I. were the boys.

'They joined together then?' Cathy queried, having suddenly gone a bit funny. They might be a pain in the bumbeleree but she was fond of those two cousins of hers.

55

'Not quite. Craig signed up first, then went home and told the family. When Ronnie heard he was furious, accusing Craig of trying to put one over on him, and immediately rushed out and signed up also.'

'Aye, that sounds just like the pair of them,' Cathy said quietly.

'Their Ma's taken it well, says she's proud of them. And that's what their Da says too.'

Cathy didn't reply to that, just got on with making her tea.

There was another face she'd never seen before, Cathy thought to herself. The man it belonged to was an ordinary working chap wearing the usual jacket, scarf at the neck and 'bunnet'.

'How are you the day then, Mrs McCracken?' a voice demanded.

The speaker was Mrs Kelly, a neighbour from across the street. Like Cathy she too was laden down with shopping, or the messages as Glaswegians tend to call it.

'Fine, and how about yourself?'

A wee bit bronchial with my chest. But tip top apart from that.'

'It's this damp weather. Bad for chests and arthritis,' Cathy nodded. 'But listen, there's something I must ask you.'

Mrs Kelly was immediately all ears. Gossip? 'Aye, what's that?'

'Have you noticed all these strange faces that have suddenly appeared round about? Recently I keep seeing folk I've never seen before in my life.' This was remarkable in what was normally a stable community. Over the space of a year only a few outsiders ever moved in, with a similar amount of the community moving out the neighbourhood. You did get a constant flow within the community like Cathy and Bobby moving to Purdon Street from their parents' houses, but that was a different thing, entirely. Moving within the community you tended to be a 'kent' or known face, whereas the strange faces Cathy was seeing were not.

Mrs Kelly laughed. 'You're right there Mrs McCracken, there are a lot of people about who're new. They're the lodgers.'

'The who?' Cathy exclaimed, surprised.

'The lodgers. Thousands of them have been flooding into

Glasgow to work in the shipyards and the like, and once here they need a place to stay. That's why so many of us have been taking them in as lodgers. I'm only amazed you haven't heard before now.'

Cathy shook her head. 'I haven't.'

'These men and women are part of the war effort, and needed to help with all the extra work that's been created on Clydeside since the war started.'

The latter was true enough, Cathy thought. The shipyards were booming, as was the iron and steel industry. Glasgow had never known anything like it.

'The new folk coming into Glasgow started off as a trickle, but now they've become a flood,' Mrs Kelly went on. 'And there just aren't the houses for them to rent for themselves. Nowadays you can't get a house of any sort in Glasgow for love nor money, they're just not to be had. Which is why those coming into the city are having to go into digs, in many cases entire families of them.'

'I see,' said Cathy. All those new faces she'd been noticing around were now explained. 'Do I take it from what you said you have a lodger yourself?'

'I have indeed. A Mr McDuff, a bachelor from Stirlingshire. And a nicer man you'd have to go a long way to meet. He has the bedroom while Archie and I make do with the kitchen.' The Kellys had a room and kitchen, same as Cathy and Bobby.

Mrs Kelly laid down a shopping bag, and rubbed a thumb and forefinger together in front of Cathy. 'The extra cash doesn't go amiss, I can tell you. Having a lodger is a nice additional income and no mistake. For as you know there's only one of us working, and not two like you and your husband.'

Cathy nodded her understanding of the situation.

'How about yourself? Would you care to take on a lodger? I can soon get hold of one for you if you want.'

'No, thank you,' Cathy replied quickly. 'I doubt Bobby would like the idea.' Nor did she, but she didn't say so in case that would sound rude to Mrs Kelly.

Mrs Kelly's lips twisted into a knowing smirk. 'With the pair of you not having been married that long you like your privacy in the evenings. Is that it, eh?'

Cathy's face flamed.

'No need to be embarrassed, hen. I was young once myself,' Mrs Kelly said, giving Cathy a dig in the ribs. Mrs Kelly was in her sixties.

'I'd better be getting along,' Cathy smiled, deciding it was time she terminated this conversation.

'Well, if you do change your mind about taking a lodger just let me know and I'll fix you up no bother at all.'

'I won't forget,' Cathy replied, edging away.

'But I do understand why you don't want one,' Mrs Kelly said, and cackled.

Cathy fled.

It was a Saturday dinnertime and as was their custom the younger lads at the coalyard had gone en masse at stopping time to the pub. All of them were in their working clothes and filthy from 'the toil', as hard graft was often referred to in the city.

They were into their third pint and chaser when Tim Murchison said, 'I have an announcement to make, fellas.'

'Don't tell us there was nothing in your pay packet because you were completely subbed out!' Bill Coltraine exclaimed, which drew a laugh. They were allowed to borrow money during the week which was then deducted from their Saturday wage packet.

'I'll buy my shout. Fear not,' Tim smiled.

'I should bloody hope so,' Bill muttered. He was only joking; if any one of them had been in temporary financial embarrassment, the others, without exception, would have been only too happy to fork out. They were all chinas together, the best of pals. They did have the odd disagreement between each other, mind, but nothing that lasted.

'Have you gone and proposed to that lassie you met at the Hogmanay jigging?' Jack Smart queried. It was now February, 1915.

Tim Murchison shook his head. 'Try again.'

'You haven't found yourself a new job? One that pays more?' Gordon Manson asked.

'You're on the right track, Gordon.'

They were all aghast, 'New job! You mean you're leaving us? Deserting us!'

Tim took a deep pull of his pint. 'A new job as such, but not

58

what you're all thinking. I've decided to join up. And in fact, when I leave you lot after this that's where I'm off to.'

Silence fell round the table.

'You're going to join up today?' Colin Baker said softly.

'That's my intention.'

'Have you told Miller yet?' Jack Smart asked. Miller was their boss who owned the coalyard.

'No, I'm going round to see him after the deed's done. That way there's no chance of him getting me to change my mind.'

They all understood that. Miller was the original silver tongue. It was said of him that he could argue black was white and you'd go away fully convinced it was so.

Silence fell again, during which some of them had a swallow or sip from their drinks.

'It's getting bad over-by, right enough,' Bill Coltraine said eventually. 'There's another big appeal out for volunteers.'

Colin Baker nodded, as did Bobby. They'd all seen the posters and read the handbills handed out on street corners.

Bobby thought of his brother Gavin who'd joined in the November. Gavin was now over in France and already a corporal, according to his letters home. A battlefield promotion.

'You're daft, Tim!' Jack Smart declared suddenly, shaking his head. 'Why go when you don't have to? I'll tell you this, a team of wild horses couldn't drag me onto a cross-Channel boat.'

Jack's little speech earned him several disapproving looks.

'Why go when I don't have to?' Tim mused. He took another swallow of his pint, then threw what remained of his dram down his throat. As he placed the empty whisky glass back on the table he said quietly, 'Well it's difficult to explain, I'm not good with words. But you see, I just couldn't live easily with myself, knowing I'd let others do my fighting for me, that I hadn't done my bit.'

'You feel strongly about King and Country?' Bobby probed softly.

Tim brought his attention to bear on Bobby. 'My pride in my King, and my pride in Scotland, yes. But most of all, pride in myself.'

Silence once more descended round the table, silence that this time stretched on and on.

59

Finally it was broken by Tim who said. 'I'll get that round of mine in now. And it'll be large whiskies, as it may be some while before I can buy all you ugly mugs another.'

Cathy was ironing when she heard Bobby's key in the outside door. Her forehead creased in annoyance. He was far later than he normally was on a Saturday; he'd be lucky if his dinner wasn't ruined. She'd added water to the stew three times now. God alone knew what it would be like. Completely disintegrated, she wouldn't be at all surprised.

Bobby swayed into the room with a sheepish grin on his face, and a bottle of whisky in his hand.

'You're late!' she snapped.

'I'm sorry.'

She laid the iron on its end, and went over to the range. 'You can wash after your dinner. Sit at the table. The sooner this gets dished up the better.'

'Forget that for now, I've got something to tell you.'

Her annoyance turned to anger. 'What do you mean forget it for now! If this stew is still capable of being eaten, it has to be eaten right away.'

He rifted, unable to hold it back. 'Sorry,' he mumbled.

She peered at him. 'Are you drunk? I mean you look as though you've had a few but are you actually drunk?'

He shook his head. 'A good bevy, but not drunk.'

She had a sudden thought. 'It's not your Gavin is it?'

'No, what I have to tell you has nothing to do with Gavin.'

Her alarm died away. 'Well, whatever it is it can be told over your stew. And I'll warn you, if the stew is ruined and inedible because of your boozing I'll be furious. I can't bide waste as you well know. And with the price of meat what it is nowadays it would be doubly sinful to chuck it in the midden.' Prices had risen considerably of late, particularly food.

While she was busy at the range he got out two thimble glasses which he filled from the bottle he'd brought in.

'Here,' he said, offering her a glass after she'd laid his meal – the stew was still recognisable as such – on the table.

'I don't want whisky at this time of the day, thank you very much!'

'I think you'd better have it all the same.'

60

'I said,' she replied emphatically, 'I don't want it!' What was wrong with the man today?

He swallowed the contents of his glass, then hers. The moment had arrived, the moment he'd been dreading all the way back to Purdon Street.

'I've joined up,' he stated.

'Eh?'

'I've joined up. All the lads from the coalyard, including Jack Smart who was completely against it but did so anyway, left the pub and went to the nearest recruiting centre where we signed, one after the other, on the dotted line. We've all to report to Queen Street Station eleven o'clock, Monday morning. We've to catch a train there that'll take us to Perthshire where our training is to take place.'

He barked out a laugh. 'Miller nearly had a canary when we all went to his house afterwards and broke the news. I think it's the first time I've ever known him lost for words.'

Cathy was dumbfounded, her mouth hanging wide open. Then a gleam came into her eye. 'You're joking, you bugger! Having me on!'

'No, I'm not.'

'Yes, you are.' She jabbed an accusing finger at him. 'For you're a married man and they don't take married men.'

'You haven't been reading the newspapers, Cathy,' he replied softly. 'They changed that rule only last week.'

She laughed. 'You can't take the mickey out of me. I won't bite.'

'It's true , love.'

'Away with you.'

He laid down the thimble glasses, then took her hand. 'I swear to God it's the truth. I've joined up.'

She looked deep into his eyes, and what she saw there brought her skin out in gooseflesh. The hand he wasn't holding went to her mouth.

'Monday at eleven, all of us at Queen Street Station,' he repeated.

'How . . . ? how . . . ?'

He tried to take her into his arms, but she pushed him away. Her thoughts were whirling, her senses numb. 'How could you?' she at last managed to whisper.

'I had to. Why don't we both sit down and I'll try to explain.'

White-hot rage erupted within her. Her hand flashed, and then flashed again. Bobby staggered back as each stinging slap cracked on his cheek.

Whirling round she ran from the room, somehow remembering to snatch up her coat from its peg before she went through the outside door to go clattering down the stairs.

Out the closemouth and into the street she ran. And ran and ran till finally she could run no more.

When the fire in her heaving chest had begun to subside a little she slipped on her coat and started walking.

As she walked she heard nothing, and saw nothing. Nor did she bother about which direction she was going.

She didn't care.

It was dark and Cathy was still walking aimlessly when she spotted something that jolted her memory, and made her come up short. A smile of recognition twisted her lips as she stared at the large stone carving of a blackbird in the process of launching itself into flight, the carving and shop front illuminated by the gas streetlight that stood in front of the shop.

The Blackbird Bookshop, she thought. She'd meant to return, but never had since that day she bought the two leather-bound volumes of *Kidnapped* and *Catriona*. Bobby had been delighted with his present, and read it on their honeymoon, pronouncing it a terrific book when he was finished. He'd also read *Catriona* but hadn't liked that quite as much. The two books, prized possessions, were at home in their bedroom with the other books they owned.

She crossed to The Blackbird Bookshop – which she was sad to see was closed, making her wish she'd arrived at this spot earlier when it was still open – and went and stood in front of the window.

The books on display were the same as they'd been when she'd been here previously, she noted. And it could all still do with a bit of a dusting! That made her laugh, and instantly feel better. She wondered how the Lithuanian-Jew owner was getting on? Well, she hoped. She'd thought him a very nice man indeed.

She stood gazing at the books on display, her eyes flicking from title to title, and author's name to author's name (those she could make out that is), which had a soothing and therapeutic effect on her.

When she finally, reluctantly, turned away from the window she was calm, and in control again.

She resumed walking, heading for home.

Bobby was sitting in his chair with a glass of whisky in his hand. He'd washed and changed she saw, as his eyes locked onto hers. The gas mantles had been turned down low which meant that parts of the room were in shadow.

'Did you go to your mother's?' he asked quietly.

She shook her head. 'I just walked. I must have covered miles.'

She went over and sat facing him. 'How was the stew?'

'I couldn't eat it. I couldn't have eaten anything, no matter what.'

'It's in the midden then?'

'Aye. A double sin as you called it.'

In other circumstances she would have laughed at that, but not now. 'Why did you do it, Bobby? That's what I can't understand. Why? What on earth possessed you?'

Bobby repeated what Tim Murchison had said about pride in King, Scotland and himself. Also about not being able to live easily with himself knowing he'd let others do his fighting for him, and hadn't done his bit.

Cathy heard his words, but didn't really understand them. How could he put himself in a position of extreme danger because of pride or guilty conscience? She thought that down-right stupid.

'But you're a *married man*!' she accused.

'Colin Baker is married also and he too felt strongly enough about this to join up. It's a responsibility, Cathy.'

'What about your responsibility to me?'

'This is a greater responsibility than I have towards you. Can't you see that?'

'No I can't!' she replied bitterly.

He sighed, 'Do you want some of this whisky now?'

She nearly told him what he could do with his rotten whisky, but didn't. She would have some she decided. A small one, with lots of lemonade.

63

She sat watching him as he mixed her drink for her. Forty-eight hours from now he wouldn't be here anymore. He'd be gone. Initially to Perthshire, and then over the Channel. When he gave her her drink she had the impulse to slap him again, but didn't do that either.

Bobby opened the firedoor of the range, and poked the fire inside. He then shovelled in some more coal, and re-closed the door.

'Can you imagine what it would be like if we lost this war and were invaded, like Belgium? Could you imagine Germans strutting up and down the streets, lording it over us? I can, and that's why I must do something to make sure that will never come about.'

A new fear clutched her insides. 'That will never happen, will it? We and the Allies will win?'

'Six months ago when war was declared the idea of us losing was laughable! Now the way things are going it's not. It could happen, and God help us all if it does.'

She tasted her whisky and lemonade, and pulled a face. It was very strong. It burned all the way down, like poison.

'But why do you have to get involved personally?' she demanded harshly.

He gave her a thin smile. She wasn't thinking rationally, he told himself. Nor was she listening. Not properly anyway. 'I've already explained that. My responsibility to my country, to Scotland, is greater than my responsibility to you. Or let me put that another way. Because of my responsibility to you I have to obey the greater responsibility. By defending my country I am protecting you.'

She started to cry.

'Cathy, I . . .' He made to rise again.

'No Bobby, don't touch me,' she said, covering her face, 'not for the moment anyway.'

He sank back into his chair again. This was proving to be even worse than he'd thought it would be. He sipped his whisky, and waited for her to speak. It wasn't as if he wanted to go to war, for Christ's sake! Some of the youngsters saw signing up as a passport to adventure, an adventure during which they would cover themselves in glory. Only it wasn't like when you were young and played soldiers. Then, when the game was over the dead got up and began a new game or went home for tea. In France and Belgium the dead stayed dead. There was no new game or going home for tea. No, he had no delusions about what he'd let himself in for. None at all.

Cathy rose, and went to the sink where a towel was hanging on a nail. She dabbed her face with the towel, then rinsed it with cold water. Then she went back to her chair, and the whisky and lemonade she'd left standing beside it.

'What about money while you're away?' she asked.

'You have your wages from Mavor & Coulson and I'll send home what I can. It won't be hellish much however, the pay's only a shilling a day.'

'Not hellish much,' she agreed.

'But you should get by all right. And don't forget you won't have me to feed which will be a big saving on what you're having to spend at present.'

Seven shillings a week as opposed to the thirty-three shillings he was bringing in at present. That wasn't just a drop in income, she thought. It was a plummet.

'And then there's the bank account for emergencies,' he said. 'That has fifteen pounds, seven and six in it.' Getting engaged, then married had depleted his original savings considerably.

She drank more of the whisky and lemonade, it still tasted like poison. 'Why do you have to go so soon? Why Monday? I would have thought they'd have let you have more time than that?'

'The officer told us that the week's recruitment always goes on the Monday morning. It was our bad luck we signed up on a Saturday. If we'd waited till Monday it would have been the following Monday before we'd have had to go. I must say it is short notice, but in some ways that's better, don't you think?'

She felt like slapping him again.

'If you're going to do something like this then . . .'

'Oh shut up!' she spat at him.

The tears came once more.

'Ahhh!' he cried out.

She clutched him to her, holding him tight now that he was still. The fourth time in one night! He'd never been so demanding before. But then he'd never joined the army and gone off to war before either.

65

'Oh Cathy!' he whispered, and kissed her neck.

Monday morning, she thought. It was Monday morning and soon . . . soon . . .

'I love you,' he whispered.

If you loved me you wouldn't bloody well have gone and signed up! she thought. No, that wasn't fair, she chided herself. She was being too harsh. He did love her. She knew that. No matter what he did it wouldn't have altered the fact.

'And I love you,' she whispered back.

He rolled off her. Reaching over he cupped her breast, his forefinger resting lightly atop her nipple.

'It was disappointing that I couldn't get into the H.L.I. but . . .'

'I don't want to talk about it,' she interrupted him. 'Nothing about the army or war.'

'I understand,' he said softly after a few seconds had ticked by.

Shortly after that a chink of light appeared where the drawn curtains met. A chink of light that seemed to Cathy to pierce her through the heart.

'It's time for you to get up and go to work,' Bobby said, and kissed her on the end of her nose.

'I'm not going.'

He pulled himself onto an elbow. 'Not going?'

'I'm coming with you to Queen Street to see you off.' She twisted her head so that she could look him in the face. 'I've never fiddled a day off work in my life, but I'm fiddling today. And that's an end of it.'

Later, when they did get up, Cathy got dressed and went down to the shops where she bought all the things she needed to give Bobby a farewell breakfast that he wouldn't forget in a hurry. The only item she couldn't get was mushrooms which annoyed her, but there were just none to be had.

'Good grief!' exclaimed Bobby in delight when she plonked his heaped plate in front of him. On the plate were two fried eggs, two sausages, three strips of bacon, a slice of fried bread, two slices of black pudding, two of white and three fried potato scones.

'Special treat,' smiled Cathy.

'What about yourself?'

She shook her head. 'A cup of tea will do me just fine.'

While he was eating she told him a funny story about an incident that had happened at Mavor & Coulson the previous week, a story she hadn't yet recounted to him.

She was determined to put a brave face on it until he was gone. A brave face and no more tears.

When she delivered the punchline he laughed so hard she had to thump him on the back to stop him choking.

They got off the tram, Bobby carrying the small suitcase he'd brought with him – and there was the station on their left.

'Quarter to, plenty of time,' Bobby smiled.

'Good,' she smiled back. She was going to pieces inside, but it didn't show, hell would freeze over first before she'd allow that to happen.

'Arm?' Bobby said, crooking an elbow at her.

'Thank you kind sir,' she replied in a bubbly voice, and hooked her arm in his.

They crossed the road. 'Where do you actually report to?' she asked, watching the station loom nearer and nearer.

'There will be an officer waiting outside inquiries. I've to speak to him.'

They passed into the station and their nostrils were immediately assailed by the combined odour of soot, grime, oil and smoke that is instantly identifiable as station smell. The atmosphere was one of hustle and bustle, to-ing and fro-ing, arrivals and departures.

'There's Jack Smart!' exclaimed Bobby, pointing to a kiosk where Jack was in the process of purchasing several items.

Cathy spotted Inquiries, and the tartan-trousered officer standing in front of it.

'Bobby!'

They both turned on hearing Bobby's name called out, and there was a very excited Gordon Manson running towards them, having followed them into the station.

When he reached them he and Bobby shook hands as though they hadn't seen one another in years. Then Gordon pecked Cathy on the cheek.

'Well this is a day and a half isn't it!' Gordon enthused to her.

'Yes,' she agreed. 'It certainly is that.' To Bobby she said. 'You go and report to the officer and I'll get you something to read. And how about a couple of bars of toffee?' She knew Bobby adored Devon Cream Toffee.

'Lovely.'

'On you two go then, I'll join Jack at the kiosk.'

Before reaching the kiosk she glanced back at Bobby – loathe to let him out of her sight for one precious second – to see that he and Gordon Manson had met up with Tim Murchison. It was going to take all her willpower and self-control to be pleasant to Tim, for it had been his idea to join up that had sparked the rest, including her Bobby, into doing the same.

She and Jack had a bit of a natter at the kiosk while she bought what she wanted, then they strolled towards Inquiries where quite a number of young men, about a dozen Cathy would have hazarded, were crowded round the officer who, from what she could make out, appeared to be handing them slips of paper.

'Train tickets and other dockets,' Jack explained to her when she asked him what the slips of paper were, he having already reported to the officer some minutes previously.

A train tooted. She'd always thought that a jolly sound before, but not now. Now it had a melancholy, hateful air to it.

An engine close by hissed, exhaling steam. A large cloud of it swirled its way upwards where it was swiftly dissipated.

Colin Baker's wife had come to see Colin off, she noted, Colin and Ishbel having appeared from the far side of the station. Even at this distance she could make out how grim faced Ishbel was. Ishbel was clinging to Colin as if she never wanted to let him go. Cathy knew exactly how she felt.

A few minutes later Bobby and the rest of the pals (with the exception of Colin and Jack, the former having told Bobby and the others to go ahead and he and Ishbel would catch up) came hurrying over to where Cathy and Jack were.

'We're to board our train,' Bobby announced to Cathy.

'I'll need to get a platform ticket,' she smiled.

'That's easily got hold of,' Bobby replied, delving into a trouser pocket.

'No one came to see you off?' Cathy asked Bill Coltraine.

Bill looked vaguely embarrassed, then replied. 'My ma

wanted to come but I said she shouldn't. It was easier just to walk out the house and shut the door behind me.'

Jack had given her a similar answer when she'd questioned him about there not being anyone there to see him off. It seemed the bachelors were of a like mind on the matter. She presumed, correctly, that Ishbel Baker had insisted just as she had done.

'The train leaves at eight minutes past the hour,' Bobby informed Cathy as they moved towards the barrier. They'd had to report for eleven to be on the 1108. He'd have thought that was neat timing himself, but there you were.

Cathy caught Bobby's hand and squeezed it. There was a coldness in her that had nothing to do with the February weather. She would have been just as cold had it been a blazing summer's day. She hoped her voice wouldn't betray her feelings. It had to remain steady she told herself.

At the barrier she contrived for the others to go on while she and Bobby got her ticket from the machine. As they went through the barrier she saw Colin and Ishbel heading for the machine, Ishbel looking wretched and even grimmer faced, if that was possible.

Her eyes met Ishbel's, and a flash of sympathetic understanding went between them. They were two women in the same awful boat. In love with their husband and seeing their man off to war.

They passed several carriages containing young men who were clearly part of that week's intake. Then they were at a carriage which the pals had claimed as their own.

Cathy glanced at the station clock. Three minutes past, five to go.

'You'll write as often as you can, won't you?' she said to Bobby.

'I'm not much of a writer, but I'll do my best.'

'Make sure you do, I want to know everything. Every last detail.'

Further along the platform a mother was weeping into a handkerchief, with her son doing his best to console her.

Beyond the weeping mother an elderly man with snow-white hair and carrying a walking stick was standing ramrod straight in a position of attention, He could easily have been a funny sight. But not there. Not then.

Cathy looked back down the length of the train, and saw the guard with the green flag. Her stomach knotted so tightly it made her wince.

'Are you all right?' Bobby asked anxiously.

'A wee bit wind, that's all,' she lied, smiling.

'I'd better get inside Cathy.'

She was forcing herself not to cling to him the way Ishbel was to Colin only a few feet away.

'Yes, I suppose so,' she managed to answer lightly.

'Thanks for the toffees and papers,' he murmured, and kissed her, his lips warm on her cold ones. They were still kissing when the guard blew his whistle.

'Come on!' Colin yelled, diving into the carriage.

Bobby broke away from Cathy and followed suit. It was Tim Murchison who banged the door shut and released the leather strap that dropped the window.

Bobby, Colin and Gordon Manson stuck their heads out. Bobby blew a kiss to Cathy, Colin the same to Ishbel while Gordon grinned like a demented idiot.

The train juddered, which brought a sort of strangled whimper from Ishbel. How Cathy was able to remain smiling and keep the tears at bay she never knew, but she did.

The train juddered again. There was a clank, followed by another, then an angry exhalation of steam.

Cathy held up her hand and waved, seeing nothing anymore except Bobby's face as it began moving away from her.

Bobby, Colin and Gordon were all waving frantically, as was Ishbel. Cathy's wave was muted, a gentle tender wave as her hand slowly moved from side to side.

The elderly man with the walking stick was saluting, but Cathy didn't notice. She only had eyes for Bobby, her husband, her love.

The train tooted, then tooted again. Seconds later it arced into a right hand curve and Bobby was lost to view.

Cathy swallowed hard. Using the hand she'd been waving with she massaged her forehead, for she suddenly had a blinding headache.

Ishbel Baker was leaning against a pillar in a state of near total collapse. Her eyes were closed, and she was sobbing.

'Ishbel?'

Ishbel's eyes fluttered open, their expression one of profound self-pity.

'Why don't we go and have a cup of tea? I know I could use one, and a sit-down.'

Ishbel tried to reply, but couldn't, the words choking in her throat.

'You look like I feel, and that's the truth,' Cathy said in a cracked voice, taking Ishbel by the arm. 'Come on, I'll help you.'

She must also try and get herself an Askit powder for this headache, Cathy thought as they began their way back down the platform, Ishbel Baker staggering and stumbling beside her.

Cathy hung her coat on its peg, then went into the kitchen. It hadn't been her intention to go to the window, but she found herself drawn straight to it. There, she looked down on the coalyard below.

In her mind she could visualise Bobby the first time they met, and again as he'd been at their wedding. Then she saw him waving to her from the train carriage window.

When she couldn't look at the coalyard any longer because it hurt so much, she turned away from the window, and leant her bottom against the sink.

He was gone, to Perthshire initially, then France, maybe Belgium. She still couldn't believe it. Didn't want to believe it.

This was some hideous nightmare that she'd soon wake from, with Bobby smiling down at her telling her everything was all right, and it had only been a bad dream.

But it hadn't been, and wasn't. It was horrible, horrible reality.

She crossed to the mantelpiece, touching it as if for the first time. Remembering how she'd done something similar the night prior to the wedding.

Leaving the kitchen she forced herself to go through to the bedroom where she stood staring at the bed they'd shared only a few short hours previously. How long before they shared it again? How long? If ever.

She shook her head. No, she mustn't think like that. Bobby would be coming back, she had to believe that. Had to!

How empty the house felt without him. Not the way it normally did when he wasn't there, when he was at work or with

71

his pals. A different kind of emptiness. It was as if the house knew he'd gone, and altered its ambience accordingly.

Sitting on the edge of the bed she let it come, everything that she'd held back since getting up that morning.

Her face was still shiny with tears when finally, exhausted, she fell asleep.

Chapter 3

Cathy was in the middle of 'The Grand Old Duke of York' when the wave of nausea suddenly hit her, nausea more intense and unlike any she'd ever before experienced.

The wave ebbed, and then a new wave struck. This one just as bad as the previous.

'Excuse me,' she muttered to her partner, one of Dougie's male relatives, and fled in the direction of the ladies' toilet.

Inside the toilet, she threw herself at the sink. She gagged and gagged, but wasn't sick. When everything started to spin she had to hold on to the sink to stop herself from toppling over.

'Cathy, what is it?'

The speaker was her sister Lily, whose wedding this was. The romance had been a whirlwind one. Dougie Mailer was a fitter at Tommy's – Thompson's Yard – where John Ford worked as a patternmaker.

Lily and Dougie had met at the dancing – didn't nearly every couple in Glasgow, the dancingest city in the Empire – and after the first birl round the dancefloor it had been a click. From that point there had been no looking back for either of them.

Cathy's reply was to gag again, and this time some evil-tasting bile came into her mouth; bile she hastily spat into the bowl.

'Don't tell me my matron of honour's pissed?' Lily teased.

'Only two drinks, that's all.'

That didn't surprise Lily; Cathy wasn't much of a boozer. 'Do you want to sit on the pan?'

Cathy shook her head.

'Can't be the food then, and no one else has complained. Has this just come on, like?'

'Yes,' Cathy croaked.

Reaching over, Cathy turned on the tap and scooped water into her mouth to rinse it out. The nausea had now passed, going as swiftly as it had come, leaving her feeling drained and

73

lightheaded. She scooped more water into her mouth, this time swallowing it.

'That's better,' Cathy said, straightening up again.

Lily indicated a deep wooden recess that was about two feet off the floor. 'Park your bum there for a minute. Do you want me to run and fetch a brandy?'

'Nothing,' said Cathy, rinsing out the sink and turning the tap back off. 'All I need is a breather.'

Lily helped Cathy to the window recess, and to sit. 'So, what do you think caused that, sis? I caught a glimpse of your face as you went past me and that was enough to bring me racing after you. You were . . .' She halted in mid-sentence as the thought struck her. A thought that brought a small smile to her lips. 'You were positively green. How long since Bobby went away?'

'Cathy frowned, unable to see the connection. 'Three months. Why?'

'How have your periods been in the meantime?'

'My periods!' Cathy exclaimed in astonishment.

'Have they been normal? Same as usual?'

Cathy's frown returned. 'Now you mention it they haven't. I put it down to Bobby's going away, and anxiety about him.' Then it dawned on her what Lily was driving at. 'You think I might be pregnant?'

'Is there any reason why not?'

Cathy shook her head. 'But I don't feel pregnant.'

'Neither do I but I am.'

Cathy gawped at her sister. 'You're what?'

'Neither do I but I am,' Lily repeated, thoroughly enjoying Cathy's look of sheer incredulity.

'But you're only just married, earlier today, I mean . . .'

'Oh, for goodness sake don't be silly. We've been doing it together since shortly after we met.'

Cathy didn't know what to reply to that. She'd always thought of Lily as a nice girl, a bit wild at times yes, but a nice girl all the same. And nice girls just didn't go to bed with a man before marriage.

Lily, smiling with amusement, took Cathy by the hand. 'I couldn't deny him Cathy, nor did I want to. To be truthful, with the housing situation as it is in Glasgow we hadn't intended getting married quite so soon, but once I knew I was pregnant we had to as quickly as possible. Shall I tell you something?'

'What?'

Lily gave Cathy a fly wink. 'The baby's going to be *premature* so it is. Not that I give a tuppenny damn myself, but to save Ma and Da's face, and Dougie's Ma and Da.'

Cathy couldn't help but laugh. Lily was a born comedienne if ever there was one. The way she'd said *premature* would have made a cat laugh.

'You'll keep my secret, won't you?'

'Of course.'

Lily patted her belly. 'I'm lucky that nothing's showing yet. And with a wee bit of jiggery pokery on my part it won't either until I want it to.'

'Does Ma know?'

'Not on your Nellie.'

'But won't she find out, or at least suspect, as you'll all be sharing the same house?' Because there were no houses available for rent on the market, it had been agreed that Lily and Dougie would stay with Winnie and John, using the bedroom that had been Lily's, and Lily and Cathy's before Cathy's marriage.

'Don't you worry, I'll be taking great care that Ma doesn't get an inkling I already have a wean on the way. She'll never have cause to feel ashamed of me, I promise you.'

'Well your secret's safe with me. You can rest assured of that.'

Lily gave a sudden laugh. 'It was the fact your face went green that tipped me off you were pregnant same as myself. Precisely the same thing happened to me one night when I was out with Dougie. He told me I went green, pea-green he cried it though I doubt it was as green as that.'

'And were you nauseous?'

'I was, and threw up with it. But only once mind, I haven't gone green or thrown up again since.'

'Let's hope it's the same with me,' Cathy said.

'It might well be. As we're sisters we could well experience the same sort of pregnancy.'

Pregnant! Cathy thought to herself, a thrill running through her. If she was, how absolutely marvellous! And the more she thought about it the more convinced she was that was the case. Her strange periods – in truth the last one hadn't really been a period at all – the nausea and feeling sick, it all added up.

'Pleased?' Lily grinned.

75

'As Punch.'

They were a further fifteen minutes in the ladies talking excitedly to one another before, reluctantly, rejoining the others at the reception.

Boomph! went the guns, and then sssssboomph! sssssboomph!

The night was chill and clear as the 16th (S) Battalion of the Rifle Brigade marched into Elverdinghe. Their orders were to camp there for the night before moving into the Ypres salient in the morning.

The 16th (S) Battalion of the Rifle Brigade had crossed the Channel three days previously. They'd come part of the way to Ypres by train, marched the rest. This would be the first taste of action for all of them, none of the men or officers having had any previous combat experience.

Boomph! went the guns again. Boomph! Sssssboomph!

The sound of the guns was frightening enough, Bobby thought as he slogged onward, but what would it be like when the shells were actually exploding around you? He was soon going to find out. They all were.

They marched round some low-lying buildings, and then on to a flat piece of ground that was in fact waste ground. Here they were brought to a halt and ordered to fall out.

They weren't the only ones on the waste ground; there were others sitting huddled in groups.

Bobby, Colin, Tim, Jack, Gordon and Bill came together, laid down their packs and then sat or squatted beside them. 'I hope we're going to get some grub,' said Bill Coltraine, peering about him. They'd had breakfast that morning, but nothing since.

'I wonder who they are?' Tim said softly, gesturing at those who'd already been there when they'd arrived.

'As long as they're not Gerries I don't care,' Gordon said, which raised a laugh.

Sergeant MacDonald appeared beside them. 'Over there!' he said pointing. 'Tea and hot rations.' And with that he moved swiftly on to the next lot to whom he delivered the same message.

The pals got out their plates and mugs and went over to where the sergeant had indicated. Behind a partially demolished stone wall they found two cooks in charge of a number of billies and urns.

76

'Get in line! Get in line!' one of the cooks was urging the men who'd started to mill about in front of the billies and urns.

When Bobby got in line he found himself behind a soldier from another regiment, one of those who'd already been there when they'd arrived. Even in the darkness Bobby could see how played out the soldier was.

'Who are your mob?' Bobby asked pleasantly.

The soldier twisted round to look at Bobby, seemed to have trouble focusing, then replied in an English country burr. 'We're the Worcesters. Who are you?'

'The 16th (S) Battalion of the Rifle Brigade.'

'Never heard of you.'

'We just arrived over here three days ago.'

'Ah!' the soldier said, and nodded.

The line shuffled forward. 'We're going into the salient tomorrow,' Bobby went on.

'Then God save you mister. God save you.'

Bobby found that unnerving to say the least. 'Have you just come out of it then?'

'That's right. We've got a spell down the road for rest and recovery, then we'll be back in again.' The soldier shook his head. 'Jesus!' he whispered.

The meal was a stew consisting of sausage bits with a few pieces of meat thrown in for good measure. There was also boiled potatoes and cabbage.

When the pals had collected their food and tea they returned to where they'd left their packs, sat and fell to. The best thing that could be said about the meal was that it was filling. Jack Smart muttered that he wouldn't have fed that bloody stew to his dog.

When they'd finished eating, Bill, Gordon and Tom lit up cigarettes. The rest, including Bobby, didn't smoke.

'Hello again mister.'

The speaker was the soldier Bobby had spoken to in the line. 'Hello again to you too.'

The soldier ran a hand across his face, then scratched amongst his bristles. 'The thing is see . . .' He shuffled uncomfortably. 'Would any of you chaps give me a fag? I finished my own days ago and am absolutely desperate.'

'He's just come out the salient,' Bobby explained.

Tim had already produced his packet. 'Here you are, Jim. Help yourself.' And with that he tossed the packet to the soldier who eagerly caught it.

The man took a deep drag, then sighed with pleasure as the smoke streamed from his nostrils.

'Take a couple for later,' Tim instructed quietly.

The soldier didn't have to be told twice, when he'd pocketed two more cigarettes he gave the packet back to Tim.

'Sit and join us for a minute,' Bobby said. 'You can tell us what we're up against. What to expect.'

The soldier felt he was obliged, and so dropped to a squatting position. 'You said you only arrived over here three days ago, does that mean this is your first time at the front?

Bobby nodded.

The soldier took another draw. 'It's all bad, the entire front is bad, the salient is the worst. By far and away so. It's like shooting fish in a barrel, and you're the fish.'

The pals glanced from one to the other.

'I've read about the Ypres salient in the newspapers,' Bobby said. 'The casualty figures have always been horrendous.'

The soldier regarded him steadily through a haze of smoke. 'Do you know what a salient is?'

'It's a bulge in our front line, isn't it?'

The soldier gave him a thin, chilling smile. 'It's more than a bulge. It's a piece of land, a loop if you like – in this instance about two miles deep at its deepest point, pushed forward into hostile territory so that the enemy is ranged round it on three sides. Do you understand what that means?'

Bobby shook his head.

'It means that a salient is a place where they can shoot at you from the front, either side, and also in the back.'

'How so in the back?' Bobby asked, his mouth having suddenly gone dry.

'The Hun guns have a perfect field of fire from their concealed positions on the shoulder of high ground that runs south of Ypres, from Hill 60 at Zillebeke, through Wytschaete to Messines. Turned inwards towards the salient they can shoot right across it, and what's more they can shoot up it from the rear so that you never know, never, from which direction the next shell is going to come.'

These names meant nothing to Bobby.

The soldier went on, his tone now bitter in the extreme. 'That's why I said it was like shooting fish in a barrel. They have the high ground and concrete pillboxes with walls three feet thick, thousands of the buggers it seems, while we have trenches that are never free of water.'

'Why's that?' Tim Murchison asked.

'Because all this area, all Flanders plain, is reclaimed bogland which quickly reverts to bog if it isn't constantly drained. In the salient the drainage system has been shelled to smithereens which means we in the trenches are in a permanent quagmire while Fritz just laughs and laughs inside those concrete pillboxes of his.'

'Why don't we shell these pillboxes?' Jack Smart questioned.

The soldier gave Jack a pitying look. 'We have done, with howitzers and field guns but the bastards are so strong the shells just bounce off. As strongpoints they're well nigh impregnable.'

'Then why don't we build pillboxes of our own?' Bill Coltraine asked.

'Search me mister, I have heard it said its because we can't afford the concrete. And you know something? I tend to believe that. Men's lives are cheaper than concrete, after all.'

The soldier stood up. 'Now you know a little about the salient. The rest you'll find out for yourselves, the hard way I'm afraid. Anyway, good luck to you all. You're going to need it.' To Tim he added. 'And thanks again for the cigarettes.'

The soldier strode away leaving a silent and very thoughtful band of pals behind him.

'Fish in a barrel,' Jack Smart said after a while, and whistled softly.

Boomph! Ssssboomph! Ssssboomph! continued the guns in the distance, somehow now sounding a lot closer than they had.

Bobby had never seen such mud; thick and glutinous it was like grey caramel. As for the smell, it was a combination of rotting sandbags, chloride of lime, the acrid stink of cordite, and fear.

'Wait here men!' 2nd Lieutenant Kidd ordered Bobby's company, knowing that he was lost and would have to seek advice before proceeding further.

Bobby gazed about him in disgust. Walls of sandbags were everywhere, and here and there breastworks of hastily thrown up mud. Over to one side were a series of ditches half sunk in the morass.

A shell went over, sounding for all the world like an express train rushing through the sky. Then another. Theirs or the Hun's? Bobby didn't know.

A platoon of soldiers, heads hunched like turtles between their shoulders, went hurrying by to suddenly disappear from sight behind a wall of sandbags, About twenty yards further on 2nd Lieutenant Kidd was in conversation with another officer not of their regiment.

Machine guns began rattling, then more took up the refrain. A shell screamed through the air to land a short distance away. There was a loud crump! and a mushroom of mud leapt into the air.

Bobby turned towards the pals, and was actually looking straight at Gordon Manson when the German sniper's bullet hit Gordon just under the helmet, blowing the other side of Gordon's face away.

Blood and bits of pink stuff spattered in all directions, and the next second Gordon slumped to the ground to fall splashing into the mud there.

Bobby stared at Gordon's body in horror, utterly transfixed. Gordon, his pal, had been killed and he'd witnessed it happen. The blood, the bits of pink stuff . . .

Another express train rushed through the sky overhead.

Cathy chewed the end of her pencil as she gazed at the blank sheet of paper in front of her. Should she or should she not tell Bobby that she was pregnant? For that she was had now been confirmed by the doctor.

On the one hand she knew how delighted he'd be to learn he was to become a father, on the other hand that knowledge might worry him in his present situation. And she didn't want him worried; she wanted him to have his mind totally on what he was doing.

Then again, if anything did happen, God forbid! at least he would have known that he had a child on the way, perhaps even his son and heir.

Cathy came out of her reverie when there was a rap on the outside door. Now who could that be? she wondered, getting up from the kitchen table where she'd been sitting. Maybe it was Winnie, round for a blether and cup of tea. Or Lily, or both.

It was neither. The woman on the landing was carrying a collecting can.

'Mrs McCracken, is it?'

The woman knew her name because it was on a brass plate by the side of the door. 'That's right.'

'I'm Mrs Ferguson and I'm collecting for the Nelsons at the top of the street. Do you know them by any chance?'

'To nod to in passing, but that's all I'm afraid. Why, what's happened to them?' Mrs Nelson was a funny wee body with a permanently grey face and gaggle of weans hanging round her skirt.

'Their furniture and belongings have been sequestrated by the landlord and them thrown into the street. I'm collecting from the neighbours to buy their things back for them.

Sequestrated! A fancy word for seized. That was awful. Cathy shivered; although it was summer it was a cold night, and a sharp wind was blowing up the close. Being pregnant she didn't want to stand at an open door in case she caught a chill.

'Come away in Mrs Ferguson and I'll get my purse.'

'That's kind of you, Mrs McCracken,' said Mrs Ferguson, following Cathy into the house.

'Shut that door behind you!' Cathy called back over her shoulder, which Mrs Ferguson did.

In the kitchen Cathy went straight to her purse lying on top of the sideboard, and opened it. 'So how did the Nelsons come to be sequestrated?' she asked.

'They fell behind with their rent and the landlord used that to exercise the Law of Urban Hypothec . . .'

'The law of what?' Cathy gasped.

'The Law of Urban Hypothec, and if ever there was an iniquitous law, it's that one. It's the law that allows the landlord to sequestrate their furniture and belongings, aye even the tools of a man's trade, and sell them off to help pay what's owing him.'

'I've heard of sequestration of course,' Cathy said, 'but this is the first time I've heard of . . . what did you call it again?'

Mrs Ferguson laughed. 'It is a mouthful right enough. The Law of Urban Hypothec.'

'Well, well, you learn something every day,' Cathy said,

shaking her head in amazement. Going to Mrs Ferguson she dropped her contribution into the can.

'Thank you very much,' Mrs Ferguson smiled.

'How did the Nelsons come to fall behind with their rent? Isn't he working?'

'He's been ill this past year, and lost his job on account of it nearly six months ago now. When the inevitable happened and they fell behind with their rent Riach their landlord had them slung out.'

'He's a hard man,' Cathy acknowledged. Riach was also her landlord.

'They were evicted this morning and he's already re-rented the house – and this is what sickens me – at a far higher rent than before. What he's asking is ridiculous but with the present chronic housing shortage, he's damned well got it.'

'So what's going to happen to the Nelsons if Nelson can't work?'

'He's got family in Inverness and it's his intention to return there. I'm hoping there's enough cash left after we get their things back to pay for their journey, otherwise it's a handcart and Shanks's pony for them.'

It was a sorry tale, Cathy thought. On impulse she reached back into her purse, extracted another coin and dropped that into the can.

'Thank you again,' Mrs Ferguson positively beamed.

'If you don't mind me asking, how did you get involved with the Nelsons? You're not from Purdon Street, are you?' Cathy probed, curious. She had seen Mrs Ferguson round and about though, she was certain of that .

'I belong to the Glasgow Women's Housing Association which Mrs Nelson came to once she realised the difficulty she was in. Unfortunately all we can do for her is this local collection.'

'The Glasgow Women's Housing Association,' Cathy mused; this was also new to her.

'Aye, we were set up by the Women's Labour League which in turn has close connections with the Independent Labour Party Housing Committee. You'll know of John Wheatley?'

'Yes indeed!' Cathy replied. Wheatley was a huge name in the Glasgow labour movement.

'He's a good friend and support to us, as is John Maclean.'

82

Cathy was impressed. The fiery John Maclean, sometimes known as the fighting domine, was a living legend. 'I've never heard him speak myself, but I do know him by reputation.'

'A great man,' Mrs Ferguson said, awe in her voice.

'A great man,' Cathy agreed.

'He believes in state housing, and argues most strongly in favour of it.'

'Is that a fact?' Now there was a novel idea, if not a revolutionary one. At least to Cathy it was.

'It's maybe a dream right now, but there's no reason why it shouldn't come about some time in the future. John Maclean has enormous vision. I see him myself like some Old Testament prophet – he's that sort of person.'

Cathy was fascinated, and thoroughly enjoying this conversation, 'Look, I was about to put the kettle on,' she lied. 'Would you have time for a cup of tea, and we can chat a bit longer?'

'Aye, well just a quick cup, mind. I have a lot of collecting left to do.'

When Mrs Ferguson did finally leave she left Cathy very taken with her and what she'd had to say, just as she'd been taken by Cathy. Mrs Ferguson made a mental note to remember Cathy McCracken.

Alone once more, Cathy picked up her pencil again and sat in front of the blank sheet of paper.

She wouldn't tell Bobby she was pregnant, she decided. And hoped that this was the right decision to make.

Bobby had never been so scared in his life; he was literally quaking with fear. He and Jack Smart were amongst a party sent out to repair breaks in the barbed wire, thus exposing themselves on the surface. It was dead of night of course; it would have been sheer suicide to be where they now were during the daytime, but that didn't mean that the Boche weren't wide awake and paying attention.

Sweat rolled down Bobby's face as he worked, sweat that was only partially from exertion. What he was doing was being made all the more difficult by the fact he was shaking so much.

Ping!

The moment Bobby heard that he knew precisely what it was. Someone had inadvertently let go of a length of taut wire which had then rushed back to spring onto the coil it was being taken from. The ping seemed to reverberate for miles.

Bobby's heart came into his mouth when the Very light blossomed in the night sky, and then another a few yards off.

He froze, as did Jack beside him. The two of them hoping against hope they'd be mistaken for the indeterminate outlines of shattered trees, of which there were a number around.

Rat a tat tat! Rat a tat tat! The German machine guns started chattering. Rat a tat tat! Rat a tat tat!

Somebody shrieked as he was hit, and at that instant the illumination of the Verys died.

Bobby threw himself flat, and stuck his head down as far as he could ram it. He heard Jack do the same.

They were called creeping barrages because that's what they were. Systematically the shells advanced over an area, and if you were on that area you could hear the explosions coming ever nearer and nearer.

Blast after blast washed over Bobby and Jack, while pieces of steel flew through the air in all directions, any one of which would cut you in half.

Bobby lay in the mud with Jack beside him, praying to live as the creeping explosions came closer and closer, and the pieces of steel whined and zinged.

And all the while the German machine guns chattered, slowly traversing from left to right, right to left searching . . . searching . . .

Bobby sat with his back against the wheel of an abandoned gun carriage. At long last he and the others of the 16th (S) Battalion of the Rifle Brigade had been pulled out of the salient and transported to a camp miles from the front where they were to have an entire week's rest and relaxation, after which they'd be returned to the salient.

How gloriously peaceful it was, Bobby thought, closing his eyes and letting the sun beat down on his face. His feet were actually *dry*, the first time they'd been so since the battalion had gone into the salient; the ubiquitous mud there saw to that.

Somebody close by began to sing, the familiar words bringing a smile to Bobby's face:

Landlord have you any good wine?
PARLEYVOO
Landlord have you any good wine?
PARLEYVOO
Landlord have you any good wine,
Fit for a soldier up the line?
INKY PINKY PARLEYVOO

Farmer have you a daughter fine?
PARLEYVOO
Farmer have you a daughter fine?
PARLEYVOO
Farmer have you a daughter fine,
Fit for a soldier up the line?
INKY PINKY PARLEYVOO

Then up the stairs and into bed
PARLEYVOO
Then up the stairs and into bed
PARLEYVOO
Then up the stairs and into bed,
Da-da-da-da-da-da-da-da
INKY PINKY PARLEYVOO

Bobby re-opened his eyes, picked up his rum ration, and sipped. Oh, but that was good, right enough! The rum was doled out daily, or supposed to be, by the Special Ration Department, the S.R.D., commonly known as Seldom Reaches Destination because the rum jars were so often destroyed by enemy fire before getting to the men to whom they were allocated.

And then, in his mind's eye, he saw it again. The German sniper's bullet hitting Gordon Manson just under the helmet, blowing the other side of Gordon's face away. Blood and bits of pink stuff spattering everywhere, and Gordon slumping to the ground to fall splashing into glutinous grey caramel.

Bobby sucked in a breath, and held it. Other moments and incidents from the salient flashed through his mind making him go, despite the sun still beating down, cold as an arctic winter inside.

Get a grip! he told himself. *GET A GRIP!* he screamed inside his head.

Taking out Cathy's letters that had been waiting for him he began at the earliest dated and read them all through again. He'd have given anything to have been home in Glasgow with her, the pair of them sitting round the fire as they did at nights, talking over the day's events, each content just to be in the other's company.

He could see her just as if she was there beside him, and seem to smell her also. See her, smell her, hear her voice.

He put her letters back in a tunic pocket, then took up the paper and pencil he'd readied with which to reply to her. Placing the paper on a tin tray to give it a firm backing, the tray on his lap, he then started to write.

Dearest darling Cathy,

I miss you terribly. You've no idea how much I think about you all the time, every single minute of the day. I'm well and so is everyone else with the exception of poor Gordon Manson who . . .

He'd intended keeping a stiff upper lip and the letter lighthearted, but that went by the board as soon as he began to write. It all came pouring out as he told Cathy what life and conditions were like in the salient.

'I'm sorry Cathy, I really am,' said Curley the foreman. 'But you know that's always been the rule. You can collect your final pay packet this Friday.'

She'd been expecting to be let go, as she'd been well aware, as Curley had pointed out, that the firm always dismissed pregnant women, and because of that had taken a leaf out of her sister Lily's book and gone to lengths to disguise her pregnancy. And that had worked too, for quite some time, but in the end it had become impossible to conceal her bump and she'd had to admit to Curley that she was pregnant when he'd asked her.

'It's a crying shame so it is, but there you are, there's nothing I can do about it. I would if I could. I hope you know that.'

'I do, Mr Curley. The last thing I would do is hold it against you personally. I fully appreciate you're only implementing company policy.'

Curley was hating this. To dismiss a woman whose husband

86

was away fighting in the war was scandalous. Outrageous! 'How is that man of yours anyway? Still well I hope?'

She had no intention of mentioning the terrible letters she'd been receiving, letters that had kept her awake night after night. 'He's fine Mr Curley.'

'Still at Ypres?'

She nodded. 'Still at Ypres,' she confirmed softly.

He thought of the recent casualty figures he'd read in the newspapers, and the new name that was beginning to be mentioned synonomously with Ypres, that of Passchendaele. The latter was a village standing on the summit of the slopes surrounding Ypres: slopes the troops fighting on them called hills.

'How's your son?' Cathy asked.

'He's fine too, I'm happy to say,' Curley replied. His son was with the Black Watch and also at the front, though not at Ypres.

'That's good,' Cathy said.

He placed a hand on her arm. 'If there's anything I can do in the future you only have to get in touch, lass. And I mean that.'

A hint of tears came into her eyes. 'You're a gentleman, Mr Curley, one of the best. All the girls here think that.'

'I'm sorry, Cathy,' he repeated.

'Don't worry, I'll get by.'

'Aye, of course you will.'

Of course she would, Cathy reassured herself.

Cathy slipped on her coat, the last time she'd ever do so at Mavor & Coulson. It was Friday night, the end of the week and end of her job.

'Right then, are we all ready for that drink?' cried Christine Drysdale gaily. She'd lost her cousin the previous September 22nd when the cruiser *Cressy* he was sailing on had been sunk by a German U-boat. Two other cruisers, the *Aboukir* and *Hogue* had been sunk by the same U-boat at the same time.

'Ready, we're gasping!' Babs Tait answered, which raised a laugh.

It had been arranged a few days previously that all Cathy's close chums at Mavor & Coulson would take her to the pub for a farewell drink.

'Are we for the off then?' Lorna McQueen queried, glancing about.

'Last one in the boozer buys the first round of bevy! Cathy excepted!' Kate Binnie shouted, which caused an immediate stampede for the door.

The girls were all laughing and joking as they streamed out into the street.

Cathy stopped to stare back at Mavor & Coulson where she'd worked since leaving school. So much had changed so quickly. The war, Bobby joining the army, her getting pregnant, and now losing her job. What else lay in store for her? she wondered. And how was she going to cope with no job and Bobby only earning a shilling a day?

Anxiety filled her, and the beginnings of panic.

She struggled to control her feelings, telling herself it was no good to anyone, least of all herself, if she went to pieces.

The anxiety drained away, the beginnings of panic ebbed. And she was her old buoyant self again.

Smiling, she turned her back on Mavor & Coulson and hurried after the girls.

On the salient the tunnelling companies were the élite. Mainly civilians who had been hurriedly drafted in from coal mines or from construction work in the sewers, they were paid the princely sum of six shillings a day.

Below and beyond the trenches, deep under the earth, twenty-one tunnels were being slowly driven forward towards the Germans on the ridge. Down there it was quiet in the dripping gloom. The men worked silently, and spoke in whispers. As the tunnels gradually lengthened they piled the sandbags of excavated clay on to bogies wth rubber wheels which could be silently slid back to the shaft along wooden rails. Only the breath of a murmured remark, the dull scraping away at the clay, the drip of water, the faint hum of the dynamo that powered the pumps, the fans and the dim electric lamps disturbed the silence.

All the time the men were listening. For the Germans were tunnelling too, honeycombing the earth with passages that splayed out from a central gallery in a dozen directions, searching for the British tunnels they knew full well must be there.

And the purpose of the British tunnelling. To thoroughly mine Hill 60, a particular thorn in the British flesh on the salient, and blow the entire hill, and all the pillboxes and men on that hill, to Kingdom Come!

It was late afternoon, the rain teeming down – which made the mud underfoot even worse than it was normally – when several tunnellers rushed past Bobby and his pals in the direction of The Cut. The Cut was an old railway line, the bottom of which was a mass of corpses and everything you could think of, that ran through the British positions and into the German ones.

'I wonder what's up?' Colin Baker said to Bobby, who shrugged.

'Commotion of some kind,' said Bill Coltraine. 'Listen!'

The pals did. And yes, Bill was right. There was some kind of commotion.

One of the tunnellers reappeared. 'You lads wouldn't have rope handy would you?' he asked.

Bobby and his pals didn't, but another group of the 16th further along did, the rope left over from repair work carried out on the trench wall.

'You should see this!' the tunneller said as he hurried back past Bobby and Co.

'See what?' Bobby called out, but the tunneller was already gone.

'Come on, let's have a gander,' Tim Murchison said, starting after the tunneller. The rest of the pals followed him.

The pals came to the side of The Cut where they found the tunnellers lying flat, all holding onto the end of the rope which had been slung into The Cut. From The Cut itself came a frantic bellowing.

Bobby and the others crawled up to the edge of The Cut and peered down into it. The tunneller who was doing the bellowing was staggering this way and that, stumbling and falling over the gruesome contents at the bottom of The Cut.

'He's drunk as a lord,' Jack Smart said.

'Must have somehow managed to save up his rum ration,' Bobby said, wondering how the man, considering the precautions taken, had managed to do that. Because the pitmen had a habit of saving up the rum ration they were given every time they came off shift, an officer was always detailed to ensure that the tunnellers drank their ration there and then.

'Drunk and fallen into The Cut,' Tim Murchison said.

'Why in hell don't the Germans shoot him?' Colin Baker queried, for the drunken pitman was in full view of the enemy.

At that point they were joined by a number of other soldiers who'd come to see what was happening.

'Grab the rope so we can haul you out you silly booger!' one of the exasperated tunnellers called to their mate.

'Why don't you slide down there and help Charlie?' another tunneller suggested jokingly to the one who'd just spoken.

'Oh aye? Well, I'll tell 'ee what, Fred Gaddas, I'll slide down and help Charlie if 'ee slides down wi' me. Done?'

Fred Gaddas grinned, 'Does 'ee mean that, George?'

'I does.'

'Then we'd both be bigger silly boogers than Charlie, and that's a fact. I'm stopping here thank 'ee very much.'

'Why don't the Boche shoot him?' Colin Baker asked again.

Bobby gazed over at the German positions where no one could be seen. But they were there all right, and undoubtedly watching Charlie in The Cut. 'Maybe they're enjoying the light relief,' he replied to Colin. It was the only answer he could think of that made sense.

More tunnellers appeared to join those already there. It was quickly explained to them what the situation was.

Charlie bellowed his loudest yet, his arms windmilling in the air. Down he tumbled, to land flat on his back.

From the German positions a cheer went up.

Charlie came onto his hands and knees, tried to stand but slipped again. This time he landed face down.

George, Fred Gaddas and some of the others tugged on the dangling rope, making it shake and jump from side to side, for they didn't think Charlie had seen it yet.

'Over 'ere Charlie! Over 'ere you daft hap'orth!' George yelled.

'I 'ears 'ee but I can't sees 'ee!' Charlie yelled back.

'We can see you Tommee,' a German voice mocked.

'They think it's pantomime time,' Jack Smart said, having arrived at the same conclusion Bobby had shortly before.

'Who are you?' Charlie yelled back.

'My name's Wolfgang. Come on up here and have some schnapps. Do you like schnapps, Tommee?'

'You're a bloody Kraut, you bastard!' Charlie shrieked, waving a fist in the direction Wolfgang's voice had come from.

'And you are one very pissed Tommee.' Wolfgang answered. A roar of laughter went up from the unseen Germans.

'Over this way! Here, Charlie!' Fred Gaddas shouted.

Charlie swivelled round, nearly fell again, but managed to recover his balance to face the dangling rope about twenty yards away. 'Who's that?' he demanded, swaying madly from side to side.

'Fred Gaddas. Now grab hold of this rope and we'll pull you out before your friend Wolfgang has a change of heart and puts a bullet through you.'

Charlie bent over and picked up something which he then brandished aloft. 'Hey Fred, look what I found!' The object he was holding was a human skull.

'Alas poor Yorick, I did know thee once!' Wolfgang called out.

Charlie glanced over his shoulder at the German positions. 'Was he a mate of yours then, this Yorup?'

'No he wasn't, Tommee. And the name was Yorick.'

'So how the f . . . do you know that?'

'Shakespeare, Tommee. Shakespeare.'

Charlie appeared to be about to make some caustic reply when suddenly he was sick, the vomit arcing out of his mouth to fall splashing on the ground. He dropped the skull which shattered into pieces.

George the tunneller groaned.

Throwing up sobered Charlie somewhat; he now realised where he was and the danger he was in. Arms windmilling again, he made a beeline for the rope.

On reaching the rope Charlie grabbed hold of it, tried to climb up but was unable to.

'Just hold on and we'll pull,' Fred Gaddas shouted down to him.

Charlie wrapped the rope round his right wrist and hung on for dear life. The tunnellers at the top of The Cut heaved and he began to be hauled upwards.

Up and up went Charlie till at last grasping hands grabbed hold of him and pulled him over the edge of The Cut, and out of sight of the Germans.

'Goodbyee Tommee! Auf Weidersehen!'

Bobby and his pals laughed all the way back to their trench. The only laugh any of them had while in the salient.

*

'Both dead?' Cathy repeated, her father John having just broken the news to her.

John nodded.

Cathy looked from her father's face to her mother's, then to Lily. Lily's husband Dougie was also present but he had never met either Big Tosh or Wee Tosh.

'Do we know how?' she asked.

'Aye. A letter from their C.O. arrived only hours after the two telegrams. It seems Craig was in a party sent into No Man's Land to try and capture a German prisoner for interrogation. Things went wrong for them and Craig was badly wounded. Only one member of the party, also wounded, managed to get back to report what had happened. When Ronnie heard that Craig was lying out there wounded he went over the top after his brother.' John paused, and swallowed hard. He then went on. 'Apparently Ronnie found Craig, hoisted him onto his back, and started back for their trench. Unfortunately they were spotted and machine-gunned. They died together.'

'Even though they fought like cat and dog they were aye close as could be,' Winnie added softly. 'And if it had been the other way round you can be sure Craig would have gone after Ronnie; that's the way they were with one another.'

'How are Aunt Evelyn and Uncle Duncan taking it?' Cathy asked, blinking back the tears.

'Not so well I'm afraid,' Winnie replied. Evelyn was her older sister.

'I'll go and see them. Pay my respects.'

'They'd appreciate that,' Winnie said.

Cathy thought of her cousins Big Tosh and Wee Tosh, remembering the day she and Bobby had bumped into them coming out of the jeweller's shop having just bought her engagement ring, and again at their wedding when the two brothers hadn't been talking to one another. Now they were both gone, and she'd never see either of them ever again.

'What a terrible pair,' Cathy said.

'A terrible pair,' John agreed, a choke in his voice. He took out his handkerchief and blew his nose. Surreptitiously, hoping the others wouldn't notice, he wiped his eyes.

Lily glanced at Dougie, and not for the first time thanked the Lord that he worked in a shipyard where, as an integral part of the war effort, he was obliged to remain. There would be no Western Front, or warship, for her Dougie.

'Well then, let's get down to you, young lady,' John stated, addressing Cathy. 'What now you've lost your job?'

'You can come and stay here if you want,' Winnie said quickly. 'We'd love to have you.'

Cathy gave her parents a thin smile. 'I know you would, and that I'm welcome. But where would I sleep? And the baby when it comes along? I can hardly sleep in the bedroom with Dougie, Lily and their wean.' Lily had announced she was pregnant as soon as it had been acceptably possible after her wedding.

'You and the bairn will sleep in the kitchen here, as your da and I will continue to do. It'll be a bit cramped to what we're used to I must admit, but we'll manage somehow.'

Cathy shook her head. 'I appreciate the offer, Ma and perhaps it'll get to the stage where I have to take you up on it. But in the meantime, as long as it's humanly possible, I want to try and keep my own house. I want it to be there, as it is, when Bobby comes home again.'

The two women stared into each other's eyes, and Winnie saw what lay behind the spoken words. To Cathy the house was a symbol; as long as she had it for Bobby to come back to then he would. Silly perhaps, and totally illogical, but it gave Cathy strength. And that was important.

Winnie nodded. 'I understand, lass.'

Cathy could see that her mother did.

She then changed the subject, and from there on it was all talk – John and Dougie left in disgust after a while and went off to the pub – about the expected babies, and baby things.

Later that evening Cathy was halfway down Purdon Street, walking home from her parents, when a voice hailed her. 'And how are you Mrs McCracken?' It was Mrs Kelly, her neighbour from over-by.

'I can't complain. And yourself?'

'Mustn't grumble. There's no point to it, it doesn't get you anywhere!' And having said that Mrs Kelly gave a gutsy laugh.

'Well if you'll excuse me I'll . . .'

'Hang on a wee. I hear you lost your job. That's a crying shame so it is. And you with your man off at the front.'

'Yes,' Cathy agreed.

'A bad business.'

'You can say that again.'

'So what are you going to do now?' Mrs Kelly probed, her expression one of genuine concern.

'Look around for another job. What else can I do?'

Mrs Kelly looked at Cathy's rounded belly, then up into her face. 'Do you mind that conversation I had with you all that while ago about lodgers? That could be the answer to your problem.'

'Lodgers . . .' Cathy mused, not at all keen on the idea, immediately resistant to it.

'Archie and I have three now. Mr McDuff, whom I mentioned to you before, and a Mr Pettigrew and Mr Guthrie. They all share the bedroom and get on just dandy together. And of course Archie and I now get three times as much money as we did when we only had Mr McDuff.'

'Very lucrative for you,' Cathy said.

A frown flitted across Mrs Kelly's face; she didn't know what lucrative meant. 'Aye, right enough,' she replied, momentarily thrown off her stride.

Then she regained her composure, affable once more. 'I know of one very pleasant chap desperate for digs. Would you like me to send him round to you?'

'A man!' Cathy exclaimed. 'I couldn't have a man to stay with me while Bobby was away. What would people say? No, but I might consider a woman. If she was the right woman that is.'

'I could ask about if you'd like?'

'But it would have to be someone nice. Someone I could get on with.'

'Aye, of course. That would be necessary.'

She wasn't at all keen, Cathy thought to herself. But as Mrs Kelly had pointed out it could be the answer, or one answer, to her problem. One thing was certain, she was going to have an awful lot of trouble finding another job in her present condition. And then what happened after the baby arrived?

Suddenly she was filled with anxiety and the beginnings of panic just as she'd been outside Mavor & Coulson the day before.

Oh, why did she have to be in this predicament! Why did there have to be a war, and why had Bobby had to feel the necessity to join up! Why! Why! Then she realised Mrs Kelly had resumed talking.

'I'll send someone round as soon as I can then. And I hope you don't think I'm interfering – I'm only trying to help.'

'I know that, Mrs Kelly and I thank you.'

'It'll be a sad day when we can't be neighbourly to one another. Isn't that right?'

'Yes indeed,' Cathy agreed.

'Cheerio for now then!'

'Cheerio!'

She hadn't really had a choice, Cathy told herself as she continued down the street.

'Mrs McCracken?'

The speaker was a balding sandy-haired man about forty years of age, Cathy judged. He had a freckly face, as sandy-haired folk often do, and a neat moustache. He was wearing a rather old-fashioned suit and holding a soft hat in one hand. He was doing his best to smile, but the smile wasn't coming off because of the worry behind it.

'Yes?' Cathy queried, wondering who on earth he was. She'd never seen him before.

'My name's Taylor and I got your name from Mrs Kelly across the street.' He held up his free hand in a placatory gesture. 'Now I know you don't want a male lodger as you feel it might not be right, but I was wondering . . .' He shifted uncomfortably. 'Do you think we could discuss the matter over a cup of tea? I'll happily take you to a teashop. It's just you see . . . I really am in desperate straits. I've been lucky enough to have been sleeping in a Salvation Army hostel since coming to Glasgow a fortnight ago, but the limited time I'm allowed there because of the demand is up after tomorrow night and despite looking everywhere I still haven't found digs.' He screwed the rim of his hat into a tight roll. 'If perhaps I could tell you something about myself. That I'm a married man, with two children. That I . . .'

It was a verbal onslaught, Cathy thought. And one that touched her. There was something rather pathetic about this Mr Taylor. Pathetic and safe.

'Well, we won't bother with the teashop,' she interjected, stopping him in mid-flow. 'Why don't you come in and I'll put the kettle on? We can discuss the matter inside.'

'Oh, thank you! Thank you!'

'That doesn't mean to say I'm promising anything, mind.'

'No, of course not.'

She closed the door behind him, then led the way into the kitchen.

'Your husband is at the front, I believe,' Taylor said.

'Yes, at Ypres.'

He shook his head, and clucked. 'I also tried to join up, but they wouldn't have me. Flat feet and varicose veins.'

Cathy wasn't quite sure what to reply to that, so she didn't. 'Please sit down Mr Taylor,' she said instead.

'Thank you.' He looked about him. 'Any preferences? I wouldn't wish to sit where I shouldn't.'

She knew he was meaning he didn't want to upset her by sitting in Bobby's chair. That was considerate of him, and sensitive of him too. 'Any chair you like,' she smiled.

As she was filling the kettle he said,' I have a croft just outside Lochbuie on the island of Mull. I keep some sheep, grow vegetables, and supplement that with a bit of fishing. The living isn't exactly a good one, but we do make ends meet. When the army turned me down I thought of coming to Glasgow to work, work being plentiful here while the war's on. Kirsty, that's my wife, can easily run the croft on her own, and what I save from my job here will pay for a few things we badly need. Or, to put it bluntly, I'm trying to take advantage of the demand for workers to provide extra for my family.'

'Well I don't see any wrong in that,' Cathy replied. 'And you've found a job?'

'No bother at all. I'm working in a steel foundry as a labourer. It's hard graft but the pay's way beyond what I'm used to bringing in. The only snag is the digs.'

'I see,' said Cathy. 'And how old are your children?'

'I've got a boy and a girl. Hamish is eleven, and a fine strapping lad he is too. A real help round the croft. And Catriona is eight.'

Catriona! Cathy immediately thought of the book through in the bedroom. 'Catriona is a lovely name,' she replied.

'Aye, it was my mother's.'

'Have you read the novel by Robert Louis Stevenson?'

'Na, na I . . .' he cleared his throat. 'Truth is Mrs McCracken, I can't read. And neither can my Kirsty. But the children can. Hamish reads quick as a trout darting down a burn, and Catriona is coming on at it very well indeed.'

Cathy set out two teacups and saucers. 'Would you be wanting meals with your digs?'

'A bite of breakfast would be enough. There's a canteen at the foundry where I can have my dinner and tea. Nor would I be home till latish every night as I'll be doing all the overtime I can get hold of.'

'What about weekends?'

'We're on a seven-day-week so Saturday and Sunday will be just the same as weekdays.'

Cathy thought of her neighbours; that a worry. Ach, what the hell! They knew her circumstances and how close she and Bobby were. She doubted they would think she was up to any hanky-panky. They'd know the idea was absurd.

'If I did consider you as a lodger, Mr Taylor . . .' she saw his eyes light up with hope, 'what would you be willing to pay?'

The figure he named came as a shock. It was far higher than she'd have thought. And made the idea of taking in a lodger very tempting indeed.

'And if I may make a point, Mrs McCracken?'

'Go on?'

He went back to twisting the rim of his hat. 'If you do take in a lady lodger you won't get nearly as much. Male wages being so much higher than female.'

She hadn't thought of that. And of course he was quite right. She would probably have to take in two female lodgers to get what he was offering.

'I'll be no trouble round the house, really. And I'm very neat and tidy,' he went on.

She smiled to see the beseeching expression on his face. But what about Bobby? What was Bobby going to say when he came home and found another man living in his house?

He was going to get one hell of a surprise, she decided. One hell of a surprise.

Mr Taylor moved in the following evening.

*

Cathy paused to wipe the sweat from her forehead. She tucked a few stray strands of hair behind an ear, then leant on her mop for a breather.

It was night-time and she was in the local school whose janitor had hired her as a cleaner. The janitor was old and his wife, who'd done the cleaning, had died several years previously. Recently he'd had trouble finding a cleaner as the women who'd normally have applied for the job preferred working in the armaments factories where they could earn considerably more than they would cleaning the school. Because of this the janitor had agreed to hire Cathy for the simple reason she was the only applicant for the job.

Cathy would have been the first to admit the wage was rotten, but it was a wage. Between it and what Mr Taylor was giving her she was getting by, if only just. There would be no new clothes or shoes for a long while to come; it was taking all her time to keep a roof over her head and food in her mouth. (She would have stinted herself on food if it wasn't for the fact she was terrified of damaging the baby.)

As for baby clothes, she'd been exceptionally lucky there. Winnie had happened on a whole stack of them at a jumble sale, and bought the lot for a song. Good clothes too, only slightly patched and darned.

And she'd also acquired a pile of nappies from the same jumble sale. These were not in such good condition as the clothes, but they'd do nonetheless. The baby clothes and nappies had been a present from Winnie and John, for which she'd been extremely grateful.

And from one of the neighbours in her ma and da's street had come a cot and hair-mattress. These too had been gratefully received.

With a weary sigh Cathy stirred herself, and resumed mopping.

Bobby had never known rain like it. For the past three days and nights it had sheeted down non-stop. As someone had remarked, it was as if some malevolent deity had opened a tap in the heavens.

The water falling from the sky on to the lower slopes of the ridges (where the 16th and other troops, a large contingent of Canadians numbered among the latter, were grimly holding on to their ragged front line) was augmented by water pouring from the high ground in front of them, in cascades that turned every stream into a torrent, every ditch into a water-course, and every trench into a creek of mud and effluent. It soaked into the earth and seeped up again from below as the Tommies who found themselves on open ground shovelled into the mud and threw up breastworks of slush for cover.

In spite of the weather – or perhaps they were trying to turn it to their advantage – the Germans had come out of their concrete strongholds and, supported by devastating machine-gun fire and terrible shelling, had gone on the offensive.

Besides being wet through Bobby was bone tired, not having had a wink of sleep for the past forty-eight hours. And what he'd had then had only been an hour and a half's shuteye.

Hell, Bobby thought wearily to himself. That was what the salient was, hell on earth. If there was a real hell it surely couldn't be worse than this. Nothing could be.

'I'm starving,' Bill Coltraine complained beside Bobby. They hadn't eaten for two days either. The supply wagons hadn't been able to get into the salient, and what rations were coming in were having to be carried. None of these rations had so far reached Bobby and his pals, who were in a position slightly to the east of Poelcapelle. If the visibility had been clear, and they'd been able to clamber up out of their trench, Bobby and his pals would have been able to see what remained of the village of Passchendaele in the distance. Passchendaele was the cork in the bottle, the taking of which the British High Command was becoming more and more convinced would allow them to burst out of the salient to advance over the plain beyond.

Someone grunted, and fell over. When Bobby looked he saw it was Sergeant MacDonald. Then he was ducking as machine-gun bullets tore into the trench wall only a couple of inches above where his head had been.

'Is the sergeant dead?' Colin Baker asked the two men crouching over MacDonald.

'As mutton,' was the grim reply.

The two men returned to their posts. Sergeant MacDonald would have to lie where he was. Perhaps, if things quietened down, they might get the body out later. But that was unlikely. As had happened to so many others the probability was that the sergeant's body would become part and parcel of the defence system.

Bobby stared down the trench at where a skeletal foot stuck out of the trench wall. Whose foot had that been? he idly wondered. Whoever, the poor bugger was at rest now. For him the horrors of the salient were over.

'Germans!' someone shrieked, and the next moment Bobby was engaged in hand to hand combat with a German soldier who'd seemingly materialised out of nowhere.

The German lunged with his bayonet. Bobby parried that, then shot the German in the chest. As the man staggered back, Bobby finished him with a bayonet thrust.

Then another was at him, this one only a boy. The boy uttered a cry of jubilation as he hooked Bobby's rifle out of Bobby's grasp, the rifle spinning away. Bobby shrank against the trench wall as the boy raised his rifle to fire.

Bang!

I'm dead! Bobby thought. But he wasn't, for it wasn't the boy who had fired, but Jack Smart. The boy's eyes were wide open in amazement as he slid to the ground.

Bobby made to grab for his rifle, but then there was another German between him and it. He snatched up a trench shovel instead.

Steel rang against steel as Bobby warded off the jabbing bayonet. Somehow, he wasn't aware how he managed it, he got himself directly up against the German, the German's rifle momentarily swivelled round the other way. Bobby seized his opportunity. The edge of his shovel sliced into the German's throat, almost decapitating the man.

Three of the Germans did for 2nd Lieutenant Kidd, the three of them bayoneting him simultaneously. Before he died the 2nd Lieutenant shot one of his assailants in the face.

Fighting was going on up and down the trench, into other trenches, onto open ground that was now relatively safe because the Germans had temporarily ceased machine-gunning and shelling round that area in case they hit their own men.

Bill Coltraine went down, shot in the shoulder. But luck was with him; the German who'd shot him didn't have the chance to complete the job with either bullet or bayonet before being caught up in another hand to hand, this time with a Canadian.

A huge Canuck, as the Canadians were called, with arms the width of tree-trunks, wrestled with an equally large German. In the end the Canadian won, stabbing his opponent to death with a Bowie knife.

And then, as suddenly as it had begun, it was over, those Germans still alive disappearing as if they'd been nothing more than apparitions, or figments of the imagination. Within a minute the machine-gunning and shelling had resumed.

Bobby sagged against the trench wall and sucked in breath after breath. He was still alive. He'd survived. Then he remembered Bill whom he'd seen go down.

Bill was wearing a Cheshire grin that threatened to split his face in half.

'A Blighty one!' Bill exclaimed gleefully to Bobby. 'I got a Blighty one!'

Bill's right arm was dangling uselessly by his side, blood still oozing from the wound. Later he would find out that the shoulder bone had been shattered.

'You jammy sod!' Bobby grinned at his pal.

Colin Baker dropped down beside Bobby and Bill. 'You all right?' Bobby asked him. Colin nodded.

'I got a Blighty one!' Bill said to Colin, and laughed. A laugh that had more than a tinge of hysteria to it.

'Where're Jack and Tim?' Colin queried glancing about.

Neither were to be seen, and then Jack came round a corner and into sight. 'Can't find Tim!' he called out.

And then, as one, they heard it. 'Help! For Christ's sake help!' The voice was unmistakably Tim Murchison's.

Leaving Bill trying to struggle to his feet Bobby, Jack and Colin raced in the direction Tim's voice had come from. They didn't have far to go, they found him in a huge shellhole, up to his waist in mud and sinking fast. There were dead men of both sides all around the hole.

'Rope! Somebody get a rope!' Bobby yelled, mind flashing back to the pitman who'd been hauled out of The Cut.

'Oh God save me! Save me!' Tim pleaded, scrabbling at the mud, trying to pull himself closer to the side of the shellhole. But all he was succeeding in doing was making himself sink even faster.

Bobby unclipped his bayonet, sheathed it, and planted a foot

101

right on the edge of the shellhole. 'Hold me', he ordered Jack, and when Jack had him firmly by the arm, he stretched out the rifle as far as he was able. But it was no use; the tip of the muzzle wasn't within Tim's reach.

Bobby brought himself back onto two feet. 'Where's that rope?' he muttered. But there was no sign of Colin, who'd run off to try and find one.

'Don't thrash about! Try to be as still as you can,' Jack urged Tim, knowing that was far easier said than done.

A shell exploded nearby, and a streak of blood splashed across Bobby's cape. The shell had claimed at least one victim.

'Please God, please! Don't let me drown in this mud! Please!' Tim gibbered, face turned up into the driving rain.

Others of the 16th were milling around. Someone had a section of duckboard which he attempted to reach Tim with, but that also was too short.

'There must be a rope! There must be!' Bobby said, glancing about him, looking for Colin coming back with one. But there was no Colin, and no rope.

'Oh Mummy, Daddy, Mummy, Daddy,' Tim mumbled, starting to cry. He had now sunk to just below his shoulders.

'Keep those hands free!' Jack instructed. For if the hands got trapped there was no hope.

Tim's eyes – eyes that were bulging in their sockets from fear – locked on Bobby's. Bobby wanted to turn away, break that eye contact. But he felt he couldn't. He knew then that Tim was going to die. And in a most gruesome fashion.

'Shoot me!' Tim begged Bobby. 'Go on, shoot me!'

Bobby swallowed hard.

There was a horrible glup! as a pocket of gas broke through the mud which imprisoned Tim, mud that was now up to his neck.

Colin reappeared, to come slipping and sliding to a halt beside Bobby, Jack and the others who were watching. He didn't have a rope with him.

'Please? One of you please?' Tim implored those staring at him, combined tears and rain washing down his face.

'I can't,' Bobby whispered, more to himself than for anyone else to hear. 'I just can't.'

'Please!' Tim shrieked as the mud reached his chin.

It was one of the Canadians who put Tim out of his agony,

several having now joined those of the 16th at the shellhole within the past few seconds. A solitary shot spat out, and Tim's face flopped forward onto the mud. His arms, which he'd been holding aloft, splashed when they fell.

A circle of blood widened round what remained of the back of Tim's head, blood that quickly became rust-coloured as it mingled with the mud.

The head vanished. Then the left arm, followed by the right. All that remained was the rust-coloured stain of blood.

Bobby turned to Jack. 'I couldn't do it. I couldn't,' he choked.

'Neither could I.'

They thanked the Canadian, then returned to Bill who hadn't been able to follow them, having passed out cold when trying to do so.

A little later the rations finally arrived. The four remaining pals divvied up Tim's rations between them.

Cathy laid Bobby's letter on her lap, and put a hand over her mouth. It was the third time she'd read the letter since its arrival with that afternoon's post.

Tim dead, and Bill Coltraine wounded. She wished she could feel more sympathy for Tim, but she couldn't. If it hadn't been for him her Bobby wouldn't be out there. He'd be home here, safe with her. Damn Tim Murchison! He'd got all that he deserved.

Instantly she was contrite. That was going too far. No one deserved to die as he'd done. But it was his own fault that he'd been there to be killed.

She glanced down at the letter again. For someone who'd claimed not to be much of a letter-writer Bobby certainly had a way with words. He was able to describe places and events so that you could actually hear and see them.

She shuddered. What an awful spot the Ypres salient must be. Hell on earth, Bobby repeatedly referred to it as. And she believed him.

She started when there was a rap on the outside door. That would be the factor whom she was waiting to pay before going off to work.

Crossing to the mantelpiece she picked up the money she'd placed there, and answered the door.

'Evening, Mrs McCracken,' said Bryce the factor.

Cathy heard the buzz of voices from the downstairs close, some clearly angry. Now what was going on?

'Here you are then,' she said, handing him the rent.

Bryce accepted the money, carefully counted it, then dropped it into the leather bag he was wearing slung round his shoulders beneath his coat. Cathy waited for him to tick her name off in his book, the tick confirming she'd paid for that week.

'I'm afraid the rent's going up,' he said quietly as he made his tick.

'Eh?'

'Instructions from Mr Riach. Starting next Friday your rent is up twenty per cent.'

For a moment she thought he was joking then she realised it was no joke. He was in deadly earnest. 'Twenty per cent!' she exploded.

'Aye, that's right. All Mr Riach's rents are going up by the same amount.'

'That's ridiculous!'

'I'm sorry, but I don't make the rules. I just carry them out.'

'Are you sure about that?' she demanded, suspicious that this might be a ploy on his part to cream off extra for himself. But then common sense told her otherwise. Twenty per cent was such a massive increase Riach wouldn't have let him get away with it.

'Absolutely certain,' he replied, meeting her gaze.

'But . . . it's so much!'

'I can't argue with you there, Mrs McCracken. But it's an owner's market, I'm afraid. If you can't pay the new rent there are those who will. You will be officially notified by mail, and told the precise amount of what will be due, before next Friday.' And with that he left Cathy and chapped next door.

Cathy's neighbours, the McLeishes, were as incredulous to hear the news as she'd been.

'That's highway robbery!' Mr McLeish protested.

'It's entirely legal,' Bryce countered flatly.

'Riach won't get away with this, so he won't!' Mr McLeish thundered.

'Go and see him and tell him that.'

Mr McLeish immediately backed down. 'He must realise we can't afford that amount.'

'If you can't, then get out.'

'To where, man?'

'That's your problem.' Bryce moved away from the McLeishes to knock on the third door on the landing.

Cathy closed her own door, and leant back against it. A twenty per cent increase in her rent!

She was absolutely stunned.

Chapter 4

Cathy recognised the woman straight away. 'Hello, Mrs Ferguson,' she smiled.

'And hello to you, Mrs McCracken. Can I come in and have a wee word?'

'Of course.'

Cathy ushered Mrs Ferguson through to the kitchen. 'What can I do for you?' She'd already noted that on this occasion Mrs Ferguson wasn't carrying a collecting can.

'It's more of what I can perhaps do for you.'

Cathy raised an eyebrow. 'Oh aye?'

'I've come about Riach and your rent.'

Cathy swore, something she seldom did. 'I'm sorry Mrs Ferguson I . . .'

'Listen, enough of these formalities. I'm Jean and you're . . .?'

'Cathy.'

'Jean and Cathy it is then.'

'Right, Jean.'

'Right, Cathy.'

They both laughed.

'Will I put the kettle on?' Cathy suggested.

'A cup of tea would go down very nicely indeed.'

Jean eyed Cathy's bump as Cathy filled the kettle. 'I didn't realise you were expecting. How long have you got to go?'

'Two months.'

'And do you have a preference, boy or girl?'

'Not for myself, Jean. I'll be happy whichever as long as the wean is fit and healthy. But for Bobby's sake I rather hope it's a boy.'

Jean nodded that she understood. 'And how is your husband?'

A cloud passed over Cathy's face. 'Still in the Ypres salient, though there's every chance his battalion will be pulled out of there soon and shipped home to Britain. They need to be brought back to strength having lost so many men. They've had sixty something per cent killed and wounded to date.'

Jean let out a soft sigh. 'The whole thing is such utter madness.'

'I couldn't agree more.'

'All those bonny lads . . .' Jean trailed off, and shook her head. Her voice turned vehement. 'And now this business over the rents. Every landlord in Partick has hiked his rents up. Talk about blood-sucking capitalists! Every one of them should be hung, drawn and quartered.'

'Very slowly,' Cathy said, which brought a razored smile of agreement to Jean's face.

'Aye, right enough. Very slowly indeed.'

Cathy wished that she had some teabread or fancy cakes in, that she could offer her visitor, but such luxuries had been out of the question for a long while now.

'You mentioned you were with Riach, last time we spoke.'

'That's correct.'

'I'm with McAusland myself. He owns nearly all of Partickhill where I am. The man must already be a millionaire, but he's not content with that. Not him, the greedy, grasping pig wants even more.'

'How much has your rent gone up by?' Cathy inquired.

'Twenty per cent, same as yours. All the Partick landlords have acted as one and raised their rents by the same amount and from the same date. It's different over in Govan where the increases vary from landlord to landlord.'

'Are the increases only in Partick and Govan?'

'Parkhead, Ibrox and St Rollox are also affected. And it's my belief that all of us are only the start. Because if these landlords get away with it you can bet your boots the others will quickly follow suit.'

'Aye,' Cathy agreed. That seemed logical.

'But that's only if they *do* get away with it.'

Cathy stopped to stare at Jean. 'What did you have in mind?'

'We in the Glasgow Women's Housing Association have decided to try and organise a resistance to these rises.'

'And how would you do that?'

'By having a rent strike.'

Cathy was intrigued. 'A rent strike?'

'If we can organise a massed refusal to pay the extra then the landlords will just have to go and whistle for their money. They can hardly throw everyone out onto the street. That would be cutting off their nose to spite their face.'

'It would that.'

'So will you help us?' Jean asked eagerly

'Any way I can. What do you wish me to do?'

Jean pointed at Cathy's belly. 'As I said earlier I hadn't realised you were pregnant. Will you be all right to help?'

'If I'm all right enough to work as a cleaner then I doubt if there's anything you're going to ask me to do that I can't manage.'

That answer satisfied Jean. 'Well for now what I want is simple enough. Can you pass the word round that I'm calling a meeting tomorrow at which I would like to speak to as many wives as I can in this street.'

'Only the wives?' Cathy queried.

'Aye,' Jean replied scornfully. 'If we're going to do this properly then it's the women we want involved. Besides, the men not off at the war are working morning, noon and night. They won't have the time, or the energy, to do what's necessary.'

'And where will you hold the meeting?'

'It's too late to hire a hall, and anyway that costs money. The street itself I suppose. We can all foregather there.'

Cathy thought about that. 'I have an idea.'

'Which is?'

'Instead of the street, why not the backcourts? The women wouldn't even have to leave their houses then. All they would have to do is open their back windows and lean out.'

Jean's face lit up. 'That's a terrific idea!'

'You stand on top of one of the middens and address them from there. They'll all be able to hear you clearly enough, and certainly see you better than if they were all ringed round you in the street.'

Tenements are built in rectangles or squares, with the backcourts being the shared common ground within the rectangles or squares. In the centre of this common ground are the middens where the ashes and general refuse go to await collection by the dustmen.

'I'll need steps or a ladder to get up on a midden,' Jean said.

'You just leave that to me. I'll arrange it.'

'This is the first place I'll be speaking tomorrow, the first shot in our Partick campaign for a rent strike. When I leave you I'm off to try and set up other meetings. I'll speak from a midden at those too.'

Cathy was chuffed that Jean was so enthusiastic about her idea.

'Tonight I'm seeing Mary Barbour,' Jean went on. 'She's a colleague of mine at the Glasgow Women's Housing Association who'll be attempting to do the same in Govan as I am here in Partick. I'll tell her about addressing the women from atop a midden. I'm sure she'll think that a terrific idea also and use it.'

'What time were you thinking of speaking?' Cathy asked.

'Well the men come home for their dinner between half past twelve and one-thirty. How about two o'clock?'

'I'd say that would be ideal.'

'That's the time then,' Jean stated.

'And you're bound to get a good response to what you have to say. Folks round here are boiling at the rent. They're talking of nothing else.'

'Then let's use that anger constructively by channelling it into positive action. We'll forge that anger into a collective weapon, a weapon with which to strike the landlords and lay them low.'

Excitement filled Cathy at the prospect of what lay ahead. She could borrow a pair of steps from the Reids on the ground floor, and she wouldn't have to go round all the doors herself. No, what she'd do was delegate. Mrs McLeish would assist her for one, and Mrs McLeish's daughter a few closes down . . .

Cathy was chapping Mrs McLeish's door seconds after she'd said goodbye for now to Jean Ferguson.

'Are you nervous?' Cathy asked Jean.

'Not in the least.'

Jean certainly looked composed, Cathy thought. Cool as the proverbial cucumber. 'Then let's away out and set the ball rolling.'

Cathy and Jean moved out the backclose into the backcourts, and headed for the most central midden where the Reids' steps were already in position.

Cathy glanced up at the windows opposite, a section of Anderson Street. At the other ends of the rectangle a section of Muirhead Street faced a section of Castlebank Street.

Rows and rows of women were hanging out their windows, and it was the same for the other three sides of the rectangle.

'Hooray!' someone shouted.

'Up the workers!' another voice cried, which raised a general laugh.

'And right up the effing landlords!' yet another voice shouted. That didn't only get a laugh but a round of applause as well.

When Cathy and Jean reached the steps Cathy helped Jean up the first couple of treads, and then Jean was atop the midden.

Cathy held up her hands for attention. 'Ladies of Partick,' she said in loud, ringing tones. 'We all know why we're here and what this is all about. It is my great pleasure to introduce to those of you who don't already know her, Mrs Jean Ferguson of the Glasgow Women's Housing Association who will speak to us today. Mrs Jean Ferguson!'

Jean got a warm and vigorous round of applause, and then the listening women fell silent.

It was a bit like one of those Greek ampitheatres she'd read about, Cathy thought. Only in this case the tiers for the audience didn't slant away but went straight up and down.

'Ladies of Partick,' Jean began, echoing Cathy. '*Working-class* ladies of Glasgow. I am here today to ask you one question. Are we going to let the landlords get away with this totally unwarranted increase in our rents, or are we, the people, going to do something about it and fight back?'

'Fight back!' came the chorus.

'But how?' a lone voice queried.

Jean singled out that woman, and pointed at her. 'I'll tell you how. If we all act . . .'

Cathy listened in rapt admiration. Jean was a tremendous orator, exuding bags of charisma and dynamism. She was quite simply a natural, a born public speaker.

'Well, do we have a rent strike?' Jean asked eventually.

'Yes!' was roared back at her.

'Do we *all* agree on that? Is there anyone against?'

There wasn't a murmur of dissent.

'Then here's how we start . . .'

'Good evening to you Mrs McCracken, and a fine evening it is too,' Mr Taylor slurred, swaying where he stood.

Cathy recoiled slightly as a wave of alcohol fumes washed over her. He's drunk as a lord, she thought.

Mr Taylor moved one of his feet, which caused a clinking sound to come from his right-hand coat pocket.

And he's got a bottle, Cathy told herself. They were both in the hallway, where she'd been busy sorting out a press when he'd arrived in from work.

'It is a fine evening for the time of year,' she agreed.

'If you'll excuse me I'll go through to my bed. It's been a very tiring day.'

'Good night then.'

'Good night.'

He clinked all the way to his bedroom door which he opened, then shut behind him.

Cathy smiled when she head a muffled curse as he tripped over something. He wasn't breaking any of her rules by bringing a bottle home with him; she'd never said he couldn't. And so what if he was drunk? Who was she to decry a working man his pint. And certainly not after a hard day's graft as he'd just stated he'd had.

Probably missing his wife and children, she thought. She could certainly sympathise with him there.

God how she missed Bobby! You would have imagined that as the months passed the ache would have eased a little, but it hadn't. It was just as intense as it had been right from the word go.

She went through into the kitchen and over to the window where she touched the oblong piece of cardboard standing on the sill. I AM NOT PAYING INCREASED RENT the cardboard stated, the message facing outwards onto the backcourts. The same message on another piece of cardboard was on Mr Taylor's bedroom window, facing out onto Purdon Street itself.

The cards in the windows had been another of Cathy's ideas, an idea that had been taken up by nearly every house in Partick, from where it had spread to Govan and the other areas that were on rent strike. When you walked down the street, or were in the backcourts, line after line of cards proclaiming roughly the same message stared down and at you.

Cathy stared into the darkness at where the coalyard was. Where was Bobby that night? she wondered. And was he well?

After a while she sat in front of the range and read again through his latest letters.

It was Saturday morning and the queue stretched from Cathy's kitchen out through the front door, and down the close stairs. The wives had come to pay their rent.

The book open in front of Cathy was one that Jean Ferguson had acquired for her. It was a proper accounts book, each page having a list of names and addresses on it. Beside the book was an open metal biscuit tin which Cathy used in the way that Bryce the factor had used his leather bag.

She glanced up to see that Mrs Noble was next. Mrs Noble was a widow with five children.

'There you are,' said Mrs Noble, placing her rent money in front of Cathy.

Cathy counted the money, placed it in the biscuit tin, then ticked off Mrs Noble's name. After Mrs Noble it was Mrs Buchanan from Anderson Street.

Partick was on total rent strike, refusing to pay their rents until the landlords stopped demanding the increase. But to safeguard themselves against prosecution it had been decided that the old rents would still be paid so that they could be handed over if necessary, when the strike stopped.

Cathy had been appointed to collect the rents for her rectangle of backcourts, payment to be made every Saturday morning between nine am and ten. Other backcourts paid their rent on a Friday night as had been customary with the factor, but it had to be Saturday morning with Cathy, as she cleaned on a Friday night.

When the rents were paid Cathy took her biscuit tin to the local bank where it was paid into a special account that had been opened there. Similar accounts had been opened in that bank and other banks in the areas that were on rent strike.

Cathy made a neat tick against Mrs Buchanan's name, and then it was the turn of old Mrs Cooper.

Cathy was mending a blouse she'd accidentally torn when suddenly there was a frenetic hammering on her front door. What on earth? she thought, laying her mending aside and hurrying to the door as quickly as she was able.

Mrs Fisher's face was flushed. 'I've come running to tell you that the Sheriff Officers are evicting Mrs Noble for non-payment of rent. When she opened the door to them they forced their way inside and now they're chucking all her things into the street!'

Cathy stared at Mrs Fisher who lived directly below Mrs Noble. What to do? What to do?

Returning to the kitchen she snatched up a large pan and wooden spoon. 'Follow me!' she instructed Mrs Fisher, and flew down the stairs.

Into the backcourts she rushed, where she immediately began banging on the pan.

'Eviction! Eviction!' she cried.

Windows shot up.

'Eviction! Eviction! Everybody to Mrs Noble's house. Everybody to Mrs Noble's house! Eviction! Eviction!'

Out of the closemouths and backcloses the women streamed, dozens and dozens of them. All with set faces and fury in their hearts. Eviction was it! They'd soon see about that.

Cathy continued banging on her pan which was now severely dented. 'Eviction! Eviction! Everybody to Mrs Noble's house!' she continued to cry.

Fat Mrs O'Mara – twice round the block, once round Mrs O'Mara, as the saying went – was amongst the leaders to burst into Mrs Noble's house where they found Mrs Noble standing crying with her youngest wean – the others at school – clutching her pinny, and also greeting.

'You would would you, you swines!' Mrs O'Mara bellowed at the astonished Sheriff Officers and barged into the nearest one, knocking him flying. The other women took their lead from Mrs O'Mara, bumping, jostling and kicking the Sheriff Officers who were very soon terrified out of their wits at this female onslaught.

Cathy had to fight her way through the densely packed throng which jammed the stairs up to Mrs Noble's house. Halfway there she was pushed back against the close wall as the first of the Sheriff Officers was womanhandled past her.

The man screeched when a well-aimed hatpin stabbed his backside. Then he was out the close and into the street where he was given a few more hefty clouts before managing to flee.

'And don't you dare come back!' Mrs Clarke yelled, shaking her fist at him.

The second and third Sheriff Officers swiftly followed the first, the two of them screeching as their colleague had done when the hatpin struck again.

When they stumbled into the street, the older of the two had a bloody lip and no shirt collar, the collar having been ripped right off him. Mrs Dyer (you couldn't have found a more gentle soul), did her bit by picking up an enamel basin – part of Mrs Noble's belongings that had already been thrown into the street – and crowning the younger Sheriff Officer with it. The two Sheriff Officers took off after the first as if Old Nick himself was at their heels.

'My, I fair enjoyed that,' Mrs Dyer confided to Mrs Clarke, who was wishing she'd thought to use the enamel bowl as Mrs Dyer had done.

'There there, it's all over,' Cathy consoled Mrs Noble, putting an arm round the still crying woman.

'They'll come back again, I know they will,' Mrs Noble sobbed.

'If they do they'll get a repeat performance. I promise you that. We all do, don't we ladies?'

Those within hearing distance shouted their agreement.

'But why me? Why me?' Mrs Noble further sobbed.

'I don't know, unless . . . Well, unless being a widow, they imagined you easy pickings.'

'Dirty dogs,' someone muttered.

'It's Riach who's the dirty dog,' Cathy said. 'It's him behind this.'

Mrs Noble was loaned a handkerchief by one of the women present. She mumbled her thanks, and then wiped her face with it.

'Put the kettle on,' Cathy instructed. 'I'm sure Mrs Noble could use a cup of tea. And we'll start bringing back up that stuff out on the street.'

Word was sent down the snake of women, and soon the first articles appeared, having been passed on up from hand to hand.

'I think we should have a sentry posted at the closemouth in case those Sheriff Officers do try and return,' Cathy proposed to those around her.

'I'll stand sentry for an hour,' Mrs McGillvary offered.'

'And I'll do an hour after her,' said Mrs Smith of the squeaky voice.

Cathy quickly had that organised; the women all too eager to volunteer.

She was going to have to have a conference with Jean Ferguson about this, she thought. She'd call a meeting for the next morning. Also they should form a committee for their rectangle of backcourts, and that committee should be present at the meeting.

When all Mrs Noble's belongings were back in their proper place, and Mrs Noble had been given a cup of tea, Cathy led the women out into the backcourts where she explained to them that she considered a committee necessary, and asked them to elect eight women to that committee, two from each side of the rectangle.

She was of course one of the two elected for the Purdon Street section.

'Riach isn't the only landlord to go on the offensive,' Jean stated to Cathy and the rest of the committee. 'Several other landlords sent out Sheriff Officers in Partick yesterday. I'm happy to report that only one lot succeeded in their eviction.'

'Who did they get?' Cathy asked.

'A Mrs Graham. Her man's away in France.'

'Evict a soldier's wife!' exclaimed Mrs Montgomery angrily. 'How low can you get?'

'In a landlord's case as low as a snake's belly,' Mrs Fyfer snorted.

'Their tactics appear to be to try and pick off a few of us, and thereby scare the rest of us into submission,' Jean explained.

'Well, it won't work,' Cathy said defiantly. 'Now we know what their game is we can use counter-measures against it.'

Jean smiled. 'Go on.'

'We had a sentry on Mrs Noble's closemouth all day yesterday, and again this morning. I suggest we draw up a list of sentries, or pickets if you like, to guard against further swoops by the Sheriff Officers. Each picket will have a noisemaker of some sort, and will use that noisemaker to alert the houses if a Sheriff Officer is spotted by them.'

Jean nodded her approval, telling herself again that Cathy had been a real find. 'You will only have to have pickets in position between ten am and four in the afternoon.'

'Why's that?' Cathy queried.

'Because I've discovered that, by law, Sheriff Officers can only evict between these hours.'

'That makes our task easier then,' Cathy said. 'We only have to be on guard six hours a day rather than twenty-four.'

'Were you thinking of pickets for every frontclose and back-close?' Mrs Fyfer asked Cathy.

'I'd say a picket for every other frontclose is sufficient, and we can forget about the backcloses because with the frontcloses covered no one can get into the backcourts without our knowing.'

'Oh aye!' said Mrs Fyfer softly, not having thought of that.

'We won't be caught napping again,' Cathy declared, which brought her murmurs of approval. For they were all in the same boat, any one of them could have been evicted for non-payment of rent to their landlord, and their belongings sequestrated.

'I think that's that then. It's up to you now to organise the pickets,' Jean said.

'We'll get that done right away,' Cathy stated. Then, looking round the other committee members, said, 'I suggest each of us take half of our street section, draw up our own list of pickets and detail who does what, where and when.'

'How long a shift?' Mrs O'Mara queried.

'I had thought of an hour's duration, but now we know there are only six hours per day to cover I'm sure we can reduce that to half an hour. Does everyone agree to that?'

The other members of the committee nodded affirmation.

'Half an hour a shift it is then,' Cathy declared.

The women rose, and began to leave. Cathy said goodbye to them at the door, the meeting having taken place in her house. Jean hung back till she and Cathy were alone.

'I'm attending a special (she heavily emphasised the word 'special') meeting in Pollokshaws this Saturday and wondered if you'd care to come with me?'

'What sort of meeting?' Cathy probed.

'Concerning the rent strike.'

Why had Jean suddenly gone all coy? And why was she speaking in a half-whisper? 'Who's going to be there?'

'Why don't you come along and find out? I think I can safely promise that you'll find it worthwhile. And I'd like them all to meet you.'

More and more mysterious, Cathy thought. 'And you're not going to tell me who *they* are?'

'I'll meet you outside the F&F at two pm.' The F&F was a local dancehall.

'Two it is then,' Cathy agreed.

Now what was this all about? she wondered after Jean had gone.

Mrs McLeish was on duty at the closemouth when Cathy came down the stairs that Saturday, en route to meet Jean. Mrs McLeish had a football rickety in her hand, the sort that makes a terrific racket when you whirl it round and round.

116

'All right Mrs McLeish?' Cathy queried with a smile.

'Right as rain.'

Cathy stepped out onto the pavement where she noted with satisfaction the other ladies on picket duty.

She laughed when she saw the noisemaker Mrs Weir had. It was the big drum her son played in a bagpipe band. Mrs Weir had the drum propped against the tenement wall ready to bash it with the bulbous headed drumstick she was holding.

Further along the street Mrs Montgomery had an old army bugle that she was quite capable of tooting loudly if the occasion demanded.

At every other closemouth a woman stood on picket duty, and that's the way it was throughout Partick and every other area on rent strike.

MACLEAN the plate by the side of the door proclaimed, the door belonging to the house in Pollokshaws that Jean had brought her to.

Cathy gave Jean a quizzical look after Jean knocked, but Jean still refused to let on who they were about to meet.

The man who answered Jean's knock had an intense, brooding quality about him. 'Hello Jean,' he said.

'Hello John.'

The penny dropped for Cathy. John Maclean! The fighting domine himself. It had to be.

'And this is Cathy McCracken whom I've told you about.'

Maclean extended a hand. 'A great pleasure Mrs McCracken. Jean speaks very highly of you.'

'The pleasure's mine,' Cathy replied, shaking with Maclean. He had a firm grip, and a sensitive one.

Maclean ushered them through to the parlour where others were already assembled.

'Will you introduce her or shall I?' Maclean asked Jean.

'We both shall.'

Maclean's eyes twinkled; he evidently found that amusing.

'This is James McDougall whom some refer to as my lieutenant,' Maclean said.

Cathy exchanged pleasantries with McDougall.

'And this is Willie Gallagher.'

The breath caught in her throat. Willie Gallagher was renowned throughout working-class Glasgow.

117

'John Wheatley and James Maxton.'

Her jaw nearly dropped open. 'Pleased to meet you both,' she stammered. She shook hands with first one, then the other.

'And this is Tom Bell and Arthur McManus.'

Bell and McManus weren't as big names as Maclean, Gallagher, Wheatley and Maxton, but they were certainly names well-known in the Glasgow labour movement.

'And Davie Kirkwood.'

Kirkwood belonged with Maclean and Co, another of the great so-called Red Clydesiders.

They moved on to where several women were standing, and here Jean took over the introductions. 'Cathy I'd like you to meet Helen Crawfurd.'

Cathy had read of Helen Crawfurd's exploits in the newspapers. Communist and suffragette, she'd been in jail three times for militant action, including smashing the windows of the Minister of Education in London and an army recruiting office in Glasgow.

Cathy felt she was in a real female 'presence'. Helen Crawfurd's lifeforce was almost overwhelming, stronger than any of the men in the room.

'Your ideas to help advance the strike have all been excellent ones. We desperately need women like you, women with a head on their shoulders and bags of imagination. Welcome.'

Cathy felt a blush stain her neck, instantly reminding her of Bobby, who was a terrible blusher. 'Thank you, Mrs Crawfurd.'

'It's Helen.'

'Thank you, Helen.'

'Are you a feminist, Cathy?'

She wasn't sure what to reply to that. 'To be truthful I've never really thought about it.'

'Then you most certainly should. But that's a subject for another time, eh?'

'Yes,' Cathy agreed.

The remaining two women were Mary Barbour, Jean's friend from Govan, and Agnes Dollan, also from Govan, whose husband was Pat Dollan who wrote for the labour paper *Forward*.

'Shall we make a start?' Maclean suggested generally, now that the introductions were complete.

The centre of the room was occupied by a long table overlaid with a brown velvet cover. Maclean took up a position at the head of the table; Cathy sat with Jean on one side of her, Helen Crawfurd on the other.

'First of all I have to tell you that as from today Kinning Park and Whiteinch have joined the rent strike . . .' He paused while Maxton and McDougall applauded. 'Those areas now on rent strike are Govan, Partick, Parkhead, Pollokshaws, Pollok, Cowcaddens, Kelvingrove, Ibrox, Govanhill, St Rollox, Townshead, Springburn, Maryhill, Fairfield, Gorbals, Woodside, and now Kinning Park and Whiteinch' – despite the strike other landlords throughout the city had gone ahead and implemented a rent increase – 'By my calculations that brings the total number out on strike to twenty thousand.'

This time, with the exception of the speaker, they all applauded.

'That's twenty thousand Glaswegians who refuse to bow to the tyranny of the landlords. Twenty thousand people of different skills, religion and sex. Aye, men and women, Protestant and Catholic, engineer and labourer uniting to fight as one; one person, one voice.'

He was mesmeric to listen to, Cathy thought. She found herself hypnotised, hanging on his every word. She recalled a picture she'd seen in a book of an Indian fakir piping a swaying snake out of a basket. She felt she was the snake, Maclean the fakir.

Maclean was well into his stride now. 'The rent strike is not a mere tenants' struggle, it is a *class* struggle. To explain that let me define my interpretation of class. Classes are large groups of people differing from each other by the place they occupy in a historically determined system of social production, by their relation (in most cases fixed and formulated in law) to the means of production, by their role in the social organisation of labour, and consequently, by the dimensions of the share of social wealth . . .'

Cathy sat riveted as Maclean's rhetoric washed over her, but Helen Crawfurd wasn't riveted; she was beginning to fidgit.

'Yes, yes, yes, John!' Helen suddenly burst out several minutes later. 'Property has made fiends of men, we all agree on that. But moralising is a waste of time. What we need is direct action.'

'I concur,' said Mary Barbour.

'We must be careful . . .' murmured James McDougall. Then, by way of explanation – 'Stevenson would love to put many of us here behind bars.' The Stevenson he was referring to was the Chief Constable of Glasgow, James Verdier Stevenson.

'May I make a suggestion?' broke in Kirkwood.

Maclean waved that Kirkwood had the floor. 'I think our next step is to compile a great petition which we can either send or deliver personally to Asquith at Number 10.'

'Deliver it personally,' Maxton said. 'And ensure that the leading newspapers in Scotland and England are there to register and report the event.'

'A great petition of a million signatures,' Maclean breathed, eyes ablaze with fervour. 'It could be done.'

'The nation as a whole must understand the cruel and heartless injustice that is happening here in Glasgow,' Agnes Dollan said.

'Capitalism as a system must be crushed, totally and utterly,' stated Tom Bell.

'That's an ultimate aim Tom,' John Wheatley said. 'For now we must deal in the specific: the matter of the rent strike.'

Cathy silently agreed with Wheatley.

'Helen?' Jean prompted.

Helen Crawfurd nodded. 'I'm not against a petition, not by any manner of means. But a petition is by its very nature a passive protest. I say we hit where it's damn well going to *hurt*!'

'What do you propose?' McManus queried.

'A general strike in Glasgow. Every last solitary worker downs tools and doesn't take them up again until the landlords retract their rent increase.'

A general strike in Glasgow! Cathy thought, and a cold shiver ran up her spine.

'There is a war on,' McDougall said softly.

'A war none of us here agrees with, I'm sure. Well, does anyone?' Helen retorted fiercely. There was no voice of dissent.

Helen continued. 'Stop the yards, bring the munitions factories to a halt, shut down the iron and steel foundries, close the pits. Aye, even have the office workers quit their desks, and you'll soon have the Government telling the landlords to retract their rent increase.'

'Why not just drag the landlords out of their houses and hang them from lamp-posts?' Gallagher said drily.

'It's a thought, Willie,' Helen replied.

'A petition first though, before we hang them,' Gallagher said in such a way that others round the table laughed. Helen wasn't one of those who did.

They got down to discussing the nuts and bolts of organising the great petition.

Cathy walked along Purdon Steet, her mind still whirling from the meeting she'd just attended. They'd all impressed her, and scared her a wee bit too. She felt she'd just participated in the making of history, and that was exciting.

Mrs Reid was on picket duty at their closemouth. Cathy had done her own stint earlier that day.

'Your lodger has just gone rushing up the stairs, and by the look and smell of him he's been drinking,' Mrs Reid stated.

Odd for Mr Taylor to be home this time on a Saturday; he should still be working, Cathy thought. 'Drinking you say?'

'Stank like a brewery. His face was all flushed and his eyes that starey, pop-eyed way some folks get when they've had a good bucket.'

Cathy thanked Mrs Reid, and entered the close. When she arrived at her front-door she found it open.

She was about to call out, then didn't when she heard a noise from her kitchen. Mr Taylor wasn't allowed in there unless invited by her.

Quietly, leaving the front door open behind her, she went into the kitchen.

Taylor was drunk, all right, that was blatantly obvious. The old tea caddy she kept her money in was open on the table and he was muttering to himself as he counted its contents.

Cathy went chill all over. 'What do you think you're doing?' she demanded. And how had he known that was where she kept her cash!

He glanced at her. 'Need more . . . need more . . .' He belched, then belched a second time.

'Put that money back this instant!' Cathy commanded.

'Away to hell!' he spat at her, scooping up the money and thrusting it into a trouser pocket. A penny piece fell to the linoleum and rolled away.

Cathy was outraged in the extreme. How dare he come into her private room, and how dare he steal her money. Every farthing of which she so badly needed.

He lumbered towards her. 'Going to the pub.'

She seized hold of him as he tried to brush past. 'Oh no you don't! You're going to . . . '

He hit her, hard in the belly.

The breath whooshed out of her as she doubled over.

'Interfering bitch!' he mumbled, and hit her again.

She crumpled to the floor, coming to rest on her side. She grabbed for his boot in front of her.

He used the other boot to kick himself free, both blows landing on Cathy's stomach. Swearing vehemently he dashed from the kitchen and ran clattering away down the stairs.

She must have passed out for a moment or two Cathy realised, coming round. Her stomach was sore, aching dully. Then she gritted her teeth as a jagged pain lanced through her insides.

She came onto her knees, then managed to get herself upright. She staggered, groggy in the head and having trouble maintaining her balance.

She went out into the hallway, and to the front door which was still open. She shut it, then bolted it top and bottom.

Returning to the kitchen she went to the sink and leaned over it. And was violently sick.

When that was finished she ran cold water and splashed some onto her face. That made her feel a little better, but only a little.

She groaned as a new pain clutched hold of her. Best sit down she thought. And made for the nearest chair.

How stupid of her to try and stop him like that she berated herself. But she'd been so incensed to see him robbing her she'd just naturally done what she had. She should have stopped to consider the possible consequences.

She bit her lip as another clutching pain occurred. Oh please God, nothing was going to happen to the baby, to her and Bobby's baby! Please God.

She forced herself to calm down, and relax. She ran her hands over her belly, gently massaging it.

An hour later the pains had disappeared, though she had a thumping headache that had come on while she was sitting in the chair. Luckily she had an Askit powder in the house which she now took, after which she went through to the bedroom.

It didn't take long to pack Taylor's few clothes and other

odds and sods into his suitcase. When that was done she carried (it wasn't at all heavy) the suitcase to the front door, opened the door and placed the suitcase outside on the landing.

Taylor would still have his front-door key on him. But by good fortune the door had two locks, only one of which she normally used. She now locked the door from the inside, using the lock that Taylor didn't have the key for, and then bolted it top and bottom again.

Going back to the kitchen she made herself a badly needed cup of strong tea.

She came awake to hear a key rattling in the front door. Taylor, she thought, as she lay in the darkness.

The key continued to rattle, and then was withdrawn. That was followed by a tapping on the door.

It was ages before she dropped off to sleep again.

Next morning she cautiously opened the front door to find the suitcase gone.

'Good riddance to bad rubbish!' she said softly, pulling her dressing gown tighter around her, as it was even more freezing cold on the landing than it was inside.

Later, she set off to visit the doctor.

'As far as I can tell, no damage has been done. Everything appears to be as it should,' Doctor McLaughlan said to Cathy, having just given her a thorough examination.

She sighed with relief. God had heard her prayer.

'However if those pains recur, or there is any bleeding, you must come straight back to me.'

'Oh don't worry doctor, I will,' replied Cathy, swinging her legs off the doctor's couch.

'What an unpleasant and traumatic experience,' Doctor McLaughlan sympathised as Cathy slipped behind a screen where those clothes he'd asked her to remove were folded over a chair.

'Yes.'

'I'll give you a prescription. Just a mild sedative to quieten your nerves.'

She didn't buy the sedative, considering she couldn't afford it. And what was she going to do now that she'd lost the money Taylor had been giving her every week?

John Maclean was standing on top of the same midden that Jean Ferguson had stood on when she'd addressed Cathy's rectangle of backcourts; backcourts that were now jam-packed with those who'd come from streets round about. Day after day Maclean was speaking non-stop in the areas on rent strike, keeping the anger of the strikers at boiling point.

' . . . The housing conditions in Glasgow are a scandal!' Maclean thundered, clenched fist punching the air. 'We have the worst housing in all Europe in this city, and the landlords are actually wanting to increase our rents! With housing conditions the way they are they should be *decreasing* them!'

That earned him a huge roar of approval.

He was about to resume speaking when a shrill voice suddenly cried out. 'Spy! There's a spy in our midst!'

Confusion immediately broke out. There were some men present at the meeting, but the one now being pointed out differed from the others in that he wore a bowler hat. Right at the back of the crowd, he had been listening intently to what Maclean had to say. Finding himself surrounded by a sea of hostile faces his own went white.

He started to push his way through to the nearest backclose, a dozen feet away, only to find his passage barred by two soldiers.

Cathy's heart skipped a beat when she spotted the soldiers; she couldn't believe she was actually seeing what she was. The two soldiers were Bobby and his brother Gavin.

At last, at long last after so much waiting and worrying he was home again, and in one piece from the look of him. Tears spurted from her eyes, tears that caused Bobby's image to blur and shimmer.

'Let me by,' bowler hat said to Bobby and Gavin.

'He's a Sheriff Officer!' someone shouted.

'And a bloody spy!'

'Who are you and what's your business here?' Bobby demanded quietly, thinking to himself that the man was an idiot. To come amongst this crowd wearing a bowler hat! Hadn't he realised he'd stick out like a sore thumb? The men of Partick wore flat caps, and occasionally a felt hat. Never ever a bowler.

'Who are you and what's your business here?' Bobby demanded again.

'He's not a Sheriff Officer,' an authoritative female voice declared. 'That's McAusland, my landlord.' The speaker was Jean Ferguson who was attending the meeting.

McAusland (for that's indeed who it was) and the other landlords knew all about these meetings of course, but he'd wanted to hear for himself what was said. He'd never dreamed he'd be recognised in this part of Partick which was a distance from Partickhill where his properties were. Even there not many would have known him, as he rarely dealt personally with property matters: his factors did that for him. Unfortunately for him Jean Ferguson was present, and she and he had met.

'A landlord!' The word rippled through the crowd, spoken as if it was the worst kind of obscenity.

McAusland tried to burst through Bobby and Gavin, but they gripped him by the arms, stopping him.

'To the middens with the swine!' a female voice shouted.

'Aye to the middens! Stick him in with the rest of the rubbish!' another voice yelled.

'Come on lads, do your duty,' a female instructed Bobby and Gavin.

McAusland struggled, but Bobby and Gavin held him fast.

'Right, Gavin!' Bobby said to his brother, and with that the two of them lifted the hapless McAusland right off his feet. The crowd parted to let them through as they headed for the middens.

'Wait a wee,' fat Mrs O'Mara said to Bobby and Gavin. Her podgy hands moved like lightning, delving up under McAusland's coat and jacket to flick his braces from their buttons, McAusland screeched as his trousers were pulled off him, and badly ripped in the process.

'And the rest!' Mrs Noble urged, remembering only too well her own humiliation, not to mention anguish, when the Sheriff Officers had attempted to evict her and her weans.

McAusland's coat was wrenched off, his jacket after that, and then his shirt and tie leaving him in semmit, pants, and hilariously, his shoes. The bowler hat had long since gone, trampled underfoot.

A group of women took McAusland from Bobby and Gavin, propelling McAusland to the midden Maclean was standing atop. On reaching the midden they forced McAusland into it, then they picked up the bins themselves and showered McAusland with the garbage and ashes they contained.

Cheer after cheer went up as a thoroughly frightened McAusland, genuinely fearing for his life, cowered at the back of the midden.

A laughing Maclean eventually gestured for quiet, and when he had it, resumed his speech where he'd left off.

Bobby twisted round as a hand crept into his, and there was Cathy smiling at him through a haze of tears. He didn't give a damn who would see them as he swept his arm round her and pulled her close. At least that was his intention, for she only came so far in before being stopped, her bump in the way.

He looked down at it, seeing it for the first time. His eyes flew open in amazement, and the breath caught in his throat.

'You're . . . you're . . .' he finally managed to stutter.

'Yes.'

'I . . .' He was completely lost for words. This was the last thing he'd expected. He'd had no idea. Why hadn't she told him?

Reaching up, he wiped the tears from her eyes. 'Oh lassie!' he mumbled in a choked voice. 'Oh lassie!'

She didn't care who saw them either. Her Bobby was home from the war, her Bobby whom she loved to distraction. Bringing his head to her she kissed him on the lips.

Time passed, neither of them, having only eyes for one another, could have said how long, and then Maclean was finished and about to move on.

'I'll see you pair later,' Gavin said to Bobby and Cathy, not having wished to intrude until now.

Bobby turned to his brother. 'Aye, fine. Tell the folks I'll be along sometime the day.'

Cathy pecked Gavin on the cheek; a far older looking Gavin than the last time she'd seen him. But then Bobby was looking older also, and so thin! 'It's grand to see you back,' she said.

'You've no idea how grand it is to be back.'

There was that in Gavin's voice told her he'd had a very hard time, just as Bobby had done. Like Bobby, he too had lost a great deal of weight.

Gavin melted into the crowd, promising himself a pint in his favourite pub, the Byres Arms, before giving Ma the surprise of her life by chapping the door. And wait till she found out that Bobby was with him! She'd be beside herself. As would their da when he got in from work.

Cathy saw Maclean coming towards them with Jean by his side. 'There are two people I'd like you to meet,' she said to Bobby.

'Aye, sure.'

She squeezed his hand, reassuring herself this was real and not something she was dreaming or imagining. It was real all right. Real as could be. Bobby was here, in the flesh. Back safe and sound. She could have eaten him there and then.

'Mr Maclean, this is my husband Bobby, home this very minute from the war.'

Maclean shook with Bobby. 'A pleasure to meet you Mr McCracken, though I don't agree with the war you're fighting.'

Anger flared in Bobby. What mealy-mouthed talk was this? In his mind's eye he saw again Tim Murchison in that shellhole, and Gordon Manson as the German sniper's bullet blew his life away. And others, so many others, friends, pals, comrades, some dead, some with missing limbs, some doomed to a life coughing their guts up, having inhaled gas and survived, some blinded, some . . .

He wouldn't argue, Bobby decided. Not here, not now. 'I've heard of you of course, Mr Maclean. I'm pleased to meet you too,' he answered – a bland enough reply.

'And this is Jean Ferguson who's become a dear friend,' Cathy went on.

'How are you Jean?'

'A lot better for seeing that pig McAusland getting his come-uppance. What a spectacle he's going to make going through the streets in his semmit and pants. He'll be the laughing stock of Glasgow, and serves him right too.'

Maclean and Jean went on their way. Cathy was supposed to have been accompanying them, but not now.

'I have so many questions,' Bobby said to Cathy.

'I'll answer them all upstairs.'

'Come on then.'

They were stopped a number of times en route to their backclose, neighbours saying how marvellous it was to see Bobby again, but finally they managed to get up the stairs and into the house.

In the kitchen she took off the shawl she'd been wearing and threw it over a chair. While she did this he propped his kitbag in a

127

corner, a kitbag he'd left in the backclose before going out into the backcourts.

They came together, he being extremely careful of her bump, and this time the kiss was a deep one, full of love and passion.

'You're still a smashing kisser Bobby,' she whispered when the kiss was over.

'I haven't had much practice lately, I'm afraid.'

'I think you're even better for that.'

He laughed.

'Before I answer any questions there's one thing I must know,' she said.

'Which is?'

'How long?'

The laughter creases faded from his face, and his lips thinned. 'Only a week. I had hoped for longer, but . . .' he shrugged, 'there you are.'

'A week!' she exclaimed softly, bitterly disappointed.

'The battalion replacements are already trained. The old hands meet up with the new a week tomorrow. We have three days of exercises, then it's back over there.'

'To the salient?'

A haunted look came into his eyes. 'It's not definite, but I believe that's where it's going to be.'

How gaunt his face had become, she thought. Gaunt, and haggard. He was a shadow of his former self.

'Why didn't you tell me?' he demanded, pointing at her bump. 'I had no idea. Not an inkling.'

She smiled. 'Pleased?'

'Pleased! That's the understatement of the year. I'm bloody ecstatic!'

'I thought you would be.'

'So why didn't you tell me?'

'I didn't want you worrying or distracted in any way. I thought you had enough on your plate without having something extra to concern you. Perhaps it was wrong for me not to write and tell you; all I can say is I did what I considered to be for the best.'

'It's eh . . .' He shook his head. 'It's a shock!' Then his face lit up. 'A father! I'm going to be a da!'

She could feel the tears coming again, tears of sheer happiness. The house was alive once more, alive as it hadn't been since he'd left it. And not only the house, herself as well. She was complete again.

'Can I touch?' he asked.

'Go ahead.'

He placed first one palm against her stomach, then the other.

'It moves all the time,' she told him. 'There are occasions when my entire stomach sort of ripples with it.'

He couldn't wait to witness that.

'I lost my job at Mavor & Coulson,' she stated bluntly.

He looked up at her.

'Expectant mothers have to go, and so I went.'

'But how are you getting by? Not on my shilling a day surely?'

'I have another job. I'm a cleaner at the school.'

'A cleaner!' he exploded, appalled.

'And fortunate to be so. It's not easy getting a job when you've a baby so obviously on the way.'

'But . . .' His thoughts were whirling. 'When are you due?'

'Next month.'

'And after that?'

'I don't know. I'll cross that bridge when I come to it. It may be that I'll have to have another lodger, or lodgers.'

Lodger! What was she talking about now?

'Although I might be forced to do that I'd certainly be most reluctant to have to. Not after Taylor and what he did.'

'Who's Taylor? And what did he do?'

He'd been appalled before, now he was even more appalled to hear of the Taylor incident.

'Actually kicked you?' he breathed, his voice cold steel.

Cathy nodded.

'The . . . the . . .' He didn't want to say what he thought of this Taylor.

Nobody's seen hide or hair of him since. Which is just as well, for when I told the neighbours several of the men swore they'd do for him if they saw him. But no one has. If he's still in Glasgow he's nowhere round here.'

Bobby had to fight to control himself. Punched and kicked Cathy! Punched and kicked a pregnant woman, his wife carrying his child! Why she could so easily have . . .

'I don't suppose you have a drink in the house?' he asked.

129

Cathy shook her head. That was another luxury that had gone by the board. 'I can make you a cup of tea though?'

'That would be nice.'

He studied her at the sink. The Cathy he knew, and yet the pregnancy made her a Cathy he didn't know. She positively shone, he thought. It was as if she had an aura surrounding her.

'Now tell me about this rent strike? We've heard a few things during the past few weeks, but very little because we were in the salient. There should have been a batch of post waiting for us when we came out, but there wasn't. The lorry bringing it up received a direct hit and that was that. There were newspapers on the boat coming over, but they were all English ones carrying a few odd references to the strike.'

She began at the beginning, and recounted everything from there. He listened with a face like fizz.

'No wonder Glasgow's hopping mad!' he said when Cathy was finished.

'We're going to beat them. You wait and see if we don't,' Cathy replied fiercely.

'And it was your idea that the women stand picket duty?'

'It was.'

He shook his head in amazement. There was so much to take in, and all at once. It was going to take him a while to digest it all.

'How is it you and Gavin got leave together?' she asked, putting a question of her own.

'Purely by chance. There was no connivance in it whatever. I got on the boat in France, and halfway across this voice says to me, "Hello. Look what the cat's dragged in." And there he was, bold as brass.'

'Has he got a week too?'

'No, a fortnight, the lucky bugger.'

'Bobby?' There were tears in her eyes again. 'Come here and give me a cuddle.'

A few seconds later she laughed. 'You don't have to be that careful. I won't break.'

'Are you sure about that?'

'Absolutely certain.'

She snuggled into his arms, and closed her eyes. She was filled with peace and contentment. She wished the moment could have gone on forever, till the end of the world.

'I love you,' he whispered.

'I know. And I love you.'

He too closed his eyes. How many times while in the salient had he thought he'd never hold Cathy again? Times without number.

'Do you want to go to bed?' she asked softly.

'More than anything. But . . .'

'That's all right too,' she interjected, knowing what he'd been about to ask.

'Then let's forget the tea. I'll have that later.'

He released her, ran a hand over her hair, then stepping back began to undress.

They made love, and slept, and made love again. It was hours later before he finally got his tea.

They stopped outside the school, for it was time for Cathy to go to work.

'I'll meet you at your folks' when I'm finished here,' she said.

'Come as quickly as you can.'

'I will.'

They stood staring into one another's eyes, each reluctant to part from the other.

'I have to go in,' she said after a while.

'Yes.'

Reaching out she touched him lightly on the cheek, then turning away, hurried inside.

He stood watching her till she'd vanished into the school. He took a deep breath, then another. He had a visit to make before he went to his ma and da's. That would be a little help for her at least.

He strode away from the school.

'Come in! Come in!' said Ina McCracken, Bobby's mother. She kissed Cathy, then ushered her through to the kitchen where the family were gathered.

There were screwtops of beer on the table, and a two-thirds-empty bottle of whisky. Bobby was sitting glass in hand, wee Sandra his sister at his feet.

'No, don't get up!' Cathy said to Gavin who'd started to rise as she came through the kitchen door.

'Mathie, let your Auntie Cathy have that chair,' Ina McCracken said to her youngest son, who immediately did as he was bid.

'Will you have a dram, lass?' Rob beamed at Cathy.

'No, thank you.'

'A taste of beer then?'

'If you've got some lemonade I'll take a shandy.'

'Right,' Rob said, and nodded to Ina to pour a shandy for Cathy.

'As you can see, we're just having a wee celebration,' Rob said to Cathy.

'It's not every day you have two sons home from the war,' Ina said, a catch in her voice despite the fact she was smiling.

'No, it isn't,' Cathy agreed.

'What a surprise!' said Rob, and smacked his thigh in delight.

'Bobby told us about this Taylor and what he did to you,' Gavin said to Cathy, eyes sparking with anger.

'Aye, well that's over and done with now.'

'Bastard!'

'Gavin! There are youngsters present,' Ina admonished him.

'Sorry, Ma.'

Ina handed Cathy her shandy, having made the lemonade in it with a press. 'The offer we made still stands, you know. You can always come and stay here with us.' The McCrackens had made the same offer that Cathy's own parents had.

'Thanks Ina, but I do want to try and keep my own house. And I will, as long as is humanly possible. I'm determined about that.'

Ina nodded that she understood.

'And I also hear you've had quite a hand in this rent strike,' Gavin went on.

'Hardly that. But I have made a couple of suggestions that have been taken up.'

'I listened to Mrs Ferguson speak the other week. She was marvellous,' Ina said enthusiastically.

'I'm against the strike,' Rob declared. 'I told Ina to have no part of it. It's a waste of time and effort as far as I'm concerned.'

'I paid him no heed,' Ina said to Cathy. 'We're on rent strike like everyone else.'

Rob threw what remained in his glass down his throat, then came to his feet. 'Anyone else for a refill?' Both Bobby and Gavin replied they'd have one.

'Why are you against the strike?' Cathy queried.

Rob collected Bobby's glass, then Gavin's. 'There's never any point in taking on the bosses, And that's all landlords are, another type of boss. They have the power behind them.'

'We're going to win this fight,' Cathy stated quietly.

'I'll believe that when it happens.'

She was becoming irritated by her father-in-law. What a negative, defeatist attitude.

'You'll end up paying the extra, just wait and see,' Rob said, pulling the cork out of the whisky bottle.

'We won't if we dig in our heels and refuse to,' Ina replied.

'Lloyd George has called for an inquiry into unpatriotic landlords,' Cathy said. 'He's been quoted as saying that if allegations on unjustifiable rent increases in Glasgow are proved then the Government will ask Parliament for powers to deal with the position. There's also the possibility he's coming personally to Glasgow, he's so concerned about the matter.' Lloyd George was Asquith's Minister of Munitions.

'If he does come and tries to speak he'll get howled down. They hate him here,' Ina said.

'Can't stand the man, myself,' Rob sniffed. 'There's something about him I don't trust.'

Cathy agreed with that, but didn't say so.

'I always think he looks shifty in his pictures,' Rob elaborated. 'Shifty and devious.'

'Twenty per cent tacked on the rent,' Ina said softly, and shook her head. 'Talk about the straw that broke the camel's back!'

'You'll find it when you have to,' Rob declared, handing round the fresh drinks.

Ina glared at her husband. 'You annoy me, so you do. You stand there and glibly tell me I'll find it when I have to. You who have no real idea of the scrimping and scraping I have to go through to make ends meet, as it is. Why, you don't even know how much our rent is now, do you?'

He didn't answer that.

'No, you don't. You just hand over your wage packet on a Friday night and leave everything else to me. It's me that has to manage on what I'm given, and it's not easy, I can assure you.'

Rob shrugged. 'Count yourself lucky you get an unopened wage packet. There are plenty of women who don't.'

'I do appreciate that. But an unopened wage packet doesn't solve all the money problems. Not by a long chalk.'

'Women! They're never satisfied!' Rob exclaimed to Bobby.

Bobby tactfully changed the subject before a full-scale row erupted.

'Here, put that in your tea caddy,' said Bobby, giving Cathy some folded banknotes.

'Ten pounds!' she breathed, having counted them. 'Where in the name of the Wee Man did you get this from?'

'All you have to know is that it's honestly come by,' Bobby replied evasively. Although she pressed him he refused to tell her where he'd got the money.

Nor did he ever.

He lay in the darkness, Cathy asleep beside him. What a homecoming – Cathy pregnant, working as a school cleaner, punched and kicked by a drunken lodger she'd been forced to take in to help with the bills, and huge areas of the city on rent strike.

Cathy needed more money, but how was he to get it for her? That was the question.

Their problems would be solved if he went back to work, but that was impossible. He was in the army with no way of getting out until the war was over.

Desertion? It was said they caught eighty per cent of those who did, and for many of these it was the firing squad. Even trying to start up in another town was no use if you deserted. When you applied for a job you had to state your past history, and those histories were now – made compulsory by the authorities – all investigated. The only way you might get away with deserting was not to work, which would defeat the object of his deserting in the first place.

He sighed, his mind churning on and on.

Bobby stared down the Clyde, its water black and forbidding at that time of year. Over on the other bank he could see the skeleton of a ship in the process of being built. Men were swarming all over and round the ship, like so many ants.

'A penny for them?' Cathy smiled.

'I was just thinking that half my week has already gone.'

The smile vanished from her face, and pain came into her eyes.

134

'It's flown by. In the salient the same amount of time would have seemed endless.'

'The difference between enjoying yourself, and not,' she whispered.

He laughed bitterly. 'You experience many emotions in the salient, but never enjoyment. Oh no! Never that.'

'It's so senseless this war, I . . .'

'None of that now!' he chided her. 'I won't hear any of that anti-war nonsense your friend Maclean was coming out with.'

She regarded him curiously. 'You still agree with the war then? Even after all that you've been through?'

'I still stand by all the reasons I gave you for joining up. I haven't changed my mind at all about those. A man must defend his own; he's not a man otherwise.'

'But so many dead Bobby?'

'Aye,' he said softly. 'So many.'

He stared again out over the Clyde, seeing countless faces of men no longer on this Earth. 'Know something?'

'What?'

'Sometimes over there it's easy to imagine that all the young men of our generation are going to go down the plughole. That an entire male section of our population is going to be completely and utterly wiped out.'

She shivered.

'It could happen, too. When the number of volunteers fall away they'll start conscription. And then it'll get to the stage where it doesn't matter what your job is, they'll want you anyway. Till in the end only the old and very young are left.'

Silence fell between them, till suddenly he roused himself with a shake of the shoulders. 'Ach, that's only a bad dream, a waking nightmare. Let's off home and sit in front of a fire, I'd enjoy that.'

Somewhere downriver a ship's horn blew, a forlorn sound full of sadness and melancholy.

It matched his present mood exactly, Bobby thought on hearing it.

Matched it exactly.

'Isn't she wonderful?' Cathy whispered to Bobby. They were at Govan Cross where an enormous meeting was being spoken to by Helen Crawfurd, a meeting called in protest against the previous

135

night's arrest of eighteen rent-striking munitions workers who were due to appear in the Small Debts Court later that day. The landlords had struck again.

Govan Cross and the surrounding streets were chock-a-block with grim-faced people, the vast majority women, listening to a Helen Crawfurd beside herself with fury and indignation.

'If we allow them to get away with this, they've won,' Helen thundered. 'So we must stop them! And stop them *now*!'

Fists were raised and shaken in agreement.

'We will march to the Court and let the Sheriff there hear and see us, and we will *make* him release our eighteen comrades!'

A great roar of approval went up.

'So who is with me? Who will march behind me?'

A tumultuous chorus greeted that. They all would.

'Not you. It's too far for you, pregnant as you are,' Bobby said quietly to Cathy.

'Nonsense.'

'It's all the way into town.'

'I'm going with them Bobby, and that's all there is to it.'

He could see he wasn't going to dissuade her, that she was fiercely determined.

Helen Crawfurd was about to get down off the barrel she'd been standing on when she saw a parked motorvan with the legend FAIRFIELD WORKS on it side. That legend gave her an inspiration. Straightening again, she held up her hands:

'We'll go to the Court, but first we'll march to Fairfield's and demand that the men there come out and march with us! To Fairfield's!'

'To Fairfield's!' hundreds of voices clamoured.

'Isn't this exciting?' Cathy said to Bobby as they were borne along by the throng.

'Yes.' He had to admit that it was.

Up the Govan Road they streamed with Helen Crawfurd at their head, till they arrived at the gates of the Fairfield Works, one of Glasgow's biggest, and certainly best-known, shipbuilding yards.

'Follow me!' Helen cried, and steamrollered in through the gates, watched by an astonished gatekeeper who could no more have stopped Helen and her people than Canute could have the tide.

Inside the yard she headed for a large open space, and was

almost there when Tommy Gibb, one of the yard's leading shop stewards, came striding up to her.

'What's all this about then, Helen?' he demanded. The two of them knew each other well, having been born and bred within a couple of hundred yards of one another.

Briefly she explained why she and those with her were there.

Tommy rubbed his chin as he gazed at Helen's followers crowding round about. Then he glanced up at a set of windows in a nearby building, behind which were the management offices.

'I want to speak to the men,' Helen repeated.

Tommy brought his attention back to her. 'I'm fully in sympathy with you Helen, but you see . . .'

'You've not become a bosses' lackey and lickspittle have you, Tommy Gibb?' she taunted.

He coloured. 'Of course not! You know me better than that!'

'Then get the men round. This concerns every one of them.'

'I'll tell you what Helen, I'll call an emergency meeting of the shop stewards committee right away. I'll need full backing before I can stop the men at their work.'

'You do that then, Tommy.'

He hurried off.

'Do you think she can get the Fairfield men to march with her into town?' Bobby queried of Cathy.

'If anyone can, Helen can.'

Meanwhile a crate had been found and pulled into a central position in the open space. Helen now climbed on top of the crate from where she waved to the Fairfield workers she could see. After that she began to address her followers again.

Some minutes later, Tommy Gibb was back beside her to report that the shop stewards' committee had voted to down tools. The Fairfield men could listen to what Helen had to say.

Gradually the shipyard noises subsided as the men left their work to make for where Helen was. To begin with they gathered in their tens, then their hundreds, then their thousands.

Helen had spoken forcefully at Govan Cross; now she spoke even more so, telling the men it was their duty to combat the evil of the landlords and authorities, and to right this terrible injustice that was taking place. If the arrested eighteen went to jail then the rent strike was as good as over, and the landlords would be laughing up their sleeves at them.

On and on she harangued till at last, with a mighty Hampden roar, the men of Fairfield's agreed to march with her and those who'd been at the Govan Cross meeting, to the Small Debts Court.

Management stood helplessly in the background as Helen Crawfurd pied-pipered their men away out of the gates in the direction of town. When the last man had gone a Sunday silence settled over the yard.

As though by osmosis word flew round the city of what was happening, that Helen Crawfurd was leading a small army of protestors to the Small Debts Court.

Maclean was with Willie Gallagher when he heard, and they immediately stopped what they were about and caught a tram, the pair of them anxious to witness events at the Court. To witness, and speak if asked.

'Are you all right?' Bobby asked Cathy.

'Will you stop worrying! I'm fine.' Though in truth she was finding it harder going than she'd thought she would.

More and more people – one of these a scrap-metal man with his horse and cart – were joining the army of protestors, continually swelling their numbers.

When Bobby spied the scrap-metal man he knew what he had to do for peace of mind. 'Come on, you!' he said to Cathy, grasping her firmly by the hand.

When the scrap-metal man heard Bobby's request he immediately replied. 'Aye, of course Jimmy. Get yourself and the missus aboard.' And with that he stopped his horse so that Bobby could help Cathy up on to an empty space on the cart, after which he jumped up to sit beside her.

'That's better,' Bobby said to Cathy after the horse and cart had resumed moving.

'You're a bonny, bonny man, Bobby McCracken, one of the bonniest,' she replied, her heart swollen with love and affection for him.

'You're not so bad yourself,' he told her.

'Will we let them put our rents up?' someone shouted, beginning a chant.

'Never!' came the response.

'Will we let them attack our wages?'

'Never!'

'Will we let them put our comrades in jail?'

'Never!'

And with that they started the chant all over again.

'Will we let them put our rents up?'

Sheriff Lee was in his chambers having a quick forty winks when he was rudely awakened by his clerk Sammy banging on the door.

'Come in!' he called out, yawning.

'There's a revolution going on outside, my Lord,' Sammy announced breathlessly.

'Eh? What are you talking about?'

'The *hoi polloi*, my Lord. They've risen in revolt.'

Sheriff Lee smiled. Sammy was well known for his exaggeration and over-developed sense of the dramatic. 'Revolution, is it?'

'It is my Lord. Hordes of them. Listen!'

Sheriff Lee's chambers were tucked away at the rear of the building in a spot that was normally deathly quiet. But now he did listen he could hear . . . Well he could hear something or other. Going to the window he pulled back the heavy velvet curtains that had been drawn, then lifted the bottom section of the window.

The normal deathly quiet was now alive with the sound of angry human voices, many, many voices intermingling to make a cacophony of noise.

Sheriff Lee frowned, and closed the window again. With Sammy at his heels he hurried from his chambers out into the warren of corridors that would take him to the front of the Court building.

A platform had been made for Helen Crawfurd that was unique. Long poster boards had been picked up from the front of newspaper shops and these placed on the shoulders of half a dozen husky, well-matched workers. Helen had then been hoisted up onto the poster boards from where she was now addressing the multitude before her.

'Good God!' muttered Sheriff Lee when he saw Helen and the multitude from the vantage of a front window. It looked as though the *hoi polloi had* risen in revolution. For once Sammy hadn't been exaggerating.

Roar after roar of rage went up as Helen, words pouring out of her rat-a-tat-tat! like some machine gun at the front, recounted incidents demonstrating the unscrupulousness and greed of the landlords.

' . . . we women who have made the greatest sacrifice at this time

139

of national crisis, thinking that a grateful country would protect our homes. This protection is not being given . . .'

And then, later. 'Rents must be frozen at pre-war level!' she ranted on.

Sheriff Lee worried a fingernail as he watched and listened. He'd despatched Sammy to summon extra police to summon those already in the building. What was keeping them? Why weren't they here? And what was going to be the outcome of this . . . this . . . anarchy?

Maclean and Gallagher fought their way to where Helen Crawfurd was. They'd arrived simultaneously with the men from Beardmore's Parkhead Forge and Barr & Stroud's.

Other Clyde yards were also on the march, converging on the Small Debts Court, while a whole host of smaller engineering firms, munitions factories, all manner of heavy and light industries, had closed their doors and set off to join the original protestors.

'The men from John Brown's are coming!' someone whispered. But they would be a while yet, having to hoof it all the way from Clydebank.

Helen Crawfurd, hoarse now, allowed herself to be temporarily replaced by John Maclean, who carried on her harangue.

At the rear of the building Chief Constable Stevenson sneaked in with a contingent of several hundred policemen. Straightaway Stevenson went into a confab with an extremely worried Sheriff Lee.

'I've never known anything like it,' Bobby commented to Cathy, shaking his head in amazement.

She nodded her agreement, then bent an ear to Maclean who was going on about the great petition that had gone to Downing Street and which, although accepted personally on the doorstep by Asquith himself, had so far been totally ignored.

This could easily lead to bloodshed, Bobby thought grimly. It seemed he'd come from one battle front right to another.

Cathy glanced down when her arm was tugged. It was Jessie McGloan who lived in the next-door close to her ma and da.

'Good to see you here!' Jessie said.

'And you, Jessie.'

'I wouldn't have missed this for the world. By the by, do you know your sister Lily went into labour earlier on?'

Cathy frowned. 'No, I didn't.'

'Last I heard, your ma had called the midwife and begun to get things ready for the birth.'

'Did you catch that, Bobby?' When he replied he hadn't, she repeated what Jessie McGloan had just told her.

'So what do you want to do?' he asked her.

'I want to stay here and see this thing through. But my place is with ma and Lily.'

'Right then,' he replied, jumping down from the cart. He then helped Cathy down, and after thanking Jessie for her news, they began, with Bobby in front, carving their way out of the multitude. Traffic had come to a standstill throughout the area where the Small Debts Court was located, but once out of that area – no easy task – Cathy and Bobby managed to catch a Partick-bound tram.

Everyone on the tram was talking excitedly about what was happening at the Small Debts Court.

'The Riot Act's to be read,' an old man declared.

'How do you know that?' a ginger-haired woman demanded.

'I heard it, missus.'

'I wouldn't be at all surprised if it is,' Cathy said to Bobby.

Neither would he, he thought.

Mrs Sharp from next door answered Cathy's knock. 'It's yourself,' said Mrs Sharp. 'Come away in.'

'How's Lily?'

'Doing just dandy, according to the midwife.'

'Is Ma in the bedroom with them?'

Mrs Sharp nodded. 'Aye, she is that.'

'Should I go through?'

'They might want you. Go and ask.'

Cathy instructed Bobby to stay in the kitchen, then went through to the bedroom, tapping lightly on the door before opening it and poking her head round.

'It's me Ma. Can I help?'

Winnie gestured her in. 'The baby's early. We weren't expecting it for some while yet,' she said softly to Cathy.

Lily, covered by a single sheet, was lying on the bed with her legs pulled back. 'The wee soul's premature, so it is,' she said to Cathy.

Cathy glanced at the midwife, but there was no contradictory look or expression on the midwife's face. She appeared to have accepted that the baby had come early. (Or if she knew better she wasn't letting on.)

'How do you feel?' Cathy asked her sister.

'Do you really want to know, with you being so close to your own time?'

Cathy grinned weakly. 'Maybe not.'

Lily tensed, then went rigid. 'Aaaggghhh!' she gargled, a tortured noise at the back of her throat.

Uttering a deep sigh, Lily relaxed again, Winnie wiped her face with a towel, then her neck.

'I'll just have another peek,' the midwife said, and lifted the sheet. She bent to peer up Lily's crotch, grunted with satisfaction, and replaced the sheet.

'How long do you think?' Cathy asked.

The midwife shook her head. 'First babies in particular are awful difficult to predict. But as a general rule they tend to be slower in coming rather than faster.'

'If you want to help you can go and do a bit of shopping for me,' Winnie said to Cathy. 'I've nothing in for your da and Dougie's tea.'

'Aye, of course. I've got Bobby with me by the way.'

'Then you'd better include him when you do your buying. Something cheap mind, that'll stretch.'

'I know something round here that's stretching,' Lily said crudely, and laughed.

Cathy had just started telling them about Helen Crawfurd's march on the Small Debts Court when Lily had another contraction.

Cathy glanced at the clock on the mantelpiece. If the men at Thompson's hadn't gone to the Small Debts Court then her da and Dougie should be in shortly; if they had then God alone knew what time they'd be home.

She and Bobby – Mrs Sharp had long since left them – looked at the wall common to both kitchen and bedroom when Lily's shriek rendered the air, Lily having begun to shriek half an hour previously. When the shriek was over Cathy returned to stirring the mince she was cooking. She was finding Lily's shrieking extremely disconcerting, but didn't want to say so.

'It can't be long now,' she said to Bobby.

'No,' he agreed. But they were just talking, neither of them really knew that it wouldn't be much longer.

'What's that?' Bobby said, cocking his head.

Cathy listened also. 'Sounds like singing.'

She and Bobby went to the window and gazed down into the backcourts where all they saw were two little boys kicking a can about, pretending it was a football.

And then, suddenly, a group of men and women burst out of a backclose, quickly followed by others out of adjoining backcloses.

All these people were singing, whooping, and generally rejoicing. A few of the men had clearly been at the drink from the way they were staggering.

Cathy threw up the bottom part of the window, and leant out on the ledge. All around the backcourts other windows were shooting up.

'We won! We bloody won!' a man shouted, punching the air.

For the space of a heartbeat Bobby thought the man was referring to the war, and that the war was over.

'They released the arrested eighteen!' another man yelled.

Cathy clapped her hands in glee. 'Who released them?' she queried.

'The Sheriff. He got the petitioner to drop his case against the eighteen, and they walked free.'

'Oh that's grand!' Cathy muttered to herself. 'That's just grand.'

'Was the Riot Act read?' Bobby shouted.

'Naw! We were waiting for that swine Stevenson to do it, but he never did.'

'Lost his nerve!' someone else called out.

'I belong to Glasgow, dear old Glasgow town . . .' That was the song being sung, and it now swelled in volume as voices from the tenements themselves took it up:

There's nothing the matter with Glasgow, except it's going
round and round.
I'm only a common old working chap . . .'

'We're home!' Dougie shouted from the hallway.

Cathy quickly pulled herself back into the kitchen, and hurried through to meet him. Dougie's face was flushed, as was her da's.

'Have you heard what's been happening the day?' Dougie demanded.

'Thompson's marched to the Small Debts Court then, I take it?'

'Every man jack with the exception of those in management. You should have seen us striding along, row upon row of us, line upon line. It was a fantastic sight.'

'I can imagine. Bobby and I were there to, but had to rush here when we heard the news.'

'What news?' John asked.

Cathy gave Dougie her reply. 'Lily's in labour. The baby's well on its way.'

Their heads swung in unison towards the bedroom door when Lily shrieked again.

'Jesus Christ!' Dougie said quietly when the shriek was over. His flush had gone, leaving him ashen.

'Is the midwife here?' John queried anxiously.

'Since the beginning. She says everything's going fine. It's only a matter of time.' She turned to Dougie. 'Do you want to go through?'

'Not me!' he exclaimed in alarm. 'No, no! No, thank you! I'll wait until it's all over before I go in and see her.'

It was the answer Cathy had expected; men were notorious cowards when it came to this sort of thing. Anyway, it was probably just as well he didn't want to go in; most midwives disapproved of the husband being present at the birth.

John closed the front door behind him, then he and Dougie followed Cathie into the kitchen where they were greeted by Bobby.

'I'll put the potatoes on. You'll both still want your tea, I take it?'

'Oh aye!' Dougie confirmed eagerly, which caused Cathy to smile. Wasn't that just like a man, his wife was in agony but he was still eager for his tea. And he would probably ask for a second helping too from what she knew of Douglas Mailer.

'I'm just away back out. I'll only be a couple of minutes,' John announced, and left them.

Lily shrieked again, the loudest shriek yet.

'It sounds like . . .' Dougie trailed off, and bit his lip. He didn't want to say what it sounded like. In fact, he didn't even want to think it.

144

'A great victory today,' Bobby said to Dougie.

'It is that.'

Cathy and Bobby listened intently as Dougie went on to describe what had occurred after they left, which was roughly the same time he and the others from Tommy's had arrived.

'It's amazing how the word got round Glasgow so fast,' Bobby commented after Dougie had finished.

'It literally swept through Tommy's. One minute we were hard at work, the next we all seemed to have heard, and the next we were out in support and marching into town.'

Lily had been shrieking throughout this conversation. Dougie now wrung his hands when she did so yet again. 'She'll be all right, won't she?' he asked Cathy.

'This is quite normal,' Cathy replied, thinking that the best answer to make. As far as she knew it was.

Several shrieks later John returned with a half-bottle of whisky.

'I could murder some of that, so I could,' Dougie said when he saw the half-bottle.

John poured the three men large drams, Cathy declining when he asked if she'd care for one.

The half-bottle was empty, the tea over and done with when Winnie barged into the kitchen. 'Congratulations, it's a son!' she cried out to Dougie.

His face lit up. 'A son!'

'A fine bouncing boy.'

The others present who were sitting jumped to their feet and crowded round Dougie, John getting there first to shake his hand.

'And Lily?' Dougie queried over John's shoulder.

'Nothing to worry about. You can see her shortly.' And with that Winnie disappeared back to the bedroom.

'I'm so happy for you,' Cathy said, kissing Dougie on the cheek.

'I'm happy for myself.'

'I should have bought a bottle of that whisky,' John said, staring over at the empty half-bottle.

And then Winnie was with them once more. 'You're not going to believe this,' she said in a strange voice.

Silence settled over the kitchen. 'Believe what?' Dougie asked hoarsely.

'It appears there's another on the way. Lily is having twins.'

'Twins!' Dougie gulped.

'That's what the midwife says.'

'But . . . but . . .' Dougie was lost for words.

This was a complete surprise, Cathy thought. There had been no indication that twins were on the way.

'Two for the price of one,' Bobby said with a laugh.

'Maybe it's even more: *triplets*!' John said mischievously.

'Oh my good God! Think how much they'd cost to feed and clothe,' Dougie breathed.

'Or quadruplets,' John went on.

Dougie realised he was having his leg pulled. 'If it's that then you're going to have to chip in and help, old yin,' he retorted. Old yin was something he called the fifty-three-year-old John when he wanted to annoy his father-in-law.

Quarter of an hour later Winnie burst in again. 'It's another boy, as fit and healthy as the first,' she announced.

'And is that it?' Dougie asked.

'That's it. No more.'

Dougie let out a long sigh. '*Two* boys!'

There was another round of hand-shaking, and another kiss from Cathy. Then Dougie was taken through to see an extremely tired and worn out Lily, who was nonetheless beaming with pleasure.

After a few minutes Cathy, Bobby and John went through also, and there was a very proud Lily lying with a swaddled baby in the crook of either arm.

'They look the spit of me,' Dougie declared, which made everyone else laugh.

'Oh, the very spit!' Winnie agreed, tongue in cheek.

Cathy bent over to view the babies more closely. 'They're smashing,' she said to Lily.

'Rare, eh?'

'Couldn't be rarer.'

'She should get some sleep now,' the midwife said.

'Aye, of course,' agreed Cathy, straightening up again.

'I am very sleepy,' Lily stated.

'Come on then, shoo!' said Winnie, flapping her hands, gesturing the others towards the door.

Back in the kitchen Dougie said to Bobby and John. 'Right, it's the pub then, to wet the babies' heads?'

'Lead on MacDuff,' smiled John.

'I don't think I will, if you don't mind,' Bobby said softly, and shot Cathy a sideways glance.

'What do you mean you don't think you will?' Dougie demanded. 'You must!'

Bobby shook his head. 'No, I don't think so.'

'On you go, love,' Cathy urged.

He gave her a small frown that said he didn't want to.

She realised at the same moment Dougie did why Bobby was hanging back: money. With things as they were he didn't believe he could afford to go out.

Cathy's lips thinned; he was right of course. They needed every farthing.

'It's my treat you know, and it's not very often I push the boat out,' Dougie said. 'I've been putting by for this. Look, I'll show you.'

He went into the hallway, delved into a jacket pocket, then he returned holding three ten-shilling notes. 'See, here it is. Money I've specially saved to celebrate the birth, or births as it's turned out. So the night is on me, and I'll have no arguing about that.'

'On you go Bobby.' Cathy repeated. 'Away and enjoy yourself.'

'You'll insult me and the weans if you don't come, so you will,' Dougie said, pretending anger.

'All right then,' Bobby capitulated with a smile. He didn't really like not paying his own way, but in the circumstances he supposed it was acceptable.

'I won't be too long,' he whispered to Cathy after he'd pecked her goodbye.

Nor would he get drunk, he swore to himself. The time left them together was much too short for him to waste it on that.

Cathy was deep in a library book, *The Cloister and the Hearth* by Charles Reade, when Bobby got home. As he'd promised, he hadn't stayed out that long.

'How was it?' she smiled.

'Fine.'

'And Dougie?'

'Aiming to get legless.'

'And my da?'

'Keeping an eye on him so he won't come to any grief.'

Bobby crossed to where Cathy was sitting, knelt beside her and kissed her.

'Hmmh!' she murmured when the kiss was over.

'Bed?'

She nodded.

'It's good that Lily had boys. I hope we have one too.'

'Your son and heir?' she teased gently.

His face darkened. 'Not just that. This country is going to need every boy it can get to replace those men we'll lose in the war.'

It was a sentiment that spoiled an otherwise marvellous day, Cathy thought.

Or then again, perhaps it didn't so much spoil the day as put it into perspective.

On this occasion, because he was going south, Bobby was leaving from the Central Station, the L.M.S. line.

Once inside the station they immediately spotted Jack Smart who waved to them, and they had just linked up with Jack when Colin Baker and his wife Ishbel appeared.

There had been six going off last time, Cathy thought grimly. Now Gordon and Tim were dead, Bill Coltraine in an English hospital somewhere. They didn't know precisely where, only that the hospital was in England.

'Here we all are again then,' Jack said cheerfully when Colin and Ishbel joined them.

Not quite, Cathy very nearly commented, but didn't. Ishbel was looking as wretched as she had last time Cathy thought. She doubted she was looking all that clever herself. She couldn't have slept for more than an hour the night before and that short sleep had been fitful and nightmare-ridden.

'Let's get our seats in case the train's busy,' Bobby suggested, thinking the last thing he, Jack and Colin needed was to have to stand all the way down south.

Bobby bought a platform ticket for Cathy, Colin one for Ishbel, then the four of them followed on after Jack, who had led the way through the barrier.

Jack found an empty compartment at the very front of the

train in which they laid claim to three seats by placing their kitbags on them.

Cathy's stomach was churning and she had the bitter taste of bile in her mouth. Despite the heaviness of her pregnancy she felt strangely ethereal, as if she was only partly there.

'Well that's the fastest week I've ever known,' Bobby said, forcing a smile onto his face.

She nodded.

'Just whizzed by.'

'Yes.'

'I eh . . .' He took a deep breath.

'Hold me, Bobby!'

He did, though that wasn't easy because of her bump.

'Keep those letters coming. I treasure each and every one.'

'I will. I promise.'

'And don't worry that you recount what goes on out there. If it helps you to put it onto paper then that's what I want you to do. Sharing the bad things as well as the good is what marriage is about after all.'

'I eh . . .' He dropped his voice to speak in a whisper. 'I love you Cathy.'

'I know that. Just as you know I love you,' she replied, also whispering.

'I wish I could be here for the birth of the baby.'

'Oh, so do I!'

He shrugged. 'We both just have to accept that I can't be. But it's hard, right enough.'

'Yes,' she agreed.

They talked for a few minutes more, and then it was time for the train's departure.

'Get on board,' she said, breaking from him – the last thing she wanted to do.

He turned to the train, hesitated, then turned again and caught her to him. He gave her a final kiss and as they kissed hot tears rolled down her face.

The guard blew his whistle, and waved his green flag.

'I love you,' Bobby repeated, then abruptly left her and jumped onto the train with Colin Baker directly behind him: Colin catching the door and banging it shut.

Bobby and Colin leaned out of the open window to wave, Jack having already lowered it for them, while Jack waved from behind another window.

'God!' Ishbel choked, waving frantically. 'God! God! God!'

Cathy had thought it would be easier second time round, but it wasn't. If anything it was more difficult.

After a while she and Ishbel, clutching one another for support, went off to the refreshments room.

Chapter 5

'Not again!' Bobby muttered in irritation as the train squealed to a halt, the umpteenth time they'd stopped since leaving the Central Station. Wiping the steamed-up window he saw they were at a small station, but couldn't spot a sign giving its name.

Jack went out into the corridor, to return a few seconds later, the corridor side of the train being against the platform.

'There's a trolley further down. I'll try and get us some tea,' he announced, and disappeared again.

'Hold on, I'll come with you! I need to stretch my legs,' Colin called out, going after Jack.

Bobby yawned. What a journey! It was proving interminable. Time after time they'd stopped for no apparent reason, and just sat there for ages before moving on again. At one point they'd stopped for almost two and a half hours before finally, with a judder, jolt and much hissing of steam, resuming their journey.

'Any seats going in here, mate?'

The speaker was a soldier standing in the open corridor door. 'Aye, come on in,' replied Bobby – he and his two pals had so far been lucky in having the compartment to themselves.

The soldier came into the compartment and looked around. 'Which can I have?' he asked.

Bobby indicated Jack and Colin's seats. 'Those are taken. Choose any of the others you like.'

'Ta!'

The soldier heaved his kitbag up onto the luggage netting, sat and pulled out a packet of cigarettes. 'Fag?'

'Don't smoke, thanks.'

The soldier nodded, placed a slightly bent cigarette between his lips, and lit up. He blew out a stream of smoke with a sigh.

Bobby hoped Jack and Colin thought to buy sandwiches if there were any for sale; he was absolutely ravenous.

'Where are we?' he asked the soldier.

151

'Garstang.'

Bobby was none the wiser. 'Where's that?'

'Just north of Preston.'

'That's Lancashire isn't it?'

'It is.'

Bobby groaned; there was a long way to go yet till they reached London. And then they had a changeover of trains there to take them further on to Wiltshire where the battalion was.

'Been on leave?' the soldier asked by way of making conversation.

Bobby nodded. 'Only a week though. Could have done with a month.'

'I know what 'ee means,' the soldier said.

The engine tooted, then tooted again. 'All aboard! All aboard!' a guard yelled.

'Damn!' Bobby muttered, thinking he wasn't going to get his tea, but he was wrong.

Jack and Colin were laughing as they piled back on board, Jack carrying two cups and saucers, Colin one.

'That was close,' Bobby said to Jack as Jack came into the compartment, the train already underway.

'Aye, we were the last served,' Jack replied, handing Bobby a cup and brimming saucer. 'Sorry about the spillage, couldn't be helped,' he apologised.

Bobby gratefully accepted the tea. 'You didn't manage to get a wad as well, did you? My stomach's beginning to think my throat's been cut.'

'Wait a wee,' Colin answered, groping in a pocket to produce a brown paper bag. 'Half a dozen *hot* sausage rolls. How's that?'

'The stuff to give the troops,' Bobby enthused. When he took the sausage roll Colin gave him he discovered it wasn't hot but piping hot.

'How about you? Would you like one?' Colin queried of the soldier who was watching them.

'No ta, mate. I had a good tuck in before I left home. Thanks all the same.'

When Bobby's sausage roll had cooled sufficiently he wolfed it down, then asked Colin for another. He was waiting for that one to cool when it struck him the soldier's face was familiar. But only vaguely so. The soldier was wearing a greatcoat so he couldn't tell from his uniform flashes what battalion the soldier belonged to, and there were no identifyng flashes on the soldier's chip-bag cap. It wasn't his own mob, the 16th (S), he was certain of that.

'That was Garstang, just north of Preston,' Bobby informed Jack and Colin.

'We know. There was a sign facing the trolley,' Jack replied.

When Bobby finished his tea he started to wish he could have a second cup. Perhaps they'd stop at another station with a trolley on the platform.

Jack laid his now empty cup and saucer on the floor, sniffed, leaned back and closed his eyes.

Good idea, Bobby thought, he'd have a zizz as well. He was just about to drift off when suddenly, in a blinding flash, it came to him who the soldier was.

'You're Charlie!' he blurted out to the astonished soldier.

'How does 'ee know that?'

'We were there when they hauled you out The Cut. It was our lot who supplied the rope your mates used.'

'Jesus!' Charlie breathed, remembering, 'but that was a close call. And you were there?'

'The three of us were.'

'I didn't recognise you at first, but I do now,' Colin said to Charlie.

'Charlie Franklyn,' he said, extending a hand to Bobby.

'Bobby McCracken, and this is Colin Baker.'

'Howdo,' said a delighted Charlie shaking with Colin.

'Wake up Jack, you'll never guess who this is.'

'Uh! Uh!' muttered Jack blearily, for he had dropped off.

'Charlie from The Cut. The drunken tunneller who fell into The Cut that day in the salient.'

'Drunk as a lord,' Charlie laughed, shaking a bemused Jack.

'You were lucky that day,' Bobby said to him.

'Luck! It was a miracle I came out of that alive. Thank the Lord that Gerry and his pals had a sense of humour.'

'Well, well, well!' mused Bobby.

'I was drunk on rum,' Charlie went on. 'Speaking of which . . .' Coming to his feet, he got up on his seat, reached into the luggage netting and opened his kitbag. There was a chink as he extracted a bottle of dark rum.

'I think this calls for a celebration, don't you?' Charlie beamed, sitting once more. 'It was your lot that supplied that rope after all.'

'A tot would go down nicely,' Jack enthused, eyeing the bottle.

'Wipe out those cups and I'll drink from the bottle itself,' Charlie instructed. When the cups were duly wiped, handkerchiefs being used for the task, he poured them each a hefty measure of rum.

'That'll warm the cockles,' Charlie said with a smile.

Bobby had a sip. Charlie was right, it did just that.

'Now, who are your mob?' Charlie queried.

'The 16th (S) Battalion of the Rifle Brigade,' Jack replied.

'I knows o' 'ee all right. You were on the salient for some while, isn't that right?'

'In for some while and going back there again we think,' Bobby said.

Charlie pulled a face. 'Tough.'

'You can say that again,' Colin agreed.

'I'm in Captain Greener's No 4 Section of the 172 Tunnelling Company, Royal Engineers,' Charlie stated.

'With Fred Gaddas and someone called George,' Bobby smiled.

'They're me muckers. Thick as shit in a bucket, we are.'

Bobby laughed – what a marvellously graphic expression! 'We heard them calling each other by name when they were trying to pull you out The Cut. Are they both still . . .' He paused, then said, 'Alive?'

'They be. It's a lot safer under the salient than it is on top of it and that's the truth,' Charlie answered.

'Anywhere is safer than the salient,' Jack muttered, which got a growl of agreement from Colin.

'We do lose men, of course,' Charlie went on. 'But nothing like those fighting above.' He gave them another hefty tot each. 'Good stuff, eh?'

'It is that,' said Bobby.

'120° proof. Knock your socks off.'

'It's certainly strong,' agreed Colin who could already feel the effect after only one tot.

The four of them chatted, and drank, talking about the salient and their experiences there. The three Glasgow lads had all taken a shine to Charlie Franklyn; he could have been one of their own. And Charlie had taken a similar shine to them.

Jack had been tired before; the rum now made him a lot more so. The bottle was only half empty when his head lolled sideways and he began to snore.

Colin followed shortly after that. And as he slept a smile crept onto his face. He was dreaming of Ishbel.

'Are you married?' Bobby asked Charlie.

'T'a lass called Sylvia. And we have six babas: four boys, two girls.'

'Six!' Bobby exclaimed, and whistled.

'The oldest is Arthur who's ten. When t'war's over and he's old enough he'll go down t'pit same as me. All the boys will.'

'A pit in Garstang?'

'Nay, in a village calles Goosclough a few miles east of Garstang. There have been Franklyns working t'pit in Goosclough for generations, and I hope will continue to do so.'

'We're all experienced with coal ourselves,' Bobby smiled.

'You are! Thou art not colliers too?'

Still smiling, Bobby shook his head. 'No, we're coalmen. We didn't dig the stuff but sold it off a horse and cart.'

'Even so,' Charlie said. It was a further bond. 'And are you wed yourself?'

'Aye. Her name's Cathy.'

'And babas?'

'One on the way. Cathy's due very soon now.'

Charlie beamed. 'That calls for another tot, eh?' He poured more rum into Bobby's cup. 'You must be a happy man?'

Bobby swallowed some of the rum. His mind had gone fuzzy at the edges, but not enough to stop himself thinking clearly. It was exactly the same with Charlie Franklyn.

'I should be, but I'm not,' he replied quietly.

'And why's that mate?'

Normally Bobby would never have told his story to a complete stranger, but the rum had loosened his tongue, and anyway, by now Charlie didn't seem like a stranger. They had The Cut, and the salient in common. Still speaking quietly he related to Charlie how he'd returned home to find Cathy pregnant, and that she'd lost her job at Mavor & Coulson because of it, about the lodger Taylor who'd punched and kicked her, and her getting another job as a cleaner in the local school, how desperately short she was of money to keep the house going . . . It all poured out.

'Ssshh!' Charlie said, a noise of sympathy, when Bobby was finally finished.

Bobby downed what was left in his cup, and Charlie immediately poured him another tot.

'So what are you going to do?' Charlie asked.

'Bobby shrugged. 'Hellish little I can do. The only solution I've come up with is to try and get myself promoted to N.C.O. level. That would help. The only trouble is . . .' He took a deep breath. 'As you probably know the casualty rate is even higher amongst N.C.O.s than it is amongst the men.'

Charlie nodded, he knew that for fact. 'It's a booger, eh?'

'It's a booger,' Bobby agreed.

'And she won't go and stay with her mum and dad?

'Won't give up our house unless she's absolutely forced to. Besides, living with her ma and da would be sheer murder now that her sister, whom as I've already said, lives there with her husband, has just produced twins. That would be five adults and three screaming weans in two rooms. And it's not just the fact it would be five adults, but it would be two married couples plus Cathy. That's where the pressure would be.'

'I understand,' said Charlie.

The train came to yet another unscheduled halt. Bobby wiped his window again, and peered out. But all he could see were winter fields. They could have been anywhere.

Charlie produced a pipe which he proceeded to fill from a round metal tin. When it was filled and tamped down to his satisfaction he lit up.

The train jolted, then resumed moving. Chuh! Chuh! Chuh! Chuh! the engine went.

'I wonder?' murmured Charlie, a faraway look in his eyes. He brought his attention back to Bobby.

'Our Captain Greener is a tremendous man, couldn't find better officer in all t'army. And our Sarn't's just as good; his name is Deeming, a miner from Backworth in Northumberland.

'Oh aye?' smiled Bobby, still thinking of Cathy and the plight he'd left her in.

'We get six shillings a day you know, while you only get a bob.'

'You do well,' Bobby agreed.

'We're all pitmen, you understand, and sewer construction workers. Hard grafters.' He paused. 'I wonder . . .' He repeated to himself.

'Wonder what?'

'I could have a word with Captain Greener and Sarn't Deeming, put it to them, like.'

Bobby was mystified. 'Put what Charlie?'

'Getting 'ee transferred into our section. The only trouble is 'ee's not a pitman or sewer construction worker. But then again . . .' He grinned mischievously. ''Ee are a coal worker are 'ee not? 'Tain't a lie to say that, now is it?'

'You mean me become a tunneller?'

'Six shillings a day; six times more than you're getting now. And as I've said, it's a deal safer down below than it is up on top.'

Elation filled Bobby, that and relief. Here was the perfect solution. 'Do you think your Captain Greener and Sergeant Deeming would agree to ask for me?'

'They could well. If I explain the circumstances to them, and point out that it was your rope saved me at The Cut.'

'It wasn't my rope exactly,' Bobby replied. 'It belonged to others of our mob nearby.'

Charlie tapped his nose. 'Captain Greener and Sarn't Deeming aren't to know that, are they? And one thing we tunnellers are to each other is loyal. We're all . . .'

'Thick as shit in a bucket,' Bobby cut in with a smile.

'That's it exactly. 'Ee has to be down below. Each man relies on his muckers for his very life.'

'If you can swing it for Bobby, do you think you could also swing it for me?' Colin Baker asked softly. Neither Bobby or Charlie had realised that Colin had wakened and been listening to their conversation.

'Or all three of us?' Bobby added, thinking of Jack. It would be rotten for himself and Colin to leave Jack.

Charlie sucked on his pipe. 'If I ask for one I suppose I can ask for all three. Why not? Like musketeers, eh?'

'Like musketeers,' Bobby agreed.

'If anyone's got pencil and paper I'll take down t'details.'

Before he did that Charlie poured Bobby and Colin another tot, then finished the bottle in one large swallow.

'Privates McCracken, Baker and Smart suhh!' Corporal Beach barked, saluting.

'Thank you Corporal, you may leave us.' Major Kandy waited till the corporal had gone, then said to Bobby, Colin and Jack standing rigidly at attention, 'At ease men. Easy.'

The 16th were camped waiting to go into the salient where they'd be relieving the North Staffs. Major Kandy was one of the battalion's new officers; it would be the first time in the salient for him, as it would be for the large majority of new men who now comprised the 16th.

Major Kandy picked up the sheet of paper in front of him, glanced quickly over it, then said, 'This is a request from the Royal Engineers asking for you three to be transferred immediately to one of their units. It says they wish you to become tunnellers because of your extensive experience in coal. Colliers, eh?'

'It's been nothing but the coal for us since we left school,' Bobby answered truthfully, if misleadingly.

'I understand the tunnelling companies are of prime importance out here, the apple of General Plumer's eye. In which case I can hardly turn down their request for you. But it's a sad loss to the 16th, we desperately need the experience of all you chaps who were here before. However . . .' Picking up a pen he signed the sheet of paper with a flourish.

'You'll report to the Royal Engineers at Vlamertinghe right away.'

'So that's me off the financial hook,' Cathy said to Lily who was changing wee David's nappy. The twins had been named David and Ewan, David being the elder.

'A tremendous relief for you, eh?'

'You can say that again.' Cathy had just received the news of Bobby's transfer that morning and had come hurrying over to tell her ma and Lily. John and Dougie were at work, and her ma was out so she'd only been able to tell Lily, who was naturally delighted for her.

'It's better pay than he was earning in Miller's coalyard,' Cathy said.

'And your cleaning job?'

'It's ta-ta to that right away.'

'Oh you bugger!' Lily exclaimed as David wee-ed over the clean nappy she was just about to pin on him.

Cathy laughed. 'Did you see the way his willie stood up before he let go. That was funny!'

'Aye,' Lily agreed, smiling.

Picking David up she kissed him, cradled him in her arm, then tossed the now soiled nappy into a galvanised bucket under the sink. Crossing the kitchen she got out another nappy.

'What's the latest on the rent strike?' she queried.

'We're standing firm. Hell will freeze over first before they break us.'

'What about this inquiry the Government has set up?'

Cathy's lips thinned. 'It has been decided that the class composition of the inquiry team is such that it is unlikely to find in our favour. So the strike goes on.'

'Wherever you go it's still the main topic of conversation. People talk about it much more than the war itself.'

'It's become Glasgow's own war, and like the one over in France and Belgium it's become one of attrition,' Cathy stated.

Lily, whose sense of humour was never far below the surface, couldn't resist jibing, 'Oh *attrition*, is it?'

'It means wearing the enemy down, weakening and exhausting them by constant friction and harassment, and it's a newspaper word that Helen Crawfurd has taken up. So there!' Cathy replied, and stuck out her tongue at Lily, which made them both laugh.

'Ohh!' Cathy gasped, grabbing her stomach.

'Are you all right?' Lily asked anxiously.

'Just a sudden pain. It's gone now.' And with that Cathy straightened again.

'What sort of pain?'

'I haven't started if that's what you mean.' At least she didn't think she had. It hadn't felt like a contraction. Not that she knew precisely what a contraction felt like, but that hadn't seemed like one.

'I'll just sit for a minute,' she said.

'Can I get you something?'

Cathy shook her head.

Lily laid out the nappy on the table and dexterously, using only one hand, began to fold it. 'I had a thought yesterday,' she said.

'That's an unusual experience for you,' Cathy quipped, getting her own back.

'It's a thought that'll take that smile off your face.'

'Well, what is it?' Cathy demanded when Lily didn't go on.

'Remember how I had that nauseous attack and went green when first pregnant, and how exactly the same thing happened to you'

Cathy nodded.

'And our pregnancies have been very similar, haven't they?'

'Yes.' She had to admit they had.

'What if you're carrying twins also, and as I was, are totally oblivious of the fact?'

'Twins! *Me!*'

Lily laughed at the expression on Cathy's face. It was simply priceless.

Could that be so? Cathy wondered. There was no history of twins on her side, apart from Lily now, and none on Bobby's as far as she knew. But then, there had been none on Dougie's either.

'Could be,' teased Lily.

It had never crossed Cathy's mind that she too might have twins. But now . . .'

'I'll tell you this, Bobby would be ecstatic if I did have twins. Particularly if they were both boys.'

Then she remembered what Bobby had said about boys, and went chill all over.

Bobby stopped digging to lean on his pick, a broad-bladed variety of pick that was ideal for digging out the blue clay that was the core of the salient. Sweat was running down him in rivers while his hair was plastered to his head. Charlie hadn't been lying when he'd warned them that tunnelling was backbreaking work. It was even more so than he'd imagined.

He was roughly halfway through his present shift, which meant he'd been at it for four hours, each shift being eight hours long. It was on for eight, off for sixteen. Four days in the tunnels, four out at rest. The tunnelling itself never ceased, twenty-four hours a day men dug and excavated continuously.

Bobby, Colin and Jack were in Captain Greener's No 4 Section, which like all tunnelling sections was split into groups. Usually the three of them worked in the same group, but not always. It depended on how Sergeant Deeming wanted the section divided up.

'It's a killer, eh?' said Jack from a few feet away on Bobby's left.

That day the three pals were digging, other days they were assigned to sandbag-filling, the filled sandbags having to be then toted to the shaft bottom where they were winched to the surface.

'Six shillings a day and no bullets buzzing round your ears, look at it that way,' Bobby replied.

'Oh I am! I am!' Jack said, his pick thunking once more into the heavy clay.

Bobby took a swig from the bottle of water he had beside him, then it was back to work.

Thunk! Thunk!Thunk!

'An idea's been put forward which I consider to be a good one,' Helen Crawfurd announced. She paused, then smiled broadly. 'It came from one of the children at Socialist Sunday School.'

Cathy exchanged amused glances with Jean Ferguson. She hadn't gone to Socialist Sunday School herself, but knew all about it. There were many such Sunday Schools in Partick, as there were many other Socialist organisations including Socialist Choirs. Socialist Choirs were every popular.

'And what's that?' Mary Barbour queried.

'We find out the address of every landlord who's trying to raise his rents and, at an agreed time and in a concerted action, we smash their windows by putting bricks through them.'

'Oh, I like that!' smiled Agnes Dollan, the other person present at Helen Crawfurd's house in Govan.

'John Maclean will disapprove,' said Jean Ferguson quietly.

'To hell with John!' Helen retorted fiercely. 'What was the outcome of his great petition? Absolutely nothing. Stony silence. I tell you, direct action is the only way we are going to win this conflict.'

Helen had certainly organised plenty of that, Cathy thought to herself. Since that day at the Sheriff Court there had been a series of marches, demonstrations, public appeals, meetings, etc. The pot had never been off the boil as Helen continued to stir matters up, trying to bring the rent strike to a head with a general strike in Glasgow, the reality of which, it was commonly agreed, was looming closer and closer as the Government persisted with its intransigence.

'I shall be amongst the brick-throwers,' Helen said. 'As you all know I have some experience in that line of work.' She was referring of course to the windows of the Minister of Education in London that she'd smashed as a militant suffragette, and those of an army recruiting office in Glasgow.

'And me! declared Mary Barbour.

'And me!' 'And me!' said Jean Ferguson and Agnes Dollan in quick succession. The only one who hadn't volunteered was Cathy.

'We won't expect you to take part in such an action because of your condition,' Helen Crawfurd said understandingly to Cathy.

'Can I say something?'

'Of course.'

'You went to jail for smashing windows, didn't you?'

A look of pride came onto Helen's face. 'I did.'

'Well if you throw more bricks and they catch you they'll jail you again.'

'If that's the case, so be it.'

Cathy frowned. 'But by going to jail, by all of you going to jail, you'd be playing straight into the landlords' hands. You ladies are the driving force behind this strike. Remove that force and the whole thing will completely collapse.'

Helen stared at Cathy, her lips pursed, eyes hooded. Slowly she exhaled. 'You're right, Cathy. We *would* be playing straight into the landlords' hands if we got ourselves locked away. But we'll have to explain clearly to those who do throw the bricks why we're not with them.'

Cathy felt she'd earned her place at the table that day with these women she so much admired.

No 4 Section raced along the twisting, turning lane of duck-boards leading to Hellfire Corner where transport would be waiting to take them to their rest billets at Vlamertinghe.

'Jesus!' Bobby muttered to himself – the noise of exploding shells was horrendous, particularly so after the quietness of the

162

tunnels. A veritable hail of shells screamed overhead, while in the background was the constant chatter of machine-gun fire.

They were forced to slow down as a party of men came hurrying towards them from the opposite direction.

'Hey up!' one of these men called.

Bobby was fascinated to see that each of these men had a large bag – each bag weighing fifty pounds – strapped to his back.

'What's in the bags?' he asked Charlie.

'Ammonal explosive. They'll be taking it to one of the tunnels.'

He paused, then said, 'The silly boogers shouldn't be so close together. If one goes west t'all will.'

Pleasantries were exchanged in passing, then No 4 Section was hurrying on with the party of Kensingtons behind them.

The explosion knocked Bobby flying, and Jack unconscious. Colin went into a mudhole but was quickly fished out.

'What was that?' Bobby gasped at Charlie. It certainly hadn't been a shell going off, the explosion had been far too great.

'Our friends with the ammonal I should think,' Charlie replied.

Bobby went to Jack, who was just coming round. 'What happened?' Jack queried groggily. 'I heard a bang and then it was curtains.'

Bobby repeated what Charlie had said to him.

'Poor sods!' Jack exclaimed softly.

When he had determined that Jack wasn't injured in any way Bobby helped him to his feet.

'Go back and take a look-see, Franklyn,' Captain Greener called out. He was squatting beside Sergeant Deeming who'd also been knocked unconscious by the blast. 'And take someone with you!'

Charlie caught Bobby's eye. 'Let's go, it'll only take a minute.'

With Charlie in the lead they retraced their footsteps till, turning a bend, they came across what was left of the Kensingtons.

There was blood, bits of flesh and guts everywhere. There were also arms, legs and heads.

Bobby had seen some ghastly sights in the salient, but somehow this was the ghastliest.

'They shouldn't have been so close together,' Charlie said. 'If

163

they hadn't been, only one of them would have gone up. They should have been at least fifty yards apart.'

'What set the ammonal off?' Bobby asked.

'God knows! A bullet, red hot scrap of shrapnel, rifle grenade, it could've been anything.' He shook his head. 'Silly boogers!'

They returned to Captain Greener and reported that there were no survivors. The party of Kensingtons had been wiped out.

Annihilated.

Cathy stood at the bedroom window staring out at the street below. Any second now, she thought. And with that the clock in the kitchen chimed midnight. The clock was still chiming when the clamour began.

The street was full of women, as was every street in Partick and all areas on rent strike. And each woman on the streets had her noisemaker with her which she would use and continue using for a full fifteen minutes.

The idea was a midnight noise protest to literally wake up those in authority, to drive home the point yet again that the strike was on-going, and that there was no escape from it for them, not even in sleep.

Two nights previously every landlord in Glasgow who was trying to raise his rents had had his windows smashed – forty-two women had been arrested as a result – and the night before every factor working for those landlords – only eighteen arrested that time.

Cathy shivered, and pulled her dressing gown more tightly about her. November was normally a bitter month in Glasgow, but it was even more bitter than usual that year. As soon as the noise protest was over she'd get into bed, she promised herself. She'd put a stone hot-water bottle in half an hour ago, so it would be nice and welcoming for her.

Eventually, fifteen minutes after it had started, the noise ceased, and silence fell once more over the city. Out in the streets legions of women disappeared back into their closes and houses.

Initially Cathy had thought that the noise protest – or to be more precise the intended timing of it – might be a bad idea as it would wake children and the elderly, but a straw poll taken in Partick and Govan had found in its favour.

Cathy ran her fingers through her hair. She normally had good hair but during the last few months all the life had gone out of it, leaving it dull and dry. It was the pregnancy of course; Lily's hair had gone exactly the same way.

From her hair her hands went to her breasts. Those too had been affected by her pregnancy, but in their case for the better. She'd always considered herself lacking in that department, but no longer. She hoped her breasts wouldn't shrink again after she'd finished feeding the baby, or *babies*!

Her dressing gown was half off when there was a knock on the outside door. Now who was that? she wondered. Must be in conection with the noise protest, she thought. But she was wrong. It was Ina McCracken.

The moment she saw Ina's face she knew something awful had happened. And then she thought further . . .

'It's not Bobby?' she queried in a harsh voice, a clenched fist having flown to her mouth.

Ina couldn't reply for the huge lump clogging her throat.

'Oh my God!' Cathy whimpered, slumping against the side of the door.'

'Not Bobby,' Ina managed at last. 'Gavin.'

Relief surged through Cathy, relief she was immediately ashamed of. 'Dead?'

'No. We had a letter . . .' Ina swallowed, then swallowed again. 'He's been blinded in both eyes.'

Cathy took Ina by the hand, and drew her into the hallway. 'I'll put the kettle on,' she said simply.

'I knew you'd want to know. That's why I came round. I knew you'd still be up because of the protest.'

'When did it happen?' Cathy asked softly.

'According to the letter the day he arrived back at the front. He . . .' Ina broke down.

It was hours later, and her bed freezing cold, before an exhausted and distraught Cathy managed to get into it.

Bobby, Jack, Colin and Charlie were working as a group, shoring up the mud walls and roof of their tunnel with timber supports when Colin suddenly stopped and said. 'Listen, do you hear something?'

The others also stopped and cocked their ears.

'I'm sure I . . .' Charlie muttered.

'I can hear it,' Bobby interrupted. 'It's coming from behind this wall.' The sound he was hearing was a faint thudding one.

'German tunnellers,' Charlie whispered. 'Has to be. Wait here.' He left them to fetch Sergeant Deeming.

When Sergeant Deeming appeared he had a geophone with him which he immediately placed against the mud wall. The geophone was a little round ball with a protruding tube out of which came two earpieces. He now listened through these earpieces.

'Not very far away. They'll break through before long,' Sergeant Deeming pronounced.

'Camouflet?' Charlie asked softly. A camouflet was a small mine containing five hundredweight of explosive.

Sergeant Deeming nodded. 'Have a camouflet sent down from up top and I'll set it myself.' He then gave the order for everyone in the tunnel to down tools.

Bobby, Jack and Colin sat together. They'd heard about camouflets but this would be the first time they would have seen one used. It was also the first time they'd made contact with German tunnellers since becoming tunnellers themselves.

Every ten minutes or so Sergeant Deeming and Captain Greener, the captain having joined his sergeant on being given the news, had another listen with the geophone. And then, just over an hour since it had been sent for, the camouflet arrived.

Sergeant Deeming had the mine placed in exactly the position he wanted it, then ordered it tamped with sandbags; the tamping to direct the force of the explosion into the mud wall rather than have 'free' explosion all round.

'They're very close now,' Captain Greener later whispered to Deeming, having had yet another listen with the geophone.

'How far would you estimate, sir?'

'A yard. Possibly a foot more.'

Deeming did some mental arithmetic. 'Right.' And with that he set the camouflet's timing device, a space round which had been left uncovered. When he'd done that he instructed the space now be tamped with sandbags as the rest of the mine was.

'Everyone fall back along the tunnel,' Captain Greener ordered in a whisper, bringing up the rear himself.

When they reached a part of the tunnel Captain Greener

considered safe he ordered his men to stop and have a sit. They waited there for the camouflet to go off.

The explosion, when it happened, was a muffled one, followed by the roar of their own tunnel collapsing in on itself. Dust and debris swirled everywhere.

When it was over Captain Greener and Sergeant Deeming strode back the way they'd come, or at least as far as they could before being halted by the blockage. Captain Greener nodded with satisfaction. 'Well done, sergeant,' he said.

'What now, sir? Do we dig that lot out or go off in a new direction?'

Captain Greener considered that. 'New direction I think. Safer for our chaps that way.'

'Very good, sir. If you'll choose a spot we'll get started right away.'

Meanwhile, Charlie was explaining to Bobby, Jack and Colin, 'The explosion brings down a large section of our tunnel but also a far longer section of theirs. It's the direction of blast you see. For every foot of ours that caves in there should be at least four of theirs.'

'And the tunnellers?' Bobby queried.

'T'explosion will have killed some, t'lucky ones. The others are buried alive.'

Bobby swallowed hard. 'How long does it take the ones buried alive to die?'

Charlie fixed Bobby with a level gaze. 'It varies. In some cases quite a while.'

There was silence between them for a few seconds, then Bobby said, 'If I do go I hope to God it's not like that.'

'Amen,' added Jack.

At long last Lloyd George, the Minister for Munitions, had done what he'd been threatening to do and come to Glasgow to address the populace. If he'd imagined it was going to be a peaceable affair with them hanging on his every word he couldn't have been more wrong. Glasgow was steaming angry, and they intended making sure that the Minister for Munitions was left in no doubt about the fact.

It was the closest thing Helen Crawfurd ever got to her general strike in Glasgow. When Lloyd George finally stepped out onto the platform that had been erected for him in front of the City Chambers he must surely have thought that all of Glasgow was present.

Men and women, young and old, they were packed into the square, tight as sardines in a can. And not only the square itself, but radiating out from the square, street upon street of grim-faced folks with fury in their hearts. It was a far, far greater multitude than had gathered at the Small Debts Court.

Cathy, in the square itself with her da, ma and Dougie – for obvious reasons Lily had stayed at home – knew the man in the police uniform flanking Lloyd George would be Chief Constable Stevenson, but didn't know who the man flanking him on the other side was.

'I think it's McKinnon Wood, the Secretary of State for Scotland,' John answered when she asked him.

McKinnon Wood, for that's who it was, introduced Lloyd George, who then opened his mouth to speak. And that's when it started, just as Ina McCracken had predicted it would.

A very loud, throaty animal sound that seemed to beat against the platform and those on the platform erupted from the crowd.

Lloyd George held up his hands, appealing for quiet, but the only effect that had was to increase the level of the sound. It was as if Glasgow was venting its anger with one voice.

It was incredible to hear, Cathy thought. An image formed in her mind, that of a huge fist being shaken at Lloyd George. That was what the sound made her think of.

And then it struck, making her gasp. There could be no doubt what the pain was. She'd never experienced that particular pain before, but recognised it for what it was the moment she did.

'What's up lass?' John said in her ear.

She pointed to her stomach. 'Baby,' she mouthed back.

He frowned.

'The baby's coming.'

John swore. What a time and place for this to happen! Winnie was already fussing round Cathy while Dougie, caught up in what was going on about him, was as yet unaware of Cathy's personal drama.

'We'll have to get home straight away,' Winnie said in John's ear.

John nodded his agreement, but it was going to be easier said

168

than done. He then prodded Dougie on the shoulder, and when he had Dougie's attention, explained what the situation was.

Common sense should have made Cathy stay at home that day. But she hadn't been able to resist coming along, not after all the work and effort she'd put into the rent strike. Whether the baby was coming at its natural time, or whether it had been brought on by the crush and excitement she would never know.

John did the only thing he could think of. He grasped Cathy by the arm, told Dougie to take her other one, and then saying, 'Excuse me, ill woman . . .' over and over again, began to make their way out of the crowd.

It wasn't as bad as John had feared. When folk saw Cathy in obvious distress they naturally parted to let her, and those with her, through. Sooner than any of them would have imagined they were out of the multitude and heading for a tramstop.

Cathy bit her lip as another pain hit her. 'Just like Lily again,' she said to Winnie when the pain had subsided. 'She went into labour the day of the Small Debts Court and here's me following suit when Lloyd George comes to Glasgow.'

Winnie smiled in reply. She was worrying about the midwife, praying the midwife hadn't gone to George Square, for that would mean she wouldn't be available.

'Ach, to hell with this!' exclaimed John, stepping off the pavement and hailing an approaching taxi.

Cathy was astonished to see her father do that. Neither she or any other member of her family had ever casually hailed a taxi in the street; that sort of thing was strictly for toffs.

Once home Winnie got Cathy ready for her bed while Dougie hurried round to fetch the midwife. But Winnie's fears proved to be justified: the midwife wasn't in. She had gone to George Square.

The pain was unbelievable; it was going to split her in two, Cathy thought, shrieking in agony. She felt as if she was being ripped right up the middle.

The pain ebbed, leaving Cathy sobbing for breath. Then it struck once more and she shrieked again.

'You're doing dandy. You're doing great,' the midwife said reassuringly. She'd come scurrying round the moment she'd read the note Dougie, on his second visit, had left tacked to her front door.

She'd returned from George Square three-quarters of an hour after Cathy had arrived home. Lloyd George had given up after only ten minutes when it became apparent to him that Glasgow wasn't going to let him speak. A very shaken Minister of Munitions was already on a train heading south to report to Asquith.

When that pain ebbed Winnie mopped Cathy's brow with a towel she'd sprinkled lavender water on. 'Not long now,' she smiled.

'The head's born,' the midwife announced shortly after that.

The rest of the baby came quickly. A slap on the bottom produced a lusty cry that was sheer music to Cathy's ears.

'Boy or girl?' she queried.

'A fine lassie.'

'Is she all there? Everything as it should be?'

'It is, Mrs McCracken. She's a wee cracker!' The midwife laughed at her own joke.

'And is that it? Is there only one?'

The midwife handed the baby to Winnie, then bent again over Cathy. She was remembering Lily and how Lily's second had caught her by surprise.

'Only the one,' she pronounced eventually.

Cathy sighed. It was all over. God, how she hurt. She never wanted to go through that again. Not ever.

'Here you are,' said a beaming Winnie, giving Cathy the baby – now wrapped in a swaddling sheet.

Cathy took the baby into the crook of her arm. A girl! She'd become convinced it would be a boy, if not two boys. But a girl was just hunky-dory. She couldn't have been more delighted.

'I'll call her Hannah,' she said. Hannah had been her granny's – Winnie's mother's – name, a name she particularly liked and always wished had been her own.

'Hannah it is then,' Winnie nodded, pleased at the choice.

Hannah, who'd been crying since being smacked, suddenly fell silent. She was fast asleep.

Winnie stuck her head round Cathy's bedroom door, her face ablaze with excitement. It was the evening of the day following Hannah's birth and Lloyd George's failed attempt to speak in George Square.

'We've won!' she blurted out when she saw that Cathy, still in bed, was awake.

She came rushing into the bedroom. 'We've just heard that Asquith is to rush a Rent Restrictions Bill through Parliament. Rents are to be frozen at their pre-war level until after the war.'

'Oh that's wonderful!' Cathy exclaimed.

'It's a tremendous victory, right enough. You should be proud of the part you played in it.'

'Every woman in Glasgow should be proud, for it's their victory. Rushed through Parliament, you say?'

'Rushed through,' Winnie confirmed.

My, my, Cathy thought. What about *that*!

The clay groaned.

The section stopped working on hearing the groan, and every eye was raised to stare at the roof of the tunnel.

The clay above them groaned again, louder than before.

'Cave in!' Arthur Shine yelled, dropping his pick and leading the stampede back along the tunnel.

Fred Gaddas trod on a water bottle, lost his balance and went tumbling down. Bobby, who was directly behind Fred, fell over him.

They were both scrambling to their feet again when the roof gave way.

'Anyone not get out?' Captain Greener queried. Sergeant Deeming did a quick head-count.

'Gaddas and McCracken are missing, sir,' he replied.

On hearing that, Jack and Colin swung round to stare at the solid wall of fallen clay behind them. Only a small part of the tunnel had caved in which was why, luckily for them, they'd managed to outrun the fall.

All Jack could think of was what Bobby had once said about if he had to go west he hoped it wouldn't be by being buried alive.

When Jack saw that Percy Throwbotham was still holding a pick, he hurried over and snatched it out of Percy's hands. He then raced back to attack the fallen clay, hacking at it like someone demented.

I'll get you out, Bobby! he promised mentally as his pick flew. I'll get you out, lad!

171

Other picks were swiftly acquired to replace those lost. The men, taking Jack as an example, dug like furies. Even Captain Greener dug, working as hard and fast as any of them.

It was Charlie Franklyn who found Fred Gaddas and Bobby. They pulled Fred out first, then Bobby. The exhausted men of No 4 Section clustered round.

'Fred's had it,' Captain Greener said heavily, then turned his attention to Bobby.

Bobby's face was waxen, his hands covered in blood. He was missing several nails which had been wrenched off as he'd desperately clawed at the entombing clay.

Captain Greener put an ear to Bobby's chest. 'He's still breathing, but only just,' he said.

Jack took one of Bobby's blood-covered hands and held it in his own. 'You're going to be all right pal. The three of us will walk down Sauchiehall Street together again yet.'

Bobby's eyes fluttered open, and the hint of a smile touched his lips.

'Cathy,' he whispered.

And died.

A weeping Jack closed his eyes.

Cathy stared at the telegram boy as if he was the Devil himself. A telegram could mean one thing, and one thing only. The boy handed her the telegram, then fled back down the stairs.

'IT IS WITH PROFOUND REGRET . . .'

After a while she went to bed, taking two books with her – *Kidnapped* and *Catriona* – and baby Hannah.

Next morning she called on Mrs Kelly across the street before going on to see Ina McCracken and breaking the news to her.

PART 2

Yesterday

Chapter 6

Hannah folded the teatowel and hung it on the length of string that stretched across the front of the sink. Going to the nearest chair by the fire, she sank into it.

'Tasty chops, didn't you think?' Cathy said from the press where she was putting away the crockery, the two of them having just washed and dried the tea things.

'Very nice.'

Cathy glanced at her daughter. 'You don't sound all that enthusiastic. Didn't you like them then?'

Hannah sighed. 'I did, they were smashing. If I didn't sound particularly enthusiastic it's nothing to do with the chops but because I'm dead beat. It's been a long, hard week.'

'Aye, you're right there. I'm feeling fair whacked myself. Thank God it's Saturday night.'

Hannah leant forward in her chair and held her hands up to the fire. Closing her eyes, she smiled softly, enjoying the heat washing over her.

'Are you going to that "do" tonight, then?' Cathy asked.

Hannah opened her eyes again and sank back into her chair. The 'do' her mother was referring to was an Empire Day dance at the Western Infirmary which she'd been invited to by her great friend Elspeth Campbell, who worked there as a nurse.

'I did promise Elspeth I'd see her there but . . .' She ran a hand through her hair which felt dirty and greasy, 'I don't think I will.'

'Elspeth will be disappointed.'

She would that, Hannah thought. Elspeth was bursting for her to meet the new man in her life, a boilermaker from Govan who she'd only started going out with a few weeks previously.

Rising, Hannah reached over to the mantelpiece where her cigarettes and matches were. Sinking back into the chair once more, she then lit up.

175

A flicker of irritation crossed Cathy's face to see that. It annoyed her that Hannah smoked, coffin nails she called cigarettes, but nearly all young people smoked nowadays. It was the done thing amongst them. The date was March 9th, 1940. War had been declared the previous September, though as yet no terrible battles had been fought. A war was on but so far it was still easy to believe that it wasn't. So far it was nothing like . . . Cathy tore her mind away from that recollection.

Hannah was thinking of Elspeth whom she'd bumped into that morning at the dairy when they'd both been out early to get fresh rolls. Elspeth lived three closes up the same side of Purdon Street from where she herself lived.

Elspeth had reminded her of the dance – again! . . . and made no bones about the fact she was dying to swank off this Peter to her. Aye, her mother was right, Elspeth was going to be disappointed when she didn't turn up true enough.

Hannah blew a perfect smoke-ring which floated ceilingwards watching it as it gradually widened and dissipated. With a fine fire going and a good book to read – she'd started *Dead Men's Morris* by Gladys Mitchell the night before and was thoroughly enjoying it – why should she bother going out? She'd be daft to, feeling as tired as she was.

Then again, if the positions had been reversed and it had been her who'd arranged to swank off a new boyfriend to Elspeth, she knew that Elspeth wouldn't have let her down. Which made her feel guilty as hell.

'It's begun to rain,' commented Cathy from the kitchen window.

'Oh, that's settled it then,' Hannah muttered, and blew another smoke-ring.

'There's a play on the wireless tonight. I'm looking forward to listening to that,' said Cathy, sitting on the chair facing Hannah.

'Oh aye?'

'It's a love story. You can't beat a love story.'

'Who's in it?'

'The cast was listed in the paper, but I didn't recognise any of the names.'

Hannah yawned, and ran a hand through her hair again. She'd have to wash her hair before she went to bed anyway, if she didn't it would annoy her during the night, and make her scratch.

'Where did you say the 'do' was?' Cathy inquired.

'In the basement of Elspeth's hospital. There's to be a live band and bar.'

'Sounds fun.'

'I'm sure it will be.'

'What dress were you going to wear?'

'My French-blue with the white polka-dot collar. But there again, I looked at it this morning and it's got crushed in the wardrobe and needs an iron.' That was another reason for her not to go to the dance.

'That dress suits you. Flatters your figure,' Cathy stated.

'That's what everyone says,' Hannah agreed. She'd only bought the dress the month before but since then it had become her firm favourite.

Hannah took a final drag on her cigarette and flicked the butt into the fire where it was consumed in a flare and crackle of flames.

'Old Mr Cameron was in today. Did you see him?' Cathy asked.

Hannah shook her head.

'Know what he wanted this time?'

'What?'

'A book on Zen Buddhism. I ask you, whatever next?'

Hannah laughed. 'He's a character, and no mistake. A fortnight ago it was Japanese paper-folding.'

'Did you get it for him?'

'Oh aye,' Hannah said.

'From where?'

'The Bearsden branch.'

Cathy nodded. Bearsden had one of the best-stocked branch libraries in Glasgow, and being a well-educated area, their stock was extremely comprehensive. She'd have a request sent to them on Monday morning inquiring if they had anything on Zen Buddhism. If they didn't she'd then try the Mitchell Library.

'According to Elspeth, this is the real thing,' Hannah said.

'You mean her new chap?'

'They looked at one another and that was it. Head over heels, the pair of them.'

'If it's that serious she really will be disappointed when you don't turn up.'

'Och, she'll live.'

'I only hope she doesn't think you're jealous.'

'Why should I be that?' Hannah exclaimed. 'I have boy-friends galore. Far more than Elspeth does.'

'Maybe that's the reason you should go tonight. She is your closest friend after all,' Cathy said softly.

Her mother was right, Hannah thought. Elspeth could easily misinterpret her not going after she'd said she would. And that would hurt Elspeth; the last thing she wanted.

'I suppose I'd better make an effort,' Hannah said reluctantly. 'Anyway, I'm not feeling quite as tired as I was. It seems to have passed off a bit.' Coming to her feet she stretched. 'I'll have to wash my hair though and . . .' She smiled at Cathy. 'How about a favour?'

'Such as?'

'Would you iron my dress while I get myself ready?'

'But I told you, I'm whacked!' Cathy protested, but with no conviction in her voice.

'Go on, Ma?'

'What I do for you!' Cathy grumbled, also rising.

When she finally left the house Hannah's mood had completely changed and she was eagerly anticipating the Empire Day dance at the Western Infirmary.

Hannah shuffled round the make-do dancefloor, her partner a young doctor who'd asked her up. He had carroty-coloured hair, freckles, an upturned nose and bad breath. He was awful. She'd ditch him as soon as the number was over.

She was enjoying herself, the dance was a good one. The band were more enthusiastic than competent, but somehow that didn't matter. By her reckoning there were several hundred people present, most of whom appeared to be having a good time.

She glanced over to where Elspeth and Peter were standing talking to a chap in uniform she hadn't seen before. Elspeth had come up trumps: Peter Kennedy was some dish. And the lovely thing was he seemed to be as mad for Elspeth as Elspeth was for him. She couldn't have been more pleased for her pal.

'Thank you,' she said to carrot-top when the dance was ended.

A hand grasped her arm. 'Stay up?'

'No, thank you.' She attempted to move away, but he held on to her.

'Oh, come on!' he urged.

She gave him what she called her 'frozen' look, and the hand fell away.

'Maybe later on?' he said.

She left him standing there. Creep! she thought.

'Hello again,' said Elspeth when she rejoined her and Peter.

'For you,' said Peter, handing her a whisky and lemonade.

'Thank you. The next round is mine.' It was unusual for Glasgow girls to buy their own rounds, but as she saw it it would be unfair to expect Peter to buy for two lassies rather than just the one he was with.

'Let me introduce you,' Elspeth said to her. 'Lawrence, this is Hannah McCracken. She and I went to school together.'

Lawrence was a soldier with a very pale complexion and dark bags under his eyes. He was a little taller than Hannah and slightly older too, she guessed. At twenty-seven he was in fact three years older than her.

'Pleased to meet you,' he smiled, and shook her hand.

A nice smile, she registered.

'Lawrence was one of my patients, but discharged from the hospital now,' Elspeth explained.

'Wounded in action?' Hannah inquired.

He smiled again, and shook his head. 'Something far more mundane, I'm afraid. I was with my regiment in France when I came down with pneumonia. They sent me home and I ended up in the Western at the tender mercies of Nurse Campbell here.'

'Are you complaining?' Elspeth exclaimed, pretending to be angry.

'Not at all, and well you know it. I think you and all the nurses here are something special. The proverbial angels you're supposed to be,' Lawrence replied.

Smooth, Hannah thought. Too much so for her liking.

'I'm still an out-patient which is how I came to hear of the dance tonight,' Lawrence said to Hannah. 'When I saw Nurse Campbell I just had to come over and pay my respects.'

'He was a terrible patient,' Elspeth smiled. 'Very difficult.'

'I wasn't as bad as that, surely!'

'Worse. You were a proper pain in the bumbeleree!'

'Well it's awful having to be in bed all day,' Lawrence said contritely. 'Even when you are ill.'

Hannah sipped some of her whisky and lemonade. She couldn't wait to tell Elspeth how much she approved of Peter – an opportunity to do so hadn't occurred yet. Then she realised Lawrence was talking to her.

'Sorry, my mind was elsewhere?'

'Would you care to dance?'

She glanced down at her glass. 'I have a drink.'

'We'll mind that for you,' Peter said. 'Away up!'

She didn't really want to go back on the floor so soon, but what the heck! 'Thank you then,' she said to Lawrence, and handed her glass to Peter.

'You still look pretty awful,' she said to Lawrence as he took her into his arms.

'Oh thank you *very* much!'

'I didn't mean it nastily, I meant . . .'

'I know what you meant,' he interjected. 'I look like something that's been dug up after being buried for three days.'

'Hardly that. But it is obvious you've been ill and aren't fully recovered.'

They danced for a little while in silence. 'My friends call me Lal,' he suddenly announced.

'Lal?'

'Short for Lawrence.'

'I'll stick with Lawrence as I'm not a friend.'

He couldn't help himself. 'Are you always so rude?'

She pulled herself out of his embrace and made to leave the floor.

'Wait!' he said, grasping her arm.

Just like carrot-top, she thought.

'It's all right for you women, all you have to do is respond to what men say. We have to initiate the conversation, do the chatting up. And I find that difficult.'

She couldn't help but warm to him for that – it was absolutely true. She wondered why she hadn't thought of that before. It must be difficult for some men, those without a natural gift for the gab. She returned to his embrace and they continued dancing.

180

'My fault. I *was* rude,' she conceded.

'I was only trying to be . . .' He paused. 'Friendly, that word again.' He paused a second time, then said. 'I think you're nice. You've got beautiful eyes.'

She blushed scarlet. She was an awful blusher: something she'd inherited from her father, Cathy had long since told her. The eyes she'd inherited from Cathy.

'Thank you,' she mumbled.

'A sort of . . . What colour would you call them?'

'Hazelnut.'

'Hazelnut,' he repeated. 'Yes, that's precisely the colour they are.' The number that was being played came to an end and they applauded. 'Please stay up?' he asked.

It was on the tip of her tongue to say no, then she changed her mind. 'All right.'

'And you'll call me Lal?'

'You're persistent, aren't you?'

'I'm not usually where women are concerned. I'm usually quite the opposite.'

She wouldn't have believed that when they first met, but now she did. 'Lal what?' she queried.

'Stuart. That's Stuart with a "u", not "w".'

'I thought that was always a Christian name?'

He shook his head. 'No, it can be a surname too. But the "w" version is far more common.'

The band struck up once more, a waltz, and they moved off. 'Are you a regular soldier?' Hannah asked.

'Not me, I'm only in for the duration. I'm a baker by trade – we have a bakery in Maryhill.'

'Your own shop?' she was impressed.

'My father's. And mine, I suppose after him. But tell me about you, what do you do?'

'What would you imagine?' she teased.

He considered that. 'I've no idea, you could be anything.'

'I'm a female navvy,' she replied.

He laughed, 'I've never danced with a navvy before.'

'The way you're moving those big feet of yours I doubt you've danced with anyone before.'

His face fell. 'Sorry, I never have been much of a dancer. And you're right, my feet are big. When I'm trying to dance I

181

keep stumbling over them which you've probably noticed by now.'

'A proper Charlie Chaplin, eh?'

He smiled. 'A proper Charlie more like.'

'I'll tell you a secret, Lal.'

'What's that?'

She whispered in his ear. 'I'm a fairly rotten dancer myself. I've no talent for it either.'

'You don't need dancing talent Hannah, you're a talent just in yourself.'

She blushed scarlet again. 'I thought you found it difficult to chat up the ladies?'

'I do. But somehow with you, now, it seems to come naturally. I feel, feel . . .' he searched for the word, 'relaxed, yes that's it. I feel relaxed with you.'

She felt relaxed with him too, but didn't say so. 'So come on then, what is it you think I do?'

He feigned innocence. 'But I believed you when you said you were a navvy! You've certainly got the . . .' He grinned impishly.

'Got the what?'

'Nothing.'

'Got the *what*?' she demanded.

'Muscles for it.'

She knew damn well he was obliquely referring to her bust, which was a large one. 'That's cheeky!'

'None was intended.'

They were both thoroughly relishing the banter that had sprung up between them. Nearly all Glaswegians love verbal cut and thrust.

'Just be careful, then.'

'Oh I will! I will!'

'I'm a librarian,' she confessed.

'Really!'

'I work at Partick Main Library where my mother is head branch librarian.'

'That's interesting,' he said.

'What is?'

'That your mother's your boss. Doesn't it cause difficulties between you?'

'Doesn't it for you?'

He frowned. 'How do you mean?'

'Well your father's your boss, isn't he? You said he owned the bakery.'

Lal's frown disappeared as he laughed. 'Touché! Of course he's my boss; it's merely that I've never thought of him as that. There's him and me, and that's it.'

'I don't suppose you read much?' she queried.

'That's where you're wrong, I love books.'

'You do!'

'I'm in the middle of one at the moment, *Practical Economics* by G.D.H. Cole. It's fascinating.'

'You prefer non-fiction?'

'No, I'll read fiction and non-fiction. It all depends what it is.'

They started chatting about books, he surprising her by the extent of his knowledge of them.

They came to a halt outside her close. 'It's very good of you to see me home,' Hannah said.

'The pleasure's all mine.'

If he tries to kiss me I won't let him, she told herself. She did find him attractive, it wasn't that, it was just . . . She didn't know what it was, but she wouldn't let him kiss her. If he suggested going into the backclose she'd say no.

'Can I see you again?' he asked.

How dreadfully white his face looked in the moonlight, she thought, the bags under his eyes like deep holes into his flesh. He'd had a very bad case of pneumonia, Elspeth had confided to her earlier. At one stage the hospital staff had actually thought they were going to lose him. But he'd rallied, and pulled through.

'Well?' he prompted.

'When would you have in mind?'

'How about tomorrow?'

'That's a Sunday! Everything's shut.'

'We could go for a walk?' he suggested hopefully.

'No, I don't fancy that. The weather's too cold. How about Tuesday night?'

'Monday night,' he countered.

She laughed. 'You really are persistent!'

'And as I said to you when we first got up together I'm not usually where women are concerned. But you're different.'

He meant that, she could tell. Truth was, she found him different too. 'Monday it is then,' she agreed.

'I'll meet you here at six-thirty.'

'Seven,' she said.

'Quarter to?'

'Seven,' she laughed. He'd been making her laugh all night.

'Seven then,' he reluctantly conceded.

He'll try and kiss me now, she thought. But she was wrong. Instead he extended a hand and shook with her.

'Goodnight,' he said, so softly it was almost a whisper.

'Goodnight.'

She turned away to go up the close.

'Hannah?'

She turned back to him.

'I like you.'

Simple words, but they went straight to her heart because of their obvious sincerity. 'And I like you too, Lal.'

When he returned along Purdon Street, heading for a tram-stop, there was a jaunty swagger to his walk.

'How was the "do"?' Cathy asked from her chair at the fire where she was sitting knitting herself a new cardigan.

'Fine.'

'What did you think of Elspeth's new chap?'

Hannah moved towards the sink. 'Care for a cup of tea?'

'Please.'

She began filling the kettle. 'I think Elspeth's come up with a winner. I was much taken with him.'

Cathy glanced at her pattern, mouthing the instructions to herself before proceeding. Her wooden needles went click-clack! click-clack! 'What about you? Did you meet anyone?'

'I was brought home, if that's what you mean.'

Cathy's gaze flicked up at Hannah. 'A friend of this Peter's?'

'No, an ex-patient of Elspeth's. He's getting over pneumonia.'

'Pneumonia! That can be nasty.'

'It can be fatal, Elspeth said. But Lal pulled through. Only not before giving them a fright at one point.'

'Lal?'

'Short for Lawrence.'

'I see.' Her needles flew. 'Lawrence what?'

'Stuart with a "u" not "w".'

'And is he . . .'

'What is this Ma, the third degree?' Hannah protested, taking the teapot from the press.

Cathy stopped knitting to stare at Hannah. 'I'm only showing interest, that's all.'

'Aye, that's what I said. The third degree.'

'Well, it's only natural for me to show interest. You *are* my daughter.'

'Your grown-up daughter.'

'At your age I can hardly dispute the fact.' Cathy resumed knitting.

Hannah placed the tea caddy beside the teapot. 'He's taking me out again Monday night. Though I don't know where we're going. I didn't discuss that.'

'And what does this Lal do?'

If she'd been tetchy with her mother it was because she'd known she was going to be asked that question. 'He's a soldier,' she replied quietly.

The click-clack of Cathy's needles noticeably slowed. 'A soldier?'

'He was over in France with his regiment when he came down with pneumonia. He'll be rejoining his regiment again when he's passed fit.'

Cathy's gaze went to the mantelpiece and the photograph in a heavy, ornate bronze frame that stood on it. The photograph was of her and Bobby, taken on their wedding day. How long ago that seemed. And yet, in another way, it might just have been yesterday.

'War,' Cathy breathed. 'It decimated my generation, now it looks like it's all set to do the same to yours.' Her eyes became slightly unfocused; in her mind she was looking into the past, remembering faces and the names that went with them. 'All those bonny men, including your da. What a waste, what a terrible, terrible waste.'

Hannah got on with making the tea. When she next spoke it was to change the subject.

*

'I wish to join the library, please.'

The voice was familiar, Hannah thought, glancing up from the list she was writing out. A smiling Lal stared back at her.

'What are you doing here?' she queried in a whisper. It was Monday morning shortly after her teabreak.

'This is a public library?'

She pulled a face. 'You know it is.'

'Then, as a member of the public, I'm perfectly within my rights in asking to become a member.'

His smile was even nicer than she remembered it. She was pleased to see him, though she'd never have admitted it. How outrageous! Confronting her at work like this. She wasn't at all displeased.

'Certainly, sir.' Producing an application form she placed it on the counter in front of him. 'Just take that home and fill it out, sir.'

His eyes were twinkling with mischief. 'Can't I fill it out here?'

'If you wish.'

'I wish.'

She made to move away.

'Excuse me, miss?'

She turned back to him.

'Can I borrow a pen?'

'Certainly sir.'

'And miss?'

'Yes?

'I can't write so you'll have to help me.'

Got you! she thought. 'If you can't write it's unlikely you can read, so why do you want to join the library?'

'Picture books,' he replied quick as a flash. Then, in a whisper. 'I couldn't wait until tonight to see you again.'

'Idiot!' she hissed, also in a whisper and further pleased with what he'd just admitted.

'I know. Idiocy runs in the family. Can you escape for a coffee?'

'I've already had my break.'

'Have another?'

'The boss wouldn't let me.'

'I hear you have influence at court?'

'The last thing I would do was to abuse any influence I might have. That wouldn't be fair on the others.'

'To hell with the others.'

186

Hannah shook her head. 'No, and that's final.'

'I dreamt about you Saturday night.'

That threw her somewhat. 'Did you now?'

'Shall I tell you what I dreamt?'

The look on his face warned her not to fall into that one. 'I'm not interested, thank you very much.'

'You were in my dream.'

She blushed furiously, cursing herself under her breath for doing so.

'Go away!' she hissed. Luckily he'd caught her while she was the only one behind the counter. It would have been mortifying if there had been anyone else to witness and perhaps overhear this nonsense.

'How about dinnertime? We could go to a pub?'

'I have a meeting dinnertime.'

'Who with?'

'A business meeting concerning the library. Now go away.'

'How about . . .'

'Go away!'

He picked up the form. 'You've still got to help me with this.'

'Excuse me,' she said, and left him to attend a woman who'd come up to the counter with two books to take out. When she'd seen to the woman she returned to Lal.

'If you keep pestering me I'll leave you standing downstairs tonight.'

'Do that and I'll come up and knock at your door.'

'I won't answer it.'

'Then I'll break it down.'

'Don't be daft!'

'What time do you finish here?'

'Why?'

He tapped his nose. 'I'm not telling you.'

Opening and closing times would be displayed somewhere, he thought to himself. Probably outside the building on a brass plate.

Picture books! she thought after he'd gone, a huge smile cracking her face. Ridiculous!

He was lovely.

As they left the library after work Hannah and Cathy were

discussing the effect the war was likely to have on the publication of books – already there was talk of paper rationing for publishers. They'd only gone a few yards down the street when Lal fell into step beside Hannah.

Hannah gaped at him. 'Where did you come from?'

'I've been . . .' he paused to emphasise the word, 'lurking outside the library. I thought I'd walk you and your sister here home.'

Hannah and Cathy both laughed. 'Flattery will get you everywhere.' Cathy said. 'I'm her mother.'

Lal's eyebrows shot up in mock amazement. 'Never! I don't believe it!'

'What are you doing here?' Hannah queried. 'I thought we agreed seven.'

'I've had a marvellous idea. Why don't I take you out for a sit-down fish tea? And after that we'll go to the pictures.'

'You mean now?'

'I think it's a brilliant idea, don't you?'

She did actually. She adored fish and chips. But wasn't going to be ridden over completely roughshod. 'I'll have to go home and get changed first. I'm not going out gallivanting in my work clothes.'

'Fine. I'll come with you and wait while you get ready. I'll chat to your ever-so-young-looking mother while you do what you have to.'

'Are you sure you're not Irish?' Cathy laughed.

'And him the same man who told me he had trouble talking to the ladies,' Hannah teased.

'There's not a smidgin of Irish in me,' Lal replied to Cathy. 'I'm Scots through and through.' He did a little dance that brought him in between the two women. Cocking his arms, he said, 'Go on, give me a treat. A lovely female on either arm.'

They walked all the way back from there to Purdon Street with Hannah on his left arm, Cathy on his right.

'Which regiment are you in?' Cathy asked – Hannah having taken herself off to the bedroom.

'The H.L.I.'

A thin, crooked smile twisted her lips. How that brought back memories. 'My husband wanted to join the H.L.I. in the Great War, but at the time he went into the army it wasn't possible. He joined a rifle brigade instead, and then after a while left that to become a tunneller. He died in a cave-in.'

'I'm sorry,' Lal said quietly.

'He never saw Hannah. That was never granted him. She was born while he was over there.'

'Whereabouts was he killed, Mrs McCracken?'

'The Ypres salient.'

'Passchendaele,' Lal nodded. Passchendaele was what the First, Second and Third Battles of Ypres had become known as collectively.

'There were six of them, pals working in the same coalyard, who all joined up together. Of those six only two survived.' The two Cathy was referring to were Jack Smart and Bill Coltraine. Colin Baker, Ishbel's husband, had been killed in June 1917, victim of a booby trap.

'Passchendaele,' Cathy repeated, her voice hollow-sounding. Almost not of this world.

'My own father fought on the Somme, and then later at Arras. He was one of the fortunate ones who came back.'

'And now it's happening all over again,' Cathy said.

'Hitler must be stopped, Mrs McCracken. There's no argument about that.'

The thin, crooked smile returned to Cathy's lips. 'You sound just like Bobby, my husband. Only it was the Kaiser then.'

'We can only hope and pray this war isn't as bad as the last,' Lal said.

'I sincerely hope not. But you know what they say about history always repeating itself?' She paused, then added bitterly, 'God help all the wives who're going to be left widows, and all the mothers who're going to lose their boys.'

When Hannah breezed into the kitchen to announce she was ready the atmosphere she encountered was positively funereal.

The big picture was appropriately *Fire Over England*, starring Flora Robson, Laurence Olivier and Vivien Leigh. Hannah and Lal were in the back row of the stalls, the courting row, at his suggestion.

They'd had their sit-down tea after which, with time to spare before the programme began, they'd gone into a pub for a couple of drinks each.

Hannah glanced surreptitiously to her right. The couple next to her were wrapped round one another, kissing intently. It was the same with the couple beyond them.

Lal was dying to make a move, she could sense it, but was still screwing up his courage to do so. Although conversation between them had become relaxed and jokey, physical contact was apparently for him another matter entirely.

He fidgeted, then fidgeted again.

His eyes slid sideways. Hannah stared fixedly up at the silver screen, pretending she wasn't aware he was looking at her.

She felt his arm begin to rise.

'Good film,' she whispered, gazing directly into his face.

The arm had stopped the moment her head had turned. It now eased down again.

She returned to staring fixedly up at the silver screen. Her face was impassive, but inside she was laughing.

A full minute passed, and another. The arm began to rise again.

'Do you mind if I smoke?' she asked him.

The arm stopped, and dropped. 'No, not at all.'

She lit up without offering him one because he didn't. She smoked slowly, taking her time over the cigarette. When it was finished she ground the butt out underfoot. Almost instantly the arm began to rise once more.

She turned to look at him, her face expressionless. The arm dropped yet again.

She was enjoying this, even if it was cruel of her. This time she let the arm get to her shoulder before saying. 'Sweetie?' as she held out the poke of lemon sherbet to him.

'No, thank you,' he husked.

She took a sherbet from the poke and popped it into her mouth.

The arm, frozen at her shoulder when she'd offered the sweets, now continued on round. She pretended not to notice until his hand came to rest on her far shoulder. She glanced down at it, then at him. Now it was he who was staring fixedly up at the silver screen.

She continued sucking her lemon sherbet until it had

completely dissolved. She considered having another and decided that would be going too far. Catching him totally by surprise she laid her head on his shoulder.

When he made no further move she sighed softly and closed her eyes.

She sighed again when his lips touched hers.

Cathy was still up playing a game of solitaire when Hannah got home.

'So what did you think?' Hannah asked.

'A nice lad . . .' Cathy trailed off, clearly leaving something unspoken.

'A nice lad *but*. But what?'

Cathy stared levelly at her daughter. 'A nice lad but a soldier,' she stated.

'Oh, for goodness sake Ma I've only met him. He's a laugh, that's all. Besides, he'll be gone soon.'

An awful lot of young men were going to be gone soon, Cathy thought grimly.

And not in the way Hannah meant either.

Hannah squirmed in Lal's tight embrace, her tongue darting and probing inside his mouth. They'd been out for the evening and were now in her backclose where, being no lighting, it was pitch-black. The kiss went on and on and on, till finally they had to break for air.

'I'll say this for you, you're one helluva kisser,' Lal gasped, chest heaving.

Hannah laughed softly in the darkness. 'My mother told me she used to always say that about my father. It must be a talent I've inherited from him.'

'Oh, Hannah!' he muttered passionately, and nibbled her ear.

'I have to go up, Lal. It's late and I've got work tomorrow.'

'A few minutes more.'

'That's what you said a few minutes ago.'

'Please?' He clutched her to him again, her full breasts – breasts he was very much aware of – squashing into his chest.

'No this time I must go up.'

'Tomorrow night, then?'

'If you want.'

'Oh, I want all right,' he replied, the implication such that it made Hannah laugh.

'Want *to go out*,' she clarified.

'You're lovely, Hannah. You're gorgeous. You're absolutely . . .' He pressed his lips onto hers. 'Hmmhh!'

She broke away. 'Sleep tight. Don't let the bugs bite. Goodnight!'

'I suppose it is getting late,' he reluctantly agreed.

'It's all right for some who can lie in as late as they like. But I'm a working girl who has to be up and on the go first thing.'

He ran a hand through her hair, then down the nape of her neck, the latter causing her to shiver with pleasure.

'I'll knock on your door at six forty-five,' he said.

'I'll be ready. Where will we go?'

'Who cares, as long as we're together?'

She smiled – he could be so romantic. She'd never known a man as romantic as Lal. And there was something else she liked about him too – the gritty single-mindedness that Hannah saw lay beneath his lovely, charming exterior. Lal Stuart was a young man who knew how to get what he wanted – just look at the way he'd gone after her! She pecked him on the lips, then with a laugh escaped the arm that tried to trap her. 'Away home,' she said, and hurried to the frontclose where she started up the stairs.

At the top of the flight of stairs she stopped to give him a wave before continuing on up.

The gas mantle had been turned down so that the kitchen was only dimly lit. Cathy was sitting by the fire which she'd been alternately stoking and staring into for hours now.

'Good time?' Cathy asked quietly.

'Very. Thoroughly enjoyed myself.'

'Do you know how old I am?'

Hannah blinked at the sheer unexpectedness, and seeming irrelevance, of the question. 'Let me see, I have to think . . .'

'I'm forty-nine. Fifty later in the year,' Cathy interjected.

'You're wearing well.'

Cathy ignored the compliment. 'I was twenty-two when I married your father, twenty-four – the age you are now – when he died. We had two and a quarter years of married life, eleven months of which he spent in the army.'

Hannah sat facing her mother, and lit up a cigarette. The eyes that pierced her own were diamond hard, and every so often flashed the way diamonds do when they catch the light. She'd never seen her mother's eyes like that before.

Cathy continued. 'We were already married when the Great War was declared, and he joined up behind my back. So you see I had no choice about either of these events.'

Hannah frowned. 'I don't understand what you're getting at, Ma?'

'I was a widow at twenty-four with a baby to look after and a house to keep and maintain. I still shudder to look back on those years, the interminable lodgers that came and went, the awful jobs I had to endure, until that day I managed to land a position with the library and my fortunes changed at long last for the better.'

'Are you saying you wouldn't have married my father if you'd known there was a war on the way?'

'I loved your father Hannah, and have never stopped loving him. After the war there was never any question of me marrying again, and despite the fact there were so many more women around than men I did get asked. Oh yes!'

This was a revelation to Hannah. Her mother had never mentioned it before. 'You had a proposal?'

'From your Uncle Gavin. We became very close after he was invalided out of the army, but it was only ever friendship as far as I was concerned, though he came to see it differently. Perhaps I became so fond of Gavin because there's a lot of Bobby in him and that's what I was drawn to. But as I've just said, it was only ever friendship on my part, nothing more.'

Uncle Gavin had proposed to her mother! There was a right turn-up for the books. She'd never have guessed that to be the case.

'I loved your father, Hannah,' Cathy reiterated, 'but if circumstances had been different I might not have married him. It's awfully difficult for me to say that because we did have a short time together, and we did have you. For me to say I might not have married him would be to wipe out you, which of course, because I love and cherish you so dearly, I could never do. But . . .' She paused, took a deep breath, then went on again. 'If I was a young woman today, in your shoes, unmarried as you are,

I wouldn't touch a soldier, or anyone in the active services, with the proverbial barge pole. I wouldn't willingly make myself a candidate for all the heartache and grief that's going to befall so many poor women before this war is over.'

Leaning forward in her chair Cathy scooped out a shovelful of coal from the scuttle and placed it on the fire. 'It may be only three weeks since you met Lal, but you've been out with him nearly every night since. More importantly, it's my guess the pair of you are falling in love with one another. All the signs are there.'

Hannah couldn't deny that. She would have been a liar if she had. She was falling in love with him, and maybe already had. And he with her.

'Are you telling me to stop seeing Lal, Ma?' she asked in a tight voice.

'I can't tell you what to do Hannah, as you've rightly said more than once you're a grown-up woman with your own life to lead. All I want is for you to be happy, and by happiness I'm thinking in the long term rather than the short. I don't want you to go through what I've had to. But then I never had the choice. You have.'

'He'll be rejoining his regiment soon. He's almost fully recovered . . .'

'That's dodging the issue, not facing it. To do that you must tell him the next time you see him that you're breaking it off. That it's finished between you.'

Hannah blew a stream of smoke at the carpet, watching it hit the carpet and bounce off in another direction.

'For your own good,' Cathy added in a whisper.

Lal stared aghast at Hannah, his face filled with hurt and shock. 'You don't mean that. You can't!' he exclaimed.

'I'm sorry Lal, really I am. But I do,' she replied. At the back of her mind she noted her hands were trembling. Her voice was steady though, she was pleased about that.

She tore her gaze away from his stricken face to glance round the Bluebird Café which was fairly empty, the reason she'd brought him in there. They were sitting at a corner table well out of earshot of anyone else.

'Hannah I . . .' He desperately searched for words, an argument that would make her change her mind.

'You've got to go away shortly, anyway,' she said. 'It could be

194

years before we see one another again.' If ever, she qualified mentally.

'But this is so sudden, so unexpected. We have to talk about it,' he protested.

'We are talking.'

'I have to think about this, then speak to you again.'

'No,' she stated flatly.

'I thought you felt the same about me as I do about you?'

'I do, Lal,' she replied softly. 'And that's precisely the reason I'm breaking it off. I'm not going to put myself in the position of being hurt the way my mother was. As she rightly put it, I have a choice; she didn't.'

'You're being heartless!' he accused, a tremor of anger in his tone.

She didn't reply, but lit another cigarette. She wished this was over. She also wished these last few minutes with him would never end. She wished someone had smothered Adolf bloody Hitler at birth.

'Another week, two at the outside, before I have to rejoin . . .'

'No,' she interjected. 'That would only make it worse, prolong the agony. We finish it here and now, cleanly.'

He slumped in his chair. 'I've never felt about anyone before the way I feel about you.'

Me neither, she thought. But didn't say so.

'We're a natural couple together.'

'I think I'd better go,' she said, stubbing out her newly lit cigarette, and rising. She was on the verge of breaking down and reneging on what she'd come here to do.

'Wait!' he pleaded, grabbing her arm.

'Lal, please don't make this any more difficult than it is,' she said, wrenching her arm free. 'Good luck, I hope and pray everything goes well for you. Now goodbye.'

'Hannah!' he called urgently after her, but she didn't look round. She walked swiftly to the café door, and out through it onto the street.

Thankfully it was raining outside. Because of that none of the passers-by realised she was crying.

Tears mingled with rainwater streamed down her face.

Hannah stared grimly at the front page of the *Evening Citizen* which carried the banner headline report of Italy having declared war that day – June 10th 1940 – on Great Britain and France. When she'd finished that article she turned to page four which carried the latest list of those killed in action, most of whom had been lost at Dunkirk between May 27th and June 4th.

What remained of the H.L.I. had been amongst the last to be evacuated from the Dunkirk beaches, many of their men being killed in a fierce rearguard engagement as the regiment tried to hold the advancing Germans to allow as many British soldiers to escape as possible.

She gave a small sigh of relief when she saw that Lal's name wasn't present in the roll of dead. Since Dunkirk she'd been checking the lists daily, heart in mouth and a sick feeling in her stomach every time she did so.

Folding the newspaper, she laid it aside. 'So Italy's against us as well now,' she said to Cathy, who was ironing.

'Aye, the pussyfooting's over. It's war with a vengeance from here on in.'

'Thank God Churchill is Prime Minister. He's the man for the job, and no mistake.' A National Government under Churchill had been formed the month before.

'A warmonger through and through,' Cathy said bitterly.

Hannah didn't agree with that, but wasn't going to argue with her mother about it.

'I bumped into Aunt Lily today when I popped out at dinnertime,' Cathy said. 'The twins have gone down to Woolwich for training.'

Hannah thought of her cousins David and Ewan, both of whom she was extremely fond. 'How's Aunt Lily taking it?'

'How do you think? She's scared stiff for them. Like me, she remembers only too well what it was like the first time round.' Cathy paused, then added. 'There was nothing I could say to help her in any way. There is nothing that can be said to help you in that situation, as I know only too well.'

Hannah had been waiting to broach the subject; now was as good a time as any, she decided. 'Ma, I've been thinking. I want to do my bit for the war effort.'

Cathy went white. Slowly, carefully, she laid down the iron. 'What sort of bit? You don't mean going into the services, do you?' A tick started up under her left eye. She didn't look at Hannah, but at the nightdress she was in the middle of ironing.

That was precisely what Hannah did want to do, but was resigned to the fact that she couldn't. If she was to join up it would devastate Cathy.

'No Ma, not the services. But something that will contribute more than being a library assistant does.'

Cathy picked up her iron again and resumed ironing. 'Fine,' she said.

Hannah's immediate boss at the Ministry of Food was Geoffrey Robb. He was of medium height, had thinning hair and a neatly clipped moustache. In his late twenties, he was still a bachelor.

'Everything all right, Miss McCracken? he inquired politely.

'Yes, thank you sir.'

He fingered his moustache, a habit of his, particularly when he was nervous. 'Quite happy with us at the M.F.?

'Very happy, sir.'

'No problems?'

'None at all.'

'Good, good!' he nodded.

At that point Hannah expected him to move on, but he didn't. He continued standing by her desk.

'Is there anything else sir?'

'I, eh . . .' He cleared his throat, and glanced around, confirming that he and Hannah were quite alone.

'There's a good show on at the Empire I'm told.' The Empire was one of Glasgow's top variety theatres.

'So I've heard.'

'I was wondering . . .' He cleared his throat again. 'I was wondering, eh . . .' He cleared his throat a third time. 'I could get tickets for Friday night if you'd care to see it? And there's a little club I belong to, very respectable you understand, where we could have supper afterwards.'

Hannah hadn't been at all aware that Robb fancied her, but it now seemed he did. She'd been out with a number of chaps since Lal, but never more than a few times with each.

'Do you think that's wise? You being my boss here?' she asked softly.

'I don't know. Do you?'

197

'Not really.'

Disappointment crept onto his face. 'You're probably right. You're turning me down then.'

'I didn't say that. I just said I didn't think it wise, not that I wouldn't go.'

The disappointment became a smile. 'You mean you will?'

'I'd thoroughly enjoy seeing a show. I'll look forward to it.'

She gave him her address when he asked for it, and they agreed a time when he'd come and pick her up in his car.

Hannah was laughing so hard it hurt. The comedian on stage was called Freddy Frobisher, and he was the funniest thing she'd ever seen and heard. Many English comedians died the death when they came north of the border, but not Freddy Frobisher. His humour was what is known in the business as low comedy which the down-to-earth, mainly working-class Glaswegians adored. It was spiced with innuendo, all of it sexual and lavatorial. His mime about the fat woman losing her knickers in a busy shop nearly brought the house down.

Hannah glanced at Geoffrey Robb who was almost beside himself. He nodded at her, the nods saying how hysterical this all was, and she nodded back her agreement.

Freddy Frobisher delivered another punchline which made a woman in the circle shriek so loudly her false teeth actually shot out of her mouth.

Hannah took a sip of the chilled Sauterne Geoffrey had ordered. She found it slightly sweet for her taste, but pleasant nonetheless. They'd both ordered fish, Dover sole, to be followed by the cheeseboard and coffee.

'The Empire was absolutely wonderful. Thank you for taking me,' Hannah smiled.

'Thank you for coming along.' He too sipped his wine, then glanced over at the door where a Royal Naval captain had just entered with a woman who looked like she was probably his wife. There were quite a few uniforms present in The Lorne Club that evening, which was only to be expected with a war on.

Geoffrey indicated the captain to Hannah. 'The navy was my first choice when I tried to join up. But they wouldn't have me. Nor would the army or air force.'

'Why not?'

He tapped his chest, 'I've been asthmatic from birth. I'm also partially deaf in one ear, the result of a childhood accident. The combination of the two meant I failed the physical examinations they put me through.'

'I didn't realise you were deaf.'

'As I said, it's only partially. The only time it really affects me is if someone I'm not aware of speaks quietly on that side.'

'And how often do you get asthmatic attacks?' she asked.

'It depends entirely on my general health, the weather, all sorts of things. There's no set pattern. Most of the attacks are minor, but every so often I have a serious one which necessitates me being off work for a couple of days. It's a pest when that happens, but something I've learned to live with.'

They paused in their conversation while they were served with brown bread and butter. When the waiter had left them Geoffrey said:

'I wanted you to know that I had tried to join up. I didn't want you to think I was somehow funking it.'

'I never thought that,' she replied.

'Still . . .' He ran a finger round the top of his glass which produced a squeaking sound. 'As the cliché goes, every cloud has a silver lining.'

She frowned. 'How do you mean?'

'Staying at the M.F. while so many of the chaps are in uniform means a splendid opportunity for me, an opportunity I shall certainly do my damnest to capitalise on. Instead of dead men's shoes, which is so often the case in the Civil Service, I shall be able to bound up the ladder. Promotion after promotion should just fall into my lap.'

She wasn't sure she approved, in the circumstances, of such a mercenary attitude. 'You're ambitious then?'

'Oh yes, frightfully so. As the forces won't take me I have no guilt feelings whatever about taking advantage of the situation. I shall be in a very senior position when this war is finally concluded, I've promised myself that.'

'What if Hitler wins?'

He'd already given deep thought to that eventuality, but wasn't about to say what his attitude would be should that catastrophe ever come about. It would hardly have been popular with Hannah or anyone else.

'Hitler will lose in the end, just as Kaiser Bill did when he took us on. I don't pretend it'll be easy, mind, but in the end we'll beat the swine. We'll see him off, and his Nazi thugs,' Geoffrey replied evasively.

'But at what cost?' she wondered, thinking in terms of lives. A very sobering thought.

The Dover sole when it came was delicious. It simply melted in the mouth.

'How long do you think before rationing comes into effect?' Hannah asked Geoffrey, the introduction of which they were already gearing up to at the Ministry of Food.

They fell to speculating about a date.

The Lanchester purred to a stop outside Hannah's close. She glanced up at the surrounding windows, knowing that folk would be surreptitiously peering out trying to see, difficult because of the blackout, whose car it was, and who was in it.

'We don't get many cars in Purdon Street,' she said to Geoffrey. 'When one does stop it's usually the doctor.'

'Well tonight it's not,' he smiled.

She touched him on the top of the hand. 'Thank you again for this evening, I had a marvellous time.'

'I did too. Thank *you*.'

She reached for the door handle.

'Hannah?'

She twisted round to look at him.

'How about next Friday? I know of a dinner dance we could go to.'

'All right.'

'I'll pick you up here same time as I did tonight. And bring your dancing shoes, we'll trip the light fantastic.'

She laughed. 'I don't know about that! But I will bring my dancing shoes.'

When she was out on the pavement she gave him a wave, then watched the Lanchester purr off down Purdon Street where it was soon swallowed up by inky darkness.

Trip the light fantastic! She liked that.

*

200

'Can you cook?'

She stared in amusement at Geoffrey. 'Why do you want to know?'

They were in his office, more of a cubby hole than an office, Hannah having just brought him some files. They'd now been going out together for six months.

'I thought we might stay in this Friday, for a change. I could show you round my flat and afterwards you could cook some tea.'

Her amusement turned to suspicion. 'You mean just the two of us?'

'Yes. There's nothing wrong with that is there?'

'Not as long as it's only tea you have in mind?'

Now it was he who was amused. 'I won't try anything caddish. You have my word on that. Cross my heart and hope to die!' As he said the latter he used a finger to make the sign of the cross over his left breast.

She'd known he had a flat almost from the beginning of their relationship – he having mentioned it very early on – and been curious about it. She'd never been inside a bachelor flat. What would it be like, a pigsty? How would it be decorated?

'What would you like to eat?' she asked.

Taking out his wallet he extracted a ten-shilling note and handed it to her. 'You buy the food, I'll lay on the booze. I'll pick you up as usual.'

She folded the ten-shilling note. 'It's a date, as the Americans say in the pictures.'

'It's a date,' he agreed, beaming.

The flat was in Sauchiehall Street, Glasgow's main artery, at the Charing Cross end. 'Voilà!' Geoffrey cried, throwing open his front door.

'Après tu, madam!'

'Less of the madam, if you don't mind,' she jibed back.

'Certainement!'

'I didn't know you could speak French,' she said stepping into a long hallway.

'I don't. Only a few phrases. Une bier, s'il vous plaît. Café au lait, that sort of thing.'

Having already switched on the electric light he now closed the

201

door behind them. 'We'll take that stuff through to the kitchen before I give you a guided tour,' he said, leading the way. The stuff he was referring to was the liver, bacon and onions that Hannah had bought for their meal. She'd learned from a past conversation with him that liver, bacon and onions was one of his favourites.

The first thing that struck her about the flat was its dimensions, far bigger than those of the Purdon Street tenements. Here the ceilings were higher, as consequently were the walls. The hallway itself wasn't only long but must have been a good ten feet wide.

When they entered the kitchen she saw at a glance that it was double the size of theirs in Purdon Street.

'Big flats,' she said.

'They are that. I was very pleased, and fortunate, to land this one when I came to Glasgow. And so central, that's another bonus. The town itself is literally on my doorstep.'

There was no range in the kitchen – that had gone, replaced by a tiled fireplace. The cooking was done on a modern cream-coloured gas cooker.

'I've never used one of those,' she said, indicating the cooker.

'Easy as pie. Nothing to them,' he told her blithely, getting out two plates.

She placed the wrapped-up liver on one plate, the wrapped-up bacon on the other. Besides these she laid the poke of onions. She then gazed more fully about her.

'What do you think?' he demanded.

So far it was neat and tidy, not the tip she'd half expected. The linoleum underfoot was new looking, and positively shone.

'Who taught you how to polish?' she asked in all seriousness.

He laughed. 'I don't do that! I have a woman come in once a week. Couldn't do without my Mrs Cowan.'

'What about your washing?'

'She does that too. Takes it away the day she cleans the house, drops it back two days later. She has her own key so she can come and go as she likes.'

'You are organised, aren't you?' Hannah teased.

'I am a manager after all. That's what a manager does, organise.'

Crossing to the fireplace, which was already laid, he lit it.

'This will soon warm the room up,' he said. Being January it was extremely cold out.

'So what else is there?'

The sitting room (what a luxury!) he ushered her into was vast. She gasped when she saw it.

'I rarely use this in winter. It costs a fortune to heat,' he explained.

She could well believe that.

'But it's lovely in the good weather. Gets lots of sun.'

'It's enormous,' she said.

'Come on, I'll show you the rest.'

His bedroom was half again the size of her own, the bed one of the largest, if not *the* largest, she'd ever seen.

'I feel lost in there sometimes,' Geoffrey smiled, seeing what she was looking at.

'I'm not surprised.'

From the bedroom he took her into the combined toilet and bathroom, prettily painted in a combination of pale blue and white. It also had thick pile carpet underfoot which impressed her.

'We have a range at home which gives us our hot water. How do you get yours?' she queried.

'The kitchen fire has a backboiler,' he explained. 'Light the fire and you heat the water.'

'Same as the range then,' she nodded.

From the toilet/bathroom he escorted her back to the kitchen where he asked if she'd care for a drink. He was having a gin and tonic himself. She replied that would be fine for her also so he mixed a brace of those.

'Cheers!' he toasted her.

'I like your flat. It's very nice.'

'You approve then.'

'Oh, very much so. Though in Partick we call tenement dwellings houses, not flats.'

'Flat is much more posh – he pronounced the "o" as "oh" – don't you think?'

'Are you telling me you're a snob?' she jibed.

'Oh, frightfully so! I would have thought you'd have realised long before now!'

Hannah laughed. Geoffrey could be such fun. She thoroughly

enjoyed his company, even if he could be somewhat pretentious. (At least he had a sense of humour about that side of himself.)

They chatted while she prepared the liver, bacon and onions, Geoffrey showing her where things were and how to turn on the cooker. She had another gin and tonic while cooking, which brought a rosy glow to her cheeks, and he set the table.

When the meal was ready she dished it out, and as she was doing this he lit two candles he'd placed on the table. When she was seated he switched off the overhead light.

'How's that?' he smiled, sitting facing her.

'Very nice.'

He poured her some burgundy, then filled his own wine glass. 'You look gorgeous by candlelight,' he said.

He didn't look so bad himself, she thought. 'You should see me first thing in the morning, not quite the same I'm afraid.'

'Is that an invitation, Miss McCracken?' he teased.

'No, it is not!' She wagged a finger at him. 'Now remember your promise.'

'I shall! I shall!' he replied, saying it in such a way as to make her laugh.

He pronounced the liver, bacon and onions a complete success, declaring that she could come and cook for him any day.

He was in the process of making the coffee – Hannah now sitting by the fire – when the attack struck. Wheezing he bent over, grabbing at the cooker for support.

Instantly she was out of her chair and by his side. 'Is there anything I can do?' she asked anxiously.

'No,' he wheezed, clutching his chest with his free hand.

'You'd better sit down.'

He allowed her to guide him over to the chair she'd been occupying, which he collapsed into, his legs curling up so that he was in a semi-embryonic position. Wheezing and choking, he struggled for breath.

After a while, Hannah had no idea how long, the attack eased and his breathing improved.

'Sorry about that,' he husked.

'Nothing to be sorry about.'

'I'd like some of that coffee if you could . . .'

'Leave it to me,' she interrupted, returning to the cooker where earlier she'd turned off the kettle he'd been boiling.

When the coffee was made she took him over a cup which he gratefully accepted.

How different he looked in the aftermath of his attack, she thought. She'd never seen him look like this before. All his veneer had been stripped away leaving him looking like . . . A little boy lost, she decided. A little *frightened* boy lost, she further qualified. Yes, that was it exactly.

Her heart went out to him.

'Asked you home to meet his parents!' Cathy exclaimed in delight.

'This weekend. Motoring through to Stranraer on Saturday afternoon after work, staying the night and returning on Sunday.'

'You've accepted, of course?'

'Yes. A trip to the coast will be a treat.'

Cathy laid down the book she'd been reading, all interest in it having now disappeared in the light of what she'd just been told. 'You appreciate what this means, don't you?'

'What?' Hannah replied, playing dumb.

'Oh don't be so dense, girl. If he's taking you home to meet his parents it's a prelude to popping the question. No doubt about it.'

That was the conclusion Hannah had already arrived at.

'So what's your answer going to be?'

'I don't know Ma,' she replied, lighting a cigarette.

'He's an excellent catch. Has a good job with prospects, earns a fair amount which will increase as he goes on, has his own flat as he calls it, and a car. What else could you ask for!'

It was a powerful argument, Hannah couldn't deny it.

'And he'll be *alive* at the end of the war,' Cathy said. 'He won't be leaving you a penniless widow, as I was left.'

'Aren't you forgetting the obvious, Ma?'

'Which is?'

'Love.'

Cathy's eyes narrowed as she stared at her daughter. 'I would be the last one to decry love. But I married for love, and look where it got me.' She paused, then said softly. 'You must feel something for him, having gone out with him this length of time?'

205

'I do Ma. I feel a lot for him actually.'

'Well then! What are you talking about?'

'I feel a lot for him, but that doesn't mean to say I love him.'

'Love isn't black and white the way it's often painted, particularly by young people,' Cathy replied. 'It can be many shades of grey. And what's more, I'll tell you this. You can't always get what you want in life, often you have to compromise. You'll learn that as you grow older, it's something we all have to learn.'

'You mean accept second best?'

'Why, is that how you see Geoffrey?'

Hannah puffed on her cigarette. Was it? 'Not exactly,' she answered slowly.

'How do you see him then?'

Her brow furrowed as she thought of the words to describe how she saw Geoffrey Robb. 'A good man . . . kind to those he's fond of, by which I mean me . . . generous . . . physically attractive . . . a bit too mercenary at times for my taste . . . intelligent . . . fiercely ambitious and determined to get ahead . . .'

'He sounds absolutely ideal, if you ask me,' Cathy interjected.

He did too, now that she came to articulate her impressions and judgement of him, Hannah told herself.

'What about his family, what's their background?'

Hannah gave her mother a thin smile. 'He told me about them and their situation after he'd asked me to meet them. They live on a farm . . .'

'Farmers!' Cathy exclaimed. 'They must be wealthy.'

Hannah's thin smile became full blown. 'Not farmers Ma, the father's a farm labourer on a farm. They live in a tied cottage and are as poor as church mice, according to Geoffrey. They're working class, same as ourselves.'

Cathy shrugged. 'Oh well, he's the one you'd be marrying after all, and he's the one with prospects.'

Marrying a man for his prospects, Hannah thought. It made her sound a right gold-digger.

Hannah sighed with contentment, and blew cigarette smoke into the peat fire she and Geoffrey were sitting facing. The light in the room came from oil lamps, a warmer light than the gas she was used to.

'I've eaten enough to last me a week. Your mother's a wonderful cook,' Hannah said. The elder Robbs had bidden them good-night and gone to bed minutes before.

'They both like you very much. Pop told me that when I was out with him earlier.'

'And I like them. They're both very genuine people. And proud of you. They think it marvellous that you won a scholar-ship to go to university.'

'I couldn't have followed my father onto the land,' Geoffrey said. 'I'm just not cut out for it.'

'Too much like hard work you mean?' Hannah jibed.

'There's no money or future in being a farm labourer,' Geoffrey said simply. 'That's not for me.'

'You don't think less of your father because of what he does?' Hannah asked, curious.

'No I do not! I respect my parents, and always have. But they're of the land, born to it. I'm not. In fact . . .' He smiled wryly. 'I've always thought of myself as something of a cuckoo. If you understand that?'

Hannah nodded that she did.

'I think they're as mystified by having me as a son as I am at having them as my parents. I'm so totally different to them. But I love them dearly nonetheless, and they me.'

'I'm glad I've met them. And been here. It's a beautiful part of Scotland.'

'Wild and cold in the winter, as it is now. Quite transformed in the summer when I've known it to be almost Mediterranean. But forget that for now. I've got some news for you. Exciting news.'

She arched an eyebrow.

'What I prophesised about promotion has started. I'm being moved up, from the beginning of next month, not just one grade but two!'

'Oh Geoffrey!' she exclaimed, delighted for him.

'I haven't told my parents yet. I wanted you to be the first to know.'

'Thank you. I appreciate that.'

'How about a kiss?' He patted his knee. 'Come on!'

As she sat his arm twined round and drew her to him. Closing her eyes she puckered her lips.

'I've got something for you,' he breathed heavily when the kiss was finally over.

'What sort of something?' When he didn't reply, but only smiled enigmatically at her she probed further. 'A present?'

'It is that, but also more than that.'

'A present, but more than a present.' She squirmed with excitement. This was fun. 'What is it then?'

He pushed her to her feet, rose and crossed to where his jacket was hung over the back of a chair. On reaching his jacket he delved into a pocket, holding the object he removed from the pocket behind his back when he turned again to face her.

And suddenly she guessed what the 'something' was. 'Let me see,' she said quietly.

The small box he handed her was black on the outside, red velvet inside. The ring was a ruby surrounded by a cluster of diamonds. It was gorgeous.

'What do you think?' he asked, a quaver in his voice.

'It's an engagement ring.'

'Right first time!' he smiled. 'Well?'

'You're asking me to marry you.'

'That's it,' he confirmed.

She pulled the ring from the velvet slot holding it and slipped it on to the appropriate finger. It was slightly large for her.

When he saw that he said, 'I can easily get it adjusted. I had to guess at the size.'

It must have cost a packet, she thought. This was no cheap ring, but a very expensive one indeed.

Coming to her he kneeled beside her. 'Will you marry me, Hannah?' he paused, then added pleadingly. 'Please?'

'You've caught me quite off-guard,' she replied, which was both true and untrue. She'd been expecting a proposal, but not that night, and not for a ring to be presented to her.

'In case you're wondering, I've never proposed to anyone before,' he stated.

'And I've never been proposed to before.' Her mind was racing. What was she to do! She hadn't yet decided one way or the other, believing she still had time before having to make a decision.

'I'll tell you this,' she said. 'A girl couldn't ask for a nicer ring. I think it's possibly the nicest one I've ever seen.'

'So, are we engaged or not?'

She took the ring from her finger and returned it to its box. 'Can I have a while to think? Would that offend you?'

His shoulders slumped. 'You wouldn't offend me. I just thought . . .' he trailed off.

'I have to be absolutely certain, Geoffrey. I don't want to make a mistake, for either of our sakes. And as I said, you have caught me off-guard.'

'How long do you want?' he queried.

'A couple of days?'

'Monday night then.'

'Make it Tuesday night. I'll come to the flat.'

He clasped one of her hands between his own. 'I do love you, Hannah. We're meant for each other. I know that.'

Which was more than she knew, she thought as his lips again sought hers.

On Monday night she went to visit Granny and Granda McCracken, only to discover they'd gone out. Uncle Gavin was home alone.

'I'll put the kettle on,' he said, having welcomed Hannah into the house.

'I'll do it if you like?'

'I can manage lass,' he gently rebuked her.

He could too, she thought. It was a marvel the way he coped without the use of his eyes.

'How's work?' she asked while he was at the sink. He'd trained as a piano-tuner after the war and earned his living at that.

'Very busy. I could work twelve hours a day, seven days a week if I wanted to.'

Hannah patted Bonnie's head as Gavin's guide dog nuzzled her. Bonnie was a black labrador, now getting on in years. The latest in a line of dogs Gavin had had since being blinded.

'How are Granny and Granda?' Hannah inquired.

'Oh just the same. In fairly reasonable shape considering their ages.' Both were now in their seventies.

'What about Granda's arthritis?'

'Not as bad as it might be taking into account the time of year and weather. Ma had a twinge of her sciatica the other day, but it didn't last long.'

They chatted while Gavin made the tea, he eventually bringing her over a cup.

'It's not too strong is it?' he asked as she sipped. 'I like it strong myself.'

'Not too strong thanks. Just right.' She knew he judged the strength of the tea by time, one of the many tricks he'd learned to compensate for his disability. Having added the water to the teapot he then mentally counted to a certain number by which time the tea would be the strength he wanted it to be.

'Do you mind if I smoke, uncle?'

'No, go ahead.'

He settled back in a chair with his own cup and Bonnie lying at his feet. 'What's wrong lass?' he asked.

'How do you know there's something wrong?'

'It's in your voice. You're worried, or troubled, I can hear it.'

She smiled, trust him! His hearing wasn't merely more acute than the normal person's, he listened very carefully not only to what you were saying but how you were saying it.

'I do have a problem. I've been proposed to,' she confessed.

'Congratulations! Or isn't that the case?'

She decided to confide in Uncle Gavin. He was the nearest thing she had to a father after all and, if Bobby had been alive, she would have spoken to him about Geoffrey.

'Can I ask your advice?' she queried.

'Fire away.'

First of all she told him about Lal, and why she'd broken off with him. Then she told him about Geoffrey, ending with his proposal two nights previously, and her promise to give him an answer the following evening.

When she was finished Gavin slowly nodded. 'Aye, I can well understand Cathy wanting you to break it off with your soldier. I mean no disrespect when I say this about her, but Bobby's death left her awfully bitter. It's understandable entirely that she doesn't want you to go through what she did. Understandable entirely.'

There was a look on her Uncle Gavin's face told Hannah he was still in love with Cathy. If she had seen that look before, she hadn't known what it meant. But now, after what Cathy had confided in her, she did.

'I'll tell you this,' Gavin continued. 'When you speak about your soldier there's quite a different tone to your voice than when you speak about Geoffrey.'

'Different how?'

'More warmth. More affection.'

She sighed. 'But Lal's gone and I'll probably never see him again. Geoffrey's here, and I have to give him my answer tomorrow night.'

'You're saying Lal doesn't come into this decision then?'

'I . . . suppose not.'

'Do you love Geoffrey? I doubt you do. If you did we wouldn't be having this conversation.'

'I don't love him uncle, but I do think very highly of him. We get on extremely well together.'

'Well enough for it to be a good marriage?'

'I think so.'

'But you don't love him?'

'No,' she reaffirmed.

'So what you're really asking me is, do you marry a man with whom you'll have a good marriage, even though you don't love him, or do you turn him down because you don't love him?'

She shook her head. 'To be honest I'm so confused. Geoffrey's an excellent catch, except . . .'

'Except you don't love him!' Gavin smiled, cutting in.

'Love isn't the be-all and end-all!' she protested. 'There's more to life than that.'

'I sometimes wonder if there is. Strange notion perhaps, but could it possibly be that *is* precisely what life is all about, the giving, taking and sharing of love. Oh not just between man and woman, but also between parent and child, siblings, neighbour and neighbour.'

Silence fell between them, silence that stretched on and on. Finally Gavin said: 'My advice to you Hannah is simply this. Follow your heart and you won't, can't, go wrong. Matters might not turn out the way you'd wanted and wished them too, but even so you'll have done the right thing. Follow your heart and be true to yourself.'

He took a deep breath. 'Can I have one of your cigarettes please? As you know I only rarely smoke but I'd like to do so now.'

After he'd lit up, by unspoken mutual agreement, they changed the subject and talked about the war. He'd given her the best advice he could.

211

It was up to her now.

Hannah stared at the back of Geoffrey's head. She was at her desk while he was about twenty feet away, talking to Mr Mowlam from another department. The two men were deep in conversation.

She started to think of the flat in Sauchiehall Street, and how lovely it would be to live there – so much more space than the house in Purdon Street. And that sitting room! She could just picture herself entertaining in there, her own friends and Geoffrey's.

And then there was the car, the Lanchester. There was no reason why she shouldn't learn to drive, which would mean she could use it herself. How grand that would be – her behind the wheel of a car, waving to the neighbours in Purdon Street and round about when she drove over to see her ma.

And then there was . . . She brought herself to an abrupt mental halt, appalled. What was she doing! What was she thinking! She couldn't marry a man just for his flat, car and other things. That would be awful. She had to think more clearly and deeply than these flights of fancy she scolded herself, glancing at the wall clock.

It was three in the afternoon. After tea at home she would get to Geoffrey's about seven. Four hours left to decide, yes or no?

Follow your heart, Uncle Gavin had counselled. But she had a mind, and a strong one at that, urging her to follow that instead.

And her mind told her she'd forever regret losing this opportunity if she allowed it to slip by.

Geoffrey opened the front door to discover a distraught Hannah standing on his landing. Her face was screwed up in anguish.

'What's wrong?' he exclaimed.

She brushed past him into the hallway, and from there headed straight for the kitchen. He closed the door and hurried after her. In the kitchen he found her dabbing at her eyes with a crumpled hanky.

'What's wrong?' he asked again.

'We were in the middle of our tea when my Granny Ford came round to tell us that my cousin Ewan has been killed in Libya.'

'Oh Hannah!' Geoffrey said softly, and going to her took her into his arms.

'My Aunt Lily, that's his mother and my mother's sister, has collapsed and been put to bed. The doctor's already seen her apparently, and given her a sedative. Ma's gone round to be with her and Uncle Dougie, that's Aunt Lily's husband, who was fetched home from work.'

Geoffrey pulled her closer to him, and she laid her head on his shoulder.

'The twins and I grew up together. We were more like brothers and sister than cousins,' she said.

He stroked her hair while she sobbed against him. 'How about a drink?' he asked gently.

'Please.' She blew her nose into her hanky when he released her.

Geoffrey poured two stiff whiskies, then returned to Hannah with them. She gulped down a mouthful from the glass he gave her, and shuddered.

'I just can't believe it,' she whispered, fresh tears springing into her eyes.

He placed his drink on the table, and gathered her back into his arms. He resumed stroking her hair.

She wouldn't give him an answer tonight after all, he thought. It would be too much to expect in the circumstances. Removing his hand from her hair he started stroking her hip.

After a while he led her through to the sitting room where he'd earlier lit a roaring fire and set out an ice bucket containing a bottle of champagne, the latter, hopefully, to celebrate their engagement. Beside the bucket were two crystal flutes.

He manoeuvred a big settee in front of the fire which they both then sat on. Hannah drank more of her whisky, and began talking about Ewan, telling Geoffrey about him.

When their glasses were empty Geoffrey opened the champagne. She'd already guessed why it was there but didn't refer to the fact, and neither did he.

The champagne, perhaps because it was on top of whisky, went to her head, but not nastily so. She became very relaxed, and woozy, and in the process of that happening her grief subsided.

She closed her eyes when Geoffrey kissed her, and soon she was kissing him back. She didn't protest when his hand came to rest on her breast, something she'd never allowed him to do before.

Why it happened she never rightly knew, the only explanation being that it was a combination of emotions and events. Geoffrey, hardly daring to believe his luck, went further and further, waiting to be stopped at every new step, and not being so.

When she was naked and stretched out on the couch he shakily rose and began to undress himself, his fingers fumbling in his eagerness.

'You will take care?' she said drowsily.

'I will,' he promised, realising what she meant.

When he too was naked he went down onto her, she smiling up at him through half-closed eyes.

Hannah lay on the wide couch, Geoffrey on the inside of her, fast asleep. They were both covered by a tartan travelling rug that he'd thrown over them afterwards.

She stared up at the ceiling, replete in the afterglow of lovemaking, and knowing she was going to turn down Geoffrey's proposal. Prior to Granny Ford arriving at Purdon Street with the terrible news she had already decided that she would accept Geoffrey, but now they'd been to bed together – which surely would never have occurred if it hadn't been for Ewan's death – she knew she couldn't.

And why? Because when Geoffrey had been doing it to her, moving so pleasurably inside her – pleasurable after that initial pain – it had been Lal she'd been seeing in her mind's eye.

How could she possibly marry a man when the first time he made love to her she imagined another in his place? She knew now it would be a mistake for her to marry Geoffrey. She might regret not marrying him, but she would regret it even more if she did.

Raising her side of the rug she slipped off the couch, and onto her feet. Geoffrey, dimly aware that she'd left him, stirred and grunted.

'It's all right. I'm only going to the bathroom to clean myself up. You sleep on,' she whispered.

He grunted again, wriggled a bit, and once more fell into deep slumber.

Quietly, she gathered up her strewn clothes and padded from the room. When she was dressed she returned to look into the sitting room where Geoffrey was still fast asleep.

Should she wake him and explain to him? she wondered. But couldn't bring herself to do that. Nor could she just walk out on him after he'd been so sweet that evening.

Going through to the kitchen she rummaged round till she found paper and pencil.

The note she wrote said she was sorry but she wouldn't marry him, that was her decision and it was final. She thanked him for the marvellous times they'd had together, but wouldn't be going out with him again after that night. To save embarrassment on both sides she'd stay off ill from work until the beginning of the following month, February, when he took up his new appointment in a different part of the building. As they would undoubtedly bump into one another from time to time she hoped their relationship would remain on a friendly basis and that there would be no unpleasantness and recriminations.

She read the note through and realised she hadn't told him specifically why she wouldn't marry him. She had to do that, she thought. He would want to know, and deserved to know.

She added that she'd come to realise that she was still in love with a chap she'd met before him, which of course made marrying him out of the question.

When she'd signed her name she left the note in a place where he couldn't fail to find it, then walked quietly from the flat, closing the front door just as quietly behind her.

It was odd, but outside on the street she felt as though a great weight had been lifted from her shoulders.

The date was March 3rd, 1942; the month after the fall of Singapore, a crushing blow to Britain and her Empire. But at least America was in the war now, even if so too were the treacherous Japanese who'd bombed Pearl Harbor in the December. Since the latter, Malaya had fallen to the Japs, as had the Philippines, Hong Kong, New Guinea and the Solomon Islands. At sea the *Ark Royal* had been sunk, so too had H.M.S. *Dunedein*, H.M.S. *Barham*, H.M.S. *Repulse* and H.M.S. *Prince of Wales*. One bright light in the general gloom was in Libya where the Eighth Army was at last on the offensive.

Hannah was hurrying along Buchanan Street when she saw him on the opposite pavement amongst a crowd of soldiers, she heading up the street, they down. He spotted her at the same moment. They both stopped in their tracks, her face flaming red.

He smiled, and would have continued with his companions except that she waved him over.

215

'Hello, Lal,' she said when he'd joined her.

'Hello, Hannah.'

They stared at one another, her heart hammering inside her chest.

'It's good to see you,' she said.

'And you.'

'Home on leave?'

'Not exactly.' His eyes flicked in the direction of the others he'd been with.

'Don't think me rude,' he apologised. 'But I have to dash.'

'Of course.'

'Goodbye, then.'

'Goodbye.'

He'd just stepped off the pavement and was about to run back across the road when she called out, 'Lal wait!'

She hurried over to him. 'If you're free this evening we could meet up? Or if not tonight, another night?'

It seemed an eternity to Hannah before he replied in a very soft voice. 'Are you sure?'

'Yes.'

He nodded. 'Tonight then.'

They agreed a time and place where they'd rendezvous.

Hannah was early, and unbelievably nervous. It was pelting down with rain, but that didn't matter. All that did was that she was going out with Lal, Lal whom she'd never expected to see again. Lal whom she loved and knew loved her.

He too was early, as anxious to be with her as she with him. 'There's a pub over-by,' he said, pointing. 'Let's get in out the rain.'

A thrill, like an electric shock, ran through her when he took her hand in his. They ran together, side by side, each acutely aware of the other's presence.

Inside the pub he sat her at a free table, then went up to the bar to order. He returned with a pint for himself and the half pint of shandy she'd requested.

'You look well,' she said, for he did.

'So do you, if perhaps a bit thinner.'

'We're all thinner nowadays, rationing has seen to that!'

They both laughed. 'How's the library?' he groaned.

216

'Fine, but I don't work there anymore. I'm with the Ministry of Food.'

'Oh?'

'And before you ask the question everyone asks, no I do not wangle any extra points for myself and family. Nor do any of my colleagues, as far as I know.'

He smiled at her indignation. 'Why the Ministry of Food?'

'I did want to join the services, but didn't feel I could. Ma . . .' She shrugged.

He remembered the conversation they'd had in the Bluebird Café when she'd broken it off with him. 'I understand,' he nodded.

'And how about you, how's the H.L.I.?'

'I'm not with the regiment anymore. I volunteered to join a new unit, the Commandoes. It's because of them that I'm here. I've been temporarily posted to Glasgow to take a course based at the university. There are thirty of us on the course.'

'What sort of course?' she probed.

'I'm sorry Hannah, I can't tell you that.'

'A secret, eh?'

'I'm afraid so,' he replied, and sipped his beer.

'The Commandoes sound very dangerous?'

'All active duty is that. The only difference between us and ordinary soldiers is that we're more specialised, that's all,' he answered evasively. That being true, if hardly the whole truth.

'How, eh . . .' She lit a cigarette. 'How long is your course for?' She tried to keep her voice neutral, and failed miserably.

'The entire course lasts a month,' he informed her.

'And how long . . .'

'Ten days,' he cut in.

Ten *wasted* days! she thought. It still left two and a half weeks. 'Are you always free at night?'

'Yes, we're only required to attend during the day. All our nights are our own.'

Something leapt inside her to hear that. 'And weekends?'

'We knock off at twelve-thirty on a Saturday, and that's it till Monday morning. Our working week is virtually office hours.'

That information pleased her immensely. 'The H.L.I. took an awful mauling before getting out at Dunkirk. I read the newspaper lists for weeks afterwards so I knew you hadn't been . . .'

She trailed off, then asked. 'Were you wounded?' So many had been at Dunkirk.

He shook his head. 'I was one of the lucky ones. I came through that entire business without even a scratch.' He smiled bleakly. 'Though to be honest, I had a few close shaves. Then, and since.'

She'd had one herself, she thought, meaning Geoffrey Robb. Imagine if she'd married Geoffrey, discovered on their wedding night what she had the night she'd slept with him in his flat, and then gone on to bump into Lal as she had! That would have been ghastly, sheer torture.

'It's *so* good to see you again,' Lal said, taking hold of her hand as he'd done out in the street.

'And to see you. So very good.'

They talked and talked, and talked and talked, till finally it was a reasonable time for him to take her home, and to the backclose they were both thinking of.

'There wasn't a day went by when I didn't think of you Hannah,' Lal whispered in the darkness of the backclose, she held tightly in his embrace.

'Nor I you.'

'I thought I'd lost you forever.'

She kissed him again, her tongue throbbing in his mouth.

'Oh Hannah!' he murmured in an agonised tone when the kiss was over. 'I do love you. I love you to distraction.'

'And I you.'

He buried his face in her hair, drinking in the smell of it, and the scent of her. 'I want to marry you,' he whispered.

And she wanted to marry him. *How* she wanted to marry him. But much as she wanted to she wasn't going to.

She pushed him slightly away. 'I won't marry you, Lal. Not now. But I promise you this, when the war's over I'll do so gladly. In the meantime from here on in, I'll see you every opportunity there is during this posting and any leaves home you might have in the future. I'll see you, and be as fully a wife to you as though we were married. The one stipulation I make is that you must ensure I don't get pregnant.'

He was taken totally by surprise. 'You mean that?'

'I wouldn't have said it if I hadn't. I'll be as fully a wife to you

218

as if we were married, do anything for you that you wish. But no marriage and no child till after the war.'

His mind began to race, considering possibilities. The situation was so damned difficult with him living in a barracks and her with her mother. Then he had the solution.

Hannah instantly agreed when he put it to her.

They got out the taxi at the front of the Marine Hotel, and Hannah stared out over the bay and Firth of Clyde beyond as Lal paid the driver. She'd never been to Largs before, but she'd liked what she'd seen of it so far during their short drive from the station.

'Right,' said Lal, picking up their cases as the taxi drove away. 'Shall we go inside?'

'After you.'

'Ladies first!'

'Age before beauty!'

'Beauty before the beast!' he riposted.

She couldn't think of a reply to that. So, doing her best to look nonchalant she went in through the large doors and headed for the reception desk, Lal following directly behind her.

The middle-aged woman at the desk, hair tied back in a severe bun, glanced up at their approach, and gave them a professional smile.

'I'll get us a newspaper,' Hannah said to Lal, and moved quickly along the desk to where a selection of that day's newspapers were on display. She didn't want a newspaper at all, but to leave Lal to deal with the woman on reception.

Lal laid down their cases. 'We'd like a double room, preferably with bathroom. Do you have one available?' he asked, the merest hint of a flush in his cheeks. As he'd said to Hannah on their way there it was highly unlikely at that time of year, and with a war on, that the hotel would be fully booked.

'Double with bathroom, yes of course,' the woman replied. 'How long for?'

'Just tonight.'

'I see.' Her eyes, as professional as her smile, went from Lal to Hannah and back again to Lal.

The woman flipped open a large book, and picked up a pen. 'The name is?'

'Mr and Mrs Lawrence Stuart. That's Stuart with a "u" and not "w".'

'Uh-huh!' The woman wrote their names into the book. 'And your home address is?'

Lal gave her his Maryhill one.

Hannah picked out an *Express*, placed the money for it in the tin provided for that purpose, then rejoined Lal. She held her left hand up at her chest so that the woman could see the gold band on her wedding finger, a ring they'd bought in Glasgow just prior to catching their train.

The woman turned the book round and handed Lal the pen. 'Sign here please,' she instructed, indicating the spot where he was to put his signature.

'Will you be down for dinner?' the woman asked, this question directed at Hannah.

She's guessed! Hannah thought. There was a glint at the back of the woman's eyes told her so. Or then again, perhaps the woman mistakenly thought they were honeymooners.

'Yes.' Hannah replied.

'We serve between seven-thirty and nine. A very limited menu, I'm afraid.' She shrugged. 'The war you understand.'

'Quite,' Hannah smiled.

'*Two* cases, is it?'

A giveaway when they were only staying for the night Hannah suddenly realised. Why hadn't she thought of that before! 'Two,' she confirmed.

The woman removed a key from a rack behind her, then beckoned over a young lad in uniform who'd been hovering nearby. 'Show Mr and Mrs Stuart to number fourteen,' she instructed. And with that she treated Hannah and Lal to another of her professional smiles.

The lad picked up their cases, 'If you'll follow me, please,' he said, and led the way to the lift.

En route to the lift Hannah glanced at Lal. He was trying as hard as she was not to burst out laughing.

Inside number fourteen Lal quickly gave the lad threepence. The moment the door clicked shut behind the lad Hannah clapped a hand over her mouth.

Lal sniggered.

'I . . . I . . .' she began, then exploded with laughter, Lal joining in.

'She knew . . .' Hannah gasped.

Lal gulped down air. 'Oh, she did that, and made it obvious too!'

'For once I didn't blush. I'd have been mortified if I had.'

Lal swept her into his arms, and they both quietened. 'Hello *Mrs* Stuart.'

'Hello Mr Stuart.'

He kissed her, a deep kiss full of passion, yet also full of great tenderness.

'We'll get unpacked and then what do you want to do?' he asked. 'We could have a walk along the front, or a drink maybe?'

'We can do those things later. Right now let's go to bed; it's what we came here for isn't it?'

He stared into those hazelnut eyes he so adored. When they'd been apart it had always been her eyes he'd thought of first when thinking about her.

'Yes,' he whispered.

She lay in his arms, her cheek on his chest. This time it had been right, the man making love to her had been the man she'd wanted to be making love to her. There had been no visions of anyone else in her mind's eye, only images of Lal.

After a while, at her instigation, they made love again.

'Now you won't cry, will you? You promised,' Lal said, voice thick with emotion.

'No. I won't cry,' she husked, fighting back the tears. She glanced along the platform and saw the guard getting ready to wave his flag.

'It was a wonderful two and a half weeks,' Lal said. He was standing behind the train door, leaning out of its open window. He and Hannah were clasping hands.

More wonderful than she'd have dreamt possible, thanks to her Ma, Hannah thought.

She'd swithered about telling Cathy she was seeing Lal again, and in the end decided to do so. Not only had she told Cathy she was seeing Lal again, but also about the agreement she'd made

221

with him, and that he'd been the 'friend' she'd gone to Largs with.

Cathy had then amazed her by pronouncing the agreement a sensible one, the best of both worlds so to speak. After which Cathy had positively astounded her by saying she and Lal could use the house, meaning the bedroom, any time they liked. All they had to do was let her know and she'd make herself scarce for a few hours.

Lal had never stayed the night of course. It would have ruined her and Cathy's reputation if he had. But after Cathy said they could use the house there wasn't a single evening passed that they didn't.

Now it was time for Lal to leave Glasgow and return south. Hannah was almost beside herself with the pain of their parting.

'I'll be back Hannah, I swear it,' he vowed, squeezing her hand.

'And I'll be waiting.'

And if he didn't return she still had these two and a half weeks to remember. Two and a half weeks of sheer bliss, the happiest two and a half weeks of her life.

The guard's whistle blew, and the train juddered.

'I love you,' she said unnecessarily.

'I love you too.' Damn it! he thought. He was going to be the one to cry. Tears were only an eye flicker away.

'God bless and keep you Lal. Come home again safely.'

'I will.'

The train juddered a second time, then started to move slowly. She walked with it, the two of them still holding hands.

Finally they had to release hands as the train picked up speed. 'Goodbye!' he choked, raising the hand that had been clasping hers in salute.

'Goodbye!' She couldn't hold them back any longer, the tears came in floods.

Aboard the train Lal was also weeping.

On returning to the barrier Hannah found a familiar sight waiting for her beyond it.

'What are you doing here?' she asked Cathy on joining her.

Cathy stared at her daughter's bright tearful eyes, and tear-stained cheeks. This was the same platform she'd seen Bobby off from that last time, she thought. That last time he went away never to return. She could remember it as clearly as though it was yesterday. 'I thought you might like a bit of support,' she smiled.

Hannah fell into her mother's embrace. 'Oh, Ma!' she wailed.

'I know lass, I know,' Cathy murmured, thanking God Hannah hadn't married her soldier love, and that there wasn't and wouldn't be, a baby. Whatever happened Hannah wouldn't be left a war widow, and a baby fatherless. Yes, Hannah had done the right thing in her agreement with Lal.

'Ishbel Baker, the wife of one of Bobby's pals, and I always used to go to the refreshments room for a cup of tea and a sit-down afterwards. Why don't you and I do the same?' Cathy suggested.

Hannah straightened herself. 'I'll have to go to the toilet first.'

'Come on, then.'

Cathy hooked her arm in Hannah's, and they moved off.

'Hold your horses! Hold your horses!' Hannah yelled, hurrying out of the kitchen into the hallway. Someone was hammering at the front door as if trying to break it down.

She threw the door open, all set to rebuke the person doing the hammering. The rebuke died in her throat when she saw who it was.

Lal was in his demob suit, and holding a bunch of flowers. 'I'm out of the army and home for good – will you marry me?' He said all at once in a rush of words.

She tried to speak, but was unable to do so. Instead she mutely nodded.

'These are for you,' he said, proffering the flowers.

She took the flowers, and kissed him. A shy kiss, after so long. Then she drew him inside.

Chapter 7

'Ready?' Lal asked with a smile having inserted the old-fashioned iron key into an equally old-fashioned (it looked positively medieval!) lock.

'Ready,' Hannah smiled in reply.

Lal turned the key and pushed the door open, the door squeaking as it moved.

Lal pulled the torch he'd brought along from his coat pocket and shone it inside. 'The electricity box and all the switches are in the rear,' he said.

'I'll wait here till the lights are on.'

'Won't be a mo'.' He kissed her lightly on the lips, then plunged into the darkness.

Hannah was thrilled. What an absolutely superb wedding present to be given! Their very own bakery and shop.

She and Lal had been married a fortnight previously and, on the eve of the wedding Harry Stuart, Lal's dad, had announced that he and Avril his wife were buying them premises of their own as a wedding gift.

The bakery and shop, which had belonged to an old crony of Harry's, had been shut for some years now, having been closed when the crony, a Danny McCormack, had retired before the war. Harry and Avril had been discussing what to buy Lal and Hannah for their wedding – terribly difficult with so few goods available in the shops – when Harry had suddenly remembered the bakery and shop that Danny McCormack still owned.

Harry had gone round to see Danny who'd been reluctant to sell even though he had no one to leave it to when he passed on, but finally Harry had talked him into it, and the necessary papers had been drawn up. Matters had been finalised that very afternoon when Lal had collected the key.

What was really nice about these particular premises was that not only were there working and selling areas – bakery, back shop and front shop – but also living accommodation above.

Since the wedding, Hannah and Lal had been staying with Cathy, which had been fine as far as it went, but how much better it was going to be to have a place of their own. And for nothing too!

Lights began flickering on one after the other, Lal having arranged for the electricity supply to be reconnected, and soon the entire front shop was illuminated.

Hannah removed the key from the lock, and closed the door behind her. She then gazed about.

There were cobwebs everywhere. All the corners were festooned with them, as were the shelves behind the counter. The counter glass fascia was broken, a long jagged crack stretching nearly three-quarters of its length. That was going to be a bugger to have replaced, glass and other such items still in very short supply.

The floor was tiled. Squatting, she examined a section. The tiles were filthy now, but should come up all right given a good scrubbing. The walls and ceiling, to her dismay, were not only extremely dirty but a nauseous yellow colour.

Lal reappeared, his face downcast. 'It's a proper tip in there.'

'What about the ovens?'

That was the big question, Lal thought. They had been lying idle an awful long while. 'All I can do is try and fire them and see what happens.'

'Let's have a look at them, then.'

The back shop was a lot worse than the front; there were boxes, baking boards, tins, bottles, and all manner of general junk strewn everywhere. The walls and ceiling were the same nauseous yellow as out front.

The bakery itself wasn't quite so bad, though it did leave a tremendous amount to be desired. The ovens were ancient, early Victorian, Hannah discovered from a date on the side of one of them.

'It could be worse,' Lal said.

But not much, she thought. Everything she'd seen so far was going to have to be done out, and where did you get the materials to do that? Her initial excitement had slumped considerably.

'Let' s have a dekko at the living accommodation,' she said.

'Up the stairs in the back shop I was told,' he replied, leading the way.

The stairs and bannister were painted a bilious green, and flaking badly. The door at the top of the stairs was the same bilious green, and flaking even more badly. They went through the door into the room beyond.

Hannah bit her lip. The room was a reasonable size with an interesting sloping roof at the far end. The floor was bare, with a number of boards missing; one wall had several holes in it. There was a small grate covered in rust.

'Ouch!' muttered Lal.

'What room do you think this is?'

He shook his head. 'No idea. Let's press on.'

There was a small kitchen, whose ceiling was badly stained by damp, with a range and other facilities, a bedroom the same size, a toilet but no bath, plus the first room they'd gone into.

'This must be a sitting room,' Lal declared when they re-entered the latter.

Hannah remembered another sitting room, and how nice that one had been. Still, any sitting room was a luxury. She was just thankful to have one.

'Da says he got the place at a reasonable price,' Lal stated.

'I should hope so too!' she retorted quickly, which made them both laugh.

'Seriously though Hannah, it does need an awful lot doing to it.'

'Now, don't be negative,' she chided. 'We must look on the positive side. I've been thinking about paint . . .'

'Damned hard to come by,' he cut in.

'But not impossible, if you know the right people.'

He regarded her shrewdly. 'Are you telling me you do?'

'I don't personally, but my grandfather might. There's a big P&O boat in at Tommy's Yard – that's the yard where Granda used to work – having a complete re-fit just now. Granda often goes back there for a natter. He could have a word.'

'I don't know that I approve,' Lal joked, tongue firmly in cheek.

'You don't have to. All you have to do is provide the where-withal. And it won't be cheap, I'm warning you.'

'As long as it isn't battleship grey! I can't have a bakery painted battleship grey.'

'You can rest assured it won't be that. P&O liners don't go in for battleship grey. And while Granda's having that word he might mention that we need a new glass fascia for the counter. There's a lot of glass in liners.'

He caught her up into his arms. 'I'm beginning to think I married a female spiv, a right wide girl.'

'Well if you don't want me to . . .'

He silenced her with a kiss.

Hannah hummed as she painted. She was up a ladder, inside the front shop, coating a wall with brilliant white paint, ten gallons of which her granda had secured for them. The glass would also be following shortly, he'd promised when delivering the paint.

She'd been cock-a-hoop to receive the paint, it made the world of difference. Without it they couldn't really have reopened. (The yellow walls and ceiling of the front shop were too far gone, no amount of washing-down would have rendered them acceptable for a public area where food was sold.)

Lal came into the front shop, carrying a new loaf and breadknife. 'The very first. I thought we'd have a slice each,' he said. The ovens had initially proved stubborn to get fired, but after a bit of work on them, and a replacement part for one, which he'd managed to find in a scrap-metal yard, he'd got them going.

Hannah came down off the ladder, laid her pot of paint and brush on a newspaper there for that purpose, then bent close to the loaf Lal was holding in front of him. 'Smells deelliicious!' she pronounced. 'Let's have a taste then.'

The bread was difficult to cut, being straight out of the oven, but Lal contrived two thin slices, one of which he presented to Hannah, keeping the other for himself. They both bit off a piece from their respective slices and started to chew.

'It really is good,' Hannah said after swallowing. 'And I'm not saying that just because my husband baked it either.'

'These ovens handle differently to those I was used to at my father's.' He then launched into some technical detail that was completely above Hannah's head.

'When are you going to try cakes?' she queried when he was finished.

'I'll stay with bread until I'm quite happy that I've got these ovens totally worked out, then I'll attempt a batch of cakes. Any preferences?'

'Eccles and french cakes, those have always been my favourites.'

'Then eccles and french cakes it is.'

He took another bite from his slice of bread. 'This flour isn't a patch on what it was before the war. But then so many things aren't a patch on what they were before the war.'

She heartily agreed with that.

'I've had an idea,' he said. 'You may think its daft, and it's certainly unusual, but I have a feeling it will work.'

He swung himself up on the counter so that he was sitting on it. 'I want to get the business off to a flying start, that's very important. But how? You see I firmly believe that if you can get customers in once, and they like what you're selling, then you should be able to get them in again.'

'So what's your idea for the flying start?'

'Free bread on opening day, as far as our allocation of flour will go. No money required, only BUs.' The latter were bread units, the coupons needed to purchase bread and cakes. It was four BUs for a large loaf. The war might be over but rationing was still very much in effect.

'Free bread!' Hannah exclaimed. That was novel.

'And we'll advertise the fact in the window. I thought you might make a poster. "Free bread on our opening day. First come first served."'

'Well, you'll undoubtedly get customers with a deal like that.'

'And hopefully keep most of them. Some won't come back, I'm sure but I'm banking that the majority will. A newly decorated front shop, a cheerful and helpful assistant behind the counter, meaning you darling: what more could they ask for?' He paused, then went on. 'Or let me put it another way. We're in an ideal spot here, perfectly located for the immediate locals who have a good five or six minutes' walk to our nearest competitors. What I need to do is get them through our door, hence the free bread, and by doing so break their current loyalties. After all, why walk to another bakery when there's a perfectly acceptable one, maybe even preferable one, right on your own doorstep?'

'I have to hand it to you, you're a clever old stick,' Hannah smiled.

'You approve, then?'

'I consider your logic to be impeccable.'

'The only snag is it will cost us the price of that first day's allocation of flour, plus overheads etc. But I think it will be well worth it in the long run.'

'So I take it we can afford that initial loss?' She wasn't at all certain of their finances. Lal had a little money of his own, and perhaps more, that his father had given him on coming out of the army, but just how much he had in the bank he'd never said. Like many Glaswegian men he was very close about his money. Not tight, never that, but close.

'I look at it this way – it's a case of spend a penny to make a pound. We can afford it.'

'Then that's what we'll do.'

He waited until she'd finished lighting a cigarette. 'Hannah?'

'Hmmh?'

'I've sort of broached this before, but now I'm asking right out. Can you get my flour allocation increased? Surely that isn't a huge problem for you? You're leaving the Ministry of Food anyway to come and work here.'

'No,' she stated firmly. 'You've applied for a new business allocation and that's what you've got. I won't try and influence the size of that allocation. It wouldn't be ethical.'

'Sod ethics! This is our future livelihood we're talking about.'

'No, Lal and that's final. If I was caught it would mean a jail sentence. Do you want me to go to jail?'

'Surely with your experience at the Ministry you're fly enough not to be caught?'

'It's not a case of being fly, but of right and wrong. I will not use my position for a criminal purpose. Which is precisely what you're asking me to do.'

'Oh for God's sake, you make it sound like I want you to rob a bank!'

'The principle is the same,' she argued defiantly.

'What about your principles when you asked your Granda to get us this paint?' He had her there, he told himself.

'Would you rather Granda hadn't got it for us?'

'No, of course not.'

'Well then!' she snapped. How could she explain that her real worry was Geoffrey Robb, still bitter about her deserting him that night they'd made love together in his sitting room. He was married now to someone else, and happy as far as she knew. But he'd never forgiven her. If he was to catch a whiff of her doing something she oughtn't to be doing at the Ministry she wouldn't put it past him to be revengeful and vindictive. Unlikely as it was that he'd find out, she just couldn't take the chance; it wasn't worth it.

'Women,' Lal said, shaking his head. 'Sometimes you lot are a complete mystery.'

'So we should be. Now if you don't mind I'd better get on with this painting.'

And having said that she collected her pot and brush, and climbed back up the ladder.

They were in bed reading, prior to going to sleep for the night. They were still at Purdon Street, their accommodation above the shop and bakery still far from being ready. At least the roof there was now fixed, they'd had a builder in the day before doing what was needed, which was mainly repositioning and clipping a number of slates that had moved.

Hannah laid her book on her lap, and pursed her lips. It might work. It was certainly worth a try.

'Lal?'

He grunted.

'I think I may know how to increase the size of your flour allocation.'

He glanced sideways at her. 'How?' he demanded eagerly. As he'd previously explained to Hannah, the more flour he was allocated the more bread and cakes he could make and theoretically sell. He would be able to increase that allocation in time, but the process, because of the rationing restrictions and related bureaucracy, would be a slow one.

'It's your idea of giving away free bread on our opening day that's given me another. I think we can safely assume the bread on that day will go very swiftly indeed. Right?'

'I'll be astounded if it doesn't.'

'Now, to be pedantic, what happens is this. We sell the bread, or in this instance give it away, collect the BUs due, and at the end of the day present the BUs at the local food office, in return for which they will sell us the next allocation.'

'That's correct,' Lal nodded. 'I buy my allocation on a daily basis, returning the BUs I've collected at the end of the day which releases the next allocation.'

'And if you are persistently underselling your allocation, which the local food office can tell from the number of BUs you return, the same food office will cut your allocation.'

'That's how it works,' he confirmed. 'It's easy for them to know when to cut your allocation, but difficult for the new baker, one just starting out, to prove he needs a larger allocation. I will be able to justify an increase in time of course, but to begin with anyway it's rather a chicken and egg situation.'

She pointed a finger at him. 'The key word you've just said is *prove*. I believe I know how we can do that.'

'I'm all ears.'

'On the opening day, the moment the last loaf is sold – you're not making cakes that day to maximise the amount of bread – I take the BUs and rush round to the food office, and the earlier I get there the better. If you're completely sold out by ten in the morning for example, then that *proves* you're badly under allocated. With me presenting your case, because I know precisely how the M.F. works – the questions they'll ask, how to correctly phrase the answers to those questions etc – I believe we stand a very good chance of having your allocation increased. And sizeably, if I have anything to do with it.'

'The more flour the bigger the turnover, and the bigger the turnover the bigger the profit,' Lal stated, eyes gleaming.

'And there's nothing wrong or unethical about what we'll be attempting. All we'll be doing is using the system as the system exists.'

'What would be awful is . . .' He took a deep breath. 'What would be awful is if we did manage to get an increased allocation and then fell flat on our faces by not getting the custom to justify it. I'd feel a right fool then.'

'You're being negative again. Don't!'

He stared at her, loving her, thankful that he'd met her and come through the war safe and sound so that they could get married. Thankful that she'd waited for him. His heart swelled with his love for her.

He gave her a sudden flashing smile. 'Know something? We make a great team, you and I.'

She returned his smile. He was right, they did make a great team. They were naturals together.

He laid his book aside, then reached for her, pulling her to him.

'Put the light out first,' she insisted, playfully resisting him.

He clicked out the light situated on the wall above their heads, then reached for her again to discover she'd snuggled down beneath the bedclothes. He joined her there, one of his hands immediately finding a fulsome breast. He thought she had the most marvellous breasts, and had often told her so. He never tired of fondling and kissing them.

'Quiet now, no noise,' she whispered when he eventually came on top of her.

That was the worst thing about having your mother in the next room. It would have mortified her to think Cathy had heard her and Lal making love.

Lal glanced at his wristwatch; it was six minutes to opening. He turned round as Hannah appeared from the back shop.

'I couldn't resist having a look out the upstairs window. You won't credit this but the queue goes right down the road and round the corner,' she told him excitedly.

'Round the corner!'

'There must be hundreds of them, all talking and laughing amongst themselves. It's a real carnival atmosphere.'

Lal ran a hand over a forehead flushed with heat. He'd been in the bakery since shortly after midnight, wanting his entire allocation to be baked for opening. Normally he would have staggered bakings, but not that day. He wanted everything sold as soon as possible. And with the queue that Hannah now said had gathered outside that was going to be even more quickly than he'd anticipated.

'Here we go then!' he declared, deciding to forget what short time was left to the hour, and strode to the door.

Hannah hurried behind the counter, ready for the onslaught. For that opening day, with all the baking already done, Lal would be serving with her.

Lal threw open the door. 'Good morning, ladies. Good morning!' he exclaimed cheerfully as a line of women streamed past him.

'Is the bread really free?' the first woman to the counter demanded.

'All we're asking today are for your BUs,' Hannah replied with a broad smile.

From there on in it was non-stop, handing out loaves with one hand, taking BUs with the other.

Lal sat in an armchair donated by his Auntie Vera and fidgeted. It was ages since Hannah had gone rushing off to the local food office. What was keeping her?

He gazed around their sitting room. He and Hannah had moved into their accommodation two days previously, but there was still a lot left to do before it could be called anywhere near finished. He should be getting on with some of that now, but couldn't.

What a morning – unbelievable! They'd sold out in fifty minutes flat.

He jumped to his feet. Come on Hannah! He was desperately tired, having worked through the night, but there would be no sleep for him till he knew the outcome of her visit to the food office. It was at times like this he wished he smoked. If he'd had a drink in, despite the hour, he would have had one.

He rushed for the door when he heard her feet on the stairs. When he saw her long face he didn't have to ask.

'Damn!' he muttered. Now he was going to have to build up the business the hard, and long, way. It would be an ongoing battle with the food office to increase his allocation, which they would no doubt do a very small amount at a time.

'I'm sorry,' she said in a little voice. 'I did my best.'

'It's not your fault. Come away in and I'll put the kettle on.'

'Are you terribly disappointed?'

'That's a stupid question. Of course I am! Damn rationing! Damn wartime bureaucracy! Damn controls and quotas and allocations! Damn . . .'

'Your allocation has been doubled,' she said over him, her face cracking into a smile.

He stopped abruptly in mid-flow. 'What?'

'I said, your allocation has been doubled with effect from this evening.'

'But your face! I assumed . . .'

'I was teasing you,' she interrupted. 'I couldn't resist it. And speaking of faces, you should have seen your own. It was a picture.'

He grabbed her, pulling her to him. 'That was very unkind,' he admonished.

'Unkind but funny.'

'Double allocation!' he breathed, and kissed her.

'I had a real stroke of luck,' she said after the kiss was over. 'The woman dealing with me recognised me, having worked very briefly in the department next to the one I worked in. When she established I was who she thought I was I got a very sympathetic hearing. She also hinted strongly that if you wish to further increase your allocation in the future then all I have to do is go and see her.'

Suddenly he was out on his feet, craving his bed and sleep. 'I love you, Hannah Stuart,' he said simply.

'And I love you.'

'Let's go to bed.'

'At this time of day!'

'Bakers keep peculiar hours. You're going to have to learn that.'

'But I'm not tired.'

'Just a cuddle till I drop off?'

'Like babes in the wood?' she smiled.

'Like babes in the wood,' he agreed.

Cuddle was all they did. And it was lovely for both of them.

Lal opened the shop door and looked out. There wasn't a queue, not a single solitary person waiting. It was their second morning.

'Bit different to yesterday,' Hannah said, trying not to sound disappointed.

'You can say that again. They were falling over themselves then.'

'It's early yet.'

'It wasn't too early yesterday.'

'I'll tell you what, if you hold the fort here I'll make us a cup of tea.'

Lal went behind the counter where he fussily rearranged cakes that Hannah had very nicely set out half an hour previously. He made a different display of them, then changed his mind and made a different one again.

'A small loaf please.'

The speaker was a middle-aged woman carrying a battered and scarred leather shopping bag, 'Certainly, madam,' Lal replied, quickly selecting a loaf.

'They're not free today, eh?' she grinned, the corners of her eyes and her cheeks screwing up into tramlines.

'I'm afraid not. I can only afford to do that once.'

The woman gave Lal the right money and BUs. 'See you tomorrow then,' she said.

'See you tomorrow!' he called after her.

That made him feel better, bucked him up a bit. He was considering going into the back shop and shouting up the stairs to Hannah that they'd had a customer when another appeared, and another behind her. After that they kept on coming.

When Lal finally locked up they were only left with a tray of large loaves and several dozen cakes. He pronounced their second day in business a resounding success.

A far better day than he'd dared hope.

'Want some balloons?' John Ford asked Hannah, who was visiting her grandparents.

'Balloons! I haven't seen a balloon since before the war.'

John went to a drawer and fished out a packet. 'These are from America. A pal of mine on the boat gave them to me, along with a bunch of bananas.'

'Bananas!' Hannah exclaimed, full of wonderment. 'I haven't seen or tasted one of those since before the war either.'

'Well, you're not going to see or taste one now either,' John retorted, eyes twinkling mischievously. 'I scoffed the lot.'

'Terrible so he is,' muttered Winnie, shaking her head.

'I knew she never cared for them much,' John said, indicating his wife. 'And once I'd started I just couldn't stop. They were a proper treat and no mistake.'

'Selfish pig,' grumbled Winnie.

'I would have kept you some if you'd liked bananas!' he protested.

'That's not the point. There are others beside me.'

'Who, for instance?'

'Hannah, for instance.'

'Oh, stop moaning at me, woman! You're always moaning at me.'

'I am not.'

'Yes you are. Everything I do nowadays is wrong. If I'd brought home the bananas that would have been wrong too.'

How very old they were getting, Hannah thought. Her granda was becoming positively stooped.

'Anyway, what does Hannah want with balloons?' Winnie retorted quarrelsomely. 'You should have given them to the children round about. She's grown up now you know!'

'I know she's grown up. I know that. It's just . . .' He shrugged. 'I suppose I don't always think of her that way.'

Very old and senile, Hannah told herself. There again, in their mid-eighties, they'd both had a good innings.

'Do you want the balloons or not?' John asked her.

'I'd love to have them. Thank you very much Granda.'

'See!' he exclaimed, flashing a triumphant look at Winnie.

Halfway home it came to Hannah what she should do with the balloons her grandfather had so unexpectedly given her.

'Oh my, aren't they pretty!' the customer enthused to Hannah serving behind the counter. The woman was referring to the blown-up balloons that festooned the corners of the front shop, and dangled from the shelves where the cobwebs had been that first night Hannah and Lal had entered the premises.

'Just something to add a bit of colour,' Hannah explained. 'Everything seems so drab nowadays.'

'Aye, that's true enough,' the woman agreed. Post-war Britain was drab, everywhere and everything seemed grey, black and dull.

'It's a lovely shop, this,' the woman said, lowering her voice as if she was imparting a secret. 'Bright white paint and now balloons. Oh aye, a lovely shop.'

'Thank you,' Hannah smiled.

'See you tomorrow, Mrs Stuart.'

'See you tomorrow.'

Those were words she was hearing more and more, words that were music to her and Lal's ears.

Balloons, she thought, smiling to herself. Commonplace before the war. Now a row of them was as though an almost forgotten rainbow had suddenly reappeared out of the darkness.

Nearly everyone who came into the shop commented on them, saying how nice and cheery they were.

A few days later Lal asked if she'd go and see her friend at the local food office to have their flour allocation increased again. Demand was such he was certain he could sell another twenty-five per cent over and above what they were already selling.

When Hannah saw her friend the increase was granted.

Lal kneaded a batch of the next day's dough, enjoying the job, as he'd always done since first doing it under his father's guidance. There was something marvellously therapeutic about kneading dough, there had been many times when he'd been in the army that he'd craved to do it. He glanced up when Hannah entered the bakery.

'So what did the doctor say?' he asked.

Her expression was one of smugness – most unlike her. 'I've been lying to you, Lal.'

'Eh?' He stopped kneading, astounded by Hannah's confession. He couldn't imagine Hannah lying to him, or why she should feel the need to.

'It's true I haven't been on top form recently, but I was pretty certain what was wrong. I just wanted it officially confirmed that's all. And tonight it was.'

He was lost. 'Have what confirmed?'

'That I'm pregnant. We're going to have a baby.'

'Going to have a baby!' he exploded, throwing his hands in the air. Bits of dough went flying in all directions.

She nodded, delighted at how overjoyed he was. She was just as overjoyed herself. That, and somewhat apprehensive.

He rushed to her and threw his hands round her. 'Oh darling, that's stupendous news! I couldn't be more pleased.'

'Watch my coat,' she chided. 'I don't want dough all over it.'

He pulled his hands away. 'The doctor is absolutely sure?'

'Absolutely.'

'When?'

'Late December, early January.'

He let out a great sigh. 'That really is marvellous.' Breaking away from her he crossed to a cupboard from which he took a half-empty bottle of sherry.

'I'm afraid this is all I've got to celebrate with,' he apologised.

'Not for me, Lal.'

'Just a taste? It is . . . well quite an occasion, after all.' She laughed. 'Just a taste, then.'

He didn't have any glasses handy, and rather than run upstairs for some he used cups instead, pouring himself a fair old dollop; for her the small drop she'd requested.

'The baby. *Our* baby!' he toasted.

'Our baby.'

When she'd had a sip she said, 'Now I've told you, I'd like to go and tell Ma. Do you mind if I go there now?'

He looked over at the batch of dough he'd keen kneading, and mentally worked out what remained for him to do that evening. 'If you'll hang on for twenty minutes to half an hour I'll come with you.'

'Right then. We'll go together.'

'We've got lots to talk over now,' he said.

She kissed him lightly on the lips. 'It's all good and getting better, isn't it?'

'Yes,' he agreed.

As they strolled down Purdon Street he stared at the tenements surrounding them, similar tenements to where they were living in Maryhill. A different part of Maryhill to where he'd been brought up, and to where his father's bakery and shop were.

'I'm going to see this baby gets the best there is,' Lal said quietly.

Hannah glanced sideways at him – they were arm in arm. 'How do you mean?'

'Maryhill's all right – it's all I've ever known, and so too is Partick, but there are far better areas in Glasgow. Areas where you can have your own detached house with garden.'

'They cost!' she exclaimed.

'Of course they do, an awful lot of money. But that doesn't mean to say that such a house is beyond our grasp.'

'You think the business can do that well?'

They walked for a few steps in silence before he replied. 'Maybe not the business as it is, or can be. But that doesn't mean to say that one day we can't afford the sort of house I've just mentioned.'

She couldn't fathom that. 'I don't understand?'

He wasn't going to explain further, not until he'd fully thought through the germ of an idea that was wriggling around inside his brain.

He gave her a smile. 'I feel quite different now I know I'm going to be a father. I may sound ridiculous, but I somehow feel more responsible.'

'Are you saying you weren't responsible before?' she teased.

'You know what I mean!'

She did, for she felt precisely that way herself.

'Oh, that's wonderful! I'm so thrilled for you,' Cathy exclaimed, Hannah having just announced her news. Taking her daughter into her arms she kissed Hannah on the cheek.

'We're both pleased as Punch,' Lal smiled.

'Tell me, has there been a point where you turned green and threw up?' Cathy asked Hannah.

'I have thrown up, several times, but as far as I know I've never turned green. Why?'

'That's what happened to your Aunt Lily and I when we got pregnant. She turned green and threw up, and so did I.' And it had been that way round she remembered, but wasn't going to say that. As far as everyone was concerned she'd been the first to become pregnant, rather than the way it had actually been. Lily's secret had remained safe with her. David and Ewan, poor Ewan, had been *premature*.

'Turn green, how peculiar!' Hannah laughed.

'As our pregnancies were so similar it made me wonder if I too was going to have twins. Thankfully, in the circumstances, there was only you.'

Hannah knew that 'the circumstances' referred to her father's death.

'Now, how about names. Have you thought about names?' Cathy demanded.

Hannah and Lal exchanged glances.

'Early days yet for that, of course.'

'We have thought of names, Ma. We discussed that on the way here.'

'And?'

'If it's a boy we'd like to call him Robert, after my Da.'

Tears sprang into Cathy's eyes. She turned away from Hannah and Lal. 'That would be nice,' she said in a tight voice.

'And if it's a girl we'd like to call her Catherine after you.'

'No!' Cathy bit her lip. 'No, I'd prefer if you didn't do that.'

Hannah was puzzled, she hadn't forseen this objection. On the contrary, she'd thought Cathy would be pleased. 'Why ever not, Ma?'

'Catherine, or Cathy as I've always had, has been an unlucky name for me. I wouldn't want it passed on to a granddaughter in case the bad luck went with it.'

'We'll have to reconsider then,' Lal said. Personally he thought that was a right load of twaddle. How could you pass on bad luck with a name? But he wouldn't have dreamt of saying so because that would have been disrespectful to Cathy of whom he was very fond.

'If you're going to call a boy after your Da, why not also a girl?' Cathy suggested. 'There's Roberta for instance . . .'

Hannah screwed up her face. 'I don't care for that at all!'

'Or, eh . . . How about Robyn with a "y" instead of the male "i"?'

'Robyn,' Hannah repeated. It was a name she'd seen in print, but didn't know anyone actually called that. 'Lal?'

'I like it,' he nodded.

So did she, she decided. 'Robert and Robyn it is then. We're agreed.'

'And what if you have twins, same as your Aunt Lily?' Cathy asked mischievously.

She laughed at Hannah's expression. It had never crossed Hannah's mind she might have twins.

Knit one, purl one, Hannah meticulously followed the pattern. She was knitting a shawl for the shortly-to-arrive baby. (It was definitely baby in the singular, the doctor at the hospital had been able to confirm that.)

Lal was at their sitting room table where he was poring over what Hannah thought were accounts. Only they weren't.

Lal pursed his lips, made a sort of sucking sound, and threw down his pencil. 'It can work,' he said softly, more to himself than for Hannah's benefit.

'What can, darling?'

He glanced over at her, then twisted his chair round so that he was facing her. 'There's a bakery and shop up for sale which I'm very seriously thinking of buying.'

She stopped knitting to stare at him. This was completely unexpected. 'Can we afford another business? And eh . . . who would run it?'

'Another baker would run it, Hannah. And, theoretically anyway, the new business would pay for itself, plus give us a profit. The only snag is it will only do that if it has the size of flour allocation that we have here.'

She laid her knitting aside, rose and waddled – that word perfectly described the way she now walked – over to the table where she sat beside him.

'Where is this shop and why haven't you mentioned before that you were thinking of buying it?'

'The shop's in Ibrox, and I haven't mentioned it before because I wanted to get all the facts and do my sums first. I've now got the facts and done those sums, and come to the conclusion we can make a go of the place.'

'Have we enough money put by to buy another business?' She hadn't realised they were doing that well.

He shook his head. 'No, I'll have to take out a mortgage.'

'A mortgage! I don't like the sound of that. It's buying something on time which I'm totally and utterly against.'

'Oh, don't be so working class!' he mocked.

'There's nothing wrong with the working class, but there is everything wrong with buying on tick and time. Don't spend what you haven't got, that's what I was brought up believing, and what I'll continue to believe.'

Reaching over he took hold of her hand which he clasped between his own. 'You're absolutely right, that's an excellent rule to live by. But only as far as it goes. What I would be doing is borrowing money in order to make money, money I couldn't make unless I borrowed in the first place.'

'I still don't like the idea of borrowing,' she replied stubbornly.

'Look, let me paint you the full picture. I take out a mortgage to buy this new business. I hire a baker to do the baking and be in overall charge, and a woman to be behind the counter. My outgoings would be the mortgage repayments, the baker's wages,

241

the woman's wages and overheads, flour, electricity, gas etc. etc. Now, providing we can make a success of that bakery and shop, get it into the position of generating the turnover we are here, I can meet all those outgoings and overheads plus enjoy a reasonable profit.'

She was far from convinced. 'What if you don't achieve that turnover?'

'Then the profit would become a loss.'

'I don't like it Lal. It's too risky.'

'No more of a risk than we took when we opened up here.'

'Yes it is,' she replied quickly. 'For a start it was you and me here; it won't be us there. And secondly, we were able, thanks to my friend at the local food office, to get an immediate doubling of our flour allocation. Who's to say we'll get that in Ibrox?'

'As I've already mentioned, that is the only snag. Will you speak to your friend and see if she can help?'

'But Ibrox isn't her area, Lal!'

'I appreciate that. But it still might be that she can help. There's certainly no harm in asking her.'

'And if she can't?'

'Then buying this particular business just isn't on.'

Hannah thought about that. 'All right,' she agreed reluctantly. 'I'll go and speak to her tomorrow. But before I do I'd like to have a look at what you call your sums.'

Later, she had to admit, on paper anyway, the idea was viable.

Lal was nursing a pint in the Brunton Arms, a pub adjacent to the local food office, where Hannah was now speaking to her friend. He thought of the bakery and shop in Ibrox, something he'd been on the lookout for ever since conceiving the notion of having a second bakery and shop. The trouble was they didn't come on the market very often, which was why he desperately wanted to grab this one while it was still going. Only it would be pointless grabbing it unless he got round the new business allocation restriction.

He glanced about the pub, a typical Glasgow boozer. It had all the attraction and charm of a pile of week-old potato peelings. Yes, it would be white paint and balloons for the new shop if he landed it, he promised himself, and free bread on the opening day as a come-on. That combination, or formula, had worked wonders the first time round. There was no reason why it shouldn't do so again.

It was just under ten minutes later that Hannah reappeared to join him. 'My legs are killing me,' she complained, collapsing onto a chair. She was suffering from puffy ankles and a varicose vein in her left calf. She was hoping the varicose vein would disappear once she'd had the baby. Certainly the puffy ankles should.

'Well?' Lal demanded.

'I explained the situation and asked if she could help. As luck would have it she does know someone in the Ibrox office whom she'll contact and sound out, someone she says she's fairly confident will cooperate. What she does suggest is we repeat the manoeuvre of taking in the BUs as soon as we can on the opening day.'

Lal nodded; he'd intended doing that anyway. 'So, in the meantime do we hang on tight or do I start the ball rolling?'

'That's up to you. But she did say she was fairly confident this person would cooperate.'

'I'll take a chance then and start the ball rolling. Now what would you like to drink?'

Hannah lit a cigarette while Lal was up at the bar. When he'd returned with her shandy and sat down again she said. 'By the way, we've been invited to a wedding.'

'Who's getting married?'

'My friend's daughter. The wedding is four weeks this Saturday, the reception at a hired hall in the Crow Road.'

'Do you want to go?'

'I think we should. Don't you?'

'Yes I do. Has the cake been ordered yet?'

Hannah raised her eyebrows. 'I haven't a clue. Why?'

'If it has, tell your friend to cancel the order. I'll make the cake – our wedding present.'

'I'll pop back and tell her just before you want to leave here then,' Hannah said.

'Ask her how many tiers she wants, and where and when the cake has to be delivered. She can leave the rest to me.'

'I still . . .' Hannah hesitated. 'I still hate the idea of a mortgage, or buying on time. It goes completely against the grain.'

'Do you think your Granda can get us some more paint and balloons?' Lal replied, changing the subject.

*

'I feel a right two-ton-Tessie,' Hannah complained as she struggled up her grandma's stairs. She was flanked by her Aunt Lily, while Winnie and Cathy were ahead of them.

'Do you want a hand?' Lily offered.

'I'll manage, thanks.'

'She's bigger than I ever was,' Cathy said, glancing back over her shoulder.

'Are you *sure* it's not twins?' Lily jibed, knowing Cathy had teased Hannah about that.

'No, it's not!'

'Doctors have been known to be wrong,' Lily went on, this a tease of her own.

'Well ours isn't. He's adamant I'm only carrying a single wean.' Hannah's tone was one of false indignation. She was aware she was being got at.

Winnie opened the door to her house. 'I'm gasping for a cup of tea.'

'I imagine we all are.' Cathy said, the four of them having been into town shopping together. Winnie had found and bought a lovely pale green dress covered with white polka dots, Lily some shirt collars for Dougie that he badly needed. Cathy herself had come back empty-handed, as had Hannah who'd been on the lookout for baby things.

Lily was the last in through the outside door which she then closed behind her. 'I hope my da's in and got a fire on,' she said to Hannah, for it was extremely cold out.

Winnie went into the kitchen where she found John fast asleep in his chair in front of a blazing fire. His eyes were closed, his head slumped forward. His hands were clasped in his lap while his feet were up on a pouffe.

'Look at that, would you!' said Winnie to Cathy, nodding at her husband.

'Don't disturb him now,' Cathy replied. 'He's having a good zizz.'

Hannah plonked herself down on the other fireside chair, and eased off her boots. Having done that she held her feet up in front of the fire. 'That's better,' she sighed after a few seconds. Her feet had been frozen.

It was Lily who twigged there was something wrong with her father. Puzzled, she crossed over and squatted beside him, from where she looked up into his face, a face she now noticed was strangely pale. Then she realised what was wrong, what was missing. He wasn't breathing.

Reaching out she took hold of the closest wrist, and felt for a pulse. There wasn't one.

'Oh dear!' she exclaimed softly.

'Shall I do some bread and marg?' Winnie asked generally.

'Ma?'

There was something in her sister's voice which caused Cathy to turn round and look at her.

'Ma?' Lily repeated, eyes suddenly bright and wet.

'What is it lass?'

'It's da. He's . . . He's . . .'

Cathy realised what Lily was trying to say. A few quick strides brought her to her father. When she touched his face it slumped even further onto his chest, but not before she'd felt how cold his flesh was.

After a while Hannah was delegated to put Winnie to bed in the other room while Cathy and Lily started to organise what had to be done.

It was a rotten day for a funeral. Her da deserved better, Cathy thought as the sleet lashed down. Despite the weather it was an excellent turn-out, for her da had been well liked.

She glanced at Winnie, who seemed to have withered like a cut plant since John's death. With her da gone she doubted Winnie would survive for long. They may have been niggly with one another latterly, but it had been a long and happy marriage; fifty-five years as man and wife. Aye, she was convinced of it, her ma would soon follow her da. They were, or had been, that sort of couple.

Her gaze drifted to where Lily was standing with Dougie and David. She and Lily were closer now than they'd ever been, and they'd always been fairly close. Losing Ewan in the war had devastated Lily, scarred her mentally for life. Thank God David, the elder of the twins, had come home safely. She dreaded to think what effect it would have had on her sister if he hadn't.

After Ewan's death she and Lily, at Lily's insistence, had spent hour upon hour together. She was the only one who truly appreciated what she was going through, Lily had said. Enough tears had been shed during that period by the pair of them – and not all hers for Lily either, but often for herself in respect of Bobby – to float a decent-sized ship. Even now Lily would come over and sit quietly with her of an evening, sometimes talking of Ewan, other times about things quite unrelated, but with Ewan really in mind.

From Lily and Lily's family her eyes went to Hannah. How proud Bobby would have been of his daughter, as she was herself. And now Hannah was about to make her a grandmother. She couldn't wait for that.

It gave her great satisfaction that Hannah had got her man after all, and a fine, go-ahead man he was proving too. She'd come to think very highly of Lal Stuart, considering him first-rate.

Not that she'd been wrong in urging Hannah to break up with Lal initially. As it had turned out Lal had come back from the war, but so many hadn't, and how easily he might have been numbered among the latter. Just as her Bobby had been in the '14–'18 war.

She wondered about Hannah's soon-to-be-born child. She was excited about the forthcoming baby as though it was her own. A boy, she secretly hoped. A boy called Robert who'd be bound to get Bobby after his grandfather.

When the service was concluded relatives and a few selected friends went to Purdon Street where – neighbours having helped with this – they were given a hot meal and a drink.

Hannah let herself into the Ibrox front shop which was ablaze with light. Lal was up a ladder painting a wall, Pat McCafferty – the baker who was going to be in charge – up another ladder doing the same.

'It looks a treat,' Hannah said.

'It will do when we've finished,' Lal replied. 'Did you get the balloons?'

John Ford had died before being able to procure paint and balloons for them, which had left them in something of a fix. It was Hannah who'd suggested they ask Dougie if he could help for he was still employed at Tommy's Yard where the original paint and balloons had come from. Dougie had said he'd be only too pleased to do what he could.

The paint had come several days previously, but not the balloons: they were proving more difficult to get hold of. Hannah had just been to Lily and Dougie's, having received word via Winnie that Dougie wanted to see either her or Lal.

'No balloons, I'm afraid. Dougie says he can't lay his hands on a single one for love or money.'

Lal swore.

'But he has got us something else.'

Hope was rekindled in Lal. 'What?'

Hannah's face cracked into a broad smile. 'Coloured streamers.' And having said that she took two fistfuls of tightly rolled up coloured streamers out of her ample coat pockets – the coat a Raglan style that Lily had made for her the previous year out of some material she'd been fortunate to come by.

'Streamers!' Lal exclaimed with a laugh. 'They're just as good as balloons. Maybe better.'

'That's what I thought.'

'Put them in the drawer under the counter and we'll get them up just as soon as we can.'

'You're doing a fine job there, Pat,' Hannah acknowledged. Pat lived in Ibrox with his wife and four children, where they would continue to stay, as these new premises had no rooms above for them to move into.

'Not long now till opening,' Pat enthused.

'Not long now,' Lal agreed, his brush slapping against the wall he was painting.

'Not long now,' Hannah echoed, crossing two fingers of her right hand. She was worried sick about this whole venture, anxious in the extreme about the repercussions should it fail. Why if the worst came to the worst . . .

'I'll put the kettle on,' she said, banishing the possibility of that to the back of her mind.

Pat McCafferty glanced at his wristwatch, then over at Hannah who was sitting on a chair just inside the tiny back shop. She'd given up working some weeks previously when it had become too much for her, her place having been taken by a young lady called Eileen Salmon.

'It's time, Mrs Stuart,' Pat said. 'Shall I open up?'

'You're the gaffer here, Pat. You don't have to ask my

247

permission,' she replied, knowing that would please him, which it did.

'Right then,' he said, squaring his shoulders. For that day, just as Lal had done when the first shop had been opened, he'd be helping behind the counter with his assistant Nancy.

When he opened the door a stream of eager women pushed past him, just as had happened to Lal.

'One and a quarter hours to get rid of the lot,' said Pat, studying his watch.

Longer than the first shop, Hannah thought. But excellent nonetheless.

'Now, we'll see you this afternoon as arranged,' Hannah said to Pat.

'I'll be along. Don't worry.'

As Hannah spoke she was gathering together collected BUs while Nancy was making another pile. When the BUs were counted and tied with string Hannah placed them in the shopping bag she'd brought along for that purpose.

Leaving the shop, she hurried as fast as she was able to the local Ibrox food office where she'd been instructed to ask for an interview with a Mrs Clark.

Lal was pulling a tray of rolls out of one of the ovens when she entered the bakery. His eyes immediately sought and fastened onto hers.

'Mrs Clark came through as we were told she would. The allocation has been doubled for now. As soon as we wish it further increased all we have to do is let her know.'

Lal let out a whoop! It had been more or less assured, but until the allocation actually was increased, you never knew. As the saying went, there's many a slip twixt cup and lip.

Lal then sat Hannah down and made her recount in detail all that had happened at Pat's shop, and with Mrs Clark.

Hannah puffed a cigarette, her eyes straying yet again to the clock on the mantelpiece. (A wire brush and blackleading had soon restored the grate to something of its former glory.) It was the second day that Pat's shop had been open, and she and Lal were waiting for Pat to bring them the day's takings. As it had been with the shop downstairs, this was the important day, the one that would give them an indicator as to what was going to be what.

'He should have been here by now,' Lal grumbled impatiently.

'Give him a chance. It's a fair old way from Ibrox, don't forget.'

Lal grunted.

'You were right about the streamers, they are even better than balloons,' Hannah said.

'See if Dougie can get us some more. If he can we'll change them for the balloons after a while.'

'I'll ask him next time I'm over there.' She glanced at the mantelpiece clock again.

'What's wrong?' Lal demanded anxiously when he saw her grimace.

'The baby just kicked.'

Lal grinned. 'Maybe it's a footballer you've got in there.'

'Judging by the kick, a rugby player more like.'

That delighted Lal. 'I'm dying to hold him or her in my arms,' he admitted.

'How about changing nappies?'

He pulled a face. 'No thanks. That's women's work.'

'Oh, I see! You're only interested in the huggy, cuddly bits while I, being a mere woman, get landed with the dirty, smelly bits.'

'Women do those sort of things so much better,' he said quite seriously.

'In a pig's eye they do! Men are just as capable.'

'You don't *really* expect me to change nappies?' he queried, suddenly alarmed.

'What if I'm ill and incapable? What then?'

He thught about that. 'I'll get Mrs Starkey from over the road in. She must be a dab hand at nappies, having three young weans of her own.'

'Anything but do it yourself, eh?'

'Well . . . I . . . I suppose I would if I absolutely had to. If there was no alternative, that is.'

Hannah laughed. From his expression you'd have thought he was volunteering to be hung, drawn and quartered. 'Don't worry. I'm sure you'll never have to do it. Anyway, knowing you, you'd always find that alternative you just mentioned.'

'Nappies,' Lal muttered, and shuddered.

A moment later the bell rang, causing Lal to shoot out of his chair and head quickly for the door.

When he was gone Hannah sat biting her lip. She forced a smile onto her face when she heard Lal and Pat coming back up the stairs.

'Pat says it went very well,' Lal burst out as soon as he had re-entered the living room, Pat behind him.

'Slow in places, but good on the whole,' Pat said.

Lal opened the bag Pat had given him, and tipped the day's takings out onto the table.

'I'll make you a cup of coffee while Lal's counting that,' Hannah said to Pat, stubbing out what remained of her cigarette.

'Ta! That would be lovely.'

Lal separated the money into its various denominations, and then began to count. Pounds first (there were no fivers), then ten-shilling notes followed by half crowns etc. etc., right down to farthings. As he totalled each denomination he wrote the amount on a sheet of paper he'd previously laid there for that purpose.

Hannah was handing Pat his coffee when Lal arrived at a final figure. Looking at Hannah he let out a sigh of relief, for he too had been worried, though he'd been trying not to show it.

'We're in business,' he stated.

'Does it match our second day here?' Hannah asked.

'Not quite. But it's still an excellent foundation to work from.' He rounded on Pat. 'Congratulations Pat!'

'It's got nothing to do with me,' Pat replied. 'I'm only the baker. If the shop's going to be a success, and personally I think it will be after today, then it's thanks to you two.'

Hannah's beaming smile became a grimace when the baby kicked her yet again.

'Lal?'

'Uh?'

'Lal, wake up.'

When he didn't move she prodded him with her finger. 'Lal, wake up – it's started.'

He began to come out of what had been a very deep sleep. 'Hmmh? What?' he replied groggily.

'It's started. The baby's on its way.'

'That'shh nice.' He wriggled, and pulled his pillow more under him. He'd been having ever such a smashing dream and wanted to get back to it.

'What?' he exclaimed, suddenly sitting bolt upright as what she'd just said filtered through.

That was so corny and clichéd it made Hannah laugh.

'What time is it?' he queried, snapping on the light situated above their heads, then grabbing for the alarm clock on his bedside table. It was three-fifty am which meant it was too late, or early, for public transport.

Hannah, who was also sitting up, made a strangled noise at the back of her throat and bent over. She straightened again when the pain had eased.

Lal hopped out of bed, came round to Hannah's side and helped her out. 'Can you manage your own clothes or . . .'

'I can manage,' she assured him, interrupting.

'Right then, I'll get dressed and warn Norm-the-lorry that we're going to need him.' Norman Niven, Norm-the-lorry to everyone, lived a little further along the street from them, and had been given his nickname because he owned and operated his own lorry.

Lal had taken the precaution of speaking to Norm-the-lorry some weeks previously, asking if they could call on Norm's services should they get caught short in the middle of the night. Nobody possessed a car where they lived, and taxis were seldom seen in Maryhill, certainly never at three-fifty in the morning. Norm-the-lorry had said he'd be only too happy to oblige.

Hannah got dressed slowly, stopping and bending over every time a pain hit her. When she was finally ready Norm-the-lorry had been roused, had taken his lorry from the secure lock-up where he kept it at night, and had it parked outside in front of the shop.

'Just take it easy,' Lal said, putting an arm round Hannah to assist her.

'How do you feel?' she asked.

'I'm all right!' he exclaimed. 'It's how do *you* feel?'

She gasped, and bent over as another pain hit her, the most

intense yet. 'Apprehensive,' she replied when that pain had passed.

Apprehensive wasn't how Lal would have described his own feelings; now the moment had finally arrived panic-stricken would have been far more appropriate.

Lal had to release Hannah at the top of the stairs as there wasn't enough room for them to go down side by side. On reaching the bottom of the stairs, and the back shop, he swiftly put his arm round her again.

Norm-the-lorry was waiting at the door, looking like the wild man of Borneo with his uncombed hair and face full of black bristles. Lal didn't look nearly so bad, Hannah told herself, she having insisted he run a comb through his hair before they left upstairs, while his unshaven face, his facial hair being a mousy colour, wasn't nearly so alarming.

'This is very kind of you, Norm,' she said as Lal shut and locked the door behind them.

'Not at all, Mrs Stuart. What are neighbours for if not to help one another, eh?'

He was a good soul, Hannah thought. She would ensure Lal gave him a drink for this.

'Now, here's the tricky part,' said Norm, opening his lorry cab door, the door being fairly high off the ground.

It wasn't easy, but with a combination of Norm in the cabin pulling, and Lal behind her pushing, she at last managed to get up into the cabin and onto the seat there.

'Squeeze over,' said Lal, joining her.

Because of her size it was an awfully tight fit for the three of them in the cabin. 'Talk about sardines!' said Norm, starting up the engine, and laughed.

It was a very fast run to the Western Infirmary, the roads being deserted at that time of the morning.

Lal had a thundering headache which, although he'd taken two lots of tablets for it, refused to go away. He chewed a fingernail, and worried about how Hannah was getting on. She'd been in labour for nine hours now.

'Any news of Mrs Stuart?' he asked a passing nurse.

'She's doing fine. Nothing to worry about,' the nurse replied, smiling pleasantly, then hurrying on her way.

That was all he'd been able to get out of them so far. 'Doing fine/well/all right/satisfactorily. Don't worry.' It meant nothing, told him nothing. He felt like a dog having its head patted.

Cathy was sitting beside Lal who had rung her at the library from one of the hospital's public phones. She'd immediately put an assistant in charge and rushed to the Western to be with Lal, and await the birth. She was hoping to see Hannah and the baby after it was born.

She was remembering Hannah's birth, and how excruciatingly painful that had been. Many mothers said they forgot the severity of the pain after a while, that it dulled with memory, but not her. She could recall how agonising it had been as though it was yesterday instead of thirty years ago.

Thirty years old! Late to have your first child, but the war was to blame for that. She hoped and prayed everything was going to be all right for Hannah *and* the baby.

'Push, Mrs Stuart! Push!' the midwife commanded.

Everything was hazy for Hannah. She couldn't focus properly anymore, the world had gone fuzzy and indistinct at the edges. She did as she was bid, pushing down there where it seemed as if a giant fist was trying to work itself out of her.

'That's good. That's very good,' Mr Ritchie muttered, busy between Hannah's bent and parted legs.

'Relax,' the midwife said.

Hannah sank back onto the bed, having arched her body while pushing. In a strange way it was as though this was happening to someone else, she thought. She was there, but wasn't at the same time. It was most odd.

'Now let's have you push again please, Mrs Stuart!' the midwife instructed.

Hannah's back began to arch as she strained.

Using his hanky Lal wiped sweat from his forehead. It wasn't hot in the hospital, but he was sweating nonetheless. Under his arms and between his legs were soaking. How much longer! Ten and a half hours now. Arriving at the Western with Norm-the-lorry seemed an eternity ago.

How he hated that unmistakable hospital smell. A combination of chloroform – he didn't really know it was chloroform but that was what he'd always imagined it to be – antiseptic, and a raw emotion, namely fear. It was a potent mixture that never failed to make his stomach turn over whenever he encountered it.

'If you're hungry, why don't you go and have a bite to eat?' he suggested to Cathy.

She shook her head. 'I'm not. Why don't you go?'

'I'm not either.'

They both lapsed again into silence.

The fist was getting bigger and more forceful all the time. The doctor was saying something, but she couldn't make out what. Then the midwife's voice was urgent in her ear.

'Push Mrs Stuart! Push!'

The doctor was speaking once more, but his words still eluded her.

'She's passed out,' the midwife stated matter-of-factly.

Something was wrong, Lal told himself. He was certain of it. The way the passing doctors and nurses looked at him wasn't natural. They were hiding something. God, he could murder a drink! A large whisky would have gone down a treat.

'Something's happened,' he muttered to Cathy.

She regarded him in surprise. 'Why do you say that?'

'I just know it.'

'Calm down Lal, you're letting your imagination run away with you.'

'It's been over fifteen hours for Christ's sake!'

'That's not unusual for a first birth.'

'How long did you take with Hannah?'

Cathy shrugged. 'Shorter than that. But there are no hard and fast rules, I promise you.'

'Nurse!' He stopped a passing Sister. 'How's Mrs Stuart doing?'

'Still in labour I believe.'

'Is there something wrong?'

'Not that I'm aware of, Mr Stuart.'

She's lying, he thought. Lying through her teeth.

The Sister studied Lal, noting how awful he looked. 'We do have a room where you could lie down if you like?' she offered.

'No, I don't want to do that.'

'How about another cup of tea then?'

'Please. And for my mother-in-law if it's possible?'

'I'll arrange it.'

She definitely was lying, Lal told himself as the Sister strode off. It was a bloody conspiracy! What was going on? What had happened? He wiped more sweat from his forehead.

'Mr Stuart.'

Lal leapt from his seat. 'Yes, doctor?'.

'Congratulations! You have a fine baby daughter.'

Elation began to surge through Lal, elation he immediately put a damper on. 'And my wife? How's she?' His voice betrayed his anxiety when he asked that.

'Very, very tired, it's been a long and hard birth.'

'But she's all right?' Lal demanded quickly.

The doctor held up a paper he was carrying which Lal now noticed for the first time. 'Complications have set in Mr Stuart which . . .'

'What sort of complications?' Lal interrupted. He'd known something was wrong. He'd *known* it.

'I'm afraid we can't get her to stop bleeding. I need you to sign this consent form so that I can perform a hysterectomy.'

'And will that stop the bleeding?'

The doctor gave a small nod. 'Yes.'

Lal took the form from the doctor and stared at it. The words were a meaningless jumble to him, they might have been written in Swahili.

'You sign there,' the doctor said sympathetically, indicating a dotted line. He then handed Lal a pen.

When Lal had signed the form and returned it and the pen to the doctor the doctor said. 'In the meantime I can arrange for you to see the baby if you'd like?'

'Please,' Lal muttered.

'I'll send someone out to you.' And with that the doctor turned and left them.

Lal closed his eyes, and not for the first time that night prayed for Hannah. A hysterectomy! he thought when the prayer was completed. That meant no more children after this one. He'd never mentioned to Hannah but had secretly hoped

255

that . . . if not this baby then the next . . . Well didn't every man?

A few minutes later a nurse appeared, to take him and Cathy through to meet and briefly hold, the white and pink bundle called Robyn.

Hannah stood completely naked in front of the large bedroom mirror they'd recently acquired. Placing her hands on her hips she slowly ran them upwards, and then in, over her flat stomach. Turning sideways she studied her buttocks which were tight and firm. From her stomach she brought her hands up to her breasts, and cupped them.

It was eighteen months now since Robyn had been born, and eight since she'd ceased breast-feeding her, the tenth month being the correct time to wean baby – as recommended by Sir F. Truby King, the leading expert on baby-care whose highly popular method of bringing up baby she was following.

Since the birth she'd struggled to regain her figure which had proved, thanks to her having been so large, extremely hard to do. But by a combination of diet and exercise she'd finally succeeded in what at times had seemed like an impossible task. If anything, and this pleased her enormously, her figure was now even better than it had been before becoming pregnant.

She moved round to look at herself from another angle, smiling at what she saw. The smile wavered when she suddenly remembered her hysterectomy, and a feeling of guilt blossomed in her as it always did when she thought of that.

Lal adored Robyn, as she did herself, but although he'd never admit it she was certain he was heartbroken he'd never now have a son. She bit her lip as the feeling of guilt intensified, a corkscrew of emotion twisting away in her gut. Sometimes the corkscrew got so bad it made her physically sick.

She extended two of her fingers to stroke and tease her dark brown nipples, and instantly desire crept in to mingle with the guilt. Ever since having Robyn she couldn't get enough sex. It was as if she was on permanent heat, always wanting it, always ready. But only with Lal, only her darling beloved Lal.

One hand left her breast to drop between her legs. She went shivery all over when she found and touched what she was

256

seeking. A hint of tears appeared in her eyes, tears for Lal, and for herself not being able to give him the one thing she couldn't.

She turned when she heard Lal enter the bedroom behind her, and held out her arms in invitation.

He kissed her on the mouth, then the neck. And while he was doing this she was delving inside his pyjama flies.

Initially Lal had been alarmed at the sexual change in Hannah, but gradually he'd come to understand why she now acted as she did, and with this understanding his already deep love for her – a love now also tinged with pity – had deepened even more.

He certainly had no complaints about her constant approaches, as long as he was up to it (and like any man he did have his limits) he was game.

With her hand still inside his flies Hannah drew him, she walking backwards, to the bed. Reclining over the side of the bed, her feet remaining on the floor, she quickly inserted him into her.

Within seconds the feeling of guilt began to ease.

Hannah ground out her cigarette, the first of the day which she always had with her breakfast cup of tea. A glance at the clock confirmed it was time to leave.

'Go get your coat,' she said to Robyn who had been seven years old earlier that month, it now being January 1954.

Lal glanced up from his *Herald*. 'I'll come with you this morning,' he announced, eyes twinkling.

'Oh?' queried Hannah, for it was unusual for him to accompany her when she took Robyn to school.

'I have a surprise for you.'

'A surprise?'

'After we've dropped Robyn off I'll take you to it.'

Another bakery and shop or shop on its own, she thought. Had to be. He'd bought another one of these on the sly and was now about to spring it on her.

Since their first bakery and shop, which they still lived above, they'd prospered tremendously. A third bakery and shop had followed the Ibrox premises, and a fourth after that. Then Lal had expanded the shop below, and the fourth, by buying next door and knocking through. After that he'd bought two further single shops which he stocked from his nearest bakeries by van. He sometimes jokingly referred to them all as his 'little empire'.

Lal didn't work as a baker himself anymore, his job was now managerial. He dealt with all the paperwork, the financial side, the hiring and firing and anything else that a managing owner dealt with. He visited each of his shops at least once a day, often twice.

'Are we going far?' Hannah probed.

He knew, as he'd planned her to think, that she thought he'd bought another business premises, which amused him hugely. He was thoroughly enjoying this.

'Not too far,' he replied casually.

'I see.'

No, you don't! he laughed inwardly.

When they'd got their hats and coats on they went downstairs to the back shop, and then through the front to the outside. From there he went to the lock-up which Lal now shared with Norm-the-lorry. Lal had learned to drive a few years previously, and on passing his test had immediately bought himself a one-and-a-half-litre Riley. Hannah helped Robyn into the back seat, then climbed into the front passenger one beside Lal who then took the car out into the street, leaving them there for a few moments while he returned and locked up again.

Hannah adored being driven in the car, but had absolutely no desire to drive herself. Lal had urged her on several occasions to learn but she'd said no, she didn't want to, each time. She was perfectly happy to leave all driving to him.

They'd no sooner set off than it started to snow, large flakes whirling and gusting everywhere.

'Beautiful,' Robyn said, staring out the car window.

The falling snow made Lal think of a kaleidoscope he'd seen for sale the other day; he made a mental note to buy it for Robyn. Hannah said he spoiled the girl, and probably he did – in fact he knew he did. But why not? He had the wherewithal and she was his one and only child.

He parked outside Laurel Bank school, one of the two most prestigious independent schools in Glasgow (the other was Park) and Hannah said she would take Robyn in. Lal leant over the back of his seat to give his daughter 'a big smacker' before she got out.

Laurel Bank! Who would ever have thought he'd be able to send his daughter there. The daughters of toffs and nobs went to Laurel Bank, not the daughter of a Maryhill baker.

He'd been worried when she'd first gone that she wouldn't be accepted by the others once they found out her background, but, much to his and Hannah's relief, she had been. He now knew for certain that Robyn was 'bi-lingual', speaking posh when at school, and like he and Hannah when at home.

Putting a hand into his coat pocket he clasped the set of keys he had there. Was Hannah in for a shock! He couldn't wait to see her face.

He opened the door for her when she came hurrying back. 'It's like the Arctic out there!' she complained.

259

He waited till she'd settled. 'Ready?'

'As I'll ever be.'

Engaging gear, he drove off. When they stopped again it was in Winton Avenue, Kelvinside, by repute the most élite area in all Glasgow.

Hannah frowned. What was he up to now? There were no bakeries or shops round here: this was strictly residential.

Lal got out, and, after a second's hesitation, Hannah followed suit.

'So where's the surprise?' she demanded.

He pointed dramatically at the large, imposing, detached house they had parked in front of. 'That's it!' he said.

She stared at the house, then back at him. 'How do you mean, that's the surprise?' He had to be taking the mickey. Surely!

'Remember I once told you that Maryhill and Partick were all right but there were far better areas in Glasgow. Areas where you could have your own detached house with garden?'

'My God!' she said softly, swallowing. 'Have you bought that?'

'No, Hannah,' he teased, pausing before adding, 'We have. It's ours as from this morning.'

'I don't believe it!' she gasped, whirling round to gaze again at the house. 'I just don't believe it.'

He produced and jingled the set of keys he'd had burning a hole in his coat pocket. 'Shall we go inside and I'll give you the grand tour?'

She was suddenly weak at the knees. A house like that, and in Kelvinside! 'It must have cost a king's ransom!'

'Well it certainly wasn't cheap,' he replied, catching her by the arm.

'Ah uh . . . we . . .'

'We can afford it, I assure you,' he interjected, guessing what she was trying to ask.

As they walked up the gravel driveway Hannah's thoughts were whirling. This was the last thing she'd expected. Over the years they'd become so settled above the bakery and shop, and now to move here! Talk about going from the sublime to the ridiculous, or more applicable in this case, the other way round.

'You open the front door,' Lal said, selecting and handing the appropriate key to her.

She laughed as she twisted the key in the lock, a laugh crackling with underlying hysteria. Surely this was a dream and any moment now she'd wake up back home in bed. Only it wasn't a dream, but incredible reality.

'Oh Lal!' she whispered from just inside the doorway. The hall she found herself in was a large square with a gorgeous inlaid wooden floor. The walls were green . . . She put a hand up to touch what she'd first thought to be wallpaper, and then seen wasn't. Silk! The walls were covered in strips of grassy-green silk.

'Do you realise Lal . . .'

He nodded. 'Yes.'

'I'm . . . I'm . . .'

'Lost for words?'

Now she nodded.

'Wait till you see the rest of the house. That will really stun you.'

'I'm already that,' she admitted. And it was true.

Her hand flew to her mouth when they moved out of the hall into a forty-two-foot – Lal proudly told her that measurement – combined dining and sitting room; dining room being one half, sitting room the other. At the far side were leaded windows and leaded French windows, the latter opening out onto a terrace. Beyond the terrace was a lawn.

She gaped about her in amazement. She'd never conceived of herself living in a house like this. What a contrast to the house she'd been brought up in!

From there Lal, bubbling with excitement, showed her room after room till she'd lost count of how many there were, and after being all round the inside of the house Lal took her out back.

To one side of the lawn were some fruit trees – come the autumn they'd have their own apples and pears he told her – while bordering the other side of the lawn were an assortment of shrubs and bushes, all of which looked delightful even though it was mid-winter.

Back in the house once more she insisted on having another inspection of their bedroom which had a small dressing room attached.

'It's . . . the whole thing is just . . . well, amazing!' she said.

'Pleased?'

'Ecstatic more like. Have you paid cash for it or . . .?'

'Mortgage,' he confessed.

'Are you sure . . .'

'Leave all that side of things to me,' he interjected. 'I promise you I really do know what I'm doing.'

She couldn't argue with that. He'd never yet been caught out, everything he touched turned to gold.

'I did swither about buying this or not, for doing so is pushing our resources somewhat, but I heard something that made me decide to go ahead and buy it.'

'And what's that?'

'Mrs Clark at the Ibrox food office tipped me the wink. Food rationing is about to end.'

'Oh, that's marvellous!' Hannah exclaimed. For although, thanks initially to her friend in the Partick food office, they'd always been able to get whatever allocations they wanted, the overall problem, or situation, had still been there nonetheless.

'When?' Hannah queried.

'In a few months' time. She didn't know precisely which month, but she thought round about Easter, or shortly after. And when food rationing does end it's going to mean I can expand even more quickly than I have been. I've got all sorts of plans.'

'Like what?'

He kissed her on the lips. 'Let's go and have a coffee and I'll tell you.'

She enveloped him in her arms. If there had been a be··· in the room she'd have had him on it. 'When do we move in here?'

'As soon as you like. All we need to do is organise the removal.'

She pulled him tight, squashing him to her. 'Oh thank you, Lal. This isn't a house, it's a palace.' She nuzzled him, nipping his neck.

'Let's get that coffee, then,' he smiled, disentangling himself.

'There's something I'd like to do first.'

'Which is?'

'Go back outside, then come in and do the grand tour all over again.'

He laughed. 'Including opening the front door?'

'Including opening the front door,' she confirmed.

And that's exactly what they did.

The party had been Lal's idea, they'd had to have a housewarming, he'd insisted. Besides – and he'd winked at her when he'd said the next thing – he wanted them to show the house off to all their friends and relations. To bum their load, as the Glasgow saying went.

'Drink, madam?' the waiter asked.

'Thank you.' Hannah took a glass of champagne from the tray he offered her. God alone knew where Lal had been able to get hold of so much champagne, but he had. She dreaded to think what it had cost him.

She sipped, and smiled. She'd discovered she adored champagne. The bubbles made her nose tickle.

'I said it earlier, and I'll say it again, this house is straight out of a fairy story,' Cathy declared, joining Hannah.

'We've been here three months now and I still can't believe it's really ours.'

'You've done well, lass,' Cathy acknowledged, grasping Hannah by the wrist. 'You knew what you were doing when you insisted it was Lal Stuart you wanted.'

Hannah caught sight of Lal across the room where he was talking to his Aunt Vera and Uncle Derek. She had known, hadn't she! Her heart swelled with love for him. She would gladly have walked over a mile of broken glass for her Lal.

Her cousin David Mailer joined them, and pecked her on the cheek. He'd married a woman called Beth after the war, and they had a little boy.

'Some bash,' he smiled.

'Enjoying yourself?'

'And how. It's lovely to be wined and dined by rich relatives.' The dining he was referring to was a stand-up buffet due to be made available later, the buffet being supplied by caterers who'd also laid on all the staff present.

Rich! Hannah thought. Yes, she supposed they were. Although she'd never thought of herself and Lal quite like that. Well off in recent years, but yes, you could hardly live in Kelvinside and not be rich.

'Do I detect a touch of the green-eyed monster?' Cathy queried, teasing more than serious.

'Not from me,' David replied quickly. 'Lal has got on through his own endeavours and that's something I admire. There's no jealousy on my part, I assure you.'

Robyn went dancing by (there were three musicians playing in an alcove), her partner Harry Stuart, Lal's father, who was having to bend over to hold her. His wife Avril had died recently, passing away in her sleep. That had been a body blow to Harry, Avril's death being completely unexpected. The autopsy had revealed a heart defect.

'How about a turn round the floor?' David asked Hannah.

'Thank you.' She had another sip of her champagne, then laid her glass on a nearby table. The dance being played was an old-fashioned waltz, a tune she was familiar with but whose name she didn't know.

Lal left his Aunt Vera and Uncle Derek to be accosted by Norm-the-lorry.

'I want to say how much the wife and I appreciate being invited here the night. It was very good of you and Hannah,' Norm said.

'We're delighted you and the wife could come.'

'You've certainly moved up in the world, Lal. It couldn't happen to a nicer couple. All the best to you both!'

'And how are you tonight?' Cathy asked Gavin, having crossed to where he was standing, after Hannah had got up with David.

Gavin turned his sightless eyes towards her, eyes only glimpsed behind dark glasses. 'Wondering when I was going to get to speak to you.'

'Did you have something specific in mind?'

He shook his head. 'I just enjoy your company, as you well know.'

'And I enjoy yours.'

He reached out, groping for her hand. When she'd given it to him he squeezed it. 'I still think you made a mistake in turning me down. Bobby would have understood. It would have given you companionship all these years, if nothing else.'

'I had Hannah until she got married.'

'Companionship with a daughter isn't the same as with a man your own age: a man who would still be with you when, as you say she has, your daughter has flown the coup.'

Cathy suddenly felt very old. How much had happened during

the sixty-three years of her life. Two terrible world wars for a start. And yet, although so many things had happened around her she, somehow, hadn't really been part of it. Not since that day in 1916 when she'd opened her front door to be handed a telegram. Something had stopped inside her then, ever since she'd merely been going through the motions.

'I made the right decision Gavin, for me that is. It may not be logical, or make particular sense, but it was the right decision for me. I'm sorry.'

'So am I Cathy. So am I.'

'But we'll always remain good friends, you and I, won't we?'

'Always,' he promised. 'Now how about giving a blind man a dance?'

'I'd love to.'

He told his dog Prince to 'stay', then moved off with Cathy.

Lal watched Hannah go dancing by with David. How happy she looked, he thought. Positively radiant. If he hadn't known it to be impossible he might have thought her to be . . . He put that thought out of his mind. How that had hurt Hannah and still did. It was like an ever-festering wound inside her. A wound they both knew would never heal.

He smiled and waved to her when their eyes met.

Hannah was looking forward to a long soak in the piping hot bath she'd just run for herself. The party had gone better than she would have dared hope. She made a mental note to use that firm of caterers again should she need caterers. They'd been excellent.

How lovely it had been to see Elspeth and Peter Campbell again, the same Elspeth who'd introduced her to Lal. Elspeth and Peter now lived in Perth, so it had been a journey for them to come. But come they had, and both sworn at the end they'd thoroughly enjoyed themselves.

Slipping off her dress she laid it over the back of a Lloyd-Loom chair that stood by their bed. Then she ran her hands over her hips.

'I'm having a whisky as a nightcap, what about you?' Lal asked, coming into the bedroom.

'Hmmh!' she smiled.

'I'll go and get them then.'

265

She crooked a finger at him. 'Come here first.'

'It was a big success, wouldn't you say?' he murmured, taking her into his arms.

'Very big. I was just thinking that.' She kissed him on the neck, the ear and then the mouth. While still kissing him on the mouth she wriggled herself up against him.

'I thought you might be too tired for that?' he said when the kiss was finally over.

'Not on your Nellie. Why, are you?'

He swirled a hand over her bottom. 'It'll be a perfect ending to a perfect evening.'

What a gorgeously romantic thing to say, she thought. But then Lal had always been a great romantic. He had a romantic streak running through him a mile wide.

'I'll have a bath first,' she informed him.

'I'll read a book until you come to bed.'

'Leave my whisky by the bedside then. I'll have it after my bath.'

'It and me?'

'It and you,' she laughed.

When he'd gone she removed her slip and tossed it over her dress. Following him out the door she then went into the bathroom which was next along the corridor. There she unhooked her bra, and was about to drop it to the floor when she noticed the stain in the right cup.

The stain, when she perused it, was unmistakably blood. Now how had that got there?

The answer was from her right nipple which had a trace of blood on its areola. How odd, she thought, wetting a finger in her mouth and wiping the trace away. Her nipple appeared to have bled. Now why should it have done that?

She looked at her bra cup again to see if there was anything there that might have snagged or rubbed against her nipple, but couldn't find anything that would do it any damage.

Taking her nipple between two fingers she gently squeezed it which produced a miniscule show of blood at the base of the teat. She then pressed the nipple all over but it wasn't painful in any way.

Just one of these things! she thought, dismissing it as a mystery.

She sighed with pleasure as she slid into the bath and the heavily scented water closed over her.

Doctor Grimley's face had been animated when Hannah had entered his surgery, but no longer. It was now an inscrutable mask.

'I see,' he said slowly when she'd concluded her tale.

'I didn't bother about it at first, thinking it would just stop. But it is persisting.'

He picked up Hannah's notes – he was her G.P. – and glanced at the top sheet. 'You're thirty-eight, is that correct?'

'Yes it is.'

'And have you noticed any other abnormalities recently?'

She pursed her lips and shook her head. 'No, none at all.'

He placed her notes back down on his desk and gave her a thin smile. 'I'll have to examine you, Mrs Stuart. Do you think you might step behind that screen and strip to the waist?' He pointed at a brown wood and leather screen standing in a corner of his surgery.

'Certainly.'

When Hannah was behind the screen he went to the gas fire and warmed his hands in front of it. His expression was severe.

'Ready, doctor,' Hannah called out from behind the screen.

'If you'll just come and sit on my couch here.'

Hannah felt self-conscious as she stepped into view. He was a doctor after all, she reminded herself. He probably saw bare female breasts, and a lot more besides! every day of the week.

When she was sitting comfortably on the edge of his couch Doctor Grimley murmured. 'You did say the right breast?'

'Yes.'

He peered at her nipple. 'I'll have to touch, all right?'

'Fine,' she replied, forcing a smile onto her face.

Using the tip of a finger he very gently pressed the nipple all over.

'Now could you please raise your arms right above your head.'

She did as he'd requested.

Using all the fingers of the same hand he began probing her breast, going over and round it methodically, bit by bit. He grunted when he discovered what he was searching for.

'You clearly haven't found this lump,' he said to Hannah.

267

Her eyebrows shot up. 'What lump? No, I haven't.'

'Here, feel for yourself.' He guided the fingers of her left hand to the lump which was right underneath her breast, back towards the ribs.

She could feel the lump quite distinctly, about the size of a pea, and fairly hard. Surely it couldn't have been there for long? She would have come across it. There again, the obvious time for her to do so was when washing and she always used a flannel for that.

A lump! The enormity of that suddenly hit her, causing the blood to drain from her face. She'd heard about lumps . . . and awful, awful operations. She flashed Grimley a stricken look.

'Both hands aloft again please,' Doctor Grimley instructed. He returned to the lump, this time moving his fingers from side to side, then sort of jiggling them. Leaving the right breast he turned to the left and gave that one a thorough examination.

'You can get dressed again, Mrs Stuart,' he announced when that was over.

'It isn't serious, is it?' she queried tremulously.

'We'll discuss matters after you've got dressed,' he said, moving to the sink where he washed his hands.

When Hannah re-emerged from behind the screen she was still very pale, and visibly trembling. Doctor Grimley gestured her to the chair, whilst he sat at his desk writing in her notes.

'It isn't serious, is it?' she repeated

The inscrutable mask was back. 'I'm going to recommend you see a specialist. There's a M . . .'

'Is it serious?' she demanded, her voice harsh.

Grimley regarded her steadily. He'd examined a great many breast lumps in his time, and doubted very much that he was wrong about this one being a carcinoma. It completely lacked the mobility of a typical cyst.

'I think you have to prepare yourself for the fact that it might be,' he replied flatly.

She swallowed hard. 'Are you saying . . .?' She stopped and took a deep breath. 'Are you saying that I have cancer?'

He could easily have opted out and let the specialist tell her, but that wasn't his way – not how he saw his job. 'It's my belief you have, Mrs Stuart. I'm sorry.'

She digested that. 'And, eh . . . what's the cure?'

'A radical mastectomy.'

Even the words sounded horrible. 'Is that removal of the breast?'

'Yes. The breast and surrounding tissue.'

Removal of her breast! Her senses swam, and for a few moments she thought she was going to faint.

'Can I get you something, Mrs Stuart? A glass of water perhaps?' Grimley asked anxiously, his mask temporarily slipping.

'No, thank you,' she mumbled. Then she promptly changed her mind. 'Yes I will please.'

This was a nightmare, she thought as she sipped the water he gave her. When she'd come into Grimley's surgery she'd never dreamt this would be the outcome.

'Better?'

She nodded. 'I know it's not the done thing, but may I smoke?'

'I'll find something to use as an ashtray.'

He left the surgery, returning almost immediately with a saucer, which he placed on his desk in front of her. When he sat down again the mask was back in place.

'Is there a way round this operation? Some other effective treatment perhaps?' she asked.

He shook his head. 'No, I'm afraid not.'

'And if I don't have the operation, what then?'

He thought before replying. 'To put it bluntly, it would only be a matter of time. These cancers, if allowed to spread unchecked, have inevitable outcomes.'

'How long, would you say?'

He shrugged. 'That I can't. It could be months, it could be years.'

'It's only a small lump,' she said hopefully.

'Size doesn't seem to come into account. I've known small carcinomas kill faster than huge ones.'

Kill! The word rang through her brain. And all because of a lump the size of a pea.

'Now I'll make an appointment for you to . . .'

'No!' she exclaimed.

He stopped speaking to stare at her.

'No, I don't want to see anyone else yet. I have to think about this. I won't be rushed into anything.'

'Time is of the essence,' Grimley said softly.

'I don't care. I won't be rushed.'

'I could be wrong,' Grimley said.

'But you don't believe you are?'

He shook his head.

Hannah stubbed out her cigarette in the saucer, and rose. 'Thank you doctor. At least I now know what's what.'

And with that she swept from the surgery.

It was just after ten pm that Lal let himself in through the front door, having been out for a drink with an old army chum. He expected to find Hannah reading in the sitting room, and was mildly surprised to discover she wasn't there.

He went upstairs to find the top level of the house in complete darkness. She must have gone to bed, he thought, striding towards their bedroom where the door was ajar. It was most unlike her not to wait up for him though, and it wasn't particularly late.

At the bedroom door he paused to gaze inside. Hannah was there all right, but not in bed. She was standing in silhouette, gazing out of the window.

'Hannah?'

She sniffed, and blew into a hanky she was clutching.

Snapping on the light he hurried over to her. She wasn't crying now, but obviously had been. Her face was streaked while the area directly below her eyes was puffed.

'What is it, love?' he queried. 'There's nothing wrong with Robyn is there?' he asked anxiously when she didn't answer.

'No, there's nothing wrong with Robyn,' she husked.

'Then what's brought this on?'

Placing her hands behind his head she pulled his face down into her bosom. He adored her breasts, how often had he said so! Times without number. Some men were bottom men, but not her Lal. He was a breast man through and through. Fresh tears welled up in her eyes to go rolling down her cheeks.

He freed himself from her grasp. 'Hannah *what* is wrong?' he demanded.

She hadn't been going to tell him, intending to keep it her secret. But now, as if a stopper had been taken from an upturned bottle, it all came gushing out.

Lal listened appalled, shocked in the extreme. He'd been

slightly drunk when he'd arrived home; he was now stone cold sober.

They stared at one another when she was finally finished.

'I won't have it done. I can't,' she said, her tone one of utter wretchedness. Crossing to their bed she sank onto it.

Lal didn't know what to think. This bombshell was so out of the blue, so totally unexpected.

'We must have a second opinion,' he said at last.

'No Lal, Grimley's right. He knows it, and so do I.'

'How do you?' he challenged.

'I just do. A second opinion is unnecessary.'

'Rubbish! To both those statements! You can't possibly know he's right. Do you feel any different? Ill in some way?'

'No, but that doesn't change the fact I know he's right.'

'Well you might believe him, but I don't accept his diagnosis as gospel. *I* want a second opinion. And if it is true then . . .' He paused, his expression one of anguish. 'I don't want to lose you Hannah. I don't . . .'

He broke down, unable to continue. Rushing at her he threw his arms round her, holding her as close as he was able while she did the same with him.

They cried together.

'I heartily concur; you should have a second opinion,' Doctor Grimley said to Lal. 'That's why I was going to recommend Mr MacKay to your wife. He's an excellent surgeon and specialist in that field.'

Hannah winced at the word 'surgeon'. It was the day after her telling Lal about her condition, the fourth since she'd originally been to see Grimley.

'Is he the best there is?' Lal queried.

'He's one of the best in Glasgow, I can assure you of that,' Grimley replied.

Lal shook his head. 'One of the best isn't good enough for my wife. If she's to see a specialist then I want the top man in his field.'

'By that do you mean Scotland or England, Mr Stuart?'

'I mean Britain. Or abroad, if needs be.'

Grimley nodded. 'You appreciate it will be expensive?'

'Money is no object. If I insist on the very best then I expect to pay for it.'

271

'Then the man you want is Sir Reginald Walcot-Hunt of Harley Street. He is considered to be the leading surgeon and authority on breast cancer at the moment.'

'Can you make an appointment for us?' Lal asked.

'I can try. Would you like me to do so now?'

'Please,' said Lal.

'Right then.'

Lal took Hannah's hand and squeezed it while Grimley looked up Sir Reginald Walcot-Hunt's Harley Street number in a medical directory. When he'd found the number he lifted his telephone receiver and asked for long distance.

Hannah was dog tired, the night before having been for the most part sleepless. She'd lain there, staring at the ceiling, listening to Lal gently snoring beside her.

Her mind had been a jumble – with memories: her as a child in Purdon Street playing peever, shops and skipping ropes, Miss Tait, a teacher at school whom she'd worshipped, her first kiss, from Johnny Boyle, occasions spent with her mother, others with Lal, the first time she'd taken Robyn out in the pram, good times, bad times. Even when she had managed a little sleep she'd dreamt – a continuation of what had been going through her mind when awake.

And in the morning, that morning, Lal had woken with the argument which had persuaded her she must have the operation, and that was simply Robyn. She had to live for their daughter's sake.

'Sir Reginald can give you a consultation this Friday morning at eleven-fifteen. Does that suit?' Grimley asked, having placed a hand over his telephone's mouthpiece.

Lal looked at Hannah, then back at Grimley. 'That will be fine,' he replied.

Grimley confirmed the appointment, then hung up. 'Number Forty-three Harley Street at eleven-fifteen, Friday morning. Can you remember that or do you wish me to write it down?'

'Number Forty-three at eleven-fifteen. I won't forget,' Lal answered.

Grimley rose and came round from behind his desk. 'All that remains now is for me to wish you good luck,' he said extending a hand to Hannah.

For some inexplicable reason she suddenly hated Grimley. When all this was over she would change her G.P.

She never wanted to see the man ever again.

'No doubt about it, that is a carcinoma,' Sir Reginald Walcot-Hunt pronounced, having just examined Hannah's lump.

Lal's hopes sank. Grimley had been right after all, as had Hannah herself. She did have cancer. Up until that moment it hadn't been definite that she had; now it was. Up until that moment there had still been an open door through which she might yet escape, now that door had banged shut.

Sir Reginald's fingers probed the rest of Hannah's breast, then moved to the other one. When he'd finished there he returned to the lump just as Grimley had done.

'How disfigured will I actually be afterwards?' Hannah asked, voice quavering.

'Oh the end result isn't that bad! There will be some scarring of course, and we often encounter post-operative swelling in the adjacent arm, but that is usually soon brought under control. With a bit of well-placed padding you'll look just as you did before. No one will guess, unless you tell them that is, that your breast has been removed.'

No one except my husband, Hannah thought.

'Right then, would you care to get dressed again, Mrs Stuart,' Sir Reginald said breezily, and going to a sink washed his hands, just as Grimley had done.

After Hannah had gone into the adjoining changing room Lal stared about him. The consulting room was certainly impressive, as was the well-appointed, plushly carpeted reception room outside. Sir Reginald Walcot-Hunt was impressive also; he positively screamed of being a 'very important person'.

'Been to London before?' Sir Reginald asked Lal as he briskly dried his hands.

'Yes, when I was in the army during the war. But it's Hannah's first visit.'

'What regiment were ye in?'

'The H.L.T. to begin with, then the Commandoes.'

Sir Reginald nodded his approval. 'And where are ye staying while in town?'

'The Savoy.'

'Damned good grill room there. Can thoroughly recommend it.'

'We ate in our bedroom last night because we arrived so late. That meal was certainly excellent.' He didn't mention that excellent though the meal might have been he and Hannah had only picked at it. Neither had had any appetite. Nor had they been hungry at breakfast, the pair of them making do with coffee and a nibble of toast.

'We'll use the grill room this evening if we're staying that long.' Lal raised an eyebrow. 'We don't know whether we are or not yet?'

Sir Reginald made a sort of harumphing sound, and crossed over to his desk. There he picked up his diary, opened it and flicked through its pages till he came to the one he wanted.

'Yes, yes, I thought that was the case,' he muttered to himself.

Hannah came out of the adjoining dressing room where she'd quickly dressed again, and went straight to Lal, who immediately jumped up so that she could have his seat. She preferred to stand.

'I can make space for you on my Monday morning list. How about that, Mrs Stuart?' Sir Reginald proposed with a kindly smile.

Hannah's heart leapt within her. So soon! She'd thought . . . Well she hadn't known what to think.

'Better all round if we get it over and done with while you're already down here, eh?' Sir Reginald went on, continuing to smile.

Fear and apprehension were clawing at Hannah's insides, that and an almost overwhelming sense of dread.

'Hannah?' Lal prompted.

'Yes,' she said. 'Monday morning.'

'Good, good!' Sir Reginald enthused. 'The operation will be carried out in the London Clinic where you will be booked in on Sunday evening. Now if you'd like to return to reception I shall instruct my secretary to give you all the relevant details and also organise various essential tests that have to be made.'

'Doctor, I . . .' Hannah paused, then asked Walcot-Hunt the same question she'd asked Grimley, wishing to be absolutely certain of the answer. 'There is no alternative to this?'

'None I'm afraid, Mrs Stuart,' Sir Reginald answered softly. 'It has to be a radical mastectomy.'

Lal took her by the arm, escorting her out of the consulting room and into reception.

'Hello Ma, it's Hannah.' She was ringing Cathy who was house-minding for them, and more importantly looking after Robyn in their absence. Harry Stuart, Lal's father, was tending the business end of things.

'What's the verdict then, lass?'

'It is cancer Ma, as I knew it was. I'm having the breast removed on Monday at some place called the London Clinic.'

Cathy sighed, then said, 'They're certainly not hanging about, are they?'

'I'm told that time is of the essence.'

'But you'll be all right afterwards?'

'That's what we're all hoping, Ma.'

There was a long pause, then Cathy said. 'Hannah?'

'Yes, Ma?'

'I'll be praying for you. With all my heart and soul I'll be praying for you.'

'Thanks, Ma.'

'As you know, Robyn's at school so you can't talk to her.'

'Tell her we'll ring tonight, round about six. Goodbye for now, Ma.'

'Goodbye for now, lass. And watch out for those English, they're crafty as foxes, most of them.'

It was a bit of banter to try and make her laugh, which succeeded. She was laughing as she hung up.

Pop! Lal had timed it perfectly, the champagne cork flew from the bottle as the telephone receiver clicked onto its cradle. He'd ordered the champagne to be sent up when they'd arrived back at the hotel.

'As we're going to be in London for the weekend we may as well make a proper weekend of it,' he said, pouring the frothing wine into first one glass, then another. He was determined to lift the atmosphere if he possibly could.

He handed Hannah a glass, then clinked his against hers. 'Here's to you and I!' he toasted.

She sipped her champagne, smiling as the bubbles went up her nose.

'I thought we might go to the theatre this evening?' Lal suggested. 'I could ask downstairs to arrange it for us.'

'That would be lovely.'

'Shall we eat before or after?'

'Before. I couldn't last till after.'

He kissed her on the lips. 'And how about some sightseeing tomorrow? And perhaps a river trip?'

'We must think of money Lal . . .'

'Blow the money!' he interrupted, placing a finger on the lips he'd just kissed.

'Talk about big-hearted Arthur!'

'Only where you're concerned.'

'And Robyn!'

'That goes without saying.'

He had another swallow of champagne, she another sip. 'I could become addicted to this stuff,' he joked.

He kept up a stream of banter and jokes before leaving her to go downstairs and order the theatre tickets. As soon as the bedroom door clicked shut behind him his expression changed completely from a lighthearted one to one haunted with worry and anxiety.

He paused for a few brief seconds to take a couple of deep breaths during which he ran a hand through his hair.

You have to be strong for her sake, he told himself. You have to be her crutch till all this is over.

He took another deep breath, then went on his way.

The variety show was called the Fol-De-Rols and was being presented at Drury Lane. There had been a play on at the Savoy Theatre, the theatre next door to where they were staying, but that had been a heavy drama, quite the opposite to what Lal had been after.

Lal was thoroughly enjoying himself, considering the show to be a real cracker. He couldn't have asked for better. Sparkle, glitter, excitement, energy and a wonderful atmosphere, the Fol-De-Rols had it all.

He glanced sideways at Hannah, expecting her face to be lit up as everyone else's was, but it wasn't. She was staring intently, and raptly, at the stage, as if something up there was fascinating her to point of her being mesmerised by it.

276

But what? Lal wondered, his own gaze flicking back to the performance. A line of female dancers with linked arms were high-kicking in a circular movement, while behind them an ensemble of scantily dressed chorus girls were . . .

Scantily dressed! The penny dropped. Not only were they that, but their costumes were deliberately accentuating their breasts. And it was the same with the dancers – their one piece outfits were doing the same.

What a bloomer! Lal berated himself. What a stupid, crass, insensitive bloomer! Here was Hannah about to have a breast removed and he'd brought her to a show where dozens of fine pairs were being flashed provocatively about.

Reaching across he took Hannah's hand and pulled her closer to him so that he could whisper in her ear.

'I've come over rather queasy, I think it must have been that fish I had earlier. Do you mind if we leave in the interval?'

'No, not at all.'

When the interval came he got her out of the theatre, and away from all those bosoms, as quickly as he could.

Lal stared out over the Strand, and the West End beyond. What a fairyland the nation's capital was, and how gloriously cosmopolitan after parochial Glasgow. When you came to London, Glasgow seemed very small by comparison.

Not that he was belittling Glasgow, he'd never do that. Glasgow was as special to him as it is to the great majority of Glaswegians who fiercely love, and are fiercely loyal to their city. But that didn't mean to say he couldn't see Glasgow for what it was, compared to London, a smaller, duller cousin. But a cousin he would never have deserted in a thousand years nonetheless.

'Lal?'

He turned from the window to find Hannah sitting on the bed combing her hair. Both of them were already in their nightclothes.

'There is one thing I'd dearly like to do while we're here,' she went on.

'What's that?'

'Go to Foyle's, the largest bookshop in the world. It's in the Charing Cross Road, wherever that may be.'

'We'll go tomorrow morning. And spend as long there, and as

277

much money on books, as you wish. You'll need some good books for . . .' He trailed off, then said softly. 'For when you're getting over the op.'

She dropped her head, and her shoulders sagged.

Crossing the room, he sat beside her. 'Hannah?'

The eyes that looked into his were tortured. 'You must understand it's you yourself I love, not your breasts, or any other single part of you.' He paused, then repeated with emphasis. '*You yourself*, your personality, character, and the many indefinables that go to make up Hannah Stuart. You must believe that.'

'I know I'm being stupid. I know it intellectually, and still . . . I feel I've let you down.'

'How can you have let me down! It isn't as if you had a choice in the matter.'

'But I did have a choice about marrying you when I did. If I hadn't put it off, made you wait until the end of the war, you might have had a son and heir.'

'What's done is done Hannah. There's no use regretting past actions.'

'But I do! It never crossed my mind that I'd only ever be able to have the one child. If I'd known . . .'

'Your decision would have been the same. Because your reasons for making me wait, us wait, were valid ones.'

She laid the hairbrush aside. 'The hysterectomy must have been hard enough for you to bear, but now this.'

'It won't matter, I promise you,' he said, enfolding her in his arms.

'It will.'

'It won't!'

'Oh Lal! I love you so much.'

'And I love you Hannah. And always will. Till my dying day.'

Her hand crept inside his flies, and round to clasp a buttock. As she was stroking the buttock she was thinking about something he'd said to her shortly after they'd been married, which was that the mere sight of her naked breasts was enough to give him a physical reaction.

'Put out the light,' she whispered.

That night the only word to describe her lovemaking was tigerish. It was hours after midnight, Lal's back streaked with blood where she'd clawed him – something she'd never ever done previously – before she allowed them, Lal first, herself shortly afterwards, the oblivion of sleep.

She slept fitfully, tossing and turning till morning.

Books, books, books beyond number. Hannah couldn't believe there were so many books gathered together under one roof, but there were.

'I knew Foyle's was big, but the reality is awesome,' Hannah said to Lal.

'I've been in a few bookshops in my time, but I've never seen the likes of this,' he replied.

Well-known publishers' names leapt out at Hannah. Michael Joseph, Collins, Heinemann, Macmillan, Hamish Hamilton, Faber and Faber, the list went on and on.

Hannah picked out a C.S. Forester, glanced through it, then replaced it in its slot to seize on a novel by Angela Du Maurier, one of her favourite writers. She'd absolutely adored *The Perplexed Heart*.

'How many can I buy?' Hannah asked Lal.

'I told you last night, as many as you like.' He laughed. 'But not so many we can't carry them all.'

Books! Hannah thought, there was nothing gave her more pleasure than a good book. Well . . . She glanced sideways at Lal, and grinned wickedly. There might be one exception.

It was some time later, and on another floor, that Lal glanced up from a green-banded Penguin crime novel he'd been dipping into to catch Hannah staring at a wall clock, her eyes riveted to the second hand going tick-tick-tick. He immediately knew what she was thinking, able to read her face as clearly as the book he was holding. Every passing second was bringing her nearer to Monday morning, and what awaited her then.

'Hannah, come and tell me what you think of this!' he called out quietly.

'Hannah!' he called again, this time a little louder and more urgently, when she didn't respond.

She broke out of her reverie to look at him.

'Come over here and tell me what you think of this,' he repeated.

He held a short conversation with her and then, without her

realising what he was doing, he moved her away, and out of sight of the wall clock.

For the rest of their lengthy visit to Foyle's he contrived to keep her away from wall clocks, of which there were a number dotted throughout.

The entrance to the London Clinic was in Devonshire Place, just off the hurly-burly of the Marylebone Road. The taxi Lal and Hannah had taken from the Savoy dropped them at its main entrance.

'Please wait,' Lal said to the taxi driver.

Hannah stood staring grim-faced up at the Regency building which seemed forbidding to her; that impression a combination of her fear, imagination and the fact it was night-time.

Lal, carrying her case, took her by the arm. 'Shall we go in?'

She entered the hospital with all the reluctance of someone going to her execution.

They'd been instructed to report to the office, which they now did. There a woman told them they were expected, and could they please take a seat for a moment.

'How do you feel?' Lal asked after they'd sat on a wooden bench.

'Do you really want to know?'

He squeezed her hand. 'I'll be in to see you as soon after the operation as they'll allow.'

'I wish you could come up with me.' They'd been warned that wouldn't be allowed. Lal had to part from her where they were.

'So do I. But it is understandable. They have to get you settled in and ready for tomorrow. And I'm sure there are tests still to be made.'

'Yes,' she agreed weakly.

'I'll ring Cathy when I get back to the hotel. Just to let her know you got here safely.'

'Good. She'll be anxious. As will Robyn.' They'd told Robyn on the Friday evening that Hannah was having an operation, but hadn't specified what type of operation. Plenty of time for that when she was home again, Hannah had insisted before they'd made the telephone call.

A young nurse appeared, and came over to them. 'Mrs Stuart?' the nurse smiled.

'Yes,' Hannah confirmed as she and Lal rose together.

'If you'd like to follow me.'

The last thing in the world Hannah wanted was to be parted from Lal. She pulled him to her, and kissed him as the nurse picked up her case.

'I'll be in to see you, just as soon as they'll let me,' Lal repeated.

There was a hint of tears in her eyes a she stared into his, drinking him in as though he was going to disappear out of her life, or she out of his, forever.

'Be brave,' he whispered.

'This way,' the nurse said, heading for a nearby lift.

Hannah tore herself from Lal and followed the nurse into the lift, staring at Lal through the closed criss-cross gates.

With a whirr the lift began to ascend. They watched one another till it was no longer possible to do so.

Then Lal, wet glistening in his eyes now, turned and went back to the waiting taxi.

It was a lovely, woozy dream-world Hannah found herself in. She'd had her pre-med an hour previously and was now on her way to theatre. A porter was pushing the trolley she was on, while a nurse was in attendance by her side.

'All right Mrs Stuart?' the nurse inquired.

Hannah dimly heard the voice as if it was coming from miles away. 'Just fine,' she slurred.

'Won't be long now.'

A blazing light bulb, like some mini exploding sun – at least that was how it appeared to Hannah's distorted senses – burst into view overhead. Then vanished. And after that a second which also quickly disappeared.

Hannah felt incredibly warm and full of well-being. She wanted to laugh and dance and . . . dancing images sprang up in her mind. Dancing images surrounded by laughter and applause.

The figures were the dancers she'd seen at Drury Lane, legs bare and high-kicking, bosoms . . . bosoms also bare. Bare bosoms bouncing and joggling. Marvellous bosoms, full, round sumptuous bosoms, the sort men drool over. The sort Lal drooled over.

And there was Lal in the audience, yes, there he was, laughing and applauding with all the rest.

281

The rest faded into nothing, leaving Lal alone. He was waving now, waving at the dancers. But where was she?

And then there she was, up on stage in the centre of the line, her breasts fully exposed, the largest and most sumptuous of all those on display.

The other dancers faded away just as the audience had done, till only she was left. She dancing, and Lal watching.

Her hands came up to cup her breasts, which she waggled provocatively at him. And then he was bursting out of his trousers, huge and grotesque like an Aubrey Beardsley drawing.

He began running towards her and she, still waggling her breasts, running towards him. But before they could reach one another a mini sun exploded between them, light bright as creation as it invaded their eyes.

Then she was falling, whirling into the sun. Lal too was there, she could hear him calling her, but couldn't see him because of the intensity of the light.

'Lal! Where are you, Lal?' she called out. And abruptly knew no more as the anaesthesia took effect.

The nurse removed Hannah's hands from her breasts which she was fiercely clutching.

The right hand proving more difficult to remove than the left.

Hannah came groggily awake to discover she had a raging thirst. 'Water!' she croaked. 'Water!'

A different nurse to the one who'd taken her to theatre bent over the bed, holding a long spouted porcelain feeding cup. 'Here you are Mrs Stuart. Just open your mouth.'

Hannah sucked greedily on the end of the spout, and would have drunk the cup's entire contents except the nurse stopped her by pulling the cup away.

'Not too much at once,' the nurse said.

Hannah licked lips dry as parchment, and realised she had a throbbing headache.

'Headache,' she mumbled. 'Bad headache.'

'The doctor will be along shortly and I'm sure he'll prescribe something.'

'More water.'

'In a minute. Too much all at once isn't good for you right now, Mrs Stuart.'

Hannah licked her lips again. The inside of her mouth had a metallic taste to it, and she just knew her breath smelled. And then, suddenly, she recalled why she'd had the operation, and what had been done to her.

Her right hand fluttered up to touch the theatre gown she was still wearing. Where her right breast had been was flat, and she could feel bandages underneath.

'Want to see!' she croaked, attempting to pull herself into a sitting position. 'Want to see!' She meant see the wound not the bandages, which the nurse realised.

'You can't do that yet I'm afraid Mrs Stuart,' the nurse said patiently, taking Hannah by the shoulders and gently forcing her back into the lying position.

'How . . . how . . .?'

'The operation was very successful I believe, Mrs Stuart. Sir Reginald will tell you that himself when he comes shortly.'

Hannah's hand was still resting on the flatness where her right breast had been. It was painful there, but strangely, her headache was more so.

'Water, please?' she pleaded.

'All right, but only a few sips now.'

Hannah sucked greedily on the spout.

'Well then, it was a complete success. Nothing to worry about from here on in,' Lal beamed at Hannah. It was mid-afternoon Monday, Lal having been waiting downstairs for several hours before they'd let him up to visit Hannah.

She was extremely pale, and haggard-looking he thought. But that was only to be expected in the circumstances. Her hair had gone very greasy, despite the fact she'd washed it just before leaving the hotel to come and be admitted.

Hannah glanced wearily – she was so tired! – at the flowers that Lal had brought her on the bedside cabinet; a large mixed bouquet that one of the nurses had put into a vase. He'd also brought fruit and a box of sweets. (Sweet rationing had ended in February the previous year.)

She brought her gaze back to Lal, tried to smile, but didn't have the energy to do so.

She was so withdrawn, Lal thought. Half the time he'd spoken to her since coming into the room it had been as though she wasn't listening. Twice he'd asked her a question which he'd had to repeat because she'd appeared not to have heard it the first time.

'Mr Stuart?'

Lal looked round at the nurse who'd popped her head in the doorway.

'You'll have to go now, Mr Stuart.'

'Oh right, fine!'

The nurse vanished, hurrying on her way to the sluice room where she had a task to perform.

Lal stood. 'I'll have a word and ask if I can come back again this evening. Now, is there anything you want? Anything I can bring you?'

'No,' she whispered.

'I'll get along then.'

She attempted another smile, and this time succeeded. She was still smiling as he kissed her on the cheek. 'Bye, bye!' she whispered.

'Bye, bye, love.' And with that he left her, heading straight for Sister's office.

Sister Blundell listened to what Lal had to say, then replied in her most reassuring tone. 'Mrs Stuart's abstraction, if you will, is a normal after-effect of anaesthesia. It'll soon pass, I promise you.'

'I was sure that was the case, however . . .' He shrugged. 'I felt I should speak to you.'

'Quite right too Mr Stuart, and please don't hesitate if there's anything else you wish to query. After all, it's a very traumatic time for you, also.'

He left Sister's office much relieved, after his conversation with her, and having been told he could visit Hannah again that evening between seven pm and eight.

Hannah sat propped up in bed, her nightdress having been slipped down to her waist. It was time for her dressing to be changed and her first opportunity to view what lay under the bandages.

'If you will please, nurse,' Sir Reginald said to the nurse in attendance.

The nurse removed the two safety pins holding the outer

bandage in place, and began unwinding. After that there was a second bandage, and finally a third.

When that last bandage was off a large pad remained, this covering the entire area where the operation had taken place.

'Now let's have a look at what's what,' Sir Reginald said, taking hold of a top corner of the pad.

He slowly pulled the pad down, slowly in case there had been bleeding after the wound had been cleaned and pad applied, which would now have resulted in the pad sticking, but the pad came away without any bother.

Hannah stared transfixed at what was revealed. Where her breast had been was now a flat expanse of partially bruised flesh, a small section of which was puckered. The dominating feature was the suture line, harsh and ugly, the stitches themselves black and horrible.

There was no nipple, that had gone. All that was left was this . . . horror. This . . . this . . .

Something snapped in Hannah's brain. Ever since she'd learned she had cancer of the breast it had all been leading up to this moment when she would see the mutilated remains of what she had once been so proud of, what Lal had adored.

Someone was shrieking she dimly noted, a high-pitched shriek that rent the air, and gave all those who heard it instant gooseflesh.

'Mrs Stuart! Mrs Stuart, please!' Sir Reginald was saying to her, but she didn't hear him. When she didn't quieten he rapped out an order to the nurse who scurried from the room.

Hannah continued staring at the bare flatness where her breast had been and shrieking, although she wasn't aware it was her doing that. It was as if her head was filled with a million crawling maggots.

She never felt the needle slide into her arm. The shrieking abruptly ceased as darkness fell upon her.

Lal peered out of the train window, intently studying a cluster of houses they were passing. Hannah was sitting opposite him, smoking a cigarette. Her face was peculiarly blank, the way it had been since the operation.

'We're in Scotland again, I'm sure of it,' Lal said to her. When he didn't get a reply he went on. 'I don't know what it is but houses on the Scottish side of the border, although they look like those of their near English neighbours, are just different somehow. It's to do with dimensions I think, for the materials they both use are the same. It's similar with the fields. Scottish fields seem to have different dimensions to them than their English counterparts. Have you ever noticed that?'

'No,' Hannah replied quietly.

He laughed. 'Stupid me! Of course you wouldn't have done! I was forgetting this was your first trip south.'

Hannah drew on her cigarette, then blew a long thin stream of smoke away from her and Lal who were the only ones in their carriage. Without realising what she was doing she pulled her coat up and out in front of her, a subconscious gesture to disguise the fact she was lopsided, with only one breast. She couldn't wear a bra yet; she was still far too tender for that.

God, how glad she was to be away from the London Clinic, and everyone there. Without exception they'd been extremely kind to her, and their caring for her had been first class, but leaving had been like escaping from some hell-hole as far as she was concerned.

She glanced at Lal who was wittering on about something else now; she couldn't be bothered to listen what. He'd stayed on in London for several days after her operation, then returned to Glasgow to take up the business reins again. She'd been in the London Clinic for three and a half weeks, and he'd come to visit her each weekend, travelling down Saturday afternoons, going back on the Sunday night sleeper. During these visits he hadn't stayed at the Savoy, but at a small hotel he'd found not far from the hospital which had not only been more convenient, but far cheaper.

Dropping the stub of her cigarette she ground it out underfoot. Less than a minute later she lit another.

'Mummy!' Robyn yelled in delight, and flew at Hannah.

Hannah squatted, and held out her arms. As the excited Robyn came into her embrace she made sure to receive her daughter, by twisting slightly away, on her good side.

'Oh my darling, how wonderful to see you again,' she said, voice clogged with emotion. She kissed Robyn repeatedly on the cheeks, nose, forehead and mouth.

'How are you, Mummy after your operation?' Robyn queried, eyes huge with concern.

'I'm all better, thank you.'

'Did they cut you?'

'Yes, darling, the surgeon cut me. He had to in order to carry out the operation.'

'And was it sore? Did you cry?'

'It wasn't that painful. And yes, I did cry.'

'I cried too. For you.'

She kissed her daughter yet again. 'Thank you, poppet.'

'And Granny, she cried as well.'

Hannah looked over at Cathy, hovering nearby, her mother's expression a combination of love, sympathy and sadness.

'How about a nice cup of tea?' Cathy suggested.

'Oh yes, please,' enthused Lal.

Hannah shook her head. 'All I want is a hot bath, and then to crawl into bed. I found that journey fairly exhausting.'

'Can I have a bath with you, Mummy?' Robyn asked. It was something they'd often done together, and which she never failed to enjoy.

'No!' Hannah exclaimed in sudden alarm. 'No, you can't do that!'

Robyn's face fell, her disappointment obvious.

Hannah rose, and retreated several steps. Her hands fluttered in front of her, then she clapsed them tightly together. So tight her knuckles showed white. 'It's a lovely idea poppet, it's just that I'm . . . I'm, eh . . .' She desperately tried to think of some plausible excuse.

'Not yet up to an energetic little girl sharing a bath with her?' Cathy offered.

Hannah seized on that. Nodding her agreement she said. 'I'm not yet up to that sort of thing. Truth is, I'm still very stiff.'

'I understand, Mummy.'

She stared at Robyn, wanting to smother her daughter with kisses again.

'There's plenty of hot water, I saw to that in case you did want a bath,' Cathy smiled.

Hannah went to her mother, and grasped her by the hands. 'We'll speak later, lass,' Cathy said softly.

Hannah put her arms round Cathy and hugged her, also

twisting slightly away in the manner that she'd done with Robyn so that Cathy only felt the remaining breast pressing into her, and not the empty space where the other had been. It was a contrivance Cathy didn't fail to notice.

Hannah released her mother, went to Robyn and tenderly rubbed her cheek. 'I'll see you later, young lady. All right?'

'All right, Mummy.'

After Hannah had left the room Cathy and Lal exchanged glances, then they all went off to the kitchen where Cathy made tea and put out some fresh scones she'd baked earlier.

Hannah let herself into their bedroom, paused for a second, then locked the door behind her. She was extremely tired; the journey had taken a lot out of her.

She sat on the edge of the bed, and ran her hands through her hair. She then thought back to the housewarming party they'd had such a short while ago. How much had happened to her since that night, the night she'd first discovered a blood stain in her bra; a blood stain that had led to the London Clinic, and Sir Reginald's scalpel. She shuddered, and went chill all over.

Rising again she took out a clean dressing gown, then stripped off all her clothes. When she was entirely naked she went to their large bedroom mirror and reluctantly looked into it.

She was filled with repugnance and revulsion at what she saw. It was as if a large part of her femininity had been sliced from her. The one remaining breast somehow seemed obscene in its singleness. The loss of a breast combined with her hysterectomy made her feel neutered. Yes, that was it exactly. Neutered.

She touched her scar, and traced its length. It was well healed now, if still red and somewhat raw in appearance. It was a scar she was going to have with her for the rest of her life, though it would fade with time.

She placed a palm against the flatness where her breast had been, how loathsome it was. Loathsome and ugly, and utterly, utterly horrible. How could Lal ever find her attractive again? He couldn't. He would be lying, have to be lying, if he said he did. It was all right him waffling on that it was her herself he loved, her personality, character, and not her breasts or any single part of her, that was fine in theory, but the cold reality was different.

She was so hideous!!! She wanted to scream the words at the top of her voice. With a sob she dropped her head and turned away from the mirror, unable to look at herself any longer.

Lal came up the stairs, carrying a cup of tea that Cathy had just brewed. Hannah had had a good three hours' sleep, if she didn't get up now she was going to have trouble sleeping through the night.

He put a smile on his face as he took hold of their bedroom door handle. He turned it, and pushed, but the door didn't open. It was locked.

'Hannah?'

When there was no reply he called again, this time louder. 'Hannah?'

There was a rustling of bedclothes, then. 'Yes?'

'It's Lal. I think you should get up now. I have a cup of tea here for you.'

After a hiatus Hannah replied. 'I'll get up in a few moments. Just leave the tea there.'

He frowned. 'Is everything okay, Hannah.'

'Everything's fine. I just want a few moments to collect myself, that's all.'

'Your tea is outside the door, then.'

He was still frowning as he went back downstairs.

Lal reached out and laid a hand on Hannah's thigh, and immediately felt her stiffen. She'd come to bed before him, lying there with the bedclothes pulled right up to her neck while he'd undressed.

Gently, lovingly , he began caressing her thigh.

'No Lal, please!'

He removed his hand. 'I thought . . . Well I wasn't sure . . . I'll be awfully careful.'

'I couldn't. I'm sorry, but I just couldn't.'

'I understand.'

She inched away from him, hoping he wouldn't realise what she was doing.

'Hannah?'

'Yes?'

'I love you.'

Tears crowded into her eyes. 'Goodnight, Lal.'

'Goodnight, Hannah.'

When he woke next morning it was to find that she was already up and dressed.

'Hannah! Hannah!' Lal yelled, bursting into the house.

What on earth? Hannah wondered, laying aside the knitting she'd been occupied with, and brooding over.

'Where are you?'

'In here.'

He came charging into the room, just as she rose from where she'd been sitting. His face was flushed, his eyes radiant.

'At long bloody last a date has been announced. All food rationing is to end on July 3rd.'

'Oh, Lal! That's fabulous.'

Mrs Clark at Ibrox had told them it was coming, but it had been longer in doing so than she'd anticipated.

'From here on in there will be no stopping me. I'm going to expand as fast as a fat woman taking off her corset.'

Hannah laughed at that image.

Lal smacked a fist into the opposite palm. 'I just had to come rushing home to tell you.'

'I appreciate that.'

He made to embrace her, but she turned away, pretending not to have been aware that was what he'd been about to do.

'Lal, I've been thinking.'

'Yes?'

She took a cigarette from her pocket and lit up. She knew this was going to hurt him, but she was going to request it nonetheless. She didn't look at him as she spoke. 'I'd like to have my own bedroom for a while. I need time to readjust to things.'

He stared grimly at her, feeling as though he'd just had his face slapped. He must try to understand! he reminded himself. He must make allowances. After all she had been through a terrible experience.

'If that's what you want, Hannah.'

'For a while anyway,' she smiled, glancing sideways at him.

'Will you . . .'

'I'll arrange everything. There's no need for you to concern yourself over any of the details.'

'I'll leave it all to you, then.' He'd been so buoyant when he'd come bursting into the house; now he was deflated as a pricked balloon.

'I'll see you later,' he said, and left the room.

Hannah watched from behind a window as he drove away, standing well back so that he wouldn't spot her.

Doctor Grimley made a pyramid with his hands as he listened to Lal. Every so often he nodded his understanding, and sympathy. When Lal was finally finished he gave a deep sigh.

'And she locks her bedroom door every night?'

'Every night,' Lal confirmed. 'I've knocked several times and asked if I could go in and speak to her, but she's never replied, presumably hoping I'll think her asleep. I've also tried the door at other times without calling out to her, and it's been locked then also.'

'Have you spoken to her about this?'

'I've attempted to broach the subject on a number of occasions, and on each one she's made it quite clear she doesn't want to discuss the situation. So far, rightly or wrongly, I haven't forced her to do so.'

Grimley nodded again. 'And you haven't seen that part of her where her breast was?'

'No, I haven't, nor has there been intimacy of any kind since her return from London. I presume there's no reason why lovemaking shouldn't take place?'

'There's certainly no *physical* reason. But psychologically? That's a different matter entirely. There's still so much we don't know about what goes on inside the brain, Mr Stuart. Or to put that another way, there's so little we do know of what goes on. Our knowledge of the brain is a bit like one of those early medieval maps – "here be dragons". In other words we're only guessing at the complexities of certain areas. Or to be totally honest, the vast majority of areas.'

'So what do I do?' Lal queried.

'I suggest you ask her to visit me and I'll have a chat with her. I might mention that I have called at the house to see how she was since she returned from London, but there was no one at home.'

'I think a chat with you might help,' Lal agreed.

291

'And if I'm unable to help I can then recommend a psychiatrist whom I'm sure will be able to.'

'That would be excellent,' Lal smiled.

'I expect to see her soon, then.'

'No!' Hannah spat out. 'I will not go and visit Grimley. I never want to see or speak to that man ever again!' Picking up her glass she threw its contents down her throat, then immediately crossed to the drinks cabinet where she refilled it.

Lal stared at Hannah in consternation. It was only early afternoon and already she was halfway to being pickled. With every passing day she seemed to drink and smoke more and more.

Hannah thought of Grimley, and the time a few weeks previously when the horrid creature had come knocking at the door. Luckily she'd recognised his car outside, so hadn't opened the door to him. Nor would she if he called again. And if by some chance she did open the door to him she'd slam it in his face.

'What's wrong with Grimley, then?' Lal asked. Her enmity towards their G.P. was entirely new to him.

'Don't like him. His breath smells.' The latter was a lie she'd just made up.

'I've never noticed that.'

'Well it does, take my word for it. And also I don't care for his . . . his manner.'

'His manner!' Lal's eyebrows shot up. 'What's wrong with his manner?'

'I don't like it.'

'You've never mentioned any of this before.'

'I am now.' She lit a cigarette, then had a large swallow of her gin and tonic. She was feeling somewhat sozzled, which was nice. In this sort of state she could dream, pretend she was other than she'd become – pretend things were still as they'd once been, before life had gone sour on her.

'Grimley is our G.P.,' Lal said slowly.

'There's no law says he has to be, for God's sake! If you have a suit and the suit stops pleasing you get rid of it and buy another. Same with G.P.s – we'll get rid of Grimley and get another.'

'And if I do arrange another G.P., will you go and see him?'

Hannah didn't answer that.

'Then again there's a psychiatrist, perhaps that's the answer?'

She waved her cigarette at him. 'I know precisely what's wrong with me. I don't need a psychiatrist to tell me what I already know.'

'But a psychiatrist might help you come to terms with it?'

'I have come to terms with it. And that's the trouble.'

He shook his head. 'No, you haven't. If you had we'd be sleeping together, instead of you locked away at nights in your room. If you had I'd have seen you naked, which I haven't since the operation.'

'Don't ask me that, Lal!' she blurted out. 'Please don't ever ask me that.'

He took a deep breath. 'I'm only trying to help, do what's best.'

'I know that.'

Going to the drinks cabinet he poured himself a hefty whisky which he considered he badly needed. 'How about going out tonight? We could have a meal, and then maybe . . .'

'No Lal, I don't want to go out.' She hesitated, then said by way of an excuse. 'There's a play on the wireless I've been looking forward to.'

'Fine. We'll listen to it together. How about that?'

'You go out, don't let me stop you because I prefer to stay in. Go out and have yourself a good old time.'

Anger, and frustration flared in him. 'That wasn't what I was suggesting at all!'

Hannah bit her lip, turned away from him and said. 'If you ever decided to take a mistress I wouldn't hold it against you. I'd perfectly understand.'

When her statement received no reply Hannah turned round again to discover that Lal had left the room.

'I'm fed up with tiddlewinks,' Robyn announced, folding her arms.

Cathy regarded her granddaughter, whom she was minding while Hannah and Lal were out at a bakers' 'do'.

'How about snakes and ladders, then?' Cathy suggested.

Robyn thought about that, then shook her head.

'Draughts?'

Robyn pulled a face.

'Chinese checkers?'

'Pontoon,' Robyn countered.

'I don't know where you learned to play that, but I for one am not encouraging it,' Cathy replied.

'I learned it at school.'

'At Laurel Bank!'

Robyn winked. 'You'd be surprised what goes on there, or what can be learned. And I don't mean lessons either.'

'I didn't imagine you did.' The maturity and worldliness of the seven-year-old Robyn never failed to amaze Cathy. What a difference between her granddaughter and what she'd been like at that age. She wasn't sure whether it was because times had changed so much, or because Robyn went to a private school, simply due to Robyn herself, or a combination of all three. Whatever, dealing with Robyn she sometimes felt she was dealing with an equal. Well . . . almost!

'Do you actually play pontoon at school then?' Cathy probed.

'Oh yes!'

'Not for money though?'

Robyn's expression became inscrutable.

'Robyn?'

The inscrutable expression vanished as quickly as it had appeared. 'Of course we do! It wouldn't be fun otherwise. How can you play pontoon except for money?'

'You could use matches?'

'There's no excitement in that. None at all.'

Cathy reached over and tweaked Robyn's ear. 'Sometimes I despair of you, young miss. Goodness knows what you're going to be like when you grow up.'

'Tall and beautiful, with men tripping over themselves to meet me,' Robyn replied instantly.

Cathy laughed. 'You're a monster, do you know that?'

'Am I?' Robyn said innocently.

'Yes, you are. And . . .' She purposefully trailed off, knowing Robyn would prompt her, which Robyn did.

'And what, Granny?'

'And I love you dearly.'

Robyn beamed. 'And I love you too.'

'I know you do, darling.'

Robyn left the table they were at and went over to a leather armchair which she threw herself into. 'If you won't play ponnies I know what else I'd like,' she said.

'What, darling?'

'The story of you and Grandad, and the rent strike.'

'But you've heard that a dozen times or more!' Cathy protested.

'I don't care, I'd like to hear it again. All of it, from beginning to end. And don't forget the bit where Grandad and Uncle Gavin helped throw the landlord who'd come to spy on your meeting into the midden.'

Cathy laughed, remembering. 'Oh aye, but that was a day and a half, right enough. Your Granda suddenly appeared from nowhere, home on leave from the war, and . . .'

'Start at the *beginning*,' Robyn chided, settling herself comfortably by pulling her feet up underneath her, and leaning on the arm of the armchair.

She listened enraptured while Cathy spoke.

Lal changed gear going into a corner, then changed back up, coming out of it. The Riley Merlin purred sweetly as it took him and Hannah home from the bakers' 'do' at which he'd given a speech that had been well received.

'How are you getting on with Doctor Davidson?' he asked. Doctor Davidson was the psychiatrist Hannah was attending.

'Okay,' she replied in a couldn't-care-less tone.

'When do you see him again?'

'Wednesday noon.'

'Uh-huh!' He paused, then said. 'What happens when you visit him? You've never mentioned.'

'We talk. Or at least I talk, and he listens. It's very boring.'

'Do you think . . .' He shot his wife a quick sideways glance. 'Do you think it's helping you any?'

'Do you?'

'It's hard for me to tell, but you do seem a little happier.'

'Do I?'

'Then again, maybe that's just my imagination.'

'Yes,' she said in that same couldn't-care-less tone.

'Yes what? Yes, you are happier? Or yes, it is my imagination?'

'Neither, just yes.'

God she was being aggravating! He drove for a way in silence, Hannah staring blankly at the passing scene, then said. 'I've had something of an idea. Why don't we go away for a short holiday? A week, say?'

'I don't want a holiday.'

'Well I bloody do!' he suddenly exploded, which made her start. He paused, then went on. 'I'm tired and run down, I could use a break, and certainly think I've earned one. I know of a cottage for rent outside Troon. We could go there.'

'What about Robyn? She's got school and we can't ask Cathy to take more time off work; that wouldn't be fair.'

He'd foreseen this objection, and was ready for it. 'I thought Robyn might stay with her friend Caroline Gibbons while we're away. Tom and Penny Gibbons would be delighted to have her, as you know, and she'd certainly be well looked after. As for Robyn, she'll jump at the chance of staying with her best pal for a week.'

Hannah fumbled for her cigarettes, and lit up. 'How many bedrooms has this cottage got?' she asked quietly through a cloud of smoke.

'Oh, don't worry. It's got two! We'll have one each.'

Her resistance melted. 'If that's the case, then we'll go,' she replied.

He could have hit her.

Lal woke to the cry of seagulls. He yawned and stretched. He'd had a marvellous sleep and felt much the better for it, he thought as he swung himself out of bed.

They'd come down late the night before, motoring from Glasgow in the Riley. On arrival Hannah had made a scratch supper with some supplies they'd brought, directly after which they'd both turned in. She to her bedroom – the larger of the two which she'd immediately laid claim to – and he to his.

When he had his dressing gown on he went to her bedroom door and knocked. 'Hannah, are you awake yet? Would you like a cup of tea?'

When he got no reply he tried the handle, and the door swung open. Her bed was made, her case unpacked, some toiletries laid out on top of a pine chest-of-drawers. He was about to close the door again when he caught sight of a bra slung over a bedside chair. Even from where he was he could see that the cup facing him was different in some way.

'Hannah?' he called through the cottage. 'Hannah where are you?' There was no reply.

Crossing swiftly to the bra he first of all stared at it, then picked it up. The right cup was filled with a spongy-feeling substance, the opening to the cup sewn over with material. The result of the spongy feeling substance was that the cup yielded to pressure, just as a real breast would do.

Ingenious, he thought, returning the bra to the chair, ensuring he placed it in the exact same position it had been in before he'd lifted it.

Leaving her bedroom, he closed the door behind him.

He stood on the dunes, surrounded by marram grass, gazing along the beach to where Hannah was walking towards him. A stiff wind was blowing, causing her hair to fly, and her coat to billow.

Raising a hand, he waved, wondering if she'd wave back? He smiled when she did, profoundly pleased that she'd done so.

'How was your walk?' he asked casually when she reached him.

'Marvellous.'

'You were certainly up early.'

'Best time to go for a stroll along the beach wouldn't you say?'

She continued back towards the cottage, and he fell into step beside her. 'If you go again tomorrow morning, give me a shout and I'll come with you.' He hesitated, then added. 'Unless you don't want me to, that is?'

'Look!' she exclaimed, pointing seawards.

A yacht in full sail had appeared, the yacht bent over dramatically as it sped through the water.

'Lovely,' he acknowledged.

Hannah took a deep breath. 'I'm starving after that. I noticed a farm near us where I'll go and try to buy some fresh eggs. Boiled or fried for breakfast?'

'Boiled.'

'Lightly, as usual?'

'Lightly, as usual,' he confirmed.

He didn't fail to register that she'd dodged answering his

question about his going with her the next morning. He didn't offer to accompany her to the farm, but returned alone to the cottage instead.

They were on the front at Troon, having just been for a fish and chip lunch, when Hannah spied the Punch and Judy show with a gaggle of laughing and shrieking children sitting in front of it.

'Can we watch for a bit?' Hannah asked Lal, eyes shining.

'If you wish.'

She practically ran over to the booth in her hurry to get to it. There they joined the other adults, parents of the children presumably, standing behind the seated youngsters.

Thump! went the truncheon. Then thump! thump! thump! thump! again in rapid succession as Judy gave Punch big licks.

Within seconds Hannah was laughing along with the children and several of the adults, her face lit up with pleasure at the antics going on in the booth.

Then it was the crocodile's turn to appear, and Punch's opportunity to wield the truncheon. Thump! thump! thump!

Lal suddenly realised it was the first time he'd seen Hannah laugh since the operation. And now she wasn't just laughing but almost falling about.

'Oh, I enjoyed that!' she said quite unnecessarily when the show was over and they were walking away.

'So did I.'

Reaching out he took her hand in his. For a moment he thought she was going to pull her hand free again, but she didn't.

They strolled hand in hand all the way back to the cottage.

The picture was an old Nelson Eddy and Jeanette MacDonald, the storyline ROMANTIC in capital letters. When Lal had noticed it was playing he'd decided, with an ulterior motive in mind, to try and get Hannah along to see it. She was now sitting beside him gazing dewy-eyed up at the silver screen.

He felt daft doing what he was about to at his age, but do it he would. His arm crept up the back of Hannah's chair, and gently onto her shoulder.

She looked at him in surprise. 'Lal?' she whispered.

'What?' he whispered in reply.

'What are you doing?'

'Frying an egg, what does it look like?'

Her lips twitched in amusement. 'We're not in the back row . . .?'

'I know that.'

'Well?'

'Do you want to go in the back row then?'

'Don't be silly!'

'All right.' He returned his attention to the screen, but didn't remove his arm.

'Lal?'

'Yes?'

'Take your arm away.'

'Don't you like it there?'

'People can see.'

'Let them.'

'I'm embarrassed.'

'I'm not. I'm enjoying myself. Anyway, why should you be embarrassed? Nobody here knows us, or we them.' Grasping her shoulder he pulled her closer.

'Lal!'

'Shut up! We're missing the film,' he hissed.

'This is ridiculous,' she muttered.

'So's all that apple blossom,' he replied. The screen was a blizzard of falling apple blossom as if every tree in sight – the scene was set in the middle of an orchard – had decided to drop its blossom all at once.

She snickered. 'You're an idiot!'

'And you're my girl. Now shut up and pay attention to the film.'

After a while she laid her head on his shoulder, just as she'd done the first time he'd taken her to the pictures all those years ago.

Her doing that brought tears to his eyes.

Later that night found Lal and Hannah sitting at the kitchen table drinking a cup of tea prior to going to bed. She'd suggested gin, he the tea they'd opted for. Since coming to Troon he'd been doing his utmost to wean her off the alcohol, and was having considerable success.

'The air down here fair shatters me. Every night when I turn in I feel I'm going to do a Rip Van Winkle,' Lal said.

Hannah smiled. 'It doesn't affect me that way at all. It gives me zip and zing.'

'Oh zip and zing, is it!' commented Lal drily, which made Hannah laugh. For he'd said it just the way, employing that same mocking intonation, as her Aunt Lily might have done.

Lal's expression became serious. 'You know you and I have an awful lot to be thankful for. An awful lot. We have Robyn, as smashing a child as ever was, we have the business which is doing extraordinarily well, we have a beautiful house, a car, money, and lastly, and in my judgement most importantly of all, not counting Robyn, we have each other.'

Hannah stared fixedly into her cup, refusing to meet his gaze.

He went on. 'All right, we have taken a few knocks, but nothing to what some people have to cope with.' He took a deep breath. 'I suppose what I'm trying to say is, at the end of the day we have far more than most, and everything to look forward to, and be positive about.'

'Are you . . . certain about that?' she husked.

'How do you mean?'

'Are you certain you still want me?'

Anger flared in him. 'Of course I want you ! That's what I've been trying to get into your skull. I want you because I love you, and always will. Having a tit removed doesn't alter that for Christ's sake!'

She smiled to herself at hearing it put so crudely.

'I don't know what you're like with your clothes off, but I can guess; a sodding great scar no doubt. But so what! Even if they'd taken both off and sewn you up down there I would still love you. So there!'

He pushed his cup from him. 'The sooner you get over all this self-pity and self-indulgence, the better. I'm getting heartily sick and tired of it. Besides which, it's cold in bed alone at night.'

And with that he rose. 'I'll leave you to lock up and what have you, I'm feeling like Rip Van bloody Winkle again.'

It was hours later before she too went to bed. Her own.

Lal let himself into the house, having just come from the bank. The manager had called him in and given him sherry and a biscuit, just by way of being friendly. He'd enjoyed that, it wasn't everyone got invited in to have sherry with their bank manager; it showed the esteem he was held in by the man and his establishment.

Humming to himself, Lal went upstairs, intending to put on a fresh shirt. It had become his practice of late to change his shirt several times a day, something he considered a tremendous luxury. Like the shirts themselves, hand made by a firm in the Candleriggs, and each costing about three or four times what a shirt in the shops cost.

Going into what had been their bedroom he stopped short at the sight which greeted him. Hannah's bits and pieces were back, the same bits and pieces she'd taken when she'd decamped to another bedroom. A quick check of the wardrobe revealed that those clothes she'd taken were also back.

He turned when he heard her enter the room. 'What does this mean?' he asked, gesturing about him.

'I would have thought that was obvious.'

'You're . . .'

'Yes,' she nodded, interjecting.

Relief bubbled up inside him. That and a feeling of elation. 'Good,' he said.

'But on conditions Lal.'

The bubbles died away a little. 'What?'

'You never touch me above the waist.'

'Not even on your good side?'

'No,' she said.

'All right, I'll agree to that.'

'And won't forget?'

'I won't forget,' he promised.

'The other condition is that you always give me privacy to dress and undress. I don't want you watching me doing either.'

'Okay, if that's what you want.'

'It is,' she confirmed.

He looked about. 'We could buy a screen, like the one Grimley has in his surgery, only nicer. How about that?'

'Excellent idea.'

'I'll start searching right away. There's a shop I know in Buchanan Street might have something suitable.'

She came to him, and stroked him lightly on the cheek. 'You're very understanding Lal. I do appreciate it.'

'As it's almost time to pick up Robyn, why don't we do so

together, and then go on to a teashop? There's a particular one I have in mind that I want to start buying from us. Do you fancy that?'

'It's a date, as the Americans say.'

'It's a date,' he agreed.

He then told her an outrageously filthy joke he'd heard earlier from one of his bakers that nearly caused her to have a conniption.

Lal switched off his bedside light, then stretched out underneath the bedclothes. Hannah had undressed and got into her nightie in the bathroom – a new nightie made of a heavy material that fastened right up to her neck. He didn't know it but it was only one of a number, all the same style, that she'd bought.

'That was a lovely time you gave us at the teashop this afternoon,' Hannah said.

'I wasn't impressed by their cakes though. Not a patch on ours.'

'No, that's true enough.'

'The éclair I had was definitely second-rate.'

'The pastry?'

'Far too heavy. And the cream could have been better too.' She was talking to put off the inevitable, he realised.

'Do you think the shop will buy from us in future?' she asked.

'As you know, I had a chat with Smellie, the owner. I'm sending him round a range of free samples, plus various loaves for him to try. I'm sure he'll taste the difference.'

'Robyn thoroughly enjoyed herself. It was a good treat for her.'

Reaching out he placed a hand on the top part of her nearest buttock.

'Lal?' she whispered anxiously.

'What, love?'

'You won't forget, will you?'

'I won't forget,' he assured her. 'Now give me a kiss.'

When it was all over he couldn't believe he'd just made love to the same woman he'd been making love to before her operation. What a change! A complete turnaround. Where before she'd been a more than eager participant she was now passive in the extreme. She'd just lain there, with her eyes closed, allowing him to do, within the bounds of their agreement, what he wished.

Still, it was progress he told himself. He was grateful for that.

Lal sat reading his *Evening Citizen*, absorbed by the 'Property For Rent And Sale' Section. He was on the lookout for additional premises – bakery with shop attached, or a shop close to one of his existing bakeries which could service it.

He glanced up to stare at Hannah, who was arranging some flowers in a Chinese patterned vase. She was singing a song he'd never heard before, her voice gay and cheerful as she sang.

How much happier she was of late, quite different to the woman who'd come out of the London Clinic. The darkness was still there, but only in patches now, patches that were becoming less and less frequent as time went by.

Her drinking had fallen right away, as had her smoking, back to what it had been normally.

Smiling, pleased with Hannah, himself and the world in general, he immersed himself once more in his newspaper.

Hannah sat nursing a small sherry while all around her long faces sat conversing quietly with one another. Lal's Uncle Derek had died of a heart attack, and been buried earlier that day. She and Lal were now at the house where, along with other relatives and close friends, they'd been invited for a buffet meal and drinks.

Hannah glanced over to where Lal was speaking with Aunt Vera, terribly old and bowed in her loss. She watched as Lal put an arm round his aunt who'd begun to weep again. She'd wept all the way through the ceremony, her expression one of stunned incredulity as though she couldn't yet believe that her man had been taken from her.

'Is this seat free?'

Hannah looked up to see a youngish chap, mid to late twenties, she judged, smiling constrainedly at her. 'Yes it is.'

The chap sat on the small sofa beside Hannah, and let out a sigh. 'My feet are killing me. Made the stupid mistake of wearing new shoes which are now pinching like blazes.'

'Then take them off.' That seemed to her the sensible thing for him to do.

'I couldn't do that! Wouldn't be right.'

'Go on, no one will realise. And I certainly won't tell anyone.'

His brow creased, giving him an intellectual, donnish appearance. 'You're sure you won't mind?'

'Go on,' she urged.

'Hmmhh!' he murmured when the second shoe was off. 'That is sheer heaven.'

'Badly-fitting shoes can be agony.'

'Not only do this pair pinch but they've started to rub the backs of my heels as well.'

Hannah pulled a face.

'Trouble is, I've got to wear them all the way home to Edinburgh.' He sighed again. 'I wonder if there's a chemist shop nearby where I can buy some plasters?'

'Why don't you have a rummage round in the bathroom first? I'm certain Aunt Vera wouldn't object.'

'Good idea, I'll do that in a few minutes,' the chap nodded. 'By the way did you say your Aunt Vera?'

'My husband's actually. She's only mine by marriage.'

The chap stuck out a hand. 'I'm Ian Dewar, pleased to meet you.'

'And I'm Hannah Stuart.'

'Ah, Lal's wife! Now I've placed you. He and I are cousins.'

'I'm surprised we haven't met before,' Hannah said. Though in truth there hadn't been many Stuart get-togethers of recent years, Lal's mother's funeral being one of the few.

'I was away studying for a long time, and then my work took me briefly abroad. I've only been back in Scotland, and ensconced in Edinburgh, for the past six months.'

'So what do you do then, Ian?'

'I'm a doctor. Or to be more precise, I'm now a radiotherapist.'

'A radiotherapist?' she repeated, raising her eyebrows. 'And what does a radiotherapist do?'

'I use a form of X-rays developed for the treatment of cancers. It's tremendously exciting, particularly as I'm working with Robert McWhirter who's a leading pioneer in the field, and for my money one of the most outstanding men in medicine today. It's a tremendous honour and privilege to be part of his team.'

Hannah had a sip of her sherry. 'What sort of cancers?' she probed.

'One of the most common is breast cancer.'

Something twisted inside her to hear that, and she went alternately hot and cold all over. 'Oh? You use X-rays to treat breast cancer? I've never heard of that.'

He regarded her quizzically. 'Are you interested in the subject?'

She decided to be evasive. 'No more than any other woman.'

He relaxed again. 'We use X-rays after minor surgery. A surgeon first of all removes the lump, and then the radiotherapist bombards the area with X-rays.'

Remove the lump! Those words rang in Hannah's ears. 'You say remove the lump only, I thought the accepted practice was to remove the entire breast and surrounding tissue?'

'What you're talking about is a radical mastectomy, or the Halstead mastectomy, as it's called in many parts of the world, named after Halstead who invented the operation. We argue that the radical mastectomy is outdated, and that the lumpectomy, as we call the simple removal of the lump, superceded it.'

Hannah stared at Ian Dewar, and forced herself to ask her next question. 'Are you saying that your lumpectomy is a tried and proven operation, and as successful as the radical mastectomy?'

'It's certainly tried and proven. McWhirter published a paper on it six years ago explaining in detail, with the facts and figures that make it so. As for it being as successful, our argument is that it is *more* successful. Not only are we effecting as many cures as there are with radical mastectomy, we have the added advantage of causing far less physical damage to the patient, for after a lumpectomy the woman is still left with her breast, or most of it anyway, depending upon the size of the carcinoma, and never suffers the painful adjoining arm swelling that so often accompanies radical mastectomy.'

She'd been lucky in that latter respect, a dumbfounded Hannah thought. She hadn't suffered the adjoining arm swelling.

'What hospital are you with?' she asked.

'The Edinburgh Royal Infirmary.'

She made a mental note of that.

'Have you heard of it?'

She shook her head. 'I know of the Glasgow Royal Infirmary of course, but this is the first time I've heard of the Edinburgh one.'

'I wish McWhirter was with the Glasgow Royal, I much prefer living here than in Edinburgh. Still . . .' He shrugged. 'You can't have everything, eh?'

'No, you can't,' she agreed quietly.

'Now tell me about yourself, Hannah. May I call you that?'

'Me? Oh I'm not very interesting. I'd much rather hear more about you and your work.'

Ian was only too happy to oblige.

'Poor Aunt Vera, she's in a terrible state. But I suppose that's only to be expected,' Lal said to Hannah as they drove home. 'There's a close friend of hers going to be staying with her for a week or so, which should be a great help.'

When Hannah didn't reply or comment on that he glanced at her. Eyes glazed, she was staring abstractedly out the windscreen.

'Hannah, is something the matter?'

'Hannah?' he queried anxiously when she didn't reply to that either.

'I'll explain when we get home,' she said in a tight, strained voice. In her mind she was going over and over again the conversation she'd had with Ian Dewar, who'd never at any point twigged that he was talking to someone who'd had the radical mastectomy it had transpired he was so scornful about.

She thought of what Ian had told her regarding the comments made by an eminent London surgeon on the subject of radiotherapy. The surgeon had said, and Ian had quoted, lips tightly pursed as he'd done so, 'I am a simple surgeon, profoundly ignorant of the recondite mysteries of radiation therapy. I have preferred a sharp knife, a stout heart and unquenchable optimism, and have regarded the widest radical surgery as the method of election in almost every case.'

The surgeon Ian had quoted had been, and still was, a close colleague of Sir Reginald Walcot-Hunt.

'I have preferred a sharp knife, a stout heart and unquenchable optimism . . .' she repeated mentally to herself.

Her hands were clenched so hard they were white from the wrists down.

They completed the rest of the journey to Winton Avenue in silence.

Once home, Hannah made straight for the gin bottle, pouring herself a very large measure which she topped up with tonic. She wafted half of that down, took a deep breath, then despatched the remainder. She immediately poured herself another, though this one not quite such a large measure as the first.

'What's happened?' Lal asked.

'Do you want a drink?'

He shook his head.

'I had a most interesting chat with your cousin, Ian Dewar. Most interesting indeed.'

'Ian! I hadn't seen him in years. He's a . . .' Lal hesitated, then said quietly, 'Doctor you know.'

'Not only a doctor, but a radiotherapist. He treats cancers, including breast cancer, about which he had a great deal to say.'

There was that in Hannah's face and voice told Lal that she was about to come out with something she considered extremely important, some sort of bombshell.

'I believe I'll have that drink after all,' he said.

When he'd poured his drink he sat and listened intently while Hannah recounted her entire conversation with Ian Dewar.

When she finally finished speaking he was as aghast and appalled as she was.

'Yes, of course I know of Robert McWhirter and his work at the Edinburgh Royal Infirmary,' Doctor Grimley admitted, his expression matching his name.

'And yet you didn't tell us about him when I asked if there was an effective treatment other than radical mastectomy,' Hannah accused, her voice a stabbing stiletto.

'The man is considered to be a heretic, his methods contradict all that is long accepted and practised in today's medicine,' Grimley retorted.

'But according to our information they work just as well, better, than those my wife was subjected to,' Lal said.

'Can you deny that?' Hannah demanded.

'I can neither confirm or deny that. I'm quite simply not in a position to do so.'

'McWhirter published a paper six years ago, giving facts and figures to support his methods,' Lal stated.

'That is very true. But publishing a paper is one thing, having its contents accepted by the surgical establishment quite another.'

Hannah frowned. 'I don't understand that?'

'The surgical establishment is conservative in the extreme. They don't just change their practices overnight because someone shouts "eureka! I've found a better way of doing something". They are highly suspicious of anything new, and rightly so in my view. As they see it, the radical mastectomy, or Halstead mastectomy as you correctly referred to it, has been around a long time, and is tried and proven. We know everything there is to know about the operation, from its execution to all possible side-effects and post-operative treatments etc. etc. The Keynes lumpectomy, to give it its proper name, is relatively new and could still be found to be full of all sorts of nasty surprises.'

'That doesn't explain why you didn't tell me about it when I specifically asked you if there was an alternative to the radical mastectomy operation,' Hannah said.

'You're not understanding, Mrs Stuart. As far as I or any other responsible G.P. is concerned, there isn't an alternative. Nor will there be until such times, should they ever come about, when the lumpectomy operation is accepted by the surgical establishment.'

'The surgical establishment sound like a pack of dinosaurs to me,' Lal said hotly.

'There are two sides to any argument Mr Stuart, and they most certainly have theirs. What would you say if they subjected you to some new-fangled idea that didn't work and left you in a worse state than when you began? You'd have a lot to say then no doubt, and probably in the presence of lawyers.'

'Is that what it boils down to, them protecting their own skins?' Hannah queried.

'That element does come into it, has to. But matters aren't, as I'm trying to explain, as clear cut as that.'

'If you had told me about McWhirter I would have used him and by doing so saved my breast,' Hannah said bitterly.

'In the short term perhaps. But in the long term you can't be sure. The lumpectomy operation just hasn't been available long enough for it to be proven otherwise. Oh yes! I know it has been proven in the short term, but there are many who argue that it is no cure at all and that the patients will eventually die as surely as if the operation had never taken place.'

'The choice should have been mine to make,' Hannah said quietly.

'If you had come to me already knowing about McWhirter then I would have fully explained the situation to you, and then arranged for you to see him, if you'd still wanted to go ahead. As it was, Mr Stuart here asked me for the top man in that field, which is precisely what you got, Sir Reginald Walcot-Hunt *is* that man. That is something about which there can be no argument. Sir Reginald Walcot-Hunt is the country's foremost specialist in carcinomas of the breast.'

'And a butcher,' Hannah spat out.

'Mrs Stuart! You have no right to say such a thing.'

'Haven't I? I believe I have.'

'I'm sorry you're taking it this way,' Grimley said.

'You're sorry? What do you think I am?' she cried back at him.

Grimley held up his hands. 'I don't see any point in continuing this discussion. If you think I've failed you then you are perfectly entitled to report me to the proper authorities. However, I can assure you right here and now that they will give me full backing for what I did. Any inquiry would totally exonerate me.'

'Like protecting like,' Hannah said.

Grimley didn't reply to that.

Lal rose, and Hannah did the same. Grimley was about to follow suit when Hannah snapped out, her voice dripping contempt. 'Don't bother, *doctor*.'

Outside in the street Hannah thought of Ian Dewar, and wished she'd never spoken with him to learn what she had.

She knew the knowledge she might have escaped the knife and saved her breast would haunt her for the rest of her days.

Lal stared out of a rear window, down into the garden where Robyn was building a snowman amidst a great whirl and swirl of snow tumbling from a leaden sky. Hannah was with her, and supposed to be helping, but wasn't. Instead Hannah, shoulders hunched inside the mink coat he'd given her, was staring into space, completely lost within herself.

Lal's lips thinned as he watched her just standing there. All the mental recovery she'd made after her operation had gone down the plughole thanks to her conversation with Ian Dewar, and subsequent visit to confront Grimley.

She wasn't the same as she'd been after the operation, but different, less emotional, less hysterical. A coldness had got into her that was now apparent in everything she said and did. He'd tried to get her to go back and see Davidson, but she'd refused point blank, insisting she didn't need a psychiatrist anymore.

She hadn't moved out of their bedroom again, which was one good thing, and had continued to allow him to make love to her, which was another.

Lal snapped two fingers in exasperation. What she needed was an interest, something to take her out of herself and stop her brooding. But what? He was damned if he knew.

He had suggested she become involved again in their business, but she'd made a face and said he was coping brilliantly by himself. He'd asked if she'd care to sign on for a course at some institution, day or night classes, whichever? All she'd done was shake her head to that proposal, and pour herself another gin and tonic.

Her drinking was bad again, her smoking quite phenomenal. When she was indoors it was rare to catch her without a cigarette or drink in her hand, and usually both.

He'd pleaded in vain with her to cut back on her drinking, but her usual response to that request was a cold, thin smile. Every time he got that smile he felt he was something being observed at the end of a microscope.

Robyn was calling to her now, gesticulating that she wanted her attention.

Hannah continued staring into space.

That evening Lal sat down with his *Evening Citizen* and began going through the 'Property For Rent And Sale Section' when a small ad seemed to leap right off the page and smack him in the eye.

He read the ad through. Then again, this time more slowly.

Could this be the answer he'd been looking for? Could it?

Next morning he made a telephone call.

*

310

'Gibson Street,' Hannah read aloud from the sign on the building in front of which they'd parked.

'Know it?' Lal queried.

Pursing her lips she shook her head. 'I think I've heard it mentioned in the past, but that's all. We're close to the university here aren't we?'

'It's not far away. A lot of students live hereabouts, which makes it one of those transient sort of areas.'

Hannah frowned. 'Do you think that's the type of place you want to open another shop in? I'm not so sure it is.' That was the reason Lal had given her for bringing her there; he was considering new premises and wanted her opinion before he committed himself.

Hannah got out onto the pavement, and slammed her door shut behind her. 'I'm surprised you're even considering a shop here. Your nearest bakery must be quite some distance away, which would make such a shop extremely difficult to service.'

'Not this shop, I don't think,' Lal said somewhat mysteriously.

She glanced at him over the roof of the Riley. 'How do you work that out?'

'Let's have a look at the shop, shall we?' Going round to her he took her by the arm.

'I can't envisage you getting a good steady trade from students you know, from what I've heard of them they mainly eat in university canteens.'

'That's true enough,' Lal acknowledged.

Hannah glanced up at the surrounding tenements which were old and grey, but nicer than those she'd been brought up in. These had a faded 'genteel' quality about them, whereas the Partick tenements had been strictly and obviously working class.

Lal steered her up the street, a small smile having appeared to hover at the corners of his lips. He was enjoying this.

'That's it,' he said, stopping and pointing.

Her attention was immediately caught by a large stone carving of a blackbird in the process of launching itself into flight, the carving on a narrow ledge above the shop's fascia.

From there her gaze dropped down to the legend proclaiming the name of the shop. 'The Blackbird Bookshop' the legend said.

'But that's a bookshop!' she exclaimed.

'Right first time.'

She twisted in on him. 'You're not going to buy a bookshop and then turn it into an outlet for bread and cakes are you!'

'Why not?'

'That would be . . . sacriligious!' she protested.

He laughed, both delighted and amused by her reaction. 'To you perhaps, but not to me.'

'Lal, you can't do it! There must be other shops.'

They walked over Gibson Street to stand in front of The Blackbird Bookshop. It was desperately run-down, Lal thought. The exterior couldn't have seen a fresh lick of paint in decades.

They looked in the window at the books on display, the books there appearing as old and tired as the building itself. Several of them, originally new books, had gone yellow from age, while the inside of the window itself screamed out for a right good dusting and general clean up.

'Shall we go inside? We're expected,' Lal said.

Hannah nodded.

'Just don't mention about turning the place into an outlet for bread and cakes, eh?'

'Buying it under false pretences are you?' she retorted accusingly.

His expression became one of benign innocence. 'I didn't say that!'

'Yes you did, you told me not to mention bread or cakes.'

'Perhaps I had another reason for that.'

'Such as?'

'Such as the fact I love you.'

That lost her, completely. She couldn't see how that tied in with his buying a bookshop under false pretences.

The door tinged as Lal opened it, and immediately the unmistakable smell of rank upon rank of books assailed their nostrils. To Hannah it was like returning to the library she'd once worked in. The smell was the same. Somewhere a clock was ticking. Tick-tock! Tick-tock!

The old man at the desk glanced up from the open book before him to regard them through gold-rimmed glasses. He had a kind face, but the eyes behind the gold-rimmed glasses, though keen and intelligent, had more than a tinge of sadness

312

about them. Hannah felt an immediate affinity with the old man who, from his facial and other characteristics, was clearly Jewish.

'Mr Katzav?' Lal smiled.

The old man came to his feet, proving to be taller than either Hannah or Lal would have guessed from his sitting position. 'I am. Are you Mr Stuart?'

'I am. And this is my wife.'

'Pleased to meet you both,' said David Katzav, extending a hand to Hannah.

The fingers that enclosed hers were long and slim, Hannah noted, with nails that gleamed whitely at their tips. But if he had one outstanding feature it was his nose, a great beak of an affair, like some bird of prey.

After shaking with Hannah, David Katzav then shook with Lal. 'You're interested in books, I take it?' he inquired eagerly.

'Oh yes, very much so. Books have always given me enormous pleasure.'

Judas! Hannah thought.

'And you, Mrs Stuart?'

'I'm an ex-librarian, Mr Katzav. I think that speaks for itself.'

He clapped his hands in approval. 'An ex-librarian, heh! Very good, very good. Though . . . 'And here his face fell, 'without libraries I might have done better business over the years. What do you say to that, Mrs Stuart?'

'I say that's a valid argument. But I for one would certainly not deny the populace at large free access to books.'

'You know something, Mrs Stuart?' He winked. 'Neither would I, though that free access must have hurt me at the till during my time here.' As he spoke he indicated an ornate brass till standing to one side of his desk.

'Business hasn't been brilliant for you then, I presume?' Lal said.

'It comes and goes, some weeks are better than others. But the state of my business isn't why I'm selling. Oh no!' David Katzav replied, shaking his head.

'So why *are* you selling?' Lal prompted.

David Katzav gestured about him, 'In truth, it is all too much for me nowadays, and has been for some while, I suppose. I will sell, and spend what days are left to me reading at home.'

Somewhere in his eighties, Hannah judged. Well past retirement. But how sad, how awful, that his bookshop was going to be turned into an outlet for bread and cakes. She resolved to talk Lal out of this. Why, the old man would be heartbroken to find out that was what had become of his so obviously beloved bookshop.

'I shouldn't really ask, but have there been many inquiries after the shop?' Lal asked.

'No, yours is the only one,' David Katzav admitted honestly.

Hannah's heart sank to hear that.

'I see,' Lal murmured, a smile stretching his lips.

'Can I show you around?'

'Please,' Lal replied.

Even though the inside of the shop was decrepit in the extreme, it was still a wonderland to Hannah, a wonderland full of jewels known as books.

'Is the stock included in the asking price?' Lal queried at one stage.

'No, that is a separate negotiation for the simple reason I shall be taking many of the more expensive books, and all the first editions, with me.' David Katzav shrugged. 'Some of these books are like children to me, we have been together a long time.'

'I understand perfectly,' Hannah said to him.

'Are you married?' Lal probed.

'I was never that fortunate, so I have no son and heir to pass this shop into.'

'The shop was your wife?' Hannah smiled.

'Exactly, Mrs Stuart! You have it in a nutshell.'

When David Katzav's back was next to her she shot Lal a murderous glance.

After showing them round the retail area, including several cubbyholes and cupboards off, David Katzav locked the front door and took them down into the basement, where there were stacks of cardboard boxes filled with books, all pre-war and second-hand.

'I would have thought the students living round about would have favoured your shop?' Hannah queried.

314

'I get a number in, mainly to browse. The stock I carry doesn't really suit them however, and I have no interest in what would be their line.' He screwed up his face. 'Paperbacks and textbooks, huh!'

He might be a darling old man but he was a terrible businessman, Hannah thought. It was a miracle the place actually earned enough for it to have kept going.

Back upstairs again, David Katzav unlocked the front door, then asked, 'Can I make you some coffee? I usually have a cup about now.'

'That would be very nice indeed,' Hannah answered quickly, hoping Katzav would leave them alone for a bit, which was precisely what he did, saying his kettle was in one of the cubbyholes they'd viewed.

'And don't worry, I'll hear the bell ting should anyone come in,' David Katzav called back over his shoulder as he hurried away.

'You can't buy this shop,' Hannah hissed at Lal, once she considered David Katzav to be out of earshot.

Lal raised an eyebrow.

'You can't, Lal. You'd break the old man's heart if you turned it into what you intend.'

'You heard him. I'm the only one inquiring about it.'

'That doesn't matter! He's bound to find a proper buyer eventually.'

'But I am a proper buyer,' Lal protested, tongue in cheek.

'Don't be dense. You know what I mean.'

Lal gazed about him. 'It's going to need an awful lot of money spent on it. I see it being totally gutted.'

'Lal!' she was getting angry now. How could he be so crass! It was totally unlike him.

'How will you do it?'

'Me!' she explained quietly. 'I'm not helping you.'

'No, no, not help me. Help yourself.'

What was he havering about. 'I don't understand.'

'I never actually said I intended buying these premises as an outlet for the business; you presumed that.'

She was lost again. 'If not as an outlet, then what?'

'A bookshop.'

Her mouth dropped open. 'A bookshop!'

'For you.'

'For *me*!'

He thought her expression absolutely priceless, and wished he'd had the foresight to bring a camera with him to catch it for posterity.

'For you,' he confirmed, adding, 'if you want it that is.'

She shook her head. 'But why on earth should I want a bookshop?'

'Because you love books just as much as that old man does. And for another reason, it would give you something other than yourself to occupy your mind and hopefully stop, or at least limit, this withdrawn broodiness you've been subjecting us all to.'

She regarded him steadily. 'So it's a plot on your part' she accused.

'It's a plot on my part,' he confessed.

'But I don't know the first thing about running a bookshop!'

'Absolute rubbish. To begin with forget all about the initial financial side of things, I'll deal with that. I'm buying the shop and making available the capital to have it done out as you want. All right so far?'

She slowly nodded.

'As for the concept and details of the refurbishment, with your taste and inventiveness they'll be a dawdle for you.'

I wish I could be so convinced of that, she thought to herself, at the same time realising that an excitement was growing within her, an excitement at the prospect of doing as he was suggesting. Her very own bookshop! The more she thought about that the more it appealed.

'From there we go to what stock you order. Again this should be relatively easy for you, having spent all those years as a librarian. You know from hard experience what is popular, and would sell. Apply that experience here and the shop can't help but be successful.'

He made it all sound so deceptively simple, she smiled inwardly. 'I know I could cope with the accounts, invoices etc.,' she said, having often helped Lal with the bakery ones in the past.

'Precisely,' Lal enthused.

'What about Robyn, though?' she queried, forehead creasing into a sudden frown.

'I'll organise my affairs so that I take her to school, pick her up

316

again and look after her till you get home in the evening. With the way things are with me that shouldn't be a problem. And should it transpire that it is, we'll find another solution. You mustn't allow Robyn to influence you in this.'

'The first thing I would introduce are the paperbacks and textbooks Mr Katzav is so contemptuous about. They would be the foundation that could make this shop commercially viable,' she breathed.

Look at her! Lal thought, elation bubbling inside him. Her eyes were glowing while her whole body had become far more alive and vibrant than he'd seen it in a long time. Yes, he congratulated himself, he'd pressed the right button. A corner had been turned, a bright new future lay ahead for both of them.

Hannah was looking about her, imagining things as they might be. She could remove those shelves there which would create more space, and if she then . . . Her mind was exploding with ideas, like a hundred Chinese crackers going off.

'So, what's your decision?' Lal demanded.

'The Blackbird Bookshop,' Hannah said softly. She liked the sound of that, it had a ring to it.

David Katzav was delighted when they told him they were going to buy, declaring that he couldn't have found two nicer people to sell to.

One month later, to the day, Hannah took possession.

PART 3

Today

Chapter 9

Ting! went the front door as it opened, causing Robyn to glance up from where she was squatting, rearranging books that had become jumbled on one of the lower shelves. The students who frequented the shop were awful at jumbling up the books, they seemed to have no sense of discipline or order whatever.

The male face that she saw just inside the door, his body obscured by a small free-standing set of shelves, was strong, eager and with a hint of arrogance about it. The hair was darkish and swept back, the eyes black-topped by dark, bushy curved eyebrows. The mouth was a good-humoured slash, the teeth a sparkling white.

'Wow!' Robyn thought. Here was real film-star stuff.

Hannah was at the rear of the shop making their morning coffee, so it was up to her to deal with him. Rising, Robyn made her way round to where he was standing.

The body matched the face. A touch over six feet tall, he was wide-shouldered and narrow-hipped with a well-developed chest that spoke of sport and exercise. He carried himself confidently and easily, a man sure of himself.

'Can I help you?' Robyn smiled, thinking she'd never seen him in the shop before, for if she had she'd have remembered him.

'I'm Guy Trecarron,' the young man stated, extending a hand, 'the new Penguin representative.'

English! she thought, the accent was unmistakable. And well-educated English at that. Public school? she wondered.

She knew Hannah had been expecting a new Penguin representative to call, Mr Dalgleish, who'd been doing the job for years in that area having just recently retired. 'Pleased to meet you. I'm Robyn Stuart.'

'The owner?'

He was teasing her; at seventeen how could she possibly be the owner? 'No, my mother is, I'm only helping out.'

'Is she about?'

'I'll get her.'

She left him to walk to the rear of the shop, and into the cubbyhole where Hannah was in the process of sugaring and milking their coffee.

'The new Penguin rep, eh,' Hannah said after Robyn had explained why she'd come seeking her. 'All right, I'll go and chat with him. What's he like?'

'A charmer, I'd say.'

Hannah raised an eyebrow. 'One of those? A bit different to Mr Dalgleish, then.' Dalgleish, a poppet if ever there was, had been old, cantankerous and crusty. They'd both adored him.

'Shall I offer him coffee?' Robyn queried. Dalgleish had always been given coffee if he'd visited while there was some on the go – not the case with all the reps, only those Hannah particularly liked.

'What do you think?'

'I'd say yes.'

Hannah nodded. 'All right then, if he does want some, you can make it while I'm dealing with him.'

Robyn, carrying her steaming cup, followed Hannah, carrying hers, to where Trecarron was waiting.

Early twenties, Hannah judged on catching sight of him. Probably new to the game, a surmise on her part that proved to be correct.

Trecarron introduced himself to Hannah, and she to him, and yes, he'd love a cup of coffee, he replied when Robyn asked if he would. She hurriedly returned to the cubbyhole where the coffee items were kept, pleased that the kettle was just off the boil.

'A great loss to the company,' Trecarron said to Hannah, referring to Dalgleish and in answer to a statement she'd made. 'He was extremely popular with those he dealt with, as I'm rapidly finding out.'

'One of the nicer things about Mr Dalgleish was that he was never pushy,' Hannah said pointedly. She found pushy reps a pain in the backside. She knew what she could sell, and how much. What was the point of her taking a title that would only lie on the shelves, gathering dust? None at all. Or taking far too many copies of a title, many of which would only have to be returned? Again, none. But that's what the pushy reps would have had her do in their supremely optimistic view that they knew better than she.

Trecarron, quick on the uptake, got to the message. 'I don't believe you'll find me pushy,' he replied slowly. 'Though . . .' He paused, then said with deference, 'I hope you won't mind me trying to interest you in titles I think might suit you and your shop?'

'Not at all. That's your job.'

'Then we are in agreement, Mrs Stuart,' Trecarron declared.

Hannah nodded. They understood one another. A bright young man, she thought. He actually listened, and took on board, what she was saying. More than many of the reps did. Yes, she and Mr Trecarron might just get on quite well together.

'May I?' Trecarron asked, lifting up his briefcase and indicating the desk they were standing beside.

That he'd asked permission before bringing out his bits and pieces again impressed Hannah. Politeness never went wrong with her.

Hannah's reply was to push to one side several papers that were lying on her desktop, and gesture he was to go ahead.

Trecarron was about to speak when the door tinged and in came a typical student type with long hair, beard and scruffy leather jacket. Behind him was a middle-aged woman called Mrs Elphinstone, a regular customer and buyer.

Hannah exchanged pleasantries with Mrs Elphinstone who then inquired after a Constable title. Excusing herself to Trecarron, Hannah took Mrs Elphinstone off to locate the book for her.

Trecarron wasn't at all perturbed to be left temporarily high and dry; that happened all the time to a rep and was something he'd been warned about at Harmondsworth where the main Penguin offices were, and where he'd been interviewed prior to being taken on. As far as booksellers were concerned the customer always came before the rep, and rightly so too.

He was leafing through a book he'd taken from his briefcase when Robyn rejoined him. 'Oh, thank you,' he said when she handed him the coffee she'd brought.

'What's the book?'

'*The Other England* by Geoffrey Moorhouse. We think it's going to be a biggie.'

'Just out?'

He nodded.

She took the paperback from him and glanced curiously at it. It was the latest in the series 'Britain in The Sixties', and a Penguin Special.

'Our powers that be are convinced it's going to be one of the runaway bestsellers of 1964,' Trecarron stated, it being April of that year.

Robyn opened the book at its first chapter and started to read. Halfway down the page she became aware of him staring at her. When she looked up she found his black eyes boring into hers, which immediately caused her to blush bright red. She was a terrible blusher, something she'd inherited from her mother and, according to Hannah, from her grandfather Bobby who'd been killed in the Great War.

Suddenly she was tingly all over, while her stomach had gone sort of mushy inside.

'Mind if I smoke?' Trecarron asked.

'Go ahead,' she replied, voice tight in her throat.

He produced a packet of Gitanes, the French cigarettes. 'Will you join me?'

'Yes, please.'

A battered silver Dunhill lighter appeared as though by magic, which he flicked into flame as he brought it to the tip of the cigarette she'd placed between her lips. In doing that he came closer to her than he'd been, allowing her to smell him.

It was a gorgeous smell, very masculine, overlaid with after-shave and the distinctive odour of French tobacco. She found it extremely sexy.

'Lovely lighter,' she commented, knowing Dunhills to be very expensive.

He grinned. 'Fell off the back of a lorry. I bought it for next to nothing in a pub one night.'

'Lucky you. They normally cost a fortune.'

'Beautiful piece of machinery. Here, try it.'

She flipped open the lighter's top, then flicked it as he'd done. It came smoothly alight giving the impression it would do so every single time.

'The Rolls Royce of lighters,' he said.

Snapping the top shut she dropped it into the palm of her hand where it nestled, smooth and sensuous. She began stroking it with her thumb when a thought flashed across her mind, making her blush again. Swiftly she returned the Dunhill to an amused Trecarron.

'How long have you worked for Penguin?' she asked, changing the subject.

'This is my first week. The normal procedure is for the outgoing rep to take his replacement round, but for all sorts of reasons I won't go into here it didn't work out that way in my case. Still.' He smiled broadly. 'Here I am.'

'And you've come up from England to take over the area?'

'That's right. First week in the job and first week in Bonnie Scotland. Don't know a soul north of Hadrian's Wall either, but I'm sure I'll soon make friends. I've been assured the Scots are a friendly race.'

'Enjoying everything so far?'

'Oh yes! Thoroughly.'

At which point more customers arrived and Robyn had to put out her cigarette and attend to one of them. Things got fairly hectic for a while after that, at the end of which Hannah had somehow dealt with Trecarron and he'd gone.

On asking Hannah, she was told that her mother had ordered six copies of *The Other England*.

One evening three weeks later Lal arrived home in an exceptionally good humour. He had two large bunches of flowers with him, one which he presented to Hannah, the other to Robyn.

'What's all this in aid of?' Hannah demanded.

'Does it have to be in aid of anything? Can't I just give you each a bunch of flowers because I feel like it?' Lal shot back.

Hannah took him into her arms, and cuddled him tight. God had given her a good man and no mistake, she could never have done better than Lal Stuart. He was a near-genius at business – his 'little empire' now comprised six bakeries and shops, five single shops serviced by the bakeries plus three kiosks selling newspapers, tobacco, sweets etc. Though it had to be admitted, there had been several hiccups along the way, one of which – buying new premises which had proved a total disaster – had given them a terrible financial fright. But they'd survived that together. And what was more important, he had stood staunchly by her during the traumas of her hysterectomy and worse, of her mastectomy. His buying The Blackbird Bookshop for her had been inspirational, and marked a turning point. No medicine or treatment could have worked the wonders the bookshop had, within six months of its purchase she was back to what he'd called 'her old self' again. She would never be sure which of them had been the more relieved by that.

'Thanks, Pa,' said Robyn, pecking him on the cheek. 'I'll put these in my bedroom.'

'The flowers aren't all,' he declared.

Hannah pushed him to arm's length. 'What else have you come home with?'

He delved into the jacket pocket of his suit to pull out a small buff-coloured envelope which he brandished in front of her. 'A surprise,' he announced.

Hannah tried to snatch the envelope from him, but didn't succeed, Lal raising it high above his head.

Robyn laughed, her Pa could be such fun. 'What's the surprise then, Pa?' she asked, still laughing.

'Guess?'

'I've no idea,' she replied.

'You're not trying very hard. What about you Hannah?'

She studied the envelope, at a loss to imagine what it contained. 'I'm afraid you've got me,' she said.

'Come on Robyn?'

'Tickets of some kind?'

'Coorrreeecct!' he announced in a wildly exaggerated manner. 'But to what?'

'The theatre?' Robyn queried.

'Coorrreeecct again!' he declaimed.

'For tonight?' Hannah asked, thinking this was short notice. There were other things she had planned to do.

'No, Friday night. Four tickets to see the new play at the Citizens', *Armstrong's Last Goodnight* by John Arden. It's had temendous reviews.'

'Oh, I'd adore to see that!' Robyn exclaimed, having read one of the reviews Lal had referred to.

'Then you shall, on Friday night. We've got seats in the stalls, best in the house I'm assured.'

'Did you say four tickets?' Hannah queried.

'I did. I thought James McEwen could come along as Robyn's escort.'

Robyn pulled a face. 'Are you at it again, Pa? I wish you'd stop trying to matchmake me with James.'

The McEwens lived several doors along from the Stuarts, Alexander and Cecily being friends of Lal and Hannah. The McEwens had two boys, James and Rory, with James, a year older than Robyn, being in his first year at Veterinary College. Alexander was a senior civil servant connected with the Customs and Excise, and a man much admired by Lal for his education, position and social standing.

'I've said it before and I'll say it again, James is a fine chap with excellent prospects. It's going to be a lucky lassie who lands him,' Lal expounded.

Robyn sighed, her and James was a relatively recent bee in her father's bonnet. 'He can be next in line for the throne for all I care. He's not for me,' she replied.

'How do you know?'

'I just do, Pa, all right?'

Lal bulldozed on. 'Personally I think he's a terrific lad. Takes after his dad.'

'Then you marry him,' Robyn retorted facetiously. She clicked her fingers. 'Oh, sorry, you can't do that! You're already married.'

Hannah put a hand over her mouth, and smiled behind it.

'I only want the best for you,' Lal muttered to Robyn.

She immediately softened. 'I appreciate that, Pa. And you've always given it to me too.'

'So you won't mind if I invite James along, will you? If only to square the numbers.'

She wagged a finger at him. 'Pa, you're an old fraud! You're still at it.'

'No, I'm not!' he protested, his expression as innocent as a new-born babe's.

'Don't fib, you are!'

'And afterwards I thought we might go out for a meal, the four of us together.'

'Talk about spiders spinning!' Robyn exclaimed, stalking towards the door. 'Well, I'm off to find a vase.'

At the door she stopped, and turned, a wicked smile on her face. 'Pa?'

'Yes?'

'Did you marry Mum for love?'

'You know I did.'

'Then why don't you allow me the same courtesy.' And with that she swept from the room.

'Touché!' Hannah said to Lal.

His brow clouded, then just as rapidly unclouded again. 'Nonetheless, it would still be a damn fine match,' he persisted.

Hannah agreed with him, but agreed far more with Robyn. How did that old Fifties Doris Day number go again? 'Che Sarà Sarà'. Yes, that was it. 'Che Sarà, Sarà' – 'What will be, will be.'

She wondered who Robyn would eventually marry? Certainly not James McEwen; Robyn just didn't see James in that light at all.

Whoever, she prayed he would be as good and kind as her Lal.

The curtain on Act 1 came down to resounding applause. Robyn had found the language – a curious blend of sixteenth-century Scots and modern Scots (not quiet Lallans but similar) – difficult to follow in places, but despite that had thoroughly enjoyed what she'd witnessed so far.

'What do you think?' Lal asked Hannah, still clapping.

She raised her eyebrows. 'Very good. I particularly like the chap playing Johnny Armstrong himself.'

'That's Iain Cuthbertson,' Robyn chipped in.

'And the mistress, she's excellent also.'

'Lisa Daniely,' said James McEwen, hastily consulting his programme, the auditorium lights having now come up.

'Right then, the bar,' declared Lal, beginning to rise. He'd placed his interval order when they'd had a drink there, prior to coming into the auditorium.

The auditorium itself was a-buzz with people commenting on and discussing the play. The buzz had an excited approval about it, clearly the play was going down well.

Robyn spied Una McLean sitting several rows behind, an actress she'd watched in the past and whose work she'd enjoyed. And was that Jimmy Logan, the famous Scottish comedian over there? He was too far away for her to be absolutely certain that it was. She'd read only recently that

Annie Ross, the well-known jazz singer, was Jimmy's sister, a fact she hadn't previously been aware of.

They could only shuffle up the clogged aisle, the extremely hot auditorium being more or less evacuated as a large majority of the audience headed out of it for a breather, and in many cases a drink.

Somehow Robyn got in behind Una McLean and a thin man talking animatedly to her. That chat was all 'darling' this and 'darling' that! Unbeknown to Robyn the thin man was an actor called Roy Boutcher, Una's husband.

The crush bar, when they finally got to it, was a heaving mass of bodies. Robyn, Hannah and James succeeded in squeezing themselves into a corner while Lal bored his way to that section of the bar where the prepaid interval drinks had been laid out, each drink order having a piece of paper with it, stating whose order it was.

'How's college going?' Robyn asked James, who was of medium height and build, with sandy-coloured hair. She genuinely liked James, and always had, but as a pal, not a boyfriend. She could no more have imagined going to bed with James McEwen than she could have done with . . . Well her own father! James didn't feel the same way about her though; noticing that had sparked off Lal's keenness for the two of them to get together.

'Hard graft. I'll be glad when the summer arrives.'

Robyn nodded. So would she.

'Our Ball is coming up soon. I was wondering if you'd care to go with me?'

Hannah overheard that and looked away, pretending she hadn't. She knew what Robyn's reply would be; a turndown.

'What date?' Robyn asked.

'June 14th.'

'Oh, that's too bad! I already have an engagement for that night.' She racked her brains trying to come up with something.

'Oh? What's that?'

'One of the girls at Laurel Bank is having a birthday party. I've been invited and have accepted. I couldn't possibly back out now. That would be frightfully rude.'

'Yes, of course,' a disappointed James agreed.

Lal rejoined them, holding a tiny tray on which their drinks were perched. Although officially too young to imbibe in public Robyn was used to having a white wine if she wanted, which was what she now had.

Warm, she thought, having a sip. It would have been far nicer, and appropriate in the circumstances, cold. Still, what else could you expect in a jam-packed theatre crush bar!

'The costumes are magnificent don't you agree?' James said to Hannah.

'Quite.'

'I've been told that the play is a reflection on the current situation in the Congo,' Lal stated knowingly.

'Really!' James exclaimed. 'You mean a *roman à clef*?'

Lal hadn't a clue what a *roman à clef* was, but wasn't going to let James know that. 'What I heard was . . .'

Robyn stopped hearing her father's words, having just spotted a familiar face about fifteen feet away. It was Guy Trecarron, deep in conversation with an auburn-haired woman about his own age – a very beautiful woman, she now noted.

Trecarron laughed, and the woman followed suit, tossing her thick auburn mane as she did. Trecarron then touched her on the cheek, after which he whispered something into her ear.

There could be no doubt they were together, Robyn thought, jealousy knifing through her. Well, it certainly hadn't taken him long to find a girlfriend, not long at all! And what a looker! She felt positively plain and dowdy by comparison. Plain, dowdy and young.

Trecarron's eyes slid away from his companion, as if he realised he was being watched, to latch onto Robyn's. His face lit up in recognition, and he smiled.

Robyn turned her back on Trecarron, completely ignoring him. As she tried to concentrate again on what her father was spouting about the play and the Congo she could feel her heart thump! thump! thumping! inside her chest.

Shortly afterwards, when it was time to leave the crush bar, she risked a sideways glance to where Trecarron and the woman had been, to discover they'd already gone.

Nor did she see either of them again during the remainder of her stay in the theatre.

'Hello? Can I give you a lift?'

Robyn gazed into the car which had drawn up beside her, and there was Guy Trecarron, smiling at her from the driver's seat. It was a fortnight since she'd last seen him in the crush bar of the Citizens'.

'I, eh . . .'

'Get in and tell me where to,' he said, opening the front passenger door for her.

Why, oh why did he have to catch her in her school uniform? she inwardly raged. His having done so made her feel the size of tuppence.

A band of friends across the road – they all caught the same tramcar together – giggled and waved at her. One of them, Isla Buchanan, wolf-whistled, the wolf-whistle directed at Trecarron.

'Saucy!' said Trecarron, meaning Isla Buchanan.

'I'm going home . . .' Robyn started to say.

'That's all right. Hop in! I'm sure it isn't far out of my way.'

'I'll have him if you don't want him, Robyn!' Isla Buchanan called out, which caused the others she was with to hoot with laughter.

One part of Robyn wanted to get in beside Trecarron, another to run a mile, the latter because of her uniform. God, what a baby he must think her.

Blushing like a bride, she got in and slammed the passenger door shut. 'I live in Winton Avenue. That's in Kelvinside,' she stated in a small voice.

'You'll have to direct, I'm afraid.'

'Go to the end of this road and turn right,' she said.

The car, a Cortina, leapt forward, and soon Isla Buchanan and those Isla was with were lost to view. Before they reached the end of the road Robyn had given Tercarron a set of simple instructions that would take them to Kelvinside, and Winton Avenue.

'I didn't realise you were still at school,' Trecarron said.

She cringed inside. 'It's my final year. I'm just about to take my Highers which are our equivalent of your English 'A' Levels.'

'And after you leave?'

'Providing I do well, I intend going to the Uni. I want to read English.'

He nodded his approval. 'When you say Uni I presume you mean Glasgow University?'

'Oh yes! Why go elsewhere when I have a marvellous university right here on my own doorstep? Its department of English is renowned.'

'Indeed!' He'd never heard of it being renowned. 'And after university, what? Any plans?'

'I'll become full-time at the bookshop. I love books and always have.'

'Me too,' he said softly.

'I suppose that helps in your job,' she replied, the hint of a smile creeping onto her face.

'It certainly does. Anyway, that's something we have in common then. A love of books.'

She could smell him again. That same masculine smell overlaid with aftershave and French tobacco. Oh, but it was yummy! She couldn't help but think of James McEwen, he always smelled of household soap and . . . No! she chided herself. She mustn't be unkind. James was a good and loyal pal, after all.

She glanced sideways at Trecarron. How worldly he seemed, and exciting. She wondered what his past was? She would have bet her savings he'd been around a great deal, and by that she included women. How many had he been to bed with? Or swived as they currently called it at school, thanks to a John Barth novel doing the rounds. Oodles no doubt. Oodles and oodles.

'Why did you snub me that night at the theatre?'

She pretended innocence. 'Snub you?'

'I smiled at you and you turned your back on me.'

'Couldn't have seen you,' she lied. 'You mean at the Citizens' Theatre?'

'That's right.'

'Where did this supposed snub take place, then?'

'In the bar during the first interval.'

'I was there all right, but didn't notice you.'

'You were with your mother and a man I presumed to be your father. Also a young chap.'

'James is just a neighbour and friend,' she replied with emphasis.

'Looked a nice lad.'

'Oh he's all right!' she said airily. 'His father and mine are fairly close chums.'

'So he's nothing special?'

'Good grief, no! Merely an escort for the night.' She paused, then asked as casually as she could manage. 'Were you alone or with someone?'

'I was with Eadie. She and I share a flat.'

That stunned Robyn. 'You've certainly been quick off the mark!' she accused, and immediately could have bitten her tongue for doing so.

Trecarron laughed. 'No, no, you've got hold of the wrong end of the stick. I said we shared a flat, not that we lived together. There are five of us in the same flat, all with our own rooms but sharing a communal kitchen and bathroom. I'm the odd one out.'

'How's that?'

'The other four are drama students attending the Royal Scottish Academy of Music and Dramatic Art. That was how I came to be at the Citizens' Theatre that night; Eadie had two tickets from a friend of hers in the cast and asked me if I'd like to go with her. The four of them have been very good at making me feel at home in the flat, and in Glasgow.'

'I see,' Robyn murmured, smiling inwardly at how she'd got things muddled, and how jealous she'd been of this Eadie.

Trecarron went on. 'Stroke of luck for me that my room came vacant when it did. It belonged to another drama student called Frank who got the bullet from the college. The remaining foursome put an ad in our local newsagent's, which I saw. I moved in a week after Frank moved out.'

Trecarron groped in his pocket to produce a packet of Gitanes. 'I don't know if I should offer you one of these while you're in school uniform,' he joked.

'Don't then,' she snapped back, cross with him for saying that.

'But I will anyway.' He shook the packet at her, several cigarettes popping out of the torn-away end.

'Thank you,' she said stiffly, accepting one.

He put one in his own mouth, returned the packet to his pocket, and flipped alight the battered Dunhill which he'd taken from the same pocket. She had to bend to the light, Guy keeping his eyes on the road.

'Doesn't your mother object to you smoking?' he queried.

'She can hardly do that when she smokes like a chimney herself. Besides, I may be still at school but I'm not a little girl. I'm . . . What?' she demanded, having heard him mutter something under his breath.

'I said I'd noticed that.'

She blushed furiously, even more so than she'd done when she'd got into the car.

If Trecarron was aware she was blushing he didn't let on or comment. 'Getting back to the flat. Besides Eadie there's Kate, Jack and Iain. Eadie and Jack live in rooms at the top of the flat which is on two floors, while Kate, Iain and myself are on the ground floor. They're a terribly nice bunch, if a trifle weird at times, particularly Jack who goes in for a great deal of introspection, a real intellectual soul-searcher.'

'And how about cooking? How do you all manage with that?'

'During the week the four of them eat mainly at college, with only bits and pieces at night. During the weekends when the college is closed they seem to survive on toast and cereal.'

'What about you?'

'There are a few cheap and cheerful places I've discovered where I stoke up at lunchtime and teatime. Sundays it's porridge, followed by bacon and eggs in the morning, with visits to a nearby café for lunch and tea, those usually, it being a café, beans on toast, spaghetti on toast, that sort of thing.'

It was on the tip of Robyn's tongue to suggest he come and have Sunday lunch one weekend with her and her parents, then she decided not to. That might appear too forward of her.

'I never did get your name?' he said.

'Robyn.'

'As in Hood?'

She could tell he was teasing her. 'No, with a "y" not "i".'

'Just as your Stuart is with a "u" and not "w",' he replied quickly.

'Right!' she laughed.

'Your mother made sure I understood that even though the name was clearly enough spelt on the order and invoice forms I inherited on the Blackbird.'

They turned into Winton Avenue. 'So from now on it's Robyn and Guy; is that all right with you?' he proposed.

He wasn't the only one who could tease. 'Is that Guy as in Fawkes?'

Now it was his turn to laugh. 'Guy as in Fawkes,' he agreed.

'Over there,' she said, pointing.

As he parked she thought how sorry she was that her lift was over, she'd thoroughly enjoyed his company.

'Is that your house?' Guy queried as she ground out her cigarette in the ashtray, gesturing at the house they were directly in front of.

'That's it.'

'Very nice too,' he said softly, and thoughtfully, staring at it.

She opened her door and got out. 'Thank you very much for the lift,' she said, closing the door again.

'My pleasure entirely.'

'No doubt I'll see you again.'

'No doubt. Goodbye for now, then.'

'Goodbye for now.'

As she walked up the gravel driveway she was still smelling the aftershave, French tobacco, and him.

'I couldn't be more delighted!' Lal said to Robyn, hugging her tightly to him. On a sudden impulse he lifted her right off the floor and, with her squealing, whirled her round and round.

Hannah watched them, her eyes shining with pride. They'd all been on tenterhooks waiting for Robyn's Highers results which had finally arrived in that morning's post, and which Lal had immediately brought round to the Blackbird as Hannah and Robyn had already left for work.

Lal deposited Robyn back onto her feet, then placed a hand on his chest. 'I'm not as young as I used to be. That fair took my breath away.'

'You'll give yourself a heart attack with that sort of nonsense,' Hannah chided, but with love and warmth in her voice.

'Well it's not every day that a father learns that his daughter's going to university,' Lal responded. For that's what Robyn's results meant; her place had been secured.

'Right then, let's get down to business,' declared Lal, going over to where he'd stood the ice-cold bottle of champagne he'd brought with him, and which had been in the fridge this past week for precisely this hoped-for celebration. Beside the Dom Perignon were three glasses he'd also brought.

He whisked the foil off the top of the bottle, and then the wire over the cork. 'I always get a kick out of doing this,' he said, gripping the bottom of the bottle with one hand while grasping the cork with the other. He moved both hands in opposite directions to one another and the cork eased out of the neck of the bottle to suddenly go bang! in a most satisfactory manner.

Hurriedly he snatched up the nearest glass as the champagne frothed over, and filled it. When he'd topped and retopped all three glasses he gave the first to Robyn, the second to Hannah, and took up the third for himself.

'To our daughter, who's done extremely well. May her days at university be happy and productive ones!' he toasted.

'Amen!' echoed Hannah.

The three of them were drinking when the door tinged open, and there was Guy Trecarron.

Guy realised the situation at a glance. 'Sorry, Mrs Stuart, I've obviously called at the wrong time. I'll come again this afternoon,' he said.

'No, wait!' Hannah replied, flapping a hand at him. 'Come in and have a glass of champagne with us, Mr Trecarron. We're celebrating Robyn's Highers results.'

He hesitated, not sure whether he should accept Hannah's invitation or not.

'Come on in,' urged Lal, waving Guy to them. Then to Robyn. 'Can you find another glass.'

'Are you absolutely certain?' Guy queried, not at all convinced they weren't just being polite and wouldn't really prefer to be on their own. Although, he reminded himself, the shop was open for business, even if he couldn't see any customers.

'Of course we are,' Hannah replied. Turning to Lal she explained, 'Darling this is Mr Trecarron, the new Penguin rep.'

Lal had already guessed from Guy's general appearance and the briefcase he was carrying, plus Hannah's having so readily invited him to join them, that he was something of the sort.

Lal and Guy shook hands after Hannah had introduced them. 'A pleasure to meet you, Mr Stuart,' Guy said politely.

'And you, Mr Trecarron.'

'Isn't it wonderful, Mr Trecarron!' Hannah enthused. 'This

means Robyn will definitely be going to the university in the autumn.'

'I'm very pleased for her, and for you, her parents. An excellent achievement.'

Lal thought of his background, and Hannah's, and how he'd pulled them both up by their bootstraps, as the expression went. Now their daughter was going to the university! He couldn't have been more thrilled.

Robyn returned with a tumbler she'd located in the cubbyhole where the kettle was kept, which Lal poured a measure of Dom Perignon into.

'To you, Robyn!' Guy toasted. 'May this success lead to many others.'

They all drank, with the exception of Robyn. 'Thank you,' she said quietly to Guy.

'What a time to be getting stuck into champagne!' Hannah laughed. It wasn't even ten am.

'Well, when we finish this bottle I'll nip out and buy another,' Lal declared. The off-licences weren't yet open, but there was an Indian restaurant further along that he and Hannah often frequented. The owner would be up and about and, he knew, only too happy to sell him a bottle at the usual restaurant price. It wouldn't be Dom Perignon, but it would be chilled.

'You look radiant. Good news suits you,' Guy smiled at Robyn.

'Although I didn't say to Mum and Pa, I honestly didn't think I'd done well. I've been dreading the results coming through.'

'I thought you were a bit unforthcoming about how you felt you'd done,' Hannah commented.

'Never mind, it's all over now. And your results are tremendous. Here's to my daughter again!' Lal said, raising his glass in yet another toast.

A few minutes later Lal was telling Guy, in response to Guy's asking what he did, about his starting off as a baker and now owning a string of bakeries and shops, when a customer appeared, inquiring if the bookshop had a copy of Kahlil Gibran's *Spirits Rebellious*. Gibran was a Lebanese poet, philosopher and artist currently very much in vogue amongst the Glaswegian intellectual esoteric set.

'Certainly,' Hannah replied. 'Follow me and I'll show you

where it is.' And with that she led the customer, a middle-aged, schoolmarmish lady, off down the shop.

Lal refilled their glasses. 'I'll pop out and get that other bottle. This one's just about had it.' He took a swig from his glass, laid it down and left the shop.

'Very nice man,' Guy said.

'A real gem. I'm very fond of my father.'

'It shows.'

'Does it?'

'Oh yes. That comes quite clearly across. And self-made, he was telling me. I admire that.'

Robyn glanced at the door when she thought another customer was about to come into the shop, but the person was only window-gazing.

'I'm glad my results came through before we went on holiday. It means I can enjoy the holiday without worrying,' Robyn said.

Guy nodded that he understood. 'When are you off?'

'This Sunday, for the Fair fortnight.' The Fair she was referring to was the Glasgow Fair when the vast majority of Glaswegians traditionally took their summer break.

'I'm told Glasgow becomes deserted during the Fair,' Guy said.

'It's just like a ghost town. Everyone has decamped en masse, usually for the Clyde resorts or Blackpool. Blackpool's a great favourite.'

'And where are you off to?'

'Someplace new for us this year. Sunny Cornwall.'

A small smile twisted Guy's lips upwards. 'Whereabouts in Cornwall?'

'Newquay.'

The smile twitched even further upwards. 'Very nice too.'

There was something in his tone made her say. 'You sound as if you know it?'

'Oh, I've been there,' he replied vaguely.

'And did you like it?'

'Very much so. Though Newquay itself can be a bit crowded. Are you renting or going into a hotel?'

'The Victoria Hotel. We're assured it's right on the front overlooking the sea.'

He had another sip of his champagne, trying to keep the

338

amusement he was feeling off his face. 'If I remember correctly, the Victoria is an old hotel, but with a very good reputation. I'm sure you won't be disappointed with it.'

'I can't wait. I'm just dying to get stretched out on a beach,' Robyn said.

'And how are you getting there? Is Mr Stuart driving or are you going by train?'

'By train, leaving early Sunday morning. Pa says he'll rent a car down there if he wants one.'

'Sensible idea.'

Hannah came back from the depths of the shop with her customer clutching not only one, but two books by Gibran.

When Guy and Robyn next spoke he changed the subject, away from that of her holiday.

'For you, from Mr Trecarron,' said Hannah handing Robyn a small gift-wrapped parcel. It was the afternoon of that same day.

'For me, from Guy!' Robyn exclaimed in delight, taking the parcel from her mother.

'I told him you were in the basement and that I'd give you a shout, but he said not to bother, and for me just to give you that when you came up.'

Robyn started to rip open the parcel which had a golden pre-tied bow at one end. She couldn't imagine what was inside.

'And since when did it become Guy?' Hannah queried with a smile.

'Since that day he gave me a lift home in his car. Remember, I told you he did? He was passing Laurel Bank as I was coming out and offered me a lift. Well, during the drive home he said I was to call him Guy and he'd call me Robyn.'

Hannah craned forward for a better look, curious as Robyn as to what the parcel contained.

'Hankies!' exclaimed Robyn when the parcel was open. 'Half a dozen of them, and pretty ones too.'

'Isn't that nice of him,' said Hannah. The hankies were small and white with lace borders. She thought them very tasteful.

'There's a note here,' said Robyn, having discovered a folded piece of paper tucked between the hankies.

CONGRATULATIONS AGAIN ON YOUR RESULTS. SEE YOU SOON – GUY.

Robyn's brow furrowed. She didn't understand that latter part. What did he mean by 'see you soon'?

'What a lovely gesture,' said Hannah.

'Yes,' Robyn agreed.

'If you wish me to, I'll embroider your initial on a corner of each?'

'Please, Mum.' Hannah did beautiful embroidery. They had several framed embroidered pictures hanging at home that were Hannah's work. One was of Edinburgh Castle, another Burns' Cottage, Ayr.

See you soon? Robyn wondered again. He must mean shortly after she returned from holiday.

She was quite wrong about that.

Robyn dumped her beach bag beside the table, and sat facing Hannah and Lal. They were in the lounge of the Victoria Hotel, a place of faded, yet still dignified, beauty. Hannah and Lal were drinking coffee.

'Care for a cup?' Hannah queried of Robyn, gesturing at the coffee pot.

Robyn shook her head. 'I think I'll have a cold glass of juice though.' She caught the eye of a waiter and beckoned him over.

'This is the life,' said Lal, stretching. The weather since their arrival in Newquay four days previously had been simply glorious, and the forecast was that it would continue.

Robyn placed her order with the waiter, asked her parents if they wanted anything further, which they didn't, and confirmed to the waiter that would be all.

Guy Trecarron entered the lounge, having been told by the receptionist that she'd just seen Robyn go in there. He glanced about, and spotted the Stuarts sitting on the far side.

'Hello, enjoying yourselves?' he smiled on reaching them.

Robyn gaped at him in astonishment, while Hannah and Lal both wore bemused expressions.

'What are *you* doing here!' Robyn exclaimed.

'Saying hello to you.'

'No, not that! What are you doing in Newquay?' And then

340

she recalled his note, See you soon. So that was what he had meant.

'This is a surprise Mr Trecarron,' said Lal, rising and extending a hand. 'Would you like to join us?'

Guy shook with Lal. 'I would, thank you.' He sat next to Robyn. 'Robyn told me you were coming here so I thought I'd drop by and say hello.'

'You're on holiday here too then?' Hannah queried.

'I am on holiday, true. But it's more than that for me, Mrs Stuart. You see I come from just outside Newquay, where my father still lives. So I am on holiday, but also paying a visit home.'

'Trecarron?' Lal mused. 'That is a Cornish name, isn't it?'

'A very old one, Mr Stuart. There have been Trecarrons in these parts time out of mind, certainly for as long as there are surviving written records.'

'Well, well, well,' murmured Hannah.

'Can we get you something, Mr Trecarron?' Lal asked.

'No, thank you. And please, call me Guy.'

'Right then, Guy,' Lal replied. 'And we're Lal and Hannah.'

'Lal?'

'Short for Lawrence.'

'I see!' Guy said, nodding.

Robyn could smell French tobacco again, though no after-shave this time. 'So you're here for the Fair as well,' she said.

'That's right. Mr Dalgleish always took his holidays at the Fair apparently, so the same fortnight was automatically allocated to me.'

'Mr Dalgleish was Guy's predecessor,' Hannah reminded Lal.

'What do you think of Newquay?' Guy asked Lal.

'Couldn't be nicer. Everyone, holidaymakers and locals, have all been extremely pleasant.'

'And the hotel?'

'First class.'

'Guy said we wouldn't be disappointed with it,' Robyn informed her parents.

'When did you come down?' Hannah queried.

'Monday night. I had some paperwork to catch up on Monday so I took the night sleeper. A change of trains at Par and I was home in time for a late breakfast.'

341

'Your mother would be pleased to see you,' Hannah said.

Guy's expression didn't change. 'My mother and father are divorced, Hannah. I haven't seen her since I was very young.'

'Oh, I am sorry!'

'I was brought up by my father and boarding school. My mother is only a distant memory.'

'How sad,' Hannah murmured, thinking she'd put her foot in it there.

'And what have you planned, for today?' Guy queried.

'Hannah and I are going on a bus sightseeing trip, leaving in . . .' Lal glanced at his wristwatch, 'twenty minutes.'

'I know the trips you're referring to. They're very good if you like that sort of thing.'

'Which I don't,' Robyn declared softly and emphatically.

'So what are you going to do, then?' Guy asked.

'Go down to the beach. I've got my things here,' she replied, indicating her beach bag. She was already wearing her costume underneath the pale blue dress she had on.

'Have you been using Great Western beach?' That was the beach directly below the hotel, and to which there was direct access from the hotel.

'Yes.'

'It'll be chock-a-block this time of year.' Great Western, because of its central position, was one of Newquay's most popular beaches.

'Like ants down there, particularly in the afternoon, for some reason. But on the other hand it is convenient, and means I can nip in and out of the hotel whenever I want to. Some of the other beaches are a bit of a trek, and Tolcarne is just as busy as Great Western.' Tolcarne was the beach adjoining Great Western.

'The reason Great Western and other beaches are busier in the afternoon is because the casual workers, of which there are a legion in Newquay during the summer, have time off then. However, I've just been thinking, I had intended going for a dip myself. Would you like to come with me? I can promise you there'll be no overcrowding on the beach I'm going to. In fact . . .' He laughed. 'I'll bet you a pound to a penny we'll be the only ones there.'

A deserted beach alone with Guy! What a delicious prospect Robyn thought.

'I'd jump at the chance if I was you,' Hannah said to her.

'You don't mind then?'

'No, why should we?'

'Is where you intend going far?' Lal asked Guy.

'Only along the coast a bit, and about three-quarters of a mile from where our house is. It's the beach our family and friends have always used, and an extremely safe one.'

'Robyn?' Hannah prompted.

'I'd love to go with you,' Robyn said to Guy.

'Right, that's settled then. And as your parents will be on their sightseeing trip for quite some while, perhaps I can give you lunch? I'll ring Pater and tell him you'll be joining us.'

'It all sounds . . . tremendous!' Robyn enthused.

'I'll just make that phone call, shan't be long.' declared Guy, rising. Quickly he strode from the lounge watched by a bright-eyed Robyn.

'Who would have thought our new Penguin rep came from here. Talk about a coincidence,' Hannah mused, shaking her head.

'Are you all right for money?' Lal asked Robyn, thinking she shouldn't really need any when with Guy but it was best to be on the safe side.

'I still have a fiver from what you last gave me.'

'That should be enough,' he nodded.

A few minutes later Guy was back. 'Pater says he'll delay lunch till half past two, which will give us a decent time at the beach, and an opportunity to work up a good appetite,' he said to Robyn.

She rose, went round and pecked Hannah on the cheek, then leaned across and did the same to Lal. 'Enjoy your trip. I'll see you this evening.'

'And you enjoy yourself too,' Hannah replied.

'Be careful, now,' Lal warned gently.

'Of course,' she answered her father, not quite sure what he was warning her to be careful about.

Outside the hotel she slipped on her sunglasses because the sun was blazing down. Everywhere were happy faces and tanned flesh, the wind wafting in off the sea, warm and balmy. It might have been the French Riviera.

'I'm over here,' said Guy, pointing to a small car park to one

343

side of the hotel. With the other hand he took Robyn's beach bag from her.

Robyn thought the car they stopped at simply gorgeous. It was a cream-coloured two-seater, looking something like a Jaguar but not a Jaguar, with the inside of its wheels painted bright crimson. It was one of the most elegant cars Robyn had ever seen.

'What is it?' she asked.

'An Allard P1 with a Buick/Rover V8 engine. It's been considerably modified from what it was originally.'

She moved from one side of the Allard round to its front. 'It's a veritable beast,' she declared.

Guy laughed. 'It is that! And smashing to drive.'

'A far cry from a Cortina, eh?'

'You can say that again.'

She stroked the shiny, cream bonnet with the vertical metal grill set into it. 'Is it yours?'

'I only wish it was,' he sighed. 'No, it belongs to Sorel. We're all having to use it at the moment, which is no hardship as far as I'm concerned, because Pater's ancient Morris is in the garage being repaired. He left it in a pub forecourt the other day only to come out and find someone had bashed him, then made off without letting on. A bad bash it was too, an entire front wing caved in.'

'That'll cost.'

'Yes, Pater was absolutely livid. According to Sorel, who was with him at the time, he went absolutely berserk when he discovered the bash.' Guy opened the driver's door, got in and opened the passenger one.

'Who's Sorel?' Robyn asked, sitting beside him.

'Pater's mistress.'

That statement shook Robyn. It wasn't that she was prudish, or unworldly, it was merely that she wasn't used to a matter like that being so casually announced.

'A long-term relationship?' she queried as Guy started up the Allard.

'About two years now. She's Canadian, from Toronto, and a lot younger than Pater.'

Robyn was intrigued. 'How much younger?'

'She's twenty-five, he fifty-three.'

Good God! Robyn thought. That sounded absolutely obscene. What was Guy's father, a dirty old man?

Guy went on. 'They met in London at an arty crafty Notting Hill Gate party, and hit it off there and then, despite the difference in their ages. Sorel came down here to live with him – or shack up with him as she persists in calling it – shortly afterwards.'

The Allard eased smoothly out of the car park, the engine a low hum that was a delight to listen to.

'Does Sorel have a job?' Robyn asked, fascinated by all this.

Guy barked out a laugh. 'Sorel, work! You must be joking. She's never had a job in her life. She recently took up photography, and witters on endlessly about selling pictures to magazines etc. But that's wishful thinking more than anything else. Her pictures are rotten, strictly amateur-night-out. Though for God's sake don't ever say that to her, she has a ferocious temper. As has Pater. When the pair of them get going at one another it's as if World War Three has broken out.'

Sorel sounded thoroughly spoilt, and not a nice person at all, Robyn thought. She doubted she'd take to her. 'Does your father keep Sorel, then?' she probed further.

'Not a bit of it. Daddy Wilks – that's their surname – is a stinking rich industrialist who gives her a yearly allowance, currently ten thou per annum. If she wants more than that, or something special like this Allard, she just bells him in Toronto and hey presto! the money appears.'

Rich, spoilt and probably a beauty into the bargain, Robyn told herself. She tried to imagine what Sorel looked like, and the image that popped into her mind was that of the gorgeous Eadie, the auburn-haired drama student, who'd been Guy's partner at the Citizens' Theatre.

'Have you met Mr Wilks?' she asked.

'He came and stayed with us last year, wanted to meet George and "check him out" as he put it. He came for a week, stayed a day and a half and then hightailed it for London and the Hilton, where he always takes a suite when in London. According to Sorel, Daddy Wilks thought George a great guy, if somewhat "screwy" – that's the precise word he used.'

'I presume George is Pater?'

'That's right. George Trecarron. Ever heard of him?'

345

Robyn shook her head. 'Should I have done?'

'He's a sculptor, fairly well known. More domestically though than abroad. He's not exactly a Henry Moore, but a damn fine sculptor all the same.'

'I'm looking forward to meeting him,' Robyn said. A sculptor! How exciting.

They came to a bend, and a hill beyond that. Robyn watched Guy expertly flick through the gears, perfectly at one with the Allard which might have been an extension of his physical and mental self. He was an excellent driver with a natural gift for it.

'I haven't thanked you yet for the hankies you left for me. It was very kind of you.'

He flashed her a broad smile, but didn't reply to that.

Robyn stared out over the sea which they were driving parallel to. It was an aquamarine colour, the sky above it cobalt-blue. Here and there puffballs of cloud punctuated the sky, puffballs all roughly the same shape but differing in size.

What a contrast to Glasgow, she thought. It couldn't have been more so. Closing her eyes, she sighed. This was sheer unadulterated bliss.

'Tired?'

'No. Just . . . very, very contented.'

He left the coast road, taking a short cut which also brought them in sight of the house. Robyn opened her eyes when he halted the car.

They were on a rise, the land to the right of them falling away. 'Hunters Moon where we live,' Guy said, pointing.

Robyn gazed at Hunters Moon, loving it instantly. It was extremely large with lots of windows, pillars and a great deal of ivy. 'It's straight out of Daphne Du Maurier,' she declared softly.

'That's been said before,' Guy smiled.

'"Last night I dreamt I went to Manderley again. It seemed to me I stood by the iron gate leading to the drive, and for a while I could not enter, for the way was barred to me."'

Realising she'd finished quoting, Guy took up where she'd left off. '"There was a padlock and chain upon the gate. I called in my dream to the lodge-keeper, and had no answer, and peering closer through the rusted spokes of the gate I saw that the lodge was uninhabited."'

'You know *Rebecca* too, then,' Robyn smiled.

'I should say! I must have read it a dozen times or more.'

'I first came across it in my early teens when I remember I had nightmares about Mrs Danvers.'

'Horrid woman,' Guy said, matching her smile.

'Have you read *My Cousin Rachel* and *Frenchman's Creek*?'

'And *Jamaica Inn*?'

Robyn laughed. 'How about . . . *The King's General*!' they both said in unison.

Robyn laughed again, and Guy with her.

'Do I take it then that representing books isn't just a job with you, but that you actually like books for themselves?'

'I don't just like them, I love them. In fact . . .' He trailed off, the laughter fading from his face.

'In fact, what?' she prompted.

He re-engaged the gears. 'That's another story, and one I'll tell you after we've had a swim.'

Robyn watched Hunters Moon till eventually they rounded a corner and it was lost to view.

From there it wasn't far to the sea again, Guy driving the car off the road and into a secluded, tree-surrounded area. There he parked.

'Come on,' he said, getting out with her beach bag.

He locked his door, then hers. After that he opened the boot from which he took a duffel bag containing his things and two rolled-up bamboo mats. That done, he relocked the boot.

They were suddenly on the edge of the cliff, causing Robyn to gasp in fright. Tentatively peering over she saw that the cliff-face was a sheer, terrifying drop to rocks and sand below.

'How do we get down there?' she queried.

'Follow me and all will be revealed.'

He led her some further yards along the cliff-top to where a natural path zig-zagged downwards. At points lengths of metal handrail had been sunk into the rock.

'Isn't there another way?' Robyn asked, not liking the look of this at all.

Guy shook his head. 'It's safe enough, I promise you. I've been up and down this path literally thousands of times without mishap. It appears far worse than it actually is.'

'You lead then, and I'll follow,' she said reluctantly.

Once she got going she found it wasn't really so bad after all, the trick was to keep your eyes on the path and what lay directly ahead.

Nonetheless, she couldn't help but sigh with relief when she stepped onto bright, golden sand. Guy had been right, they were the only ones in sight. Apart from them the beach as far as could be seen in either direction was deserted.

Guy spread out the two bamboo mats side by side, placing her beach bag beside one, his duffel bag beside the other.

Robyn gazed about her. The base of the cliff-face was dotted with small caves, or at least caves with small entranceways, while the cliff-face itself seemed even higher looking up it than it had looking down.

Guy rummaged in his duffel bag to pull out a pair of trunks. Sitting, he quickly removed his shirt, shoes and socks. 'I'll nip into the nearest cave and put these on,' he said, waving the trunks at her.

'Fine.'

As he walked away she began stripping off her dress which she neatly folded and laid alongside the beach bag. From that she took out suntan oil and her towel.

'Not in yet? What's keeping you?' Guy said on his return, chucking his trousers and underpants carelessly down.

Grasping her by the wrist he pulled her towards the latest wave to tumble and hiss up the shoreline.

'Wait a minute! Wait!' she protested, throwing her sunglasses back onto her mat, but he was having none of that. It was straight in for both of them.

She squealed when she splashed into the water, but only as a reflex not because the water was cold. Quite the opposite, it was Mediterranean warm.

When they were waist deep, Guy let go and dived underwater. Seconds later he bobbed up again with such force water fountained off him in all directions.

He had a lovely body she'd already noted, with a bottom that was even sexier in trunks than in trousers.

'You can swim, can't you?' he queried.

'Of course.'

'Then let's see you. Don't just stand there like a ding-dong!'

Ding-dong, was it! She launched herself into the water, then crawl-stroked away from him, her yellow hair, now dulled to almost brown, streaming out behind her.

She sensed him before she saw him. A strong pair of hands grabbed her by the waist and pulled her down. She struggled, to no avail, the hands continued pulling her till with a bump she sat on the sea bed. She glimpsed Guy's grinning face as he twisted, kicked out and shot past her.

She floundered to the surface having completely lost her composure. Greedily, she sucked in air.

Then the hands were back, this time one of them grasping her by the ankle while the other tickled the sole of the same foot.

She writhed, threshing the water with her flailing arms, at the same time laughing from being tickled. Using her other foot she stabbed repeatedly at where he must be until, with satisfaction, she connected hard with what transpired to be his chest.

Guy shot out of the water, mouth wide open, gasping for breath.

'Serves you right!' Robyn told him, and swam in the opposite direction.

Flipping over, she backstroked, watching Guy as she retreated from him. She headed out to sea a little way, then turned so that she was swimming parallel to the beach.

Guy went after her, knifing swiftly through the water.

'No more monkey business or I'm going home!' she cried out as he got close to her.

He trod water. 'You swim well for an emmet,' he acknowledged.

'What's an emmet?'

'A tourist. In Cornwall we call them emmets, in Devon they're grokels.'

'How patronising!' she jibed. 'Why shouldn't a so-called emmet swim well? There's lots of sea outside Cornwall, you know and plenty of swimming pools.'

'I meant it as a compliment.'

'I'll have you know I represented my school at swimming, and Laurel Bank has one of the best girls' teams in all Scotland.'

'If you're that good, how about a race, then?'

She wasn't about to do that, in case she lost. 'All right. To that rock then!' she replied, pointing to a jagged finger of rock protruding from the sea about two hundred and fifty yards further out.

'You're on.'

'One, two, three, go!' she yelled, and threw herself in the direction of the finger of rock.

Almost instantly she twisted round, and leisurely swam back to the beach while he, going flat-out, powered towards the proposed mark.

Touching bottom, Robyn stood up and waded ashore. When she was clear of the water she ran to where her towel was and picked it up. Gazing out to sea she smiled to see that Guy, still swimming flat-out, hadn't yet realised he was on his own.

She wiped her face, then dabbed her shoulders and bosom. She was squeezing out her hair when Guy finally reached the finger of rock. She laughed softly to herself as he glanced about him, looking for her.

'Coooeee!' she called out, waving.

Guy turned, to stare back at the beach.

'Ever been had?' she yelled, and sniggered. She sniggered again when Guy shook a fist at her.

Flopping onto her mat she groped in her beach bag for cigarettes and matches. When she'd lit up she put her sunglasses back on, then stretched out to soak up the sun.

'That was a rotten trick!' Guy reproached Robyn, on rejoining her.

'Serves you right for being patronising and half drowning me out there.'

'I didn't half drown you, I was only being playful.'

'Then, so was I.'

He dropped onto his mat to lie facing Robyn. 'Okay, even Stephen. Can we start again?'

'If you like.'

He reached out and for a wild, heart-thumping moment she thought he was going to caress her cheek. Instead he pulled the cigarette from her lips and placed it between his own.

'Do you always take without asking?' she queried.

'Depends what it is.'

A thought flashed through her mind, making her blush. 'You promised me a story,' she reminded him.

350

'I did?'

'When you were showing me Hunters Moon you said you loved books but that was another story which you'd tell me after we'd had a swim. Well, now we've had a swim.' She retrieved her cigarette.

'I'd put some of that suntan oil on, you don't want to burn,' he suggested.

'I will, when I'm completely dry. I'm not yet.'

'Suit yourself.' Rolling onto his stomach he stared out to sea. His brow furrowed, while his eyes took on a sad, introspective look.

'Well?' she prompted, after almost a minute's silence.

'Pater is very artistic, which he inherited from his mother, and I believed I was too. Though in my case the ambition wasn't to be a sculptor, but a writer. A writer of "Literature" with a capital "L".' Guy began, speaking slowly as if he was reliving the past in his mind, and commenting on what he was inwardly seeing there.

He went on. 'I too had the opportunity of going to university, but decided against that. My idea was to go out and actually live life, to give me the experience from which to draw for my writing. Pater was excellent; when I explained to him what I intended he gave me every encouragement, and wasn't at all disappointed in my not going to university. He said he understood, which I'm certain he did. And so I packed a case and left for London; the Big Smoke.'

'When was this?' Robyn queried softly.

'Three years ago when I was eighteen. For a fortnight I stayed with a group of Newquay girls I know who then had a flat in Coleherne Road, which isn't far from Earls Court. I slept on their couch while I scouted round for work and a place of my own. I became a barman at the Nell Gwynne pub in the Fulham Road, and also found myself a room which was disgusting, but cheap.'

Guy shook his head. 'I think disgusting is too nice a word for that room, it was worse than that. The ceiling was badly flaking due to damp, as were the walls, thanks to the same thing. There was green mould in one corner, and I swear to God various fungi in another. There was a threadbare carpet on top of linoleum, both of which could have been a hundred years old, and mice.

The entire house was infested with the little buggers who scurried hither and yon twenty-four hours a day.'

His face lit up in a sudden smile. 'At the time I thought that room absolutely marvellous, an ideal habitation for a budding writer. A real "garret" in which to suffer, and work.'

He laughed. 'And work I did. No one could have accused me of being slack. Poetry, short stories, books, they flew off my typewriter like falling snowflakes in a blizzard.'

He paused, and shook his head again, his eyes far away in time and distance.

'So what happened to them, the poetry, short stories and books?'

'They were all, without exception, rubbish. A load of old codswallop. It took me a long time to learn the truth about myself, but eventually I did. I just didn't have any writing talent, none whatever. In desperation at one point I even took a position writing copy for a third-rate advertising agency, and got the boot from that. I couldn't even pen a jingle that didn't jangle.'

'Perhaps you didn't give it long enough?' Robyn suggested quietly.

'No! It wasn't a case of developing my talent, because there wasn't any talent to develop. I could have continued writing for the rest of my life and still wouldn't have produced anything halfway decent, unless by accident. And so I decided to chuck it and try my hand at something else, which is where my job with Penguin comes in. You'll know *The Bookseller* I presume, the so-called organ of the book trade?'

'Of course, Mum has it delivered every week to the shop.'

He nodded. 'I picked up a copy in Paddington Station the day I was leaving London to return home, and there it was. "Sales Representative wanted for Penguin Books". I thought, why not? If I can't write books then why not represent a company that sells them; at least that would be something I'd enjoy.'

'So you applied, and got the job.'

'I wrote a letter of application as soon as I got to Hunters Moon and posted it that very evening. The reply came a week later asking me to present myself at Harmondsworth, which I did. I later learned there were nine applicants for the post, but despite my not having a degree or previous experience of any kind they chose me. There was a short training course at

Harmondsworth, after which it was straight up to Glasgow to take over from Dalgleish.'

'And are you enjoying the job?' Robyn queried.

'Very much so, even more than I anticipated I would.'

'I'm sure you're going to be very successful at it, Mum says you have a way with you that makes you a good and sympathetic salesman.'

'If that's so, it's because I'm selling the right product for me; books,' Guy answered.

Robyn buried what remained of her cigarette in the sand, and picked up her suntan oil. Opening the bottle she slopped some onto her legs, and began spreading and smoothing it in.

'Do you wish now that you'd gone to university?' Robyn asked.

'Part of me does, and part of me doesn't. However, there's no use regretting past mistakes that can't be undone. You just have to learn to live with them, and build on them.'

'How old did you say you were; twenty-one? You could still go.'

He scooped up a handful of sand, then let it dribble away through his fingers. 'I could, but have no intention of doing so. I've been given an opportunity with Penguin which I shall maximise to the fullest.'

'You mean you're ambitious?'

'I've only been with Penguin, and in the world of selling books, for a few short months, but during that time I have developed aspirations, yes.'

'To become what?' she probed.

He laughed. 'I don't know yet. Successful, get to the top I suppose. Whatever that may be.'

She was having trouble getting oil onto the centre of her shoulder blades, and just below there.

'Here, let me,' he said, coming to his knees, and taking the bottle from her. She shivered when his hand made contact with her flesh.

'I'd like to read something of yours, sometime,' she stated, a husk having come into her voice.

'I told you, it's all rubbish.'

'I'd still like to read something.'

'Well, you can't, I burnt the lot.'

'You didn't!' she exclaimed.

'I damn well did. I loaded every last page I'd written into a metal dustbin, poured a pint of white spirit over it, and tossed in a match. When there were only smouldering ashes left I peed over them, then went out and got stinking drunk.'

Robyn laughed. 'You actually peed over the ashes?'

'And most satisfying that was too. Vulgar and ridiculous perhaps, but most satisfying.'

'Not even a teensy poem left tucked away somewhere?'

'Not even a teensy poem,' he confirmed. 'At least not that I know of.'

She stiffened slightly, and closed her eyes as his hand ran down to the small of her back. Her lips thinned, and parted when he drew a finger up the length of her spine.

'There you are. Finished,' he said, returning the bottle to her.

'What about you, would you like some?' She tingled inside at the prospect of rubbing oil onto his back.

'I put some on earlier in anticipation. That should do me.'

Pity, she thought, disappointed.

'Have you been out on a Malibu board yet?' he queried.

'Is that one of those things the surfers ride?'

'That's right. If you haven't I could let you use mine one day.'

'Sounds fun,' she said.

'It can be, if you don't take it too seriously, as many of the surfers do. The élite among them view surfing as akin to a religion.'

Guy talked at length about boards and surfing, after which they had another swim, this one without the previous skylarking. When they waded ashore again it was time to leave for Hunters Moon, and lunch.

'Just wipe yourself off with your towel and we'll get changed back at the house,' Guy said.

'Good idea,' Robyn nodded considering that much more preferable to changing in a horrid old cave.

After towelling themselves they gathered their things together and returned back up the path to the cliff-top. At the Allard, Guy draped his towel over the driving seat, and Robyn followed suit, draping hers over the passenger one. When the boot was loaded Guy got in beside Robyn, and they were off.

Robyn found herself suddenly nervous at the prospect of

meeting George Trecarron and his mistress, Sorel Wilks. She forced a smile onto her face as she listened to Guy telling her a little of the history of the surrounding countryside, and pointing out a flower farm along the way.

It was only a short drive to Hunters Moon, a matter of minutes, and then they were swinging round in the carriage driveway to park in front of the main door, an elaborate oaken affair.

'Hungry?' Guy asked, pulling up the handbrake.

'Starving.'

'So am I. Let's go round to the rear and say hello before we change. That's where Pater and Sorel will be.'

Guy removed his duffel bag and Robyn's beach bag from the boot, carrying her bag for her as they made their way round the side of the house.

There were trees everywhere, including a massive yew that seemed to stand guard over the house. There was a broad sweep of manicured lawn. With an orchard beyond that. They found George and Sorel there, he presiding over a brick-built barbecue.

Robyn's eyes went to Sorel first, to discover the Canadian woman wasn't at all the beauty she'd imagined. Sorel was short, with a bulky body that had only the hint of a waist to it. The heavy legs were unshaven and bare, her broad feet – with red painted toenails – in flip-flops. The face was pleasant enough, but wore a scowl, the eyes large and calculating, her hair mousy, hanging in a shoulder-length straggle.

George Trecarron was a different kettle of fish entirely, being a magnificent specimen of manhood. His head was large and leonine, his white hair a shaggy mane. He had the same black eyes as Guy, and the same bushy, curved eyebrows. He was shorter than Guy, and stockier.

'Pater, I'd like you to meet Robyn Stuart,' Guy said.

George wiped his hands on the black and white striped apron he was wearing, then extended a meaty paw. 'How do you do, Robyn.'

'Pleased to meet you, Mr Trecarron.'

'George, please! Do you want me to feel geriatric?'

She smiled at his pretended indignation. 'George, then.'

'That's better. And this is Sorel.'

'So you're the schoolkid Guy was telling us about,' Sorel said in a strong Canadian accent.

Robyn flushed. Schoolkid indeed, bitch! 'I've left school now, actually,' she replied.

Sorel's gaze flicked over Robyn's figure in a way that made Robyn wince. She'd been right in thinking she wouldn't like Sorel; she didn't.

'Chicken, chops and sausages coming up shortly,' declared George, gesturing at the barbecue.

'Pater is the best barbecue-er in Cornwall. Or at least, so he claims to be,' Guy said to Robyn.

'I claim to be, because I am,' George stated, reaching for a glass of white wine. He downed half the glass, and sighed. 'Can I get you two a drink?' he asked Robyn and Guy.

'We have to change first,' Guy replied. 'Then, I don't know about Robyn, but I certainly will.'

'We have some Pepsi,' Sorel smiled.

'White wine would be lovely,' Robyn smiled back.

'Come on, I'll show you where to change,' Guy said to Robyn.

She followed him to the back of the house, and an entrance there. That led to a covered-in area, which in turn led to a hall.

'You can use my bedroom and I'll use one of the other rooms,' Guy said, taking her upstairs.

She wasn't sure what she'd expected the inside of the house to be; grand probably to match its exterior. Well it certainly wasn't that.

There were a great many pictures on the walls, and strange objects everywhere. They passed some ancient farming implements, at least that's what Robyn guessed them to be, propped against a wall, and why on earth was there a large terracotta dish on the floor, filled with water with a yellow plastic duck floating on it?

'Here we are,' announced Guy, opening a stripped-pine door, then handing her her beach bag which she'd packed her dress into before leaving the beach.

'I'll come back for you,' he said as she entered the room.

'Fine.'

He closed the door behind him, and she heard him walk away.

His bedroom! Eagerly she gazed about her. The single bed was covered with a fairly ancient green quilt, old fashioned pre-war blankets below that. The pillowcases were brick-coloured, as were the sheets.

There was a stripped-pine fireplace which had a tiled hearth, with photographs on the mantelpiece. These were all of Guy when younger she discovered, peering at them.

How old was he in this one? she wondered, picking up a brass frame. Nine? Ten? Certainly not much older. What a cheeky grin he was wearing, and what an endearing-looking little boy. She replaced the photo with the others.

The lampshade dangling in the centre of the room was a huge white paper globe, filthy on top, with Chinese characters printed on it. She wondered what the characters said.

She smiled to see a bookcase, spilling over with hardbacks and paperbacks. A quick inspection revealed his taste to be more classical than popular. Homer, Balzac, Gogol, Sartre, Dostoyevsky, Delderfield, D.H. Lawrence . . . *Lady Chatterley's Lover*! and a well-read and thumbed copy too, she noted leafing through it.

She was slotting Lady C. back from where she'd taken it when she caught a whiff of French tobacco. He must have been smoking in the room earlier, she thought.

On the shelf above the wash basin that stood opposite the bed was a bottle of aftershave. Opening the bottle she sniffed the contents, the smell that assailed her nostrils one she'd come to associate closely with Guy.

Crossing to the bed she laid her beach bag on it, then took out her underclothes and dress.

She had just finished combing her hair when Guy returned to escort her down to lunch.

Hannah stepped from the shower, picked up the towel she'd placed in readiness, and began briskly drying herself. She could hear Lal moving about next door, their hotel bedroom being en suite.

When she was completely dry she began examining her remaining breast, something she did regularly once a week.

The breath caught in her throat when she thought she'd found a tiny lump on the underside of her breast, only for her to laugh when on looking she discovered the lump to be in fact a pimple.

She gently stroked the scar tissue where her right breast had been; even after all these years she was still profoundly bitter and angry that it had been removed when it needn't have.

Then she thought of the hysterectomy she'd had after Robyn's birth. What a body blow that had been to Lal who'd desperately wanted the son and heir which the hysterectomy had denied him. Dear lovely Lal, for what might have been the millionth time she told herself how lucky she was to have a man like him. He'd put up with a lot, never wavering in his love for her, always the perfect partner. The door from the bedroom opened and there he stood, smiling.

'Finished your shower?' The business of his not seeing her naked, or touching her above the waist had been done away with years ago.

'Yes.'

'I thought you might care for a drink?'

She shook her head. 'Maybe later.'

'I'll pour myself one then.'

He was turning away again when she said, 'Lal?'

He turned back to her.

'Come here.'

He went to her, and she wrapped her arms round him. 'Thank you,' she whispered in his ear.

'For what?'

'Being you. Being my husband.'

He stroked her bottom, which made her smile. 'Do you remember what I was like after my hysterectomy? My God, I was forever at you.'

'Remember? How could I ever forget? Morning, noon and night, you were insatiable.'

'I used to do all sorts of brazen, whorish things. Like this.' She pulled down his flies, and slipped a hand inside.

'I hope you're not going to start something you don't intend finishing?' he teased.

She kissed him on the neck, then nibbled the same spot. When she looked into his face there were tears in her eyes.

'I love you, Lal.'

'And I love you too.'

Removing her hand from his flies – that had only been a joke – she curled it round his neck, and kissed him.

She said far more with that kiss than she could ever have articulated, and he understood.

*

'So what did you think of Sorel?' Guy asked. They were in the Allard, he driving her back to the hotel.

Robyn glanced sideways at Guy, but didn't answer.

'She was jealous of you. It was purely and simply that.'

'I must say she could have been more . . . pleasant.'

'Being pleasant isn't her style, not to other women anyway. She's strictly male-orientated and sees all other females as opposition, particularly young, pretty ones.'

Robyn blushed.

'You are you know.'

'What, young?'

'No, pretty, very much so.'

Her blush deepened.

'Do you mind me saying that?'

'Of course not.'

'It's been said to you before, surely?'

She muttered something inaudible.

'Eh?'

'I said, yes,' she whispered.

'Who by? That young chap you were at the theatre with? Your neighbour.'

'Don't pry, it's rude.'

'That means he has.'

'No, it doesn't!' she snapped in reply.

'So who has then?'

'I said it's rude to pry. I don't pry into your affairs.'

'But you'd like to, wouldn't you?'

She turned to look at him. 'How much of that wine did you have?'

'Only a few glasses. Why, am I embarrassing you?'

'Not at all,' she lied.

'Shall I tell you something?'

'What?'

'Pater fancied you rotten. He said you were as delectable a piece of crumpet as he'd seen in a long day.'

This time her face went positively scarlet. She waited till that, and her confusion had died down a little, before saying, 'Can I ask you a question?'

'Fire away!'

'What does he see in Sorel? He's a very handsome older man while's she's . . . well hardly Marilyn Monroe.'

359

He couldn't resist it. 'Now who's prying?'

'I knew you'd say that. I just knew you would!'

Guy laughed. 'The answer to your question is that I don't know. Though he certainly sees something in her, otherwise he wouldn't have kept her around for so long.'

They drove for a short distance in silence, then Robyn said, 'It's a gorgeous house. Does much land go with it?'

'There are only a few acres left in our possession, but at one time the Trecarrons were among the largest landowners in Cornwall. We owned thousands of acres.'

'What happened?'

'Bad blood came into the family, according to Pater. Anyway, the Trecarron men who'd been used to making money started losing it. We owned two tin mines that ran out of tin – that no one's fault – then business losses began to occur; the results of bad judgement. Then there were gambling debts, and latterly death duties. Bit by bit, section by section, the land was sold off to keep the family in the style to which it had long been accustomed, till now there's only Hunters Moon left, plus those few acres I mentioned.'

'I hope your family never lose Hunters Moon. That would be tragic!' Robyn exclaimed.

'It would that. If only Pater was a stockbroker or some such instead of a sculptor. He does make money at it of course, but nothing like the amount of money he would make if he was in the City, say.'

'I can't imagine George in the City. He's just not the type!' Robyn laughed.

Guy pulled a face.' I suppose not. Far too eccentric and bizarre for that lot. Besides, the only talent he has with money is to spend the stuff, not make it.'

Robyn laughed again. 'What about you? Shouldn't you have tried the City instead of attempting to be a latter day D.H. Lawrence?'

'D.H. Lawrence!' he spluttered. 'Who said I wanted to be another D.H. Lawrence?'

'I came across Lady Chatterley in your bookcase, well-read and -thumbed it was, too. I thought maybe he was your hero, the writer you'd tried to fashion yourself after?'

'I do believe you're taking the mickey, Robyn!' he smiled.

'It is a lovely book, if a bit . . .' She shrugged. 'You know?'

'Dirty?'

'Explicit is how I would have put it.'

'I certainly wish I had written Lady C. . . . it's made an absolute mint since we published it four years ago. Sold by the boxload, they told me at Harmondsworth. But to get back to the idea of my working in the City . . . I could no more do that than George could. I'd die of boredom and mental suffocation.'

'Then to ensure that Hunters Moon is safeguarded in your lifetime you'll just have to make lots of money in the book trade,' she said.

'You mean become another Allen Lane?' Allen Lane was the creator of Penguin Books, and its majority shareholder.

'Why not? Anything's possible if you want it, and strive for it hard enough.'

Another Allen Lane! he mused, thinking of the nine-ton cutter he'd been told the great man had bought on Penguin's first birthday, after a fantastically successful debut year. (A cutter Lane had fitted out with items being sold from the royal yacht, *Britannia*.) Now there was a thought! A rather fanciful one mind you, but a thought nonetheless.

'Come in!' Hannah called out when there was a tap on their bedroom door.

'It's only me,' Robyn announced on entering. 'Just to let you know I'm back.'

'How was your swim and lunch?' Lal inquired.

'Terrific! I had a fab time. How about you two?'

'A very enjoyable trip: we both enjoyed ourselves,' Hannah replied from the vanity table where she was applying the finishing touches to her make-up.

Lal glanced at his watch, then at Robyn. 'You'd better hurry up and get changed if you're not going to be late for dinner.'

'I won't be late. It'll only take me a couple of minutes to do the necessary.'

There was that in Robyn's tone made Hannah study her daughter in the mirror before her, and in which Robyn was reflected. 'Are you seeing Guy again?'

'Yes, he's asked me out tomorrow night for a drink. That's okay, isn't it?'

'Of course. I take it you got on well together, then?'

'Extremely. He's good fun. And I believe he thinks I'm the same.'

'What about the father – what's he like?' Lal probed.

'I'll tell you everything over dinner. Byeee!' And with that Robyn vanished from the bedroom, hurrying to her own across the corridor.

Lal glanced at Hannah who was smiling into her mirror. 'The start of a holiday romance?'

'Could be.'

Lal frowned. 'Guy is considerably older than her. How old do . . .'

'Lal!' Hannah interjected. 'Stop being over-protective. She's a big girl now, going to the university in the autumn. Give her a bit of rope.'

'I suppose you're right,' Lal admitted with a sigh. 'I only wish she'd sound so enthusiastic about James McEwen.'

Hannah laid down the brush she'd been using. 'I think you'd better accept the fact that that idea of yours is a dead duck. She's just not interested in James romantically.'

'Pity. But I haven't given up all hope yet!'

Over dinner Robyn gave her parents an account of her day's events, nor did she try to fudge George's relationship with Sorel, or the age difference between them, but didn't mention that Sorel had been less than warm towards her. She spelled out the relationship in case Guy mentioned it at some point, or Hannah and Lal were invited to Hunters Moon in which instance they were bound to demand afterwards why she hadn't explained the situation to them.

'Sounds quite a set-up,' Lal commented drily.

Hannah, uncertain whether she approved or not of Robyn moving in such company, pressed Robyn for further details about Hunters Moon, which had captured her imagination.

Robyn sipped her half pint of lager, and gazed about her. She liked The Sailors' Arms; it had a great deal of charm and atmosphere, and wished there were similar pubs in Glasgow. Glasgow pubs weren't exactly the most salubrious in the world, although there were one or two almost reasonable ones round about the university.

'A hazelnut colour,' Guy said beside her.

She turned her attention back to him. 'I beg your pardon.'

'I've just been looking at your eyes. They're a hazelnut colour.'

She wasn't quite sure what to reply to that, so didn't.

'It's odd that I've never noticed their colour before.'

She smiled, and had another sip of lager.

'See that chap over there, him with the cutaway jeans and faded pink shirt,' Guy said in a whisper to her, surreptitiously pointing up at the bar.

Robyn's gaze latched onto the chap in question. 'Uh–huh!'

'He's an American, and a world-renowned surfer. I've watched him in action, and he's absolutely amazing. And see that fellow just along from him, wearing beige trousers and a sports shirt, standing beside the adoring brunette.'

Robyn nodded.

'He's the Aussie champion, over here for the summer. He and the Yank are great rivals.'

The Australian was ginormous, one of the largest men Robyn had ever seen. She judged the circumference of each of his biceps to be bigger than her waist.

'Either of those two could have his choice of women among the legion who follow the surfing scene,' Guy went on.

'Really?'

'Oh yes. The top dogs are run after and chased the same way pop stars are.'

'Why, hello Guy.'

The speaker was an extremely tanned, attractive girl, roughly the same age as Guy. She was with a taller, dark-haired female companion.

'Hello Simone, hello Mary,' replied Guy, rising to his feet.

'We heard on the grapevine you were home,' the dark-haired Mary smiled.

'For a fortnight's holiday, then it's back to Glasgow, where I'm based nowadays. Had you heard about that?'

'Yes, we had,' Mary answered.

Simone was staring curiously at Robyn.

'This is Robyn who's also down on holiday from Glasgow,' Guy introduced.' Then, to Robyn. 'Simone and Mary are local girls I've known all my life. It was Simone's flat in Coleherne Road that I stayed at when I first went to London.'

The three girls shook hands.

'Are you still living in London?' Robyn asked Simone.

'No, I didn't like it there. In fact, I hated it. I couldn't wait to get back to Newquay.'

'You're looking marvellous,' Mary said to Guy. 'Things are obviously going well with you.'

'Very much so. I adore my new job. I miss Newquay of course, but . . .' He shrugged.

'We must get together for a good old chat before you return to the frozen north,' Mary suggested to Guy.

'Yes, we must.'

'In the meantime,' said Simone, 'I'm having a party tomorrow night to which everybody who is anybody in surfing, and who's in the locality, will be coming. Consider yourself invited.' When Guy hesitated she added, 'By that I mean the pair of you, you and your girlfriend.'

A thrill ran through Robyn to hear herself described as that.

'Robyn?' Guy queried.

'I'd love to go.'

'We'll be there, then,' he told Simone.

'It's good to see you again, Guy,' Simone said to him, and pecked him on the cheek. After which Mary did the same.

'Nice girls,' Robyn commented when Simone and Mary had moved on.

'Both mad keen on the surfing scene, Simone in particular. I believe she's currently going out with some bloke from Hawaii she's dotty about. We'll probably meet him tomorrow night.'

Guy's girlfriend, Robyn repeated mentally to herself. How she liked the sound of that!

Later, on leaving the pub, he took her by the hand. The moment his hand clasped hers she knew their relationship had taken on a new dimension.

And that he was aware of it also.

The lively exhuberance of the Beachboys gave way to an oldie: Johnny Mathis singing 'Smoke Gets in Your Eyes', real smoochie music if ever there was.

It was getting late, Robyn thought, nestled in Guy's arms as they shuffled round the sitting room; she'd have to leave soon. It had been a wonderful party, Simone and her friends couldn't have made her feel more welcome and part of the crowd.

Early on she'd met Simone's chap, Delbert, whom she'd thought super, ever so nice, but not a patch on her Guy. None of the fellows present were that. At least, not in her opinion anyway.

'Robyn?' he whispered.

She looked at him, his face a shadowy outline in the dimly lit room.

The face moved closer, and then his lips were on hers as he kissed her for the first time.

The kiss went on and on, as though their mouths were glued together, till at last, with the utmost reluctance, they pulled them apart.

She'd been kissed many times in the past, but never like that she told herself. It wasn't the mechanics of the kiss that were different, but who was doing it with her. That was what made it different, and elevated the kiss above all the kisses she'd had from chaps before.

'Again,' she whispered. 'Kiss me again.'

Amazingly this second kiss was even better than the first. When it was finally over she laid her head against his shoulder, closed her eyes, and sighed with happiness.

She felt she was overflowing with happiness. Positively oozing with it.

Sorel was sitting cross-legged on the floor, studying a batch of photographs she'd developed the previous day. Her eyes were slitted, their pupils huge, both effects of the dope she'd been smoking. She was, as the expression went, high as a kite.

George too was high, having also been smoking. It was he who'd brought home the Lebanese Gold which he'd purchased from a contact in Newquay. He often smoked dope, or pot as he preferred to call it, as did Sorel.

Guy and Robyn were sitting on a couch together, he with his arm round her. Both were drinking rum and coke. They'd been offered dope, but had declined in favour of alcohol.

The Beatles were singing on the radio. The Beatles were Robyn's favourite group, followed closely by the Stones. It was her great ambition to see either in concert.

Sorel suddenly, petulantly, threw the photographs from her which ended up in a jumble on the carpet.

'Know what I'd like to do right now?'

'What?' George asked her.

'Go down to the beach and watch the sunset. How does that idea grab you?'

George swung his legs onto the floor; he'd had them over an arm of his chair, and rasped a hand over his unshaven chin. 'Yes, why not? Guy?'

Guy glanced at Robyn, and raised an eyebrow.

Go down to the beach and watch the sunset? Yes, as George had put it, why not? Anyway, she was tired of just sitting about which they'd been doing for the past couple of hours. That would be a nice change.

'Okay,' she said to Guy.

Five minutes later they were on their way – squashed into George's ancient Morris, now home from the garage. They couldn't have all got into the Allard which was only a two-seater.

George parked more or less where Guy had when he'd brought Robyn here previously, and they all piled out. From there they went to the zig-zag path, and down they started, with George in front.

Robyn wasn't quite so worried about descending the path this time, but it still worried her nonetheless. With relief she reached the beach behind Sorel, Guy bringing up the rear.

Guy was carrying a large canvas bag containing torches, two blankets and several other hastily assembled items. He now shook out the blankets and laid them side by side on the sand.

George gazed up at the sky. 'About twenty minutes to sunset,' he gauged.

'And a cracker it's going to be too, I'd say,' Guy smiled at Robyn.

Sorel squatted on one of the blankets and proceeded to roll herself another joint. While she was doing this Guy asked Robyn to help him gather up whatever driftwood there was about so they could make a fire.

There was plenty of driftwood and other bits and pieces to be found, which they stacked into a large pile. Guy then set about making the fire which was soon ablaze, thanks to the firelighters he'd had the foresight to put into the bag.

'I'd have brought marshmallows if we'd had some at home, but unfortunately we didn't,' he said to Robyn.

'You toast them on sticks, don't you? I've never had toasted marshmallows, but have read about them in books.'

'You don't know what you've missed; they just melt in your mouth and taste absolutely delicious. Quite out of this world!'

It was the same as it had been the last time they'd been here, Robyn thought. Not another soul in sight in either direction. They might have been castaways on a desert isle.

The temperature was cooler on the beach than it had been at Hunters Moon, but still lovely and warm. There was no wind; the sea a flat calm.

Robyn sat on the free blanket, and Guy joined her there. George had meanwhile taken off his shoes and socks and was paddling in ankle-deep water.

Sorel had a drag on her joint, drawing the smoke deep into her lungs. 'Aaaahhh!' she crooned, exhaling.

'Come on, do yourself a favour,' she said to Robyn, offering her the joint.

Robyn shook her head.

'Come on kid, don't be such a goddamn party pooper!'

'I said no, thank you,' Robyn replied firmly. She wasn't going to let the Canadian bully her into anything. She'd decided earlier she wasn't going to try marijuana, and wouldn't change her mind.

'Guy?' Sorel queried, her tone a tempting teasing one.

He'd refrained so far because Robyn hadn't wanted to indulge, but his resistance was crumbling. 'Do you mind?' he asked Robyn.

She was disappointed by that, but didn't let it show. 'No, you go ahead.'

Guy accepted the joint from Sorel, stared at it for a moment, then placed it between his lips. He repeated what Sorel had done, drawing the smoke deep into his lungs.

'Are you sure, honey? Don't you want to join the grown-ups?' Sorel smiled sweetly at Robyn.

Robyn smiled back, wishing she could think of some crushing retort, but couldn't.

'I only do that once in a while,' Guy explained to Robyn after returning the joint to Sorel.

'How do you feel?' Robyn asked, curious.

'It's a sort of "floaty" sensation.'

'Like having a stiff drink?'

'Better.'

'Like having a stiff something,' Sorel muttered, and laughed at her own joke.

Robyn ignored the crudity, pretending she just hadn't heard.

Guy reclined on one arm, and gazed at the sky which had gone a deep red colour where the sun had begun to sink over the horizon.

George came out of the water, removed the old Panama hat he was wearing, and ran a hand through his hair. The bottoms of his trousers were soaked because he hadn't bothered to roll them up. Turning his back on the others he stared out over the water at the sinking sun.

The sun was half gone, the sky on the horizon even redder than it had been, when Sorel screwed her roach out in the sand beside her. Standing, she started to strip.

Robyn stared curiously at Sorel, wondering how far the Canadian was going to go. (She knew Sorel didn't have a swimsuit on underneath her clothes.) The answer, to Robyn's utter amazement, was all the way.

When Sorel was stark naked she lifted her arms above her head, threw them out in supplication, then dropped her head backwards so that her straggle of hair hung free from her shoulders.

An Inca priestess, praying to the Inca god, or gods, that was what Sorel made Robyn think of. There was a wild alienness about the Canadian that Robyn had never seen before, and which frightened her a little.

Sorel rounded on Robyn and Guy, her eyes that had been shut snapping open.

She was better undressed then dressed, Robyn noted. She didn't appear quite so bulky, while her waist definitely had more form to it. Her breasts were extremely large, and conical, each with a huge dark nipple at its tip, the nipple stalks at least two inches long. From her crotch to her belly button and round onto her buttocks was a veritable forest, a spread of pubic hair that was far more like a man's than a woman's.

Guy stared at Sorel, never having seen her naked before. He

368

found her body both attractive and horribly repulsive at the same time.

'I'm going for a swim. Why don't you come in too?' Sorel said in a strangely ethereal voice. Her eyes glittered as she spoke.

Without waiting for a reply Sorel whirled and dashed for the water. She gave an animal-type cry on reaching it, then she'd thrown herself forwards, her buttocks seeming to twinkle and shimmer before they, and she, vanished from sight.

George, who'd been watching this from about a dozen feet away, gave a loud booming laugh and began taking his clothes off.

'Don't be shy, boy!' he called out to Guy, tossing his shirt aside.

Guy looked at Robyn. 'What do you say? It's a harmless bit of fun.'

'Do you want to?' Her heart was racing, her stomach fluttering at the thought of taking her clothes off in front of Guy and George. She glanced up at the cliff-top, but that was already lost in gloom. Anybody up there, if they could see anything, would only see very indistinct figures. And the sun would be gone within minutes.

George was nude now, and hurrying to the spot where Sorel had gone in. She had reappeared further out, floating on her back.

'You don't have to if you don't want to,' Guy said.

'But you do?'

'It'll be fun. But if you don't want to then I won't either.'

Should she, shouldn't she? It would be fun and, as Guy had said, it was harmless enough.

Nor was anyone trying to bully her into it as Sorel had with the marijuana. The decision was entirely up to her, without any attempted pressure being brought to bear.

'Let's!' she said, jumping to her feet and kicking off her shoes.

She shivered when she dropped her bra, not because she was cold but because she was now bare above the waist, and Guy only inches away.

She removed her knickers a fraction after Guy stepped out of his underpants.

'Last one in's a rotten egg!' she shouted, haring for the cover of water.

George was bouncing up and down, windmilling his arms. Laughing he fell backwards, causing a fountain to go shooting up into the air, then cascade down again.

When she was up to the middle of her ribcage Robyn pinched her nose with two fingers, and lifted her feet. The warm water closed over her as she temporarily sank.

What an odd sensation it was to be totally naked in the sea, she thought. And a pleasant one, oh yes, very much so. She felt tremendously daring, and wanton.

When she surfaced there was no sign of Guy. And then suddenly he was beside her, popping out of the water also.

He grabbed at her, but she managed to evade him. She struck away, heading seawards, he catching up with her after several powerful strokes to grasp her by the leg, just below the buttock.

She twisted and turned, but couldn't free herself. Then his arms were round her, pulling her close.

They both went under, and were still under when his lips found hers. Continuing to kiss they rolled over and over, he using his feet to keep them below the surface.

Eventually they had to come up for air, she breaking away from him when they did. She was now in a playful mood, thoroughly enjoying this romp.

The sun had almost gone, the red sky beginning to dim to darkness. Somewhere Sorel squealed with laughter, and Robyn wondered what she and George were up to. She was trying to see when Guy pounced on her again.

His hand found her breast, closing over it to hold it. She could have made him let go, but didn't.

'Oh!' she said softly when his seeking mouth closed over her nipple. A smile creased her mouth as his tongue flicked and licked.

They stayed in the water till the sun had disappeared, and their fire had begun to die down. The first thing Guy did when they returned to the blankets and fire was to build the fire up again.

Robyn squeezed out her hair, then threw herself down on the nearest blanket. From there she blatantly stared at Guy's backside as he worked on the fire. His backside was a thing of beauty, she thought. She found herself desperately wanting to touch it, caress it, kiss it.

She blushed furiously, imagining herself doing the latter. Such a thought had never entered her head before. But then she'd never known a Guy Trecarron, far less been naked with a Guy Trecarron, before.

He dusted off his hands and came to lie beside her. 'What I didn't bring were towels. I'm sorry about that,' he smiled.

'It doesn't matter. We'll soon dry off.'

She glanced about. 'Where are George and Sorel?' Neither were in evidence.

'Oh, around somewhere. Forget about them.'

She cocked an ear, but there was no splashing or other tell-tale noises from the sea, which meant George and Sorel must have come ashore before them. But if so, why not to the blankets and fire?

Guy saw her puzzled expression. 'Don't worry about it. They've probably gone off to one of the caves.'

'But why should they do that?'

'Why do you think?' Guy replied softly.

Her puzzled expression cleared as the penny dropped. 'You mean they . . . that they've gone off to . . .?'

'Knowing Pater and Sorel I'd say that was highly likely. They've gone off to be alone for a while.'

Guy fumbled in his clothes to produce an opened packet of Gitanes and his Dunhill. 'Fag?'

'Please.'

He lit two, then gently inserted one between her lips, making an implied sexual connotation out of the act, that wasn't lost on her. Their eyes locked together.

A hand came slowly over to rest on her thigh. When she didn't protest the hand began to stroke her there.

After a few moments she reached across to stroke him in the same place.

'Robyn?' he husked.

'Yes?'

His mouth was suddenly on her neck, his hot tongue pressed against her flesh. She'd turned to a mushy soup inside, soup rapidly coming to the boil.

He flicked his cigarette away, and she did the same. Now his hands were everywhere, touching, feeling, and she was doing likewise.

'I don't want George and Sorel to see,' she croaked, snatching up the other blanket and pulling it over them so that they were now both covered.

And soon, the mystery she'd wondered about for so many years was solved.

Later, the four of them used the torches that had been brought along to illuminate their way back up the zig-zag path, and to where the ancient Morris awaited their return on the cliff-top.

'No regrets?' Guy asked Robyn, slightly anxiously, when he kissed her goodnight.

'None at all. And you?'

'If you've none, then I haven't.'

He held her tightly in his arms where she could have stayed forever, if that had been possible. Guy Trecarron, no matter what the future might hold, was a name she would never forget.

As she'd never forget that night.

'Mrs Stuart, telephone,' the waiter said.

Hannah glanced up from her breakfast in surprise. 'For me?'

'Yes, madam.'

She looked at Lal, then at Robyn, then at the waiter again. Surely it was Guy ringing Robyn? 'It must be for my daughter, Miss Stuart.'

The waiter shook his head, 'No madam, I took the call myself, as the receptionist was tied up elsewhere. The lady on the end definitely said *Mrs* Stuart.'

'Who can be ringing me here?' Hannah queried of Lal.

'The best way to find out is to go and speak to whoever it is,' Lal replied drily.

'I suppose so.'

Hannah laid her napkin on the table, and rose.

'If you'll follow me, please,' the waiter said, and led Hannah away.

Robyn glanced at her watch. Guy would be coming for her in half an hour; they were going to play tennis and have coffee together after that. Lal and Hannah were taking them out to lunch, but nothing was planned for the afternoon. She smiled to herself, it would probably be Hunters Moon and his bed there. They'd managed to make love every day since that first time on the beach, each bout of lovemaking better than the previous. She was head over heels in love with Guy Trecarron and, although he hadn't said so yet, she was certain he was with her.

'Another scorcher by the looks of it,' Lal declared, glancing out of a nearby window, where the morning sunlight was streaming down. They'd been very fortunate indeed with their weather.

'Yes,' Robyn agreed.

Lal and Robyn chatted for a few minutes about this and that, then Hannah was back in the dining room heading in their direction. As soon as Lal saw how pale she was, he knew something was wrong.

Hannah sat, her lips thin and tight. 'That was Ma. I mentioned the name of the hotel we were coming to and she had the Glasgow operator look up its number, and ring through.'

'What's happened?' Lal asked quietly.

'Uncle Gavin's dying. According to Ma I'll have to go right away if I want to say goodbye to him.'

Lal's expression became grim. He liked Gavin, a fine man. 'Of course we all must go. He's the closest thing you've had to a father. You've told me that many a time.'

'Oh Pa!' Robyn exclaimed. 'Surely I can stay on till our fortnight's up?' The last thing she wanted to do was leave Newquay, and Guy.

It was Hannah who answered. 'No,' she stated firmly. 'You'll come home with us.'

'Surely you can trust me to be a few measly days on my own?'

'It isn't a matter of trust Robyn, but of respect. If he's the nearest thing I've had to a father, then I'm the nearest thing he's had to a daughter, and you a granddaughter. I know how much he'll appreciate us going to him now, particularly in the circumstances.'

'But . . .'

'I'm not asking you, Robyn,' Hannah interjected, her tone steely. 'I'm telling you.'

Robyn bowed her head in defeat, knowing of old that when her mother adopted this attitude there was no swaying her.

'I'll set matters in motion. We'll catch the first feasible train,' said Lal, rising.

'And I'll begin packing. You can help, Robyn,' Hannah said, also rising.

373

A miserable Robyn followed her parents from the dining room.

'I'll ring you tomorrow evening,' Guy promised Robyn, squeezing her hand. He'd arrived at the hotel fifty minutes previously, to be informed of the Stuarts' sudden departure. He'd said he'd stay on and accompany them to the station, which was where they now were. Lal and Hannah had already climbed aboard the local train which would take them to their connection at Par; Robyn had remained on the platform with him.

'Oh Guy, I wish I didn't have to go, but Mum insists,' Robyn replied.

'It's not the end of the world,' he laughed softly. 'I'll be back myself at the weekend and be right over to see you as soon as I can. Now cheer up, for goodness sake!'

His own manly smell mingled with aftershave and French tobacco was strong in her nostrils. She inhaled it deeply into her lungs, the way Sorel, George and Guy inhaled dope.

'I've no cigarettes,' she said suddenly. 'Can I have yours?' That was a lie, she had a full packet in her pocket. What she wanted were his French ones.

'Of course.' He gave her a packet of Gitanes that had only a few missing from it.

'Thank you,' she whispered.

Guy glanced down the platform. 'You'd better get inside. The guard's already slamming the open doors.'

'Kiss me, then.'

He knew Lal was watching them through a window, which disconcerted him slightly. Subsequently his kiss wasn't as passionate as either he or Robyn would have liked, but he couldn't really bring himself to give her the full works with her father staring on.

When the kiss was over he helped her into the carriage, and closed the door behind her. She immediately pulled the window down, and leaned out.

'Don't forget to ring tomorrow evening,' she said.

'I won't.'

Putting two fingers to her lips she blew him a kiss.

'Safe journey!' he smiled. 'And you, Lal and you, Hannah!'

Lal and Hannah waved to him as the train started to move off slowly.

Robyn waited a few seconds, then blew him a final kiss. She then closed the window again, and dropped into her seat with a sigh.

'You seem to be getting very close to that young man,' Lal commented quietly.

'Do you object?'

He shook his head. 'Not in the least.'

Clutching the packet of Gitanes to her, Robyn gazed out of the windows at the far side of the carriage, seeing Guy instead of the scenery that was now flashing past.

Lal looked at Hannah, and raised an eyebrow.

Hannah smiled back at him, thinking to herself that there was no harm in a holiday romance. On the contrary, at Robyn's age it was a very healthy thing to have. And Guy was such a nice, clean-cut chap.

She wished she'd met the father though. It had been mooted on several occasions but somehow had never quite come about.

'Stop crying, woman. I've had a good run for my money. I've no complaints,' Gavin said, his voice weak, and weary. The doctor had wanted him to go into hospital, but he'd insisted on staying in his own house and bed. That was where he wanted to die, not in some impersonal hospital amongst strangers.

Cathy dabbed away a tear.

'I'm the last, you know,' he said.

She frowned. 'Last of what?'

'I've been thinking, remembering. All the lads that were there the night of Bobby's stag night; I'm the last.'

That was true enough, Cathy thought. Bill Coltraine had gone in the mid-Fifties, Jack Smart a couple of years back.

'I can visualise that night, and them, as though it was only the day before yesterday,' Gavin went on. 'Your Bobby, Gordon Manson, Colin Baker, Sandy House, Kenny Tamm, Tim Murchison, Jack Smart, Bill Coltraine and Greg Wylie, all dead and gone. We all fought on the Western Front, and only Jack, Bill and myself came home. The rest stayed behind, as poppies.'

The tears were streaming down Cathy's face now.

Gavin gave a sudden low laugh. 'And the two whores that stag night of Bobby's! I thought Bobby was going to murder me for bringing them over. But he didn't let you down, Cathy. Oh no, not Bobby! I knew he wouldn't. The whole thing was just a joke like, you understand?'

'I understand,' Cathy answered.

'It was a grand night that. One of the best I've ever had. If I'd ever married that was the sort of stag night I'd have wished for.'

His sightless eyes turned to stare at Cathy. 'I wish I could see you, Cathy. I wish God would grant me that before I die.'

Lady, Gavin's dog lying on the floor at the bottom of the bed, whimpered.

'She knows,' Gavin said. 'Dogs always do. Will you look after her when I'm gone? I'd be obliged if you would.'

'Of course I will, Gavin.'

Lady whimpered again, and placed a foreleg over her head.

'I hope there are dogs in Heaven. After all these years I'd be lost without a dog,' Gavin said, his voice now so weak it was almost a whimper.

'Rest a bit Gavin. Try and sleep.'

His bloodless lips drew back wolfishly. 'I'll soon have all the rest and sleep I want.'

Cathy was about to reply to that when there was a knock on the outside door. When she answered the knock she found it to be Hannah, Lal and Robyn.

Cathy kissed her daughter. 'You're in time. Come away through,' she said.

Guy lay in the darkness, staring at the ceiling. It was that same night, and he was thinking of Robyn. What a sweet, adorable girl she'd turned out to be. He couldn't wait to be with her again.

He smiled, recalling the day before when she'd been in this bed with him, and what they'd done together. More on the floor than the bed really; the bed being a single had its drawbacks where that was concerned.

He heard a noise elsewhere in the house. That would be Sorel, it certainly wouldn't be Pater. George and Sorel had gone out earlier on to have drinks with their friends, Nigel and Moira Tangye who owned the Glendorgal Hotel. Nigel was the brother of the well-known writer Derek Tangye who lived with his wife Jeannie, further down the coast at Minack.

The damage had been done at another hotel George had insisted on stopping at after they'd left the Glendorgal. When they'd finally arrived back at Hunters Moon, George had been so legless Sorel had had to ask his assistance to get him upstairs. That had been over an hour ago, since when he'd come to bed himself.

He was about to turn over and go to sleep when his bedroom door swung silently open.

'Are you still awake?' Sorel asked in a quiet voice.

Guy came onto an elbow. 'Just. Why, what's up?'

She closed the door behind her, and crossed to his bed to stare down at him. 'Thinking of your little friend who's gone home to Glasgow?'

'I was, actually.'

'I thought you might be. Pretty piece of ass, isn't she?'

'Very.' Indignation filled him. Indignation and hostility towards Sorel. How dare she call Robyn a 'piece of ass'! George had referred to her as a delectable piece of crumpet which was one thing, piece of ass was quite another.

Sorel, eyes glinting in the pale moonlight that dimly lit up the bedroom, sat on the edge of Guy's bed. Her breathing, he now noticed, was deeper and more laboured than normal.

'How's Pater?' he asked pointedly.

'Pissed out of his skull. The stupid son of a bitch was mixing brandies and vodkas. He'll have one goddamn awful head, come morning.' Reaching across she placed a hand on Guy's bare chest, he being naked beneath the bedclothes.

'You shouldn't be here, Sorel,' he admonished.

She found a nipple, put her fingertip on it, and rotated the fingertip.

'I don't like that!'

'But I do.'

He sighed. 'Sorel, what do you want?'

'The same thing you've been giving Robyn,' she purred in reply.

'You're being ridiculous! You're my father's woman!'

She chuckled throatily. 'I don't see that's a problem. Anyway, what George doesn't know about won't harm him.'

She removed the fingertip from Guy's nipple, and slipped out of the cream silk negligée she was wearing, the nightdress underneath matching the negligée. Taking his hand she brought it to her breast.

'Sorel, I . . .'

'I've decided to have you, Guy. And I *always* get what I set my heart on.'

He gave her a thin, contemptuous smile. 'Then this is the exception to the rule.' And with that he pulled his hand away.

A quick flick, and the nightdress went the way of the negligée, whispering to the floor.

'Jealousy, Guy. I suppose you could call it that. Every time you brought that Robyn in here it made me pea-green with envy. Now it's my turn.'

He shook his head. 'You really are amazingly arrogant, Sorel! What makes you think I would even consider going with you, after Robyn? If you want it straight, physically you aren't a patch on her.'

'I want it straight all right, and I'll get it too,' she jibed in reply and began sensuously moving her hips.

Guy ignored both the jibe, and movements. 'Even if I did fancy you, which I don't, I wouldn't betray Robyn, and I most certainly would never betray Pater.'

She laughed. 'Wouldn't you?'

'No, I wouldn't! Now please stop this absurd farce and leave.'

'Robyn may be prettier than me,' Sorel said slowly. 'But I think you'll find me far more exciting, and satisfying, in the sack.' And with that, continuing to move her hips, she started stroking him through the bedclothes.

He wriggled away, but her seeking hand soon found him again.

'Sorel, there is absolutely nothing you can either do or say will change my mind. I am not going to make love to you, and that's that.'

'It wasn't making love I had in mind, but that good old four letter Anglo-Saxon word with *-ing* tacked on the end.'

He knocked her hand aside. 'Get out, before I lose my temper.'

'Tell Pater on me, will you?' she mocked, her insistent hand finding him yet again. Despite his protestation she could feel she was getting a response.

'Only if you force me to.'

'He might find it amusing.'

'He might. There again, he might just chuck you out on your

backside. Trying to seduce his son could be too much, even for him.'

Using her free hand Sorel suddenly ripped the bedclothes down so that Guy lay exposed. 'When I want, I get,' she hissed.

'Not this time,' he said, scrabbling for the bedclothes to pull them back up again.

'I'll give you the Allard.'

That stunned him into immobility. 'What?'

'I said, I'll give you the Allard if you will. That and the promise I'll never let on to your father.'

He swallowed hard. The Allard! What a prize that would be.

She laughed at his expression, certain now that her judgement of him had been correct.

'But how . . . how could I explain your giving me the Allard?'

'You work, don't you? We can say I became tired of the Allard, wanted another car and made a deal with you whereby you bought it from me. What could be more normal than that?'

Guy licked his lips, his resolution crumbling within him. Pater would never know, Robyn would never know, so where was the harm? And he'd have the Allard as his own.

'You bitch!' he breathed.

She knew then she'd won, that her ace card had taken the trick, as she'd imagined it would. 'Thirty pieces of silver, Guy. That's your weakness. For you there will always be thirty pieces of silver, in the shape of an Allard or whatever.'

'You won't renege?'

'I won't renege. And I have my own reasons for that.' She didn't elaborate what these reasons were.

He caught her by the waist, to draw her down onto the bed, but she resisted that, pushing him flat instead.

'No, Guy,' she smiled, climbing astride him. 'You may now have the car, but for this it's me that's in the driving seat.'

After she'd gone, leaving him utterly exhausted – a limp washed-out rag – Guy reflected that he now understood what Pater saw in Sorel. Sexually she was sheer dynamite, a voracious shark to Robyn's goldfish.

Next morning, a smirking Sorel handed him the keys to the Allard for keeps.

'Cathy?'

Cathy came abruptly awake with the realisation she must have dozed off. She was sitting by Gavin's bedside in a comfy chair she'd placed there.

'Cathy?'

'I'm here Gavin, what is it?'

'Your hand. Give me your hand.'

His thin one clasped hers tightly when she'd done as he'd requested.

'Would you like some water? Or a nice cup of tea perhaps?'

A joyous smile that wasn't of this world lit up his face. The sightless eyes swung round to stare at her. 'Aaahhh!' he sighed softly.

The pressure on her hand increased. 'Kiss me, Cathy.'

His forehead was cold when she kissed it, as was his cheek.

'Even though you've aged so much, I would have recognised you anywhere,' he said.

He was havering, she thought. Imagining he could see her as he'd earlier wished he could.

His sightless eyes roved over her face, then down over the upper part of her body.

'Black suits you,' he muttered. 'Gives you great dignity.' He was still smiling joyously as his eyelids closed in death.

Cathy sat transfixed in wonder. For she *was* wearing black, a colour she only wore occasionally.

Had his last wish been granted? For the rest of her own days she liked to believe that it had.

When they buried Gavin her wreath contained ten poppies, one for each of the men who'd attended her Bobby's stag night. She thought Gavin would have approved of that.

380

Chapter 10

'I love Edinburgh, particularly during festival time,' Robyn enthused to Guy. He had temporarily stopped the Allard so they could look out over Scotland's capital which lay spread below them, a sparkling jewel of a city that positively oozed history and romance.

'Have you heard what they say about Edinburgh women?' Guy asked her, tongue in cheek.

'No, what's that?'

'All fur coat and no knickers.'

Robyn laughed, thinking that very funny. She would have bet a pound to a penny it was a Glaswegian had made that up. The two cities, and populaces, were deadly, if good-humoured, rivals.

'Ever been to Rose Street?'

Robyn shook her head,

'We'll go there before the play for a drink and hopefully a bite to eat.'

They'd come to Edinburgh to see *The Sport of my Mad Mother* by Ann Jellicoe, being performed by members of the Royal Scottish Academy of Music and Dramatic Art. Included in the cast were Iain, who stayed in the same flat as Guy, and Stuart, a pal of Iain's, whom both Guy and Robyn had often met. It was at Iain and Stuart's insistence that they had motored through to see the production.

When they reached Edinburgh they found it, as could only be expected during festival time, busy as a beehive. Guy had trouble parking, every kerb a jam-packed line of bumper to bumper vehicles, but eventually he was lucky when a car pulled out directly ahead of him and he was able to nip into the space vacated.

When he'd locked the Allard Guy took Robyn by the hand, and they headed for the fabled Rose Street, which he'd been to several times before, during the course of business – for his Penguin territory included Edinburgh as well as Glasgow.

There were placards and posters everywhere, advertising plays, musical recitals, late night cabarets, performances of dance, painting exhibitions, and of course, the Military Tattoo.

'What's the theatre we're going to?' Robyn inquired.

'It's not a theatre but a hall called The Tron. And don't worry, Iain gave me explicit directions on how to get there.'

There were sights aplenty to be witnessed en route to Rose Street. People in outlandish clothes, various street performers including a troupe of jugglers and a fire-eater dressed in motley, wide-eyed Americans wearing stetsons, a group of Japanese ladies in colourful kimonos, gay men walking hand in hand just as Robyn and Guy were doing, and so on and so forth.

Rose Street was full of pubs, yet another every few yards it seemed – the reason for its reputation – all well filled and doing a roaring trade. The Bag O' Nails appealed to Robyn and Guy, so in they plunged and battled their way to the bar.

'Any idea what this play's about?' Robyn asked Guy as she tucked into haggis, neeps and mash, which she was eating standing up as all the tables were occupied. Guy had settled for the Lanchashire hot-pot.

'Not really. Iain was a bit vague about that when I questioned him about it. He did say it was set in London however, and avante garde. Apparently his part is that of a bongo-drum player.'

'A bongo-drum player!' Robyn exclaimed, almost choking on her haggis.

'It seems there's a band on stage throughout which he plays in, besides acting one of the lesser characters, or as his own character in the piece.'

'Sounds most confusing.'

'It does that,' Guy agreed.

The door to the pub burst open. 'Don't miss Strindberg's *The Father*!' a long-haired chap yelled at the top of his voice, grinned at everyone, then departed the way he'd come.

'Must catch that, Caroline,' an upper-crust English voice said.

'Oh yes, rather!' an equally pukka female English voice replied.

'Rather!' repeated Robyn quietly to Guy, taking the mickey.

'I don't speak like that!'

'Thank God. Though you are very public school.'

'And you're very Laurel Bank, so there!' And with that rejoiner he poked out his tongue at her.

He was gorgeous, she thought. Absolutely gorgeous. It was only a few short months since Newquay, but already she couldn't imagine life without Guy Trecarron. How lacking she'd been before she'd met him, and how fulfilled she now was.

'Penny for them?' he smiled.

'I love you.'

His fork stopped halfway to his mouth, her eyes boring into his. 'And I love you too,' he whispered back, something he'd first admitted to her shortly after his return from Newquay.

Reaching across, she touched him lightly on the arm, and even in that completely non-sexual contact she felt she was at one with him. Their bodies and minds joined, two halves making up a whole.

'We'd better hurry,' he said, glancing at his watch. 'We don't want to be late.'

They didn't speak again, neither feeling the need to do so, till they were outside the pub, heading for The Tron.

'I thought it was absolutely marvellous,' Robyn said to Maurice, one of the drama students who'd had a leading role in the play. 'You were terrific.'

Maurice positively glowed at this praise. 'Thank you very much. We're all enjoying it, aren't we Iain?'

Iain, sipping a pint of heavy, nodded.

'Pity it was such a small audience though,' Guy said.

Stuart shrugged. 'That's the trouble with the festival, if you're part of the Fringe as we are, audiences can be sparse due to the sheer volume of what's on offer.'

They were in Bennets Bar, not far from The Tron, where they'd all repaired to – Robyn, Guy and everyone connected with the play – after curtain-down. The place was chock-a-block, bedlam at the bar where the bar staff were working flat-out.

Robyn glanced about her. For some reason the inside of Bennets reminded her of a Toulouse-Lautrec painting; it had that sort of ambience about it.

'Would you like to go to the Festival Club?' Maurice asked Guy. 'A few of us are going on there after here.'

Robyn brought her attention onto Guy, having overheard what Maurice had said.

Guy turned to her. 'I'm sure the Festival Club would be fun, but what I'd rather do, if you're in agreement, is go and visit a client of mine, Jim Haines who owns The Paperback Bookshop. He's having a poetry reading on the premises later on.'

Robyn had heard of The Paperback Bookshop and Jim Haines, its eccentric – that's how he'd been described to her – American owner. He was making quite a name for himself on the Scottish literary scene.

'The Paperback Bookshop, please,' she smiled to Guy, thinking this was too good an opportunity for her to miss.

'Sorry, but thanks for the invitation anyway,' Guy replied to Maurice who was 'giving the eye' to a very attractive blond-haired girl who'd caught his attention.

'What's the poetry?' Stuart asked Guy. He was a devotee of Yevtushenko, the Russian poet.

'I've no idea, I'm afraid. All I know is that poetry's to be read.'

'I fancy that,' Stuart said to Iain, who replied he did too.

An amused Robyn watched Maurice, like some bird of prey homing in on its victim, move in for the kill.

> Garlic and sapphires in the mud
> Clot the bedded axle-tree.
> The trilling wire in the blood
> Sings below inveterate scars
> Appeasing long forgotten wars . . .

The poem was *Burnt Norton* by T.S. Eliot, the reader an earnest young academic sort with thick pebble glasses.

Robyn's gaze drifted round the room. The Paperback Bookshop was packed tight as sardines in a can, all types, all ages, hanging on the reader's every word. She knew, having witnessed it happen, that others had been turned away at the door because no more could be squeezed inside. At half a crown a head The Paperback Bookshop's taking for the week would be very nicely boosted indeed.

The speaker continued:

At the still point of the turning world. Neither flesh nor
    fleshless;
Neither from nor towards; at the still point, there the dance
    is,
But neither arrest nor movement . . .

'I was surprised that a poetry reading was so popular,' Robyn
commented to Guy as they sped home to Glasgow.

'So was I, I must admit. But you heard what Jim said, he'd
had the same response every night he's had a reading.'

Guy gave a sudden grin. 'And the good news is that he's given
me an increased order for our current publications of poetry, and
those on our backlist which he says are selling, if not exactly like
hotcakes, then in far larger numbers than they ever have previously. *Nine*! copies of *Metaphysical Poets*. Tony Godwin at Harmondsworth should be most impressed when he hears of that.'

'And who's Tony Godwin?' Robyn queried.

'The biggest name in Penguin, next to Allen Lane himself,
and an extremely clever man who's bringing about a great many
innovations within the company at present.'

Robyn thought again of The Paperback Bookshop, which
she'd been extremely taken with. It had a marvellously contemporary feel about it, one of being 'right up to the minute'. As for
decoration and display, both had been excellent, the latter just
screaming for you to reach out and pick up a book.

Yes, she'd been extremely taken with Mr Jim Haines and The
Paperback Bookshop.

And the poetry reading.

'So my idea was, do you think a similar thing would work at the
Blackbird?' Robyn said to Hannah. Cathy was also present, over
visiting, while Lal was sitting reading his newspaper. Or at least
had been reading his newspaper; he'd switched his attention
from it to Robyn to listen to what she'd been saying.

Hannah shook her head in disagreement. 'I shouldn't imagine
so. I can understand poetry readings being an attraction at the
festival, which is a unique venue and of limited time span, don't
forget, but in Glasgow? That's another kettle of fish entirely.'

'Gran?' Robyn prompted.

'It's hard to say, lass. Edinburgh is a cultured city whereas

Glasgow, bless its socks, is basically working class with working-class likes and dislikes . . .'

'That doesn't stop the Citizens' Theatre making a good go of it,' Robyn interrupted, recalling her visit there to see *Armstrong's Last Goodnight*.

'That's true enough, according to the newspapers and from what one hears,' Cathy conceded. 'But I'm sure if you went into the figures you'd find that the number of people who go to the Citizens', as opposed to the variety theatres, is only a minute proportion of the city's population.'

'Maybe so Gran, but even a small percentage of that minute proportion would be sufficient to fill the Blackbird regularly once a week. And don't forget the student potential; I can't believe we wouldn't draw considerably from that.'

'What would be the advantages to the Blackbird? Are there any?' Lal asked quietly from his chair.

'Yes, Pa. First of all there's the half crown charge at the door which would bump up the week's takings, providing the readings were well attended. And secondly, as Jim Haines through in Edinburgh is discovering, the readings are stimulating poetry sales. I know that for a fact, from the order he's given Guy.'

Lal's lips curled upwards in a smile. 'So this proposal isn't merely altruistic, a furthering of the arts so to speak? But also has a sound business motivation behind it.'

She returned his smile, knowing precisely why he'd given her it. 'Like father like daughter, I suppose. This is a way to make money, and create a lot of enjoyment for all concerned.'

'But mainly a way to make money?' he teased.

'You brought me up to believe there's nothing wrong with that, as long as the customer gets fair value for cash and goes away happy.'

'I still think it's a risky proposition,' Cathy muttered.

'What's at risk?' Robyn queried. 'There's no outlay, other than a bit of electricity and a few hours of Mum's time. If it's a flop it's a flop; no big deal. But it's a chance worth taking, in my opinion.'

'Well I'm not interested,' Hannah stated firmly. 'Poetry readings aren't me at all. I wouldn't dream of going to one, far less running one'

'I thought you liked poetry!' Robyn exclaimed.

'I do, some. But for me it's a personal thing, something I would read by myself, for myself. I don't view it as a shared pleasure at all. Besides, who wants to work nights at my age! It's not as if we *need* extra money. We don't.'

'I was thinking of the shop as you well know,' Robyn retorted. 'A successful run of poetry readings wouldn't do it any harm whatever; it would only do it good.'

'So what's wrong with the shop?' Hannah demanded, taking offence.

'Nothing at all, Mum. But, if you want the truth, you have been running it for a long while and perhaps become a little staid in your ways?'

'Staid, is it!'

Cathy laughed. 'You'd better watch yourself,' she warned Robyn.

'Times move on and you have to move with them. You should go through to Edinburgh and have a dekko at The Paperback Bookshop; it's a real eye-opener, I can tell you.'

'Listen to her, telling me what it's all about and her still wet behind the ears,' Hannah complained to Lal.

'Nonetheless,' mused Lal. 'She does have a point.' He wasn't thinking of the bookshop now, but his own business. How long since he'd looked at that, as a whole and on an individual unit basis, with a critical eye? Quite some time.

'I'm not telling you what anything's about,' Robyn said softly to Hannah.

'Where's your sense of humour, girl!' Cathy chided her daughter.

'Maybe so,' Hannah conceded, softening. 'Perhaps I am being somewhat touchy.' Going to Robyn she put her arms round Robyn, and held her close.

'Poetry never went well in the library. It was always a dead loss,' Cathy said to them, it being now eight years since her retirement. She paused, then added, 'With the exception of Rabbie Burns that is. We had two books of his poems that did pretty well.'

Lal was about to declaim. 'Wee sleekit, cow'rin, tim'rous beastie, O, what a panic's in thy breastie!' when he suddenly thought the better of it, on account of Hannah.

'Why don't *you* organise these poetry readings, then?' Lal suggested to Robyn.

'Me!'

'If your mum doesn't object to you using the bookshop to hold them in, that is?'

'I wouldn't object,' Hannah replied.

'I hadn't thought of me doing it,' Robyn said slowly.

'But it's obvious, isn't it?' Lal went on. 'And if it does take off you can keep the profits which will, in turn, help *me*.'

Robyn frowned. She didn't follow that. 'How so?'

'I give you an allowance, don't I?'

She nodded.

'If the poetry readings are a success then what you make will be your spending money, and will save me doling out to you every week.'

Robyn laughed. 'Trust you to think of that!'

His eyes twinkled. 'Good experience for you too. If it does work, you'll have more in your pocket than I was giving you, and if it doesn't we'll go back to our previous arrangement.'

'You can't lose,' Cathy smiled at Robyn.

She couldn't either, Robyn thought.

'But!' said Lal, pointing a finger at Robyn. 'You don't attempt this until you've had at least one full term at university. I want you properly settled in there before you take on any further commitments.'

'I agree with that,' Hannah nodded.

'All right, I'll do it,' Robyn told them, making a decision. 'And I also agree with my having a full term to settle in first. That's good advice. Besides which, by the end of the term I'll know lots of people reading English as I'll be, many of whom I'm sure I'll be able to interest in coming along. And there will be other students I'll have met whom . . .'

Lal roared with laughter. It might have been himself speaking.

Hannah opened her medicine cabinet and began searching for some codeine. She had a blinding headache which had just suddenly come on, and codeine was the only thing that ever helped her headaches.

'Blast!' she muttered when she realised there wasn't any. Lal, out at an all male bakers' 'do' must have used the last ones and forgotten to either buy a fresh supply or tell her one was needed.

A glance at her wristwatch informed her it was ten past eight at night; the chemist shops shut at six.

She closed the medicine cabinet again and gently massaged her temples, trying to think where she could get some codeine. The McEwens might be able to help, yes she would . . . And then she wondered if Robyn might not have a couple? Only Robyn was out with Guy and wouldn't be home for at least several hours yet. She'd try Robyn's medicine cabinet she decided.

She groaned on entering Robyn's room. What a tip! Honestly, that daughter of hers was so untidy. There were clothes strewn everywhere, including a pile of dirty things stacked up beside the bed. No wonder Mrs McLaughlan their cleaner was forever complaining about it. Hannah realised then it was a considerable time since she'd been in Robyn's bedroom, which could do with a bit of an airing she thought, sniffing.

The bedroom was en suite, the bathroom a present to his daughter from Lal – he'd had a large cupboard turned into a bathroom/toilet – which was where she now went, straight to the medicine cabinet above the pale green sink.

'Ah!' she exclaimed with relief in finding an almost full bottle of what she was after. She quickly popped two tablets into her mouth, and washed them down with a glass of water.

She was replacing the tumbler in its plastic holder when she noticed Robyn's opened make-up case. The make-up case was something Robyn usually carried round with her, only tonight she must have forgotten it and left it behind. Hannah remembered then that Robyn had been in a dash when she'd left the house.

Now what was that? Hannah wondered, spying a section of foil-wrapped card protruding from a slit pocket inside the case. Being nosy she went over to the case to find out.

Mon . . .Tues . . .Wed . . .With a shock Hannah realised that the card of pills she was holding was The Pill. And as a number were missing she could only conclude that Robyn had taken them.

Her Robyn, her baby, taking contraceptives! That could only mean that Robyn was sleeping with Guy.

Hannah sucked in a deep breath, then slowly exhaled. It was the Sixties after all, quite different to her day. Permissiveness was all the rage, you saw and read about it everywhere. But when it applied specifically to a member of your own family, your daughter, it really struck home.

Mind you, she and Lal had slept together before marriage, but there had been a war on at the time, and their circumstances had been unusual. And another thing, they'd been in love. Was Robyn in love with Guy Trecarron?

Now that she thought about it, the answer was probably yes, though at seventeen was it a love that was going to endure, or something that was transient? The latter surely. Why she'd been . . . how old? She had to cudgel her memory. Twenty-six, that was it, twenty-six years old when she'd gone to bed with Lal for the first time. Twenty-six and . . . Good God! twenty-four when she'd lost her virginity to Geoffrey Robb. It was years since she'd thought of Geoffrey, and to think how close she'd come to marrying him.

She'd been twenty-four; Robyn seventeen. Quite a difference in ages, but the Sixties were so different to the Forties. Everything was so much faster now, everyone in such a hurry. And Robyn was a child of her time, just as she'd been of hers.

Should she tell Lal about this? No, she decided, he'd go through the roof and insist on confronting Robyn, which she didn't think would be a good thing.

Robyn might be only seventeen, but she was mature, and had a sensible head on her shoulders. If Robyn had decided to sleep with Guy then that was her decision, and one she wouldn't interfere with.

It seemed only yesterday that Robyn had been in nappies and cutting teeth, Hannah thought sadly as she replaced the card from where she'd taken it, only slipping it right into the slit pocket so that there was no protruding, giveaway, section of foil.

When she returned downstairs to make herself a cup of coffee it surprised her to discover her hands were shaking. Then again, maybe it didn't.

Within a short while the codeine had worked its usual magic and her headache was gone.

Later, when Robyn arrived in from her date with Guy, she saw her daughter in an entirely new light. Up until her discovery in Robyn's bathroom it had been a woman/girl relationship between them: now it was woman/woman.

*

Robyn came up to Guy who was taking money at the door, and glanced at her watch. 'Five minutes till we start,' she said. It was February 1965, the first Friday of the month and the first poetry reading to be held at The Blackbird Bookshop.

'We're doing all right,' Guy replied, glancing at the rows of chairs that had been set up, two thirds of which were occupied.

'A lot of faces from the uni,' Robyn said. That pleased her, and so did the fact that one of them belonged to her favourite lecturer, Mr Arnott. He was there with his wife.

Another couple arrived, paid their half crowns, and went inside. And then a single female arrived, looking as though she'd been hurrying.

To Robyn's amazement Mr Singh who owned the Indian restaurant along the street turned up. 'Good evening, good evening,' he said to Robyn and Guy, folding his hands together in front of him and giving them each a bow.

'Good evening, Mr Singh. I didn't know you liked poetry?'

'Is that because I'm an Indian, run a restaurant, or both?' he queried.

'I don't know. You've just never struck me as the poetry sort, I suppose.'

Mr Singh wagged a finger at Robyn. 'That shows you how wrong you can be about people. I adore poetry. I even write poetry. Not very clever poetry! But I write it nonetheless.' He produced a half crown which he dropped into Guy's tin. 'Now where do I sit? Am I shown to a seat as in my restaurant, or do I find my own way as in most rude British establishments?'

Robyn laughed. 'Everyone else has been finding their own way Mr Singh, but in your case I'll personally show you to a seat. How's that?'

He gave her a beaming smile that displayed dazzling white teeth. 'Pretty damn good I think.'

They started on the dot at nine pm, having decided that was a better time for their situation rather than the late night start there had been at The Paperback Bookshop; the latter was undoubtedly better for the festival.

Robyn made a speech of welcome, saying she hoped this would be the first of many poetry readings held at The Blackbird Bookshop, and if they enjoyed themselves she hoped they'd all come back, and meanwhile tell their friends. She also announced that the shop would remain open for a while after the reading was over, and that books could be purchased by anyone wishing to do so. She pointed out a specially made-up bin of books containing poems that were going to be read that night.

Guy was the first reader. Thanks to his public school education he was quite used to speaking in front of others, and had confided to Robyn it was something he got a considerable buzz from.

Determined to push Penguin, he'd chosen as his first piece *Vampire* by the Yorkshireman Ted Hughes, the volume he was reading from *The New Poets*, selected and introduced by A. Alvarez. He began, his voice rich, deep and resonant, and lovely to listen to:

> You hosts are almost glad he gate-crashed: see,
> How his eyes brighten on the whisky, how his wit
> Tumbles the company like a lightning stroke-
> You marvel where he gets his energy from . . .

While Guy was reading Robyn was counting heads. The number she arrived at was very satisfactory indeed for a first night. And, she was pleased to note, as it had been in Edinburgh so it was here; all types were present, including a minister and several women who were clearly ordinary housewives.

Guy read three poems, then it was Robyn's turn. Like Guy she was used to standing up and speaking, having done masses of it at Laurel Bank – though to be honest she wasn't nearly as comfortable doing it as Guy was. But that didn't show, she appeared perfectly relaxed and at ease as she read. She'd decided the audience would appreciate having some Scots poets included in the programme, so she started with *December Day, Hoy Sound* by George MacKay Brown.

After Robyn, Hamish McDermott, a chum of hers from university, whom she'd dragooned into reading, took up where she'd left off.

When it was all over, the applause enthusiastic, Robyn thanked the audience for coming and said the reading for the following Friday would be at the same time.

'Congratulations. We thoroughly enjoyed ourselves,' Mr Arnott beamed at Robyn, Mrs Arnott nodding her agreement by his side.

'Yes, I thought it went rather well.'

'And a good turn out.'

Robyn saw that Guy was already ringing up the till, the buyer being one of those from the university. Only a few had left the shop, the remainder had stayed on to browse, and hopefully buy.

'Just one small criticism,' Mr Arnott said.

'Yes?'

'It would have been nice if a cup of tea or coffee had been available for afterwards.'

'And a biscuit,' Mrs Arnott added.

Tea, coffee and biscuits! Now why hadn't she thought of that. She'd charge for them of course, which would increase the takings.

'Next time you come I'll see there's some available,' Robyn assured the Arnotts.

It was a full hour after the end of the reading before the last member of the audience left and Robyn was able to lock up.

'We took five pounds, seven and six at the door, and sold twenty-one books!' Robyn announced jubilantly to Lal and Hannah who'd stayed up to hear how she'd got on.

'Five pounds seven and six,' Lal repeated quietly. 'You did well.'

'And twenty-one books, don't forget about those.'

'All poetry?' Hannah queried, curious.

'No, but sixteen were. The rest were novels.'

Sixteen poetry books in one go! Hannah was impressed. Poetry books were notoriously slow movers.

'The big question now is, they came tonight but will it be the same next week and the week after that?' Lal said.

'Only time will tell. But quite a few of those there tonight said they would come again. Were quite definite about it,' Robyn replied.

'Five pounds seven and six,' Lal repeated again. 'A very nice little side line for you. Most lucrative.'

'Money for old rope really.'

'Don't get over-confident and cocky now girl,' Lal admonished. 'Take my word for it, that's the quickest way to lose out in business. Over-confidence, cockiness and taking the customers for granted. It'll sink you every time.'

'I'm none of these things Pa, I promise you. Just excited and thrilled that's all.'

Maybe so, he thought. But he was right to make the point all the same.

'Guy must have been delighted as well,' Hannah said.

'Oh, he was! Fourteen of those twenty-one books were Penguins. He sent you the message that he'll be in tomorrow to take a new order.'

Hannah laughed. 'Well, whatever else you can't accuse him of being slow off the mark.'

'He's certainly not that,' Robyn agreed.

'You know what all this reminds me of?' Lal said to Hannah. 'The day we opened our first bakery.'

Hannah smiled in memory. 'It does, doesn't it.'

'Remember your granda got us ten gallons of white paint to do out the front shop with, and how we gave the bread away free on our opening day?'

'And you . . .'

Robyn had heard it all countless times before. As Lal and Hannah reminisced her mind was on the poetry reading earlier, and Guy.

She couldn't get enough of that man.

Robyn ran a finger down Guy's cheek, then gave the cheek a lingering kiss, licking the flesh as she did.

'Hmmh!' Guy smiled. 'I would have thought you'd had enough.'

'I'll never get enough of you.'

His eyelids flicked open, and he glanced sideways at her. 'Or me of you.'

A thrill ran through her to hear that.

Twisting his head he brought his mouth to hers, one hand running up and down her naked body. They were in his room, lying in front of the gas fire which was turned up full. They'd decided to stay in that night, rather than go out as they'd originally planned to do.

'Ooohhh!' Robyn sighed when the kiss was over, and snuggled up as close to him as she could.

'What have you chosen to read this Friday?' he asked. 'I've come up with some real cracking stuff from America. It's written by a chap called Rod McKuen who, as far as I can make out, isn't published over here yet.'

'I don't know. I've still to decide,' she muttered in reply.

'I must mention McKuen when I'm next in Harmondsworth. I think he could do well in the U.K.'

'I've been wondering if perhaps we shouldn't branch out a little on Friday nights,' Robyn said slowly. It was now April and the weekly poetry readings had been going from strength to strength.

He regarded her quizzically. 'How do you mean?'

'Give the evenings something other than just poetry, add a new dimension.'

'What sort of dimension?'

'Well, we're doing all right as it is, that can't be denied. But it doesn't mean to say we can't make the evenings even better, even more interesting.'

Guy sat up and reached for his packet of Gitanes. They both smoked Gitanes now, Robyn having been doing so since her return from Newquay. 'How?' he queried.

'I thought we might incorporate excerpts from plays into the programme?'

He lit two cigarettes, and passed her one. 'Excerpts from plays? That could appeal.'

'Particularly if we chose the poetical playwrights. Shakespeare, Christopher Fry, Dylan Thomas, to name but a few.'

He liked the idea of Shakespeare, Penguin published the entire Shakespearean canon. So too did Signet mind you, but he would ensure that only Penguins were featured in the bin.

'I don't mind reading excerpts from plays; it'll be fun,' he said.

'Poetry is one thing, dramatic works quite another. It would be better if we got professionals to do that job for us. Or if not professionals exactly, trainee professionals.'

He realised what she was driving at. 'Our friends Eadie, Jack, Iain and Kate?'

'Do you think they'd do it?'

'I'm sure of it. They'll jump at the chance to perform in public. But you'd have to pay them. You couldn't ask them to do it for nothing, that wouldn't be fair.'

'What about five bob each? Would that be reasonable?'

He laughed. 'Talk about last of the big-time spenders!'

'Five bob is five bob when you're a starving student. And it does give them an excellent opportunity to practice their art. Frankly, they profess to being so keen about acting I'd have thought they'd have done it just for the love of it, and the experience.'

He reached across and tweaked her nipple. 'Anyone ever tell you that underneath that beautiful breast beats a heart of solid brick?'

'Soft hearts don't take you far in business. I heard Pa say that once.'

'But didn't you tell me he also once said that it was self-defeating to exploit your staff, for if you did they'd only work against you instead of for you.'

'That's why I'll pay them five bob instead of asking them to do it for love and experience.'

He studied her face, seeing something there he'd also noticed in the past. 'You enjoy being a boss, don't you? Enjoy the feeling of power?'

'Are those questions or accusations?' she countered, her tone a teasing one.

'Come on, don't prevaricate. You do, don't you?'

'I certainly don't mind being in charge. I am my father's daughter after all and there is a lot of him in me. As for enjoying power, I've never really thought about that.'

'I believe you do.'

Placing a hand on the inside of his thigh she began to stroke him there gently. 'Would that be a fault, if I did?'

'No, but it is interesting.'

'Why?'

'Because it would be a factor we'd have in common.' His eyes gleamed. 'It must be marvellous to have oodles of power, don't you agree?'

'I suppose so.'

'Oodles and oodles and oodles.'

She laughed, and moved her hand upwards. 'How about noodles and noodles and noodles?'

He laughed too. 'Noodle in the singular I'm afraid. I can't manage more than that.'

'One's enough for me,' she said softly.

A few minutes later, when he started to pull himself on top of her she suddenly crossed her legs.

'What was that you said about me enjoying the feeling of power?' she smiled.

'I knew I was right.'

'Say, pretty please?' she teased.

'Pretty please,' he replied solemnly.

She uncrossed her legs again. 'Remind me to put Lysistrata on that list of plays,' she said a moment after he'd entered her.

'My husband!' Eadie cried out. She was reading the part of Lady Macbeth, Iain that of Macbeth himself. The scene was the one between the pair, directly after the murder of Duncan. Iain had already read the famous 'dagger' speech which preceded the scene.

'I have done the deed,' Iain replied as Macbeth. 'Didst thou not hear a noise?'

'I heard the owl-scream and the cricket's cry.
Did not you speak?'

       'When?'

          'Now.'

             'As I descended?'

                'Ay.'

Eadie was excellent as Lady Macbeth, Robyn thought. With a bit of luck she should go far after she left drama college. This was the third Friday they'd included play excerpts in the programme, the previous two having proved most successful.

Robyn glanced about her. The numbers were up yet again. She hadn't turned anyone away at the door so far, but if the numbers continued to increase that wasn't far off.

As for her mother, Hannah was ecstatic about the amount of books being sold on Friday nights. Last week they'd excelled themselves and sold forty-three! Nineteen poetry books, seventeen copies of *Under Milk Wood* by Dylan Thomas, publisher J.M. Dent & Sons Ltd., the remainder seven novels unconnected with the evening.

Iain continued as Macbeth:

There's one did laugh in's sleep, and one cried 'Murder!'
That they did wake each other. I stood and heard them.

But they did say their prayers and addressed them
Again to sleep.

Robyn's eyes locked onto Guy's as he stood across the shop from her, and, as one, they smiled at each other.

As they continued to smile the idea came to her.

'As you know, we ran out of chairs tonight. Can your father get us some more?' Guy asked Robyn, turning the Allard out of Gibson Street in the direction of Kelvinside, and Winton Avenue. Lal had acquired the chairs they used on Friday nights from a second-hand dealer he knew. When not in use the folding chairs were kept down in the basement.

'I'll ask him. I'm sure he can.'

Guy was thinking with satisfaction of the number of Macbeth sales the bookshop had had, when Robyn said, 'I had an idea tonight.'

'Uh-huh?'

'Why don't I move in with you?'

Her proposal took Guy completely by surprise. 'Move in with me?'

'Wouldn't that be absolutely super! Then we would be together every night, all night. We'll have to buy another bed of course, a bigger one, and a second set of drawers wouldn't go amiss either. So what do you say, eh?'

Their living together had never crossed his mind. 'Have you thought this through, Robyn? What about your mother and father, for example. What's their reaction going to be when you announce you're leaving them to come and stay with me?'

'I'm eighteen: I can do as I like,' she replied defensively. She'd been eighteen that January. 'And anyway, lots of people at the uni live in rooms, alone and with members of the opposite sex.'

'Not ones, I'm sure, with beautiful homes only minutes away from the university. And you have to admit, yours is a beautiful home.'

Her lips thinned. 'Are you turning my offer down?'

'Not at all. What I am saying is we must consider the matter carefully before making a decision.'

'But you would like me to be in your bed every night, wouldn't you?'

'That's a daft question, as you well know. Of course I would! I love you after all, dammit!'

And how she loved him. God how she loved him! There were times when that love was an almost unbearable ache. Times she wanted to scream out loud with frustration because she wasn't with him. Times of sheer, unadulterated ecstasy.

'What about Lal and Hannah, what *would* their reaction be?' he queried.

Robyn considered that. 'I doubt they'd jump for joy. Not that they've anything against you personally – quite the contrary, they both think very highly of you – but I doubt they'd jump for joy nonetheless. They can be rather old-fashioned about certain things.'

'So are most parents, regarding their offspring,' Guy smiled, thinking that his Pater was an exception to that rule. But then George was exceptionally liberal and broad-minded.

'They'd be hurt, probably,' Robyn said. 'Particularly Pa.'

'There you are, then. Do you want to hurt your parents?'

'Not at all. But what I do want is to move in with you. That way we can be far more of a couple than we are now.' Moving her body sideways she kissed him lightly on the neck, savouring that combination of smells she'd come to so identify with him.

It was tempting! Guy told himself. It was most certainly that. Having Robyn around on a permanent basis would be no hardship whatever. And yet . . .

'I will think it through. But I already know I won't change my mind about this,' Robyn declared, laying her head on Guy's shoulder.

Would the others in the flat object to Robyn moving in, he wondered? He couldn't imagine they would. Nor Bernie the landlord, who might increase the rent for his room, however.

Living with Robyn! Very, very tempting indeed.

Guy sat in darkness, staring into the hissing glow of his gas fire. Did he wish Robyn to come and live with him, or not? That was the question, and his decision to make.

He was in love with her; he hadn't lied about that. But at the same time he had to remind himself that she was only eighteen, he twenty-two the previous month of March.

If she did move in, with the pair of them feeling as they did about one another, would that be the start of something irreversible? Would moving in lead to an engagement and that to wedding bells? He suspected it would.

And why shouldn't he eventually marry Robyn? On the one hand there was his love for her, and her for him, on the other the fact she came from a wealthy family. Wealth that would some day become hers, she being an only child, and his if he was married to her.

There again he was twenty-two, with his whole life before him; a life in which anything or anyone could happen. He was doing well with Penguin, they were pleased with him and had told him so. He had prospects within the company, no doubt about that.

What if they suddenly asked him in a few months' time, or a year say, to move on elsewhere? That would be devilishly tricky if Robyn was living with him, or they were engaged, and she still at the university. In that case she'd be a definite complication, and one in the circumstances he could well do without.

And who was to say his future lay with Penguin? As he was doing well for them there was always the possibility he could be approached by another company with an offer he might want to jump at. Poaching between companies went on all the time.

He ground out his cigarette, and immediately lit another. This was indeed a dilemma. Part of him yearned to come home to her every evening, and for her to be in his bed every night. Another part was screaming 'Beware! Be careful! Don't take on something, no matter how enticing, you'll come to regret!'

As for love itself, he didn't believe, couldn't, that there was only a single pre-ordained love in your life. That notion was ridiculous, farcical! An individual was capable of falling in love many times over. If he was never to see Robyn again, then surely there would be someone else, another love, in the not-too-distant future.

To rationalise things even further, he might be in love with Robyn now but would that still be so years hence, after he'd married her? There was no certainty about that. No copper-bottomed guarantee.

Perhaps he was thinking too deeply about this, he told himself. After all, couples lived togther all the time nowadays, it was no big deal. It didn't have to lead to anything if he didn't want it to. No one could force him to the altar against his will.

There again, looking at another aspect of the situation, what if

Robyn did move in and her parents were so outraged they decided to make trouble for him? Hannah in particular could do that by complaining to Harmondsworth, the powers that be there were notoriously strait-laced. A complaint of the type Hannah would make would be a definite black mark against him with the company, with who knows what repercussions affecting his future.

Guy sighed, so many pros and cons, all swirling and whirling in a confused, interlocking mass round and round inside his head. Yes or no? Yes or no!

Later, his mental tussle still unresolved, he rolled himself a joint which helped relax him.

And come to a decision.

'Well?' Robyn demanded eagerly. She'd come to Guy's for his answer about her moving in.

'From your expression I presume you haven't changed your mind about this?'

She shook her head. 'I told you I wouldn't.'

He pulled the cork out of a bottle of Beaujolais and filled two glasses he'd laid out in readiness. He handed her one, then had a long pull from his.

'Well?' she repeated.

'How are your studies going?'

She frowned. 'Fine. What's that got to do with it?'

'Quite a lot really. Look around you, at the size of this room. It's tiny.'

'So?'

'I have a lot of paperwork to do at home which usually means files and invoices strewn everywhere and, if you were here studying with your books, papers etc., it would just be chaos.'

Her stare was hard, and filled with bitter disappointment. 'You're saying no, is that it?'

'And then there are the others in the flat,' he bulldozed on. 'Lovely folk as you well know, but extremely noisy. I'm certain you'd find their screams and shouts and general carryings-on most disturbing when you were trying to concentrate. I mean, you were here the other evening when Iain and his friend Stuart got roaring drunk and started chasing Eadie about. That sort of nonsense happens all the time.'

'It wouldn't bother me Guy, honestly.'

He drank more of his wine. 'I don't want you to fail any exams, or do badly, on my account.'

She blinked away a tear. She'd convinced herself his answer would be yes.

'It's for the best, Robyn. I know it is.'

She swallowed some of her Beaujolais, tasting nothing. 'If that's really all that's bothering you, we could get a larger room, or even a flat of our own. They're not impossible to find.'

'Not impossible, but almost at this time of year. The university students plus the thousands of other students in the city have seen to that.'

'Where there's a will there's a way, Guy,' she stated softly.

He drained his glass, and refilled it. 'I'd prefer things to remain just as they are between us. For now anyway. We're both young, with our entire lives ahead of us, so why rush matters? I think that would be a mistake, and one we might both regret.'

'I see.'

'I do love you, Robyn. I swear before God, I do.'

Her lips twisted into a cynical smile. 'But not enough for us to live together?'

'I didn't say that. I said let's not rush matters, which is hardly the same thing.'

'Maybe you're right,' she said heavily.

'In the meanwhile I have a suggestion to make.' He'd thought of this while under the influence of the joint. A sop that he would enjoy just as much as her.

Robyn raised an eyebrow.

'Why don't we go away for our summer holidays together, just the two of us. Do you think that's possible?'

Her heart leapt within her, and her disappointment receded a little. 'I don't know. Why, where do you have in mind – Hunters Moon?'

He had no intention of taking her to Hunters Moon while Sorel was still on the scene. The Canadian bitch had promised him never to let on that he'd slept with her in exchange for the Allard, but that promise had been in respect of Pater and no one else. It would be just like Sorel to come up with a way of telling Robyn without Pater finding out. No, Hunters Moon, which he hadn't been back to since the previous summer, was far too much of a risk.

'How about a package holiday abroad? Spain, or Portugal perhaps?'

A fortnight alone in either place was something she would have given her eye-teeth for. 'Sounds terrific.'

'What about Lal and Hannah, have they planned anything yet?'

'Pa is talking of touring the Highlands by car during the Fair. It's assumed I'll be accompanying them.'

'Can you get out of it without telling them the truth of what we intend? I don't think it would be a good thing for them to know.'

Robyn agreed with that. 'What we need is a plausible story. Or at least I do.'

Robyn remained with Guy for some hours after that, but it was one of their few ever evenings in the flat together when they didn't make love. He didn't expect her to, nor did she propose it.

The tears rolled down Cathy's cheeks, while her face was contorted with pain and memory. She'd come along to the Blackbird that Friday night after learning that the poems and prose to be read were those relating to the Great War. The experience was proving most harrowing.

Guy, reading *The Sentry* by Wilfrid Owen, began the second verse. Other than his voice, not a whisper of sound could be heard in the bookshop. It was as if the audience was collectively holding its breath.

> Those other wretches, how they bled and spewed,
> And one who would have drowned himself for good –
> I try not to remember these things now.
> Let dread hark back for one word only: how
> Half-listening to that sentry's moan and jumps,
> And the wild chattering of his broken teeth,
> Renewed most horribly whenever crumps
> Pummelled the roof and slogged the air beneath –
> Through the dense din, I say, we heard him shout
> 'I see your lights!' But ours had long died out.

'Here you are, Gran,' Robyn said to Cathy, handing her a cup of tea. They were in the cubbyhole at the rear of the shop where the tea and coffee were made. Guy, Hamish McDermott, Jack and Iain were at the front of the shop helping sell books, and in Jack and Iain's case also copies of *Journey's End* by R.C. Sherriff, the famous play about life in the trenches from which that evening's excerpt had been taken.

Cathy accepted the cup, and sipped at its contents. 'I'm sorry I made such a fool of myself lass. I . . .'

'You did no such thing, Gran,' Robyn interrupted.

'Bubbling like a big wean!'

'I cried a bit myself. The whole programme was very moving.'

'All those bonny lads. Such a waste. Such a waste!' Cathy said quietly, shaking her head.

'It was a terrible war,' Robyn agreed.

'I can see them all still, you understand,' Cathy said, her mouth thinning into a narrow slash. 'Bobby, your granda, my cousins Craig and Ronnie McIntosh who aye got Big Tosh and Wee Tosh, the pals from Miller's Coalyard, other chaps I went to school with and grew up alongside . . .' She trailed off, tears back in her eyes.

'Is there anything else I can get you?' Robyn asked gently.

'No lass, this tea's lovely.' She had another sip.

Cathy went on, now in a whisper. 'So long ago. Fifty years next year since Bobby died. Fifty years!'

'You must have been very much in love,' Robyn said.

'Oh aye. We only had a short while together, but it was a great love story while it lasted. A great love story.' Cathy took a deep breath. 'How I wish we'd had longer together. Damn Kaiser Bill and all warmongers. Damn them to hell and everlasting perdition.'

Robyn had never heard so much hatred in a voice, or so much sadness. Love might be the most marvellous thing in the world, but it was also a double-edged sword.

Her gran was living proof of that.

'Another bakery, with shop attached!' said a smiling Lal, rubbing his hands. 'And for a song as well. They were almost giving it away.' He had just returned home to announce his latest acquisition. That meant he now owned seven bakeries with attached shops, five single shops serviced by the bakeries plus three kiosks.

'Congratulations!' said Hannah, kissing him on the cheek. 'From strength to strength, eh?'

'From strength to strength,' Lal agreed.

'Does this one need much doing to it?'

'Gutting out completely.'

'Does that mean new ovens?'

Lal nodded. 'The present ones are totally clapped out, which is one of the reasons why the price was so low. But I know where I can get two excellent second-hand ones that were sold for scrap. I'll get those for a song too, and they'll replace the clapped-out ones and give us many years of service.'

'If you keep on the way you have been you're going to rival the City Bakeries before long,' Robyn said – the City Bakeries being a large chain of bakeries and shops.

'Why not?' replied Lal. 'If you don't aim for the moon you'll never get there. Now, how about a celebratory drink?'

'Yes, please,' enthused Robyn, while Hannah nodded that she'd have one also.

Lal disappeared, to return with a cold bottle of champagne. When the cork had been popped, and three flutes filled, they toasted the new premises.

Robyn had been waiting for a suitable occasion when her mother and father were both in a good humour, and judged this was now it. She let Lal burble on for a few minutes about the new bakery and shop, then said, 'Pa, I've been asked by a couple of female friends at uni if I'd be interested in going with them to Estapona on the Spanish Costa Del Sol for the Fair. What do you think?'

Lal frowned. 'Spain?'

'Yes, it would be a package holiday and not all that expensive. I could pay for it myself out of what I've saved from the poetry readings.'

'I thought . . . Well, I presumed you'd be coming with us,'

'Touring the Highlands would be all right Pa, but to be honest I'd much prefer to go to Spain with the girls.'

'You feel we're too inhibiting for you now, is that it?'

'I am eighteen, Pa, and at university. There does come a time when, no matter how much you love them, you don't always want to be with your mother and father. When you want to strike out on your own. Or in this instance, with friends.'

Lal glanced at Hannah. He knew that was reasonable, but didn't like it nevertheless.

'I would have been happier if it had been somewhere in this country, and not abroad.' Hannah said slowly.

'Oh Mum, thousands of people go to Spain every year! I'm told the British are like locusts over there.'

'And who are these girls who want you to go with them?' Lal asked.

Robyn had been prepared for that question, and had her answer ready. 'Ann Morrison, Shirley Banks and Patti Angus. They're all very nice girls from good, respectable homes, reading English same as I am.'

'And would you be in a hotel, or what?'

'In a hotel, two rooms with two of us sharing each room.'

'Full board?'

Robyn nodded. 'Breakfast, lunch and dinner. The works. So you wouldn't have to worry about me starving to death.'

Hannah was staring at Robyn, her eyes thoughtful. 'And do we get to meet these girls before you give them your answer?'

Robyn pulled a face. 'I'm not asking them here to be vetted; they'd be black affronted. Just as I would if their parents demanded to vet me. No, just take my word for it, you'd thoroughly approve. None of them is wild, or anything like that.'

Lal couldn't see how he could refuse to let her go. Not without being unreasonable, that was. 'Oh well!' he shrugged.

'Thanks, Pa!' She went to him and kissed him on the cheek.

'And I'll pay. You keep what you've got saved for your pocket.'

'Thanks again, Pa.' She kissed him on the other cheek.

'We'll miss you mind. Won't we darling?'

Hannah nodded, her eyes still thoughtful.

'That's settled, then,' beamed Robyn.

Hannah had a sip of her champagne. 'Where's Guy going this year?' she asked casually.

'Back to Newquay to visit his father. He hasn't been home since last summer, so he's spending his hols there, again,' Robyn lied smoothly.

'Well, he won't have you to keep him company this year,' Hannah said, watching Robyn closely.

'No. And I've warned him he's not to get off with any other female down there either. Or else!' And with that she laughed.

A smiling Hannah remained unconvinced.

'Right then, that's it,' said Guy, having loaded Robyn's suitcase into the boot of the Cortina – he still had his company car which he used for business: the Allard was for pleasure. Back at the Stuarts' door Robyn was saying goodbye to Lal and Hannah. The story was that Guy was driving Robyn to the airport, the reality being that he would pick up his own suitcase after this, and then they'd drive to the airport where they'd both catch the plane.

'Be careful now, look after yourself,' Lal said to Robyn.

'Don't worry Pa, I'll be fine. You just see that you and Mum enjoy your tour of the Highlands.' Lal and Hannah were leaving Glasgow later that morning.

Robyn kissed Lal, then Hannah, who was strangely quiet. 'Goodbye Mum.'

'Goodbye, Robyn. Have a good time.' Her eyes flicked over Robyn's shoulder to Guy. '*And* you Guy. You have a good time too.'

Guy force himself to meet her gaze, wanting to look away.

'Let's go, you've a plane to catch and I don't want you to miss it,' Guy said to Robyn.

'Watch those Spaniards and their roving hands!' Lal joked to Robyn as she and Guy made for the Cortina.

Her reply to that was to hold up her hands and wiggle her fingers, which made Lal laugh.

Guy helped Robyn in, then went round to the driver's side and got in himself. Robyn waved as they drove off.

Robyn let out a long sigh as they turned the corner of the road and Lal and Hannah were lost to view. 'Spain here we come,' she smiled at Guy.

'Your mater knows.'

Robyn's smile disappeared. 'No, she doesn't!'

'I'm telling you, she does. I could see it in her eyes.'

'Are you sure?'

'Absolutely. She's guessed that all this business about you going off with some girls is a pack of lies, and that we're actually going off together.'

Robyn thought about that. 'Well if she has guessed, she hasn't told Pa. There would have been ructions if she had.'

Silence fell between them for a while, then Guy spoke again, changing the subject.

Robyn lay beside Guy who was asleep, and gently snoring. They were both naked, having just made love; it being afternoon siesta time, a custom they assiduously adhered to for the obvious reason.

She glanced over at the open window through which streamed a shaft of intense, bright sunlight. There was the distinctive odour of frying sardines in the air, mingled with the smell of the sea itself.

She sighed with pleasure, and sexual contentment. How happy she was, how gloriously ecstatically mind-blowingly happy! Being with Guy night and day, sharing every moment, was sheer, utter bliss.

How she adored waking in the night to find him lying beside her. She'd reach out and touch him, and often kiss him on the arm or shoulder while he slept. Sometimes he snored as he was now doing, other times he made snorting noises that she found hysterically funny to listen to.

And how he moved when asleep! He never seemed to remain in the same position for more than a minute. From his back he'd go onto his side, then his back again, and onto his other side after that. Then he'd repeat the whole business all over again.

What fun Fuengirola was proving to be. They spent endless hours down on the beach, sunbathing, swimming, sitting in the shade at the Sugar Shack, a palm-leaf topped bar on the beach itself, drinking Barcardis and Cokes or San Miguel beer.

One day they'd gone to Marbella, strolling hand in hand along the quay admiring the rich people's yachts tied up there, and wondering what it would be like to be fabulously rich as the yachts' owners clearly were. They'd taken coffee in the Marbella Beach Club where they'd spotted a famous American film star whom, Robyn was quick to note and comment on, was far, far shorter in the flesh than he appeared on screen.

'A bloody dwarf!' she'd whispered to Guy, who'd almost choked with laughter on the coffee he'd been drinking at that moment.

Another day they'd taken the coast bus to Estepona, which was completely unspoiled and very Spanish. They'd eaten a marvellous paella there which they'd washed down with a bottle of Rioja, and after that gone to a street market where Guy had bought himself a belt and her a small handbag, both of brown leather and excellent value for money.

God, it was warm, Robyn thought, wiping sweat from her brow. No wonder the Spanish took to their beds in the afternoon; you needed to in weather like this. And how lovely it was when the cool of the evening arrived, and you got your second wind.

After dinner it was drinking and dancing, some nights in the hotel itself, other nights in the many bars that abounded hereabouts. Her favourite of the latter was The Scots Bar run by a Glaswegian named, appropriately enough, Jimmy, who poured them whiskies large enough, as she'd said, to float the Queen Lizzie on. Jimmy came from Pollok and was married to a local girl called Juanita.

They'd go to The Scots Bar that evening, she decided. And afterwards a moonlight stroll along the beach before returning to the hotel, and bed.

How romantic it was here, she thought. Straight out of the pages of a Mills & Boon novel. If only it could go on and on forever. An eternity of Fuengirola, this hotel room, and Guy.

But of course all holidays had to come to an end, as theirs would shortly. Then it would be back to Glasgow, she to Winton Avenue and university, Guy to his flat and Penguin.

If only he had agreed to her moving in with him they would have at least retained something of what they were experiencing on holiday. They would have had each other during the nights, and oh, how she was going to miss that now!

Reaching over she lightly placed a hand on his buttock, a buttock hot and slippery with sweat. Twisting herself round, and down, she kissed where her hand had been. Then licked off some of the sweat, smiling at the salty Guyish taste of it.

Guy muttered under his breath, moved a leg, then flopped onto his back. Muttering again he scratched himself in the groin, cleared his throat, and snorted.

'You're beautiful, my love,' Robyn whispered to him. 'The most beautiful man ever.'

How she craved to move in with him! But he was adamantly against it. She'd broached the subject several times during their stay in Fuengirola, but his reaction had always been the same. He thought it for the best that she didn't. His room at the flat was too tiny, there was his work at home to consider, and her studying. Then there was . . . He'd trotted out his original objections on each occasion, and when she'd again suggested a larger room or flat of their own he'd . . .

The thought came to her in a flash that made her want to leap out of the bed and whoop for joy. There *was* a way she could have him in bed if not every night then most nights, and without moving in with him.

Simple really. So awfully, awfully simple. Why hadn't she thought of it before!

She'd implement matters directly she returned to Glasgow.

'Rent a room of your own! Don't be absurd, lassie,' Lal spluttered.

'There's nothing absurd about it, Pa.'

'Of course there is! Why on earth should you want to rent a room when you have a perfectly good home only minutes away from the university?' Lal said, echoing Guy's words when she'd first broached moving in with him.

'A home, with everything in it you could want,' Hannah qualified quietly.

'Is it us, your father and mother? Have we done something?' Lal, rapidly getting red-faced, demanded.

'It's nothing to do with either you or Mum. And it is a perfectly good home, a brilliant one compared to many. It's just that . . . I want a little bit of freedom.'

'Freedom!' Lal exploded, and swore.

'Lal!' Hannah admonished.

'You're only eighteen . . .' Lal started to say.

'And a half,' Robyn interjected.

'All right, eighteen and a half then . . .'

'And going into my second year at uni. Don't forget that,' Robyn cut in again.

'I'll try not to,' Lal said sarcastically. 'Eighteen and a half and going into your second year at university, and completely lacking in common sense, it seems to me. For God's sake Robyn, why make life difficult for yourself when you already have it easy. Why live in a rotten old room when you have all this!'

'You're not understanding Pa, it's the freedom I want, freedom I can only get by cutting the umbilical cord and trying to stand on my own two feet. It's a stage of growing up, if you like.'

'When I was a lad, we didn't need to go and live in rooms in order to grow up! We did that quite naturally, at home.'

'Times change, and so too do circumstances. When you were a lad you didn't have the wherewithal to leave home and set up on your own. Your background and environment didn't encompass such things. But Pa, different lads of different backgrounds and environments *were* doing just that. It is, and always has been, amongst certain sections of society, a quite normal and accepted process.'

Hannah stared grimly at her daughter. Robyn could say whatever she liked, put forward any argument; she knew the real reason why Robyn wanted to leave home. Guy Trecarron.

'I could see the point if circumstances necessitated it, you attending university in another city say. But that doesn't come into it,' Lal riposted.

'I'm going to take that room, Pa, with or without your permission. But preferably with,' Robyn stated defiantly.

Lal had an almost overwhelming urge to hit Robyn, smack her hard across the face. Caution! he warned himself. He could very easily lose a daughter here, the last thing he wanted.

'You feel that strongly about it, then,' Hannah said quietly to Robyn.

'Yes.'

'And how do you intend paying for this room?'

'With the money I make from the poetry readings. That's enough to pay for a room and support me.'

'What if I say you can't use the Blackbird anymore?'

'Hah!' exclaimed Lal, believing that had clinched the argument in their favour.

'Somehow or other I'll find a way to manage, Mum. Poetry readings at the Blackbird would make it a lot easier though,' Robyn replied, as defiant and determined as ever.

Hannah lit a cigarette, thinking it was going to be most odd not having Robyn round the house any more. It was a day she'd known would come eventually, but hadn't imagined it would be this soon.

411

'Well, Mum?' Robyn queried.

'I won't stop you using the Blackbird for poetry readings.'

'Pa? Do I have your permission to rent a room?'

Lal's shoulders were slumped in defeat. 'Yes. But *reluctantly*, mind you. Reluctantly. And you will come home often, won't you?'

'Often,' she agreed.

Bernie Rabinovitz was an American Jew from New York City, now settled in Glasgow. He'd arrived in Glasgow some years previously with his wife Rachel and baby daughter Miriam, and immediately started buying up properties which he then renovated and let out. It was rumoured amongst those who'd rented from Bernie for a while that he now owned dozens of houses, and was a very rich man indeed.

The nice thing about Bernie was he charged a fair rent, and his properties were always in good condition. Subsequently, they were much sought after.

Robyn had learned of Bernie from Guy, whose landlord Bernie was, and on approaching Bernie had been told, as it was still some weeks till the students came crowding back into the city for the autumn term, that of course he could fix her up, and she could have the pick of what was available.

Bernie turned the key in the lock and the heavy door swung silently open. A quick flick of his finger and an overhead light snapped on.

The room was large, with a high ceiling, all the proportions generous ones as is often the case amongst older Glasgow buildings. It had recently been redecorated – Robyn could smell paint and size – the ceiling was a gleaming white, the walls tastefully papered.

There was a washbasin on one wall, and a cooker in a corner, while the bed was a double. The carpet had seen better days, but was far from threadbare.

'I like it,' Robyn pronounced to Bernie. It was exactly what she'd been after, including being on the first floor which meant she could come and go – or more importantly Guy could – without anyone being aware of the fact.

'It's a month in advance, and a month's notice if you decide to leave,' Bernie stated.

'Fair enough.'

'And *no* noisy parties. I draw the line there.'

'I understand.'

'The meters are over here,' Bernie said, going to a cupboard and opening it.

'What about telephone?'

'On the landing upstairs. The usual coin in the slot, okay?'

'Okay,' Robyn nodded. 'Now when can I move in?'

Before leaving the room she had a little bounce on the bed, which was neither too hard or too soft.

Just right, she thought, smiling.

Guy sat staring out of the window as the train sped south. He was on his way to Harmondsworth, having to visit and report in there on a regular basis. He would stay the night in London, and return to Glasgow the following day, getting in early evening.

Nor was he to go to his flat from the Central Station, but straight to a mysterious address that Robyn had given him where he was to meet her and be given a surprise!

Groping in his inside jacket pocket he took out the sheet of paper, torn from a pad, that she'd given him with the address written on it. Now why was he to go there, and what was the surprise awaiting him?

Mysterious, mysterious, he thought, and laughed softly to himself. Robyn up to one of her tricks. Well, it was something to look forward to.

And fun.

Robyn threw open the front door, having spotted Guy crossing the street. 'Hello, how was your trip?' she said, kissing him on the cheek.

'Fine,' he replied, his gaze stabbing over her shoulder into the hallway.

'Come in! Come in!'

When he was in the hallway she shut the door behind him.

'Who lives here?' he whispered.

'Aha! That's the surprise I promised you.' Grabbing him by the hand she hauled him along the hallway and into her room, closing that door also.

'What do you think?' she demanded.

413

He gazed about him, his expression puzzled. 'Very nice.'

'Only *very nice*. It's absolutely fantabuloso!'

He smiled at her made-up word. 'All right, it's fantabuloso. Now who lives here?'

'I do.'

He gaped at her. 'You what?'

'I do. As from yesterday morning.'

'You've left home?'

She nodded.

He gazed about him again.

She explained. 'It's the perfect answer, which came to me one afternoon in Fuengirola. Now I don't have to go home at nights. You can either sleep here with me, or I can sleep at your place. Pleased, eh?'

He fumbled for his cigarettes and lighter. 'You wouldn't have a drink in, would you?'

'Of course. Drink, and a special meal for the occasion. I'm cooking paella, which will hopefully taste something like the ones we had in Spain, and also have a bottle of Rioja in to go with it.'

'I'll have a glass of Rioja then.'

'There's gin if you prefer?'

'Even better. A big dollop of that is just what I need.'

She frowned. 'Are you all right? You suddenly look ghastly.'

He noted his hands were trembling as he lit a cigarette. 'The train was very crowded coming up, with a lot of screaming kids on board. It wasn't exactly the most pleasant journey.'

Her frown immediately became a crease of concern. 'Poor dear. You must be worn out.'

'I am rather.'

She hurried over to where the gin bottle was, and poured him a hefty measure which she topped up with tonic. 'Here you are,' she smiled, handing it to him.

He took a deep swallow, then another.

'Here, let me,' said Robyn, and began undoing his tie. When she had that off she removed his jacket and hung it in the wardrobe.

Guy bit his lip, then finished his drink. 'Can I pour myself another?'

'Go ahead. And do a small one for me.'

414

The drink he poured for himself was even heftier than that she'd poured.

'How was Harmondsworth?' she asked, as he gave her her drink.

'Fine,' he replied quietly.

'Are they still happy about your work up here?'

An odd expression came onto his face. 'Very. I'm doing far better than Dalgleish ever did. They're extremely impressed. Funny thing is . . .' He had another swallow of G & T. 'I have The Blackbird Bookshop in particular to thank for that. The rise in sales, due to the poetry readings, hasn't gone unnoticed, and was specifically mentioned. They're delighted with the number of poetry books and Shakespeare plays your mother's selling.'

'You must tell Hannah when you next see her!' Robyn exclaimed. 'She'll enjoy hearing that.'

Guy gave a thin smile, and swallowed more G & T.

'I haven't started the paella yet. Should I do so now, or leave it for a while?'

'Leave it for a while,' Guy answered.

Robyn made a sweeping gesture with her arm that encompassed the entire room. 'I've brought lots of things from home with me, including my hi-fi. Pa was a poppet and had one of his drivers bring everything over in one of the delivery vans.'

'How did Lal take the news that you were moving out?'

'He was furious to begin with, but became resigned once he realised there was no stopping me. I told them I needed a bit of freedom, which is true enough. Only what I didn't say was that I meant the freedom to spend nights with you.'

Guy had another swallow. The gin was going straight to his head, as he'd only had a biscuit and a cup of tea coming up on the train. But perhaps that was a good thing; it could help make matters easier.

'Double bed,' said Robyn, pointing. 'Come and try it.'

She gave him a wicked smile when he sat beside her. 'Comfy, eh?' He nodded.

'I was hoping . . . But if you're worn out.'

'Hoping what?' he queried, realising he'd slurred his words.

'That we might try it out before we eat?'

He finished his second G & T. 'I, eh . . .' He trailed off to stare down into his empty glass.

'Well?'

'I'd like another of these. They're hitting the spot.'

She took his glass from him. 'You stay there and I'll get it for you.'

Jesus! he thought. Or should it have been Judas. For that's what he was, a betrayer.

'Thank you,' he mumbled when she returned with his refilled glass. '

'I can't even begin to tell you how excited I am about this room and what it'll mean to us. When Bernie gave me the keys I went cold all over, cold with gooseprickles.'

'Robyn I, eh . . . I . . .' He couldn't say it. He just couldn't! Damn you for a coward, he raged inwardly.

'Something's wrong isn't it?' she said, her face suddenly clouding over.

He nodded.

She waited, but he said nothing.

'Guy?'

'I'm going to Australia,' he at last managed to blurt out.

She stared at him in disbelief, then a huge grin arced her mouth upwards. 'You're having me on! Taking the michael!'

He couldn't look at her. 'No, Robyn, it's true. I leave just as soon as everything can be arranged.'

Her grin faded. She was completely stunned, her body and brain numb as if shot through with novocaine. 'Australia?'

'I've to go initially to Melbourne, where I'll meet everyone and learn about our Australian set-up. I'm to be the rep for New South Wales, which as you know includes Sydney, Australia's largest city. If I do well at that I'll be very seriously considered for the top post, Head of Sales for Penguin Books Australia Pty., which will fall vacant in a few years, due to retirement. I would have thought my age would have been against me for such an elevated position, but not so apparently. The Australians it seems, prefer young people with lots of drive and get up and go, as opposed to the more middle-aged managerial types we favour here.'

Robyn couldn't believe she was hearing this. Guy, going to Australia, the other side of the world!

'It's a tremendous opportunity Robyn, you have to understand that. When it was offered to me I just couldn't turn it down. It

416

would have been madness, rank stupidity to have done so. There would have been other chances for me in time, but . . .'

It dawned on her what he meant by that last bit. 'Are you saying you had a choice?' she broke in. 'That you didn't *have* to go? That you weren't ordered there?'

He dropped his gaze, shrinking away inside from that terrible look of accusation she was levelling at him. 'How could I refuse and stay on here? It's something I would have lived to regret for the rest of my days. And to be offered the possibility, the carrot, of Head of Sales at my age! Why I could . . .'

Her hand twisted into a claw that shot out to sink into his cheek. She raked the length of his cheek with her full strength behind the action.

Guy screamed, as blood spurted in all directions. His G & T went flying.

'You bastard!' Robyn hissed through a haze of tears. 'You fucking bastard!'

Guy jumped up, clutching his lacerated cheek, blood oozing from between his fingers.

Robyn, tiny pieces of torn flesh protruding from under her fingernails, glared at him. 'Get out. I never want to see or hear from you ever again. *Get out*!'

He'd known she was going to take it badly; but hadn't dreamt it would be as badly as this.

'I do love you, Robyn. You must believe that.'

She did believe him; that was what made the whole thing so horrible. He loved her but was still prepared to ditch her like this.

'Get out right now, Guy or so help me God I'll kill you.' Realising there was a pair of scissors on her bedside table she snatched them up and brandished them at him.

She would kill him too; staring into her face he didn't doubt that. 'I'm sorry, Robyn, honestly I am,' he said, backing towards the door. Halfway there he remembered his jacket. Dashing to the wardrobe he opened it, pulled his jacket out from inside, then walked swiftly to the door.

He opened the door and looked back at her for the last time. The pain in his cheek was horrendous. He'd have to go directly from there to the nearest hospital and have it stitched.

Robyn, tears now streaming from her eyes, had almost caved in on herself. She was a picture of abject misery and despair.

'Robyn, I . . .'

'Just go!' she whispered, her voice cracked and riven.

When he'd left she collapsed onto the bed, and curled up into a tight ball.

Hannah was sitting studying the new Corgi stocklist, Lal having gone up to bed some twenty minutes previously with a splitting headache, when she heard a noise outside in the hall.

'Is that you, Lal?' she called out, glancing up from the stocklist.

'No, Mum,' Robyn replied, entering the combined sitting and dining room. 'It's me.'

'Robyn!' Hannah exclaimed in astonishment.

'I tried to let myself in quietly. I didn't want to . . . Oh, Mum!' Robyn suddenly wailed, staggering where she stood.

Hannah was instantly on her feet and at her daughter's side. She exclaimed again when she saw the state of Robyn's face. There were tear stains on her cheeks while the areas under her eyes were dark and swollen.

'Oh Mum!' Robyn repeated, falling into her mother's arms.

A bewildered Hannah held Robyn tightly to her bosom. 'What's wrong darling? What's the matter?'

Hannah listened grimly as it all came tumbling out, the story of the night's events.

'If only he'd asked me to go with him I would have done. But he didn't. He never asked,' Robyn ended up by saying.

Robyn hadn't mentioned that she and Guy had been lovers, but then Hannah knew that already.

'I understand lass. I understand,' Hannah declared softly, stroking Robyn's hair. And she did.

After a while Hannah gave Robyn a mild sedative she luckily had in the house, then put Robyn to bed in her old bedroom.

The next day Lal gave Bernie Rabinovitz another month's rent, and brought all Robyn's things back to Winton Avenue.

Chapter 11

Robyn was thinking about the tights she'd just been into town to buy as she hurried along Winton Avenue. Normally she would have been driving but her Mini was in having a service.

She'd left The Blackbird Bookshop early to do her shopping, as being a Monday, it was invariably a slack day, and one on which Hannah could easily manage on her own.

'Hello Robyn, haven't seen you for absolutely ages.'

Being called by name snapped her out of her reverie, and there was James McEwen by her side, smiling at her.

'Oh hello, James! Yes it is a while since we've seen one another.'

'Thank you for the invitation to your twenty-first, but as I explained in my reply I was away in Austria ski-ing for almost the whole month of January.' It was now June 1968, a year since Robyn had left the university where she'd won an honours degree. She'd been working at the Blackbird since.

'Did you enjoy your ski-ing trip?'

'Very much so, thank you. Particularly the aprés-ski!' He laughed at that.

'How's your brother Rory doing? I haven't seen him either.'

'Still grafting away at medicine, when he's not chasing women, that is.' He gave her a salacious wink. 'Terrible man for the women, my brother. The despair of us all.'

Unlike you, Robyn thought. She could never imagine James being a ladykiller.

They made small talk until they reached Robyn's house, where she was about to bid James goodbye, when he suddenly said. 'I'm throwing a gay-and-hearty this Saturday night to celebrate my leaving vet college. All the gang from college, plus various other nefarious characters should be there. If you'd like to come, you'd be most welcome.'

Her refusal was automatic. 'I'm sorry James, but I'm already booked for Saturday night.'

He shrugged. 'Pity, but there we are.'

'I would have loved to come,' she lied.

'Anyway, it's nice seeing you again. Take care now.' And with that he was off, striding down the street towards his own home.

She liked the thick moustache he'd grown, she thought. It suited him. How long was it since she'd last seen James and they'd spoken together? She couldn't remember. She must ring Lesley McKay, she reminded herself as she hurried indoors. Lesley was her great chum, whom she'd palled up with at the uni, a small, dark-haired girl with a vivacious personality who lived with her parents out in Newton Mearns. Lesley's father was a bank manager with the National Commercial Bank of Scotland.

James McEwen and his party were soon forgotten.

Robyn replaced the telephone on its receiver. 'Buggeration!' she swore. That was Lesley to say she was coming down with another of her interminable colds and would have to call off that evening – they'd planned to go to the pictures together. Well she wasn't going to the pictures by herself, not on a Saturday night she wasn't!

'Everything all right?' Hannah inquired, appearing out of an adjacent room and noticing Robyn's thunderous expression.

'That was Lesley cancelling out. Another cold coming on.'

'Poor love,' commiserated Hannah. 'She does suffer from them, doesn't she.'

'What about you, what are you and Pa doing this evening?'

'Staying in and watching TV.'

'What's on?'

'A variety show from Bournemouth, and a thriller thing that your Pa has been watching.'

A variety show and a thriller thing, yuch! Robyn thought. Still, there might be something decent on the radio. When she looked it up in the paper she discovered there wasn't.

They ate about seven o'clock, as was their custom, then after the dishes had been washed and dried, repaired to the television room where Lal settled himself into his big easy chair that no one else was allowed to sit in.

The variety show was even worse than Robyn had anticipated. There was a Russian juggler followed by a dog act, the compère an awful English comedian who cackled every few seconds he was on, like some demented hen.

'Drink, anyone?' Robyn asked.

Lal replied he'd have a whisky mac, Hannah a glass of Madeira. Robyn poured herself a vodka and tonic and hoped it would help relieve the gloom that had settled on her.

She picked up a novel she'd brought home from the bookshop, and tried to read that. But she couldn't get interested in it at all.

Lal laughed, and pointed at the T.V. set. 'That's hysterical!' he said.

Hysterically bad. Robyn thought, lighting a Players. She'd stopped smoking Gitanes shortly after her break-up with Guy. Or Guy's defection, as she always thought of it to herself. After three years, and quite a few boyfriends, none of whom she'd been really serious about, that pain was now a thing of the past, something she'd come to terms, and learned to live with.

She sighed. Boring! Boring! Boring! What a rotten Saturday night. And then she remembered James McEwen's party, and invitation.

She could still go to that, she thought. It couldn't be any worse than this. And there might be some interesting men there. You never knew.

She would go! She decided. Why not! And she'd wear those new purple tights she'd bought at the beginning of the week. The purple tights and . . .

Rory McEwen answered her ring of the bell. 'Hello Rory, I was invited,' she smiled.

'Robyn! How lovely to see you. Come away in!'

'I was supposed to be going out, but there was a change of plans. So here I am!' she explained as she stepped inside.

A girl came up to Rory and wound herself round him. 'This is Stephanie, a friend of mine,' Rory said.

'How do you do,' Robyn nodded.

Stephanie extended a limp hand. 'Welcome to the madhouse.' Then, continuing in a mock upper-crust English accent. 'We're all friiiightfully gargled. Aren't we Rory dear?'

'Some are. Others are taking their time about reaching that state.'

Stephanie narrowed her eyes. 'Do I detect a jibe there? Just a teensy bit of disapproval?'

After a few seconds Robyn slid past and away from Rory and Stephanie who were rapidly building towards a contretemps.

There was music playing, but relatively quietly, which pleased her. She didn't care for parties or situations where you couldn't hear yourself think, or conduct a conversation, because of the music or general noise.

There were lots of chaps present, she quickly saw; the usual mixed bunch to be found at parties. One or two 'smashers', one or two 'uggers', the remainder somewhere in between.

'Well hi, who are you?' said a male voice.

The speaker was wearing an Aran sweater and sandals over socks. Goodbye! she thought immediately. One thing she couldn't abide at any price were men who wore sandals over socks.

'I'm Robyn, I live in the street,' she replied.

'And I'm David. Have you just arrived?'

'Yes.'

'And no drink yet?'

'Perhaps you'd care to get one for me. What is there?'

'Wine, wine, wine and wine. What would you like?'

She groaned inwardly. How often had she heard that old chestnut? ' A glass of wine sounds fine.'

'Red or white?'

'No rosé?' she teased.

''Fraid not,' he answered seriously.

She nearly giggled out loud suddenly wondering if he had dirty underpants on. For some reason he looked the sort. 'It had better be red then,' she said.

'Right! You just wait here. I won't be a tick.' And with that David scuttled off in the direction of the kitchen.

Rory came up to her. 'Sorry about that. Steph's had a proper skinful, doesn't know which end is up. Have you seen James yet?'

Robyn shook her head.

'Well he's about somewhere. When I see him I'll tell him you're here. I know he'll want to welcome you. Now, how about a drink?'

'Somebody called David has gone off to do that.'

'David Hartington?'

'He didn't mention his last name.'

'Sandals and socks?'

Robyn laughed. 'You've got him in one!'

'He's a *Liberal*!' Rory said in such a way it made Robyn laugh again. She knew precisely what he meant by that.

'Good sort really, if somewhat academic.'

'Friend of James's?'

'No, mine actually. Brilliant at medicine and – this will surprise you – the best filthy joke teller I've ever encountered.'

That did surprise her. But only by the fact she wouldn't have thought David to have much of a sense of humour.

Robyn and Rory nattered for a few minutes, and then an eager David was back with a glass of red wine for Robyn.

'There's dancing in the dining room should you feel in the mood,' said Rory, and left them to answer the doorbell which had rung again.

'And what do you do, Robyn?' David inquired intently.

She talked about the bookshop, and a little of her time at the university. He was telling her about life as a medical student when she suddenly spotted James.

He was with an exceptionally pretty elfin-faced girl who appeared to be hanging on his every word. An elfin-faced girl with quite some figure Robyn now noticed. The girl was slim, but deceptive with it.

The girl's face was familiar, Robyn thought. She'd definitely seen it before. But where? University? Possibly. The bookshop? Could be. But she had seen it, she was certain of that.

'Would you like to dance?' David Hartington asked.

'Not really. But don't let me stop you.'

His eyes filled with disappointment at this obvious brush off. He'd begun to believe he was making an impression on Robyn, but clearly not. He was being given the big E.

'Speak to you later perhaps?' he smiled.

'Perhaps,' she replied, meaning no, not if she could help it.

David moved away in the direction of the dining room, then halfway there pounced on another unattached female.

A little later Robyn went to the toilet, where she had to queue, and was coming out of there when she walked straight into James.

'Rory mentioned you were here. I'm glad you could come,' he said.

'Change of plans. I suddenly became available.'

'Are you enjoying yourself? Meeting people? Do you want me to introduce you around?'

'Please, no. I shan't be staying too long anyway.'

'Ah!' he said, as if he'd been expecting that, and nodded.

'I hope you don't mind me asking, but who was that girl you were chatting with earlier? The one with the elfin face. I feel I know her but can't place her somehow.'

'That's Caroline who goes to the L.S.E., London School of Economics. You may have seen her in the newspapers last week? She was pictured at a demonstration with Tariq Ali and Martin Tomkinson. The picture a lot of rags carried on their front page, featured the three of them. Tariq Ali on one side, Martin Tomkinson on the other, and Caroline in the middle.'

That clicked with Robyn. 'I did see the picture! Yes of course, I remember her now. She and the other two led the demo. There were thousands and thousands there.'

'That's right. She's frightfully interesting if somewhat radically Left Wing.'

'Surely you aren't?' Robyn queried.

'Not me!' James laughed. 'But that doesn't mean I can't sympathise with many of their points of view.'

'And this Caroline, she's a friend of yours?'

'Oh yes.'

'*Girl*friend?' Robyn couldn't stop herself asking that.

'Caroline doesn't agree with such tags, considering them sexist. Anyway, she spends most of her time in London,' James replied, evasively Robyn thought.

'She is from Glasgow, then?'

'Born and bred. And a real firebrand, if ever there was.'

Robyn recalled her gran's stories of the rent strike, of Mary Barbour, Helen Crawfurd, Jean Ferguson and Agnes Dollan. 'Glasgow has a history of producing female political firebrands. Not to mention male ones,' she commented drily.

'That's true enough!' James laughed.

Someone shouted and hallooed! which turned out to be Rory with a female other than Stephanie draped round him. James waved back, as did Robyn.

'Terrible man for the women,' said James, shaking his head.

'He certainly appears successful with them, from what I've seen anyway.'

'Take my word for it, he is.'

And might there not be something of that in James too? she wondered. Were there depths to James she'd never been aware of before?

About three-quarters of an hour later when she went to seek out James to say goodbye and thank him for the party Robyn found him in an out of the way corner with Caroline, the two of them holding hands while talking earnestly together.

She changed her mind and left without saying goodbye.

'I don't believe it!' exclaimed Robyn angrily, slamming down the phone.

'Don't believe what?' queried Hannah, returning to the counter from further down the shop where she'd been restocking the latest James Bond, which was selling like hotcakes.

'That was Lesley and she's come down with yet another cold! I swear that girl spends more time in bed with a cold than she does on her feet, being well.'

Hannah grinned. 'I must admit, it certainly seems that way at times. What does the doctor say?'

'Only that she's susceptible to them. She's getting worse you know, she never used to be as bad as this.'

'So does that mean she's cancelled out on you, again?'

'Yes, and for tonight's opera too. Geraint Evans singing Falstaff in *The Merry Wives of Windsor*. The tickets were ever so difficult to get hold of, not to mention costing an arm and a leg each. I don't suppose you'd like to come with me, would you?'

Hannah pulled a face. 'No, thank you very much. You might enjoy opera, but for me its sheer purgatory. And it's the same with your Pa so there's no point in asking him.'

'I suppose you'd jump at the chance if it was John Hanson in the *Desert Song*?' Robyn said sarcastically.

'You're dead right, if it was John Hanson in the *Desert Song* you wouldn't have to ask me twice. But as for *The Merry Wives of Windsor*, wild horses couldn't drag me to that.'

'But Geraint Evans is brilliant, Mum!'

'So's John Hanson. No, you stick to what you like, and I'll do the same.'

So who could she ask in place of Lesley? Robyn wondered. The last thing she wanted to do was go alone, or waste the tickets.

She began to rack her brains.

Robyn was in the bath, an hour and a half before curtain-up, when she thought of James McEwen. He liked opera, she remembered him telling her that once. But would he be free to go? No one else she'd rung had been.

She'd buzz him as soon as she was out of the bath, she decided. And if he wasn't available she would have to try and sell the other ticket back to the box office.

She gave a sudden grin at the irony of it. Her ringing James McEwen to ask him out!

Wonders would never cease.

Evans was singing wondrously, Robyn thought. The emotion he could convey with that voice of his was unbelievable. And what a stage presence! Whenever he came on it was as if the stage lit up, then faded down again when he left it.

She turned to look at James, sitting beside her and as she did he turned to look at her. They smiled simultaneously.

She brought her attention back to the performance, and he did the same.

'That was simply superb!' enthused Robyn as she and James left the theatre.

'All those curtains calls! They just went on and on.'

'They did, didn't they.' Robyn was feeling all bubbly inside, a combination of euphoria, excitement and pleasure. She was very much on a 'high'.

'Would you like a drink before we go back?' James suggested.

She would, she thought. In fact that was precisely what she'd like. 'Yes, please.'

'There's a pub just over the road then,' said James, pointing.

The pub was a bustle with regulars and people like themselves who'd just come from the opera. Despite this they were fortunate in finding a free table, where Robyn sat while James went up to order.

The moustache James had grown really did suit him, Robyn thought, staring at him standing at the bar, waiting to be served. It was amazing how such a small thing could change what she had always considered to be a fairly plain face into an attractive one. Or was there more to it than that? Was it that James himself had changed, matured, lived a bit, and that was what was being reflected in his face? She didn't know. But what she did know was that she wasn't seeing him as she'd always seen him in the past.

'Here you are,' said James on rejoining Robyn, placing the glass of cider she'd requested in front of her.

'I'm glad you could make it tonight. I hate going to these occasions on my own,' Robyn said, after she'd had a sip of cider.

'I'm delighted you thought of me. What was going to be a very dull evening turned out to be a memorable one.'

'I thought you might have been going out with Caroline?' Robyn smiled, a smile with an edge to it. Just as there had been an edge to her voice when she'd asked that.

'Caroline's in London.'

'But it's the summer breaks.'

'She has things to do down there.'

Robyn leaned closer to him. '*Revolutionary* things?' she queried in a mocking tone.

James gave her an exaggerated wink. 'Knowing comrade Caro, I should expect so.'

They both laughed.

'Do you sleep with her?'

James's face went blank, while his eyes took on a piercing quality as he studied Robyn. 'Isn't that rather a personal question?'

'Which means you do,' Robyn stated instantly. She hadn't meant at all to ask him that. But it was something she'd wondered about, and somehow it had just sort of popped out.

James had a slow pull of his pint. 'Yes, we do actually,' he admitted. 'From time to time, that is.'

'Do you love her?'

'No. I have a great fondness for her though. As she does for me. We get on well together.'

Robyn was smiling, but there was a strain to her smile. She was annoyed, though she certainly had no right to be. James was

427

nothing to her, or she to him. He could go to bed with whoever he liked. Good luck to him!

'So she is your girlfriend,' Robyn said.

James sighed. 'I told you, Caroline doesn't agree with such tags.'

'I'm not talking about her, but you now. Do *you* consider her your girlfriend?'

'No, I don't. She's a mate I sleep with occasionally, all right? Now can we change the subject.'

'Why, am I embarrassing you?'

'Not in the least. It's just not something I think we should, or I should, discuss. What happens between me and Caroline is precisely that, between me and Caroline. I mean, if I was sleeping with you, would you like me discussing the matter with someone making a casual inquiry about it? I shouldn't think so.'

Robyn blushed bright red. The idea of her sleeping with James was preposterous. She couldn't even imagine such a thing.

'I appreciate this is the so-called permissive swinging Sixties but that doesn't mean manners have to go out the window. Don't you agree?'

'Yes, I'm sorry.'

He stared at her, his brow creased. 'I'm curious. Why did you ask?'

'Just that, curiosity.' She fumbled for her cigarettes, feeling she'd made a right fool of herself. For the first time ever she felt she wasn't in a position of dominance over James. Why – and this astounded her – she actually felt vulnerable!

'Cigarette?' she asked, offering him her packet.

He accepted one, and they both lit up. 'So you've left vet college. What happens now?' she asked, changing the subject, as he'd requested.

'Now I start work and earning my way. My father has bought me into a practice located out in Anniesland. It's a thriving practice, and I believe I'll do well there.'

'When do you start?'

'The first Monday of next month. I can't tell you how much I'm looking forward to it. I had considered going for a country practice, dealing with livestock etc., but as my real interest is large dogs I've decided to stay in town. There's also more money in a town practice, which is another attraction over a country one.'

'I didn't know you liked large dogs?' Robyn said.

'I adore them. Great Danes in particular.'

'But you don't have a dog at home? Least, I've never heard of you having one.'

'The reason for that is simple. My father is allergic to dogs; they bring him out in an itchy rash. That's why we don't, and never have had, a dog. It broke my heart when I was a lad, as I desperately wanted one. But there you are, we can't have everything we want in life, can we?'

'No,' she agreed, thinking briefly of Guy Trecarron.

'I intend specialising in large dogs, and hopefully to make my name in that field. My idea of heaven would be a practice where, ultimately, I dealt solely with large dogs. Feasible I suppose, but it would take a long time to bring that situation about.'

They chatted till they'd both finished their drinks, then left the pub and headed for James's car, which they'd come in. The car was an old Zephyr, long in the tooth but, as James put it, a marvellous runner.

They continued chatting all the way back to Winton Avenue where James parked the Zephyr outside his house.

'I'll walk you to your front door,' he said when they were out of the car and the car was locked.

'There's no need.'

He hesitated, then said. 'It's no trouble, Robyn.'

She smiled at him. 'Manners again, eh?'

He matched her smile. 'Quite.'

He walked on the outside, she on the inside, but he didn't attempt to take her by the arm or touch her in any way.

'Right then,' she said when they reached her front door.

'Thank you for a tremendous evening. I can't remember when I've enjoyed myself more,' he said softly and sincerely.

Surprisingly, neither could she. At least, not for a long time.

'Are you sure you won't let me pay for that ticket?'

'My treat. I insist.'

'That's very kind of you.'

He's going to try and kiss me! she thought as he moved closer to her, but she was wrong.

James held out his hand. 'Goodnight, Robyn.'

She shook with him. 'Goodnight, James.'

'See you about.'

'See you about,' she echoed.

He swung suddenly on his heels and strode back down the gravel driveway, gravel scrunching under his feet as he went.

She waited, ready to wave if he turned and did. But he didn't.

Who would have imagined she would have enjoyed a night out with James McEwen as much as she had! she thought as she went inside.

Not her. Not in a million years.

'I was thinking,' Robyn said casually. 'That I might throw a small dinner party. I've never done that before, and the idea appeals.'

Hannah glanced up from her knitting. 'A dinner party? For how many?'

Robyn pretended to consider that. 'How about four? That's not too many is it?'

'Not in the least. And you'd cook?'

'Oh yes, I'll do everything. It wouldn't be any trouble to you.'

'Are we invited to this dinner party?' Lal, tongue in cheek, asked from where he was sitting doing the crossword puzzle in that day's *Glasgow Herald*.

'If there are only to be four how can you be!' Robyn replied, knowing her leg was being pulled.

'Oh I see, it's like that, is it? You entertain your friends and we get the heave for the night.'

She wagged a finger at him. 'It'll give you a golden opportunity to take Mum out. You haven't done so for ages.'

'You're doing *us* a favour, now!' Lal riposted, keeping up the banter.

'That's one way of looking at it. You can take Mum out for a slap-up meal, and perhaps go on somewhere else afterwards.'

'And what if she doesn't want to go out for a meal?'

'Yes, I do!' Hannah said quickly, which brought smiles to all their faces.

'There you are,' Robyn said to Lal.

'And just who are you thinking of inviting to this dinner party of yours?' he queried.

'The McEwen brothers and Lesley, say,' she replied lightly.

Lal stared at his daughter in disbelief. Then he stuck a finger in an ear and waggled the finger up and down. 'Could you please repeat that? I must have misheard you.'

430

Robyn couldn't help but grin at her father's antics. 'I said the McEwen brothers and Lesley.'

'You mean *James* McEwen?'

'That's right.'

'Good God!'

'I thought you weren't interested in him?' Hannah queried.

'I'm not! But I do think his brother Rory might click with Lesley who, as you know, hasn't had a boyfriend for ages.'

'Lesley and Rory? I see,' said Hannah thoughtfully.

'And I've nothing against James, never have had. He's always been nice enough, if not exactly my sort. And as I want to try and get Rory and Lesley together, he's the obvious one to make up the foursome.' Robyn said, so convincingly she almost convinced herself it was true, instead of a right load of twaddle.

'Wasn't it James you took with you to the opera?' Lal queried.

'Yes, he was the only one free. We had a good night, too.'

'What date did you have in mind for this dinner party?' Hannah asked.

'That depends. I'll have to consult with James and Rory first before I can name a date.'

A little later, when Robyn's back was turned to them, Lal caught Hannah's attention and raised an eyebrow.

She shrugged in reply.

'I'll get the next course,' said Robyn, rising and reaching for James's plate.

'And I'll help you,' said Lesley, also rising and reaching for Rory's plate.

'Top up the glasses,' Robyn instructed James.

'Everyone want some more?' James queried, picking up the claret jug.

'Yes, please,' replied Lesley, and giggled.

'Please,' smiled Robyn.

'Can I smoke?' a very relaxed Rory asked. They were all that, and thoroughly enjoying themselves. The evening had started off rather stiffly, but after a few aperitifs that had soon disappeared.

Lesley followed Robyn out of the room to the kitchen where she plonked down the plates she was carrying.

'That Rory!' she choked. 'What a card! An absolute riot!'

'I thought I was going to wet myself when he told that one

about the wide-mouthed frog,' said Robyn. It had been the most innocuous of jokes imaginable, but hysterically funny.

Lesley pursed her lips. '"Not many of those about" said the wide-mouthed frog to the crocodile.' And exploded with laughter at her repeat of the joke's tag line.

Robyn laughed too. 'They're tremendous company, aren't they?'

'Yours is certainly sexy. No wonder you've been keeping quiet about him. I don't blame you.'

'James?'

'Hmmh! Sexy-lexy. He can give me a how's your father any day.'

'Lesley! Don't be so crude.'

'Same goes for Rory. He can do push-ups with me any time he likes.'

'You're being disgusting now.'

'No, I'm not. Just honest. I think the pair of them are dishy as all get out.'

Robyn opened the fridge and took out the fruit brûlée she'd made for dessert. It was a great favourite of hers, and one she'd thought would go down well.

'That looks delicious!' exclaimed Lesley, peering at it.

'I just hope it tastes as nice as it looks.'

As they returned to the dining room Robyn thought about Lesley and Rory. She'd never really believed they'd click together – that had merely been an excuse for Lal and Hannah – but from the way things were going she wouldn't be at all surprised if Rory asked Lesley out. She made a mental note to warn Lesley about Stephanie and the others. She didn't want Lesley getting hurt because of an introduction she'd brought about.

Robyn was sitting in front of her dressing-table mirror brushing her hair, something she did most nights. The dinner party had ended about an hour previously, and there could be no doubt, it had been a roaring success. Both James and Rory had been most effusive with their thanks when they'd left.

And Rory *had* asked for Lesley's telephone number, which Lesley had given him, quick as wink. Rory had promised to be in touch.

She'd warned Lesley about Rory's reputation, but Lesley had shrugged that off, saying she'd play it by ear. She wasn't going to shoot Rory down right at the off just because he was a womaniser.

Robyn picked up the cigarette that had been resting on an ashtray by her elbow, and had a puff, her mind going back over the evening.

After the meal and liqueurs, at her suggestion, they'd played Monopoly, and that had been even funnier than what had gone on during dinner. James, much to her amazement, had cheated blatantly, and usually at her expense.

He'd attempted to pinch her money, knocked the dice to change the numbers, tried to shortchange her paying penalties, and so on and so forth.

At one point she'd pretended to lose her temper and biffed him over the head with a cushion, his reaction being to fall flat on the floor and pretend to be dead.

And then, something that had become a running joke, every so often he'd reach across and squeeze Lesley's knee while leering lecherously at her. The poor girl's knee was going to be black and blue in the morning.

She'd been sorry to see him go but by the time he and Rory had left Lal and Hannah had been home for a good hour, and midnight come and gone.

How odd, she thought. The James McEwen she was recently discovering was quite different to the conception and perception she'd always had of him.

Entertaining, witty, charming – fair do's he'd always been that – fascinating and sexy-lexy?

Yes, she realised. She now found him that as well.

She blushed furiously at a sudden thought she had. A thought concerning push-ups.

It was nearly six weeks before Robyn saw James again. She was returning in her Mini from the newsagent where she'd been collecting the Sunday papers, when she spotted him coming out of his house and heading for his car, parked in the street. She drew up beside the Zephyr.

'Hello! Off for a Sunday drive?' she smiled.

'To work, believe it or not,' he replied.

'Work. On a Sunday?'

He nodded. 'An Alsation belonging to one of our clients has been accidentally hit by an arrow, and needs attention right away. As I'm the one with the stated interest in large dogs, I've been called out.'

'How did it get hit by an arrow?' Robyn asked.

'By the owner apparently, who was target shooting. It was an accident, needless to say and the owner's quite beside himself with worry and guilt.'

'So where exactly are you going to now?'

'My surgery, to operate on the dog. The client is already on his way there, as is my assistant.'

She was about to say 'good luck' when she had an idea. 'Any chance of my coming with you? I'd love to see where you work and what the set-up is.'

That clearly took him by surprise. 'I don't suppose there's any reason why you shouldn't come along. I'm leaving right away though. I can't hang about.'

'Just let me park the car and bung these papers indoors and I'll be with you.'

'Quick as you can, then.'

She smiled inwardly to hear the ring of authority in his voice. It took her less than two minutes to do what she had to. On returning to the Zephyr she slid into the front passenger seat, and the moment her door was shut the car moved off.

'Is the dog in danger of dying?' she asked.

'Very much so, from what I've been told. But of course I can't tell precisely what's what until I examine the animal.'

He drove fast, but well and safely. Being a Sunday morning there was little traffic about, so they made good time.

The practice transpired to be in the Crow Road, one of Anniesland's main thoroughfares, and a prime position for any business. The building that housed the practice was old and somewhat dilapidated in appearance on the outside, but very modern and up-to-date once you got inside.

Miss Peterson, James's assistant, was already there, as was the client, a Mr Wark, with the wounded dog. Miss Peterson and Mr Wark had taken the dog through to the surgery where it was laid out on the operating table with a distraught Mr Wark trying to soothe the whining beast.

James didn't introduce Robyn who followed him into the surgery; there wasn't time for that. Swiftly he examined the dog, the dog yelping in agony as he did.

'Sorry boy, this has to be done,' James said softly.

'I never saw him, you understand,' Wark explained to James. 'I wouldn't hurt Roscoe for the world.' Wark was a wealthy scrap-metal merchant who lived in a big house surrounded by land on the outskirts of Glasgow.

James straightened and rapped out an instruction to the hovering Miss Peterson. He then removed his jacket, hung it up, and slipped into a freshly laundered operating gown.

He washed and scrubbed his hands, put on a pair of rubber gloves, then returned to the operating table where Miss Peterson was waiting with the pre-med.

James administered the pre-med, then said they'd have to wait a short while until that took effect. He told Wark to continue stroking and generally soothing Roscoe.

When he judged Roscoe ready, James injected the dog with a barbiturate anaesthetic which knocked it out cold. 'I'm going to ask you to leave us now please,' he said kindly, but firmly, to Wark.

'Yes, of course,' replied the agitated Wark.

Miss Peterson showed him to the surgery door, where he had a last look at Roscoe, before leaving the surgery and going on into the waiting room.

As soon as Wark was gone James said to Miss Peterson, 'Shave the wound site.'

Robyn made sure she was well out of the way, but in a position to see all that was happening. She watched Miss Peterson shave a fair sized area round the spot where the arrow had penetrated. Miss Peterson cleaned and dried the now exposed flesh, using paper towels which she discarded in a bin.

James had another visual examination of the wound, then instructed Miss Peterson to drape Roscoe.

'Scalpel,' James said when Miss Peterson had finished that. She handed him one, and he bent to his task.

'Scissors.' Miss Peterson gave him a pair.

'Rat-toothed forceps.'

Then almost immediately. 'Artery forceps.'

Robyn gazed on in fascination as James worked on Roscoe.

She'd thought he would have removed the arrow right away, but he didn't. It was ten, perhaps fifteen minutes before he finally pulled the shaft free, the dog's back legs jerking convulsively as the arrow came out.

'Lucky it wasn't a hunting arrow,' James said to the hovering Miss Peterson, laying the arrow aside. 'That would most certainly have killed the poor bugger.'

The arrow James had removed was a practice one, which meant it had a stubby, slightly pointed end rather than barbs. The latter were usually a little less penetrating, but caused far more damage over a wider area.

Robyn watched entranced as James continued with the operation. His brow was furrowed, his attention total. His largish hands seemed to alternately float and dance over the wound site. But it was his extreme gentleness that impressed her most. He seemed to have an aura about him which for some reason made her think of – odd, as she wasn't Catholic – St Francis of Assisi.

'A no 5 curved triangular suture needle and monofilament nylon,' James said after a while, discarding his bloodied scalpel.

For a brief second his eyes met Robyn's, and he smiled. It was a smile that went straight to her heart.

Then Miss Peterson was by his side with needle and nylon, and he bent again to Roscoe.

'I thought Mr Wark was going to burst out crying when you told him that Roscoe would live,' Robyn said to James as they sped back to Winton Avenue in his Zephyr.

'He was a bit overcome, wasn't he.'

'A bit! I'd call it a lot more than that.'

James gave a soft laugh.

'It must feel marvellous to have just saved a life.' Robyn said.

'Oh it does! I can assure you.'

She stared at him in undisguised admiration. 'Thank you for letting me come today and witness what I did. It's much appreciated.'

He didn't reply to that.

'Can I tell you how I feel?' she said.

'How do you feel?'

'As if I've just been to church.'

He gave her a strange sideways look. 'I know precisely what

you mean by that. I sometimes feel that way myself after an operation, or series of operations.'

They drove in silence for a short distance, then Robyn said casually. 'How's comrade Caro, as you called her?'

'In Germany.'

'Oh?'

'She has friends and connections over there.'

'How long is she away for?'

'Till it's time for her to return to the L.S.E., which is soon, now.'

Robyn looked at his hands on the driving wheel, remembering how they'd floated and danced over Roscoe's wound site. She was suddenly very dry in the throat, while her breathing had turned shallow as if there was a heavy weight pressing on her chest.

'What have you got planned for this evening?' she asked in a croaky voice.

'Nothing much.'

'Me neither.'

He gave her another sideways look, this a searching, slightly puzzled one.

'We could do something together if you fancied it?' she suggested,

'That would be nice.' His voice was now strained, while hers remained croaky. 'What?'

'Whatever.'

He thought about that. 'There's a funfair at Milngavie. We could drive out there?'

'A funfair!' she exclaimed. 'Perfect!'

'We'll do that, then.'

'Lovely.'

They arranged the time when he'd pick her up.

Something slimy slapped Robyn in the face, causing her to shriek. She and James were on the Ghost Train, and had just rattled round the first bend into darkness.

Green lights flickered, and a skeleton appeared to shake its bones at them. Above them a bat swooped, then another.

The green lights died away, and it was darkness again. But not for long. A weird pulsating light lit up an opened coffin, out of

437

which a hairy hand rose. The decomposing body sat bolt upright to stare straight at Robyn: at least that's how it seemed to her.

'Oh, my God!' a female voice said from further up the train.

'It's our Ronnie,' commented a male voice, which got a huge laugh.

Robyn was amongst those laughing when a hissing snake suddenly reared up and lunged at her.

She propelled herself away from it, and into James who instinctively threw his arms round her in a protective manner. He pulled her close, as more snakes and other horrors rose up all around them.

When they finally emerged from the tunnel his arms were still around her, and they were staring at one another.

'Shall I win you a kewpie doll?' he asked as they came upon a shooting gallery.

'Can you shoot?'

'I'm a regular Dead-Eye Dick.'

'Go on, prove it then,' she challenged.

'I shall. You just watch this.'

James paid his money, and accepted a loaded .22 from the stallholder. He sighted on the paper target, and fired.

'Missed altogether,' said Robyn, trying to keep a straight face.

James glared at the target, then at her while the stallholder reloaded the gun.

'Dead-Eye Dick?' she taunted, raising a scornful eyebrow.

James sighed again, and fired. 'Ah!' he exclaimed.

The stallholder inspected the target. 'Outer ring sir, that scores one point, he said. Going to the now fuming James he reloaded the gun.

'Last shot?' queried James.

'Last shot, sir,' the stallholder confirmed.

James sighted a third time, and fired.

'One again sir, tough luck,' announced the stallholder.

Robyn almost burst out laughing, but managed not to.

'Another go!' exclaimed James, putting more money on the counter in front of him.

'Certainly sir,' smiled the stallholder, reloading the .22.

This time James hardly seemed to sight at all, snapping off the shot.

438

'Bull!' said the stallholder in surprise.

James grinned at Robyn. Again he hardly seemed to sight.

'Bull!' said the stallholder.

James grinned even more widely at Robyn.

'And a third!' the stallholder announced seconds later. 'You win a prize sir. What's your choice?'

'A kewpie doll please,' James replied. When he was given the doll he handed it to Robyn.

'You deliberately did badly that first go!' she accused him.

He winked at her. 'Got you going though, didn't it?'

'You've shot before.'

'Shall I let you into a secret?'

'What?'

He whispered into her ear. 'I belong to a rifle club and shoot at least once a month.'

Now she did burst out laughing.

She clutched her kewpie doll to her as they moved on.

James pulled the Zephyr into the kerb in front of Robyn's house.

'It was great fun at the funfair. Thank you for taking me,' she smiled.

He hesitated, then said, 'We should go out together again sometime.'

She stared levelly at him. 'When?'

'How about next Friday night? There's a dance on I know of that should be quite good.'

'We'll go then.'

'Right.'

She placed a hand on his thigh. 'Thank you again, James.'

He wanted to place a hand over hers, but didn't. 'Friday at eight, then?'

'Friday at eight,' she confirmed, and got out of the car.

As she hurried inside she realised that her heart was thumping wildly.

The band was a rock 'n' roll one, it's members dressed as Teddy Boys. They were tremendous.

Robyn and James applauded enthusiastically when the number they were dancing to came to an end.

'Enough for the moment,' said Robyn. 'I'm puffed.'

'I'm the same,' replied James, taking her by the crook of the elbow and guiding her from the dancefloor.

They were at the Dawsholm Park Tennis Club, the building they were in a grey stone affair surrounded by tennis courts.

'Would you like some juice?' James asked when they were off the floor. The club wasn't licensed to sell alcohol.

Robyn screwed up her nose. 'I suppose so. What I could really use is a proper drink though.'

'I wouldn't mind one myself. If you care to come out to the car I've got a bottle there.' When he saw her expression he added, 'It's been in the boot for ages, left there by Rory after he'd borrowed the car one night.'

'Let's go sample the contents then,' said Robyn.

They left the building and music behind, going down a flight of stone steps that led into the jam-packed car park. It was dark in the car park, the only light coming from the stars, of which there weren't many out that night, and a slight overspill from the building at the opposite end of the car park where the Zephyr was.

James opened the front passenger door for Robyn, who slipped inside. He then went to the boot, took out the three-quarters-full bottle of whisky, relocked the boot and got into the driver's seat.

'Hope you like malt?' he queried.

'What's the brand?'

'Macallan.'

'Yes, please!'

'You know your whiskies do you?'

'I know that Macallan is reputedly the best malt there is, and I also know I like it.'

He removed the top from the bottle and handed it to her. 'You have the first slug.'

She laughed. '*Sip* please! Ladies don't have slugs.'

'You sip then and I'll slug.'

She laughed again, had a sip from the bottle and gave the bottle back to him. 'Hmmmhh!' she murmured in appreciation.

'Good?'

'Nectar.'

He had a large swallow. 'I agree. Sheer nectar.'

'Let's have another sip then.'

He passed her the bottle, and she had a second sip.

'That feels a lot better,' she said, handing him the bottle again.

He had another of his so-called slugs. 'I definitely agree,' he concurred.

Robyn giggled. 'How absolutely decadent! Sitting in a car drinking from a whisky bottle.'

'And how very, very Glasgow.'

She giggled again. 'True! But not for people who live in Winton Avenue.'

'Oh no, not for those!' he agreed, shaking his head.

'We're posh.'

'And posh people don't do common things like that.'

'Definitely not,' she said, wagging a finger.

'Posh people . . .' she started to add, but didn't finish for suddenly his mouth was on hers, and he was kissing her deeply.

She went stiff, resisting for only a brief second, then she yielded herself to the kiss, and James.

They kissed and kissed, and continued kissing.

And never returned to the dance.

Robyn closed her front door behind her, then leant back against it. She felt wonderful. All sort of zingy on the inside. She and James were courting; that's what it had become. She wanted to shout at the top of her voice, and drum a little dance on the floor. She wanted to do cartwheels. She wanted . . .

'Are you all right?'

The speaker was Lal who was staring at her in concern. She'd neither noticed or heard his silent approach.

'Yes Pa, I'm fine. Why?'

'You're looking very odd. As if you'd suddenly been taken ill or something.'

'Not ill, but definitely something,' she replied mysteriously. 'Mum already in bed?'

Lal nodded. 'She went up about twenty minutes ago.'

'I'll away up as well then.'

She was heading for the stairs when Lal called after her. 'How did tonight go?'

'Very well. I enjoyed myself.'

'Are you seeing James again?'

She turned to give him a funny smile. 'Yes, tomorrow night.

We're going to the pictures.' She paused, then added softly. 'Goodnight, Pa.'

'Goodnight, Robyn.'

Her feet pitter-pattered on the stairs, then she was gone. Lal gazed after her. Was it happening between Robyn and James, after all? He couldn't have been more pleased if it was. James was the man he'd wanted for Robyn for years now, a man she hadn't been at all interested in romantically.

He mustn't count his chickens, he told himself. It was early days yet.

He mustn't count his chickens, but he could keep his fingers crossed.

'Have a good time!' Hannah cried out to Robyn and James who were just leaving, off to a new year's party.

'We will!' Robyn shouted back, and blew her mother a kiss.

'See you tomorrow,' said Lal, emerging from their combined dining and sitting room. He and Hannah were spending a quiet night at home. They'd watch the special edition of The White Heather Club on T.V., and see the new year in. That would be it.

'See you tomorrow, Pa!' Robyn replied, and closed the door behind her. She immediately shivered, for it was freezing out.

'Brrr!' she complained. 'Somewhat chillsome, eh?'

'Somewhat,' James agreed, taking her by the arm.

She stopped, to stare at him. 'What's wrong?'

'What makes you think there's something wrong?'

'Oh come on James, I know you well enough by now. Your face is absolutely tripping you.'

He shrugged. 'Aye, well you're right. I had a call out today that has really upset me.'

'Tell me about it in the car. It'll be warmer there,' she said, not wanting to hang around outside in that weather. They hurried to the Zephyr, and got inside.

'Now what's this all about?' Robyn asked.

'You remember I told you I adore all big dogs, but Great Danes in particular?'

She nodded.

'Well, I had a phone call from the Anniesland police early this afternoon, requesting me to go round to the station and attend to a Great Dane they had there. Apparently they'd arrested a man

442

for burglary shortly before, and the Dane belonged to him. As the man was arrested at home where he lived alone, they had to take the Dane as well.'

James's expression changed to become extremely grim. 'That dog Robyn, you should have seen the state of the beast. It was matchstick-thin and covered in scars where it had been beaten. According to the information the police were able to give me, the bastard kept it tied up in the flat where he lived, hardly ever taking it out for exercise. He fed it very irregularly, and would find an excuse to beat the damned animal nearly every day. I . . .' James swallowed hard. 'I nearly cried when the police showed it to me.'

'Were you able to help it?'

'A bit. But what it needs more than anything is feeding up, and love of course. Both of which it will get now, thank goodness as one of the policemen has volunteered to keep the dog as his own.'

James clenched and unclenched his hands. 'How anyone could treat an animal like that is beyond me. If I had my way I'd flog the bastard to within an inch of his life. And I'd make sure the dog was watching.'

He sniffed, and fell into a moody silence.

'How old is the dog?'

'Three, I believe. How it's managed to survive so long is a miracle. The man got it as a pup, he said. Paid good money for it as well.'

Robyn frowned at a sudden thought. 'Why did the police ring you and not the R.S.P.C.A.?'

'They did ring the R.S.P.C.A. first, and it was McCorkindale there who suggested they contact me. Nearly the entire unit is down with the flue it seems, which is why they wanted me to deal with the matter.'

'Poor dog,' whispered Robyn, shaking her head.

'Well, that's why I'm upset and my face tripping me. Sorry.'

She leant over and kissed him on the cheek. 'We don't have to go to this party you know. We could stay in if you wish?'

'But you've been looking forward to it?'

'True enough. But I wouldn't enjoy myself if you were miserable.'

'Are you sure you wouldn't mind?' he queried.

'Not at all. We can have a few drinks by ourselves and play some music. How about that?'

He kissed her lightly on the lips. 'The way I feel, a party is the last thing I want to go to.'

'Right then, that's settled. We stay in,' she said with finality.

They got out of the car again. James crooking his arm around hers as they made for his front door.

'Heard anything yet from your parents?' Robyn asked when they were inside. Alexander and Cecily McEwen had gone off to spend five days in Salzburg, Austria. Five days that would include New Year's Eve and day.

'I had a phone call this morning. They're having a whale of a time, and are tremendously pleased with the hotel. They said there's lots of snow there, though that hasn't tempted them to try any sporting activities. They're both spectators born and bred.'

Having hung up their coats James ushered Robyn into a comfy sitting room where there was a fire all made up, just waiting to be lit.

'The central heating is on, but I think we'll have the fire as well,' James said. Central heating was still a novelty, with the McEwens having had it installed only recently. The Stuarts on the other hand had had it for a number of years.

James put a match to the fire which was soon roaring away. 'Now, how about a drink?' he said to Robyn.

'Please.'

'And Schubert?'

'Whatever you wish will be fine by me.'

'Schubert it is then.'

James poured them both whiskies, and after giving Robyn hers crossed over to the hi-fi standing in a corner. Robyn settled herself on a settee facing the fire as Schubert's piano quintet opus 114 (the Trout) stole into the room.

James came and sat beside her. 'This is perfect. Thank you for being so understanding.'

She had a sip of her whisky, and smiled at him. Reaching out, she stroked one side of his moustache, then the other. Which made him smile also.

Putting an arm round her shoulders he drew her close. She shut her eyes, and so too did he, as they listened to the music.

After a while James got up and turned the record over. He

poured himself more whisky, Robyn declining when he asked her if she wished a freshener.

'It's beautifully warm in here now,' Robyn murmured when James rejoined her.

'Hmmh!' he agreed. The fire was throwing out a great deal of heat which, combined with two radiators, made the room warm as toast.

With her free hand – she was holding her glass in the other – she sought out his. 'I'd be happy to stay here forever, just like this,' she said softly.

'I'd be happy to stay anywhere forever, as long as it was with you,' he replied, his tone matching hers.

'That's a lovely thing to say James.'

'I mean it. You must know I love you, and have done for years.'

She squeezed the hand she was holding. 'I love you too. I haven't always, but I do now.'

They stared at one another. 'This is the first time we've ever had a house to ourselves,' he said.

'I know.'

He opened his mouth, but before he could speak further she said, her voice a velvet caress. 'Why don't you switch off the lights. That would be better, don't you think?'

A little later they moved off the couch to lie in front of the fire.

Robyn came dreamily awake to find a smiling James sitting by her side staring at her. He as naked as she.

'I woke up a couple of minutes ago,' he said.

They'd made love twice, she remembered. Both gentle, tender, loving experiences. She felt languorous in the extreme, and completely satisfied.

She stretched, and yawned.

'Will you marry me?' James asked.

Marry James McEwen? She couldn't think of anything that would please her more. If she'd had any lingering doubts the events of that evening had completely dispelled them. 'Yes,' she replied.

'Are you . . .'

'Yes, I'm, certain,' she interrupted.

'Oh Robyn!' he husked. 'You've no idea how happy this makes me.'

'But I do. For it makes me just as happy.'

Sitting up she wrapped her arms round him, and kissed him. Then he kissed her.

Dawn was creeping over the rooftops when she finally got home.

'Engaged!' Lal exclaimed in delight, Robyn having just broken the news to him and Hannah. It was New Year's day afternoon and, by agreement, she'd waited till James had come round before announcing their engagement.

'I haven't bought the ring yet, but I will, just as soon as the shops open again,' a beaming James said.

Hannah had her fist in her mouth. She was as delighted as Lal by this news.

Lal went to Robyn and, eyes glistening, kissed her on the forehead. Then, grabbing hold of James's hand he pumped that furiously up and down.

Hannah grasped her daughter by the shoulders. 'This is marvellous Robyn. Simply marvellous. You're doing the right thing, I just know you are.'

'Champagne! That's what this calls for, champagne,' said Lal, and charged from this room.

'And all this happened last night?' Hannah queried.

Robyn nodded.

'What a marvellous night to propose James. That was quite inspired of you.'

'Not as inspired as you might think,' he admitted modestly.'I hadn't planned to. It just sort of came about.'

'Well, planned or not, proposing on New Year's eve is ever so romantic!'

'You and Pa are the first to know,' said Robyn. 'James will be ringing his parents later on.'

'And when is the wedding going to be? Have you discussed a date yet?' Hannah asked eagerly.

'We need a little time to get organised, but we don't want too long an engagement. We thought August would be about right,' Robyn replied.

'A church wedding of course. Your father won't hear otherwise.'

'Yes, a church wedding,' Robyn laughed. She glanced at James to note the love shining from his eyes as he gazed at her.

Then Lal was back with a bottle of Krug and four flutes. 'I'm so excited I feel I'm going to burst with it,' he burbled.

'For God's sake don't do that, you'd make an awful mess of the room,' Hannah teased.

'Now when . . .'

'August,' Robyn said, pre-empting her father's question.

'August!' he nodded. 'Good, good.'

What a relief, Hannah thought as Lal handed the glasses round, accepting one when it was offered to her. How she'd worried after Guy Trecarron had broken with Robyn, worried herself sick but done her best not to show it. Now everything had come out all right in the long run. Robyn was in love again, and marrying James McEwen, as fine a young man as you could find.

'To the happy couple. May all your problems be little ones!' Lal toasted when the bottle was popped and glasses filled.

The four of them drank to that.

'Just wait a minute,' said Cathy, stopping to catch her breath. Beside her, Lady, Gavin's dog who was now hers, immediately sat. She too was getting on and glad of a breather.

'Are you all right, Gran?' Robyn asked anxiously. They were three flights up a close in Woodside Terrace, a stone's throw from Charing Cross. She'd brought Cathy to see the flat she and James were in the process of buying.

'Just a bit peched, that's all,' Cathy replied.

'Do you want me to give you a hand?'

'No thanks. I'm old but not entirely decrepit yet. I'll manage under my own steam.'

A few seconds later Cathy started up the stairs again, soon arriving at what was to be Robyn's door, the next flight up.

'It's very handy here for both James and I. We'll be within easy striking distance of his practice and the Blackbird,' Robyn explained as she slid the key into the Yale.

'And a nice area,' Cathy added. 'Very nice indeed.'

'This is the hallway,' Robyn said quite unnecessarily once they were inside, which made Cathy grin. She could see it was *that*!

'Oh aye,' Cathy nodded.

'And this is the spare bedroom,' said Robyn, throwing open a door on their left.

It was a decent-sized room, Cathy thought. And light. 'When did the owners move out?' she asked.

'A couple of weeks ago. His firm suddenly shifted him to Manchester. The wife didn't want to leave Glasgow – was quite miffed about it apparently – but had to go with the husband who had no choice about the matter. It was either relocate or be out of a job.'

'Are you going to have to do much painting and decorating?' Cathy queried, thinking this room didn't need anything doing to it.

'Just the bathroom. The rest of the flat has been done fairly recently, and tastefully too, as far as James and I are concerned. So why bother changing it?'

'You're lucky,' said Cathy. 'That's a considerable saving for you.'

'We're more than lucky with the flat. Pa is insisting on buying everything we'll need to furnish it fully. The beds, carpets, a three-piece suite, curtains – he's going to foot the bill for the lot. It'll cost him a packet, but as I said, he's insisting he does it.'

Robyn ushered Cathy out of the spare bedroom and into the kitchen which was more or less opposite. 'Cooker, washing machine, kitchen table and chairs – he's buying all those as well. It's to be our wedding present from him and Mum,' she added.

'It's a fine big kitchen, and bright, like that bedroom.'

Cathy could see what Robyn meant about the bathroom needing to be redecorated when she was shown it.

'We're having this gutted. A new bath, w.c. and basin in what I call sludge green, but which the man in the shop has a fancy name for. And then once they're installed, a Sanderson print for the walls that I've already chosen.'

'Lal paying for that as well?'

Robyn nodded.

'And what about James's parents? What's their wedding present going to be?'

'They're giving us the honeymoon. A fortnight in Lanzarote; that's in the Canary Islands. We're flying there and back, and are booked into the best hotel on the island. It should be idyllic.'

Cathy shook her head in wonder. 'It's a far cry from my day, I can tell you. With Bobby and I it was a room and kitchen in Purdon Street – outside toilet as you well know – and the

448

honeymoon a week in Largs. But still . . .' Her face lit up with memory. 'I wouldn't have changed it for the world. By our times we did well, you have to remember that.'

Cathy took a deep breath. 'It's amazing how the family's come on. Hannah and Lal living in Kelvinside, him with all those bakeries and what have you, and of course your mother's bookshop which I know for a fact is doing terribly well. And now you marrying a professional man from another Kelvinside family.' She shook her head again. 'Aye, the family's come on all right, a long way indeed.'

'Thanks to Pa,' said Robyn.

'Thanks to Lal, true enough. I was against him at the beginning, you know. Not because of himself – I aye liked him as a person – but because he was a soldier and there was a war on. He survived, thank God, to marry your Ma, and look at how happy they've been. I only hope you and your James are even half as happy.'

'We will be, Gran. I'm sure of it.'

'That's all right then,' said Cathy, wiping away a tear that had blossomed in her eye.

On impulse Robyn kissed her gran on the cheek.

'I'm proud of you, lass. And of your ma and da. I know your granda would also have been proud. Proud as Punch.'

Linking arms with Cathy, Robyn continued showing her round the flat.

Hannah lit a cigarette. 'As we now have a children's department I think you should go to the Bologna Book Fair,' she said to Robyn, who glanced at her in surprise. They were in Robyn's Mini travelling home from work.

The children's department had been Robyn's idea. Noticing how their volume of sales had increased in that area over the past few years, she had suggested to Hannah that they might increase the volume even further if they had more on offer. She had then suggested they enlarge their retail space by incorporating the basement, turning that into a separate children's department.

The snag had been, where to keep the stuff they then stored in the basement, a snag quickly overcome when Robyn had found that a neighbour down the street was willing to rent them part of his premises which he didn't use, and which now housed all their storage.

Hannah had put Robyn in charge of the newly-opened children's department, and taken on another member of staff, a Juliet Symons, who worked upstairs with her.

The Bologna Book Fair Hannah was referring to was an event that occurred annually in the northern Italian city of Bologna where the world's publishers of children's books assembled to show, sell and buy. As a book fair Bologna was getting bigger, and more important within the trade, every year.

'If we're going to have a children's department then let's do it properly,' Hannah went on. 'The Blackbird is considered by many, myself included, but then I'm obviously biased, to be the best bookshop in Glasgow. That being so, let's ensure our children's department is also the best. If you go to Bologna you can have an overview of all that's currently on offer, and about to be on offer, from British and foreign publishers, which can only be to our advantage. Now what do you say?'

'I agree that a trip to Bologna would be of tremendous help in raising the standard of the department. In a couple of days I could see more titles than I normally would in months, and of course many titles I would never see at all.'

'Exactly,' Hannah nodded.

'But it'll be an expensive trip, particularly considering we're only one outlet.'

'As you're aware the Blackbird makes a damned good profit for me, money that is mine and mine alone, as your father won't touch a penny of it. So let's say this will be my personal wedding present to you, and also a thank-you for all the hard work you've put into the Blackbird since joining me from university.'

'Bologna!' Robyn mused. Italy in the spring! (The fair was held at the beginning of April.) She could probably pick up a few clothes when she was there, and shoes. Italian shoes were absolutely divine. With her wedding and honeymoon looming she was certainly in the market for new clothes and shoes.

'Well?' Hannah demanded.

'Yes, please.'

'Good. I'll get Lal to arrange everything. He's a whizz at that.'

James's reaction to Robyn telling him about Bologna was that he was madly jealous, and only wished he could accompany her. But that was impossible because of the practice.

She promised she'd bring him back a souvenir.

Robyn arrived at Bologna by a train which she'd caught in Milan, having flown to Milan from Heathrow. (There wasn't a direct flight from Glasgow.) The train journey had been a relatively quick one as she'd travelled *rapido*, the fastest service.

A porter carried her luggage out to the taxi rank, and there she had her first proper glimpse of Bologna, or *la Dotta* (the learned) as she was later to hear it called, and *la Grassa* (the fat) – the latter a reference to the city's gastronomic delights.

Her initial impression was of elegant architecture, classical in design. Many of the buildings she could see were of a burnt-orange colour that she thought must be quite dazzling on the eye in mid summer.

The taxi driver was very Italian in appearance with raven-black hair, brown eyes and an olive skin. He was also extremely excitable, continually gesticulating with both hands, even, frighteningly, when he drove. He took it upon himself to give Robyn a running commentary, his English limited but capable of that, en route to her hotel.

'The beautiful galleries of the Via dell'Indipendenza,' he said, pointing and waggling his hand up and down.

They were beautiful too, Robyn thought, craning to get a better look.

'Piazza Nettuno!' he announced, kissing the tips of his fingers afterwards.

'Pretty,' Robyn commented.

Then, a little later, in loud strident tones. 'The Basilica of San Petronio.'

Robyn stared out at a huge Gothic structure.

'It would have been bigger than St Peter's in Rome had not the Holy Father intervened,' the driver said, scowling into his overhead mirror.

'Most impressive, all the same.'

The driver muttered something in Italian, his scowl deepening.

Robyn spied a cluster of Romanesque churches that were

quite austere in appearance, which made them stand out from what she'd seen so far.

'The Basilica of Santo Stefano,' the driver explained when she inquired about them.

The driver pointed, and waggled his hand again. 'That round church is the Santo Sepolcro where San Petronio, the patron of Bologna, is buried. And in yard behind is Basin of Pilate.'

It was a gorgeous city, Robyn mused. Somehow soft and feminine, unlike the Glasgow she was used to which was hard, tough and very masculine. The air seemed to hum with energy, air filled with all manner of exotic smells quite alien to her nose.

Finally they arrived at the Hotel Baglioni, having nearly had a bump on the way which caused great vocal outbursts and arm waving from both parties concerned.

The man on reception oozed charm and reeked of garlic. He effusively welcomed Robyn to Bologna and the hotel, then asked her to sign the residents' book.

'Are you here on holiday?' he asked.

'No, business. I'll be attending the book fair.'

'Ah!' he exclaimed, eyebrows shooting up. 'The Fiera del Libro per Ragazzi!'

Robyn frowned. 'I'm sorry. I don't speak Italian.'

'That is the book fair. The Fiera del Libro per Ragazzi. We have many people staying who are going there. We are, how you say, jam-packed with them!'

That should be interesting, Robyn thought. 'Lots of British people?'

'Lots. And Spanish, and French and Portugeeses, and several Egyptians . . .' He trailed off, then added quickly. 'Very popular book fair, very popular hotel.'

When she was finished at the desk a bellboy, carrying her luggage, escorted her upstairs in the lift and showed her into her room. When he was gone, suitably tipped, she gazed about her.

There was only one word to describe the room, and that was charming. It reminded her of the man on reception, but without the garlic.

The room was a double, and en suite. She'd have a bath, then get ready for dinner, she decided. She could hardly wait for the next morning and the commencement of the book fair. It was all tremendously exciting.

She was stripped and about to get into the bath when her telephone rang.

'Hello,' said a most familiar voice, sounding as if he was right there in the room with her.

'James!'

'I thought I'd give you a surprise.'

When she finally sank into the bath she was smiling broadly, thinking of something intimate that James had whispered to her during the course of their conversation.

'Does madam mind sharing a table?' the head waiter inquired in a curious combination of Italian and cockney accents.

'Not at all,' Robyn replied.

'As you are English I shall put you with other English guests. We have found in the past that the English prefer that.'

Robyn felt like saying she wasn't English, but Scots. 'You speak our language extremely well,' she said instead.

The head waiter looked pleased at this compliment. 'I worked for a number of years in London's Soho. I learned your language during that time.'

There were three people already at the table the head waiter ushered her to. Two men and another woman. The two men rose politely at her arrival.

Introductions were soon made. One of the men was a literary agent with David Higham Associates, the other a senior member of the publicity department at Arrow paperbacks, while the woman was a translator. And the subject under discussion was naturally enough, books.

Robyn thoroughly enjoyed the meal and conversation, and learned a great deal about the fair in particular (which the other three had all been to before) and publishing in general.

At the end of the meal she was introduced to sambuca, a sweet Roman potation with coffee beans in it.

Before going up to bed she gave her promise to her new-found friend at Arrow to visit his stand next day, he promising in return to introduce her to other British publishers in the adjacent and surrounding stands.

The book was a real find, Robyn thought. *Celtic Fairy Tales* published by Dover Publications Inc. of New York. Excellently produced and exquisitely illustrated, she knew she could sell quite a few of these at the Blackbird. A Mr Schmitz, chewing a thick cigar, was only too happy to take her order and give her a catalogue to go away with.

She was laden down with catalogues and posters, not to mention give-aways. Thank goodness for the two plastic carrier bags she'd acquired from a Dutch publisher which had come with a glass of Dutch gin and nibble of cheese.

Her feet were killing her, and she was thinking she should call it a day and return to the Baglioni for a bath when she turned round to find a man staring at her. With a shock she recognised him as Guy Trecarron.

Her face flamed, and she went weak all over. He was staring at her with an incredulous expression on his face, clearly as thunderstruck as she.

Whirling round she began to walk swiftly away. A walk that got faster and faster till it was almost a run. She was in front of the very large Italian Mondadori stand when a hand grabbed her arm, forcing her to stop.

'We must talk,' said Guy quietly, aware that several folk were gazing curiously at them.

'Why?' she spat in reply.

'I . . . I just can't believe it's you! After all these years, to suddenly bump into you like this. It's incredible. We simply can't ignore one another.'

'I can,' she stated defiantly.

'You're exactly as I remembered you. You haven't aged a day,' he said.

'Don't try and soft-soap me. It won't wash!'

'I wasn't soft-soaping you. It's the truth.'

She gazed into his face. 'You *do* look older. More crease lines than I recall.'

He laughed. 'It's responsibility has done that.'

'You became Head of Sales for Penguin in Australia, then?'

'No, I got passed over in favour of a local chap. But I'm not with Penguin anymore. I'm U.K. Sales and Marketing Director, with a seat on the board of Orbit Books. I'm here in connection with our Mushroom imprint, the children's side of our organisation.'

'Orbit Books?' she repeated quietly.

'Yes, we have offices in Bedford Square.'

'So you now live in London?'

'We came over fourteen months ago, for me to take up my present position.'

That one word was like a knife being stuck into her. Stuck in, and twisted. '*We?*' she queried.

His lips thinned, while the skin of his face seemed to stretch and thin also. 'Myself, my wife Daniella and little boy, Ben. We have a house in Hampstead.'

She forced herself to smile, but mentally she was reeling. 'Congratulations! Wife and son. Well, well, well!'

'And you?'

'I'm engaged to be married in August.'

'Congratulations to you, then. Anyone I'd know?'

'A vet whose family are very old friends of my family.'

'Not that McEwen fellow you used to always make jokes about! He was a vet wasn't he? Or training to be one.'

Her face flamed again. 'It is James, actually. And I did make jokes about him, but that was before I got to know him properly. I discovered he's a wonderful, wonderful man. And I love him dearly.'

'I'm sorry,' Guy muttered. 'I didn't mean to be . . . disparaging.'

She caught a whiff that triggered her memory, and made her catch her breath. That manly smell Guy had overlaid with aftershave and the distinctive odour of French tobacco. Nor was the aftershave different; it was the same brand he'd been wearing that first day he'd walked into the Blackbird . . . how long ago was it now? Five years, she calculated. Five long, long years.

'U.K. Sales and Marketing Director, with a seat on the board. You have come up in the world, haven't you?' she smiled.

'Yes, I've been very fortunate. But then, I have to admit, it does help when your father-in-law owns the firm.'

She raised an eyebrow.

'My father-in-law is Big Ben Linehan. You must have heard of him?'

'The Australian tycoon and multi-millionaire?'

'That's him. He owns all sorts, including Orbit. But that's another story. Listen, how long are you here for?'

'I'm leaving the day after tomorrow.'

'And where are you staying?'

'The Baglioni.'

He laughed. 'Snap! So am I.'

'I didn't see you in the restaurant last night?'

'I was out to dinner with some Americans I'm trying to put a deal together with. Nor was I there at breakfast.'

'Too hungover?'

He gave her a wry smile. 'You get a lot of those when you're a Sales and Marketing Director. Anyway, why don't we have dinner together tonight? We have a lot to catch up on with each other.'

She immediately shook her head. 'No. I don't think that's a good idea.'

'Why not?'

'I just don't.'

'But I want to hear all about you, and Glasgow. How are Hannah and Lal?'

'Both fine. Thrilled about my forthcoming marriage.'

'I bet Lal is. I remember he always wanted you to marry the vet.'

'His name is James,' Robyn said a little more coldly than she intended.

'That's right, James. I recall now. So what about dinner, eh?'

She hesitated. It wouldn't really do any harm after all. And she was dying to hear more about what had happened in Guy's life since she'd last seen him, and about this Daniella he'd married.

'For old times sake?' Guy cajoled.

'I'm not sure. Where did you have in mind, the hotel?'

'We wouldn't be able to talk properly there, far too crowded. I'll take you to the restaurant I went to last night. It's reasonably quiet, and the food is sublime.'

Still she hesitated.

'Please?' he pleaded in a whisper.

She relented. 'All right then. What time and where will we meet?'

Robyn left the fair complex shortly after that, still weak all over and stunned that she'd met up with Guy again.

The smell of him stayed with her, even after she'd had a bath and dabbed on a liberal amount of her own strong perfume.

*

456

'Red or white?' queried Guy, meaning wine.

'Either suits me.'

'Then we'll have a bottle of each.' He consulted the Ristorante Franco Rossi's wine list. 'What's Est! Est! Est!!! like?' he asked the hovering waiter.

The waiter made an appreciative gesture with his hand, and a sort of hissing sound with his mouth. 'Wine of Lazio. She ver' nice. Ver' nice.'

Guy smiled. 'We'll have a bottle of that then. And also of Barbera d'Asti.'

The waiter nodded enthusiastically. 'Ce good, ce good.'

'Now what starter do you favour?' Guy inquired of Robyn.

Robyn chose a fish antipasto; for her next course, the primo piatto, zuppa di cozze, which was mussel soup; and for her secondo piatto, osso buco, a veal concoction. Guy insisted she follow that with gelato, saying that he'd been told the local ice cream was unbelievably good.

Guy ordered the same fish antipasto as Robyn; pasta e lenticchi, pasta and lentil soup, for his second course; and stufato di manzo alla Romano, a beef casserole, for his main dish. He too would have ice cream.

'Do you object to me smoking?' Robyn asked after the waiter had left them. She was terribly nervous, her stomach alive with butterflies.

'Have one of mine.'

She smiled in recognition when a packet of Gitanes and the battered Dunhill appeared.

'Same lighter, I see,' she commented, accepting a cigarette.

'Yes. Still giving sterling service.'

He lit her, then himself. 'Now I want . . .'

'You first,' Robyn interjected, her tone firm. 'How did you meet Daniella?'

'At the famous Bondi Beach, would you believe. Through a surfing friend of mine I knew in Newquay. It was a fun day that in turn led to other fun days, and eventually marriage.'

'When was that?'

'April '66.'

She smiled thinly. 'You didn't waste much time once you got there, did you?'

He was saved from replying to that by the arrival back of the waiter with their two bottles of wine.

Robyn said she'd have a glass of white Est! Est! Est!!! to start with, and Guy declared he'd have the same. The waiter filled their glasses, then departed again.

'How old is your son?' Robyn queried.

'Just coming up to two. I'm very proud of him, a real chip off the old block. Would you like to see a photograph.'

She wasn't at all sure that she did. 'Please.'

He delved into an inside jacket pocket to produce a paper wallet of photographs. 'That's Ben,' he said, passing Robyn one of the photos.

Ben *was* a chip off the old block, she thought jealously. He looked very much like Guy.

'And here's another taken only recently on Hampstead Heath,' Guy said.

This could have been her child! she suddenly realised with a shock. Now her child, or children, if they were so blessed, would be James's. 'He's a handsome lad,' she smiled, returning the photo to Guy.

'There's one here of Daniella and I. Would you care to see that?'

This time she had to force the smile onto her face. 'Of course,' she answered, trying to keep her voice neutral.

With huge relief she saw there was nothing special about Daniella, certainly not the beauty she'd been dreading. Roughly five feet high with dark, wavy hair and, from what she could make out, though she could be wrong, not much of a bust. And thick ankles she noted gleefully, which cheered her no end. The face was an Irish one, and rather plain.

'She looks very nice,' said Robyn, handing the photograph back to Guy. 'What does she think of England?'

He shrugged and put the wallet of photos away again. 'The usual complaints that all Aussies have when they go there. The weather is too cold, everything seems so dirty etc, etc. But she does seem to have settled in, and started enjoying herself. What she does love are the London shops! She's mad about those.'

'That must cost you.'

'I get extremely well paid in my job. Big Ben sees to that. He wouldn't allow his daughter to miss out on anything.'

Robyn drank some of her wine, which was delicious. And very more-ish. 'It was a big wedding, I presume?'

'Almost a national event. Why, the Prime Minister himself was there. When Big Ben does something, he does it in a big way. That's how he got his nickname.'

'Boing! Boing! Boing! teased Robyn.

Guy screwed up his face. 'I don't understand?'

'Boing! Boing! Boing! Big Ben.'

His face relaxed again. 'Very droll.'

'Is he really as fabulously wealthy as I've read?'

Guy nodded. 'Daniella is fourth-generation Australian, the family originally coming from Enniscorthy, County Wexford. It was Daniella's paternal grandfather who started to make the money, and Big Ben has very successfully furthered the cause from where the grandfather left off. He owns two vast cattle and sheep stations, and when I say vast, I mean precisely that. They're both bigger than Wales. Then there are the oil wells, copper mines, the manganese and rutile workings, and the brewery. He also owns *The Sydney Gazette*, a daily newspaper, and three magazines. And now there's Orbit Books.'

'Amazing. I'm extremely impressed,' Robyn replied.

'Lovely man. But for God's sake don't ever cross him. The word ruthless might have been invented just for him.'

'I suppose you have to be ruthless to get to that position in life.'

'Mind you, I'm never quite certain who's the more ruthless, Big Ben or his wife, Goldie. Not many women terrify me, but my mother-in-law does. I think I'd rather tangle with a great white than take on Goldie.'

'Great white?' Robyn queried.

He laughed. 'It's a type of shark, the most ferocious and vicious of the breed. In tropical waters it's every swimmer and diver's nightmare to meet up with one of those monsters.'

'Charming!' Robyn muttered. 'And you say your mother-in-law is worse than that?'

'She can be. Nothing stands in Goldie's way, ever.'

They stopped talking while being served their antipasto. 'Hmmh!' Robyn exclaimed in appreciation on tasting hers.

'I told you the food here was sensational.'

'How did you discover the restaurant?' Robyn queried.

'One of the Americans I was with last night knew of it. He's been to Bologna many times before. We came here on his recommendation, and certainly weren't disappointed.'

The restaurant had a lovely ambience about it, Robyn thought, glancing around. And how well dressed the Italian women present were, they positively exhuded style and glamour.

'So why did Big Ben decide to buy Orbit Books?' she asked.

'Orbit was in financial difficulties and struggling. Big Ben learned of that and decided to make a bid, which was accepted. Acquiring Orbit was an opportunity for him to break into the U.K. – something he had long wanted to do, as having a U.K. business is prestigious for him, particularly in the élitist world, as the Australians would see it, of British publishing.'

'Go on,' said Robyn.

'When he knew he had Orbit he offered me the top sales job, which I jumped at.'

'But you're not the boss?'

'Ah!' Guy smiled. 'There's a huge difference between being the Head of Sales for Penguin in Australia, and M.D. for a publishing company in the U.K. The Australian job is purely a sales one, Penguin don't actually publish books down there but import them from the U.K. then sell them. Whereas in the Orbit situation the M.D. is in charge of the company actually buying in, commissioning and producing the books, a different kettle of fish entirely. I'd need to get a lot more experience of the other sides of publishing – especially of how the editorial decisions are taken – before I could become an M.D.'

'I understand,' said Robyn, nodding.

'But! Although I'n not the M.D. – Harry Webber is that – I, as Big Ben's son-in-law, naturally have an awful lot of clout within Orbit. Far more than someone in my position would normally have. In other words, if I make a suggestion it tends to be carried out.'

'You're the power behind the throne, is that it?'

'That's it, exactly.'

'This Harry Webber must love you,' she teased.

'Harry is a pragmatist. We also, perhaps surprisingly in the circumstances, get on well together. Besides which he's an excellent M.D., Big Ben wouldn't have appointed him if he wasn't.'

Robyn had another sip of wine, studying Guy over the rim of her glass. Her butterflies were gone; she was totally relaxed now.

'There is something I'm curious about?' she said.

He pushed his empty plate away. 'Oh?'

'Daniella being who she is I'm sure she could have had the pick of more or less anyone she wanted. She is a fantastic catch, after all. So why you?'

'She fell in love with me. It was as simple as that.'

'And you? Did you fall in love with her?'

'I married her.'

A cynical smile twisted Robyn's lips. 'That doesn't answer my question.'

Guy dropped his gaze. 'I also fell in love with Daniella.'

'Or her father's money?'

He shot Robyn a filthy look. 'You've no right to say such a thing, make such an accusation. No right at all. I love Daniella, and I love my son, Ben. I'd give my life for that child.'

Robyn could hear the sincerity in his voice, which made her cringe inside.

'Sorry if I've misjudged you,' she said softly.

Guy ground out his cigarette, and immediately lit another. After a few seconds' hiatus he said. 'Anyway, that's my tale, now it's my turn to hear yours. Did you finish university?'

The conversation lightened after that, and soon they were laughing together.

Just like old times, Robyn thought at one point. Just like old times.

It was well past midnight when they returned to the Hotel Baglioni where, from the reception area, they could hear that the bar was still open.

'How about a nightcap?' Guy suggested.

Robyn considered that, then shook her head. 'I think I've had enough. What I want now isn't another drink, but a hot bath and hairwash.'

He couldn't conceal his disappointment. He didn't want the evening to end.

'But you go ahead if you like,' Robyn said.

'Can't I tempt you? How about another sambuca? Or a grappa, we haven't had one of those yet?'

461

'No thank you, Guy. I've honestly had enough.' Which was true – she was feeling decidedly squiffy.

She held out her hand. 'Thank you for a marvellous evening. I've thoroughly enjoyed myself.'

'And I've thoroughly enjoyed myself too. It's been a long while since I've enjoyed myself as much,' he replied, shaking with her.

'Goodnight then. I'll see you at the fair tomorrow, no doubt.'

'Or perhaps at breakfast?'

'Perhaps.'

She extricated her hand, he reluctant to let it go, and walked to the lift with him watching her. At the lift she gave him a wave. 'Go and get that grappa!'

He returned her wave, more of a salute than a wave actually, then turned and headed for the bar.

He didn't order grappa, but a large whisky instead. Which he followed with another, and another.

Robyn lay wide awake, thinking of Guy. She'd been dog tired when she'd come to bed, expecting to drop off right away, but hadn't. Instead her mind had become filled with Guy, of that evening with him, and past events. The poetry readings, Newquay and Hunters Moon, his flat.

With a sigh she switched on the bedside light, glanced at the clock beside it to see it was almost two-thirty am, and reached for her cigarettes.

She was still squiffy, but not unpleasantly so. It was not being able to get to sleep that was unpleasant.

Rising, she went through to the bathroom where she splashed cold water over her face, which made her feel fractionally better.

Going back to the bedroom she poured herself a glass of fizzy bottled water, and drank that. Perhaps if she read a bit, that might help, she told herself. But when she tried all she saw was Guy's face staring back at her, the words behind and surrounding the face a meaningless jumble.

Abandoning the book she crossed to her window and gazed out over the city. A cluster of multi-coloured lights flickered and winked, and somewhere nearby a car horn tooted angrily. She was still gazing out of the window when there was a soft knock on her bedroom door.

'Robyn?' Guy's voice whispered.

She hastily put on her dressing gown, and while she was doing that there was another knock on the door, this one slightly louder than the previous.

'Robyn, are you awake?'

She opened the door to find Guy standing there looking distraught.

'I saw the light on under the door,' he said.

She raised an eyebrow. What was he doing outside her door when his room was on the floor below?

'Can I come in and speak to you?'

'About what?'

'I just have to talk to you, that's all.' Having said that he brushed past her into the room.

She closed the door, and turned to face him, her heart suddenly thumping like a piston.

'I couldn't sleep,' he explained. 'I went to bed but all I could do was toss and turn.'

Same as her, she thought.

'I wouldn't have knocked if I hadn't seen the light, but . . .' He trailed off, and bit his lip.

'Sit down, Guy. I'd offer you a drink but I don't have anything here.'

'I do.' He produced a hip flask. 'Whisky. Will you join me?'

'No, thanks.' Then she changed her mind. 'Yes I will, but only a little one.'

There were two glasses which came with the complimentary bottled water; she set them out for him.

'Whooa!' she exclaimed as he poured hers. 'I said a little one.' He had his neat, she topped hers up with bottled water.

'Now, what's bothering you?' she asked, sitting on the edge of the bed.

He swallowed some of his whisky. 'I lied to you tonight, and just had to tell you,' he confessed in a cracked, emotional voice.

Robyn didn't reply to that, merely stared at him.

'About Daniella and me. I don't love her, and never have. You were right, I married her because of who she was and what she could do for me. I do love little Ben, though. I was being truthful about that. It's funny, I would never in a million years have

463

imagined myself as the doting father, but that's what I am. I think the sun rises and sets on that little chap.'

'Why the compulsion to tell me this, now?' Robyn queried.

'Because I love you still. I've never stopped loving you. And I swear before God, on my son's life, that's true. I made a terrible mistake leaving you, which I've regretted ever since.'

Robyn heard this as though in a dream. 'And yet you married Daniella?' she said slowly, her thoughts whirling.

'Yes, but as I just admitted, because of who she is and what she can do for me. I wouldn't have the job I have now if it wasn't for her. Or more correctly, her father.'

'You sold yourself, then?'

He went white, and saw off what remained of his whisky. Pulling out his flask again he refilled his glass.

'You sold yourself then?' Robyn repeated.

'I never thought I had a chance with her, and have often thought since that might have had something to do with it. I didn't chase her, or even appear interested in her in that sort of way. She was fun, and that was it as far as I was concerned. Next thing I knew, to my utter amazement, she was head over heels and I'd won the jackpot. She's an only child, you understand – when Big Ben and Goldie die it all goes to her. And *me*. Christ, Robyn, you must appreciate the temptation.'

'I don't blame you for marrying her Guy, not at all. What I do hold against you is leaving me in the first place.'

'That was temptation again Robyn! A temptation I succumbed to, and lived to regret.'

'If you'd asked me to go with you I would have done.'

'But you were at university!'

'That meant nothing compared to what I felt for you. At the time I was so in love with you, I do believe I'd have cut off my arms and legs if you'd asked me to.'

He hung his head in shame, and silently began to weep. 'What a cock-up. What a mess I've made of things. On the one hand I've got everything, on the other, nothing.'

'You have your son. That must be an enormous compensation.'

'Yes,' Guy whispered. 'It is.'

Watching him cry, she wanted to reach out and touch him, to wipe away his tears, and draw him close to her bosom. 'I believed you earlier when you said you loved Daniella, but I realise now the sincerity I heard in your voice was in regard of young Ben, and not her.'

'She's not a bad wife, or anything like that,' Guy replied. 'It's just that . . . I don't love her. Towards her I feel nothing like the way I used to feel about you, and still do.'

'Have you got a hanky on you?'

He shook his head.

She didn't have a hanky either, but there was a box of tissues in the bathroom. Rising from the bed she laid her glass down, then went through and got him a handful.

'Thank you,' he mumbled when she gave them to him.

She was about to return to the bed when he reached out and grasped her dressing gown. 'You must think me an awful fool,' he husked.

'Not at all.'

'Tonight just sort of broke me apart. It was so marvellous being with you again, laughing the way we used to, it was as if . . . as if we'd never been apart. And then I said goodnight to you downstairs, after which the world seemed to crumble in on me, somehow.'

She bent down to kneel beside him, everything still happening as though in a dream. 'Oh Guy!' she whispered.

'I'd give anything to turn back the clock, Robyn. Please believe that.'

'I do.'

She wasn't sure who took who into whose arms, but suddenly they were entwined, feverishly kissing one another. His smell was strong in her nostrils, a smell so well remembered, and at that moment acting as a most potent aphrodisiac upon her.

She continued kissing as a hand went inside her dressing gown, and then down the front of her nightie to find and hold a breast. It was a hand that was like fire against her flesh.

All reason was gone, flown from her head. All that mattered was that this was Guy and she wanted him as much as she knew he wanted her.

'Let's go to bed,' she whispered, the words thick in her throat.

When they were both naked she pressed him to her, holding him like that while ever mounting passion threatened to engulf them both.

Then they were on the bed, and he almost instantly inside her.

'It was like coming home again after a long absence,' he crooned in her ear when it was all over.

She smiled, knowing precisely what he meant by that.

She was still smiling as he began making love to her a second time.

Robyn came lazily and contentedly awake, but kept her eyelids closed. What a remarkably vivid dream she'd had. Guy had come to her room in the small hours and . . .

Her eyelids flew open with the realisation it hadn't been a dream, but reality. Guy *had* come to her room, and was now lying beside her.

She stared at him in horror. What had she been thinking of? She must have been mad! She was getting married to James. It was James she loved, not Guy.

Panic welled in her, panic she desperately fought to control. Then she saw the time.

'Guy! Guy!' she said urgently, shaking him by the shoulder.

He mumbled something incomprehensible, and yawned.

'Guy, we've slept in.'

'Hmmh?'

'We've slept in.'

He swore, and sat bolt upright. When he saw what time it was he swore again. 'I've got a meeting in ten bloody minutes!'

She swung herself out of bed and hurried to her dressing gown, which she quickly threw on. When she glanced again at Guy he was already pulling up his trousers.

Robyn ran a hand through her hair. She felt dreadful. She'd betrayed James, the man she loved and was going to marry. Or did she love him? She was so confused, bewildered. Why in God's name did she have to run into Guy Trecarron! And why, oh why had she allowed herself to get drunk! That was the word for it, she thought with appalling feelings of guilt. And what had possessed her to allow him into her room when he'd come knocking in the middle of the night? And most pertinent and shameful of all, why had she let happen what had?

She stared at the bed and blushed to think of some of the things they'd got up to the night before, her blush deepening to remember just how much she'd enjoyed it. Abandoned, that's what the pair of them had been, totally and utterly abandoned.

'Can you make one o'clock at the Orbit stand?' Guy queried. 'I'll take you to lunch.'

She smiled, a smile that seemed to her to quiver on her face. 'Fine.'

'You'll be there?'

'I'll be there,' she lied.

He slipped into his loafers, and stuck his tie into a pocket. 'I have to run. No time for niceties,' he said.

He pecked her on the lips, then dashed for the door. 'Remember, one o'clock!' he called out.

One o'clock!' she repeated.

She slumped in on herself the moment the door had slammed shut behind Guy. She must have been insane! She berated herself. Guy was married, with a family, and the past. James was now and the future.

She had to get away from here, she thought. She certainly had no intention of meeting up with Guy at one o'clock, that was the last thing she'd do.

No, she had to get away, from the Hotel Baglioni, the book fair and Bologna itself.

Spying a packet of cigarettes she extracted one, and lit it. She drew smoke deep into her lungs, which made her feel better, and helped her marshal her thoughts.

Crossing to the telephone she picked it up and rang reception. The man who answered was the same one who'd greeted her arrival.

In a few terse sentences she explained that she'd had a change of plans and would be leaving within the hour. Could he please make up her bill for her and she'd pay when she came down.

He expressed disappointment that she wasn't completing her intended stay, and yes he would prepare the bill right away.

She was shaking, she noted as she cradled the receiver. Which was hardly surprising. A swift shower, then dress and begin packing she decided.

Twenty-five minutes later, having first taken the precaution of ringing Guy's room to make sure he'd already left the hotel, she was downstairs in reception settling her bill and asking for a taxi to be called.

*

She gazed out at Bologna as the *rapido* pulled away from the station. Initially she'd thought to go straight back to Glasgow, then decided against that, as it would mean she'd have to concoct an explanation for her early arrival home. Instead she would stop over in Milan for the night, and next day catch the flight that she was already booked on. When she got home no one need know she'd only spent two nights in Bologna rather than the three she was supposed to have.

A picture leapt into her mind of her and Guy in bed making love. Her stomach contracted so hard, and with such sudden intensity, it felt as though it must surely implode.

The train was only minutes out of Bologna when she had to dash to the toilet where she threw up what remained of her dinner from the evening before.

'I'll get it!' yelled Robyn when she heard the front door bell ring, guessing that would be James who'd telephoned earlier to say he'd be round about this time. It was the evening of her return from Italy.

She charged across the hall to the front door, and threw that open.

'Hello,' smiled James.

She grabbed him, drew him inside, closed the door behind him, and fell into his arms.

'Oh my darling! My darling!' she whispered, clinging to him as though for dear life.

James was astonished at the intensity of her welcome. He was about to comment on the fact when her eager lips pasted themselves to his, and her hot seeking tongue darted into his mouth where it writhed and wriggled, like some demented creature.

'Hey, it's only been a few days, not months,' he laughed when the kiss was finally over.

She squeezed him tight, and nuzzled him. 'I know, but how I missed you,' she said softly.

'And I missed you.'

'I love you. I love you. I love you!'

'And I love you, Robyn. That's why we're going to get married.'

'I thought of you every single minute,' she lied, nibbling his neck.

He laughed again. 'Well I can't say I thought of you *every* single minute but I did for an awful lot of them.'

She ran a hand over his chest, then up to his jawline. She would have put a hand on his crotch if it hadn't been that Hannah and Lal were home, with the likelihood of either appearing at any moment.

'Come on in,' she said, pulling him towards the combined dining and sitting room.

'Did you have a good time?' he asked.

She launched into a strictly edited account of where she'd been, and what she'd seen and done.

Nor did she mention later on, giving him his promised souvenir, that it had been bought in Milan, and not Bologna.

'There you are, madam, thank you very much,' said Robyn, handing the customer the book she'd just wrapped up for her.

'Thank you. Bye, bye!' replied the customer, and left the children's department.

Robyn was about to attend to a task she'd been meaning to get down to all morning when there was a clatter of feet on the stairs and Juliet Symons, the assistant Hannah had taken on, appeared.

'There's someone on the phone for you,' Juliet said.

It didn't cross Robyn's mind to wonder who it might be, she was phoned at the Blackbird all the time. Usually the calls were concerning business, but sometimes it was James or friends, particularly Lesley McKay. (The Lesley/Rory thing hadn't lasted long, much to Lesley's chagrin.)

Robyn picked up the telephone, idly noting that Hannah was further down the shop talking to a customer. 'Hello?'

'Robyn, it's Guy. Can you speak?'

She caught her breath. 'Yes,' she said slowly.

'I'm up in Glasgow and in your area. Can we meet for coffee?'

'No!' she exclaimed.

'Why did you run out on me in Bologna?'

Lifting the telephone base she turned her back on the shop. 'It, eh . . . It was all a mistake. My leaving was for the best.'

'If you're sorry about what happened, I'm not. Meet me for coffee? There's that café just round the corner from you.'

'Impossible, I'm afraid. I haven't got the time.'

'Then I'll come to the Blackbird.'

'You musn't!' Robyn answered sharply, thinking what Hannah would make of it if he did.

There was a pause, then Guy said, his tone pleading. 'Please Robyn, I've come up specially to see you.'

Something twisted inside her to hear that. And she softened. 'You have?'

'I needed an excuse, and one finally presented itself. Please meet me?'

She had an hour due for lunch, she thought, and often spent it outside the shop, as did both Hannah and Juliet.

'All right,' she relented. 'But not the café you're referring to. Do you remember The Papingo?'

'Yes.'

'I'll meet you there.'

'When?'

She named a time, and immediately hung up.

Damn! she thought. She shouldn't have agreed to that. She shouldn't have!

Despite herself she couldn't wait to see Guy again.

He was already there waiting, and rose as she approached his table.

'Hello,' he smiled shyly when she'd sat.

'Hello Guy.'

He offered her a cigarette, and they both lit up. 'It's cappuccino in here, same as Bologna,' he said.

'But not as nice.'

In a small, flat voice he asked. 'Did you run out on me there to pay me back for my breaking it off with you and going to Australia?'

'Don't be daft!'

He reached across and laid the tips of his fingers over the tips of hers, which sent a thrill racing through her. 'Then why?'

'Because I realised after you'd gone that what had happened was a mistake, and shouldn't go any further. You're a married man, for God's sake Guy, and I'm due to get married next month.'

They halted their conversation when a waitress appeared beside them. They ordered two cappuccinos which the waitress then went off to get.

'Did you really come up to Glasgow just to see me?' Robyn queried.

He nodded. 'As I said on the telephone, I needed an excuse to do so and one finally presented itself. You must know Billy Fulton, the Orbit rep?'

'Of course. Quiet chap, very efficient.'

'Well his wife had a sudden stroke, and died. The funeral was earlier today.'

'Oh I'm sad to hear that! How old was she?'

'Thirty-six, a young woman. It's hit Billy very badly, as you can imagine.'

She could. 'And you travelled up to attend the funeral?'

He gave her a thin smile. 'A Sales and Marketing Director wouldn't normally attend a rep's wife's funeral, but I saw it as the opportunity to see you. He believes it's because I think so highly of him and his work.'

She removed the tips of her fingers from under his. 'So, why do you want to see me?'

'To find out about Bologna and . . . Because I desperately wanted to. Christ, Robyn! How I wanted to. If you haunted me before Bologna it's been ten times worse since. I just *had* to see you again.'

Truth was, she thought wryly, she was just as pleased to see him as he was to see her. And that was wrong! wrong! wrong!

She noticed something then she hadn't in Bologna. 'Those white marks on your cheek, what are they?'

'You should know, you put them there.'

She recalled only too clearly how she'd gouged and raked his cheek with her nails when he'd admitted to her he'd had a choice about going to Australia. 'I scarred you?'

'The surgeon who stitched them up did an excellent job. Nowadays they usually only catch the eye in a certain light. Or if you're looking for them.'

'I was beside myself with fury that evening,' she said by way of explanation.

'I know.'

'I wanted to lash out, to hurt you. In fact I wanted to kill you. And might well have done if you hadn't got out when you did.'

'Robyn, what I did to you was rotten. But if it's any consolation I hurt myself as much as I hurt you.'

Their coffee arrived, with a bill to be paid at the cash desk on leaving.

'Why don't we drink this then go back to my hotel?' he suggested quietly.

She couldn't believe she'd heard what she had. Talk about nerve! 'Don't be absurd Guy. I'm getting *married* next month.'

'You were getting married when we were in Bologna. That didn't stop you then.'

She stared at him, eyes narrowed. 'What are you trying to do? Make me feel cheap?'

'That's the last thing I intend, Robyn.' He lowered his voice to a whisper. 'I love you, for God's sake!'

She wanted to riposte that *she* loved James. But for some reason the words stuck in her throat.

'One last time? What do you say?'

She glanced at her watch. 'I must get back to the shop.'

His hand shot out to grab her wrist. 'Not yet. Please?'

'How's Daniella?' she queried.

'Fine. Why do you ask?'

'I just wondered.'

He dropped his gaze. 'I'll tell you something that's absolutely true. That night in Bologna was the first time I'd cried since I was a little boy. Since a very little boy.'

'Take your hand off my wrist,' she commanded softly.

When the hand was removed she picked up her coffee cup and sipped at its contents, studying him over the cup's rim as she did.

'You could leave Daniella, you know,' she stated.

He looked up quickly at her. 'Are you saying leave Daniella for *you*?'

She didn't reply to that.

He drew heavily on his cigarette, his face contorted.

'Well?' she prompted.

'It wouldn't bother me to leave Daniella herself, but it's not as simple as that. I've told you what Big Ben and Goldie are like, Christ knows what they'd do to me for ditching their one and only. I'd lose my job for a start, and would consider myself very, very lucky if that was the only repercussion. Big Ben, don't forget, is tremendously influential and can bring that influence to bear in all manner of ways. It might possibly be that I'd never get a decent job ever again, in publishing or out. He really is that influential and powerful.'

Guy had another deep drag on his cigarette. 'But I'd take the risk of that happening if it meant getting you in return. I swear I would. Only . . .' He trailed off, his expression crumbling into one of absolute wretchedness.

'Only what?' she asked so softly, it was almost a whisper.

'I'd give up anything for you Robyn, except my son Ben. I couldn't do that. Not for you, not for anyone.'

This time it was she who reached out and touched his hand. 'Thank you for being honest with me.'

'Funny things, kids. They can get to you in ways I'd never have believed. You know, I get the biggest kick in the world out of reading him a bedtime story. I feel like I'm floating on air after I've done that. And when there's something wrong with him – he had croup last winter and that was awful – I'm frantic with worry.'

Robyn allowed a knowing smile to creep onto her face. 'You've become a family man, Guy. I find that admirable.'

'Do you understand, Robyn? I couldn't give him up. He's meat and drink to me.'

'So you won't, or can't, leave Daniella.'

'What's the clichéd expression, "hoist by my own petard!" well that's me.'

He was quite right about having no one but himself to blame, she thought. But that didn't stop her feeling sorry for him.

'One last time, Robyn?'

She shook her head. 'Even if I wanted to I couldn't. I can't just take the afternoon off work; that wouldn't be fair on Mum. I won't do it to her.'

'How about this evening then? I'm at the Lorne Hotel in Argyle Street, room three hundred and thirteen. There are several very large parties of tourists staying there at the moment, with a great deal of to-ing and fro-ing going on. You wouldn't merit a second glance walking in and taking the lift.'

She ground out what remained of her cigarette, noting that her hand was trembling as she did. James, I must think of James, she told herself. She'd already let him down once, she wouldn't do so again. And yet . . .

'Please?' Guy pleaded.

473

'I have to go, Guy,' she said, rising abruptly to her feet.

'I'll walk out with you.'

'No!'

They stared at one another, their eyeballs locked together.

'I'll be in my room from six o'clock onwards. I'll leave the door unlocked so that you don't even have to knock but can walk straight in. Room three hundred and thirteen. Don't forget the number.'

He watched her walk out of The Papingo, a beautiful young woman he'd foolishly discarded when she could have been his wife and partner for life.

Would she come to his hotel room that night, or wouldn't she?

He had absolutely no idea.

Robyn toyed with her ham salad, not in the least bit hungry. Since leaving The Papingo she'd thought about nothing other than Guy's proposal. She couldn't possibly go, she told herself for the umpteenth time. Couldn't possibly. So why didn't she just accept the fact and forget about Guy and his hotel room?

'Are you going out tonight?' Lal asked Robyn.

'Why?' she snapped back in alarm.

Lal gazed at his daughter in surprise, wondering what had made her so touchy. And preoccupied; she'd been that ever since arriving home from work.

'I only thought you might be seeing James,' he said.

'Oh!' Relief flooded through her. Of course Lal knew nothing, how could he? 'No.'

'So you're not going out,' he smiled.

'I didn't say that. Just that I'm not seeing James.'

Lal looked at Hannah, then back again at Robyn. 'You're going out with someone else then?'

She threw down her knife and fork. 'What is this, the Spanish Inquisition? I didn't say that I was going out, or staying in, because I don't know yet. All I did say was that I didn't have an arrangement to go out with James. All right?'

'Sorry, I was, eh . . . Only making conversation,' Lal said.

She bit her lip, then pushed her plate away from her. 'If you'll both excuse me I've had enough.' And with that she rose and stalked from the room.

'Nerves,' Hannah said quietly to Lal. 'With the wedding so close it's only to be expected.'

'Nerves,' Lal agreed, nodding. It had to be that.

Guy sat slumped in front of the small television set he'd had put into his room. There was a glass and bottle of whisky by his feet, the bottle, which he'd opened at the beginning of the evening, almost half consumed. The curtains were closed, the bedside light on.

He glanced at his wristwatch. Ten past nine, more than three hours now that he'd been sitting there waiting. He ran a hand across his face, and sighed. She wasn't going to come. If she'd been going to she would have been there by now. Surely!

Picking up his glass he had a swallow of whisky, then returned the glass to its spot on the floor. He should have known she wouldn't come; she'd said she was getting married next month, after all!

Jealousy rose in him to think of another man with Robyn, another man putting his hands on her and . . .

Guy shook his head in despair. He had no right to be jealous, none whatever. He'd forfeited that right when he'd chucked her over to go to Australia. But he felt jealous nonetheless, jealous as hell!

He started thinking yet again of the night they'd spent together in Bologna, something he'd found himself doing at least once a day ever since.

That night had been sheer heaven, a night to remember for the rest of his life. And not merely for the sex either, but for the emotion involved. They'd come together in mind and body to fuse as one in a way he never had, or would, with Daniella.

And the reason? Because he loved Robyn. He hadn't lied to her about that. He loved her as much now, probably more, as when he'd left England.

He lit another cigarette; he'd lost count of the number he'd smoked since beginning his vigil, and tried to concentrate on the television programme, but couldn't. His mind kept wandering, back again to Robyn. Always back to Robyn.

Nine-twenty, his watch now informed him. He'd never known time pass so slowly. Each minute was like an hour, each hour a day.

She wasn't coming. She was probably with that James character she used to make jokes about, Guy tortured himself. She'd
probably forgotten by now that he was waiting in for her as he'd
said he would. She'd probably dismissed and forgotten his
proposal the minute she was out of The Papingo.

Oh Robyn! he thought in anguish.

He was having another swallow of whisky when the door
opened.

Hannah looked up from the book she'd been engrossed in,
thinking she could do with a nice cup of tea and an Abernethy.
The smile died on her face when she caught sight of Robyn
sitting over on her right.

Robyn, book open on her lap, was gazing blankly into space. Her
eyes were glazed, and unfocused, her features pale and drawn.

Robyn had lost weight recently, Hannah suddenly realised.
Quite a bit too, now that she noticed it. She glanced over at Lal
in a corner, where he'd been working at his bureau, to find him
staring at Robyn, his expression worried and perplexed.

'Would you care for a cup of tea and a biscuit, dear?' Hannah
asked him.

'Please,' he answered.

'And what about you, Robyn?'

Robyn gave a little all-over shudder, and breath hissed out of
her mouth. 'Sorry Mum, I was thinking.'

'Would you like a cup of tea and a biscuit?'

Robyn considered that as if it was some weighty matter. 'Yes,
I think I would,' she replied eventually.

'I'll make the tea, then,' Hannah said, coming to her feet.

'Hmmh!' Robyn murmured to no one in particular, and
immediately retreated back inside herself.

'I'll come with you,' Lal said to Hannah, also rising.

'Won't be long,' Hannah smiled at Robyn from the door. She
got no reply, or even an indication that Robyn had heard.

'It's getting worse,' Lal said to Hannah when they were in the
kitchen.

'Five days to the wedding Lal. It'll soon be over.'

'I hope so.'

Hannah hesitated, then said quietly. 'I'll tell you something I
wasn't going to.'

'What?'

'I passed her room the other night after she'd gone to bed and heard her crying.'

'What sort of crying?'

Hannah shrugged. 'Just crying. I nearly knocked on the door, but then decided not to. That it was best to leave matters alone.'

'Do you think she's worried about married life, about making a go of it with James? Or perhaps she's scared stiff of the first honeymoon night? I believe some women are like that. Absolutely terrified of it.'

Hannah's lips thinned into a sudden smile. Dear, lovely Lal, how like a doting father to be so naive about his daughter, to think her still a virgin at twenty-two and a half years of age, and engaged to be married.

'No, it's definitely not the honeymoon. I'm sure of that.'

Lal took up the kettle and began filling it at the sink. While he was doing this Hannah started laying out cups, saucers and side plates.

'Let's hope that everything's back to normal when she and James return from Lanzarote,' Lal said.

'Amen,' Hannah agreed.

'Can I have one of my fags please, Pa?' Robyn requested. She and Lal were in a hired limousine taking them to church. Because she was wearing her wedding dress she'd asked Lal to carry her cigarettes and lighter for her.

'Here,' he said, handing them over.

Robyn looked positively ghastly, Lal thought. Quite the opposite to how she should look on her wedding day. The make-up she had on wasn't helping at all; if anything it only accentuated her ghastliness.

'He's a good man,' said Robyn.

'Who?'

'James.' She turned to frown at her father. 'A good man.'

'Of course he is, darling.'

'He'll be there by now. Waiting.'

Lal nodded.

Robyn lifted her forehead as though in surprise. 'Mrs James McEwen, that's what I'll be shortly. Mrs James McEwen.' She giggled, a giggle that had more than a touch of hysteria to it.

Lal stared at her in concern. 'I have a hip flask with me. Would you like a drink?' he asked.

She shook her head.

'You look a complete knockout Robyn,' Lal lied, if only partially so. Her dress was indeed that, but she herself wasn't. 'James is a very fortunate chap.'

She twisted her head away from Lal when she felt tears come into her eyes, not wanting him to see that she was crying. She felt as if she was going to her execution rather than her wedding. She was cold and empty inside, and feeling utterly wretched.

Lal groped in a pocket to produce the flask he'd mentioned. Robyn might not want a swig but he could certainly use one.

'This should be the happiest day of my life,' Robyn said dully.

'*Should* be?' La queried. 'Are you saying it's not?'

There was a pause, then Robyn said in a strange, disjointed voice. 'Do you know they have black sand in Lanzarote? It's because the whole region is volcanic.'

'No, I didn't.'

'Black sand! That should be fun.'

Lal reached over and took his daughter's hand in his. He squeezed it, then squeezed it again. 'What do you mean, it's not the happiest day of your life?'

She didn't reply to that.

'Robyn? Robyn look at me.'

'Please, Pa,' she mumbled.

'Robyn?'

When she turned to face him her eyes were brimming with tears, while others ran down her cheeks.

'Oh, lass!' he whispered, fumbling for his handkerchief.

She dabbed her eyes and cheeks, not really caring whether her make-up was ruined or not.

She was stubbing out her cigarette when the church appeared ahead of them. Their was Lesley waiting outside. The other two bridesmaids, both a lot younger than Lesley and from James's side, were undoubtedly in the vestibule.

And in that moment all her indecision and doubt vanished. There was only one honest thing for her to do.

'Pa, I can't go through with it. I thought I could, I really did, but now I know I can't.'

Lal's expression became long and grim on hearing that. 'Are you certain it's not just last minute nerves?' he asked quietly.

'It's not that Pa, believe me. I thought I loved James, but don't.'

'He loves you,' Lal said in the same quiet tone of voice.

'Yes, I know that. But he's a good man who deserves better than a wife who doesn't love him. He'll find someone else eventually.'

Lal glanced at the rapidly approaching church, then back at Robyn. 'You're my daughter and I want what's best for you. I'm not going to try and bring any pressure to bear – I'll agree to whatever you decide – but you do appreciate this will gut him, don't you? Gut him and humiliate him before his friends and family.'

'Oh God!' she whispered.

'Well?'

She closed her eyes, and thought of Guy. It was Guy she loved, and always had. For a while she'd believed she'd loved James, but that so-called love had vanished as soon as Guy had reappeared. By going to Australia and marrying Daniella, Guy had dug a hole for them both. If she married James she'd be digging that hole even deeper, compounding the original error. And if she didn't love James she was certainly extremely fond of him. What she was doing now was right for him and her. He wouldn't see it that way of course, but he might in time.

She sniffed, dabbed at her face again, and took a deep breath. 'No wedding,' she stated firmly.

'Are you abso . . .'

'Yes!' she interjected.

Lal sighed. What a mess! What a bloody, gory mess. And he was the one who was going to have to break the news to James and the McEwens. He had a huge swallow from his flask that made him splutter afterwards.

Leaning forward, Lal opened the glass partition between them and the chauffeur. 'There's a change of plan,' he said. 'You're dropping me off at the church, then taking Miss Stuart straight back to Winton Avenue. Okay?'

The chauffeur flashed them a startled look in his overhead rearview mirror.

'Okay?' Lal repeated.

'Yes, sir.'

'Do you want Lesley to come with you?' Lal asked Robyn as the limousine drew into the kerb.

'Yes. That's a good idea.'

Lesley listened incredulously when Lal explained there wasn't going to be a wedding after all, and that she was to accompany Robyn back to Winton Avenue.

After he'd bundled Lesley into the limousine and the limo had moved off again Lal had another long pull at his flask. He'd done some difficult things in his life, but nothing as difficult, and certainly never as embarrassing, as this.

When he walked into the church with the two bewildered young bridesmaids trailing alongside, every eye in the place fastened onto him, while the partially unsighted organist, believing Robyn to have arrived, struck up 'Here Comes The Bride'.

'I'd happily marry you even if you don't love me,' James said. He and Robyn were in the Stuarts' garden where she'd been waiting, knowing that he would come to demand a personal explanation.

He looked dreadful, she thought. But then what else could you expect in the circumstances? Or perhaps defeated was a more appropriate word: defeated and totally crushed. When she'd first seen his face on his arrival in the garden she'd cringed inside. And she was still cringing.

'No,' she replied, shaking her head. 'It wouldn't work.'

'But why! It would if we wanted it to!' he cried, falling onto his knees before her.

She wished he hadn't done that. It demeaned him. 'Get up,' she commanded softly. 'I appreciate what it must be like for you, but for God's sake don't go on your knees to me.'

'We can still have the ceremony today. The minister said he can fit it in later,' James babbled.

'There will be no marriage. Not later, not anytime.'

James shook his head from side to side. 'I don't understand what went wrong. It was so good between us. I've never been so happy, and I thought it was the same with you. And now . . . this.'

'It's entirely my fault, James. I should have realised earlier. I

480

should never have allowed things to go on as they did. But you see, right up until the last moment I really did believe I could go through with it.'

He blanched to hear that.

'I'm sorry James. I couldn't be more so.'

He grabbed her arm, and pulled her close. 'Please, Robyn?' he whimpered. 'Please?'

She wanted to wrench herself free and run away, run far away and never come back. She wanted to be a million miles from where she now was. A million miles away from that face staring, pleading, up at her, and the man it belonged to. How could she be doing this to another human being, how could she?

It was a case of being cruel to be kind, she told herself, latching onto that. She was actually doing him a favour. And though it hurt unbelievably, that was something that had to be endured by both of them.

'No James, it's over between us. Finished.'

'You can't mean that! I won't accept that you do!'

'I do mean it James. Now get up for Christ's sake.'

He lurched to his feet. 'This is a nightmare. The whole thing, since your father walked down the aisle to where I was standing with Rory and told me, has been a nightmare.'

'I think you'd better go now, James.'

'I refuse to go. You're mine and you're going to be my wife.'

'No James. No!'

She never saw his hand coming, but when it hit her jaw it sent her flying. He immediately leapt after her, and hit her again, the crack of that blow reverberating across the lawn like a pistol shot.

Her head swam, and she was seeing stars. But she didn't go down. 'I suppose I deserved that,' she said thickly.

James went to hit her a third time, but didn't follow it through. His arm dropped to his side, and his head drooped.

'Robyn! Robyn!' Lal yelled, racing towards them. For he had been watching the confrontation from the house and had reacted the instant James had hit her.

James started to walk away from Robyn, gutted as Lal had predicted he would be. He wasn't even aware of Lal charging past him.

'It's all right, Pa,' Robyn said to Lal when he reached her side. 'In fact I'm glad he did that. Makes it easier somehow.'

481

After a while Lal took Robyn inside, and she went up to bed.

Robyn brought her Mini to a halt, preparing to turn left when the traffic permitted. She and Hannah were on their way to work.

Waiting her opportunity to move off again, Robyn suddenly became aware of two women staring at her from the pavement opposite. They were both neighbours from Winton Avenue.

She automatically smiled, but received no smiles in return. Instead the two women turned away and hurried off, muttering between themselves. About her and James, she had no doubt. It was the talk and scandal of Kelvinside.

'Don't bother about them,' Hannah counselled, having noted what had happened.

They drove for a little way in silence, then Hannah said, 'I've been waiting to tell you, and this is as good a moment as any, that I agree with what you did.'

Robyn's eyebrows shot up in surprise. 'You do?'

'Well, not quite the way you did it. It would have been far better if you'd stopped matters before they went as far as they went. But be that as it may, I agree you made the right decision in not marrying a man you didn't love.' She was thinking of Geoffrey Robb, her boss at the Ministry of Food, and how close she'd come to making a mistake with him – though not as close as Robyn had with poor James.

'Thank you. I appreciate you saying that, Mum.'

'Though heaven knows, I'll never be able to look either Cecily or Alexander McEwen in the eye ever again. That's one friendship that's gone completely by the board.'

'I am sorry about that. I do know how Pa valued Mr McEwen as a friend.'

Hannah was gazing out at the passing scenery when Robyn asked tentatively, 'Mum would you mind if I took a few days off? I really would like to get away from everything for a short while.'

'Get away? Where?'

Robyn shrugged. 'I don't know. Up north perhaps, or maybe London. It doesn't matter.'

'Well, I don't see why not. I can get Cathy to cover for you. As you know she adores helping out in the shop.'

'Isn't she a bit old for that now?' Robyn queried.

'She might be seventy-eight but you'd never know it. She's as fit and active as a woman twenty years younger. No, no! She's still quite capable of doing a stint in the shop if she has a mind to. I'll ring her this evening and see what she says.' Cathy had had a telephone in Purdon Street for years now, Lal having paid for it to be installed. He also took care of her quarterly bills. 'When do you want to go?'

'As soon as possible, Mum.'

Hannah nodded. She understood that.

Robyn emerged from Hatchard's in Piccadilly, the last of the famous London bookshops she'd promised herself the treat of visiting. And what a treat it had been. Foyle's, Collet's, Zwemmer's, Better Books, the Russian Bookshop in Museum Street which had both fascinated and intrigued her, and Dillon's University Bookshop.

Now her list of bookshops was complete, and she'd fulfilled her excuse for coming to London. Now she could do what she'd intended all along, contact Guy Trecarron.

'Taxi!'

The cruising black cab pulled alongside. 'Bedford Square, please,' she instructed the driver.

What a marvellous place London was, she thought as the cab sped on its way. How cosmopolitan. Though in truth, the sheer enormity of England's capital did frighten her a little. No matter in which direction you went, it seemed to go on endlessly.

And what a conglomeration of different types and races. Black faces, brown faces, Chinese, Americans, Europeans of every kind, Japanese, all manner of combinations – it just went on and on.

'Here you are, miss,' the driver said, stopping in a most elegant Georgian square of tall, terraced houses.

She got out, gave him what she considered to be a reasonable tip, and then watched him drive off.

She gazed about her, extremely impressed by her surroundings. The place positively reeked of history. She strolled round the square, reading the blue plaques en route of the famous people who had lived there, until she came to the number she was looking for, that of Orbit Books.

There was a railinged garden in the centre of the square, with various public benches outside the railings. Crossing to the nearest bench, she sat on it and from there gazed at the building where Guy worked.

She must have sat there for about twenty minutes, during which a number of people came and went from number forty-four – none of them Guy – before deciding what she was going to do next.

She went hunting for a public telephone which she found in nearby Goodge Street underground station.

'Mr Trecarron, please,' she requested of the receptionist at Orbit when asked whom she wished to speak to.

'Who's calling, please?'

'Miss Robyn Stuart.'

'One moment, please.'

Her heart was hammering as she waited. What if he didn't want to see her? What if . . .

'Robyn?' his voice eagerly queried.

'Yes it's me. How are you?'

'Couldn't be better. What's up?'

'Nothing's up. I just rang to say hello, and ask if we could meet?'

'Meet!' he exclaimed. 'Where are you?'

'Round the corner in Goodge Street underground station. I'm ringing from there.'

'My God,' he breathed. 'Are you down for the day, or what?'

'I'm having a break to visit all the big London bookshops. I'm staying at the Grafton Hotel in . . .'

'I know it!' he interjected excitedly. 'Now listen. Go outside the underground station again, turn left and just along a bit, less than a hundred yards is a coffee shop. I'll meet you there as soon as I can get away. Ten to fifteen minutes, say.'

'I'll be waiting.'

'This is wonderful Robyn! Absolutely wonderful.'

She was smiling as she hung up.

He was at the coffee shop in under ten minutes. He burst in through the swing doors, spotted her at the corner table she'd bagged, and came hurrying over.

'What a marvellous surprise,' he beamed, kissing her on the cheek. 'Welcome to the smoke.'

'I hope I didn't drag you away from anything,' she said, not caring whether she had or not.

'Nothing that can't wait. Now tell me, what are you doing here when you're supposed to be on your honeymoon?'

'Hadn't you better get yourself some coffee first,' she replied, for it was counter service.

'Another for you?'

'No, thank you.'

'Won't be a mo'.'

On returning he plonked himself down again.

Robyn dropped her gaze to stare into her cup. 'I didn't get married after all. We called it off,' she stated softly.

That rocked Guy. 'Called it off?'

She nodded.

'Buy why?'

She didn't reply.

Suddenly he knew the answer to his own question. Her failure to reply had told him. 'Me?'

Robyn continued staring into her cup. 'I realised in the end it just wasn't going to work out between James and myself.'

'Oh Robyn!' he said, reaching over and clasping her hand.

She lifted her gaze to stare straight into his eyes.

'What now?' he queried.

She didn't reply to that either.

He caught his breath. 'Am I getting the right message? Would you consider coming to London?'

'Are you asking me to?' she replied in a velvet whisper.

'I've explained my position regarding Ben. That hasn't changed. But if you did come there's no reason why we couldn't see a lot of one another.'

'You'd like that?' She had to be absolutely certain.

'Don't be stupid! Of course I'd like it. I'd be bloody ecstatic about it. I love you.'

A warm glow filled her, while her skin went all prickly and tingly at the same time. This was of course what she'd hoped would happen, what had been at the back of her mind since conceiving the idea of a trip to London.

'It would be a terrific wrench leaving the Blackbird,' she answered slowly. 'But in the circumstances it might be the best thing if I was to up sticks for a while. It's not as if I'm irreplaceable, after all! Mum will just have to find someone else to take over the children's department.'

He couldn't conceal his joy. 'Does that mean you will come down?'

'If there aren't any doubts in your mind?'

'None at all.'

'Then I'll come,' she agreed.

'If there weren't people about, I'd kiss you!' he declared, bubbling with pleasure.

'Since when were you shy?'

'Goddamnit then, I will!' He half rose, leaned across the table and kissed her full on the lips.

'Hmmh, nice!' she murmured in appreciation when he'd sat down again.

His thoughts were racing now. 'You'll have to get a job and . . .' He broke off as an idea came to him.

'How would you fancy working in publishing?' he asked.

'As what?'

'A junior editor?'

'But I know nothing about editing,' she protested.

'You have an honours degree in English haven't you?'

She nodded.

'Well, that combined with your knowledge of bookselling is qualification enough.'

'Which company are we talking about?' she asked.

His face broke into a broad smile. 'Orbit Books, of course. If you're coming to London, then let's work together. Or if not exactly together then at least in the same company.'

'Is there a position going?'

His smile took on a different dismension. 'Not yet. But I can arrange for one to fall vacant in the immediate future.'

'How, Guy?'

'Leave the details to me. Just remember the influence I have with Harry Webber, our M.D., and the board itself, should it come to that – which it won't. Watch *The Bookseller* during the coming weeks and when you see a junior editorial position advertised for Orbit Books apply for it with a c.v. I shall be one of the interviewers, and can assure you that no matter who else is after the job you'll end up with it.'

'That's corrupt!' she admonished.

'Of course, I could get you a sales job under me, but I think it preferable that you're on the editorial side. You'll feel far more at home there, and it's better we're not too tightly linked.'

A junior editor for Orbit Books! That appealed, very much so.

'I'll see you get taught all there is to know by Maggie Pendle, one of our senior commissioning editors. You couldn't find a better teacher anywhere.'

He rubbed a hand across his jaw. 'And then there's a place to live. I'll have to think about that.'

That evening he came to her at the Grafton Hotel just as she'd gone to him at the Lorne in Glasgow.

Robyn was all of a tremble as the train eased its way into Euston Station. It was a Thursday afternoon, and she was due to start her job at Orbit Books the following Monday. Everything had gone just as Guy had said it would. The position had appeared in *The Bookseller*, she'd applied enclosing her c.v., she'd been summoned to Bedford Square where she'd been interviewed by Harry Webber, Maggie Pendle, a chap called Colin Motley, and Guy. Three days later a letter had arrived at Winton Avenue stating that the position was hers, and giving her the date of her commencement.

Hannah and Lal had been extremely upset to learn that she was going to London, but they did understand – or at least thought they did, as she hadn't told them anything of Guy – why she wanted to leave Glasgow for a while. It had been a tearful farewell at the Central Station when she left, Hannah and Lal having insisted on seeing her off. Accommodation had been arranged through Orbit, she assured them. Which was true enough, in a way.

There was a sailor who'd been sitting opposite who kindly helped her with her two heavy suitcases. He was placing the second on the platform when Guy appeared with a trolley.

Robyn thanked the sailor, then Guy was by her side, sweeping her into his arms and kissing her.

'Hey be careful! You're a married man,' she whispered when the kiss was over.

'This is London. The chances of someone being around who knows me are one in a million.'

'All the same.' How pleased she was to see him; almost overwhelmingly so.

'That it?' he queried, indicating the two suitcases.

'That's it,' she confirmed.

He loaded the suitcases onto the trolley, and then they started for the barrier.

'I've been counting the days and hours,' he said as they went through the barrier and headed for the taxi rank.

'Me too.'

'All set for Monday morning?'

'Nervous as a kitten about it.'

He laughed. 'You've got nothing to worry about. They're a very friendly bunch who'll take you straight to their bosom. Within a couple of weeks you'll probably feel you've been with Orbit forever.'

They waited in a queue, shuffling forward until finally it was their turn for the next taxi.

Guy loaded the suitcases onto the taxi, while the driver watched him, then he gave the man an address in Camden Town.

'Camden Town is fairly close – you might even say adjacent – to Hampstead, which is to our advantage,' Guy explained once the taxi had moved off. Hampstead of course was where he and Daniella lived and Robyn got the point.

They held hands during the journey, talking animatedly with one another, each thrilled to be in the other's presence again.

When they arrived at their destination Guy unloaded the suitcases, and paid the driver.

'Come on,' he said, picking up the suitcases and leading the way into a yellow brick purpose-built block of flats. Hers was on the third floor.

'Here you are,' he said, giving her the set of keys he'd used to open the downstairs main door. 'The key with the piece of green thread tied through the centre hole is the one you want.'

The door to the flat swung open, and she went inside, Guy following with her suitcases. He closed the door behind them with a flick of his heel.

There was a bedroom with a large double bed, built-in wardrobes, chest-of- drawers and a vanity table.

The lounge had modern units, and everything else she could possibly want including a colour TV.

From the lounge they went to the kitchen which was tiny, but contained all the necessary. The crockery, which particularly caught Robyn's eye, was by Habitat.

The final room Robyn inspected was the combined toilet/bathroom whose carpet was, to her delight, a fluffy white one. She thought that great fun.

'What do you think?' Guy asked eagerly.

'It's lovely. Can I afford it?'

'You don't have to. That's taken care of.'

'Taken care of?' she queried with a frown.

'The flat's rented, the rent paid for one year in advance. That's been paid for by Orbit, as has everything else in the flat, which now belongs to you.'

She was incredulous. 'How did you manage that?'

'As Big Ben's son-in-law no one would dare question my expenses. Besides, I have ways and means of losing money amongst all the genuine expenses incurred by myself and department.'

'I'm amazed,' she said, shaking her head. 'I wasn't sure what to expect. This is just terrific!'

'I've kept a set of keys for myself. Is that all right?' he asked softly, and mischievously.

'You know it is.'

He took her into his arms. 'This means so much to me, Robyn. So very much.'

'As it does to me,' she answered.

He nibbled her neck, then kissed the lobe of her ear. 'Oh Robyn, I do love you!' he breathed.

His smell was strong in her nostrils making her head swim. 'I'd better get unpacked,' she sighed.

'After.'

She didn't have to ask what he meant by that, she knew fine well. '*After* then,' she readily agreed.

Hand in hand they went back to the bedroom.

Chapter 12

Guy exploded the moment Daniella came into the room. 'What time is this to come home, for Christ's sake? Half-past midnight. Half-past sodding midnight!'

Daniella regarded him through narrowed eyes.

'You've been drinking, haven't you? You look pissed as a newt.'

'I have had a few glasses of wine, so what?' she countered, irritated in the extreme. Guy was irritating her more and more nowadays.

'A few glasses, huh! More like a few bottles, by the sight of you.'

'Why don't you just stuff it where you sit,' she hissed, crossing to a handsome silver-mounted tantalus and pouring herself a large brandy to which she added lovage. She adored brandy and lovage.

'You forgot, didn't you?'

She rounded on him. 'Forgot what?'

'There was a film on television tonight that you promised you'd sit and watch with Ben. He kept assuring Sibby right up until the damned thing started that you'd be there to join him. According to her he cried all the way through it because you didn't show.' Sibby, short for Elisabeth, Rainbird was their Australian nanny who'd been with them now for two years. She was their third Australian nanny since moving to London eight years previously; it now being 1976.

'Shit!' Daniella swore. 'I did forget. It went clean out of my mind. Shit in a bucket!'

'So where have you been?'

She gazed balefully at him. 'Since when do I have to give an account of where I go and what I do?'

There were times when he could have slapped his wife silly, and this was one of them. 'I'm not asking you to account for your movements, at least not the way you mean. I'm merely curious about what you've been up to that was so important and mind-absorbing as to make you forget the date you had with your own son?'

'I was out, okay? That's all you need to know buster. O – U – T, *out*!'

He took a deep breath to try and cool his anger. 'I see,' he said when he was once more fully in control of himself.

'Come to that, where the hell were you?'

'I had a late night meeting with Harry Webber, I told you. It did go on longer than I expected though, which is why Ben was in bed asleep when I got back.'

'People in glass houses shouldn't throw stones,' she muttered.

This had all the makings of a classic ding-dong between them, Guy thought, of which there had been an increasing number over the past few years.

'Forget the rest then, it's the fact that you've let Ben down which annoys me,' Guy said.

Daniella threw what remained of her brandy and lovage down her throat, and immediately poured herself another.

'You're out so much of late the wee chap is becoming positively neglected,' Guy went on.

'Nonsense! Anyway, he's got Sibby to care for him.'

'And a great job she does too. But she's not his mother, *you* are.'

Daniella shrugged. 'I get bored looking after a kid. I want to enjoy myself before I'm past it. Besides which, if you're so concerned about Ben, you stay home more often.'

'I've been trying to. But you know damn well being Sales and Marketing Director entails putting in a lot of hours, both day and night, as well as being away from home a considerable amount.'

Daniella, eyes narrowed again, stared across the room at Guy. 'Whatever happened to the Guy I met on Bondi? I tell you this, husband mine, and I tell you true, you are very rapidly becoming one boring old fart.'

He gazed back at her in contempt. 'Why? Because I love and worry about my son?'

'It's nothing to do with Ben, but with you yourself. Middle

age is settling over and round you like some blanket you're enveloping yourself with.'

'I'm only thirty-three! How can I be middle-aged?'

'Some people acquire it prematurely, and I reckon you're one of those. Middle-aged, pedantic and *boring*!'

Guy stuck a Gitane in his mouth, and lit it with his Dunhill. There was no point arguing with Daniella when she was like this, all she would do was become more and more abusive.

'I'll sleep in a guest room tonight,' he said.

'Good!'

'The least you can do to make amends to Ben is take him to school in the morning,' Guy suggested.

'I'll think about it.'

'Which means you have no intention of doing so.'

'I said I'd think about it. Now leave it alone will you!'

He mentally ran through his next morning's appointments. 'Don't you bother. I'll take him instead.'

'Do that!'

She'd been getting fat from drink for a while, he thought. And now her backside was beginning to blow up like a balloon. Horrible! Her figure had never been brilliant, but at least when he'd first met her she was able to appear in public wearing a bikini. She wouldn't dare do that now.

'I'm going to bed. You lock up,' she said.

Guy nodded. 'All right.'

Daniella looked at the tantalus, considered topping up her glass, then decided not to. She was going to have a bad enough hangover next day as it was.

'Goodnight,' said Guy.

Daniella muttered something Guy couldn't make out, and left the room.

He sighed when she was gone. Boring old fart! Middle-aged, pedantic and boring! What a load of garbage, he was none of those things. He paused for a moment; at least he didn't think he was? No, of course not.

He toured the front, side and back doors checking that they were properly locked and secured, doing the same with the downstairs windows as he went along. When he'd finished that, ending up in his study, he activated the alarm system sited there.

492

These precautions completed, he returned to the sitting room where he'd confronted Daniella and poured himself a small whisky nightcap from the tantalus, the latter a fine Georgian piece and a gift from Big Ben and Goldie.

Crossing to the nearest window he gazed out into darkness, in his mind visualising the large amount of ground that stretched out behind the house.

And what a house it was too! Big Ben had decided during one of his frequent trips to the U.K. that their old house in Hampstead Village (Peter O'Toole the actor had lived close by) didn't have a big enough garden for little Ben to play in, and had immediately set about finding a house that did.

The Bishop's Avenue is arguably the most prestigious address in north London, and probably the most expensive. The house Big Ben had finally selected for them, but bought in Daniella's name, was at the Hampstead as opposed to Finchley end, and massive. Many of their neighbours were extremely rich Arabs and Jews.

Big Ben had told Guy at the time, giving him a broad wink as he did, that not only was it one helluva house, but also a shrewd investment. Guy had afterwards cynically wondered if Big Ben had really been concerned about little Ben and a decent-size garden, or had all along been manipulating the situation to his own benefit. For didn't this new house give Big Ben and Goldie a place to stay and entertain while in London that was far far better than the Hilton and Inn On The Park in Park Lane, where they'd previously put up?

Not only had Big Ben and Goldie bought the house but also supplied and paid the resident staff. There was a butler, cook and three Spanish maids. The only exception was Sibby, whom Guy and Daniella had personally hired, and whose wages he met out of his own pocket.

Besides the staff quarters the house had seven bedrooms, a dining room, two sitting rooms, a billiards room, library, study and kitchen facilities that would have been the envy of any West End chef. Mrs Grierson the cordon bleu cook, turned out the most mouth-watering meals imaginable.

The butler was called Henry and never ever smiled. His dry sense of humour, when he deigned to use it, was devastating. Guy thought the world of Henry who'd been in service all his life, as had his father before him, and his father's father before that.

Guy smiled as he remembered that tomorrow was Friday. Friday was his favourite day of the week, when he visited Robyn at home and they had a few hours together.

Just the two of them.

Robyn laid the manuscript aside, and rubbed her tired eyes. The manuscript was an excellent one, she would certainly bid for it in the forthcoming auction that the author's agent, Pat White at Deborah Rogers Ltd., was holding. Should she establish a floor with topping up rights, she wondered? She would ponder that before making a decision on the matter.

She glanced at a brass carriage clock. Two-thirty; Guy was late. He was usually here by now.

In the seven years that had passed since she'd come down to London Robyn had flourished at Orbit Books. From junior editor she'd quickly progressed – a combination of natural ability and flair plus help from Guy – to becoming a commissioning editor, and then senior commissioning editor. Although she deferred to Maggie Pendle because of Maggie's greater experience, the pair of them in reality had equal standing within the company. Between them, and one rung below Harry Webber, they ruled the editorial department.

Robyn too had moved. Believing that owning was better than renting, she'd bought a two-bedroom conversion in Roderick Road, South Hampstead. When traffic wasn't too heavy it was roughly a five minute car drive between her flat and Guy's house in The Bishop's Avenue. Her location was therefore a most convenient one.

Friday was her reading day at home. She read for work purposes all week of course, but that could be extremely difficult at the office when the phone was forever ringing and heads were continually popping round her door, asking advice about this and that. And then there were the interminable meetings, with authors, agents, publicity, sales, the art department and so on and so forth. Friday was therefore her day set aside to concentrate solely on reading, without these perpetual interruptions. It was also the day Guy visited her when in London. *Their* day, or afternoon as it was, together.

Her excuse for being away from Bedford Square was catching up on her reading, with Guy it was simply a case of disappearing off on firm's business. As a matter of precaution he always tried to ensure that everything in his department was battened down for the weekend before he left. And as he was Sales and Marketing Director, who, providing everything was going smoothly, was going to question how or where he spent his time? Only Harry Webber, and Harry had never been given cause to do so.

Going through to her kitchen Robyn opened a bottle of chilled Piesporter and poured herself a glass. 'Hmmh!' she murmured after she'd had a taste. Divinely delicious!

She had some pâté in, bought from a local delicatessen, and smoked salmon she'd had delivered from Harrods which she'd serve with small buttered brown bread squares. Friday afternoons she and Guy always had a little feast in bed after they'd made love. And after the feast they always slept, invariably twined in one another's arms.

How she looked forward to Fridays and her time together with Guy. It was the high point of her week.

The old magic leapt inside her when she heard her front door click shut. Guy had arrived.

'I'm in the kitchen!' she called out a few seconds later, pouring a second glass of Piesporter.

It had been a long, tedious flight and Robyn felt positively shattered. She couldn't wait to have a hot bath followed by a few hours' sleep. Proper sleep that was, in a bed, not the uncomfortable dozing that was all she could ever manage in a plane.

She glanced at Guy who was also sitting in an aisle seat, but five rows further along from her, and on the other side of the aisle. They had considered sitting together during the flight, but as there would have been another Orbit employee beside them it would have been impossible to talk or act freely, and so they had elected to keep apart. There would be occasions enough for them to be together in Singapore.

A short series of musical notes played throughout the plane indicating that an announcement was about to be made.

'Ladies and gentlemen this is your captain speaking. In a few minutes' time we will be arriving in Changi International Airport. We hope you've had a good flight and would remind you that . . .'

Guy twisted in his seat to gaze back at Robyn. He didn't smile, but his eyes said everything.

He'd arranged it so that his room was directly across the corridor from hers.

The Equatorial Hotel where the Orbit employees would be staying during the course of their Autumn sales conference was a modern building, superbly appointed. The staff, a combination of Europeans, Eurasians, Singaporians, Chinese and Malays couldn't have been more friendly or helpful.

Robyn had been flabbergasted when informed that their next sales conference, of which they had two a year, was to be held in Singapore. Publishing sales conferences were more and more being held in foreign resorts, Minorca was a favourite, and she had heard of one company going as far afield as Miami, Florida – but Singapore, almost halfway round the world!

It was Big Ben himself who'd chosen the spot as a reward for how well Orbit Books was now doing, thanks to the hard work, dedication, professionalism, know-how and even inspiration of its employees. And so what if it cost an arm and a leg, he'd said to Goldie, he could well afford it. Besides which it was bound to make others in the trade jealous as hell. He'd have spent the money for that alone.

Robyn tipped handsomely the two young bellboys who'd brought up her luggage. One suitcase contained her personal belongings, the other her presentation material for the conference, which included a slide projector.

A sales conference was basically an in-house affair during which the entire national sales force assembled to meet up and converse with the editorial people. (A time to complain, exchange ideas etc. etc.) The editorial people for their part took this opportunity to 'sell' the books due to be published by the company during the forthcoming half-year. In other words it was their task to transmit their enthusiasms for what was in the pipeline to the sales force whose task in turn would be to transmit that enthusiasm to the bookseller.

A sales conference was also an excuse for employees to get

away from home, let their hair down and generally whoop it up at the expense of the management.

Robyn gazed about her room which she couldn't have faulted in any way. A huge basket of fruit sat on a teak coffee table, with a bottle of Dom Perignon beside it. The card accompanying them said 'compliments of Big Ben Linehan'.

There was a small fridge in the room which Robyn popped the D.P. into. Then she set about unpacking. The first company rendezvous was dinner that evening. The conference itself would start with a bang directly after breakfast next morning.

She had just completed her unpacking – the slide projector had arrived unscathed she'd been pleased to discover, though no doubt it would have been relatively easy to find a replacement had it not – when her telephone rang.

'Hello, gorgeous, can I join you for a drink?' Guy asked when she answered it.

She laughed at the word gorgeous. 'I'm about to take a bath.'

'That's all right. I'll be quite happy to watch you, and will even scrub your back. Your duty frees or mine?'

'Mine if you like.'

'I bought you some perfume on the plane. I'll bring that with me.'

'Perfume? What make?'

'I can't remember. But it was *veerry* expensive. I only got a few pence change out of a quid.'

She laughed again. 'Idiot!'

'Hong chong, ping pong dong.'

'Come again?'

'Hong chong, ping pong dong.'

'What does that mean?'

'It means I love you in Chinese.'

'Well, I don't know about the dong part, but ping pong to you too,' she replied.

'I'll be right over and we'll practice being inscrutable together.'

She knew precisely what he meant by that. 'No, we won't. After my bath I'm going straight to sleep. And I mean *sleep*.'

'Want to bet?' he chuckled.

'No, because you'd lose.'

As it transpired, he wouldn't have done.

The functions room in the Equatorial Hotel where the Orbit contingent was having its dinner was awash and piled high with drink and food. A lot of the food was Chinese, the Equatorial boasting one of the finest Chinese restaurants in Singapore, which was saying something. It also had a Japanese restaurant, French restaurant, American restaurant and basement snack bar. On learning of the Japanese restaurant Robyn had promised herself a meal in it before returning home, wondering what on earth that would be like.

She was sitting beside Paul Young, one of the regional managers, two reps (the younger of whom was absolutely paralytic) and an editor (for their Mushroom imprint) called Caro Shelton. Guy was at the top table with Big Ben, Harry Webber, Colin Motley, a stunning blond creature who was Big Ben's personal secretary, and a man whose name she didn't know, but who was part of Big Ben's organisation, having flown to Singapore with Big Ben and the secretary in Big Ben's private Lear jet.

Big Ben let out a great roar of laughter and thumped the table in front of him with a balled fist the size of a small joint of meat. Big Ben was as Irish-looking as they come. He might have been Australian by birth, but only a blind man would have failed to see he was unmistakably of Paddy descent.

Gross, was how Robyn would have described Big Ben Lineham. Guy had told her Big Ben had been slim in his youth, but no more. His trousers bulged in all directions, and it must have been years since he'd seen below his waist without the aid of a mirror.

In a crowd Big Ben stood out. Not only because of his size – a twenty-two inch collar – but also because of his personality. He positively exuded power and charisma; that and success. Robyn, who'd met him many times previously, found him both awful and fascinating.

'More vino?' queried Paul Young, waving a bottle at Robyn.

He was rapidly getting three sheets to the wind as well, she noted, shaking her head. But then that was all part and parcel of being at a sales conference.

Big Ben came to his feet – he was a surprisingly quick and

agile mover – and held up his hands for silence, which he quickly got. He jabbed a massive cigar at those looking at him. 'Are ye enjoying yourselves sports?' he asked in a loud bellow.

'Yes!' came back the concerted reply.

'Good on yez all then. Good on yez.' He took a draw on his cigar, then slowly blew out a stream of smoke.

'I'm pleased, mightily pleased, couldn't be more so. You've not only turned Orbit about, but made a success of it, a success that's gathering momentum with every passing year. The latest figures to hand are by far and away the best yet, forty per cent increased turnover on this same quarter last year . . .'

He had to pause as a great cheer rang out.

'You bunch of beauts!' he smiled, which got another cheer.

He continued. 'Which leads me to believe we'll have a thirty per cent increase overall when we close the yearly figures. One helluva achievement in anyone's book!'

Somebody got the pun, and laughed.

'Anyone's *book*,' Big Ben repeated, and this time the laugh was general, which pleased him. He liked to think of himself as having a humorous side.

Big Ben had another draw on his cigar, savouring the moment, and the bombshell he was about to drop.

'These figures are terrific, boys and girls, but we're going to better them, knock them into a cocked hat. And you know how?'

No one answered, but then how could they. The only person in the room, other than Big Ben himself, who could have done was Ray Toomes his chief accountant, the man at the top table whose name Robyn didn't know.

'By expanding our set-up, that's how. Boys and girls we're going to publish hard as well as soft.'

A gasp of surprise greeted that. Hard and soft meant hardback and paperback.

Guy leaned forward in his chair to gaze up at Big Ben. He couldn't wait to hear what was coming next.

'To put you out of your suspense,' Big Ben went on tantalisingly slowly. 'As from noon today, G.M.T. time.' He glanced at his wristwatch, 'that's forty-five minutes ago, I became the owner of Munthe & Platt Ltd. They and Orbit are now, metaphorically speaking, under the one roof.'

Guy led the applause. A hardback tie-in was just what Orbit needed. It opened up all sorts of possibilities.

Munthe & Platt was a very old, and prestigious, company which had been sliding downhill of recent years since the death of Joe Munthe, last of the line, who'd kept the company financially viable during his long lifetime. Munthe & Platt had a rock-solid reputation as a quality house, with a history that went back to the mid-Victorian era.

Big Ben was beaming, thoroughly pleased with himself. But then he was always pleased with himself when he made a new business acquisition.

'One more item, folks!'

When he had hush again he continued. 'As you know this little jaunt to Singapore is my way of showing appreciation for all your efforts. To this I would add a money bonus. Each of you will be given at tomorrow's conference an envelope containing two hundred and fifty pounds cash to be spent while you are here in Singapore. Now what about that, eh?'

The cheer that now rang out was the loudest yet.

Two hundred and fifty pounds spending money! Robyn thought. Very nice too. There were some marvellous shops in Singapore she'd been told. She'd have no trouble whatever spending her two hundred and fifty.

'Now drink up, eat up. Enjoy, enjoy!' Big Ben said, then dropped back down into his seat.

Everyone began talking excitedly about the two hundred and fifty pounds bonus, and Big Ben buying Munthe & Platt.

'Come in!' Big Ben called out when there was a knock on his suite door. He was sitting with Ray Toomes on one side of him, Charlene his personal secretary on the other.

Guy entered the suite, closing the door behind him. 'You asked me to come up after dinner,' he smiled at Big Ben. It hadn't actually been a request, but an order.

Big Ben pointed at a chair. 'Park your posterior, Guy. Want a drink? I'm on scotch myself.'

'A scotch would be lovely.' Creep! he thought of himself.

One glance from Big Ben and Charlene was on her feet and hurrying over to the cocktail cabinet.

'So what did you think of my announcement?' Big Ben demanded.

'I had heard rumours on the grapevine that someone was after Munthe & Platt, but had absolutely no idea it was you.'

'It was me all right,' Big Ben said, and gave a great booming laugh.

'I got it for a good price, too. A damn good price!' He stuck a paw inside his half-opened shirt and scratched a hairy chest.

Guy thanked Charlene when she handed him his whisky.

'I have plans for Munthe & Platt, big plans,' Big Ben said.

Guy nodded.

'For a start we're going to make their list more commercial. I don't want to lose all the up-market literature they do now, though pruning will take place, but what I want to bring to that list are books that will *sell*. Respectability on the one hand, underpinned by profit. A Booker Prize author will be just dandy, but I also want the Wilbur Smiths of this world. Do I make myself clear?'

'Very,' Guy replied.

'As you know, at the moment Orbit buys in laterally from hardback houses, with the exception of when we do a paperback original. Well, that will continue but decrease as time goes by. From now on I want to publish the same author hard and soft, which is to the author's advantage as well as ours.'

'Publish vertically,' Guy nodded. Vertical publishing was when the same company – or companies jointly owned as it would be in their case – did both hard and soft. Lateral publishing was when a paperback house bought from a hardback one who had already secured the rights from the author.

'Now, how would you feel about being Sales and Marketing Director for Munthe & Platt? The bloke they have now is a proper klutz who'll be out on his ear, along with a number of his colleagues, just as soon as I have organised my intended shake-up.'

'You mean move over from Orbit?'

'No, do both jobs,' Big Ben said, stabbing a finger at Guy.

'Both jobs,' Guy mused.

'There will be a board of directors at Munthe & Platt; that was part of the deal. Accept the position and you'll be on that board, as you are on the board at Orbit.'

'It's a bit unusual isn't it? I mean, I don't know of any other Sales and Marketing Director who works simultaneously for a hard and soft house.'

'You're missing the point Guy, although you are correct about that. Don't view them as two different houses, but as the opposite sides of the same coin. For that's what we'll be aiming for. Eventually the lists will be more or less the same, which is why I want the same sales force selling both.'

'A united sales force under my command?'

'I wouldn't call it united exactly, as I expect you to give most of their blokes the sack. The same sales force you have now, with perhaps one or two additions which might or might not come from the sales force now existing at Munthe & Platt.'

'Hiring and firing at my discretion?'

'Completely.'

'Hmmh!' mused Guy. The prospect was exciting, and challenging.

'Well, what do you say?'

'A criticism?'

'Go ahead.'

'Munthe & Platt are located in Bayswater, with Orbit in Bedford Square. It would be far better all round if . . .' He stopped when he saw that Big Ben was grinning at him. 'Have I said something funny?'

'I'm already way ahead of you, Guy. There's a new building under construction in Covent Garden that'll be up for sale on completion early next year. Covent Garden is an ideal situation, don't you think?'

'Ideal,' Guy agreed. 'You'll be buying it, then?'

'I certainly hope to. But if that did fall through there are other satisfactory options. As long as it's a *big* building, centrally located.'

There was something in Big Ben's voice that made Guy wonder. 'Would I be right in guessing that you're not going to stop with Munthe & Platt, that you're considering adding to that and Orbit?'

Big Ben flashed Ray Toomes a thin smile. 'I told you he had a head on his shoulders.' To Guy he said. 'You are right, but keep that strictly to yourself. I like being in the U.K. publishing business, and see it going through a period of consolidation and ultimate expansion. At the moment, as is often the case where you Brits are concerned, publishing in the U.K. is strictly amateur night-out, a pastime for gentlemen and blue-stockinged ladies. Well, I prophesy that's going to change, and when the dust finally settles yours truly is going to be one of the players left at the table.'

Guy was intrigued. 'And you saying the day of the small publisher is over?'

'I'm saying that things in publishing are changing. For any publisher to survive he's going to have to adopt a hard-nosed approach and publish for profit rather than sentiment or idealism.'

Charlene was staring at Big Ben as though he was Moses just come down off the mountain. Guy couldn't help but wonder if Big Ben was sleeping with her. If Big Ben was, he was jealous of his father-in-law.

'Anyway,' said Big Ben, breaking the spellbinding ambience he'd created when speaking, 'your taking on Munthe & Platt merits an increase in salary. And a new, bigger car. Isn't it a B.M.W. you have at present?'

'Yes.'

'Order a Mercedes. The most expensive model.'

'Thank you.'

'Don't thank me,' Big Ben said, eyes glittering with amusement. You'll earn both the increase and the car.'

Guy knew that to be true. He couldn't wait to report all this to Robyn.

Five minutes later, having ironed out a few more details, he left Big Ben's suite.

'Are you sure you wouldn't have preferred to go with Freddy and Mike to a massage parlour?' Robyn teased. Freddy and Mike were two of the reps who'd been drinking with her and Guy on the Equatorial's roof terrace where there was a bar, pool and a spectacular view of Singapore's skyline. It was their second night in the city.

'Why should I go to a massage parlour when I can get what's on offer there from you?' Guy leered in reply.

'Don't be rude.'

'On the other hand I wouldn't have minded going along as a spectator. For the experience.'

'Spectator!' Robyn laughed.

'Well then . . . just the massage and nothing else. No extras.'

'You make it sound as though you know about these things?'

'Who me?' Guy exclaimed in mock surprise.

'Yes, you.'

'I'm innocent m'lud. Totally innocent. I've never been to a nookie parl . . . I mean a massage parlour or house of ill repute in my life. On my son's head, I swear it.'

'I'll believe you. Thousands wouldn't. By the way, how is Ben?'

Guy's face clouded over. 'I'm worried sick about that child.'

'Still as bad as ever?'

'Worse. I just don't know what makes him behave the way he does. I do my best, but it doesn't seem to have any effect on him. Of course it doesn't help that Daniella contradicts me all the time when I'm trying to deal with him. If I say he can't do something she immediately tells him he can.'

'What about the new school?' She knew from previous conversations that Ben had been expelled from his previous one.

'Norfolk House appears to be able to exercise more control over him than Parkhall was able to. It's early days yet, but I'm keeping my fingers crossed that N.H. is going to work out. So far we've only been called in once, which is an improvement on Parkhall where we were being called in every week.'

'Doesn't Daniella worry about him, as you do?'

Guy shook his head. 'Her only comment is that boys will be boys. Even when he was accused of bullying it didn't faze her. She said she was sure the whole thing was exaggerated, and left it at that.'

'Poor Guy,' Robyn whispered. He so loved his son who was nothing but a constant source of trouble and worry to him.

Guy ground out his cigarette. 'I have an idea for Sunday.' The conference straddled the weekend, and Big Ben had given everyone Sunday off to sight-see or do as they wished.

'What's that?'

'Why don't we hire a car and drive into Malaysia?'

'Malaysia!' That sounded marvellous to her.

'It's only a spit from here, and I believe there are facilities called rest houses where you can put up for the night. I can get details, if you're interested.'

'I am. If we can keep our going together a secret from the others.'

'Leave that to me, I'll work something out. We'll spend the day and night there, rising early Monday morning to be back at the hotel for the re-start of the conference.'

Robyn immediately began to plan what she'd wear and take with her.

Guy drove off the causeway that joined Singapore to the mainland and into Malaysia proper. They'd already been through barrier control and customs. The hired car they were in was a Volvo estate.

Guy started laughing to himself.

'What's amusing?' Robyn demanded.

'I was thinking of Paul Young and what he told me yesterday.' Guy shook his head. 'Hysterical!'

'Well come on, share the joke.'

'Paul and a couple of others went out the evening before last, ending up someplace where there's apparently a street market during the day, dancing and other entertainment in the evening. According to Paul there were dozens of knockout females floating about, one of whom Paul, naughty man, got off with and took back to the Equatorial.' Guy stopped to laugh again.

'Go on.' Robyn urged.

'This will kill you. When the "female" undressed Paul discovered to his horror that it wasn't a female at all, but a fella in drag!'

'No!'

'But not only that, this fella had all his bits and pieces tucked up inside himself.'

Robyn was thunderstruck. 'You're kidding! You mean his . . .'

'Penis and testicles all somehow tucked up inside himself so that nothing showed. Paul later found out they're called Kai-Tais, and that where he'd been was a favourite haunt of theirs.'

'How horrible,' Robyn muttered, quite disgusted.

'Paul swore that before the fella took his clothes off you wouldn't have been able to tell the difference between him and the real thing.'

Robyn had to smile, thinking what a shock the awful discovery must have been for Paul. 'So what did Paul do?' she queried.

'Paid the fella and got rid of him as quickly as he could. He said he was absolutely shaking afterwards, and drank nearly three-quarters of a bottle of whisky before the shaking finally stopped.

'Kai-Tais,' Robyn mused, thinking Paul's face must have been a picture the moment the penny dropped.

Soon Paul Young and Kai-Tais were forgotten as the incredible beauty that was Malaysia began to unfold before them.

On advice given him by a member of the hotel staff Guy had decided to head for the village of Mersing on the east coast overlooking the South China Sea. Besides being just the right distance for their purposes from Singapore it also had one of the best rest houses in that part of Malaysia.

They drove through lush green forests, alive with strange and exotic creatures who cried and screeched in a seemingly endless cacophony of sound. The road they travelled on was originally British built, and reasonably well maintained. It was a road the Japanese had also used when they'd occupied the area during the Second World War.

Eventually they burst out of the final forest on their route, to descend a long incline that brought them into Mersing, a picturesque native village where many of the houses had palm-frond roofs and all were built up off the ground on either stilts or piles.

The rest house was in a prominent position, and well signposted in English so they had no trouble finding it. Guy booked them in as Mr and Mrs G. Trecarron, which gave Robyn a thrill. It was lovely to be Mrs Guy Trecarron, if only for a day and night.

'This way, Tuan. This way, Puan,' the Malay who'd picked up their two holdalls said, leading the way into a cool, shady corridor.

The room they were shown into was in stark contrast to the luxuriousness of their rooms at the Equatorial. This was simplicity itself. White-washed brick walls, wooden floor, a single chest-of-drawers and a brass double bed with a mosquito net tied above it.

Guy tipped the Malay who then left them, bowing unnecessarily and grinning hugely as he did.

'I adore the mosquito net,' said Robyn, going to it and untying it so that it dropped over the bed.

'Very nineteen-twenties, what?' joked Guy in a frightfully pukka accent.

'Very.' She pulled up one side of the net and squirmed in under it to lie flat on the bed. Sadie Thompson and *Rain* by Somerset Maugham she thought, that was what all this made her think of.

'What's the bed like?' Guy queried.

'Soft.'

'Shall I join you there?'

She laughed, and wriggled out from under the net again. 'No, thank you. We've got all tonight for what you have in mind.'

'And how do you know what I have in mind?'

'Because it's what you *always* have in mind. A bit of how's-your-father!'

She was right he told himself. Even after all these years he couldn't get enough of her.

'Bags me the shower first,' she said, starting to strip. The shower room was off the main one, and was reached through an entrance with no door. The unit itself, when they came to use it was positively ancient, but still in good working order. The shower room had a grey stone floor and white tiled walls.

'No, me first,' declared Guy, deciding to make a game of it.

Robyn beat him to it, but allowed him to join her underneath the shower head.

He washed her back, then she washed his.

The banyan boat, about twenty feet in length, chugged away from the wooden jetty, making for the open sea. Guy was sitting in the prow of the gaily decorated craft, Robyn behind him.

Earlier they'd strolled all round Mersing, and along the beach of golden sand on the village's seaward side. They'd gone hand in hand, thoroughly enjoying one another's company, each laughing occasionally at something the other had said.

Returning to the rest house for a drink they'd fallen into conversation with two Australian girls who'd told them of the banyan boats that could be hired, and of the island, a number of miles offshore, that they'd been to the previous day where they'd spent several hours and had a fabulous picnic.

Guy and Robyn had decided they'd like to do that also, so a picnic had been made up for them in the rest house kitchen.

Guy lit a pair of Gitanes, and passed one back to Robyn. She smoked that while trailing a hand in the water.

She'd never seen water that shade of green before, or so thick with salt: the water was completely opaque with it. When at one point she experimentally licked her hand she screwed up her face at the bitter, salty taste of it.

The banyan boat was long and narrow, and powered by an American outboard motor. It stank of fish and tar and other unidentifiable, at least to Guy and Robyn, odours. They both thought it quite delightful.

The mainland vanished from view, and then shortly afterwards a strip of land appeared on the horizon. They were in sight of the island they had come to visit.

To Robyn's surprise – it had appeared such a long way off – they very quickly reached the island where the two men drew the banyan boat up onto the sandy shore.

Their picnic was offloaded, and the holdall containing the other items they'd brought with them.

'Six o'clock I come back for you,' the boat owner said, tapping his cheap watch as he spoke.

'Six o'clock,' Guy nodded.

'You be here that time,' the boat owner went on, pointing at where they were standing.

'We'll be here, I promise you.'

'Have lovely picnic then,' the boat owner said and, returning to his boat, shoved it back into the water. As soon as the boat was floating free he scrambled aboard and restarted his outboard. The three of them waved to one another as the boat chugged away.

Robyn took a deep breath, and gazed about her. 'Paradise,' she proclaimed.

Guy also gazed about. She was right, that's precisely what this was. Paradise.

'Let's explore,' Robyn suggested.

'Okay.' Guy picked up their picnic basket and holdall which he carried to the nearest palm tree, where he placed them at its base. He didn't see any point in carrying these things around with them.

'Let's get our bearings, we don't want to get lost,' Robyn said, gazing about again.

Guy wished he'd thought to bring a compass, but he hadn't. Anyway, they wouldn't wander all that far from where they now were.

'Come on,' he said, as taking her by the hand they started inland.

Robyn gasped with pleasure when some minutes later they emerged from trees into a large natural clearing dominated by a cascading waterfall that fell into a rockpool.

Running to the edge of the pool she stared into its clear crystal depths which glittered and glistened as if containing a million miniature suns.

'How beautiful,' she whispered.

'Look!' said Guy, gesturing upwards.

At the top of the waterfall was a shimmering rainbow that stretched from one side of the cascade to the other.

'Gorgeous,' Robyn breathed.

'Shall we have our picnic here?' Guy queried.

'We're certainly not going to find a better spot.'

'I'll get the picnic basket and holdall then,' he said.

'Guy!'

He stopped, having taken a few steps back the way they'd come. 'Yes?'

She crooked a finger at him.

He came into her arms, and she kissed him. A kiss full of love, tenderness and passion. 'Thank you for bringing me here.'

'Thank you for just being you.'

Now he kissed her, a kiss that perfectly matched the one she'd given him.

'I won't be long,' he said, breaking away when the kiss was over.

She watched him vanish into the trees, then turned again to the rockpool. Taking a deep breath, she then slowly exhaled, after which she languorously stretched herself. How good life could be. How very, very good.

She gazed again into the depths of the rockpool, and tested the water with the tips of her fingers. It was cold, but not prohibitively so. A dip would be just the ticket to counter the

509

heat and humidity that was making her perspire, and be sticky, all over.

When she was naked she stood on the very edge of the pool, ran her hands over her breasts, down her sides, and then down her thighs. With a springing dive she arced forward to knife below the surface.

Down and down she went, then twisted onto her back to stare up at the surface. The myriad miniature suns were all around her now, she part of the universe they inhabited. A profound happiness filled her as she floated upwards, happiness and the most sublime feeling of contentment.

She was still in the pool when Guy returned. 'Come on in, it's lovely,' she called out.

He stared at her, drinking her in, devouring her with his eyes. 'Eve,' he husked. 'Eve, in the Garden of Eden.'

'Which would make you Adam,' she smiled. Then, looking round and pretending puzzlement. 'But where's the serpent?'

She roared with laughter when Guy showed her.

They lay side by side on the sand, gazing up at the sky. It was ten to six, while out at sea the banyan boat was heading in their direction.

'I wish this didn't have to end, but could go on and on forever,' Robyn said dreamily.

'I wish it would, too.'

She turned to stare at him, her expression soft and warm. 'I think this has been the happiest day of my entire life. I want you to know that.'

'A day to remember for always,' he murmured in reply.

Neither spoke again, savouring those last few minutes, and finally seconds, until the arrival of the banyan boat.

'I want to go to the toilet to do number twos,' Ben announced to his mother. They were in a taxi taking them from Changi International Airport to the Equatorial Hotel.

'You should have gone aboard the plane. You'll just have to wait now,' Daniella replied, voice crackling with irritation. It had been a long, tedious flight, and an uncomfortable one as far as she was concerned. As for Ben, he'd been a non-stop fidget. Blast Sibby for being down with the flu and not able to travel with them!

'But I didn't want to go aboard the plane,' Ben protested.

The child's logic washed over her. She was convinced he was just being difficult to annoy her. 'We'll be there in a few minutes, just hold on,' she said.

Ben made a face and glared out at Singapore. Although it was past two am the streets were still blazing with light, and alive with people.

Daniella's trip to Singapore was a surprise one; neither Guy or her father knew she was coming. After Guy's departure for the sales conference she'd had the bright idea, it being half-term, that she'd like to pay a flying visit home to Sydney with Ben, so why not hitch a lift at least part of the way with Big Ben in his Lear jet!

She hadn't been invited to go to Singapore with Guy, as spouses and partners were traditionally excluded from sales conferences, which were strictly employee and management junkets. Why even Goldie hadn't been asked, and it was well known she went nearly everywhere with Big Ben.

Daniella thought of Sydney, and smiled. She couldn't wait for the blazing sunshine that would greet her on arrival. How she craved that. And how bloody sick and tired she was of dreary England with its seemingly never-ending cold and damp. She absolutely loathed the damp. Loathed and detested it.

Big Ben would of course be delighted to see her. As for Guy, she mentally shrugged, she didn't give a jumbuck's spit whether he was or not.

The sales conference was scheduled to finish early the following afternoon, directly after which Big Ben would be flying back to Sydney where she knew he had pressing business to attend to. If Guy wanted to link up with them fine; he was due some time off anyway. If he didn't, well that was his loss, not hers.

She yawned. Damn, she was tired, and stiff from sitting that amount of time. She couldn't wait to slide into a hot bath.

Guy stirred, coming slowly out of a deep sleep. What was that noise? Telephone, he realised groggily. The telephone was ringing.

He sat up, and reached for the bedside light which he snapped on, then for the telephone beside it.

'Hello?' he queried, blinking horribly gummy eyes.

'Mr Trecarron, this is the desk clerk speaking. I thought you would like to know that Mrs Trecarron and your son are on their way up.'

'Thank you very much,' mumbled Guy in reply, still disorientated.

'One of the maids will be along shortly with a folding bed for your son.'

'Yes, good, okay.'

'Goodnight, Mr Trecarron.'

'Goodnight.'

Guy was replacing the receiver when what had just been said to him sank home. Daniella and Ben! Jesus Christ!

He leapt from the bed, pulling the bedclothes with him. 'Robyn! Robyn! For God's sake get up! Daniella's here!'

The lift rose smoothly and silently upwards. Daniella glanced at Ben who'd gone to the toilet when they were in reception, much to the relief of both of them. The bellboy attending to their luggage was coming up in another lift.

They passed the fifth floor, then arrived at the sixth, their destination. The lift silently came to a halt.

Daniella was about to open the criss-cross metal gates when suddenly a partially-clothed female figure came flying out of a door down the corridor facing, to fumble at a door opposite to the one she'd emerged from, then vanish inside.

Daniella looked down at Ben, but he didn't appear to have noticed the incident.

Someone up to hanky-panky, Daniella thought to herself with a smile, as they left the lift.

Her smile died when arriving at Guy's door she realised it was the one the female had come out of.

Turning, her expression thoughtful rather than angry, she stared at the door the partially-clad woman had vanished through.

'Mrs Trecarron would like to speak with you in the east reception room,' Henry the butler announced to Guy as he took Guy's overcoat from him. Guy had just returned home from work.

'Thank you very much, Henry,' Guy replied lightly. He was in a terrific mood, things couldn't have been going better for him and his department.

He found Daniella sitting with a closed folder on her lap and drink in her hand.

'Evening, dear,' he said, kissing her on the cheek. Crossing to the tantalus he poured himself a stiff whisky.

'You wanted to speak with me?' he said after a sip.

'I thought you might care to see this,' she answered, opening the folder and extracting a photograph.

'Oh?' Crossing to Daniella he took the photo from her and glanced at it. What he saw made him go ashen.

The picture was black and white, and somewhat grainy. Despite the quality, there could be no mistaking the two people in it. He and Robyn were in her bedroom, on her bed. He was on top of her, her legs wrapped tightly round his waist.

'Pretty, isn't it?' Daniella said, giving him a razored smile.

He had to clear his throat before he could speak again. 'How did you manage to get this?'

'Professional photographer, long-range lens with a special light intensifier of some sort. I don't really know the details. But your friend, Miss Stuart, made the mistake of leaving her curtains ajar, and that was the result.'

Guy, mind whirling, thought of Robyn's bedroom and bed, the bed on the other side of the room from the window. She did occasionally leave the curtains ajar in the afternoons when the weather was fine, the buildings opposite just far enough away for that not to be a problem. At least, that was so under normal circumstances. They hadn't bargained for a long-range lens and light whatsit.

'Before you lie to me, you should know that I've had a private investigator following you for the past month. Fridays are when you have your regular sessions, I believe?'

Guy swallowed hard. 'How, eh . . .how . . .?'

'Singapore. As my lift arrived at your floor I saw her running from your bedroom to her own. I wanted to know if it was only a sales conference fling or what. So I hired the private eye to watch you. How long has it been going on for, Guy? Not that it makes the slightest difference to the fact I want a divorce, it's merely that I'm curious.'

'Divorce! Now look Daniella, I . . .'

'How long, Guy? And I want the truth.'

He swallowed his whisky, and poured himself another. 'A while,' he muttered.

'How long! Weeks, months, years?'

When Guy didn't reply she said in a voice that dripped honey. 'Or perhaps you'd prefer my father to ask you?'

It was as though he'd been thumped hard in the guts. The thought of Big Ben asking him how long he'd been cheating on Daniella scared the living daylights out of him. His skin was suddenly alive with imaginary scuttling ants. If only he'd had some idea he was going to walk into this. If only he'd had time to prepare answers. If only he'd had some inclination she was onto him and Robyn!

'Well?' Daniella demanded.

'A few years.'

'How many years?' she pressed.

Guy ran a hand over his mouth. 'Seven,' he stated quietly.

That shocked Daniella to the core. What a slap in the face. How humiliating! And how incredibly stupid of her not to have twigged. 'Seven years,' she repeated in as quiet a tone as he'd used.

'Where's Ben?' Guy queried.

'Out with Sibby. They won't be back till later.'

He groped for his cigarettes, noting his hands were trembling badly as he lit up.

'Do you love her?'

'Robyn?'

'Who the hell do you think, you stupid bastard!' Daniella screamed. Then, regaining her composure. 'Unless there's someone else?'

'No, only Robyn.'

'Whom you've been rooting for the past seven years.' She wanted to laugh, but didn't, knowing it would have been a hysterical laugh if she had.

'It's not quite what you think, Daniella. I knew Robyn long ago. I met her originally when I was a rep with Penguin in Scotland. She and I were . . . well, were involved then.'

She stared at him through slitted eyes. 'I asked a question; do you love her?'

He opened his mouth to say yes. 'No,' he said instead.

'Liar!' Daniella hissed.

He pocketed his lighter, then picked up again the photo of Robyn and him that he'd temporarily laid down.

'You can keep that as a memento. My lawyer has the negative.' Daniella said.

'You weren't serious about the divorce, were you?'

'Too right I was, mate. And that was before I knew you'd been screwing this sheila for the past seven years.'

He swallowed hard. The inside of his mouth had become hot and feverish. 'I'm sure we can work this out Daniella. Make a fresh go of things.'

'Not a hope. This is the end of the line for you and me. We're finished. Through, Kaput!'

Desperation welled up in him. 'I'll never see Robyn again. I promise you. I'll show you she means nothing to me.'

'Too late, Guy. Far too late.'

'It's never too late if . . .'

'Oh, shut up!' she exclaimed scornfully. 'You sound just like the original whinging pom. God knows what I ever saw in you. I must have been mad. Stark raving looney!'

Desperation gave way to panic. Everything he had, and had achieved was poised to vanish down the plughole. The house, the servants, the car, the job, everything! And what about Ben, his son and heir whom he loved to distraction?

She was going to enjoy this next bit, Daniella thought. Having stuck the knife in, she'd now twist it. 'I can imagine how my father is going to react when I show him that picture and the contents of this folder. He's going to go berserk. Particularly when I start to weep and call you all the bastards under the sun.'

An icy fist gripped Guy's heart, and a weakness invaded him that turned his body to jelly. 'Big Ben will crucify me,' he whispered.

'Oh yes! You can bet on that. After he's finished with you, you'll be lucky to get a job cleaning out lavs.'

He had to sit down before he fell down, Guy thought, seeking the nearest chair.

She'd twisted the knife, now she'd waggle the damn thing! 'Knowing my father, there's no saying how far he'll go. He

515

could have you framed for embezzlement, for example. I happen to be privy to the fact he's done that in the past. Or something more crude and violent perhaps, like having the offending equipment removed.'

Sweat burst out all over Guy's forehead with the realisation of what she meant.

'That's right Guy. He might have your balls shot off. I did hear him threaten someone with that once, but I can't say whether or not it was actually carried out.'

His balls shot off! The very thought made Guy want to throw up.

Daniella paused for a few seconds, then said. 'But . . . On the other hand, I could square you with my father. Ensure he doesn't exact any kind of revenge.'

'Why would you do that?' Guy croaked in reply.

'Because, heaven help me, I was fond of you once. So I'll make a deal with you.'

'What sort of deal?'

She pointed a finger at him. 'You will agree to my divorcing you, the Stuart sheila to be cited.'

He nodded.

She now got down to the most important items as far as she was concerned, the ones she and her lawyer had talked long and hard about.

Her finger stabbed. 'I inherit when Big Ben and Goldie are gone. Ben from me in due course when I go. In the meantime I know my father intends to settle a sizeable amount on Ben when he reaches his majority. You will sign a waiver regarding both. You will relinquish all claim to Linehan finances, holdings, etc., either now or in the future.'

Guy thought of the cattle and sheep stations, the oil wells, copper mines, the manganese and rutile workings, the whole Linehan empire. An empire he could have one day shared with Daniella.

Daniella went on, now vehemently. 'You won't get a zack through our divorce, I swear it. Attempt to do so and I'll set my father onto you, and God help you then.'

'A settlement of some sort at least?' he said quietly.

'No.'

'Show some charity. As you said, you did love me once.'

'No Guy. Not a zack, not even a penny piece.'

He finished his whisky, staggered to the tantalus and poured himself another. 'All right,' he whispered.

Elation filled her. That was what she'd wanted to hear. The bastard could cheat on her, but he damn well wasn't going to profit by her. Not from here on in.

Those were the terms, after consultations with her lawyer, she'd come prepared to lay before Guy, but now since the revelation that he'd been sleeping with Robyn Stuart for the past seven years she was going to add another of her own. And one that would probably hurt him most of all. It was her personal condition to offset her humiliation.

'A final condition,' she said.

He looked sideways at her, but said nothing.

'No access.'

He frowned. 'I don't understand. No access to what?'

'Not what, *who*. No access to Ben.'

'No!' he cried.

'Yes!' she spat back. 'You've seen your son for the last time because you're leaving this house tonight before he returns.'

'No Daniella, please, not that?'

'I've already decided that he and I are returning to Australia just as soon as possible. I don't know what will happen about this house, even though it is in my name. I'll have to speak to my father about that. He might wish to use it himself as a London base, if not it's going on the market. Whatever the outcome I'll be buying a place for Ben and me in Sydney. Possibly out at Avalon or Whale Beach, I've always had a notion to live up there.'

Not see Ben, his son, again? Guy couldn't conceive of the idea. Why Ben was his flesh and blood, he had a right!

'Go and get packed. I want you out of here an hour from now.' She glanced at her watch. The locksmiths would be arriving to change all the locks in an hour and a half. Once out, Guy wouldn't be able to sneak back in again.

'Daniella . . . anything but Ben. You know how I love that child.'

'Precisely,' she smiled, thinly.

He sank to his knees, not caring how ridiculous he appeared. 'Please?'

517

Her upper lip curled in contempt. She couldn't imagine an Aussie male begging like that. He would have died first.

'Please?' Guy whimpered.

'Get up, and get out.'

Anger broke in him that almost immediately transformed itself into a rushing surge of white-hot fury. He came to his feet, and took a stride towards her.

'I wouldn't if I was you,' she said hurriedly. 'Lay one finger on me and I'll set Big Ben on you for sure.'

His fury, and the anger it had sprung from, disappeared as swiftly as they'd appeared.

'Goodbye Guy. Don't slam the door on your way out,' she said.

When he was gone from the room she closed her eyes, then smiled. She'd have this divorce rushed through as quickly as possible; she yearned for her freedom. The business of seven years had been an awful shock, but she'd repaid him in full. In full, and more. And the Linehan fortune was totally safeguarded; Big Ben would be pleased when she explained that to him. Not that Guy would have won a claim against her. But then, even with Big Ben's backing, you could never be absolutely certain. This way, she was. And about any claims he may have attempted to make at a later date against Ben, they too were now nipped in the bud.

From here on in she would also ensure that Ben thought of his father as she wanted him to think, which was in the worst possible light. She'd turn Ben against Guy so that he would never have the notion to seek his father out at any time in the future. She would poison Ben's mind against Guy. Totally and utterly.

She smiled again to think of Tim O'Connor, the young man she'd met when she was home the last time. He'd interested her, very much so.

She'd get Goldie to throw a party when she got back to Sydney, she decided. One to which Tim would be invited.

Robyn had to pass Guy's car before she could draw in to the kerb. She saw him sitting hunched at the wheel, a most dejected figure with his head in one hand.

He got out of his car as she got out of hers, and went to her.

Even in the extremely unflattering streetlight she could see how haggard and drawn his face was.

'What's up?' she asked.

'I have something to tell you,' he replied in a strange, tight voice.

Later, he came back out for his suitcases.

Robyn woke to the realisation it was still dark outside. A glance at her luminous dialled clock/radio informed her it was three-fifty-three am.

Guy's back was towards her. From his breathing she was certain he too was awake.

'Guy?' she whispered.

'What?'

'How long have you been awake?'

'I haven't been to sleep.'

She was amazed at that, considering the amount of alcohol he'd consumed earlier.

'Would you like me to make you a cup of tea?' she offered.

'No,' he husked.

'Or . . .'

'Nothing, Robyn. Nothing at all.' His tone was distraught, full of pain and self-pity.

Reaching across, she placed a comforting hand on his side.

'Never see Ben again. I can't believe it, I still can't take it in,' he husked further.

'Oh, Guy!'

His body shook, then shook again.

'Come to me darling. Let me hold you close.'

He turned round, and she drew him to her breast as though he was a child.

He was still there, and the pair of them wide awake, when dawn came up.

The Marlborough Gallery was in Old Bond Street; it had a name as the top gallery in the country, and that evening was the opening of an exhibition of George Trecarron's sculptures.

Guy and Robyn arrived by taxi, and made their way into the gallery where they were immediately offered Bucks Fizz. It was a glittering occasion with many luminaries from the art world

519

present, plus a sprinkling of showbusiness personalities to add bezazz and glamour.

Robyn spotted the large, leonine head, topped by a shaggy white mane she remembered so well from Newquay; she and George hadn't met since then. 'There's your father,' she informed Guy, pointing.

'We'll wander over, shall we?'

Robyn was glad that George was no longer with Sorel; that relationship had foundered years ago. There had been several women since, the latest being someone called Wendy.

'Hold on a second,' said Robyn, stopping to look at one of George's sculptures.

She didn't know what to make of it. She didn't dislike it, but there again, she didn't particularly like it either. The two entwined figures were (realistically anyway) all out of proportion, the female's thighs exaggerated beyond belief.

'What do you think?' Guy asked with a smile.

'Would make an awful good, if large, doorstop.

Guy sniggered. 'For God's sake, don't say anything like that either to, or in front of, Pater. He's a real prima donna where his work is concerned. Sensitive as all get-out.'

'Of course I wouldn't! What do you take me for?'

Robyn caught sight of a well-known television face, deep in conversation with a most distinguished looking gentleman in a velvet jacket. The latter, unknown to Robyn, was connected with the Royal Academy.

'What does the red spot on that sculpture mean?' Robyn queried of Guy, the red spot she was referring to a small red sticker.

'Sold,' Guy replied.

'Ah!' she exclaimed. She'd look for more red stickers.

'My dear Guy, how are you?' George enthused when they reached his side.

'Excellent, Pater.'

'And Robyn. I'm so pleased to see you again.' And with that he gave her a kiss on the cheek.

It was three weeks now since Guy had been told to leave the house in The Bishop's Avenue. He'd spoken to George on the telephone since then, so George knew all about the break-up with Daniella. George had been in London for the past ten

520

days, but this was his first meeting with Guy as he'd been totally immersed in his forthcoming exhibition which was frightfully important to him, and a definite step-up in his status.

Guy's invitation had originally been for himself and Daniella, but as he was now living openly with Robyn he'd brought her instead.

'And this is Wendy Petworth,' Guy (who'd met Wendy a number of times previously) said to Robyn, indicating a pleasant-faced middle-aged woman whom Robyn took an instant liking to.

'Wendy, Robyn Stuart.'

Robyn and Wendy shook hands. What a contrast to the odious Sorel, Robyn thought. Chalk and cheese. This one was a lady, and an exceptionally nice lady too, if she was any judge.

'Pleased to meet you Robyn,' Wendy smiled.

'And I to meet you.'

'Quite a turn-out, eh?' George said, clearly pleased about that.

'Very good,' Guy acknowledged.

George dropped his voice to a whisper. 'Don't look now but that character over there talking to the black chappie is Sir Anthony Blunt. A *very important man* in the art world.'

While Guy was glancing surreptitiously at Blunt, Robyn said to George, 'Tell me, do you still claim to be the best barbecuer in Cornwall?'

'Indeed! Because I am. That right Wendy?'

There was a warmth and loving in George's voice when he spoke to Wendy that Robyn had never heard when he'd spoken to Sorel.

'That's right, George. Nobody in the entire country to beat you.' To Robyn she then said, 'He's concocted a wonderful new sauce that's just out of this world. A sheer gastronomic delight!'

George preened with pleasure to hear that.

'And how's Hunters Moon?' Robyn inquired of George. 'I thought that the most fabulous house.'

'A little older since you last saw it, like me. Otherwise just the same.'

Twelve years, Robyn suddenly realised. It was twelve years since that summer she and her parents had holidayed in Newquay. That made George . . .? He'd been fifty-three then, she seemed to remember, which would make him sixty-five now.

'George!' an American voice boomed out. 'How are you, you son of a gun?'

'Nat!'

The two men fondly embraced, then slapped each other on the back. The American was accompanied by a very pretty girl in her early twenties.

Having embraced and slapped one another, the two men now pumped hands.

'Wendy, I'd like you to meet Nathaniel Bartholemew LeRoux, the biggest crook unhung,' George said.

'And a good customer of his. Don't forget that, George.'

'And a good customer of mine, in the past,' George agreed.

'Pleased to meet you ma'am,' Nat said, shaking hands with Wendy. 'And this here is Fiona, a friend of mine.'

'Hello, pleased to meet you,' murmured Fiona in an upper-crust, Sloaney, voice.

Nathaniel Bartholemew LeRoux could never have been described as handsome. Of middle height, he had a pigeon chest with a face that could easily have belonged to a failed boxer. His hair was carrot-red and cut in the style Americans call a flat-top. Robyn judged him to be fortyish; he was in fact thirty-seven.

George then introduced the others present, after which he asked. 'How long are you over for this time, Nat?'

'A couple of weeks more. I got in last Thursday.'

'I sent your invitation to New York on the offchance you might be able to come. It's been a while since you were here,' George said.

'Oh I've been here George. But not in touch. I've been kinda busy with personal matters.' And with that Nat smiled at Fiona.

'Nat is a stockbroker,' George explained. 'Filthy rich, owns a skyscraper.'

'*Part* of a skyscraper,' Nat laughed. 'Only part: the first eighteen floors.'

'The critic for *The Sunday Times*,' Wendy whispered to George having spied that worthy carving a path in their direction.

Guy took Robyn by the arm. 'We'll circulate, Pater. Catch up with you later.'

'Fine,' George nodded in reply, hoping that the critic from *The Sunday Times* was going to be kind to him; now, when they spoke, and later in print.

Guy steered Robyn away.

*

Robyn stared at the extremely large abstract piece entitled *Woman*, and wondered what on earth it had to do with the female of the species? The only vaguely feminine thing about it was the hole sited slightly off centre.

'Guy?'

She and Guy turned round to find Wendy smiling at them. 'Nat and Fiona are taking us out to a meal afterwards and we wondered if you'd care to come along?'

Guy glanced at Robyn and raised an eyebrow.

'Sounds great.'

'Count us in then,' Guy replied to Wendy.

'It'll be a while yet. Is that all right?'

'We're happy to hang on,' Robyn replied. 'How's it going, by the way?'

'Extremely well. A number of firm sales already, plus a lot of important people saying very nice things. People who *count*. This exhibition is going to be a watershed in George's career, I'm absolutely convinced of it.'

A tinkle of laughter pierced the air.

'Everyone certainly seems to be enjoying themselves,' Robyn commented.

'A good sign,' Guy said to her. 'If people don't like what they see, the atmosphere is quite different. I've been to enough exhibitions in my time to know that.'

'None of them George's, I trust?' Wendy queried, tongue in cheek.

'None of them Pater's, I assure you,' Guy smiled.

Wendy noticed that Robyn's glass was empty and signalled a waiter to come over. 'Must dash back to George. He gets all of a twitter if I'm not there by his side. Drink as much as you like.' She lowered her voice. 'The gallery is paying for that.'

Robyn laughed.

'Your father has fallen on his feet, there,' Robyn said after Wendy had left them.

She accepted a fresh glass of Buck's Fizz from the waiter, who was carrying a tray of them. Guy drained his glass, and exchanged it for a full one.

'I've never known him go for the mother type before. But whatever, I couldn't agree more with you. She certainly seems good for him. And he appears exceptionally fond of her. Let's just hope it lasts between them, eh?'

'Let's hope,' replied Robyn, holding up her glass in a toast.

They both drank to that.

'As we've been on champagne I suggest we stick with that,' Nat said as he led them to the bar.

Robyn gazed about her. Nat had brought them to the Wellington Club in Knightsbridge, of which he was a longstanding member. He adored the place, he'd confided to them en route.

George's face was flushed with a combination of alcohol and success; the opening of his exhibition had gone far better than he'd dared hope. He felt a door he'd long been knocking at had finally opened for him.

'Mr LeRoux, sir,' the white-coated barman beamed.

'Champagne for my guests,' Nat ordered.

'Can we have pink, darling?' Fiona asked winsomely.

'Do you have pink? Nat queried of the barman.

'We do indeed, sir.'

'Then we'll have a bottle of that.'

They sat at a table to await their champagne, and while there, a large bowl of peanuts was placed in front of them. After that they were given menus.

During this they chatted about the exhibition – it was George's night after all – Nat declaring he'd thought the whole thing had gone just 'real swell'.

'I hope you'll visit us at Hunters Moon,' Wendy said to Robyn.

'I'd enjoy that. Very much.'

'Then make it soon.'

They continued to chat and indulge in small talk, Nat cracking jokes when not topping up glasses.

They were excellent company, Robyn thought. She felt very much at ease with them.

After a while they were requested to go to the restaurant which was now ready for them, so down a flight of stairs they trooped into a wood-panelled Victorian room where they were shown to a table laid for six.

'Another bottle of pink bubbly, we're celebrating,' Nat

instructed the wine waiter who came over to inquire politely about their order, their previous bottle having been killed before they left the bar. Like all the waiters at the Wellington the wine waiter was an older man, and a professional to his fingertips.

Already merry from what had gone previously, they became even merrier as the champagne continued to flow. They were in the middle of their main course when Fiona said to Guy. 'Tell me, what do you do?'

'Nothing at the moment I'm afraid. I'm in publishing, and looking for a new job. As is Robyn.'

'Oh?' queried Nat through a mouthful of steak.

'He worked for his father-in-law who gave him the boot,' George explained, and hiccuped.

'Do tell all,' murmured Fiona, intrigued.

Guy glanced at Robyn, who nodded her assent. And so he launched into their story, editing it in parts so that some of the more sensitive details were excluded, concluding with Daniella ordering him from the house in The Bishop's Avenue and letters terminating their employment landing on his and Robyn's desk the following week.

'I've heard of Linehan. Hard bastard,' Nat commented.

'As nails,' Guy agreed.

'He might have kept you on, though. What harm would that have done?' Fiona said to Guy.

Guy shook his head. 'No, Big Ben was right. In my case my position with the firm would have been untenable after Daniella and I split up. My only complaint is that he might have given me time, a breathing space, in which to look around for another job.'

'Surely finding one won't be difficult for you?' Nat queried.

'More difficult than you think. I was at the top of the tree in my side of things. Positions at that level don't exactly come on the market every few weeks. So it's a case of waiting, biding my time until one does.'

'Which could take some while,' Robyn added gloomily.

'Quite a while in fact. And then there's . . .' Guy trailed off.

'Then there's what?' Wendy prompted.

'Despite my reputation in publishing – and it's considerable believe me – potential employers might worry about the risk of taking me on. Big Ben is a very, very influential person, and not one you would wish to make an enemy of. That might prey on some minds when considering me to fill a vacancy.'

'Particularly when you take into account the fact that Big Ben is beginning to make inroads into the British publishing world,' Robyn further spelled out.

Guy pulled a face. 'This is speculation on our part, of course. We'll just have to wait and see what transpires. Our fears may be totally groundless, on the other hand, however, they may be completely justified.'

He took a deep breath, then swallowed what had remained in his glass. He was worried sick about what he'd just spoken of.

'Have you actually been up for anything yet?' Fiona asked Robyn.

'Two jobs, both of which I thought I might have got, but didn't.'

'And do you think that could have been because they were wary of Linehan?'

Robyn shrugged. 'Who knows? But it could well be. There again, perhaps I just wasn't what they wanted.'

'She's a damn fine commissioning editor. Anyone with half a brain in their head would jump at the chance of getting her,' Guy grumbled.

'You're both that good, eh?' Nat said, the hint of a twinkle in his eyes.

'Ask around the publishing scene if you doubt my word!' Guy replied immediately.

Nat, smiling now, held up a hand. 'Only a joke Guy, cool down.'

'So there's the possibility you two could be out of publishing for keeps?' Fiona said.

Robyn glanced at Guy. That was something they'd studiously avoided articulating to one another. 'Yes, that is a possibility,' she replied.

Guy pushed his plate away; he wasn't hungry anymore. If he had to leave publishing what would he do? He hadn't the foggiest.

'Why don't you start your own company?' Fiona suggested.

Guy laughed. 'Oh sure, just like that!'

'That's not impossible, is it?'

'Not at all,' said Robyn. 'A chap called Paul Hamlyn did that a few years back when he launched a brand new imprint.'

'Well then!' exclaimed Fiona, quite caught up with this idea.

'It's not as easy as that,' Guy stated morosely.

'Nothing worthwhile ever is,' Fiona ploughed on.

'I should imagine it's a question of capital,' said Wendy astutely.

'Precisely,' agreed Guy. 'Where on earth would Robyn and I get the sort of money needed to start up our own publishing company?'

'Speak nicely to Nat, he's got venture capital he's looking to invest,' Fiona said.

'Hold on a minute!' protested Nat. 'I only invest in what I know about, and I know nothin' from nothin' about publishing. Why, I can't even recall the last time I read a book. My reading nowadays consists solely of stock market ticker and the business news in *The Wall Street Journal*.'

'Publishing can be profitable if you go about things the right way,' Robyn said softly.

'But from what I've heard you can also lose your pants if you're not careful,' Nat countered.

'Isn't that the same in any line of business, publishing or otherwise?' Robyn went on. 'Don't tell me profits on the stock market are guaranteed?'

'Damn tooting and they're not. Guys go down the toilet all the time.'

'But not you, darling. You're far too clever for that,' Fiona smiled at him.

'Don't give me no soft-soap now,' Nat replied. Then his face lit up. 'But goddamnit if what she's saying's not right enough!' He was sending himself up rotten.

'Anyone who owns a skyscraper must know what they're on about,' George mumbled.

'*Part* of a skyscraper George, I keep telling you that.'

'Yeh, yeh, eighteen stories or whatever. I haven't forgotten.'

Fiona would have continued with the idea of Guy and Robyn forming their own company, but Nat gave her a look which clearly said he didn't wish that line of country pursued further.

More champagne was ordered, and soon that topic was completely forgotten.

For that night, anyway.

'No wonder she's as popular as she is; she tells a fabulous story,' Guy said from the chair where he'd been reading, having temporarily laid his book aside to light a cigarette.

'Who?' Robyn queried from the ironing board.

'Catherine Cookson. A fabulous story, rooted in reality, told at a cracking pace. A sure-fire combination.'

'She certainly sells; no one can deny that.'·

'And despite the fact she insists, I believe, that she doesn't write love stories, I would disagree. They *are* love stories, which are what your average female buyer wants to read.'

'I think I understand what Cookson means,' Robyn said. 'They're not *just* love stories, there's a great deal more to them than that. They are also a documentation of the period she writes about.'

'I agree. But there again, her stories aren't all period, she does write contemporary ones as well.'

'But in my opinion the stronger ones are those with a period background. Have you read the Mallen trilogy?'

Guy shook his head.

'Cookson at her best. A period setting combined with a compelling love interest – or lust interest in some parts. Worked a treat.'

'I would have given my eye-teeth to have had Cookson on our list for a bit,' Guy sighed.

'Or . . .' Robyn was about to expound further when the telephone rang.

'Get that, will you,' Robyn said, waggling the iron at him.

Guy pulled himself out of his chair. He wanted a break and a cup of coffee anyway.

Robyn didn't listen as Guy talked on the telephone, more concerned with getting the creases out of one of his best Jermyn Street shirts, which were a proper pig to iron.

'You'll never guess who that was,' he said quietly when he'd hung up again.

'Who?'

'Nat LeRoux's Fiona asking us over to her place for a chinwag with Nat.'

Robyn stopped ironing. 'What sort of chinwag?'

'She didn't say.'

'Well, when then?'

'Tonight.'

Robyn up-ended her iron, and ran a hand through her hair. 'Tonight!'

'As soon as we can pop over. It's a Chelsea address.'

'And she didn't say about what?' That was mysterious.

'Nope. Only that Nat would like a word with us.'

'*Us*, you and I?'

'The "pair of you", were her exact words.'

'Curiouser and curiouser,' mused Robyn, thinking she'd have to wash her hair before she went anywhere.

Forty minutes later they were in her car – Guy had lost his company vehicle when sacked – heading for swinging Chelsea.

Paulton's Square was directly off the King's Road, an exclusive rectangle of Georgian terraced houses that only the very well-to-do could afford.

The King's Road itself, which they'd partially driven along, was its usual carnival of assorted drop-outs, freaks and would-bes. Robyn had never liked the King's Road, finding it pretentious in the extreme.

'Basement flat,' Guy said to Robyn as they drew up in front of the number he'd been given.

They got out and locked the car, then went down a very steep flight of brick and concrete steps. The door was bright yellow. 'Worsley' stated the pale blue nameplate fixed to the centre of the door. Guy pressed the bell.

Nat himself answered the bell, shaking them both warmly by the hand and inviting them inside.

'Good of you to come at such short notice, but I've had a sudden change of plan and have to fly back Stateside sooner than I'd intended. And I did want to speak with you before I go.'

The room Nat ushered them into had a low ceiling and a distinctly 'county' feeling about it. Cosy, was Robyn's overall impression.

Fiona appeared, wearing a fawn jumper and tartan skirt, the latter knee-length and pleated at the back. All she lacked was a string of pearls and a Hermes headscarf, Robyn immediately thought.

'Lovely to see you both again!' Fiona cried out, and going to Robyn, kissed her on the cheek. She then did the same with Guy.

Robyn and Guy had already divested themselves of their coats in the small hallway, and now Nat asked them what they'd like to drink. He and Fiona were on Portuguese rosé he said, but not to let that influence them. Robyn replied she'd have the same, as did Guy.

When everyone was sitting and settled Nat said, 'I've been doing a bit of homework on you two, and it's just as you said Guy. You are both highly respected and well thought of within your profession.'

Robyn shot Guy a look. She and Guy had dismissed the chat in the Wellington Club as just that, alcoholic chat and speculation. She concentrated again on Nat as he went on speaking.

'Not only have I done my homework on you two, but British publishing in general.'

'At my insistence,' Fiona broke in, smiling sweetly at Nat.

'Okay, at Fiona's insistence, I admit. But I did the homework anyway. And what I've discovered is that a new imprint, to use one of your words, is viable. There is space for one, or several, within the existing publishing galaxy.'

Robyn could feel the excitement mounting in her. 'You're saying you're interested in backing such a venture?' she queried, a slight tremble in her voice which Guy didn't fail to notice.

Nat sipped his wine. 'Fiona was quite correct when she said I had some spare capital to invest. I must admit I had never thought of publishing, but it may, and I emphasise the word *may*, be precisely the sort of undertaking which would suit my purposes.'

Guy was as excited as Robyn. This was unbelievable, a golden opportunity. One to be grabbed with both hands.

'Do you think you two could successfully run your own company?' Nat asked.

Guy lit a cigarette, taking his time before answering. 'To be truthful we haven't really considered the prospect, but I don't see why not. We both have a great deal of experience in the trade, and know it inside out. With me heading sales and marketing, and Robyn in charge of the editorial side I think we have an excellent chance of making a go of it. It would take a considerable amount of capital of course to give us a reasonable chance to get the thing off the ground.'

Nat glanced over at Robyn. 'And what's your reaction? Do you agree with Guy that the pair of you could do it?'

'I believe so,' she replied.

'You don't sound too sure of yourself?'

'Would you be more impressed if I was brash and over-confident?' she answered softly.

Nat laughed. 'You mean like an American?'

'We may speak more or less the same language but we are nonetheless very different peoples, you know. We British tend to be more reserved and conservative about our opinions and abilities.'

'Ouch!' exclaimed Nat. 'I think I've just had my hand slapped.'

'Not at all,' Robyn said. 'I'm merely explaining why my reaction may not be the kind of one you're used to getting in America.'

Nat *was* impressed by that, and realised there was a lot more to Robyn than he'd seen hitherto. He also, shrewdly, guessed that she was the dominant partner in her relationship with Guy – which was quite right, though Guy would have been horrified, and highly amused, if that had been suggested to him.

Guy, meanwhile, was frowning at Robyn, thinking she was going about this entirely the wrong way. You didn't 'cheek' someone like Nat LeRoux; you were deferential and obsequious to him.

'So you do agree that you and Guy could make a go of this?' Nat asked Robyn again.

'Yes, providing we have the proper back-up and can make everything come together correctly, I don't see why not.'

'And the company will make a profit?'

'Not right away Nat, but eventually it should. And hopefully an on-going and increasing one.'

Nat signalled to Fiona who got up and poured them all more wine. 'Let's just say I am interested and willing to go further, if you are.'

'We most certainly are,' Guy confirmed.

'Robyn?'

She nodded. 'Very much so.'

'Right then. I propose that the next step is this. The pair of you draw up a masterplan. A total initial costing broken down into its component units. The number of staff you'd need, salaries, premises, overheads etc, etc.; the type of books you'd wish to publish; the market you'd be aiming for. In other words the whole shebang. Can you do that?'

'It'll take a while,' Guy said.

'I'd expect it to. But when you have finished it, send it to me, or a copy of it, in New York, and when I've studied and digested the contents I'll fly back over here, and we'll discuss it all in detail. How's that?'

'Just dandy,' said Robyn, which made Nat laugh. As she'd known it would.

Robyn and Guy were sitting round a scarred wooden table in their local, a pub in South End Green, where they'd come directly from Paulton's Square.

'I'm stunned,' said Guy, shaking his head. 'Absolutely stunned.'

'It is a bit of a turn up for the books, eh?'

'Our own publishing company. Christ!'

'If we can pull it off,' Robyn cautioned.

'Do you have any doubts? Do you think we can't?'

'If I'd have thought so I would have said. Why waste our time after all? But by the same token we do have to appreciate that neither you nor I have ever run a company before. There's a huge difference between being an employee and shouldering the ultimate responsibility of employer. The person with whom, to paraphrase President Truman, the buck stops.'

'We're not totally inexperienced at management level. Don't forget we did organise and run those poetry readings, which were a great success.'

He was pulling her leg, she thought. 'Be serious!'

'I am,' he protested.

'That was kid's stuff compared to what we're about to embark on.'

'Maybe so. But between us we did make a success of those readings, both artistically and financially. If we can do it at that level, then why not at a far greater?'

'It's like saying if you can ride a bicycle you can also drive a Formula One.'

'No,' he said, stabbing a finger at her. 'It's saying that if you can ride a bicycle then you are also capable of riding a far bigger, more complex machine. At the end of the day they're both bicycles.'

'You're daft!' she answered tenderly, thinking he was grossly over-simplifying matters. However, she did appreciate his point.

Guy had a long pull of his pint, then said, 'Nat did his homework on us so I think it only right we do ours on him. Just because Pater knows him, doesn't mean that he's bona fide. And how did Pater introduce him again, "the biggest crook unhung", wasn't it?'

'If he's an accredited member of the New York Stock Exchange, as he claims to be, then inquiries about him should be relatively easy to make,' Robyn said.

'I'll ring Pater tonight and find out just what he really does know about LeRoux,' Guy declared.

Excitement bubbled up in Robyn again. 'This could turn out to be a night we'll remember for the rest of our lives,' she said.

'Or one we'll more or less have forgotten about in six month's time,' he countered.

They fell to discussing preliminary details.

'Excellent. A truly excellent piece of work,' Nat enthused, referring to the masterplan Guy and Robyn had sent him in New York a fortnight previously and which he now had before him.

The four of them were in Fiona's flat, Nat having jetted into Heathrow the previous evening.

'It's as comprehensive as we could make it,' Guy stated.

'Hoxton? Where the hell's Hoxton?' Nat queried.

'Within striking distance, by which I mean minutes of the City and general West End area,' Robyn replied.

Nat glanced down at the opened folder containing the masterplan. 'These proposed premises seem awful large to me.'

'Gives us space in which to expand, and that means we can remain there for quite some time to come,' Robyn answered, it being she who'd dealt with this particular matter. 'The lease is up for sale, and negotiable. The price range is very reasonable as it's now a fairly run-down part of London, though as I've just emphasised, a most convenient one.'

'Hmmh!' murmured Nat.

'More coffee?' Fiona quietly asked Robyn and Guy who both shook their head.

Guy was tense in the extreme; he and Robyn had put a horrendous amount of effort into this compilation of facts and figures which had taken them two and a half months to complete.

'The Anchor Press Ltd. Tiptree, Essex. Tell me about them,' Nat asked.

'One of our leading book printers and binders who come thoroughly recommended. Their prices are fair, they deliver on time and their quality is high. I could put forward cheaper firms, but not ones I'd have the same confidence in,' Guy replied.

Detail after detail was gone into, explanations given, views aired, until at last Nat closed the folder before him. 'Enough! Anything further right now would just be quibbling on my part.'

'You accept it then?' Guy asked with bated breath.

'I do.' Nat paused, then said. 'There's only one drawback. It need only be temporary, but it's a drawback all the same.'

'Which is?' Robyn queried.

'Your total costing comes out at half a million sterling. I can't meet that. It's a larger amount than I had anticipated.'

Robyn went very still inside. 'You surely must have realised that setting up a publishing company isn't a tuppence ha'penny affair?'

'Of course I did. I just didn't imagine I was going to have half a mil thrown at me.'

Was he trying to pull a fast one? Robyn wasn't sure. 'As far as I could ascertain your American assets are somewhat in excess of forty-three million dollars,' she stated quietly.

Nat's eyebrows shot up his forehead in surprise.

'And it would be logical to assume there's more than that in various accounts and investments outside the United States?' Robyn went on.

Nat smiled, a thin smile that twisted his lips upwards.

'Homework works both ways,' Robyn said.

'Do you think I'm trying to flim-flam you?'

'You're a businessman, and an extremely clever one from what we've heard.'

His smile widened. 'Shall I explain?'

'Please do,' said Guy, anxious to get in on the act.

'You will recall I originally stated I had venture capital to place. That was precisely true. *Venture* capital, not my entire goddamn bankroll, a huge chunk of which is tied up in real estate anyway. Now, I could raise the half mil required, but am not going to because that is more than I wish to stake at present. It's as simple as that.'

Robyn nodded, his explanation was acceptable.

'How much can you put up?' Guy queried.

'Three hundred thousand, which leaves us with a shortfall of two hundred thousand. Can you cover that?'

Guy thought of what he had in the bank; just enough to keep him solvent for another six months at most. After that, to keep his head above water, he'd have to flog off the few items of jewellery that Daniella had given him over their years together. The gold cufflinks with tiny pearl insets, the gold and bloodstone ring and the gold medallion with his, and her, name inscribed on it. He hadn't a clue how much they would realise, but probably a lot less than he would have liked.

'No,' said Guy.

'No,' added Robyn.

'Okay then. But it's not a problem. All we have to do is find another investor, or several, to make up the shortfall. Leave that to me.'

'You mean another partner?' Robyn queried. The partnership was something they hadn't gone into yet.

'Depends, Probably.'

Robyn contemplated her own assets. There was the flat, with a mortgage on it, and car – nothing she could even begin to raise the necessary amount with.

'Any objections to that?' Nat asked.

Guy glanced at Robyn, then shook his head. 'Not if that's the only way.'

'I can't see another. Can you?'

'What about the City?' Guy suggested hesitantly.

'What have you two got to offer the City other than an idea? Why, you haven't even got a job between you. No, if we approached the City the only way we'd get a loan was through me, and as I've already stated I don't wish to take on any further financial commitments at this time other than the amount I've already offered.'

That was true Robyn thought. In the present economic climate the City wouldn't entertain her and Guy without collateral. Whoever they approached would probably just laugh at them.

'Have you anyone in mind?' Robyn asked Nat.

'A couple of guys I know over here who might be interested. As I said, leave this bag to me. Okay?'

Driving back to Hampstead through the January snow Robyn said the meeting had been a bit of an anti-climax really. She'd been hoping for the green light, instead of which they'd got an amber.

There was a shock waiting for her when she arrived home.

Hannah had been on the phone during their absence and left a message for Robyn on the recording machine. Her Great-Aunt Lily, Cathy's younger sister, had passed away, having suffered a fatal stroke while asleep the night before. The funeral would be the following Friday; could Robyn manage to get up for it?

Robyn rang her mother straight back, and caught Hannah in. Yes of course she'd come up, she said. She'd catch a train on Thursday that would arrive in somewhere round about teatime. Hannah said that Lal would be at the Central Station to meet her.

It was a sad Robyn who finally hung up; she'd been very fond of her Great-Aunt Lily who'd had such a marvellous sense of humour. Mind you, Lily had never been the same since Dougie had died five years previously. She'd gone into decline after that, the two of them having been so close.

'Do you want to come with me?' she asked Guy.

'As they don't know about you and me, I don't think this is an appropriate time for me to make a reappearance. It will give you the opportunity to tell them about us, though.'

It would that, she thought. She'd kept her relationship with Guy from them in the past while he'd been with Daniella, but now they were separated and he was living with her there was no further need. She just hoped her mother and father understood, that was all.

She was sure they would.

*

536

'Well, that's that,' said Lal, warming his hands at the sitting room fire. He, Hannah and Robyn had just returned from the funeral which had gone off as well as could be expected.

'Lots of lovely flowers,' Robyn commented.

'Aye, they were that,' Hannah agreed. They'd sent a large wreath from the three of them.

'I thought David was looking a lot older,' Lal said. David was Lily's son, the twin who'd survived the Second World War in which his brother had been killed.

'Well, there's none of us getting any younger, and that's a fact,' Hannah said. She was sixty that month, while Robyn, whose birthday was also in January, had just turned thirty.

'Mind you go and see your gran tomorrow, as you promised,' Hannah said to Robyn.

'I won't forget, Mum.'

'She'd be heartbroken, if you did.'

'Speaking of ages, she's amazing isn't she?' Cathy was eighty-five, eighty-six that year.

'Aye,' said Hannah, nodding her agreement. 'She gets around like a woman half her years.'

'Anyone for a drink?' Lal queried.

Hannah said she'd have a sherry, Robyn a whisky. They were all cold through from standing in the cemetery where a bitter, biting wind had been blowing.

Lal left them to get the drinks which he brought back on a small tray.

'A toast,' proposed Hannah when she had her sherry. When the other two were looking at her she raised her glass and said. 'Here's hoping that Robyn will have had enough of London soon and come back to Glasgow, and her ain folk!'

Robyn lowered her glass which she'd also raised. 'Oh, Mum!' she said softly.

Hannah drank, then said, 'You know it's your father's and my fondest wish that you come home again. We never dreamt when you originally told us you wanted to go away for a while that it would be anything like as long as it's been!' She held up a hand when Robyn opened her mouth to speak. 'I appreciate you've got a good job down there, and your own flat. But you can easily get a flat up here, and as for a good job, I'm sure something could be sorted out if you didn't fancy the shop anymore.'

537

Robyn took a deep breath. She'd been awaiting a chance to tell them about Guy, their being sacked from Orbit, and the proposed new company. This was a perfect opening.

She began with the fact she'd actually gone to London to be Guy's mistress.

And took it on from there.

'What time are you going to visit Cathy?' Lal asked Robyn at the breakfast table. Robyn had said she'd be catching a mid-afternoon train back to London.

'She said she'd be in all morning, so any time then,' Robyn replied, spreading marmalade on a slice of toast.

'Right, I'd like to have an hour with you before you go. So why don't you spend that hour with me directly after this, and if you want I'll drop you off in Purdon Street?'

'Fine.'

Hannah opened her mouth to say something, then changed her mind.

'Will you ring Gran and tell her what's what?' Robyn asked Hannah.

'Of course, I was going to ring her anyway. Lily's death was an awful blow to her you know. It affected her deeply.'

'Do you want to meet me there?' Robyn queried.

Hannah thought about that, then shook her head. 'I'm sure Ma would prefer to have you all to herself. I'll drop by there later, after you've caught your train.'

'And what's this hour to do with Pa?' About her and Guy, she thought – which was partially true, but not at all in the way she'd imagined.

'I want to take you sightseeing. Down memory lane,' Lal replied, which surprised her.

'Down memory lane.'

Reaching over, Lal picked up Hannah's hand, and kissed it. The unexpectedness of that, and with Robyn present, made Hannah blush furiously.

'Down memory lane,' he repeated to Robyn with a smile.

Lal drew his Rover into the kerb. 'Come on,' he instructed Robyn, and got out.

Robyn smiled in recognition. 'The first shop,' she said.

'The first shop which we lived above before moving to Winton Avenue,' Lal elaborated. 'You should have seen it the day we got the key to go inside. What a mess! We painted the shop white with paint your great-granda "acquired" from Tommy's Yard – now closed down – where he'd worked all his life. And on the opening morning we gave the bread away free, all a customer needed for a loaf were her BUs – bread units to you. That was the start of it, the start of my chain of bakeries, shops and kiosks.'

'You've done well for yourself, Pa. No one could ever say otherwise.'

'I did well for *us* Robyn. It was all for your ma and you as much as it ever was for me. It took us out the slums and gave us Winton Avenue. In your case it gave you an education at Laurel Bank which is second to none in Glasgow. It gave us the sort of lifestyle your mother and I could only have dreamed of before.'

Lal stopped speaking to gaze at the shop he had so many fond memories of. The balloons John Ford had given Hannah which had taken such a big trick at the time. The night Hannah had gone into labour and Norm-the-lorry had driven them, all squashed into the cab of his lorry, to the Western Infirmary where Robyn had been born. The day that . . .

'Pa?'

He turned to Robyn. 'Yes, lass?'

'I know you Pa, there's a point to all this. What is it?'

'The word *us* Robyn.'

'Go on?'

'Let's get back into the car, it's brass monkey weather out here,' he grumbled.

When they were once more in the car she lit up a cigarette.

'I was awake most of last night thinking about what you told us,' Lal continued.

She gave him a sideways look, but didn't say anything.

'You never are going to come back to live in Glasgow again, are you?'

'It's highly unlikely, Pa.'

That was what he'd thought. 'I like the idea of your proposed new company. Do you really think it'll work?'

She shrugged. 'Any new venture is a gamble, Pa, you know

that. But yes I do believe it'll work. I'l tell you this, if it goes down the Swanee it won't be for lack of effort or commitment on my part, or Guy's.'

'Knowing you, I certainly believe that. And yet, neither you nor Guy will have control of this new company; that will be in the hands of Mr LeRoux and whatever partner, or partners, he takes on.'

'Only financial control,' Robyn argued. 'We will be in control of everything else.'

Lal smiled thinly. 'There is only *one* control, and that is the financial one.'

She had to admit he was right. 'Guy and I have to agree to such an arrangement, Pa, neither of us has any capital of our own to invest.'

'You have,' Lal stated softly.

'I do?'

'Of course you bloody well do. *Us* remember! Like the three musketeers, what's mine is yours.'

She regarded him in astonishment. 'Are you saying you'd give me two hundred thousand pounds?'

'Why not? Everything I and your mother have will come to you eventually anyway. If you can put a part of that to good use now, then now is when you should have it.'

'I . . . I don't know what to say. I had never even considered such a possibility.'

'Or the entire half million? We could go to that if you wished? You fund the whole kit and caboodle, which may be the best thing when we go into the details.'

'You have that much available to you?' Robyn queried.

'Of course. I'm a very rich man. Far richer than I think you must realise. Don't forget how much I've expanded, just since you went to London. I've almost doubled my operation between then and now.'

Her thoughts were whirling; this was so unexpected.

'Naturally I'll have to consult my accountant,' Lal went on. 'I don't keep that sort of money lying in the bank. But I can easily come up with it, given a week or two.'

Half a million pounds if she wanted it! The concept was mind-boggling. 'You certainly have faith in me and my judgement,' she said to Lal.

'Faith founded on knowledge. You're my daughter, and I'm quite convinced you've inherited my business ability. Just as I believe you've inherited your mother's flair.'

They sat and talked for a while longer, then Lal drove Robyn to Purdon Street. After that he went to see his accountant.

Cathy had shrunk since the last time she'd been up in Glasgow, Robyn thought, as Cathy, after the doorstep kiss and cuddle, ushered her inside. She'd noticed that at the funeral, but had thought it might be to do with the circumstances, or her imagination. Now she was certain it was neither. Cathy had definitely shrunk, but then that wasn't unusual in someone her gran's age.

'You look wonderful. Absolutely wonderful!' Cathy enthused, filling the kettle at the sink.

'You don't look so bad yourself.'

'Och, away with you!' Cathy admonished, but clearly delighted with the compliment. 'I've got some fancy cakes in specially. You'll take a cake, won't you? I love a cake myself. A real treat.'

'A cake would be lovely.'

Cathy plonked the kettle on the stove and lit the gas underneath. 'Tea or coffee? I've got both.'

'Whichever you prefer.'

'Not at all, you're the guest!'

'Tea then,' Robyn chose, knowing Cathy drank tea far more often than coffee.

'Right! Tea it is.'

'The funeral went well, don't you think?'

Cathy's happy expression vanished. 'Yes, it did. I still can't believe it, you know. I never imagined Lily would go before me. But there you are!'

They talked about the funeral till the tea was masked, when Cathy poured and changed the subject. 'Now I want to hear all about you being back with Guy Trecarron. Your mother told me on the phone when she rang, and about this new company you're thinking of starting. Give me all the details, about everything!'

Robyn laughed. 'There's been a development concerning the company that Mum doesn't know about yet. But I'll start at the beginning, and bring you up to date.'

Cathy sat entranced as Robyn recounted the same story she'd told her parents the night before, bringing the very end up to date with what she and Lal had discussed earlier in his car.

'Well, well!' Cathy muttered when Robyn was finally finished.

'Exciting, eh?'

'About the company, yes. But imagine you being Guy's . . .' She hesitated, then said, 'ladyfriend all these years. None of us up here had any idea. We believed you'd become terribly hard to please, and that there wasn't anyone special. The two of you will be getting married now, of course?'

'I presume so. When Guy's divorce comes through.'

A strange expression came over Cathy's face which prompted Robyn to ask. 'Do you disapprove of what I did?'

'About Guy you mean?'

Robyn nodded.

'Not at all. If I'd been in your position I'd have done exactly the same.'

'You would?' Robin exclaimed in surprise.

'Most certainly. I'd have done anything to have had another year, month, day or hour even, with my Bobby. Anything at all. So I can understand you accepting the situation you did in order to have some time at least with Guy.'

Robyn had a sudden inspiration. 'Yours was a great and tragic love story, Gran. You should write it as a novel and Guy and I will publish it when we get the new company going,' she suggested.

'Me! Write a novel! Havers, lassie.'

'Why not? You might even become another Catherine Cookson, a number one bestseller!'

'Now you're being preposterous.'

'No I'm not. I've heard the story often enough, don't forget. Two young people madly in love against a backdrop of the rent strike and Passchendaele; very powerful ingredients indeed.'

'They were powerful times,' Cathy agreed. 'Powerful in the extreme.'

'So, why don't you have a bash?'

'I wouldn't even know where to start,' Cathy protested.

'At the beginning, where else? Pick a point before the war, where Granda Bobby had just proposed say, and away you go!'

'Nineteen-thirteen.' Cathy said. 'He proposed in nineteen-thirteen. I was twenty-two at the time. And a widow at twenty-four.'

Cathy had a sip of tea, then continued, speaking slowly. 'You know the rent strike is almost forgotten about nowadays, few people outside my generation are even aware there was such a thing. It just never got documented the way it should have been. And why? My own guess is because it was fought and won by women. Ask any Glaswegian who John Maclean was, or James Maxton or Willie Gallagher, and they'll be able to tell you. But I doubt if one in a hundred has ever heard of Helen Crawfurd, Mary Barbour or Jean Ferguson, which is a crying shame.'

'Then you rectify the matter,' Robyn said. 'Put them all in your book. Tell us what they did, and what they were like. Who better than you? After all you were there and knew them personally.'

'Oh aye, I did that,' Cathy smiled.

'Well, then?'

'It's a thought. If only I could write.'

'How do you know you can't unless you try?'

Which was true enough, Cathy couldn't argue with that. But there again! 'I'm too old a dog to learn new tricks, Robyn. Far too old. Now . . .' she made a gesture of dismissal, 'let's get back to you. Tell me more about this Daniella. I find her intriguing, if somewhat nauseous.'

Robyn laughed at that. Nauseous fitted Daniella to a T. But then she was prejudiced.

She began to speak further, drawing a fuller (and even bitchier, it has to be admitted) picture, of Guy's wife.

When Robyn was gone Cathy gathered up the dirty crockery and piled it in the sink. She'd wash and dry later, when she was more in a mood to do so.

Glancing out of the window behind the sink she stared down at where Miller's coalyard had once been, now long gone. The stables were still standing, if only just. They'd been used for something else for a while – she didn't know what – then abandoned again. The rest of the yard was covered in weeds and assorted rubbish, which made it look a right tip.

She sighed, thinking that Purdon Street itself had gone the same way. Many of the closes were condemned, their houses empty and windows boarded up. Dirt and filth were everywhere, while over Purdon Street and surrounding roads the smell of decay and despair hung like a pall. The entire area was on its knees, a pale shadow of its former robust self, waiting for the *coup de grâce* that the bulldozers would finally bring. And not a day too soon, many folk said.

She could have moved away donkey's years ago; Lal had offered her a new house any number of times. All she'd had to do was say and he'd happily have bought her one. But she didn't want that. She wanted to remain in Purdon Street where her memories were.

Again in her mind's eye she could see Bobby coming out the yard gates on his horse and cart as she stood on that very spot waving to him, and he waved back.

So vivid was the image, it was as if she'd stepped back in time. She was young again, with everything before her. She had Bobby, and this house, and the world was their oyster. She half raised her hand to wave just like she'd used to, then dropped it again as the image faded, crumbling and withering into nothingness.

Leaving the sink, she went from the kitchen through to the room. From a tallboy there she took out an ancient shoebox which she carried back into the kitchen. Laying the shoebox on the table she then sat in front of it.

The letters inside the box were yellow with age, the writing on them a light brown, when originally it had been black.

'Dearest darling Cathy . . .' the letter she'd selected at random began.

A few paragraphs later she smiled to read, ' . . . everyone is talking of a new hit musical currently running at Daly's Theatre in London called *The Maid of the Mountains*. It has a marvellous show-stopping song in it which you hear hummed and sung everywhere. Even I, with my awful voice, have taken to singing it – though only when alone! – upon occasion! Do you know it darling? It goes like this.

At seventeen he falls in (the rest of this line had arrived smudged and indecipherable)
With eyes of tender blue.

> At twenty-four he gets it rather badly
> With eyes of a different hue.
> At thirty-five you'll see him flirting sadly
> With two or three, or more,
> When he fancies he is past love,
> It is then he meets his last love,
> And he loves her as he's never loved before.

'Lovely song, but not at all like us. For you, Cathy are my first love, and my only love . . .'

She had to blink away the tears that suddenly filled her eyes. Damn you for joining up, Bobby McCracken! Damn you! Damn you! Damn you for the gorgeous, adorable, loving patriotic man you were!

As the letter continued its tone changed. Now he was telling her of the horror of being caught in a creeping barrage, the description of which made her go cold inside.

She'd instructed him not to spare her any details in his letters home, to unburden himself fully to her if that would be of help, which was precisely what he'd done. His letters contained a full and explicit account of his life at the front that would have made a novel in itself.

Write a book about her and Bobby, she wondered? One thing was certain, she had more than enough material to do so. Why with these letters she could describe accurately, precisely what he was going through while she was fighting the rent strike here in Glasgow.

Could she write a book? Was she capable of such a thing? Heaven alone knew. It wasn't as if she didn't know about books. She'd loved and been around them all her life. But that was hardly the same as writing one!

Then she thought again of Helen Crawford and the others who'd been involved in the rent strike. It was criminal to think that their efforts and achievements might soon be totally forgotten, for once the last of her generation died away there would be no one left to recount their heroic exploits. As she'd said to Robyn, documentation of that episode had been negligible, why even those so-called Glasgow historians who'd actually heard of it had only vaguely done so, and knew little, if indeed any, detail.

She refolded the letter, put it back in its envelope and returned that to the shoebox. She then began to read another letter, this one of the very last she'd received.

It was hours later when she finally replaced the cardboard shoebox in the tallboy having reread every single letter it contained.

Robyn was packing her case when there was a soft knock on her bedroom door. 'Come in!' she called out.

It was Hannah with a forced smile on her face. 'I was wondering if I could have a chat with you?' she said, closing the door behind her.

'Of course mum. What is it?' She folded a favourite Janet Reger slip and placed it on top of a matching pair of French knickers. Both had been a present from Guy the previous year.

'I've been trying to have a private word with you ever since you got home. But between one thing and another I haven't had a proper chance up until now.'

'Well, here we are,' Robyn smiled.

'Do you really think this . . .' She hesitated, then continued more forcefully. 'Do you really think this new company idea is a good one?'

Robyn stopped what she was doing to stare at her mum. 'Yes I do.'

'It's just that . . .' Hannah wrung her hands.

'Just what, Mum?' Robyn prompted.

'Helen McEwen, James's wife has had another baby boy.' James had married four years before to a girl he'd met through his brother Rory.

'Good for her. Are they still happy together?'

'Very, according to Alexander and Cecily. They're living at Craigendoran down the coast, but then I wrote and told you that.'

'Yes, you did.'

'Beautiful bungalow. Cecily has shown us pictures of it.'

'I was always pleased that you, Pa and the McEwens managed to remain friends. After all, what happened was entirely my fault, no one else's.'

'They're calling this boy Alexander after James's father,' Hannah said.

Original! Robyn thought drily, but didn't say so.

'If you'd gone ahead and married James they might have been your two boys,' Hannah went on.

Robyn was lost. 'I don't understand. What has James and his family got to do with me and the new company? I fail to see the connection?'

'I, eh . . .' Hannah fumbled in her cardigan pocket, pulled out a packet of cigarettes and lighter, offered the packet to Robyn who declined with a shake of her head, took out a cigarette and lit up.

Robyn was becoming exasperated. 'What Mum?'

'Don't you think it's high time you settled down to having children? There aren't all that many childbearing years left to you, you know.'

Robyn's exasperation melted away. 'Yes, Mum, I do appreciate that.'

'You do want children don't you?'

'Of course, I'd love to have some. It's just that my life hasn't quite worked out that way.'

'All the while you've been in London I've been waiting, hoping, that one day the telephone would ring with you announcing your engagement or forthcoming marriage, but that call has never come.'

'Perhaps I should have told you about Guy before, Mum, But I hardly thought you or Pa would have approved.'

Hannah sat on the edge of the bed. 'You're right. I would have understood, but not approved. As things were you were most certainly getting the short end of the stick don't you agree?'

Robyn thought back to her earlier conversation with Cathy. 'The short end of the stick is better than no stick at all,' she replied.

Hannah's expression became grim. 'If you start this new company you're going to be fully tied up in it for God knows how long to come. There won't be time for pregnancies and children, will there?'

'It's a fantastic opportunity, Mum, particularly now that I'm going to be involved financially.'

'I wish your father had spoken to me about that first. I would have told him not to do what he did,' Hannah muttered darkly.

'Why, Mum?'

'Because I want you married with a family. And best of all married with a family and living up here!' Hannah exclaimed.

'Isn't that somewhat selfish on your part?'

Hannah puffed agitatedly on her cigarette. 'Maybe so. But it grieves me to think you might end up a spinster.'

'That's not likely now Guy's getting divorced.'

'And how long will that take to come through?'

'I've honestly no idea.'

'And when it does and you do get married will you start a family straight away?'

'I can't answer that either. Everything depends.'

'I know damn fine what'll happen!' Hannah said, stabbing her cigarette at Robyn. 'By the time you get round to the family bit it will be too late for you'll be too old to have one!'

'That's always a possibility,' Robyn agreed.

Hannah's face contorted. She dropped her head so that she was staring at her lap.

Robyn, experiencing a medley of emotions, sat beside her mother.

Seconds ticked by, then Hannah said in a tight, choked voice. 'I've always felt guilty about not being able to give your father a son. Although he's never said anything, I know he desperately wanted one.'

She looked up suddenly at Robyn. 'Not that that makes him think any less of you; it doesn't. But it's a male thing Robyn, a son to carry on his name.'

Robyn had known her mother had been given a hysterectomy directly after her birth, but had never before appreciated just how profoundly Hannah had been affected by it.

Hannah reached over and grasped Robyn by the wrist. 'Lal can never have that son, but it's been my dearest wish for as long as I can remember that you would give him the next best thing, a grandson.'

Now Robyn understood what this conversation was all about. 'And me living locally so that Pa can regularly see and play with that grandson?'

'Aye lass, just that.'

Robyn enveloped Hannah in an embrace, and held her tight. She could distinctly feel her mother's prosthesis which was less yielding than the real breast.

'I wasn't being selfish for my own sake. It was Lal I was thinking of,' Hannah whispered.

'I realise that now.'

Hannah pulled herself free and had another puff on her cigarette.

'I'm glad we've had this conversation, Mum. But at the end of the day I must live my life as I see fit,' Robyn said softly, and with great tenderness in her voice. 'I'm sorry, but I can't give you any promises or assurances.'

Hannah's shoulders drooped in failure. She considered she'd failed Lal again, just as she had done so often. That was something Lal would have derided, but nonetheless her belief.

'I have a present for you before you go,' she said, knowing further argument and attempted persuasion were useless.

The present, when Robyn came to open it, was of course a book.

There were five of them in the hotel room, Lal, Robyn, Guy, Nat LeRoux and Fiona, Nat having been invited to the Savoy by Robyn to meet Lal and hear Lal's proposition.

Robyn had suggested to Lal that he stay in Hampstead with her and Guy, but he'd insisted on booking into the Savoy, an hotel he knew. He'd done this for two reasons, the first being that he hadn't particularly wanted to stop with Robyn and Guy, preferring to be on his own; the second that an hotel room became 'his' territory, thereby giving him psychological advantage when doing business with LeRoux – always a good bonus to have.

'Fifty-one per cent of the company will belong to Robyn, forty-nine per cent to you if you decide to remain in. She has to have the majority holding; that's how it must be,' Lal stated quietly to LeRoux.

'And what if I find that unacceptable?' LeRoux challenged.

Lal shrugged. 'I am quite prepared to put up the entire half million. Which, incidentally, is what I want to do. But Robyn feels that as Miss Worsley conceived the idea, and you were prepared to implement it, it would be wrong for us now to squeeze you out.'

Nat did a quick mental calculation. 'Fifty-one per cent is two hundred and fifty-five thousand pounds. Correct?'

Lal nodded.

'And forty-nine per cent is two hundred and forty-five thousand.'

Lal nodded again.

'What about the guy I've found to cover the two hundred thou I believed to be our shortfall?'

'If you still wish to include him that's up to you, but whatever his portion, it comes out of your forty-nine per cent,' Lal replied.

'I see.'

'As I just said, Robyn must maintain an overall majority.'

'Hey!' exclaimed Nat good humouredly, swinging round on Robyn. 'I thought you told me you had no dough!'

'I didn't then, but I do now.' A twinkle was in her eye when she added. 'My father specialises in it.'

'You're a banker?' Nat queried of Lal.

'No, Mr LeRoux. A baker by trade,' a smiling Lal replied.

Nat got the gag, and slapped his thigh. 'I like it! I like it!'

Guy was elated by this general turn of events, and had been since Robyn had dropped her bombshell. For the moment however he felt slightly excluded.

'So what do you say, Mr LeRoux?' Lal asked.

'Nat, please.'

'All right. So what do you say, Nat?'

'I say I'm not in a position to argue. Robyn and Guy, should they so desire, are entirely within their rights to walk away and set this company up by themselves. I have no hold over them, or their proposals, whatever.'

Lal had by now come to the conclusion he wasn't going to have any trouble with LeRoux; the man was both reasonable and likeable. He was further aware from what Robyn had told him that LeRoux was also extremely shrewd and clever. An ideal partner for her.

Nat came to his feet and extended a hand. 'Count me in for the full forty-nine per cent.'

'Does that mean you're excluding your friend who was going to accommodate us with the shortfall?' Robyn queried, going to Nat.

'It sure does.'

Robyn took Nat's hand in hers. 'Our lawyer will be in touch

with yours to draw up the necessary papers. When that's done and both lots of money are lodged in the company account, we can get started.'

'Which bank had you in mind?' Nat asked as he continued to pump Robyn's hand.

'Coutts, I thought. If it's good enough for the Queen then it's good enough for . . .' She trailed off, to frown. 'What should we call the company?' Then generally, 'Anyone any suggestions?'

'Yes I have,' said Lal from the room's mini-bar. Inside the fridge mini-bar were several bottles of champagne that he'd had sent up earlier.

Holding a bottle in one hand and five chilled up-ended glasses by their bases in the other he crossed to where Robyn and Nat were standing.

'Well, Pa?' Robyn prompted.

'Can you open that?' Lal requested, handing Nat the champagne.

Lal looked straight into Robyn's hazelnut eyes, almost identical to her mother's, and smiled. This had come to him during the train journey south, but so far he'd kept it to himself.

'Roederer Cristal,' said Nat with approval, glancing at the bottle's label. 'You have excellent taste in fizz, Lal.'

'Come on, Pa, stop teasing. What's your suggestion?' Robyn urged.

'Your mother has always had good luck and success with her shop, The Blackbird Bookshop. Why don't you borrow the same name for your company and call it The Blackbird Publishing Company?'

Fiona squealed as the champagne cork popped extraordinarily loudly and frothing wine cascaded out.

The five glasses Lal held up were quickly filled

'The Blackbird Publishing Company,' Robyn mused. As far as she was concerned that was perfect.

'What do you think?' Lal asked her.

'Spot on, Pa. Absolutely spot on. Nat?'

'I'm happy with that. Let's just hope the name is as lucky and successful for us as it's been for your mom!'

'The Blackbird Publishing Company!' Lal toasted.

A tinge of anger prickled inside Guy as he drank. Someone

might have asked his opinion of the name. But no one had. Not even Robyn.

Robyn came awake to find Guy tossing and turning beside her. He muttered something she couldn't make out, then rolled completely over, whipping the duvet right off her.

'Guy?' she said, shaking him by the shoulder. Then, more loudly when she had no response. 'Guy!'

Breath whoofed out of him, and his eyes flicked open. 'Wh . . . What is it? What's wrong?'

Robyn glanced at the clock/radio and saw it was hours yet before they were due to get up.

'You seemed to be having a nightmare,' she said to Guy.

'I, eh . . .' He reached for his bedside glass of water and drank all of it. 'I was.'

'You've also pinched the duvet.'

'Sorry.' He sat up and flicked her side of it back over her. 'You all right now?'

He ran a hand across his forehead. 'The sweat's just lashing off me,'

'Wait there.'

She got out of bed and padded away. When she returned she was carrying a towel. 'Let me,' she said, sitting beside him.

She patted his face, then rubbed his hair which was sopping wet. And after that she wiped inside his pyjama jacket.

'How's that?'

'Better, thank you,' he acknowledged.

'What was the nightmare about?'

'Ben. He was being eaten alive by a shark.'

Robyn laughed. 'You and your sharks! That was what you compared your mother-in-law to once, if you remember.'

'A great white. I remember all right. Maybe she was the shark that was eating Ben, I don't know. Dreams are funny things, imaginings can get so twisted and convoluted in them. Not to mention bizarre at times.'

'Poor Guy,' murmured Robyn, stroking his forehead which although now dry was still hot.

'I miss that kid so much, it's unbelievable,' Guy said softly.

'I know.'

'I day-dream about him too. I'll be doing something, working away or whatever, and then suddenly he pops into my mind and that's me gone for minutes on end.' Guy sighed. 'Perhaps it wouldn't be so bad if I wasn't so exhausted. I expected starting up a new company to be a hard slog but nothing like as hard as it's turned out to be.'

Robyn had every sympathy with him, she was just as exhausted. Her muscles had a permanent ache to them, as did her brain. Many nights she went to bed with a thundering head, only to wake next morning with the damn thing still thundering. She hated to think how many pills she'd swallowed since that day four months ago at the Savoy.

'And we're not even halfway to the launch yet,' she said, attempting a smile.

Guy groaned.

'But look on the bright side, another fortnight and we *are* halfway . . .'

'What's "bright side" about that!' he interjected. 'There's still a mountain of work – and I'm talking about Mount bloody Everest – still to be done!'

'It'll get done in time, never fear,' she said soothingly.

'I wish I could be so optimistic.'

'It will be, you'll see.'

'I'm meeting a chap from W. H. Smith tomorrow who . . .' He had to stop when she laid a hand firmly across his mouth.

'Not now, Guy. First thing in the morning, if you like. But not now.'

He caught her in his arms. 'I love you, wench. Every delectable pink square inch of you.'

She gave a low, sultry laugh. 'And I love you. To total and utter distraction.'

He kissed her tenderly on the lips, then nibbled her neck. 'You know what we haven't done for absolute ages,' he whispered.

'I thought you were exhausted?'

'I am.'

'But not *that* exhausted?'

He pulled her over to lie beside him, and kissed her again, after which she kissed him.

Their lovemaking on that occasion was brief, intense and blissfully satisfying.

Both were smiling when they fell asleep once more.

'If the amount of alcohol being consumed is any indicator then the launch is a runaway success,' Fiona said to Robyn.

Robyn laughed. 'Publishing people are like that. They can drink it by the bucketful, and often do.

'They'd tried to have the launch at the zoo, but for various reasons that hadn't come off. So they'd opted instead for the Café Royal in Regent Street, another first-class venue.'

'It's all terribly exciting!' enthused Fiona who'd come to work for Blackbird early on, to begin with as a shorthand-typist, and then, because of her intelligence and ability, as personal secretary to Robyn. She was now Robyn's indispensable right hand.

The company was officially registered as The Blackbird Publishing Company, but Robyn had wanted to shorten that, give it more immediate impact, make it snappier, and so it was now simply known as Blackbird, their logo a copy of the stone carving above the shop in Gibson Street, the blackbird launching itself into flight.

Robyn gazed about her. An excellent buffet had been laid on which was proving extremely popular, while the two bars were doing, as Fiona had pointed out, runaway business.

She glanced over at a huge cardboard display featuring the Blackbird logo plus covers of the four books published that day, which, in conjunction with this party, constituted their launch.

It was certainly a glittering occasion, she thought. And how gratifying that so many of the people they'd invited had come along.

She spotted Tom Maschler from Jonathan Cape talking to Graham C. Greene, another Cape employee and bigwig. And there was Maggie Pringle from Michael Joseph, someone she particularly wanted a word with before the evening was over.

'Robyn, I'd like you to meet Maureen Rissik from Hodder & Stoughton,' a male voice declared, interrupting her reverie. The speaker transpired to be Steve Canterbury, Blackbird's Art Director.

'How are you?' smiled Maureen Rissik, a good-looking brunette whom Robyn judged to be in her late twenties, possibly early thirties.

While Robyn was chatting to Maureen Rissik, Guy was getting

himself another drink. He'd been speaking with an editor from Gollancz who'd left him to move on.

The band was going well, he thought. At the far corner of the room Kenny Ball was giving it big licks. He'd personally chosen Ball, a favourite of his. And of many others present too, from what had been said to him, and what he'd overheard.

Someone was waving at him, and he realised it was George and Wendy. He waved back.

Something he'd never told Robyn was that he'd contacted George while she was up in Glasgow attending her Great-Aunt Lily's funeral to see if he could put the bite on his now affluent father in the hope that he could buy into the company, securing at least part of what had then been their two hundred thousand pounds shortfall for himself.

He'd got a flea in his ear for his trouble. George did have money as a result of the exhibition at The Marlborough Gallery, but had plans for all of it. Hunters Moon desperately needed a new roof for a start, did Guy realise how much that was going to cost? And then there was a ten-acre field coming up for auction shortly that had once been Trecarron property and which George was going to endeavour to buy back. And so on and so forth.

What a shock it had been when Robyn had returned from Glasgow with the news that Lal was prepared to give her the entire half million if she wanted it. Christ, talk about being dumbstruck! He'd never been rendered speechless in his entire life prior to that. It must have been a full minute after she'd told him before he could offer a congratulatory reply.

Nat LeRoux was speaking with a man from Simon & Schuster delighted he'd found a fellow American to chat to. They were discussing what they considered to be the correct mix for a martini, New York style.

Fiona introduced herself to agent Tim Corrie of Fraser & Dunlop (Scripts) Ltd. whose offices were situated just across the street from the Café Royal. Agents and hardback publishers would be the lifeblood of Blackbird, their prime source of material.

Robyn spied Ian Chapman in conversation with Anthony Blond and a female she didn't know. Beyond them Lal and Hannah were chatting to John Calder of Calder & Boyars. Lal was asking fellow Scot Calder about the Milnathort Festival which Calder held annually at his baronial home in Milnathort.

Robyn's roving gaze latched onto Anthony Cheetham. Cheetham was with Futura and had recently acquired the British rights for *The Thorn Birds*, an Australian novel by Colleen McCullough which Macdonald had brought out that year in hardback. Robyn knew the figure he'd paid for these rights, which was scandalously high. The general opinion in the trade was that Cheetham clearly had enormous faith in *The Thorn Birds* and Futura's ability to sell it.

Robyn didn't know why a paperback publisher, and rival, should be present, but someone had obviously invited him.

Barbara Briskin from publicity brought a smiling man to Robyn.

'Robyn, this is Henry Glover from John Menzies.'

'Pleased to meet you Mr Glover,' said Robyn, matching the man's smile.

When the party was finally over the entire Blackbird staff agreed that it couldn't have gone better, while Nat declared the night a resounding triumph!

Guy was at his desk when he heard Robyn's office door slam so hard it shook the entire floor.

'Come in!' she spat out in reply to his knock.

'I don't have to ask how your lunch went. I can see,' he said. Her face was dark with fury.

'I wanted that book. I wanted it so bad I could taste it!' Robyn exclaimed, plonking herself down on her desk. Her hands were shaking when she took out her cigarettes.

'What happened?' queried Guy, flicking his Dunhill alight.

'The same old story. I got a polite listening to, a load of waffle about this, that and the next bloody thing, and the assurance that "of course we would be considered".'

'But we won't be?'

Robyn shook her head. 'It went unspoken, but was said nonetheless. My guess is that this one will go to Pan.'

'We are getting books,' Guy said, lighting up a cigarette himself

'Oh sure! The damn books no one else wants or cares about. What we need, as you know only too well, is a bestseller, one with which we can establish a reputation.'

556

'Catch 22,' smiled Guy. 'They won't sell us a potential bestseller until we've already proven ourselves with one. But how can we prove ourselves if they won't sell us an appropriate vehicle!'

'Precisely.' Robyn made a fist and punched the air in front of her. 'It's all so frustrating!'

'Didn't have this trouble at Orbit, eh?'

'Orbit might have been in financial difficulty when your father-in-law took it over, but it had long been part of the establishment.'

'All you can do is keep on trying, plugging away at both the agents and the hardback companies,' Guy commiserated. 'As for the lunch itself, how was it?'

'Lovely. Just don't ask what it cost.'

'That much?'

'*That much*,' she confirmed.

Guy was laughing as he left her office. Though, on reflection it was nothing to laugh about, he thought.

'Thin, isn't it,' muttered Robyn, gazing down at their Autumn catalogue spread before them.

'Thin is a description that flatters it,' Guy replied.

'The cookbook might do well?' she said hopefully.

'The advance orders are most promising.' He paused, then qualified, 'Well, reasonably so.'

Robyn sighed. 'Then there's the espionage story.'

'The cover for that is quite good.'

'That's what I thought,' Robyn agreed. 'It might be a go-er.'

'Might be.'

She pulled a face. 'Who the hell are we trying to kid? You know as well as I do we only bought it so that the catalogue wouldn't be even thinner.'

'I'll shift enough copies so that it earns out and makes us a profit. But Le Carré and Deighton it is not.'

'Le Carré and Deighton! I'd give my right arm to sign either of those two!'

'Only your right arm?' he gently teased.

He yelped when her elbow dug hard into his ribs.

Guy sat glowering into a large glass of whisky and sparkling Malvern water. He was incensed to say the least. Robyn had overruled him regarding a sales promo, which she was perfectly entitled to do as Managing Director, but it was infuriating nonetheless.

It was an argument he should have won, being totally convinced his side of it was right, but as always, he'd felt at a disadvantage when disagreeing with her. He might be a partner, but she was the majority owner. It was the same as it had been with Daniella – she had the money, he was the poor relation.

'Damn!' he swore softly.

When the idea of Blackbird had been mooted it had never crossed his mind that Robyn would end up being his boss. If anything, he'd seen it more as a partnership of equals, the pair of them acting in concert.

Well, it might have been like that if Lal hadn't given her the capital that had bought her fifty-one per cent of the company, but Lal had. And now she was the boss, whom even Nat LeRoux deferred to.

Nor would it make any difference to him or his position when he and Robyn eventually got married; the fifty-one per cent majority wouldn't become a joint holding but would remain in her name.

It was Daniella all over again, he told himself bitterly. Only he loved Robyn which he never had Daniella.

He crooked a finger at the barman and ordered himself another double.

When one of a group of girls sitting at a nearby table smiled at him he smiled back.

'Guy?'

When there was no reply Robyn called out again. 'Guy?'

'You're late,' he said, coming into the room.

'I had, and still have, so much to do. It seems neverending.'

Going to him she threw her arms round his neck. 'Still cross with me?'

'Who said I was cross?'

She laughed. 'Do you think I don't know when you're cross? At one point this afternoon I actually thought you were going to hit me.'

When he didn't reply she kissed him on the lips. 'Well?'

'I still think your decision was the wrong one.'

'I don't. Have you been drinking?'

'Only wine,' he lied. 'I have a bottle opened. Would you like a glass?'

'Hmmh! Please.'

'By the way there's a parcel for you,' he said breaking away from her and heading for the kitchen.

'Where?'

'On the couch. It's got your grandmother's name on the back.'

She was intrigued. What on earth had Cathy sent her? She took off her coat and put that away first, then went to the sofa and the parcel lying on it. She was opening the parcel when Guy reappeared with her glass of wine.

'What is it?' he queried.

'I don't know yet. But whatever, it's heavy.'

Inside the wrapping paper was a pale blue folder/wallet containing a thick wad of A4 paper filled with old-fashioned copperplate writing. The top page stated:

THE DAY BEFORE YESTERDAY
By
CATHERINE McCRACKEN

'Good Lord!' Robyn exclaimed. She'd completely forgotten suggesting that Cathy write a novel. It appeared Cathy had taken up that suggestion, and this was the result.

There was also a letter which said:

Dear Robyn,

I don't know whether this is any good or not. But what I can say is that I've enjoyed, if that's the right word, writing it. The title is something your Great-Uncle Gavin said to me just before he died, and which stuck in my memory. I thought it made an appropriate title.

If you decide you can't publish the manuscript because it isn't up to standard I will quite understand. You are under no obligations whatever.

How fascinating it was to . . .

When she'd finished the letter Robyn laid it aside, then flicked through the manuscript. She couldn't wait to read it. Though she had to admit she was nervous at the prospect.

She explained to Guy, now sitting across the room watching her, about the book and how it had been penned at her instigation, then asked, 'Have you eaten?'

'Nope.'

'What would you like?'

'Anything you'd care to cook. I'm easy.'

'How about I make us a special treat. That North Sea prawn and avocado salad you always say is so scrumptious?'

'A peace offering?' he queried, a slight mocking tone to his voice.

'What we had was a professional disagreement, Guy. It shouldn't be brought home by either of us.

'Pax?' she smiled when he didn't reply to that.

'Okay then. Pax,' he relented.

She cuddled and kissed him again before going off to prepare the salad.

Guy reached for Robyn intending to snuggle up to her, only to discover she wasn't there. Further groping revealed her side of the bed to be empty.

He snapped on his bedside light to see that her nightie was still slung over the chair, which meant she hadn't yet come up. What was she doing? he groggily asked himself as he shrugged on his dressing gown.

He found her sitting on the couch immersed in her grandmother's manuscript. 'Do you know what time it is?' he demanded.

She glanced up at him, excitement glowing in her eyes. 'I can't lay this down Guy. It's enthralling!'

He yawned, 'Enthralling, eh?'

'A real compulsive page-turner. And *I* already know most of the story. What would it be like for someone coming to it for the first time?'

'It excites you that much?'

Robyn nodded.

'Are you sure it's not just because Cathy wrote it?'

She considered that. 'The fact Cathy wrote it made me, if anything, resistant at the beginning, a resistance that soon disappeared. This really is good! A terrific combined-tale-and-love-story that bowls along, holding your complete interest. You can't wait to find out what happens next.'

'Hmmh!' murmured Guy, rubbing a stubbly chin.

'It needs a fair amount of editing, mind you. Her grammar and punctuation leave a lot to be desired. But these are minor things, easily rectified. The story itself is a winner. I'm certain of that.'

'I'd like to read it when you're finished,' Guy said thoughtfully.

'I'll tell you this, I'm not coming to bed until I have.'

Nor did she.

'This could be an extremely important book for Blackbird, so I want each and every one of you to give *The Day Before Yesterday* your best shot,' Robyn announced to the gathering in her office.

She pointed at Steve Canterbury, the Art Director. 'Steve, you have double the usual budget on this one. And if you feel that to get the high results I'm expecting it's still not enough, then come back and talk to me. Okay?'

A delighted Steve Canterbury nodded.

'Who's editing?' Linda Khwaja asked, hoping it might be her.

Robyn had anguished over this decision. On the one hand she desperately wanted to edit it herself, on the other she was worried about being too close to the story and many of the characters it contained. The question was, could she retain her objectivity and be as ruthless and professional in the editing as she normally was?

'I am,' she informed a disappointed Linda Khwaja.

'And it's to be billed as a paperback original?' Barbara Briskin from publicity queried.

Robyn nodded. She could have sold it to a hardback house, then published the paperback a year after the hardback had come out. But all that would take time, and she wanted Blackbird's *The Day Before Yesterday* in the shops as soon as possible. Publishing it as a paperback original, without the prestige of a hardback edition behind it, was a calculated gamble but one she'd decided to take.

'Now Guy,' she said smiling at him. 'Tell us what you have planned.'

'The works,' Guy declared to the gathering. 'Thirty-six copy dumpbins, full custom colour headers for the dumpbins, posters, streamers, half-page colour adverts in at least four major mags, adverts in Scottish and English newspapers, plus, hopefully radio, and possibly even television interviews with the author.'

A hum of approval ran round the room; that really was pulling out all the stoppers.

'Any further questions?' Robyn asked.

'Have you scheduled the date of publication yet?' That came from Jackie Curtis, another of the editors.

When the meeting broke up ten minutes later those who'd been present left buzzing with excitement and enthusiasm.

Robyn entered the wine bar where she'd arranged to meet Guy for lunch, to find him staring morosely into space.

'What are you so happy about?' she asked, having first pecked him on the cheek.

'What do you think?'

Her face set with concern; she knew him to be worried about Cathy's book. 'That bad, eh?'

He shrugged, and poured her a glass from the bottle of claret he was already well into. 'I've got a hamburger coming, what about you?'

She glanced across at the menu written on a wall-mounted blackboard. 'A slice of quiche I think.'

'Nothing else?'

She shook her head.

He rose and crossed to the bar where he spoke to an assistant. On returning to his chair he slumped into it.

'Still having trouble with the advance orders?'

'You know the old adage about the futility of kicking a ball of cotton wool? Well, it's just like that. Half our reps are tearing their hair out, the other half contemplating suicide.'

'Surely they're having more success than we've had with our other titles to date?'

'Oh yes! But they're securing nothing like the orders we need to turn the book into a bestseller. They try to get the bookseller to take a dumpbin, he says no and orders four measly copies. This is a bookseller quite capable of shifting forty or fifty! When we ask the smaller booksellers and other outlets to take a dozen they order three, and if we ask them to take six they order two, or in some cases one.'

'They've been informed about the advertising etc. etc?'

Guy gave her a 'don't be so bloody stupid, woman!' look. 'Of course they have. If we were Pan, Corgi, Fontana, Penguin or Orbit they'd be ordering them by the boxload. But the plain fact of the matter is we're, "Who again? Blackbird? New, aren't you"? And then inevitably, "Oh I don't know, I'm not sure."'

'What about the radio and television interviews?'

'I've tried every programme which might be interested, rung every contact I know. Not a nibble,' Guy replied heavily.

'It's a scunner,' Robyn said.

'A what?'

'Scunner. It's a Scottish word. Sickener I think would be about the closest translation.'

'It's a scunner,' Guy agreed.

Robyn reached across and laid a hand over Guy's. 'Just remember the Robert the Bruce and the spider story. If you keep on trying and never give up you'll get there in the end.'

'I hope you're right.'

So did she, Robyn thought.

So did she!

Cathy was boiling a nice fresh egg for her breakfast when there was a knock on the front door.

'Parcel for you, missus.' said the postman. Not Tommy her regular, but one who'd come in a van.

'Thank you very much.'

She took the parcel through to the kitchen where she placed it on the table. The Blackbird logo which dominated the sticky paper her name and address had been typed on told her where the parcel had come from.

She needed scissors to cut the well-taped parcel open. Eventually the wrapping paper fell away to reveal six spanking new copies of *The Day Before Yesterday*, the complimentary ones that were her due.

The breath caught in her throat when she saw them. 'By Catherine McCracken,' she said aloud, thrilling at the sound of her name. Then again. 'By Catherine McCracken.' How grand that suddenly sounded she thought. Grand and highfalutin'!

563

She picked up a copy and parted it somewhere in the middle. She began to read, words she herself had actually written.

As she continued to read a warm smile lit up her face.

'I went into all the town's main bookshops today and only saw Cathy's book in three of them,' Lal said to Robyn. They were on the telephone, he having rung her at home.

'How many copies in each shop?'

'Three, three and two.'

Robyn swore, which startled her father.

'What's the problem, lass?'

Robyn launched into a comprehensive explanation which soon had him frowning.

'I see,' he said when she finally stopped speaking. 'I hadn't realised how important this book was to the company as a whole.'

'It's the potential springboard we desperately need. If we can get it into the Top Ten bestsellers Blackbird will become a viable proposition in the eyes of agents and hardback publishers, who will then feel confident enough to deal with us in future at the more lucrative end of the market.'

'And if Cathy's book fails to make the Top Ten?'

'We wait until we get another suitable vehicle with which to try again.'

Lal understood perfectly now. 'And that could be some time, from what you've just said.'

'Exactly, Pa. In the meantime the company's ticking over, but only just.'

'In other words, at the moment you're playing second division when you want to be in the first!'

Robyn laughed. 'Substitute third division for second and you've got it right.'

A little later, after further probing and ascertaining of details Lal said, 'I believe your mother wishes to speak to you. She's loitering here with intent.'

'What Lal didn't tell you was that my shop is one of the three carrying Cathy's book,' Hannah explained when she went on the phone.

Robyn swore again, but this time under her breath.

*

'What are you looking so thoughtful about?' Hannah asked Lal later that night.

'Hmmh?'

'I said the house is on fire and your flies are undone.'

'What!'

Now she had his attention. 'What are you so thoughtful about? From the look on your face you were a million miles away.'

'A lot closer to home than that, Hannah,' he smiled. 'I was considering ways and means of breaking into the first division.'

Hannah frowned; she'd missed that part of his conversation with Robyn. 'Are you talking football?'

'No, books. Cathy's in particular. What do you think of this idea?'

'That's cheating!' she exclaimed when he'd told her.

'So too, it could be argued, was giving away free bread on our opening day.'

'That wasn't cheating!' she protested. 'That was a business ruse.'

He laughed. 'Let's just say this is too, shall we?'

When he asked her to help she didn't hesitate in agreeing.

The Job Centre sent along fifteen men and women prepared to do temporary travelling work on a daily basis. The pay was excellent, all relevant expenses would be met. Furthermore there would be a bonus when the job was concluded.

Lal gazed at the eager faces staring back at him. They were waiting to hear the details of what was expected of them.

'You will each be assigned a specific area within the U.K. that will be your territory until further notice,' Lal began. 'Once established in that territory I want you to go from bookshop to bookshop and outlet to outlet – all addresses and locations will be provided to you before you set off – buying single copies of this book.' He held up a copy of *The Day Before Yesterday* which all fifteen stared at curiously.

Lal went on. 'In the case of the very large bookshops and outlets you may return twice, or even three times, in the one day, your guideline being that the number of shop assistants is such that you are not recognised as having bought the same book earlier. Regarding the smaller shops and outlets, I suggest you visit them every second or perhaps third day, or depending upon the size of your territory, which varies amongst you, and your mobility within that territory.

'To summarise. Using your own discretion I wish you to travel throughout the territory assigned you buying up copies of this book, always single copies, without it becoming apparent to any of the shops you're purchasing from that you have a specific interest in this particular book.'

A hand went up.

'Yes?' Lal queried.

'Is this a market research programme Mr Stuart?' the owner of the hand asked.

Lal knew the speaker was being polite, fully aware that this couldn't be a market research anything.

'The truth is,' Lal replied smiling disarmingly, 'my mother-in-law, a very old woman, much loved by her family, has just published this book, which as you can see is called *The Day Before Yesterday*'. Unfortunately, to her great disappointment, it isn't doing as well as it might and so I, a relatively rich man, have decided to do something about that.'

'Ah!' a female breathed, nodding approval.

'Of course I wouldn't want what I intend being done getting out and possibly back to her, which is why I am prepared to pay such a handsome bonus for your combined loyalty and discretion.'

'Besides . . .' this time his smile was broad, beaming and ever so slightly conspiratorial, 'it really is a damn fine book – as I'm sure you'll all agree once you've read it – that merits a helping hand.'

He paused, then declared softly, 'If anyone isn't interested in the job now is the time to say so.'

None of the fifteen wanted to back out.

He hadn't lied to them, he'd told them the truth, Lal thought to himself when they'd gone.

The truth, if not the whole truth.

It was mid-morning, several days after Lal's newly recruited troops had swung into action, that the first re-order for *The Day Before Yesterday* was phoned through from Doncaster, and shortly after that the second from Exeter.

From there on in, with ever-increasing frequency, re-order followed re-order.

Fiona's shriek was so loud it caused Robyn to start and score an unintentional line through cover copy she was marking. Seconds later her office door flew open and a flushed Fiona came charging in.

'*The Day Before Yesterday* is to be number eighteen in next week's *Bookseller* when it comes out!' she cried.

Robyn, heart suddenly thumping, came to her feet. 'You're sure about that?'

'I've just had it from the horse's mouth.'

Guy rushed into the office while others piled up at the door behind him. 'What's going on?' he demanded.

When Fiona saw that Robyn had her hands clamped over her mouth she replied, repeating what she'd just told Robyn.

'Number eighteen!' breathed Guy, while one of the members of staff crowding the doorway let out a cheer.

Fiona gestured for silence and attention, she wasn't finished yet. 'And . . . and . . .' she teased, drawing it out.

'*And* what?' Guy prompted.

Robyn was so excited she was almost dancing on the spot.

'And number seventeen on the W. H. Smith list!'

'Yahoo!' Barbara Briskin from publicity screamed in a most unladylike manner.

'We're on our way. We're on our bloody way!' Guy exclaimed to Robyn, who could only nod in reply.

It was hours before any serious work was got down to again.

Guy was going through his reps' weekly reports and figures when his telephone rang.

'Hello?'

'Guy, it's Lal Stuart in Glasgow. How are things?'

'Improving all the time Lal. Cathy's book is really starting to take off. We're all highly delighted by that of course.'

Lal smiled, then said, 'Robyn mentioned that you were going to try and fix up some radio and T.V. interviews for Cathy. How's that going? When I spoke to Cathy yesterday she said she hadn't heard anything.'

'That's proving stickier than I'd anticipated Lal, though with her now at number sixteen in *The Bookseller* list I'm hoping things will improve in that direction.'

'Have you tried Davey Dallmeyer? I know his show is local to Scotland, but he's very big up here.' The Davey Dallmeyer Show went out on Monday to Friday between twelve noon and quarter to one.

'I've attempted to get through to him three times now, Lal but on each occasion got no further than his secretary. She tells me they're spoilt for choice when it comes to having guests on the show.'

'As I said, he's very big up here. Didn't you once tell me you played golf?'

Guy frowned at this sudden switch of subject. 'I have done in the past, but not for a while now. Why?'

'How about a round with me this Sunday?'

'What, up in Glasgow?'

'That's right, I'm a member of the Bishopbriggs Golf Course. A terrific course, you'd enjoy it.'

Guy was mystified at this invitation out of the blue. And why should Lal think he'd want to go all the way to Glasgow for a game of golf! The idea was preposterous. 'I'm sorry Lal, I'm up to my neck in work and . . .'

'Davey Dallmeyer will be playing with me,' Lal interrupted softly. 'He and I often play together. Have been doing so for years.'

The penny dropped with Guy. Why the conniving old bugger!

Lal went on. 'You can fly into Glasgow Airport Saturday night, and out again early Sunday evening. I suggest it might be worth your while.'

Guy didn't need any more persuading. This was an excellent opportunity for him. 'I'll be delighted to come up, Lal.'

Lal told Guy to let him know what flight he'd be on. He'd be at the airport to meet him.

'You might mention to Davey that the B.B.C. in London have shown an interest in interviewing Cathy,' Lal said casually as he swung his car into the drive that led to the club house.

Guy turned to stare at Lal. 'Since when?'

'Whenever you like. Friday? Thursday? Take your pick.'

Guy's eyes narrowed as he continued to stare at Lal. 'If I told Dallmeyer that he might have it checked up on, and find out it's a lie.'

'If the B.B.C. really was interested in interviewing Cathy do you think they'd admit the fact to an Independent? Not on your Nellie Duff. Nobody from one station gives anything away to another, everything is strictly secret. Davey himself has told me so. So if you say that the B.B.C. is interested in interviewing Cathy he has no option but to take you at your word.'

Guy laughed. 'You're a right twister Lal, as devious as they come.'

Guy didn't know how true that was, Lal thought, laughing also.

'How was I?' Cathy asked having just come off the set of The Davey Dallmeyer Show.

'You were fabulous. Couldn't have been better,' Lal assured her, and kissed her on the cheek.

'You're a natural, and I mean that sincerely. I wouldn't be at all surprised if every member of the audience, and every single person watching, didn't go straight out and buy a copy of *The Day Before Yesterday*,' Guy said to her.

Cathy's eyes shone to hear that.

The following day she had interviews on Radios Clyde and Forth as a direct result of appearing on The Davey Dallmeyer Show.

'Thank you,' said Fiona, and hung up.

'Well?' Robyn and Guy demanded in unison.

'Number five next week in *The Bookseller*,' Fiona announced excitedly.

Breath hissed from Robyn's mouth. It just got better and better. 'Now W. H. Smith,' she said.

It transpired that *The Day Before Yesterday* was to be number four on that list.

'We'll have to rush through a reprint,' Robyn said to Guy.

'How many do you think?'

'Twenty-five thousand?'

He thought about that. 'The way it's climbing the lists I'd tend to stick my neck out and go for more.'

She made it fifty thousand and prayed she wasn't being over-optimistic.

She wasn't.

Cathy gazed up at Broadcasting House, the epicentre of B.B.C. radio broadcasting. 'It's a lot smaller than I imagined,' she said.

'And a bit of a dump inside,' Guy informed her. 'I've heard that parts of it are positively antediluvian.'

'Just like me,' Cathy said, and giggled.

'You're looking like a young thing today, and that's a fact,' Robyn smiled at her grandmother.

'I have to admit all this excitement over the book does seem to have given me a new lease of life.'

And *Blackbird* the start of one, Robyn thought.

They crossed Portland Place and in through swing doors where they were immediately approached by a commissionaire asking if he could help.

Guy explained to the commissionaire who Cathy was, and who he and Robyn were, after which the commissionaire consulted a sheaf of papers he had to hand.

'Mr Wogan is expecting you. If you'd care to have a seat I'll ring and inform the studio that you've arrived.'

This has to be worth a further twenty thousand copies at least, Robyn thought as they rode up in one of the bank of elevators that serviced the building. Perhaps a lot more: Wogan had a huge following.

Petula Clark, the singer, in the elevator with them, smiled at Cathy who smiled back.

Robyn cradled her telephone, then sat back in her chair. That had been Mort Zahl of Zahl Associates Ltd, who'd just rung asking her out to lunch at Bertorelli's. He had a manuscript he wished to discuss with her he'd said. Would she be interested in a tie-in with Weidenfeld & Nicolson?

Would she ever!

The lovely thing was it was the third such request she'd had that week.

Their success with Cathy's book – as she and Guy had known would happen – was opening vital doors that had hitherto been closed to them.

*

'What's so funny?' Hannah asked Lal who was sitting across from her, chuckling to himself.

'I was just thinking of all those copies of Cathy's book that went into the oven at St Kilda Street. God knows how many batches of bread and cakes they made!' St Kilda Street was where Lal had one of his bakeries, the oven an extremely old one that normally ran on coal, but recently on loads of books Lal had delivered there to the baker in charge. The books had come to Lal from his troops, who'd been parcelling and sending them back to him by post at the end of each day.

'And now *The Day Before Yesterday* is number one,' Hannah said.

'Aye, number one. It's a tremendous achievement for Cathy and Robyn.'

'With more than a little help from you.'

'All I did, Hannah, was to get the ball rolling. Once it broke into the lists it started to pick up a momentum all its own. A momentum that's taken it – and don't forget I paid off the temporary workers three weeks ago now – right to the top. Every copy that's put it in the number one slot is a genuine sale with no hokery-pokery on my part.'

'You're a marvellous man, Lal Stuart. The best day's work I ever did was in marrying you.'

'And mine in marrying you.'

'Even though I never gave you a son?'

'You can't have everything in life, Hannah. If that wasn't to be, it wasn't to be. I just thank God for what I do have; it's a lot more than most.'

Dampness crept into Hannah's eyes. 'How about a nice cup of tea before we go up?'

'The very dab.'

As she was passing him he reached out, grasped her by the hand, and gently squeezed it.

'I'll get the tea,' she husked when he let her hand go again.

Robyn poured herself and Guy large whiskies. It was ten pm and they'd only minutes previously arrived home from work. Guy was reading a letter that had been awaiting him.

'From Daniella?' Robyn queried, having noticed that the letter bore an Australian stamp.

'No, her lawyer. The divorce has been finalised. I'm a free man again.'

The breath caught in her throat. 'Oh Guy, that's wonderful!'

Going to her he swept her into his arms. 'Will you marry me?' he asked softly.

The smell of him was dancing in her nostrils. The combined odours of the same aftershave he'd worn all these years, French tobacco and his own personal scent. 'I can't think of anything I'd like more,' she smiled in reply.

He kissed her, then she kissed him.

Placing the tip of a finger on her cheek, he slowly drew it down to her chin. 'You're the right woman for me, Robyn, just as I'm right for you. We were born for one another.'

Having said that he kissed her again, a kiss both fierce and tender at the same time.

'I love you Guy,' she stated simply when that kiss was over.

'And I love you.'

She sighed with contentment and happiness. 'Why don't we go to bed and discuss the wedding plans?' she suggested.

'I have a better idea.'

They did both.

Cathy stared into the glowing embers of the now dying fire. She was sitting in darkness, something she often did. It could be very enjoyable when there was a fire on.

A great wave of tiredness washed over her. Tiredness and a strange, light, ethereal feeling that made her think of a leaf floating on a gentle wind.

'He's still breathing, but only just,' a voice said.

She didn't know how, but suddenly she found herself in a tunnel alongside a group of soldiers crowded round a man lying prostrate. Then she recognised the man kneeling beside the prostrate man as Jack Smart.

Jack took one of Bobby's blood-covered hands and held it in his own. 'You're going to be all right pal,' a weeping Jack said.

Bobby's eyes fluttered open, and the hint of a smile touched his lips.

'Cathy,' he whispered, his eyes staring directly into hers.

And in that instant, after all the years apart, they were together again.

Flower of Scotland

PART ONE

Twilight

Chapter 1

He was quite simply the most gorgeous man she'd ever clapped eyes on. Just the sight of him had the amazing effect of sending a thrill through her entire body, a phenomenon she had never experienced before. She found the inside of her mouth had gone suddenly dry.

'Charlotte, may I introduce my colleague Second Lieutenant Geoffrey Armitage,' her brother Andrew said.

Geoffrey gave a small bow of his head, then held out a hand. 'Delighted to meet you, Miss Drummond.'

'And to meet you, Lieutenant.'

He smiled as they shook. 'Geoffrey please.'

'Then you must call me Charlotte.'

She reluctantly released his hand, furious with herself to find she was blushing, something she rarely did. And never where men were concerned.

Andrew Drummond noted her blushing with amusement. Well well, he thought. This was a turn up for the books.

He turned towards his younger sister who was standing a little apart. 'And this is Helen,' he declared.

Helen, shorter than Charlotte and plumpish, also shook hands with Geoffrey. 'May I too call you Geoffrey?'

'Of course.'

'And what's all this formal Helen nonsense? It's been Nell since I was a child,' she admonished Andrew.

'Nell's far nicer. More you somehow,' Geoffrey stated.

Nell beamed. 'Thank you.'

Andrew rubbed his hands together. 'Now what about a dram after that journey, Geoffrey. I know I could certainly do with one.'

'The family whisky naturally.'

'Naturally.'

Andrew moved to a long oak sideboard on top of which were various decanters and glasses. 'Girls, will you take sherry?'

Charlotte glanced at the ornate grandfather clock situated in a corner of the room. It was just past three in the afternoon. 'A little early for me, but why not?' She decided to shock this Geoffrey Armitage who had just walked into her life and from whom she could hardly tear her eyes. 'Make mine a dram as well.'

Geoffrey was momentarily taken aback, then laughed. 'By Jove!'

Nell wasn't to be outdone, emulating her elder sister as she so often did, or tried to do. 'Same for me, Andrew.'

Charlotte crossed to a red velvet-covered chaise longue and sat, her mind whirling and filled with confusion. There she rearranged the ankle-length skirt of the white cotton day dress she was wearing, already mentally flicking through her wardrobe wondering which gown she would choose for that evening. Something stunning; she wanted to look her best for Geoffrey. She glanced coyly over at him. About five foot nine or ten she noted. With raven black hair and matching eyes. He was broad shouldered, his body suggesting exceptional physical strength. He appeared to be roughly the same age as Andrew, who was twenty-six.

Geoffrey produced a silver cigarette case. 'May I?' he asked Charlotte.

'Carry on. Pa smokes, though in his case it's a pipe.'

'Tried smoking once but found it beastly,' Andrew declared, handing Charlotte a cut crystal glass. He then gave a second one to Nell, now sitting on a chair adjacent to the chaise longue.

'Did McPhie pick you up from the station?' Charlotte enquired of the men. McPhie was the family chauffeur.

'No, we came in Geoffrey's car. It's quite a corker!' Andrew replied enthusiastically.

'A Humber T. Splendid machine,' Geoffrey declared.

'I'm going to ask Pa to buy me one. It would be so convenient to tootle around in,' Andrew said, passing Geoffrey his drink. He raised his own glass in a toast. 'Chin chin!'

'Chin chin,' Geoffrey echoed, and they all took a sip.

'I say, this is sheer ambrosia,' he declared, black eyes shining.

'Twelve-year-old Drummond single malt. Pa says there isn't another in all of Scotland to beat it.'

'I must agree. Wonderful stuff.'

'We've been brought up on it. It's like mother's milk to us,' Nell informed him.

'Really?'

'Oh yes. I can't remember when I had my first drop.'

Charlotte laughed. 'Nell, what will Geoffrey think of us after such a confession?'

Nell was instantly dismayed. 'But it's true.'

'That's all very well. But it makes us sound so . . . awful I suppose.'

'Not at all, Charlotte,' Geoffrey hastily reassured her. 'It is the family business after all.'

'And a damned good business it is too. We're all extremely proud of our whisky,' Andrew declared. 'As for the girls being brought up to take a dram, that's a family tradition. My mother had one every single night before going off to bed.'

His face momentarily clouded. 'God rest her soul.'

'She died in childbirth,' Charlotte softly explained to Geoffrey. 'A baby some years after Nell which was still-born.'

'I'm sorry,' Geoffrey sympathised.

Andrew stared into his glass, then quickly saw off the remains of his drink. It was still painful for him to think of his mother of whom he had such fond memories. It hadn't been quite so bad for the girls who'd been extremely young at the time, but he, several years older than the girls, had known her a great deal better. In his mind's eye he quite clearly saw a vision of Louise Drummond, she and Pa together, the pair of them laughing as had been so often the case. His father had been inconsolable when she'd died and had never looked at another woman since.

'How about the other half?' he queried of Geoffrey.

'Rather.'

'Not for me. One is quite sufficient at this time of day,' Charlotte smiled.

'For me also,' Nell said.

Geoffrey finished his dram, Andrew taking his glass and refilling it along with his own.

'Pa and Peter won't be home till six. You'll meet them then,' Andrew said.

'Jolly good. I'm looking forward to that.'

Peter Drummond was the eldest of the Drummond children and worked with his father at the distillery which he'd eventually run by himself and inherit.

'Pa has a car which he bought last year,' Nell piped up, making conversation. 'A Rolls-Royce.'

'I say!' Geoffrey exclaimed.

'A Silver Ghost tulip back limousine with a body by Lawton,' Andrew elaborated. 'It's his pride and joy.'

'I can well understand that.'

'He doesn't drive himself. McPhie does that.'

'Have you driven it?'

Andrew gave his friend a conspiratorial wink. 'Several times though Pa doesn't know. He'd have a fit if he did. As I said, it's his pride and joy.'

'How long are you home for?' Charlotte casually inquired of her brother, holding her breath as she awaited his reply. What she really wanted to know was how long Geoffrey would be with them.

'A week.'

A whole week! That was wonderful indeed. It would give her time to get to know the fascinating Geoffrey better. There would be walks, and conversations, and . . . She experienced an inner shudder of delight at the prospect.

'It's my first time in this part of the country,' Geoffrey stated. 'Perthshire is quite new to me.'

'And where are you from?' Charlotte asked.

Geoffrey pushed back his hair which had partially flopped over his forehead. 'Glasgow.'

'Oh?'

'I'm a town chappie, I'm afraid.'

'I went to Glasgow once,' Nell said.

'And what did you make of the Dear Green Place, which is what Glasgow means.'

Dear Green Place! That was a joke. She'd thought Glasgow horrid but of course couldn't say so as that would have been rude. 'Interesting.'

'Very different to what you're used to.'

'Very,' Nell agreed.

'I love it there. But it's what you're brought up to, I suppose. And you, Charlotte, have you been to Glasgow?'

'On several occasions with my father when he had business there. I enjoyed the shops.'

'What you really need is to be shown the city by someone who knows it back to front as I do.'

Her heart leapt. 'Is that an offer, Geoffrey?'

'It would be an honour to escort you, Charlotte,' he beamed in reply.

'Perhaps some time then,' she murmured.

He nodded. 'I'll look forward to it.'

'Now,' Andrew declared, their glasses empty once more. 'How about a stroll, Geoffrey? I need to stretch my legs after that car journey.'

'Excellent idea,' Geoffrey answered, trying to put enthusiasm into his voice. He'd much rather have stayed with

Charlotte, a spiffing girl if ever there was. Quite a stunner in his opinion. He was glad he'd come to Drummond House.

Charlotte was also disappointed, wishing him to remain, but at least his absence would give her a breathing space in which to regain her composure.

'Are you all right?' Nell asked when the men were gone. 'You seem somewhat flushed.'

Charlotte fixed her sister with a level stare. 'Do you believe in love at first sight?'

Nell gaped in astonishment.

'I must say, old boy, your sister Charlotte is a corker.'

The two of them had just left the house, an imposing edifice of grey stone topped with slate and many chimneys. Andrew glanced sideways at his friend. 'I thought you were taken.'

'Quite bowled over. Quite. Is she spoken for in any way?'

Andrew laughed. 'She's entirely free. Most of the eligible young bachelors in the area have been after her to no avail. She hasn't been interested in any of them.'

Geoffrey sighed with relief.

'Smitten, eh?'

'Smitten indeed.'

'And she seemed rather taken by you,' Andrew mused, remembering how she'd blushed.

'Do you really think so?'

'Believe me, I know my sister. She was interested all right. I've never seen her so thrown by an introduction to a chap before.'

Geoffrey couldn't believe his luck.

*

'And whereabouts in Glasgow do you live?' Murdo Drummond inquired of their guest, tucking into poached salmon which was a great favourite of his.

'Park Crescent, sir.'

Murdo nodded his approval. That was an excellent address. He turned his attention to Charlotte, resplendent in a black silk sheath dress inlaid with narrow strips of blue satin that fell elegantly to her ankles where it flared slightly. Directly below her bust was a matching blue ribbon tied at the back from where the remainder of the ribbon dangled. 'What's wrong with you, gel, you're not eating?'

'I don't have much of an appetite, Pa.'

'Unlike you. You usually eat like a horse.'

Charlotte blushed bright red, the second time in one day.

'Hate to see good food wasted,' Murdo grumbled.

'I'm sorry, Pa.'

Murdo beckoned to the maid in attendance to replenish their glasses. 'And what does your father do?' he enquired of Geoffrey.

'Senior partner in an accounting firm, sir. He wanted me to follow him into the firm as Peter has done with you, but accountancy held no attraction for me.'

'Not exciting enough, eh?'

'That's right, sir.'

Murdo grunted.

'Would you like me to show you round the distillery tomorrow, Geoffrey?' Peter smiled. He too sported the auburn hair which ran in the family, the exception being Charlotte who was golden blonde, though in Peter's case it had begun to recede. He also had the beginnings of a double chin, unlike his brother who had a firm jawline and finely chiselled features. Peter's were becoming rounded and fleshy.

'I'd like that, thank you.'

'Not very exciting, mind,' Murdo said drily, a twinkle in his eyes. 'Though I've always found it so.'

'I'm sure I will too, sir.'

Charlotte found herself mesmerised by Geoffrey's hands, wondering what it would be like to be touched, caressed by them. What it would be like to . . .

Rousing herself from her reverie she had a sip of wine.

'Any news of the regiment being posted?' Peter asked Andrew.

'None. At least not that I've heard.'

'Let's hope it isn't India. That's a long posting,' Murdo said.

'Five years.'

Five years! Charlotte thought in alarm. An eternity.

'Did you go straight to the Watch from Sandhurst?' Peter queried of Geoffrey. He was referring to the Black Watch, Andrew and Geoffrey's regiment.

Geoffrey shook his head. 'I was with the Middlesex for some time and was only transferred several months ago. Much to my pleasure, I might add. Nothing wrong with the Middlesex but I'd far rather be with a Scottish regiment.'

'Well said,' Andrew declared.

Geoffrey glanced across at Charlotte who was being very quiet, having contributed hardly a word to the dinner conversation. Was she always this quiet? He doubted it. God, she was beautiful.

For a brief couple of seconds their eyes met and locked, then Charlotte, with a small cough, looked away.

'I made my mind up during dinner, I'm going to marry Geoffrey Armitage,' Charlotte informed Nell.

Nell was stunned. 'But you don't know him,' she protested.

'This is going to sound silly, I appreciate that, but it's as though I've known him all my life. We were meant for one another, I truly believe that with all my heart.'

Nell shook her head. This was so unlike her sister. Charlotte was acting completely out of character. 'You're mad,' she said softly.

'No I'm not. I've never been saner in my life. It's as if I've been waiting for Geoffrey, and now I've found him I'll never let him go. He's mine, now and for ever.'

'He's certainly handsome, I'll give you that,' Nell conceded.

'Isn't he just!' Charlotte beamed.

'But what of his character? You've still to find that out.'

'His character's fine. A gentleman through and through. And I love him.'

'Suppose he doesn't want you?'

'Oh he does all right. I could see it in his eyes tonight.'

Nell had a sudden thought. 'It's possible he already has a girlfriend, he might even be engaged.'

'He isn't. I had a quick word with Andrew before dinner. Andrew thought it highly amusing and laughed, but I got the answer I was hoping for.'

'Will you like being an army wife, Charlotte? It can be quite hard by all accounts. You could end up in the most God-forsaken of places.'

'It won't bother me,' Charlotte declared defiantly. 'As long as Geoffrey and I are together, that's all that matters.'

'You won't always be together, there are bound to be separations.'

Charlotte's lips thinned in a grim line. 'They'll have to be endured somehow.'

'Oh, Charlotte!' Nell sighed. 'In a way I'm quite jealous of you.'

Charlotte went to her sister and clasped her by the arms. 'Don't worry, dear Nell, your prince will come.'

'I've never had anything like the suitors you have. Just Willie McCall come to think of it, and he's awful with smelly breath.'

True, Charlotte thought. Willie's breath did stink.

'I'm plain Jane compared to you, and fat . . .'

'You are not fat,' Charlotte interrupted.

'I am. It's horrible.'

'A trifle chubby perhaps, but certainly not fat.'

Nell slowly exhaled. 'Chubby,' she muttered. That was a nice way of putting it. But there was more to it than chubbiness and being plain; she didn't have any allure. Men simply weren't attracted to her. She lacked that something which Charlotte had in abundance.

'You'll be my chief bridesmaid of course,' Charlotte said.

'I think you'd better get him to propose first before you start making plans like that,' Nell counselled.

'I'll get him to propose all right. You can count on it.'

She would too, Nell thought. Charlotte had a long history of getting what she wanted.

*

Nell woke with a start to find her face and forehead slick with cold sweat while her body was shaking almost uncontrollably. She'd come out of a nightmare that had been ghastly beyond belief.

She gulped in a deep breath, the scenes of carnage in her mind still crystal clear.

Men in khaki uniforms, thousands of them, engaged in a dreadful war. Men being blown to smithereens, men missing arms, legs, others shrieking in agony.

Guns flashing and booming, shells whistling through the air to land with mighty explosions. And hanging over it all a terrible pall, the rank smell of fear.

Nell shook her head and the ghastly pictures began to fade, till at last they blipped into nothingness.

'Dear God,' she whispered. What a nightmare. It had all been so very real, as if she had actually been there. What did it mean?

It resembled one of her waking visions, only this time she'd been asleep. Visions that had been with her for years but which she'd never told anyone about, not even Charlotte, in case they thought her insane.

Visions that had always been set in the past, unlike this nightmare which she was certain was of the future.

Reaching out she picked up the glass of water by her bedside and greedily drank, noting as she did that her shaking had subsided. As she snuggled back down into bed a cold, dark tremor of deepest apprehension and despair ran through her.

It was hours before she finally drifted off again to sleep.

*

Charlotte didn't sleep well that night either, rising from bed and putting on her negligée as dawn was breaking. She shook out her long blonde hair that reached almost to her hips and crossed to the window.

'Geoffrey,' she murmured, and a smile crept onto her face. She'd never been more sure of anything than that she and he were fated. She wondered if he'd slept well and hoped he had.

What time would he go down for breakfast? she further wondered, for of course she wanted to take it with him.

'Mrs Geoffrey Armitage,' she said aloud, her smile widening. What a grand sound that had to it. 'Geoffrey and Charlotte Armitage.' That sounded even better.

It was going to be another fine day if she was any judge, a day with Geoffrey after he'd completed his visit to the distillery. Pity about that. But afterwards . . .

A plan began to form in her mind.

'This is a mash tun,' Peter explained to Geoffrey. 'The dried malt is ground into a coarse flour, or grist as we call it, which is mixed with hot water as it is poured into the tun. The mash is then stirred helping to convert the remaining starches to sugars . . .'

Geoffrey was only half listening, though trying to give Peter the impression he had his full attention. He was really thinking of Charlotte who'd been absolutely radiant at breakfast.

He couldn't wait to get out of the distillery and back to Drummond House, and her.

*

'He seems a personable enough young chap,' Peter commented to his father on rejoining him in the large office they shared.

Murdo glanced up from the figures he was studying as Peter sat at his desk. 'It went all right then?'

'Oh aye. Gave him the usual tour and a dram afterwards. I have to say though, he did seem a bit keen to be on his way.'

Murdo couldn't resist the jibe. 'Maybe he found it boring.'

Both men laughed.

Murdo tapped the sheets of paper in front of him. 'If this keeps up, and I can't see why it shouldn't, 1912 is going to be our most profitable year in the history of the distillery.'

'We're only half way through the year, Pa, don't tempt fate.'

'Aye,' Murdo agreed. 'Maybe I am being a bit hasty.'

They fell silent as each got on with the work in hand.

Charlotte was furious with her brother who'd got to Geoffrey first on his return from the distillery.

'Fishing,' Geoffrey mused. That wasn't what he'd had in mind at all.

'There are some excellent salmon to be caught round here this time of year. I'll kit you out and have Cook pack a hamper. Now what do you say?'

'I, eh . . . don't fish, old bean. Never handled a rod in my life.'

Andrew was relishing this, having purposefully suggested the fishing expedition just to annoy Charlotte. The look on her face told him he'd succeeded.

'Not to worry,' he enthused. 'I'll soon teach you the rudiments. I'm certain I can promise you a fine day of sport.'

How could he get out of this? Geoffrey wondered. 'I'm not sure, Andrew, fishing has never really appealed.'

'How do you know you won't like it unless you try?'

He was sunk, Geoffrey thought disconsolately. He'd so wanted to spend the rest of the day with Charlotte. Now this damned fishing nonsense had been proposed. Damn and blast!

Andrew was laughing inwardly.

'What will you be doing, Charlotte?' Geoffrey queried softly. Perhaps she might care to come with them.

'I had thought of having McPhie drive me into Pitlochry. That's a small town not too far away. I have a few things to pick up from the shops there.'

Geoffrey's face brightened. 'I've heard of Pitlochry. It's supposed to be lovely.'

'Oh, it is.'

Geoffrey rounded on his friend. 'Look here, Andrew, don't take this amiss, but I'd much rather trot along with Charlotte to Pitlochry. If she doesn't mind that is.'

'No of course not,' she replied swiftly. 'I'd enjoy some company.'

'What about Nell?' Andrew suggested, keeping the pot boiling. Oh, this was fun.

'She's busy,' Charlotte snapped in reply.

Andrew pretended astonishment. 'You must do as you wish, Geoffrey, you're our honoured guest after all. But I find it incredible you'd rather go to some pipsqueak little town where there isn't all that much to see as opposed to an afternoon's salmon fishing. Particularly on such a perfect day, what?'

'I would rather,' Geoffrey replied.

'Oh well, that's up to you then.'

Relief washed through Charlotte. 'I shall leave in half an hour. Is that all right with you, Geoffrey?'

'I'll be ready and waiting. But say, instead of McPhie driving us, why don't we go in the Humber?'

Better still, Charlotte thought. That way there would be just the two of them.

'Good idea. I'll meet you right here in half an hour.' And with that she swept from the room before there was any more discussion.

Andrew turned away so that Geoffrey couldn't see the broad smile he couldn't keep from his face.

Wonky was dumbfounded. 'She's what?'

'Intent on marrying this Geoffrey Armitage.'

Wonky sat and stared at her cousin who'd just dropped this bombshell. 'Are we talking about the same Charlotte?'

Nell nodded.

'I don't believe it. You're pulling my leg. It's some sort of joke. She only met the man yesterday.'

'Love at first sight, according to Charlotte.'

'But . . . the whole thing's preposterous!'

'I entirely agree. But you know Charlotte, once her mind's made up there's no changing it. She's adamant. She says she's in love and going to marry him.'

Wonky, whose mother was Murdo's younger sister and father the local minister in Dalneil, simply couldn't believe this. It had quite taken her breath away.

'Love at first sight,' she said slowly. Their Charlotte!

'What's he like?' she queried, thinking he must be really something to have swept Charlotte off her feet. She couldn't wait to meet him.

'Handsome of course.'

'He must be an Adonis.'

'Hardly that. But certainly handsome.'

Wonky listened wide eyed as Nell launched into a description of Geoffrey Armitage.

Charlotte had never felt so much at ease in a man's company as she did in Geoffrey's. Everything was so natural between them. It was as though she'd known him all her life.

When they reached Pitlochry they parked and together went shopping for the items Charlotte had referred to earlier. Items that weren't really urgently required but which Charlotte had used as an excuse to lure Geoffrey away from Drummond House and to be alone with her without fear of interruption.

'Well, that's that,' she declared eventually, handing Geoffrey the final parcel.

'I say, how about some afternoon tea?' he suggested.

Her eyes sparkled with pleasure. 'That would be most agreeable. There's a teashop just down the street that does mouth-watering cream cakes.'

'Then that's the place for us.'

In The Atholl they chose a table and sat, Geoffrey placing their order with the waitress who was almost immediately in attendance.

'So,' Geoffrey smiled when the waitress had departed.

Charlotte returned his smile. 'I want you to tell me all about yourself. And I mean *all*.'

They remained over tea for two hours that flew by.

During the drive back Charlotte reflected that she couldn't remember ever being so ecstatically happy.

Chapter 2

'And this is our cousin Wonky Comyn,' Charlotte declared.

Charlotte and Geoffrey had just returned from their outing.

Geoffrey extended a hand. 'Delighted to meet you, Miss Comyn.'

He *was* a dish, Wonky thought. 'And I to meet you, Lieutenant Armitage.'

'Geoffrey, please.'

'And I'm Wonky.'

Geoffrey raised a quizzical eyebrow. 'It's a rather strange name, is it not?'

She laughed. 'My real name is Veronica which when I was small I pronounced as Wonky and it's stayed with me ever since.'

Not unattractive, Geoffrey mused, though not a patch on Charlotte. He could see the family resemblance, however.

Wonky noted how Charlotte was staring at Geoffrey. A look of admiration and far more. Yes, it was love all right. Anyone with two eyes in their head could see that.

'Wonky arrived earlier and is staying to dinner,' Nell announced. That at Wonky's insistence, as she had no intention of missing the chance to meet Geoffrey. 'I've already informed Cook.'

'How did your trip to Pitlochry go?' Nell now enquired.

'Excellent. Tip top,' Geoffrey beamed, glancing fondly at Charlotte.

It had obviously gone extremely well, Nell thought. Just look at the pair of them, like a couple of love birds. She wouldn't have been at all surprised if they'd suddenly started billing and cooing.

'We took tea in The Atholl,' Charlotte stated.

'Ooh, those scrumptious cream cakes,' Nell sighed.

Geoffrey produced his cigarette case. 'May I?'

'Of course you may,' Charlotte replied, having to stop herself at the last moment from adding, darling.

'And what did you think of Pitlochry?' Nell asked Geoffrey.

'Charming.' In fact he'd hardly taken anything in having had eyes only for Charlotte. What a truly splendid gel she was.

After a while of idle chatter Geoffrey reluctantly excused himself to bathe and get dressed for dinner.

'Nell's told me your news,' Wonky declared excitedly when Geoffrey had left the room.

'And?'

'Not only cream cakes can be scrumptious.'

The three young women laughed.

'Did it really happen just like that?' Wonky queried, snapping her fingers.

Charlotte nodded. 'A bolt completely out of the blue.'

'Heavens,' Wonky breathed.

Charlotte had a sudden thought that made her laugh again. 'Andrew wasn't the only one who went fishing this afternoon. I've well and truly caught my fish, now all I have to do is land him.'

She paused, then added, great determination in her voice, 'Which I most certainly will.'

Murdo was sunk deep into a leather chair, morosely puffing on his pipe, with a large whisky balanced on the arm. He was in his study which was forbidden to the rest of the household, with the exception of the maid who cleaned it. He was thinking of his wife Louise.

He glanced over at a photograph taken the year before she'd died, his most treasured possession. Picking up his glass he silently toasted her.

'To you, darling,' he whispered. And in his mind he heard her voice replying.

He'd never get over the loss of her. She hadn't only been his wife and lover, but dear friend and companion. He missed her dreadfully.

He suddenly gasped and clutched at his chest, spilling some of the whisky in the process. Damn these pains, crushing ones that always left him breathless afterwards. He felt sweat pop onto his brow.

He really should go and see Dr McAllister, he thought when the pains had finally subsided. They were becoming more frequent. When was the last attack? The previous month he recalled.

He decided to call on McAllister, a lifelong friend, during the next couple of days.

'Hmmh,' McAllister murmured on completing his examination. 'I think the best thing for you, Murdo, is for me to refer you to a specialist in Glasgow.'

Murdo frowned as he began rebuttoning his shirt. 'Is that necessary, James? Can't you do something to help?'

'It's your heart, Murdo, and dealing with that is beyond me. I'm only a simple country practitioner. Ask me to deliver a baby or deal with gout and I'm your man. But when it comes to what's ailing you specialist advice is required. There's a chappie in Glasgow who's top notch in his field. He's the one to speak to.'

Murdo sighed. 'Then you'd better arrange the consultation.'

McAllister was more concerned than he was letting on. The symptoms Murdo had described, and his subsequent examination, were very worrying indeed.

He'd keep this to himself, Murdo decided. There was no point alarming the children.

A full moon and a million glittering stars shone brightly above them. The mood couldn't have been more romantic.

'Andrew and I are leaving after breakfast tomorrow,' Geoffrey stated quietly.

'I know.' That was something Charlotte was only too well aware of.

'I've, eh . . . come to think a lot of you, Charlotte. I appreciate it's only been a week, a short time really, but that's the truth of the matter.'

'And I of you, Geoffrey.'

He took her hand and gently squeezed it. 'Can I come back?'

'Whenever you wish.'

'Then I will. As soon as I can.'

He gazed deep into her eyes. 'You're beautiful, Charlotte, but there's more to it than that. I simply don't have the words to express what I feel.'

'I understand perfectly, Geoffrey.'

'Do you?'

'Very much so.'

'Good.'

'How long before you can get further leave?'

'I'm not certain. In the meantime may I write?'

'That would be lovely.'

'And you'll write to me?'

'Yes.'

He took a deep breath. 'That's settled then. In the meantime there's another matter. I don't know if Andrew has mentioned or not but there's a regimental ball next month. Would it be at all possible for me to take you to it?'

'You mean in Perth?'

'That's correct.'

'I'd love to go, naturally. But I'll have to ask Pa. I'll need his permission.'

'Of course.'

A ball with Geoffrey! How truly wonderful. And Pa

would agree, for hadn't she always been able to wind him round her little finger?

Geoffrey leant closer, drinking in the sweet smell of her. Dare he on such short acquaintance?

Guessing what was going through his mind Charlotte closed her eyes in compliance.

Their lips met, and then she was gloriously in his arms.

'I'll write tonight, that's a promise,' Geoffrey said.

'I wish you could stay longer,' she whispered.

'So do I. Oh, how I wish that.'

Andrew, lounging by the side of the Humber, watched their parting with amusement.

'Take care, my darling.'

'And you.'

He touched her gently on the cheek. A kiss in the circumstances, there being spectators, would have been quite out of order. Turning abruptly he jumped purposefully into the car.

A heavy-hearted Charlotte stood staring after the vehicle until it was finally lost to sight.

'I'm off to Glasgow on business next week,' Murdo announced at breakfast a few mornings later.

Peter frowned. He knew nothing of this. 'Business?'

'Nothing to do with the distillery. It's private.'

'Oh.' Peter couldn't think what that business might be but from his father's tone knew better than to inquire.

'Can I come with you, Pa?' Charlotte asked eagerly.

Murdo glanced at her in surprise. 'Why would you want to do that?'

'I need a new gown for the ball, Pa, I've simply nothing in my wardrobe that's suitable for such a grand occasion.'

'You've got masses of dresses and gowns, gel,' Murdo protested.

'But nothing suitable, I swear. You don't want me to look as if I'm straight off the farm, do you?'

Murdo laughed. 'I can't imagine anyone ever thinking that of you.'

'Well, they might.'

Murdo considered the idea. Why not? There couldn't be any harm in her accompanying him and he'd enjoy the company. She wouldn't find out about his visit to the specialist, he'd keep that secret, the 'business' that was taking him to Glasgow.

'And how much is this new gown going to cost me?' he queried lightly.

'Oh, lots, Pa. Lots and lots!'

He laughed again. 'Don't you know we Scotsmen are supposed to be a tight-fisted bunch?'

'Not you, Pa.' Rising, she crossed and kissed him on the cheek. 'Please, Pa. Pretty please?'

'Couldn't you have it made locally?' he teased. 'As you and Nell have always done.'

Her face fell. 'It wouldn't be the same, Pa. I want something very special for this ball, right up to the minute in style. The Glasgow dressmakers will be far superior and knowledgeable than our local ones.'

'Oh, all right,' he conceded, a twinkle in his eye.

The previously long face now lit up with delight. She kissed him a second time. 'Thank you, Pa.'

Murdo harumphed and got on with his breakfast as
Charlotte returned to hers.

Something very special indeed, Charlotte promised herself.

They were leaving the breakfast room when Charlotte had
another idea. She flew upstairs where she wrote a letter to
Geoffrey.

'There he is!' Charlotte exclaimed excitedly, and waved.

'Contain yourself, lassie,' Murdo muttered.

Geoffrey came striding along the platform to meet them.
It hadn't been easy but he'd managed to get the day away
from the barracks, arriving from Perth three quarters of an
hour previously.

Murdo was beckoning to a porter when Geoffrey
reached them. 'Hello, Charlotte,' he beamed.

'You made it then.'

She was even more beautiful than he remembered.
'With some difficulty. But I'm here now and that's all that
matters.'

Murdo instructed the porter where to find their two
overnight cases, then turned to Geoffrey who immediately
extended his hand. 'It's good to see you again, sir.'

'Hmmh,' Murdo muttered, shaking with Geoffrey. It
had been quite a surprise when Charlotte had informed
him she hoped to meet up with the young man, he'd had
no idea they'd formed a relationship. Anyway, it was harmless him escorting her round the city. If they wanted to
spend time together then let them get on with it.

'Where are you staying, sir?'

'The Station Hotel. We will be going there to register and freshen up, I'm sure you won't mind waiting for Charlotte in the foyer.'

'Oh, Pa, I don't need to freshen up and you can register for me.'

'I see,' Murdo commented wryly.

'Is that all right, Pa?'

He exhaled slowly. 'It seems it'll have to be.'

'Now where do you wish to go?' Geoffrey asked her as their little group proceeded along the platform.

A thoroughly shaken Murdo faced Mr Gillespie, the specialist, across his large wooden desk littered with paraphernalia.

'I can prescribe pills,' Gillespie went on. 'They'll help. But the main thing is for you to take life a lot easier. Do you smoke?'

Murdo nodded. 'A pipe.'

'Well, that has to stop. Now what about drinking?'

'I'm a distiller, so of course I drink.'

'From here on it'll have to be very much in moderation, I'm afraid.' Gillespie made a face. 'I always hate saying that to my patients as I enjoy a decent dram myself.'

'What do you consider moderation?' Murdo queried.

'A dram a day, perhaps two. Certainly no more. I also recommend gentle exercise, a daily stroll of about half a mile would be ideal.'

Walking, he loathed walking.

'That's it, Mr Drummond. All the advice I can give you except cut back on work if you can. Better still, give it up altogether if that's possible.'

'Give up work,' Murdo muttered. The thought appalled him.

He needed time to come to terms with this news.

On returning to the Station Hotel the first thing Murdo did was go into the bar and order a large Drummond which he despatched in a single gulp. The moderation could start tomorrow, he thought, ordering a second.

Should he put Peter in the picture? he wondered. He could do that and not tell the others.

No, he decided. He'd keep them all in the dark. Best that way.

The dressmaker was situated in Holland Street, just off Sauchiehall Street, and was expecting Charlotte to call as she had made an appointment by telephone.

Geoffrey insisted on coming in with her where he had to wait patiently in an ante-room while Charlotte was measured and she and the dressmaker, a Miss Sinclair, fussed over patterns and fabrics.

'Well?' he demanded when she reappeared some while later, her face radiant.

'I couldn't be more pleased.'

'Good. Now what about a spot of luncheon? I know the very place. And then I'll give you that tour I promised you.'

'Everything hunky dory?' Murdo enquired when Charlotte joined him at dinner.

'The gown is going to be fabulous, Pa. It's—'

He held up a hand, silencing her. 'Spare me the details.

Women's fripperies aren't my line of conversation.'

'Sorry, Pa.'

'And what did you do with the rest of the day?'

He listened quietly as she rattled on about all the things she and Geoffrey had done.

'Tell us all about it, every single detail,' Wonky demanded.

'Was Geoffrey there to meet you?' Nell queried.

Charlotte nodded. 'He managed to make it after all.'

Nell clapped her hands with pleasure.

'What about the gown?' Wonky asked. 'What colour did you choose?'

'There were so many wonderful colours but in the end I settled for a pale green chiffon.'

'Lovely,' Wonky breathed. 'That'll beautifully complement your blonde hair.'

'And what about the style?' Nell prompted.

'Very full sleeves caught at the wrist, masses of material that ends in a train, otherwise simple and flowing. You'd have to see it to understand the overall effect. It's going to be simply divine.'

Wonky sighed. 'Expensive, I take it?'

'Extremely. Pa's going to have a seizure when the bill arrives.'

'And what about fittings, are you going to have to go back?' Nell enquired.

Charlotte shook her head. 'Miss Sinclair understood the situation perfectly. She'd have liked fittings of course but in the circumstances says she'll manage without which was why she was so particular about measuring me. The gown will arrive by post in plenty of time for the ball.'

'Now what about shoes?' Wonky asked.

'I've found a pair in matching green that I've left out in the hall.'

'I'll fetch them,' Wonky declared, and quickly left the room.

'Do you still feel the same about Geoffrey?' Nell asked quietly.

'Oh yes, Nell. Being with him again was quite exquisite.'

'Did you kiss?'

Charlotte nodded. 'Discreetly, mind. As he was leaving to catch his train.'

Nell briefly closed her eyes wishing she'd been to Glasgow to meet her prince, whoever he may turn out to be. Please God there would be one, she prayed.

Please God.

Murdo replaced the top of his fountain pen and laid it aside. 'I'm off for a walk,' he announced.

Peter stared at him in astonishment. 'A walk? But you hate walking. You've said so many times.'

'It's good for you at my age. I've been suffering from indigestion recently and that's what Dr McAllister has recommended.'

'I see.' That seemed reasonable to Peter.

'Another thing, I'm taking the day off tomorrow to go fishing. I presume you can cope by yourself?'

Peter rocked back in his chair. 'But you never take a day off! Even when you're ill, which is rare, you insist on coming in.'

Murdo had known this was going to be difficult, and so

it was proving. He was changing the habits of a lifetime after all. He was a grafter, and always had been, a trait Peter had inherited.

Murdo made a pyramid with his hands and gazed at Peter thoughtfully over the tips of his fingers. 'I'm not getting any younger, son, and some day you'll be taking over. It seems to me I should start easing off and delegate more. A wise man looks to the future. Besides . . .' He allowed himself a soft smile. 'Who knows? I might actually enjoy having some time to myself.'

Peter was mystified and confused; this was so unlike his father. 'Is there something you're not telling me, Pa?'

Damn! Murdo thought. 'Nothing,' he lied. Rising, he crossed to the door. 'I'll be gone about an hour, perhaps longer.' And with that he left, clicking the door shut behind him.

Peter shook his head. Wonders would never cease.

'Taking the day off tomorrow!' Charlotte exclaimed.

'That's right.'

Charlotte glanced at her sister, then back at Peter. 'But he never does that. It's unheard of.'

'That's what I said and his reply was that it was time he eased off a bit and delegated more responsibility to me in preparation for when I take over.'

'And he went for a walk?' Nell queried.

'Said McAllister had recommended it for recent bouts of indigestion.'

'He's never mentioned indigestion to me,' Charlotte commented.

'Or me,' Nell added.

'Cook won't be best pleased if she hears,' Charlotte said.

Nell laughed. 'She'll be downright furious.'

When Murdo joined them prior to going through to dinner he refused a dram which none of the children could remember him, at that time of night, ever having done before.

'We'll go to Perth together. McPhie will drive us,' Murdo declared, thinking how much he'd enjoy a pipe right then.

'Pa?'

'Oh don't worry, I won't get in the way. I haven't been to Perth in years and fancy seeing it again. Besides, I have friends there I'd enjoy calling on.'

'You're not doing this just for my sake, are you, Pa?'

'Not in the least.' He paused, then said, 'I'll book us into an hotel I know. We'll stay the night and then come back next day as we did in Glasgow. That all right with you?'

'Yes, Pa.'

'Good.'

'What about Jenny, can I take her? She's a marvel at doing my hair.' Jenny was one of the household maids.

Murdo nodded. 'She can travel in front with McPhie.'

Charlotte thought of her gown which had arrived that morning and was now hanging in her room. It had more than lived up to her expectations.

Charlotte swept into the hotel foyer where Geoffrey was waiting. He stared at her in open admiration.

'You look . . . incredible,' he breathed, hurrying over to join her.

She stopped herself giving a little twirl as she'd done when showing off the gown to Nell and Wonky. 'I'm glad you approve.'

'Approve! By Jove I most certainly do. I'll be the envy of every man there.'

'You look fairly dashing yourself.' The kilt suited him, she thought, he had the figure for it.

He extended an arm. 'Shall we? Your carriage awaits, Miss.'

She gave a low laugh as she accepted the arm. It was the start of what was to be a memorable evening.

'Murdo, how lovely to see you. It's been far too long.'

The speaker was Jean Ritchie, a school friend of Louise's who'd moved to Perth when she'd married. Forbes Ritchie had died four years previously and now Jean lived alone as they'd never been blessed with a family.

'You don't look a day older than the last time we met,' Murdo declared gallantly.

'You old flatterer. I'd forgotten that about you.'

His eyes twinkled. 'I don't need to use flattery in your case, Jean. Simply tell the truth.'

She laughed. 'You're incorrigible. Now come and sit down and give me all your news.'

Murdo stayed far longer than he'd intended. It was almost midnight before he left.

Charlotte and Geoffrey were in the middle of a slow waltz, the pair of them well aware that she'd been turning heads all night. On a number of occasions she'd been approached and asked to dance, her reply the same every time, her card was already full. She had no intention of dancing with anyone other than Geoffrey.

'You're the belle of the ball, you know that?' Geoffrey smiled.

'Nonsense.'

'You are, darling.'

His use of that word thrilled her.

'Would you care for some punch after this? I'm parched.'

'That would be nice.' She paused, then added mischievously, 'Or how about a whisky? That would go down well.'

'Don't you dare even think of it!' he retorted. 'You'd cause a scandal.'

'Well, I certainly can't do that. It might adversely affect your career, Lieutenant,' she teased.

On they danced, she seeming to float over the floor as gracefully as thistledown.

'What a night,' Charlotte sighed, as they once more stood in the hotel foyer.

'It isn't one I'll forget in a while.'

'Me neither.'

'I wish I could see you again tomorrow. But unfortunately that's impossible.'

'Never mind.'

He desperately wanted to kiss her, positively ached to do so. He drew her behind a pillar that masked them from reception, and there he got his wish.

And she hers. For it was what she too had desperately wanted.

*

Murdo lay in bed reflecting on how satisfying it had been to have good female company again, and Jean Ritchie was certainly that. Not that he lacked feminine company at home, but Jean was of his generation and that made all the difference.

It wasn't as though he was thinking of taking another wife, Heaven forbid. No one could ever replace Louise in his affections. But company and a right old blether was something else.

Yes, he thought. The evening had been most satisfying and uplifting.

Chapter 3

Wonky laid aside the book she'd been trying to read, realising it was a hopeless business. She just couldn't concentrate. She gazed around the parlour in distaste, hating the manse in which she'd been born and brought up. It was so dark and gloomy, like a mausoleum. It exhuded an air of genteel poverty, her father's stipend being a fair rate of pay for the job, but nowhere near a fortune.

She thought with envy of Drummond House, wishing she lived there. There was nothing dark and gloomy about it and certainly no air of genteel poverty, for the Drummonds were rich. She was further envious of the fact her cousin Charlotte had a man in her life, and a handsome, well-off one at that. She'd have given anything to have gone to the regimental ball in Perth, for there must have been stacks of eligible bachelors present.

That was the trouble of living in the country – the opportunities to meet new people, and by that she meant men, were few and far between. If only she could go to one of the big cities and get a job, but her father wouldn't hear of it. She was a nice, well-brought-up young lady whose place was at home.

She laid her head back against the anti-macassar and closed her eyes, thinking of the ball and what it must have been like, for Charlotte had described everything to her and Nell in detail.

The gaiety, the glamour, the uniforms, which had apparently been a glorious sight as had the gowns and jewellery worn by the women. There had been a dance band and piping and a sumptuous meal washed down with oodles of wine.

Oh, why couldn't she have been born a Drummond and not a Comyn, getting all the things that Charlotte and Nell did. Why, that gown alone had cost the earth and Uncle Murdo, against all expectations, hadn't complained about the price. There again, why should he? He could well afford it. And it was well known he spoiled Charlotte and Nell rotten. Maybe he wouldn't if their mother hadn't died, but she had and he did.

'Veronica!' her mother trilled outside in the hall. Only her mother and father called her that. 'Where are you?'

Wonky rose and made for the partially open door. 'Here, Ma.'

Moira Comyn was in her late forties and had long since run to fat, in complete contrast to her husband Tom who was painfully thin.

Moira was holding a cloth-covered bowl. 'I want you to take this to old Mrs Murchie. It's a wee bit of potted hough.'

Wonky's face fell. 'But, Ma, you know what she's like. She'll want to talk and never knows when to stop. I'll be there for ages and she's so boring.'

'That's a most unchristian thing to say, dear.'

'But it's true, Ma. She can talk the hind legs off a donkey and half the time forgets what she's just said and repeats herself.'

'A little charity, darling. The poor soul is so terribly lonely.'

'I can't help that. Can't you take it yourself? You don't mind the way she goes on.'

Moira did but would never have admitted to the fact. 'I'm busy, Veronica. I'm baking.'

Wonky could see there was no way out of it. Reluctantly she accepted the bowl. 'Oh all right,' she conceded with bad grace.

'There's a good girl.' And with that Moira hurried back to her kitchen.

'Blast!' Wonky muttered.

Charlotte stared expectantly out of a front window. Geoffrey had written informing her he had a spot of unexpected leave and would like to spend it with her at Drummond House. She was awaiting his arrival which should be any time now.

'Any sign yet?' Nell queried, glancing up from her embroidery.

Charlotte turned to her sister and shook her head.

'No doubt he'll be along shortly.'

Charlotte suddenly squealed as the Humber came into sight. 'He's here,' she informed Nell, and hurried from the room.

What a to-do, Nell thought. Charlotte had been on tenterhooks all morning. There again, wouldn't she have been in the same state if it had been her young man who was due.

Geoffrey leant out of the car and waved to Charlotte when he spotted her. It was going to take all his self control not to sweep her into his arms, but that would never do.

'Hello there,' he smiled when he'd brought the car to a standstill. 'How are you?'

'All the better for seeing you,' she admitted frankly.

He laughed. 'Exactly how I feel for seeing you.'

'Are you tired after your journey?' she asked as he got out of the car.

'I was a bit so I stopped off at a pub and had a pint of beer. That soon put things right.'

He touched her on the arm. 'I say, you look positively spiffing.'

She was wearing a light rose-coloured day dress edged at the bodice and cuffs with cream lace.

'Why thank you, kind sir.'

'How are the family?'

'Fine, though Pa's been acting queer of late.'

'Oh?'

'Let's go inside and I'll explain.'

There was a tap on the office door.

'Come in!' Murdo called out.

It was Isobel, one of the staff, with their morning coffee and biscuits. Murdo took out his gold pocket watch and snapped it open. Dead on eleven as he'd expected. He leant back in his chair and thought of the pipe he'd normally have had after the biscuits. He'd come to terms with only one or two drams a day, even the walking which was becoming more endurable, but his pipe! He still craved that.

Peter stretched and yawned after Isobel had gone.

'Tired, son?'

'Not really. It's just a bit close in here.'

'Then open a window.'

'Tell me something,' Murdo said when Peter was reseated. 'What do you make of Charlotte and Geoffrey Armitage. Is it really serious?'

So, Charlotte hadn't spoken to her father about Geoffrey. He'd wondered about that. But it was hardly surprising she hadn't confessed to her father her love for the chap.

'I think it might be,' he prevaricated.

'Seems a decent sort, eh?'

'Seems.'

'Good family as well, by all accounts.'

Peter had a sip of coffee and nibbled at a digestive. He preferred fancy biscuits himself but they invariably had digestives as those were Murdo's preference.

'How long is he here for?'

'No idea, Pa. I don't think Charlotte knows either. Unless he's arrived and told her.'

'Hmmh,' Murdo mused. Perhaps it was time he had a chat with Geoffrey Armitage, found out what the lad's intentions were. He didn't want his daughter's affections being trifled with. On the other hand, it might be early days for that. Perhaps it was best to let matters ride for the moment, see what happened. The whole thing might fizzle out after all.

'I've made a decision,' Murdo declared, changing the

subject. 'As from next Monday I shall be working mornings only.'

Peter carefully replaced his cup on its saucer.

'Can you cope with that, son?'

Peter eyed his father speculatively. There *was* something behind all this, he was certain of it. But what, he had no idea. If and when Murdo wanted him to know he would say.

'I think I'm quite capable.'

'So do I.'

'And what do you intend doing with all this free time, Pa?'

'Well, for one thing I'm going to learn to drive.' He glared at his son. 'You seem amused?'

'I just . . . well, I suppose I am if I'm being honest.'

'And why's that?'

'You've never shown any interest before.'

'Well, I am now. McPhie can teach me.'

Murdo chuckled inwardly. McPhie wasn't going to be pleased, in fact he was going to be downright outraged as he regarded the Rolls as his own personal property. Not that McPhie would articulate his displeasure or outrage, he knew better than that.

Murdo couldn't wait to see McPhie's face when he told him.

'It's such beautiful countryside round here,' Geoffrey observed. It was the middle of the afternoon and he and Charlotte had decided to take a stroll. He glanced round to make sure they weren't being observed, then took her hand. 'I've missed you.'

'And I you.'

'Letters are fine, but they're a poor substitute for the real thing.'

'Well, you have ten days of that ahead of you.'

'Sheer bliss,' he smiled.

And for her, she thought.

His smile vanished. 'There's a rumour going round that we might be posted overseas soon.'

Her face darkened. 'Oh, Geoffrey!'

'It's only a rumour, mind. And it's only *might*. But if it does happen it can happen quickly.'

'Any idea where to?'

He shook his head. 'Not the foggiest. It could be anywhere.'

She'd known this could happen of course, he was in the army. But so soon after their meeting! She suddenly felt sick.

'Are you all right, Charlotte?'

'I've just come over a bit faint, that's all.'

'I say, I'm sorry.'

He had said *might*, she must cling on to that, she told herself. A rumour was hardly fact. Far from it.

'If you go you will still write?' she asked.

'You have my solemn word on that.'

She turned away so he couldn't see her face. 'Have you ever considered leaving the army, Geoffrey?'

'You mean resign my commission?'

'That's right.'

'No, I haven't. I intend the army to be my career.' He barked out a laugh. 'I don't really know what else I could do. I have no other training or skills.'

'I can't bear the thought of you going away,' she said huskily.

'Now that we've met the prospect would be pretty dreadful for me too.'

Damn his being an army officer! she thought. Of all things why did he have to be that? It so complicated matters. But it wouldn't change things, how she felt, not one iota.

'I'll wait for you,' she said, knowing she was being fast but not caring.

He took her by the shoulders. 'I was praying you'd say that. I didn't dare ask.'

'I'll wait, no matter what,' she repeated.

'I think I love you, Charlotte,' he whispered.

'Only think? Aren't you sure?'

'Yes I am. And how do you feel about me?'

'The same. I knew we were meant for one another the moment we met.'

'Oh, my darling.'

He closed his eyes, and she hers, as they kissed. And it seemed to her they were already one.

'May I speak with you, sir? Alone that is.'

It was after dinner that night and Murdo had intended going to his study to read the day's papers. He suddenly guessed what this was all about and it explained Charlotte's nervousness during the meal, an uncharacteristic mood he'd put down to the young man's presence. 'Come with me,' he said.

Geoffrey didn't know the honour he was being accorded when Murdo ushered him into his study, the holy of holies.

'Care for a dram, lad?'

'Yes please, sir.' That would help keep up his courage. When Murdo handed him his drink he swallowed half of it straight off.

'Well, Geoffrey, what can I do for you?'

'Sir . . .' He took a deep breath. 'I'd like to ask for your daughter's hand in marriage.'

'I see. That would be Charlotte presumably.' He'd said the latter as a little tease.

'Oh yes, sir.'

'I presume she knows you're asking me this and have her agreement on the matter?'

'Indeed, sir.'

Murdo crossed to the fireplace to gaze at the photograph of his beloved Louise standing in pride of place on the mantelpiece. 'A bit sudden, don't you think? I mean, you've only known each other five minutes.'

Oh God, Geoffrey thought. He was going to be refused. 'That's true, sir, but we're very much in love.'

He'd wondered what the lad's intentions were, now he knew. But what to answer?

'I think we'd better have Charlotte in on this. Will you go and fetch her.'

'Certainly, sir.' Geoffrey rushed out to fetch Charlotte.

Marriage? He wasn't against that but it worried him they'd only been acquainted such a short time. Marriage was a lifelong commitment after all.

A few minutes later Geoffrey returned with Charlotte who halted in the doorway. 'Am I to come in, Pa?'

'Well, I'm not going to shout at you across the room.'

She entered hesitantly, closing the door behind her. This

was the first occasion she'd ever been in the room. She glanced curiously about her.

'Drink, lass?'

'Please.'

He stared at her, noting how nervous she continued to be, a nervousness he now interpreted as a good sign. She wanted this marriage and was worried he might object or cause problems.

'Whisky please, Pa.'

'Geoffrey has just asked for your hand,' he informed her as he handed her her drink.

'I know, Pa.'

'Says you love him.'

'I do, with all my heart.'

Geoffrey beamed.

'I see,' Murdo mused. He sipped his own drink. 'As I pointed out to him it all seems a bit sudden. You hardly know one another.'

'When something's right it's right no matter the time involved. And that's how it is with Geoffrey and me.'

True, he thought. Quite true.

'There's no doubt in your mind then?'

'None whatever, Pa. I want to marry Geoffrey.'

'And I Charlotte,' Geoffrey stated.

Murdo turned his attention again to Geoffrey who boldly stared him straight in the eye. 'And what are your prospects, Geoffrey?'

'The army, sir. My prospects are what I make of myself. As an only child I shall also inherit a considerable amount in due course when my parents pass on.'

'Hmmh.'

'I've given it careful thought, Pa. Being an army wife isn't ideal but if that's required to be with Geoffrey then I'll put up with it.'

'Even if it means long years in various stinking hell-holes?'

Charlotte blanched, then stuck out her chin. 'Even so, Pa.'

That seemed to be that, Murdo thought. He wasn't one to stand in the way of his daughter's happiness. If she wanted Geoffrey Armitage, then so be it.

'When would this wedding take place?' he inquired.

'Oh, not for at least eighteen months, sir. I'm not allowed to get married, rules and regulations you know, until I'm thirty and I'm twenty-eight and a half now.'

Murdo replenished his glass thinking he'd have more than two that night. It was a momentous occasion after all.

'Do we have your permission, Pa? I'll only elope if we don't.'

'Don't threaten me, gel,' he growled. 'I won't have it.'

'Sorry, Pa.' She wasn't sorry at all, she'd meant what she said. She would elope come hell or high water if he refused permission.

There was a few seconds hiatus, then Murdo said, 'Tell you what, let's play safe on this by having a breathing space.'

'Breathing space?' Charlotte queried quietly.

'It still worries me that you've known one another such a short while so I'm going to ask you to humour your old father by putting the engagement off for six months. Come to me again in six months, Geoffrey, and my answer will be yes. This way, should it so happen that either of you does change your mind there won't be any loss of face or embarrassment. Now what do you say?'

'You *will* say yes, Pa?'

'You have my word on that, Charlotte.' He stared from one to the other. 'Well?'

Geoffrey looked at Charlotte who nodded.

'Agreed, sir. Six months it is and you may rest assured that I will be back.'

'I think a top up is in order all round, eh?'

Charlotte went to her father and kissed him on the cheek. 'Thanks, Pa.'

'And no more talk of eloping. If a marriage is to take place I want it to be done in style as befits the daughter of Murdo Drummond.'

When their glasses had been recharged Murdo silently saluted the happy couple and they all drank.

Nell clapped her hands with glee when Charlotte and Geoffrey told her.

'Congratulations to the pair of you!' Nell swept her sister into her arms and hugged her tight.

'It's unofficial of course,' Geoffrey said. 'We can't make a formal announcement for six months yet.'

'That's Pa's suggestion as we've only known one another a short time,' Charlotte explained.

'Is it to be a secret then?'

Geoffrey's brow furrowed as he reflected on that. 'I suppose so. I presume that's what your father meant when he said about there being no loss of face or embarrassment.'

'We must let Wonky in on it though,' Nell said.

'I'm sure there can be some exceptions,' Charlotte mused.

'Your brother for instance. I shall jolly well want to tell him.'

'Wonky and Andrew then . . .'

'And Peter,' Nell added, interrupting her sister.

Charlotte nodded her agreement.

'I can't tell you how pleased I am for the pair of you. It's so wonderful.'

'To begin with I thought he was going to refuse outright. It fair put the wind up me,' Geoffrey said.

Charlotte laughed and the other two joined in.

She'd said she'd land her man and so she has, Nell thought. How like Charlotte.

Wonky screamed with delight when told the next day by Nell and swore to keep the secret.

Murdo halted to lean on the stick he sometimes carried when out walking. He was doing a loop that would eventually bring him back to Drummond House.

He glanced up at the sky wondering if it would rain. He didn't think it would. Summer had definitely gone and now there was a nip in the air. He was thinking of Jean Ritchie and the most pleasant evening he'd spent with her. He'd been mulling over the idea of asking her to Drummond House for a spell. It would be a nice break for her and a pleasant interlude, he hoped, for them both.

Why not? he thought. He decided to write to her on his return.

*

Charlotte and Geoffrey were also out walking, following the bank of the burn that fed the distillery, hand in hand.

'Only a couple of days left, I'm sorry to say,' Geoffrey sighed.

'I know.'

'I'd give anything for it to be longer.'

As would she. 'Any idea when you might get some more leave?'

'None at all.'

They strolled a few steps in silence. 'Geoffrey, what happens if you are posted abroad before the six months is up? You can hardly speak to Pa if you're overseas.'

'I've already thought of that. I'll have to write to him.'

'And what if you're overseas for years and years?'

'You can join me and we'll marry wherever I am. But let's not worry about that. It's a bridge we'll cross if and when we come to it.'

'Look!' Charlotte exclaimed, pointing over to their left. 'A stag.'

Geoffrey had never seen a stag before. 'It's magnificent,' he breathed.

The stag raised its muzzle and sniffed the air. Then slowly, proudly, began walking away.

'He reminds me of your father,' Geoffrey stated.

Charlotte laughed.

'No really, I'm serious. He has that same regal quality about him. The same sort of bearing.'

'I'm sure Pa would be flattered to hear that.'

They resumed walking. 'Talking of fathers, you'll have to meet mine. Both my parents that is.'

'I suppose I shall.'

'They'll like you, I'm certain of it.'

'I certainly hope they do. It'll be awful if they don't.'

He patted the hand he was holding with his free one. 'The three of you will get on like a house on fire. I have no worries in that direction.'

Charlotte prayed he was right.

'Are you happy about this proposed engagement, Pa?' Peter asked, as he and Murdo took their morning coffee in the office.

Murdo, who'd been lost in thought, came out of his reverie to stare at his son. 'Perfectly. Why, do you have doubts about the match?'

Peter shook his head.

'Then why ask?'

'The six-month postponement. I wondered if there was more to it than the reason given?'

'There isn't. Geoffrey is a fine chap and they assure me they're very much in love. It was simply a case of being cautious, that's all.'

'Everything's all right then?'

'Quite.'

Murdo had a swallow of coffee and finished his biscuit. 'What this engagement business has made me think about is you, son.'

'Me?'

'Isn't it about time you started courting? *Tempis fugit* and all that, and none of us is getting any younger.'

Peter dropped his eyes to gaze at the papers on his desk, not wanting Murdo to see his alarmed expression. How did you explain to your father that you had no interest whatsoever in women, that they left you entirely cold. The thought of actually entering their bodies was totally repugnant to him, revolting in the extreme. He didn't mind them being around, or their company, but that was as far as it went.

Not that he was homosexual, he had no inclinations in that direction either. There had been one incident at school which had been nauseating in the extreme. He recalled it now with an inward shudder. Sandy McPherson had talked him into it and he'd hated the bastard ever since. He'd been physically sick afterwards and was convinced he'd have the same reaction if he was to go to bed with a woman. If he managed the act that was, which he doubted.

'Well?' Murdo queried.

Peter, mind racing, refocused on his father. 'It's important to you that I produce an heir, isn't it, Pa?'

'Very much so.'

'But you would want me to be happy, as Charlotte now is?'

'Naturally.'

'I couldn't marry just for the sake of it, Pa. I'd want to be in love as you and Ma were. Or as Charlotte and Geoffrey now claim to be.'

'I understand that,' Murdo conceded.

'I don't know when it'll happen, Pa, or indeed if it ever will. But I refuse to get wed simply to produce an heir. It has to be love or nothing.' He then added craftily, 'I learnt that from you.'

A lump came into Murdo's throat remembering the day, that glorious day never to be forgotten, when he'd met Louise. A day that had changed his life for ever.

'I'll say no more on the subject, son.'

Peter breathed a soft sigh of relief. There never would be an heir from him, that task would fall to Andrew and would have to satisfy his father.

Chapter 4

Jean Ritchie carefully folded Murdo's letter and replaced it in its envelope. The contents had surprised her.

A visit to Drummond House for a break, as Murdo had called it, the prospect certainly wasn't unappealing. Her life since Forbes's passing had been humdrum to say the least.

Her brow furrowed in thought. Was there more to this than met the eye? Murdo had always been devoted to Louise, virtually worshipped her. But Louise had been gone a long time now and perhaps he was thinking of remarrying and she was a candidate. It was a possibility.

Marriage to Murdo? He was a fine, upstanding man whom she'd always admired. It wouldn't be difficult at all sharing the rest of her days with him.

Forbes would have approved, she was certain of that. He'd always spoken highly of Murdo Drummond.

But here, she mustn't get ahead of herself. Perhaps the proposed visit was simply that, a break and nothing else. She mustn't put two and two together and come up with five.

Naturally she'd go, it would be lovely seeing the girls again. Now they were grown up the three of them could have some right old blethers together.

She decided to wait a few days before replying. She didn't want to appear too eager.

Nell was staring out of her bedroom window when the familiar tingling took hold of her, and then the trembling of her hands. The amazing thing was these visions always occurred when she was alone and never when with others.

Her sight wavered and then cleared. The countryside she was now seeing wasn't that she'd been looking at before. The land was wild and heather covered, somewhere further north, though where she had no idea. There were mountains in the background, several of the taller ones with snow on their peaks.

And then *he* came into view, the same Highlander as in all her visions. Tartan wrapped and armed with broadsword, dirk and pistol, he was wearing a blue bonnet that sported the eagle feather which proclaimed him to be a chief.

There was no sound, there never was. All was silent in her vision as the Highlander's weary horse plodded stoically forward.

He was closer now and she could see his face more clearly. He appeared drawn and haggard, ill almost. He shivered and drew his plaid more tightly about him.

He'd lost the beard he'd had the last time she'd seen him, but of course she had no way of knowing whether or not these visions were in chronological order. He'd always appeared to be roughly the same age.

A group of men came into sight, Highlanders like himself but wearing a different tartan, and went hurrying towards him. He pulled up his horse and dismounted.

When they reached him a discussion took place with one, who gave the impression of being the men's leader, pointing off into the distance.

Her Highlander – oh how she wished she knew his name – nodded, said something further to the men and remounted. The group started off in the direction he had pointed to.

The vision faded and then suddenly blinked out of existence and she was left gazing at the usual view from her window.

Nell took a deep breath, turned and crossed to her bed where she sat, drained as she always was after a vision.

She had tried looking up the ancient tartans but had never been able to discover the one he wore, so even his surname, or the clan he belonged to, remained a mystery.

She knew he lived in a big stone house with his wife and children where she'd often watched him.

Nell shook her head in wonder. Why did this happen to her and what did it mean? Why was it this particular man she always saw? How did these visions come about?

At least she wasn't frightened any more as she'd been when the visions started all those years ago. The only thing that frightened her now was the idea of anyone finding out about them.

She didn't want to be thought of as mad.

'I'll drive, McPhie,' Murdo declared. He was setting out to pick up Jean Ritchie from Pitlochry station.

McPhie groaned inwardly. He'd thought this might happen. He hated it when Murdo drove, the man was a bloody menace.

'Jean! How wonderful to see you again.'

She pecked him on the cheek, then regarded him speculatively through new eyes.

'How was your journey?'

'Uneventful. A little boring really.'

Murdo had a swift word with McPhie who climbed into the carriage Jean had just emerged from to get her cases. Why pay a porter when McPhie was on hand?

'It's most kind of you to invite me, Murdo. I've been looking forward to it and meeting your family again.'

'They all know you were a good friend of their mother's.'

They proceeded towards the barrier. 'I've told Cook to hold luncheon until we arrive.'

'Will the girls and Peter be there?'

'Not Peter, he'll be at work in the distillery.'

'Of course.'

Murdo felt very relaxed with Jean as he'd known he would. 'I drove the car here,' he declared proudly.

'I didn't know you could drive?'

He can't, McPhie thought sourly following in their wake and party to the conversation.

'I'm learning. And coming along fine, eh, McPhie?' The latter he said over his shoulder.

'Handsomely, Mr Drummond,' McPhie tactfully lied.

'I've stopped working in the afternoons and decided to learn as a sort of hobby,' Murdo explained.

'Good idea.'

Bad idea, McPhie thought.

'Are you finding it easy?' Jean enquired.

'Oh yes. I have a natural ability with mechanical things.'

McPhie nearly choked. Talk about self delusion! He made a face remembering the gear-grinding on the way there. That and the few hair-raising moments when Murdo had very nearly lost control. Some natural ability.

When they arrived at the Rolls-Royce McPhie was extremely relieved when Murdo assisted Jean into the rear of the car where he joined her.

Thank you, God! McPhie silently prayed as he began loading Jean's cases onto the roof rack.

'My, what fine young ladies you've turned out to be,' Jean declared to Charlotte and Nell, thinking Charlotte prettier than her plumper sister. 'You were only bairns the last time I saw you.'

Charlotte and Nell had been discussing Jean before her arrival, both puzzled as to why she'd been invited. She'd been a friend of their mother's, of course, but why invite her now after so many years? Was Pa up to something? they'd wondered.

'How do you do, Mrs Ritchie,' Charlotte replied, giving a small curtsy.

Nell merely smiled as she curtsied.

'I see their mother in both of them,' Jean proclaimed, which delighted Murdo.

'Peter's the one who takes most after Louise. You'll meet him at dinner.'

Jean gazed around her. 'This sitting room is exactly as I

remember it. Why I do believe that even the aspidistra is the same.'

Murdo laughed. 'You're wrong about the aspidistra. That's a new one though bought some while back.'

'Well, it looks the same,' Jean said, and laughed with him.

'Now how about some luncheon. I don't know about you but I'm starved.'

Charlotte and Nell led the way to the dining room.

'He's done what!' Charlotte exclaimed that evening shortly after dinner.

'Taken her to his study,' Peter repeated, pouring himself a dram.

'But no one's allowed in there,' Nell protested.

'Charlotte went in with Geoffrey,' Peter commented drily.

'Ah yes, but that was different,' Charlotte retorted. 'It was an exception. And the only occasion I've ever been in there, I'll remind you.'

Peter's expression became thoughtful. 'Ma was allowed in. I remember that quite distinctly.'

Charlotte glanced at Nell who raised an eyebrow.

'Makes you think, doesn't it?' Peter said quietly.

'That meal was delicious. The beef quite superb,' Jean declared, sitting on Murdo's comfy club chair, the only chair in the study.

'We're very fortunate to have Mrs Clark for a cook. If she has a fault it's that she can be a little adventurous for my taste. But on the whole she's excellent.'

'Has she been here long?'

Murdo paused in pouring out the sherry he'd previously brought into the study, having noted in Perth that that was Jean's preference. 'Five or six years, I can't recall exactly. She came from the Duke of Strathearn's household. It seems she and the Duchess didn't see eye to eye which doesn't surprise me; I've met the Duchess on occasion and she can be something of a dragon to say the least. As Mrs Clark is a very self-willed woman I suppose a collision of personalities was inevitable.'

Jean laughed.

'Well, the Duchess's loss was our gain.'

He handed Jean her sherry then crossed to the mantelpiece on which he placed his own glass. 'I don't know if you've seen this,' he said, picking up Louise's photograph in its ornate silver frame and giving it to Jean.

Jean studied the photograph, a soft smile on her face. 'Louise was a good friend to me, I still miss her.'

'As do I,' Murdo declared, a catch in his voice.

'You two were so much in love.'

'So much,' he repeated in a whisper.

Jean regarded him keenly. 'But life goes on, Murdo, we must always remember that.'

'Aye,' he agreed.

'That's what I told myself after Forbes died. Life goes on and we must go with it. The past is the past which can never be taken away from us. But it is the past.'

Murdo sighed and sipped his whisky. It had recently become a pretence with him not to notice he was pouring larger measures than he'd done before his trip to Glasgow and consultation with Mr Gillespie, the heart specialist, since when there hadn't been any recurrence of the chest pains.

'Do you get terribly lonely?' Jean asked quietly.

He glanced at her in surprise. 'I suppose I do. There's work, and the girls and Peter of course, and Andrew when he's home. But yes, I suppose I do get lonely. I miss . . . well, the companionship of someone my own age. Just being able to relax and chat about the day's events.'

'I understand that perfectly. At least you're fortunate enough to have your family and the distillery. I have nothing apart from bridge and whist afternoons, and the occasional bit of charity involvement. The days can seem interminable at times.'

She returned the photograph of Louise wondering if she'd been a little too honest. Trouble was, it was true. They were both roughly in the same boat.

Murdo replaced the photograph on the mantelpiece and gazed lovingly at it for a moment. 'I have a favour to ask.'

'Oh?'

He cleared his throat. 'This is rather difficult, Jean. A trifle delicate, shall we say.'

'I'm all ears, Murdo. If I can help you in any way . . .' She trailed off and waited for him to go on.

'Charlotte has a young man who was recently in this very room asking for her hand.'

Jean beamed. 'That's wonderful.'

'He's one of Andrew's fellow officers, a splendid chap called Geoffrey Armitage. They both assure me they're head over heels in love.'

'She's extremely pretty, Murdo. And by the by, you were quite right. Peter does take after his mother the most.'

Murdo glanced again at the photograph, then back to Jean. He explained about the six-month postponement in the engagement announcement.

'Very wise of you,' she nodded.

'The thing is, Jean.' He cleared his throat again. 'Charlotte doesn't have a mother to talk to her about . . . you know, the intimacy of marriage. What actually happens.'

'And you won't explain?' Jean teased.

'Heavens no! I couldn't possibly.'

'And you wish me to have a chat with her?'

'Exactly,' he smiled. 'Though not straight away. Get to know her first, and she you. Then possibly towards the end of your stay here you might have a word. I'd be awfully obliged.'

Murdo saw off the rest of his whisky, noted Jean's glass was still half full, and poured himself a second, even larger than the first. He was most uncomfortable about asking this particular favour, but had seen Jean's presence as the perfect opportunity to do what had to be done.

'Tell me, Murdo,' Jean asked softly. 'Was this the reason you wanted me here?'

'Not at all. I didn't get the idea until after you'd accepted my invitation.'

'I see.'

'Of course if you feel that you can't . . .'

She held up a hand to stop him. 'I shall, Murdo. If the positions had been reversed I'm sure Louise would have done the same for me.'

Murdo breathed a huge sigh of relief. 'Thank you, Jean. I'm in your debt.'

*

'Andrew!' Charlotte exclaimed.

'Five days' leave, sis. Didn't know until this morning so it's been something of a rush. Took a taxi from the station.'

Nell popped her head round the door. 'Andrew! I thought I heard your voice.'

'It's me all right. Home for five days. Terrific.'

His eyes twinkled mischievously as he turned to face Charlotte. 'I've got news.'

'Oh?'

'It was only announced just before I left.' He smiled. 'The Battalion's being posted.'

Charlotte's face fell and she was filled with dread. 'Where to?'

'Jolly old India which is what the majority of us expected. The Battalion will be gone for years.'

Charlotte swallowed hard, crossed to the nearest chair and sat. Nell hurried to her and put a consoling arm round her sister's shoulders. This was awful. Poor Charlotte.

It wasn't the end of the world, Charlotte told herself. It simply meant she and Geoffrey would get married over there.

'The second Battalion that is,' Andrew added quietly.

It took a few moments for that to sink in. 'The second Battalion?' Nell queried.

'That's right.'

'But you're in the first.'

'Yes, we're remaining. Geoffrey and I aren't going any-where.'

Relief surged through Charlotte and she found herself breathing heavily.

'You horror!' Nell snapped. 'That was downright cruel.'

'Just my little joke, that's all.'

'Some joke,' Charlotte hissed, furious with her brother. Nell was right, that had been cruel.

'I didn't realise you'd take it so badly,' he protested.

'How did you think I'd take it,' Charlotte retorted, voice icy cold. 'You know the situation, Geoffrey's told you.'

'That's why it was so funny.'

Charlotte resisted the urge to go and slap Andrew, reminding herself he'd always had a peculiar, some might even say perverted, sense of humour.

'So it's wedding bells, eh? Ding dong and all that malarkey. Congratulations,' Andrew smiled to Charlotte.

'Would you like a drink?' Nell asked Charlotte, seeing how shaken she still was.

Charlotte shook her head.

'I'd like one,' Andrew said.

'Then pour it yourself and I hope it chokes you,' Nell riposted.

'Doubt it'll do that,' he replied, heading for the decanters and glasses.

Charlotte took a deep breath to steady herself. 'Those were a few very nasty moments,' she murmured, shooting Andrew a filthy look.

'Thought I'd pop over and see Pa and Peter,' Andrew declared, taking a deep swallow.

'Pa doesn't work afternoons any more. He's out some-where with Mrs Ritchie.'

Andrew stared at them in amazement. 'Not working in the afternoons any more, what's come over the old bugger? And who's this Mrs Ritchie?'

'Mrs Ritchie was a friend of Ma's who's staying as a

house guest. As for what's come over Pa, who knows! He even goes walking nowadays which was unheard of until recently.'

Andrew gaped at them. 'Walking? I simply don't believe it.'

'It's true,' Nell said. 'And he's given up his pipe.'

Andrew whistled. 'Well, I never.'

'You haven't been home for some time and a lot has happened in the meanwhile,' Nell went on.

'I'll say. You'll tell me he's stopped drinking next.'

'Not quite, but he has cut back considerably,' Nell informed him.

'This is serious. Something must be wrong for him to do all these things.'

'If there is he hasn't said.'

'Hasn't one of you asked him?'

'You know Pa. If he hasn't volunteered the information then he doesn't want to tell us. Asking him would be pointless.'

'Hmmh,' Andrew mused. 'What does Peter think?'

'He's as mystified as we are,' Charlotte replied. Then, eagerly, 'How's Geoffrey?'

'You should know, he writes to you almost every day from all accounts. Lover boy is fine, in the pink. Getting set to go out on some jolly manoeuvres which I'll also be doing when I return.'

At which point voices in the hallway announced the arrival home of Murdo and Jean Ritchie.

Jean crawled into bed and pulled the bedclothes up to her chin. What a stunning young man, she thought, like a

Greek god descended. Amusing too; he'd made her laugh repeatedly over dinner and afterwards.

She then found herself thinking of him in a sexual way, wondering how he'd look undressed. How he'd make love.

·Don't be ridiculous, she chided herself. She was old enough to be his mother – indeed, his mother had been her best friend. It would almost be like incest.

She smiled wryly. If Murdo did have marriage in mind that's exactly what she would end up, Andrew's stepmother. What a lark!

It had been so long, so very long, not since Forbes in fact. There had been times when she'd almost screamed from frustration. She was a passionate woman who needed a man in her life, desperately so.

Oh, the memories of the lovemaking with Forbes, he had been excellent in that department, a man who knew how to pleasure a woman.

She thought again of Andrew, that dear sweet boy. She groaned imagining him fondling her, moving within her. Those brown eyes boring into her, those finely chiselled features gazing down at her.

'God,' she moaned. She shouldn't be thinking like this, it was all wrong. She'd come hoping for the father and now all she could think about was the son, and certainly not platonically either.

She couldn't help herself. She needed release. She pulled up her nightdress and then slid her hand between her legs.

And all the while until release came it was Andrew she thought of.

*

'She didn't!' Wonky gasped.

'She did, at Pa's request. I nearly died of embarrassment. Though I have to admit some of the things she had to say were pretty informative.'

Nell giggled.

'Well, come on, tell us everything,' Wonky urged Charlotte.

Charlotte became coy. 'I don't know if I can bring myself to repeat what she said.'

'Of course you can. I'll kill you if you don't.'

Nell, face a trifle red, giggled again.

'Well, she started off by asking me if I knew what a man and woman did in bed, how babies were made.'

'And?' Wonky's eyes were huge and she'd moved forward to sit right on the edge of her chair.

'I reminded her that I was a country girl and that one couldn't help but observe things.'

Nell covered her mouth with a hand. This was priceless.

Charlotte continued. 'She said that was good. Then she said I wasn't to worry if Geoffrey was too nervous on our wedding night and nothing happened. That occurs quite frequently apparently. I simply wasn't to worry and that nature would take its course in due time.'

Wonky was fascinated. 'Go on.'

'She told me that making love should be a pleasure and not merely a duty. That the woman should enjoy herself as much as the man. She advised me to take a large white handkerchief to bed with me as lovemaking can be pretty messy at times.'

Nell's face was now almost beetroot. 'A large white handkerchief,' she repeated, thinking about that.

'So she advised. She also . . .' Charlotte broke off and took a deep breath. 'She also said I wasn't to be scared when I saw a man's erect penis for the first time. Some of them can be rather large and give an unexperienced girl quite a fright.'

'How big?' Wonky demanded.

'She didn't exactly say. Only that I wasn't to be put off by size.'

'Anything else?' Wonky queried.

'Well . . . she did mention that it isn't always done in the same way. I mean, there are various ways of doing it.'

'No!' Wonky breathed.

'She didn't go into great detail but according to her some men like doing it like the animals.'

Wonky frowned. 'I don't understand?'

'Well eh . . . You must have seen a bull with a cow?'

Wonky nodded

'Like that.'

'Aaahhh!' Wonky exhaled.

'How demeaning,' Nell declared.

'Exactly what I thought. Quite humiliating. But not nearly as humiliating as what she said next. Even she was embarrassed when she told me, which is something. She was quite matter of fact about what she'd said previously.'

'And what was that?' Wonky queried.

Charlotte shook her head. 'I can't repeat it.'

'Please, cuz?' Wonky pleaded.

'It's too awful for words and doesn't bear thinking about. It had never entered my mind that men could do such a thing.' She shuddered.

'Charlotte!'

Charlotte stared at her cousin. 'Honestly, Wonky, you don't want to hear.'

'But I do. What if my future husband wants to do it to me? I should be prepared in advance.'

'I swear, Wonky, it's too awful to repeat.'

'Then whisper in my ear.'

Charlotte considered that. 'She said it was something boys sometimes did to each other at school and then got a liking for.'

Boys to boys? Wonky couldn't imagine what. Neither could Nell.

'Geoffrey's never doing it to me I can assure you of that,' Charlotte stated firmly, and shuddered again.

'Please, Charlotte?'

She sighed. 'Oh all right. But you'll be revolted, it's quite ghastly.'

Wonky went pale as Charlotte whispered in her ear. Her eyes had been huge before, now they almost popped out of her head.

'That's disgusting!' she exclaimed in horror.

'Do you want to hear?' Charlotte asked Nell, for if she'd told Wonky she might as well tell Nell.

Curiosity got the better of Nell who nodded.

Charlotte crossed to her sister and repeated her whisper.

'Dear God!' Nell said in a strangled voice. 'Surely not?'

Now it was Nell's turn to shudder. The thought was horrendous beyond belief.

'What else did she tell you?' Wonky croaked.

'Nothing as bad as that.'

'Thank the Lord.'

Chapter 5

Tom Comyn might normally be the dreariest of men but all that changed the moment he stepped into a pulpit where he was transformed into a hellfire preacher.

Murdo groaned inwardly. Would Tom never stop! His sermon, as usual, was going on and on, seemingly without end. Tom's voice reverberated round and round the church, at times a mighty roar as he condemned the sins of humanity.

Murdo glanced sideways at Jean, wondering what she was making of all this. She seemed transfixed.

Charlotte was bored to tears, she'd heard all this countless times before. She'd have done anything to miss coming to church but for her to do so, unless she was ill, wasn't allowed. Murdo, as a pillar of the community and believer, insisted they attended without fail.

Nell shifted on the family pew with the beginnings of cramp in her legs. Surreptitiously she reached down and massaged them through her dress.

Peter was thinking about business, pleased with himself at how he was managing without his father there full time.

He wished he wasn't sitting beside Mrs Ritchie whose strong-smelling perfume he found irritating. She must be doused in the stuff he thought.

Murdo was wrong about Jean being transfixed, she was only giving the appearance of being so. She too was thinking, about Murdo.

So far, to her disappointment, nothing had happened between them and she was rapidly coming to the conclusion that her invitation to take a break at Drummond House had been precisely that with no ulterior motive. Murdo had been friendly enough, a perfect host, and they'd spent considerable time together, but conversation and company were all he appeared interested in.

Her thoughts then turned to Andrew sitting beyond the girls. How handsome and dashing he looked that morning, almost good enough to eat. A little shiver ran through her, and she quickly banished some carnal images from her mind; she was in church after all. No place to be thinking such things.

And then she had an idea that brought a soft smile to her face. She'd speak to Murdo about it later.

'Can I have a word with you apart, Murdo?' Dr McAllister requested on the way out. He had hung back to wait for Murdo.

'Aye, of course,' Murdo replied. To Jean and the others he said, 'I won't be a moment.'

McAllister and Murdo moved away from the congregation still streaming out of the church.

'As you haven't been to see me for a while I presume you haven't had any more attacks?' McAllister queried.

'That's right.'

'You're still taking the pills and doing everything Gillespie advised you to do?'

'A pill every morning without fail and I walk miles every afternoon. I still miss my pipe dreadfully, mind, there isn't a single waking moment when I couldn't cheerfully light up. But I don't. And only a couple of drams a day as ordered.'

McAllister nodded his approval. 'How do you feel within yourself?'

'Never better. Fit as a flea in fact.'

'That's grand, Murdo. Just make sure you keep up the regime and hopefully these attacks will be a thing of the past. He's a good man that Gillespie, knows what he's doing.'

'You must come up to the house sometime soon, James, and we'll have those two drams together.'

'I will indeed.'

They shook hands and parted, Murdo rejoining his party and McAllister his wife and family.

The Comyns had come to Drummond House for Sunday lunch. Murdo felt obliged to invite them several times a year, occasions he didn't look forward to. What Moira saw in Tom Comyn was, and always had been, beyond him. The man was dry as a stick and humourless. But there you are, who was to say what one person saw in another. And the pair were happy together, or so Moira had told him often enough.

'Perth is such a lovely city I always think, Jean,' Moira said. They of course knew one another from when Jean had lived in the area.

'It is.'

'I can well understand why you've never thought of moving back.'

'I might have done if I'd any relatives still here, but as you know my parents are both dead and my brother is in Australia.'

Moira nodded. 'Taken so young too. You never know the moment, do you?'

'Amen,' Tom intoned.

Moira's eyes flicked from Jean to Murdo, and she wondered about Jean's visit. Murdo had always sworn he'd never remarry, but people, even her brother, had been known to change their minds. And Jean was such an attractive woman too, she'd worn well. Murdo could do a lot worse.

Murdo stared at his empty wine glass contemplating indulging himself. Then he remembered his conversation with McAllister and put temptation firmly behind him.

'And how's the army treating you?' Tom Comyn asked Andrew.

'Fine. Our second Battalion's off to India shortly while my Battalion, the first, is staying behind.'

'Exotic place India,' Tom commented. 'Lots of disease there though I believe.'

'So I understand.'

Jean glanced at Murdo and smiled, he smiling in return.

Smiles Moira didn't fail to note. Perhaps there was something in the wind.

'I'm told you have a beautiful house in Perth, Mrs Ritchie,' Andrew said. 'Pa mentioned.'

'It is rather beautiful. You must come and see for yourself one day. Bring a friend, I always have a bottle of Drummond in the house.'

Murdo beamed. 'Well said, Jean.'

'Well, I could hardly buy any other brand, could I?'

'Most certainly not. By the by, Andrew, Mrs Ritchie has suggested that you and she travel back to Perth together. Good idea I thought. You can keep each other company.'

Jean had presented her idea to Murdo before luncheon and he'd instantly agreed.

'I hope you don't mind, Andrew?'

'Not at all, Mrs Ritchie. It will be charming.'

She hoped they managed to be alone in their carriage and then she'd have him all to herself. She shivered at the prospect.

'I say, are you cold, Jean?' Murdo queried.

'Not at all.'

'Are you certain of that?'

'Absolutely.'

Murdo glanced over at the roaring fire and wondered if he should instruct more coal be put on. The dining room seemed warm enough to him.

'If you wish to come up this way again perhaps you'll stay with us at the manse, Jean,' Moira said provokingly, watching Murdo for his reaction.

Murdo frowned.

'That's a very kind offer, Moira, which I shall perhaps take you up on sometime.'

'Nothing so grand as Drummond House mind, plain fare I'm afraid. But you will be welcome.'

Jean was also wondering at Murdo's reaction. He seemed none too pleased. She had no intention of ever staying with the Comyns whom she found boring in the extreme.

A little later, and not for the first time, Murdo marvelled at Tom's appetite. The man ate like a horse, several horses, yet never put on an ounce.

He watched as Tom waded through three helpings of pudding after having had two full helpings of the main course.

'Well, I did enjoy my time at Drummond House,' Jean declared to Andrew as their train pulled out of the station. As she'd hoped they were alone in the carriage.

'I know Pa enjoyed having you there.'

She thought of Murdo who'd come to see them off. She was now more or less convinced that there hadn't been an ulterior motive behind his invitation which was a great pity. Life with Murdo could have been most fulfilling.

'Tell me, Andrew, do you have a lady friend?'

He laughed. 'No such luck, Mrs Ritchie.'

'I find that surprising considering you're such a handsome young chap.'

He regarded her with amusement. 'Not that handsome,' he replied modestly.

'Get away with you, Andrew. You're hiding your light under a bushel. I'm sure you're well aware that you're extremely so.'

Andrew glanced out the window, suddenly embarrassed. There was something about Jean Ritchie which unsettled him. Something he couldn't quite put his finger on. Perhaps it was the way she had of staring so directly at him.

'You're a handsome woman yourself, Mrs Ritchie,' he replied gallantly.

'Ah! A flatterer just like your father,' she teased.

'He can be, can't he?'

'Like father, like son.'

Andrew decided to change the subject. 'Whereabouts in Perth do you live?'

She told him the area and her address. 'Which reminds me, don't forget I've invited you to call on me. I'll take great delight in showing you round my house.'

'I haven't forgotten,' he smiled. 'And there's always a bottle of Drummond in residence.'

And more, she thought to herself. Much more.

'This is a pleasant surprise, Moira,' Murdo declared, pecking his sister on the cheek.

'I hope I'm not intruding?'

'Not at all.' He'd been preparing to go out for his daily walk but that could now wait for a while.

Moira crossed to a comfy chair and eased herself into it. 'I suppose you're wondering why I'm here having had luncheon with you last Sunday.'

'You're not exactly a regular visitor, Moira.'

'Nothing personal, Murdo, as you're well aware. Being a minister's wife can be most exacting.'

'Quite.'

'So many good works to be done. A whole host of tasks that fall on my shoulders.'

She was becoming more and more pious with the passing

of the years, Murdo thought. It didn't suit her. Where was the carefree laughing lassie he remembered? No more, unfortunately.

'So how can I help you?' he asked. 'I presume there's a reason for this.'

'I'm simply being nosy,' she stated baldly. 'Is there something going on between you and Jean Ritchie?'

He stared at her in astonishment. 'How do you mean?'

'It could be you're thinking of remarrying and I wanted you to know if that's the case you have my full approval. Jean Ritchie's a fine woman who'll do you proud. She also has the advantage of being wealthy in her own right so you can be assured it isn't your money she's after.'

Her approval! How bloody impertinent. 'Tom's approval too I take it?' he queried.

'Of course.'

'Well, I'm sorry to disappoint you, Moira. There's nothing of that nature between Jean and myself. I merely asked her to Drummond House because she's such damned good company.'

'Language, Murdo!' Moira exclaimed, wagging a disapproving finger at him.

'I don't know where you got such an idea.'

'I saw the way you two were looking and smiling at one another during luncheon. She's certainly set her cap at you.'

'That's preposterous,' Murdo protested.

'Why should it be? You're a widower, she's a widow. It would make complete sense for the pair of you to get together.'

'I swear to you, Moira, it never even entered my mind.

I'll never remarry. Louise was the only woman I'll ever love.'

'Who's talking about love? You said yourself she's good company which means the two of you obviously get on well. Wouldn't another marriage make sense? Do you want to end up on your own in your old age?'

'Peter will never leave this house which goes to him. When he marries he'll stay here with his wife.'

'That's not the same, or won't be, as having someone of your own. Someone to share with.'

She had a point, he thought. It was a fairly grim prospect. But remarry? Never. He was adamant about that.

'And while I'm here, what's all this about you not working afternoons any more. Work is food and drink to you.'

Dammit he thought. He was going to have a dram. 'Would you care for a drink, Moira?'

'No I would not. You know Tom disapproves of strong drink. A little wine from time to time, yes. But no spirits.'

'There is sherry.'

'No thank you, Murdo,' she stated firmly.

He poured himself a hefty one.

'Well?' she demanded.

'Well what?'

'Not working in the afternoons.'

He sighed. 'This is beginning to sound like the Inquisition.'

'I know you, Murdo. You're up to something. Come on, admit it.'

'I'm nothing of the sort. I simply want Peter to take

more responsibility. It's common sense as he'll inherit one day.'

Moira harumphed. 'I don't believe a word of it. You're fibbing, Murdo Drummond.'

'Not so.'

'You've also given up your pipe I hear, and you go walking. *You* walking! I nearly fell over when I heard.'

'There's nothing wrong with walking. It's good for you.'

'But you *hate* walking, always have. It's a well-known fact. And now here you are, walking all over the place apparently. Being sighted everywhere, up hill and down dale. What's going on?'

'Suppose I told you to mind your own business?'

'You're my brother, that makes it my business.'

'I don't pry into your affairs.'

Her face softened. 'I'm worried, Murdo. What's wrong? Are you ill?'

'Do I look it?' he prevaricated.

'Not in the least. To be honest I've never seen you look so fit and well.'

'There you are then!' he declared triumphantly, swallowing the remainder of his dram and pouring another.

'That still doesn't answer my question. Why the changes in the habits of a lifetime?'

He eyed her over the rim of his glass. She was right about being nosy, and knowing Moira she'd persist unless he gave her an acceptable explanation.

'It's poor circulation,' he lied.

She studied him intently.

'I'm doing all this on McAllister's advice. He said I was sitting down too much and not getting enough exercise.'

'Ahh!' she exhaled, believing him.

'And don't you go saying anything to the rest of the family. I don't want them worrying. Have I your word on that, Moira?'

She nodded.

He decided to elaborate a little. 'I was getting pains in my legs which is why I went to McAllister in the first place.'

'Are you still having them?'

'Not a twinge for ages. Nor will I go back to working full-time. What I said about Peter is right enough, it was time I let go of the reins a little. This simply gave me a reason for doing so.' Murdo made a mental note to speak to McAllister, it would be just like Moira to quiz the doctor on his story.

'I still think you should reconsider remarrying, Murdo. I'm sure Louise would have approved.'

'No,' he stated defiantly. 'And that is an end of that. I'll hear no more on the subject. Understand?'

A few seconds ticked by, then Moira replied in a gentle, caring voice, 'I understand.'

'Good.'

Moira rose. 'Now that's settled I'd better be on my way. I have a great deal yet to do this afternoon.'

'I know, good works,' Murdo said, a trace of sarcasm in his voice.

'Precisely.'

He saw her out.

'I called you all in here because there's something I wish to clear up,' Murdo announced later that day after dinner. Towards the end of his walk he'd dropped in on James

McAllister and put him in the picture. Moira would get nothing out of the good doctor other than affirmation of the poor circulation nonsense.

Peter, Charlotte and Nell looked at him expectantly.

'Your Aunt Moira was here having got some idiotic notion into her head about Jean Ritchie and myself.'

He glared about him. 'Just in case you too are fostering the same delusion I wish to state categorically that there is nothing between Jean and myself. Nothing whatsoever. I enjoy her company, nothing more, nothing less.'

Charlotte glanced at Nell. 'We had wondered, Pa.'

'Well, now you know. Your mother's memory is sacred to me and always will be. There will never be another Mrs Murdo Drummond.'

He paused as a lump came into his throat, and turned away.

'Never,' he repeated quietly.

'Are you awake?' Andrew queried, having crawled into the tent he was sharing with Geoffrey on manoeuvres.

Geoffrey opened his eyes. 'Yes.'

'It's damned cold out there. I think we'll have snow before morning.'

Andrew shivered. Another five days before they returned to barracks. It seemed a lifetime away.

Geoffrey closed his eyes again. He'd been thinking about Charlotte and wishing he was with her. The image in his mind was so clear and sharp he could almost smell her personal scent.

'Supper was appalling. Those cooks should be hung, drawn and quartered,' Andrew complained.

'They're doing their best, old boy.'

'Well, their best isn't good enough. I feel as though I've been poisoned.'

Geoffrey chuckled. 'It wasn't that ghastly.'

'To me it was. Muck, pure and simple. When we get back to Perth the first thing I'm going to do when I get the chance is go out for a slap-up meal. Want to come?'

Geoffrey thought how he'd love to go out for a slap-up meal, but with Charlotte not Andrew.

'Well?'

'Certainly.'

'We'll have champagne, the lot. Put this misery behind us.'

Andrew turned out the hurricane lamp and crawled into his cot. 'I'd give anything for a lovely hot bath.'

'Fat chance out here.'

Andrew yawned, thinking how the cold was really sinking into his bones. He was terribly tired.

'Turkey's not doing well. The Bulgarians and Serbs are giving them a proper pasting by all accounts.' He was referring to the current war between Turkey and the Balkan League.

'So I hear.'

'Thousands dead apparently. Poor sods.'

'Who do you think will win?' Geoffrey asked.

'Well, it won't be the Turks unless they buck their ideas up somewhat. Just shows you how an army can be overrated.'

'Do you think we are?'

Andrew laughed. 'Don't be daft. The British Army could take on anyone and win. And the Watch is one of its finest regiments. We're with the cream.'

They were, Geoffrey thought. They most certainly were. A regiment to be proud of.

'I wonder when I'll get my next leave?' Geoffrey mused aloud.

'Straight to Drummond House and Charlotte, eh?'

'As fast as the Humber will take me.'

'Missing her?'

'Of course. She's the woman I intend marrying.'

'I hope you're going to ask me to be your best man. I'll be frightfully slighted if you don't.'

'I fully intended asking you, nearer to the date that is.'

'Then you're on. I accept.'

'Good show, Andrew.'

'Now let's get some sleep. We're up before the crack.'

'Goodnight, Andrew.'

'Goodnight, future brother-in-law,' Andrew teased.

Geoffrey smiled in the darkness.

Jean Ritchie opened a letter that had arrived with that morning's post, a smile coming onto her face as she read it.

The letter was from Andrew proposing a visit. If he didn't receive a reply from her he would know she'd agreed the arrangements.

She felt light as air and extremely happy as she refolded his missive.

'It really is a splendid house, Mrs Ritchie,' Andrew enthused. He and Geoffrey, whom he'd brought along, had just completed the grand tour.

'Why, thank you.'

She escorted them down to her drawing room. 'Now how about some of that Drummond I promised you?'

'Yes please,' both young men chorused in unison.

She gestured towards a solid oak sideboard. 'In the right-hand side, Andrew, perhaps you'd do the honours.'

'Of course.'

Geoffrey took up a position in front of the roaring fire.

'And what about yourself, Mrs Ritchie?' Andrew queried.

'A little sherry would be agreeable.'

Her heart leapt when, on giving her her glass, his hand brushed hers.

'Now tell me all about your manoeuvres, Geoffrey,' she smiled.

'Too boring for words. You don't want to hear about them. Ghastly things.'

'The food was awful,' Andrew chipped in. 'On several occasions I thought I'd been poisoned.'

Jean gave a tinkling laugh. 'Well, I hope my cook does better by you tonight.'

'She certainly couldn't do any worse, and that's a fact.'

This time they all laughed.

They continued making polite conversation until informed that dinner was served.

Jean hooked each by an arm as they went through.

Jean took her opportunity after dinner when Geoffrey excused himself and left the room.

'It's been delightful having you here tonight,' she purred.

'I can assure you, Mrs Ritchie, we've both thoroughly enjoyed ourselves. An enchanting evening.'

'I think you can call me Jean when we're alone.'

He sat further back in his chair and stared at her. The suggested informality surprised him; she was an older woman after all. There were conventions.

'If you wish.'

'I do.'

'Then Jean it is when we're alone.'

'I hope you'll come again soon, Andrew, I'd like that. And perhaps next time without the chaperone.' She emphasised the word *without*.

By God, she was flirting with him he realised with shock. He hurriedly glanced down into his drink.

'Well, Andrew?'

'That would be most pleasant.'

'These long winter evenings can be most tedious, don't you agree? Or perhaps you don't?'

'Oh but I do. Especially in the barracks.'

'Then you must think of this as your second home where you're welcome any time day or night.'

He was beginning to see Jean Ritchie in a new light. He had to admit she was attractive, still attractive, considering her age. He swiftly worked out how old his mother would have been. Forty-eight, he calculated which would make Jean Ritchie the same age. Old, but not impossibly so. And terrifically well preserved.

He glanced at her quizzically. 'The family thought there might be something between you and Pa, Jean, but he called us all together to refute that. Said mother's memory was sacred to him and there would never be another Mrs Murdo Drummond.'

There it was, she thought. Confirmation that Murdo

was out of the question. So why not his son? A dalliance instead of marriage, if Andrew was interested that was.

She laughed. 'Murdo and I are friends and no more, I assure you, Andrew. I'm well aware he would never look at another woman. He worshipped your mother.'

'Yes,' Andrew agreed.

Jean heard the sound of approaching footsteps. 'Now remember what I said. A second home, any time day or night.'

She'd given Andrew a great deal to think about.

Chapter 6

'How wonderful to meet you at last, Charlotte, Geoffrey has told us so much about you,' Mrs Armitage gushed. Geoffrey had decided it was time Charlotte met his parents and so it had been arranged she'd travel down to Glasgow by train where he'd be waiting for her at the station. She was nervous as a kitten.

Charlotte shook hands with Mrs Armitage while Mr Armitage smiled on.

'How was your journey?' he enquired politely.

'Uneventful, thank you very much. Quite pleasant really.'

'I believe you have snow in Perthshire at the moment.'

'That's right. The first flakes fell early last week.'

They were in the Armitages' parlour, a large room with heavy flock wallpaper and thick floral-patterned curtains. There was a welcoming, cosy atmosphere about it.

'Would you care to sit, Charlotte?' Geoffrey asked.

'Please.'

Mr Armitage rubbed his hands briskly together. 'I

thought a little refreshment might be in order. Will you take something?'

Geoffrey shot her a warning glance. His parents would be shocked beyond belief if she asked for whisky and probably deem her a most unsuitable young lady for their son's affections.

'A small sherry would be nice.'

Geoffrey heaved an inward sigh of relief.

'Certainly. And you, Gillian?'

'The same thank you, Robert.'

Mrs Armitage sat facing Charlotte. 'Geoffrey informs us that he's already requested your father for your hand in marriage and that your father has asked he wait six months and then request again.'

'That's correct, Mrs Armitage,' Charlotte replied.

'A wise precaution,' Mr Armitage said, handing Charlotte her sherry.

'Most wise,' Mrs Armitage agreed.

'Better safe than sorry,' Mr Armitage went on. 'Marriage is a huge step after all.'

'We both love one another dearly and that won't change,' Geoffrey declared stoutly.

'I understand your mother has passed on,' Mrs Armitage said, sympathy in her voice.

'Quite some time ago. In childbirth.'

'Your father must have been devastated.'

'He was, Mrs Armitage. They were devoted to each other. He's never got over her loss.'

Mrs Armitage nodded her understanding.

'So your father brought you up,' Mr Armitage stated.

'Yes he did. There were various nannies along the way

because of Pa's business commitments but he did the best he could.'

Geoffrey produced his silver cigarette case which caused Mrs Armitage to screw up her nose in disgust. 'Dreadful habit, don't you agree, my dear?'

Charlotte smiled. 'I can't say it bothers me.'

'Well, I wish he'd stop. The house always reeks after Geoffrey's been home.'

Geoffrey lit up.

'Can't say I approve either. But there you are. Chap's too old now for me to forbid him.'

'So, Charlotte,' said Mrs Armitage, settling herself deeper into her chair. 'Tell us more about yourself. We'd like to know all.'

'Isn't she a stunner!' Geoffrey declared enthusiastically to his father, the women having retired and the men staying on for a nightcap.

'She is, I'll grant you that. But looks aren't everything, Geoffrey. They often fade all too soon.'

'There's more to it than her looks, Father, it's Charlotte herself.'

'Are you certain about that?'

'Indeed I am.'

'Hmmh.' Robert Armitage mused into his brandy glass. 'Have to admit I was taken by the lass as was your mother which she'll no doubt confirm when I join her shortly.'

'I have your approval then?'

'I can see no reason why not. She'll make a welcome addition to the family.'

Geoffrey beamed, which he'd been doing on and off all evening. That was that out of the way. Not that he'd doubted Charlotte would make a good impression on his parents. He hadn't. It was simply good, and a relief, to have his judgement confirmed.

Charlotte was sitting at a vanity table in the room she'd been allocated staring at her reflection in the mirror and thinking about the evening which had gone off even better than she'd hoped.

What a lovely couple the Armitages were, so kind and understanding. It was foolish of her to have been so nervous beforehand, but despite Geoffrey's reassurances they might have turned out to be complete horrors.

She wondered what Geoffrey and his father were saying. Talking about her undoubtedly, Geoffrey getting his father's reaction to meeting her. She was certain, and there was no arrogance about this, that it would be favourable.

She unpinned her hair and shook it loose, then slowly began brushing it. She'd considered bringing Jenny along but had decided against that. She'd just have to do her own hair in the morning.

How long she wondered before the taps on the door? For she and Geoffrey had agreed a code before entering the house. Two taps meant all was well, three and it wasn't.

She thought of the following morning when she and Geoffrey were going shopping before she took the train back to Pitlochry. There were all manner of items she wanted to buy and what fun it would be doing so, especially with Geoffrey accompanying her.

She wished there had been an opportunity for a good-night kiss but that had been impossible. Closing her eyes she imagined it instead.

She didn't hear any footsteps but suddenly there was a double tap on her door.

Charlotte smiled at herself in the mirror. As she'd thought, they'd taken to her as she'd taken to them.

All was well.

Murdo paused beside a pile of wooden boxes to watch with approval the bottling taking place. The women, all local of course, were doing the menial tasks, the men the semi-skilled labour.

The gaffer in charge came over and touched the brim of his cap. 'Good morning, Mr Drummond.'

'And how are you today, Jamie?'

'Just dandy, sir.'

'Everything going well?'

'As you can see, sir. No problems here.'

Murdo cast his eye along the line of workers. 'Where's Isa McFarlane? She appears missing.'

'Down with the flu, sir. I sent her home yesterday in a terrible state. Her cousin Mary says Dr McAllister has called and confined her to bed until better.'

Murdo made a mental note to send round a wee some-thing. This common touch was one of the many things that endeared him to his workforce who considered him a good boss. It was often said that, as employers went, there didn't come any better than old man Drummond.

Not that he was a soft touch, far from it. And as he paid a fair day's wages he expected a fair day's graft in return. But fair was the operative word, Murdo Drummond was always that.

'Carry on then, Jamie,' Murdo instructed, and went on his way.

Andrew was surprised when Jean Ritchie answered the door herself. She smiled at him. 'Come in. Come in.'

'I've given the staff the night off,' she explained, helping him out of his coat.

Andrew still wasn't convinced he was doing the right thing. What if he'd misinterpreted her? Whatever happened, he was determined not to make a fool of himself. Jean would have to make her intentions absolutely clear.

'You'll need a dram to warm you up. It's cold out there,' she said.

'It certainly is.'

They went through to her drawing room where a cheery fire blazed.

'I've had a little supper laid in the dining room for later,' she said, opening the door on the right-hand side of the oak sideboard.

'You look very pretty tonight,' he declared gallantly.

'Why, don't I always?' she teased.

That flustered him. 'Well yes, of course. I mean eh . . .' He broke off in confusion.

'Prettier than usual, is that it? I have gone to a lot of effort.'

'Yes, precisely.'

She could see how nervous he was, and on edge. When she gave him his glass she noted the hand that accepted it was trembling.

'Now come and sit beside me here on the sofa and we'll talk,' she said.

Slowly she began to calm him and put him at his ease.

Andrew didn't know how it happened, one moment they were chatting, the next she was in his arms, the two of them kissing. She was an expert at that he soon realised.

'Why don't we go upstairs?' she suggested after a while.

His nervousness returned and he didn't reply.

'Andrew?'

'I, eh . . . I . . .'

'Tell me something, and don't be shy,' she said, taking his hand and placing it on a breast. She'd already guessed. 'You've never known a woman, have you?'

He shook his head.

'I thought as much. Well, you're not to worry. Leave everything to me. I have been married don't forget.'

'Jean, I'm not certain we should be doing this.'

'And yet you came tonight. You may be inexperienced where women are concerned but you're hardly naive, Andrew. You knew full well what I intended.'

He swallowed hard. 'Yes,' he whispered.

'Is it my age?'

'Partly, I suppose. And that you were a friend of my mother's.'

'The friendship is true enough. But I get so lonely, Andrew, so very lonely. Surely there's no harm in us seeing one another?'

'Seeing, no. But what you're proposing is beyond that.'

'You're a grown man, Andrew, and I'm a woman. Surely that's all that matters. A woman who wants you very much.

And don't think our involvement will give you cause for concern. I know nothing can come of this in the long run but in the meantime why not just enjoy ourselves.'

'You'd be discreet?'

'Totally, I swear. I have my reputation to think about after all. I've presumed you'd be the same.'

'Oh yes,' he assured her.

He squeezed her breast and immediately felt his manhood twitch and start to rise. He knew then there was no drawing back, that he'd go through with it. Going to bed with a woman was something he'd dreamed of for a long time.

Jean lifted the hand from her breast and rose, drawing him off the sofa.

'You won't have any regrets, I promise you.'

And with that she led him towards the door.

'It's not a race, Andrew, slow down,' she whispered throatily.

'Sorry.'

'There's nothing to be sorry about. Just slow down, make the pleasure last.'

He stared down at the naked body writhing beneath him, unable to believe this was actually happening. What a figure, her breasts large and voluptuous. The first naked breasts he'd ever seen.

So long, so very long, Jean thought. How she'd missed this. And what a stallion Andrew had turned out to be. Oh, she would teach him, many many things that Forbes had taught her.

'Stop for a moment,' she instructed.

'Can't.'

'Yes you can, but stay inside me.' She offered him a nipple

which he greedily took into his mouth like a starving baby.

She smiled as she stroked the back of his head. Dear Andrew, dear sweet Andrew.

'Now the other one,' she said.

He groaned and, despite her having told him to stop, started to move again.

Her lips drew back and shudder after shudder racked through her. When they'd subsided she brought her legs up round his waist as he plunged, though far less vigorously than before, on and on.

Then Andrew cried out, arched his back and then collapsed onto her sweat-slicked body, his own heaving from exertion.

Jean closed her eyes, in seventh heaven. 'That was wonderful, darling,' she whispered.

Andrew pulled himself up and out of her.

'Well?' she queried, a smile of sexual satisfaction on her face.

'I can't describe . . . I can't even begin to describe . . .'

She gave a low laugh. 'Not as you'd imagined, eh?'

'Far, far better.'

He was hers, she thought. There was no saying for how long, but for now he was hers. That was all that mattered.

A little later he mounted her again.

'I've got news, Miss Charlotte,' Jenny the maid, eyes shining, stated. Picking up a silver-backed brush she began grooming Charlotte's hair.

Charlotte stared at her in the mirror she was sitting facing. 'Oh?'

'I'm to be wed, miss.'

Charlotte's face lit up. 'Congratulations, Jenny. Who's the lucky chap?'

'Hamish Bell, miss. We've been stepping out for a while now.'

That was news to Charlotte who'd had no idea the maid was courting. Rising, she warmly embraced Jenny. 'I couldn't be more delighted for you. I know Hamish, he's a splendid young man.'

Jenny giggled. 'The ceremony will be next June, miss, when I'll move into Hamish's cottage. Oh it'll be grand right enough.' The cottage came with Hamish's job – he's a ghillie.

'Have you told Pa yet?'

'No, miss. I wanted you to be the first to hear seeing how I'm more or less your personal maid and all.'

Hardly that, Charlotte thought. The majority of her duties were general ones.

'Will you come to the wedding, miss?'

'Wild horses wouldn't keep me away, Jenny. I expect we'll all be there if asked.'

'Oh yes, miss.'

Charlotte resumed her seat and Jenny her brushing. 'Now the dress, what will you do about that?'

'Well, miss, I thought . . .'

Jenny's plans tumbled out of her as she dressed Charlotte's hair.

'What's wrong with you today?' Geoffrey enquired casually having come across Andrew standing staring distractedly out across the parade ground.

Andrew blinked and brought himself out of his reverie. 'Pardon?'

Geoffrey repeated himself. 'You've been like it all day I've noticed. Something up?'

Andrew's expression became sheepish. 'I have got a lot on my mind I'm afraid.'

'Want to talk about it?'

Andrew shook his head. It was Jean he'd been thinking about, Jean whom he couldn't keep out of his thoughts. His whole world had changed, a new dimension added, since taking up with her. He was rapidly becoming obsessed with Jean Ritchie. That body, that magnificent body. The experience of making love to her had been as though Heaven had come to Earth.

'Well I'd look a bit more lively if I was you, you don't want the C.O. breathing down your neck.'

'Yes, you're right.'

'Certain there's nothing you want to discuss?'

Andrew would have loved to tell Geoffrey about Jean and what it was like being with her. But discretion, discretion.

'I'd best get on,' Andrew declared.

'And so should I.'

They parted, each going his separate way.

Murdo was in the study savouring his second dram of the evening and thinking about Jean Ritchie. He'd always sworn . . . But was Moira right? It wasn't that he was after sex. But the company . . . Aye well, that was something else.

If he did speak to Jean, and it was a big if, the nature of the relationship would have to be clearly spelt out.

She was alone after all, and so was he.

*

It was Andrew's third visit alone to Jean and he'd only just arrived. He was impatient to get upstairs to the bedroom.

'I had a letter from your father today,' Jean announced.

That startled him. 'Really?'

'He's asked me to Drummond House for Hogmanay. Says your family always has a gathering at that time.'

Andrew nodded. 'We do.'

'Should I accept?'

Andrew considered that. 'I don't see why not. Though it's hardly my decision to make.'

'I don't want you feeling embarrassed in my presence.'

He grinned. 'What I'll be feeling won't be embarrassment, Jean, and I won't be able to do anything about it.'

'No?' she teased.

'Hardly in the family home. Wouldn't be right somehow. And what if I was seen coming or going? What a scandal! Pa would be outraged.'

'You could always be very careful coming and going,' she further teased.

'Not worth the risk, old thing.'

She wagged a finger at him. 'Less of the old if you don't mind. That's a touchy subject.'

He went to her and took her into his arms, thinking how gorgeous she smelled. 'I didn't mean it that way. Figure of speech that's all.'

'I should hope so too.'

'Oh, Jean,' he whispered, and then his mouth was on hers, she melting against him.

Hogmanay is Scotland's greatest festival and celebrated with enormous enthusiasm, the revelries always accompanied with copious amounts of alcohol. Murdo had already made up his mind that he wouldn't be sticking to his daily quota. 'To hell with it,' he'd muttered to himself on making that decision.

Andrew and, to Charlotte's enormous delight, Geoffrey had managed leave, so they were in the throng now filling the Drummond drawing room.

Also present were Geoffrey's parents who, at Murdo's written invitation, had travelled up from Glasgow and would be spending the entire holiday at Drummond House.

The Comyns were there and the McAllisters, the good doctor turning a blind eye and not making comment as dram after dram vanished down Murdo's throat. He understood, Hogmanay was Hogmanay.

Jean Ritchie was chatting to Donald Skene, a local landowner and widower like Murdo. His grown-up daughter Alison, a spinster in her late thirties, stood listening on. The reason she was a spinster, despite the fact her father was a wealthy man, was obvious. She was extremely unattractive to the point that not even her father's wealth had ever tempted a suitor.

Peter went over to talk to Jack Riach, a friend of his, now in conversation with Wonky. Jack and he often went shooting together.

'Enjoying yourself?' he asked Jack on joining them. A glance at the clock en route had told him there was still a little over an hour till midnight.

'Extremely. A splendid "do", but then it always is.'

Wonky had on a plainish blue taffeta dress that she'd worn countless times before and which she now hated. But, due to lack of family cash, her wardrobe was limited and would remain so. She looked over at Nell in a new cream-coloured gown. What she wouldn't have given for a gown like that! It not only suited Nell to a T, it somehow made her appear slimmer.

Wonky brought her attention back to the men and Jack in particular. She'd been wildly attracted to Jack, a bachelor like Peter, for years but so far he hadn't shown the slightest interest. She lived in hope.

'Go on, ask him now,' Charlotte urged Geoffrey.

'He's busy chatting.'

'He'll be that all night. You'll just have to break in.'

Geoffrey had a swallow of whisky to give him courage, then set his glass aside.

'Good luck,' Charlotte breathed, squeezing his hand.

Geoffrey headed for Murdo.

'Excuse me, sir, may I have a private word?'

Murdo noted the look of determination on Geoffrey's face. Glancing round the room he spotted Charlotte watching them intently. 'If you wish.'

'Thank you, sir. Could we go somewhere perhaps?'

Murdo guessed what was coming. 'Follow me.'

They went to the study where Murdo closed the door. 'Yes, Geoffrey?'

'Sir, I'll get straight to the point. I know I agreed to wait six months before again requesting Charlotte's hand which I will honour if you insist. However, I can assure you, sir, neither she nor I will change our minds no matter what.'

Murdo nodded. He fully believed that.

'The thing is, sir, tonight would be, with my parents here and your family present, an ideal opportunity to announce our engagement.'

Murdo nodded again. The lad was right. It *was* an ideal opportunity.

'There's such a short while left to the end of the six months?'

'Whose idea was it you speak to me?' Murdo queried softly.

'Charlotte's, sir.'

'I see.'

Murdo crossed to the mantelpiece and leant against it, gazing at Louise's photograph. He remembered only too clearly what it was like to be newly in love. 'Have you bought a ring yet?' he asked over his shoulder.

'No, sir.'

Murdo knew Louise would have approved of what he was going to do next. 'Would you humour an old man, Geoffrey?'

Geoffrey frowned. 'Yes, sir. Anything, sir.'

Murdo sighed and went to his bureau where he opened one of the drawers. He reached for a small black box that lay inside. Opening the box he stared at its contents. He sniffed.

Geoffrey was mystified. Whatever was going on? He waited patiently while Murdo continued to gaze into the box.

Murdo fumbled in the box which he then snapped shut and replaced in the drawer. Turning to Geoffrey he smiled.

'This was my wife's engagement ring,' he explained, showing it to Geoffrey. 'If you agree I would very much like it now to be Charlotte's.'

Geoffrey accepted the ring when Murdo handed it to

him. When it caught the light it was a blaze of diamonds, a large centre stone surrounded by smaller ones.

'I, eh . . . I don't know what to say, sir.'

'Yes or no would do.'

'Oh yes, sir, thank you, sir. But are you certain about this?'

'Quite, Geoffrey.'

'Then thank you, sir. I take it we now have your consent?'

Murdo nodded, suddenly afraid to speak because of the huge lump in his throat. He turned away and waved Geoffrey to leave him.

'Thank you again, sir,' Geoffrey said at the door. 'I promise you I'll be a good husband to your daughter. She'll never have a moment's regret marrying me.'

Murdo found his voice again. 'Just one thing, don't say anything to anyone, except Charlotte of course, until I make the announcement.'

'I understand, sir.'

Geoffrey left Murdo alone with his thoughts.

Murdo had always had a theatrical streak. He waited till five minutes to midnight before calling the gathering to order and attention. He then broke the news.

Wild applause erupted as Geoffrey slipped the ring onto a blushing Charlotte's finger.

As he kissed her, the clock chimed the hour heralding the arrival of 1913 and the room erupted with cheers.

Chapter 7

Andrew couldn't sleep; for hours he'd tossed and turned and even tried his old childhood trick of counting sheep, to no avail. The trouble was Jean Ritchie who was in a bedroom a few doors down the corridor. He simply couldn't stop thinking about her.

He groaned with frustration. He'd had no idea her close proximity would affect him like this. Visions of her naked voluptuousness and of them making love kept flashing through his mind.

If he'd known this was going to be the case he would have told her not to come to Drummond House. And she was going to be with them for another three whole days and nights! The thought of that was . . . well almost unendurable.

The party had gone extremely well, he reflected. But then as Jack Riach had commented, their Hogmanay ones always did. And what a surprise Geoffrey and Charlotte getting engaged like that. It had certainly leant an added zing to the occasion.

What would 1913 bring for him? More of the same he supposed. His duties at the barracks and . . . Jean.

He drew in a deep breath. He daren't go to her, that would be foolhardy in the extreme. What if he was seen? Though that was highly unlikely on this morning of all mornings. It would be a lie-in for everyone, including the servants who'd had just as late a night as the family and guests. The whole house was undoubtedly fast asleep with the exception of him.

Dare he risk it? Even a short while with her would suffice, rid this fever that had gripped him.

'To hell with it,' he muttered through clenched teeth. He had to have her, simply had to.

Murdo woke with a headache and the desperate need to go to the toilet. He shivered as he slipped into his dressing gown. If it was cold in the bedroom it would be damned freezing in the toilet. But needs must.

Murdo paused outside Jean's door and frowned on hearing muted sounds coming from within. What was she up to? And then it dawned on him what those sounds were the product of.

Dear God, she had someone with her! The woman was being rogered, no doubt about it. He flushed with embarrassment when she gave a low moan of pleasure. The sort of moan he remembered only too well from his marriage.

But *who* was with her? That was the question. It certainly couldn't be Robert Armitage, he was tucked up with Gillian. And it certainly wouldn't be Geoffrey. So, apart from himself, that left . . .

He swallowed hard. Peter and Andrew were the only other males in the house which meant it had to be one of them. That staggered him. Why, she was old enough to be their mother!

Murdo shook his head in bewilderment. How could he of all people so misjudge someone. He would never have believed Jean Ritchie capable of behaving like this. Not only sleeping with one of his sons, but under his own roof.

For a brief moment he considered throwing open the door and confronting the pair of them, finding out which one of his sons it was before ordering the baggage from his house. Then discarded that idea for what possible purpose would it serve.

Then, 'Oh, Andrew!' he distinctly heard.

Well, that was that problem solved. It was his younger son in there with Jean Ritchie. The thought of them together was obscene. He found the thought of a woman her age with his younger son quite repugnant.

And to think he'd actually considered marrying her, making her his wife while all the time she was sleeping with his son.

He moved silently on towards the toilet.

'You're quiet, Murdo,' Jean commented over breakfast.

He eyed her coldly. 'Am I?'

'Hardly a peep out of you.'

He grunted.

'Well, it is New Year's Day,' she burbled on. 'The morning after the night before.'

His fork halted halfway to his mouth. She was certainly right about that, though the party wasn't what he had in mind.

Andrew breezed in. 'Sorry I'm late. Just couldn't get myself out of bed.'

Murdo noted the look that passed between Andrew and

Jean. A conspiratorial one if ever there was. His stony expression became even harder.

It wasn't that he disapproved of Andrew having a sexual relationship – young men had to sow their wild oats after all. He'd done so himself. There had been several women before Louise. It was the fact Andrew had done it under his roof with a woman who'd once been his mother's friend.

He glanced again at Jean. Just look at her, a picture of innocence, as though butter wouldn't melt in her mouth. And what, if he had taken Moira's advice, would have happened when they were married – he was fairly certain she would have accepted – would she, lovemaking denied her by him, continue on with Andrew? Would Andrew have continued with the affair, cuckolding his own father with his stepmother? The thought sickened him.

'Bit liverish today, Pa?' Peter asked. 'You took more on board last night than you have for a while.'

'A bit,' Murdo grunted.

'I say, these kippers are excellent,' Geoffrey enthused which won him an admiring glance from Charlotte.

Andrew sat facing Jean. 'And how are you this morning, Mrs Ritchie?'

'Couldn't be better,' she smiled in reply.

'I feel on top form myself.' His time with her had been wonderful, and he had been totally drained when he'd eventually crept back to his room where he'd instantly fallen into a deep sleep. He was already wondering if he dared a return visit that night.

'Pa.'

Murdo looked up at Charlotte who quite clearly was

radiantly happy. 'I did say to you last night, but thank you again for Mother's ring.'

Murdo's expression softened. 'Been in my mind for years.'

Charlotte twisted the ring. 'It fits so perfectly. And . . .' She hesitated. 'I never knew you'd kept it. You've never once said.'

'I kept a number of your Mother's things that I've never mentioned. Personal things, you understand.'

'What about her wedding ring, Pa?' Nell queried.

He nodded. 'That's one of them.' It resided in the same black box from which he'd taken the engagement ring.

'Any other jewellery?' Nell further asked.

'Bits and pieces. Your mother was never a great one for jewellery.'

'She did have a beautiful pearl necklace. I recall that quite distinctly,' Jean said.

Murdo regarded her with an icy stare. When she left after her visit she would never enter his house again. Not while he was alive.

'That's in my study along with the other items,' Murdo said, directing his reply to Nell. What he didn't say was that he occasionally took out these various bits and pieces and fondled them in memory.

'I love pearls,' Nell declared.

It was daft keeping these things shut away, Murdo thought. Far better, now the girls were grown up, for them to have them. It wasn't as though they'd be leaving the family after all. With the exception of the wedding ring that is, he'd hold onto that.

'Then you shall have the necklace,' he stated gruffly.

Nell's eyes flew open. 'Oh, Pa!'

'And there's a cameo brooch she was fond of. You can have that, Charlotte, if you wish.'

'Please, Pa.'

Murdo pushed his plate away and laid his napkin aside. 'I'm going out for a walk to clear my head. I'll see you all later.'

He had to stop himself shooting Jean Ritchie a withering look as he left.

Murdo gasped and clutched his chest, his face screwing up in pain. It only lasted for a few seconds, and then the agony eased.

Murdo staggered over to a large rock and sat. He sucked in breath after breath.

'Damn,' he muttered. 'Damn damn damn.' This was because he'd overdone it the night before, had to be. It was his first attack since seeing Mr Gillespie.

He'd have to be more careful in future he told himself. No more exceptions to the rule, not even at Hogmanay. He didn't want to be pushing up the daisies quite yet.

He sat for a good ten minutes to recover before getting to his feet again and returning the way he'd come.

'I wonder when I'll get engaged and who it'll be to?' Wonky mused to Nell. She'd come to Drummond House to have another look at Charlotte's ring only to find that Charlotte and Geoffrey had gone out for a spin in his car.

'Only time will tell,' Nell replied.

'Or when you'll get engaged and to whom,' Wonky further speculated.

Nell sighed, 'If I ever do get engaged that is.'

'Of course you will!' Wonky assured her. 'It's only a matter of when.'

'I sometimes wonder . . .' Nell trailed off. Would her prince come one day? She fervently hoped so. It would be ghastly ending up as an old maid. She thought of Alison Skene, and shuddered. There was no doubt in Alison's case.

'When I get married I wish it to be to someone fabulously rich,' Wonky declared. 'And we'll have six children, three of each.'

Nell laughed. 'Does he have to be rich?'

'Oh yes, most definitely.' She became introspective. 'You forget I've been relatively poor all my life, Nell, a minister's stipend doesn't go all that far, believe me.' A trace of jealousy crept into her voice. 'Unlike you and Charlotte. You've had everything from a doting, wealthy father.'

True, Nell thought. Murdo had spoiled them, though the reason for that was obvious. 'And what about love?' she asked softly. 'Suppose you fall for a poor man?'

Wonky bit her lip.

'Well?'

'I shall try very hard only to fall for a rich man,' Wonky replied defiantly.

Nell had intended telling Wonky about the pearl necklace Murdo had promised her, but now decided not to. She didn't want to rub her cousin's face in it.

'Jack Riach would be perfect,' Wonky stated dreamily.

'He is a nice chap.'

'He's more than that. He's scrummy.'

Jack didn't appeal to Nell at all. Oh, he was pleasant enough, but that was as far as it went where she was concerned.

'Except he's never shown the slightest interest despite my making it clear I was interested in him,' Wonky went on.

'Not the slightest?'

Wonky shook her head. 'I obviously don't appeal to him. God knows why.'

'Why does anyone appeal to anyone else? It just happens that's all. It's either there or it isn't. Look at Charlotte and Geoffrey, that was love at first sight.'

'Lucky thing,' Wonky said, meaning Charlotte.

'Yes she is, I agree.'

'So handsome too,' Wonky mused, thinking what she wouldn't have given for it to have been her Geoffrey had fallen for.

'Oh, how I wish I could get away from here,' Wonky went on. 'But as you know, Father won't hear of it. I have to stay at home and be the dutiful, well-brought-up daughter.'

'There are worse things in life than being that.'

'Are there?' Wonky sighed wistfully.

Peter was standing staring out of his bedroom window when Geoffrey and Charlotte arrived back in the Humber. They were both laughing as they emerged from the car, Geoffrey dashing round to open Charlotte's door and assist her out. Geoffrey quickly pecked her on the cheek.

What made him so different to other men? Peter wondered. It wasn't as though he wasn't manly, no one could ever accuse him of that. But when it came to women . . . They simply left him cold.

Grizelda McPherson had been after him again the previous night. Grizelda had the sort of figure most young women would have died for. She was intelligent too, you could always have a good conversation with Grizelda.

At least he had his job, he thought. He enjoyed that. And his friends, Jack Riach for example. They were a spiffing lot. Great fun most of the time.

Ah well, he was as the good Lord had made him. He could only presume there must be a reason for that.

Murdo entered his study and sat down. He was dying for a dram but forbade himself from having one. That incident out on his walk had frightened him more than he cared to admit. He again told himself he'd have to be more careful in future.

He thought again of Jean and Andrew. Should he say something to the lad? He pondered that.

No, he decided. It might cause a rift between Andrew and himself which he didn't want. Best let things go on as they were.

How on earth had Andrew become involved with Jean? he wondered yet again. And how could she possibly bring herself to go to bed with her friend's son? Why, it was almost like incest. Louise would have been horrified.

Had it happened during Jean's previous visit? Then he remembered they'd travelled back to Perth together. Had the relationship been sparked off then? He supposed he'd never know for he'd never ask and Andrew would hardly volunteer the information.

What, though, if the lad was serious? Surely not. The age difference was far too great for anything to come of the relationship. It was a transitory thing, had to be.

Please God.

'I can't tell you how delighted we are with your engagement,' Gillian Armitage said to Charlotte, having found her alone in a small sitting room, Geoffrey temporarily off tinkering with the Humber.

'Why thank you.'

Gillian beamed at her future daughter-in-law. 'Such a good match I think. The pair of you are so well suited.'

'I believe so.'

Gillian sat beside Charlotte on a floral-patterned sofa and took one of Charlotte's hands in hers. 'I'm looking forward to being a grandmother. I hope you won't keep me waiting too long after you're married.'

Charlotte blushed. 'That's entirely up to nature, Mrs Armitage.'

'Of course it is, but you know what I mean.'

'I will certainly be doing my duty, Mrs Armitage, you can rest assured of that.' She recalled her conversation with Jean Ritchie, not a duty but something to be enjoyed. However, duty seemed the correct word to use in these circumstances.

'His father always wanted him to follow him into the firm you know, but Geoffrey had other ideas.'

'Yes, he's mentioned.'

'A very strong-willed person is our Geoffrey. And he adores the army. Simply adores it. Both Robert and I are quite certain he'll go far.'

Charlotte smiled. 'Andrew speaks highly of him. One who's well liked by his fellow officers and men alike.'

It pleased Gillian to hear that. 'It was so kind of your father to invite us here. We're both having a wonderful time. I must say, I like your family. All of them without exception.'

'And we all like you and Mr Armitage. Nell remarked on that earlier.'

At which point they were interrupted by Geoffrey's return.

After a further short conversation Gillian left the young lovers to themselves.

It was all very satisfactory, she thought. Very satisfactory indeed.

'I'll call in next Wednesday evening,' Andrew whispered to Jean as he escorted her to the Rolls-Royce which would take her to the station.

'I'll be expecting you.'

He wished he could kiss her goodbye, but that was out of the question.

Jean climbed into the Rolls to which her luggage had already been strapped. She waved to Andrew as the Rolls purred away.

She leant back against the leather upholstery and frowned. Murdo had wished her a gruff goodbye at the conclusion of breakfast and that had been that. His manner had been distinctly cold over the past few days, something she hadn't mentioned to Andrew and Andrew hadn't seemed to have noticed.

Did Murdo suspect, or even *know* about them. She

couldn't imagine how. Andrew had only come to her room that one night and assured her afterwards he hadn't been seen.

So why the change in Murdo's attitude? Was he merely guessing or was there more to it than that? He'd been friendly enough when she'd arrived, and then the change.

Perhaps he wasn't feeling well. Perhaps . . . No, it wasn't that, he'd been friendly enough to the Armitages. It had only been her he'd been chilly towards.

So why?

If he did know then how he'd found out was beyond her.

Charlotte found Miss MacQueen in the linen cupboard where she was counting out sheets. Miss MacQueen was their housekeeper, an austere woman in her fifties who ran the house smoothly and efficiently. The staff, with the exception of Cook and McPhie, were said to be terrified of her. A hard woman, though fair and not unkind.

Little was known of Miss MacQueen other than she came originally from the Isle of Skye, but rumour had it she'd had a beau in her youth, a fisherman who'd been drowned at sea. A tragedy she'd never fully recovered from.

'How are you today, Miss MacQueen?' Charlotte enquired. As the elder female of the family it was her task to act as the lady of the house and deal with the house-keeper and cook.

'Fine thank you, Miss Charlotte. Though displeased with McPhie.'

Oh dear, Charlotte thought. Here we go again. Miss MacQueen and McPhie didn't get on.

'What is it this time?'

'I've asked him twice to mend the runny tap in the laundry room which he still hasn't done.' Besides being chauffeur McPhie was also the odd job man round Drummond House.

'I see.'

Miss MacQueen sniffed. 'He's a law unto himself that man.'

'Quite,' Charlotte agreed.

'Would you care to speak to him. He'll take far more notice of you than me.'

Which was true enough, Charlotte thought. 'I'll do that right away. I'll see if I can find him. Is there anything else?'

'Not for the moment thank you.'

'Right then,' said Charlotte, turning to go.

'Oh, Miss Charlotte!'

Charlotte stopped and turned again. Miss MacQueen's usually stern features softened. 'I haven't had a proper chance to congratulate you on your engagement. I'm very happy for you.'

For a moment Miss MacQueen's eyes took on a faraway look and Charlotte wondered if she was thinking of her long-dead beau. Then the look was gone.

Charlotte smiled. 'Exciting, isn't it?'

'Very.'

Charlotte didn't know why she did what she did next, but somehow it seemed right. She went to Miss MacQueen and kissed her on the cheek.

'Thank you. I appreciate your congratulations.' And with that she hurried off to try and find McPhie.

When she was gone the faraway look returned to Miss

MacQueen's eyes and it was some minutes before she returned to what she'd been doing.

'What do you think of women having the vote, Pa?' Nell asked. The family were in the drawing room, Murdo reading while Charlotte and Peter played a board game.

Murdo glanced up at his daughter and frowned. 'I'm not certain really. One thing I am certain about is that I don't believe in violence.'

'You mean Mrs Pankhurst?' Emmeline Pankhurst was due in court the following day on bomb charges relating to the attack the previous week when an explosion had wrecked Lloyd George's new golf villa at Walton Heath in Surrey. No one had been hurt but workmen had been due to start only twenty minutes after the bomb went off. According to newspaper reports the explosion was so strong some local residents had thought it an earthquake.

Murdo nodded. 'Dreadful woman to have done what she did. A quite outrageous act. It's a mercy no one was killed.'

'There are many think she's a heroine.'

Peter glanced across at Nell. 'She could easily have been a murderess and there's nothing heroic about that.'

'It's what she stands for I'm asking about. Not the woman herself.'

'Women and the vote!' Peter laughed. 'Stuff and nonsense. What do women know about politics and the like? They should leave all that to men.'

Charlotte regarded him coldly. 'I don't see why women shouldn't have the vote. They comprise half the population after all. Your ideas are quite outmoded, brother dear.'

'Are they indeed,' he replied, voice dripping sarcasm.

'Pa, you haven't answered my question,' Nell prompted.

'It's something to which I haven't given a great deal of thought,' Murdo confessed. 'But yes, I believe the day will come when they will get the vote. Though I think that day is still far off. Considerably so in fact.'

Peter laughed again. 'They'll never get it, Pa. Not in a thousand years. You mark my words, it simply won't be allowed. The whole thing is quite preposterous.'

'I suppose you think we're all feather-brained idiots,' Charlotte accused hotly.

Peter shrugged.

'And I'm included in that generalisation.'

'And me,' pouted Nell.

'Maybe Mrs Pankhurst should have tried to blow up you and your beliefs,' Charlotte muttered.

'That's enough,' Murdo admonished her.

'Do we have a couple of budding suffragettes here?' Peter teased.

'Fat chance we have of being suffragettes in Dalneil,' Nell retorted.

'You could always chain yourself to the distillery,' Peter further teased. 'That would be a fine sight. Or how about the pub? That would be a laugh.'

Charlotte and Nell glared at him. 'For someone who's reputedly, by gender that is, supposedly so intelligent you don't half come out with some stupid suggestions,' Charlotte said.

Murdo sighed. 'I think we should terminate this conversation, don't you?'

Peter stood and crossed to the whisky decanter. 'I've had enough of the game, sis.'

'Only because I'm beating you.'

He smiled as he poured a dram. It was true, he didn't like losing. 'No, because it's boring me,' he lied.

'Hah!'

Peter waved the decanter at Murdo. 'Pa?'

Murdo stared enviously at the whisky, but he'd already had his quota. 'No thank you, son,' he replied reluctantly.

'If I lived in one of the big cities I'd be a suffragette,' Nell declared.

Murdo sighed again. 'Would you really?'

'Oh yes.'

'And so would I,' Charlotte added.

Peter regarded his sisters with amusement. 'I doubt Geoffrey would be pleased about that,' he said to Charlotte.

Charlotte had no idea what Geoffrey thought of the matter. It was a subject they'd never discussed. She didn't reply.

'Well?' Peter prompted.

'There are times when you can be quite horrid,' she snapped.

'Game, set and match I believe,' Peter murmured, and had a sip of his drink.

'Enough,' Murdo said sternly. 'Enough.'

'I think . . .' Charlotte began.

'I said *enough*,' Murdo repeated in a voice that made Charlotte blink and shut up.

'I'm going to bed,' Nell declared.

'Me too,' said Charlotte, rising.

They heard Peter chuckling as they left the room.

Chapter 8

'I say, you chaps, I'm drunk as a lord,' Bobby Baxter declared.

His three companions, out on the town celebrating Geoffrey's engagement, laughed.

Andrew knew he was fairly tipsy as well, but then he would hope to be considering the amount of alcohol he'd consumed. Geoffrey was in a similar state.

'Why don't we move on?' John Blair suggested. All four of them were equal-ranking officers in the Watch.

Bobby hiccuped. 'Jolly good idea. But where to?'

They all thought about that. They'd already done several pubs and were now in the bar of the St Johnstoun Hotel.

Andrew ran a hand through his hair and tried to think, a difficult process as his mind was quite muzzy.

John leaned across to Geoffrey. 'Enjoying yourself, old bean?'

'Thoroughly. Though the room keeps going round and round.'

They all laughed and Bobby slapped his thigh which

caused several of the other patrons to glance across at them.

'Ssshhh!' John counselled. 'Don't want to get thrown out, what? Regimental honour and all that.'

The other three nodded sagely.

'I know where we could go,' Bobby declared.

His companions looked on expectantly.

'Mulligan's.'

Andrew rocked back in his seat. He'd heard of Mulligan's, a gaming salon, but had never been there.

'What do you chaps think?' Bobby queried.

'Mulligan's,' Geoffrey mused. 'Don't you have to be a member or something?'

Bobby tapped his nose. 'In the know, old boy. My father's a member and I've been a few times with him. They'll let us in all right. Might cost a couple of bob at the door, but so what.'

'Then let's go there,' John declared, finishing his whisky and standing up. The others did likewise.

'Cab or walk?' Andrew queried when they were outside the hotel.

'Cab, of course,' said John. 'We're officers and gentlemen, bad form to be seen staggering down the street.'

That produced another laugh for they all knew it would have been the case.

'Now sober up,' Bobby said when they arrived at Mulligan's, a detached house indistinguishable from any of the others in the area. There was no outward sign that it was a gaming salon. Stepping forward he tugged on the bell pull.

The man who answered the door was smartly dressed in a double-breasted pin stripe. His face had the battered look of an ex-pugilist. 'May I help you?' he asked in a gravelly voice.

Bobby explained who he was and enquired politely if he and his friends could come in.

The man's keen gaze swept over them. 'There would be an entrance fee, sir,' he said. And stated the amount.

'That all right, chaps?'

Wallets were produced and money changed hands. Then the man stepped aside and gestured they should enter.

Their coats and hats were taken by a maid who then disappeared off into a side room.

Bobby rubbed his hands and led the way while the man followed the maid.

The main room was formed from two large ones that had been knocked together. Andrew judged there to be roughly thirty patrons present, most of them at the various gaming tables. Elegantly dressed young women who Bobby explained worked for the establishment were there to assist or simply chat if that was what was required. One of these, a pretty dark-haired girl, now approached them.

'What would your pleasure be, sirs?' she asked.

'A drink to start with if you don't mind,' Bobby, who'd temporarily become their leader, replied.

'Certainly. Champagne?'

'That would be wonderful.'

'I shan't be long, sirs.' And with that she walked off.

Andrew gazed about him. The wallpaper was flock and

two large crystal chandeliers dangled from the ceiling. If it hadn't been for the gaming tables he might have been in a decent drawing room. He felt quite relaxed and not nearly as tipsy as he'd been earlier.

'These girls go upstairs if you wish,' Bobby whispered to them.

Andrew raised an eyebrow. He hadn't been aware *that* activity took place at Mulligan's. He glanced with new interest at the girls wondering what it would be like to go to bed with someone other than Jean. He had to admit he was tempted.

The girl returned with a silver tray on which there were four flutes of champagne. 'Will you be playing tonight, sir?' she asked Bobby as he took a glass.

'Certainly shall. Though not quite at present.'

'I understand, sir.' She gave them all a sweet smile and went off again.

'What a corker!' Geoffrey breathed.

'Down, boy, you're engaged,' Andrew, eyes twinkling, told him.

'Can still look though, can't I?'

'No harm in that, dear chap,' Andrew agreed.

They crossed to a sofa where they sat and observed the proceedings. After a short while Bobby declared he was going to play cards and John said he would join him.

'Are you going to play?' Geoffrey asked Andrew after they'd gone.

'Might do. You?'

'I fancy a couple of spins at roulette. I'm feeling lucky tonight.'

Andrew thought he might try that as well.

After another glass of champagne they rose and went to the roulette wheel.

Andrew collapsed onto his bed, rolled over onto his back and laughed. He'd won a hundred pounds, a whole hundred! He could hardly believe it.

What fun the evening had been. He'd thoroughly enjoyed himself. They all had. A spiffing celebratory night out.

As for Mulligan's, well . . .

His head dropped sideways as he abruptly fell asleep. Seconds later he began to snore.

Nell was returning from Dalneil where she'd been on an errand when the familiar tingling and trembling of the hands took hold of her. She came up short and stared out over the winter landscape.

Her sight wavered, and then cleared. There he was, the Highlander and his wife, in a room she recognised as belonging to his house. A door was thrown open and another man hurried in, obviously agitated.

The Highlander, who'd been sitting, immediately came to his feet and went to the newcomer. A short conversation took place during which the Highlander also became agitated. At the conclusion of the conversation he crossed to his wife, who had a tartan shawl draped round her shoulders, and warmly embraced her.

The Highlander's two young children came running into the room through another door that was open and were immediately scooped up by him who held one in each arm.

The Highlander threw back his head and roared with laughter. He was still laughing when the vision started to fade. And still laughing when it blinked out of existence and Nell found herself back in the present.

She shivered, a shiver that had nothing whatsoever to do with the extremely cold day.

It was a Friday night and Andrew was at a loose end. Normally he and Geoffrey would have gone out somewhere together but Geoffrey was on duty as was Bobby Baxter. He'd already knocked on John Blair's door, getting no reply. Nor could he find John anywhere else.

'Damn,' he muttered to himself. It would have been lovely to go and see Jean except it wasn't an agreed night for him to visit and he never called unless it had been arranged.

What to do? he wondered. He could go to the officers' mess, he thought, but that had been almost deserted when he'd looked in a short while previously.

And then he had an idea. Why not go to Mulligan's? The man on the door had already let him in once so why not twice?

Yes, he decided. Mulligan's it was.

Andrew reluctantly left the roulette table. Best to finish while he was ahead, he told himself. This time his winnings amounted to just short of a hundred and fifty pounds. He crossed to one of the sofas dotted round the room and sat.

'You did well again, sir.'

He'd been so bemused by the situation he'd neither seen or heard her approach. It was the same girl who'd greeted him on his last visit.

Andrew nodded. 'Yes I have. Jolly good, eh?'

'Jolly good indeed. Can I get you anything, sir?'

He could certainly use a drink. 'Champagne would be pleasant.'

'I'll fetch it for you.'

He studied her as she walked away and, to his surprise, suddenly found himself aroused. He again wondered what it would be like to sleep with someone other than Jean. He was still thinking about that when the girl returned.

'Will you join me for a while?' he requested with a smile.

'Certainly, sir.'

She sat beside him.

'I should have told you to get a drink as well.'

'I couldn't do that, I'm afraid. It's forbidden while on duty.'

He nodded his understanding. 'I'm Andrew by the way.'

'And I'm Tina.'

A somewhat common name he thought, though she was fairly well spoken. He wondered what her background was that it had brought her to work in a place like Mulligan's.

'I'm an army officer,' he explained.

'Oh?'

'With the Black Watch.'

'I must say you look the officer type. It's the bearing that gives it away.'

He gazed into her dark, intelligent eyes. 'How old are you, Tina?'

'Nineteen.'

He'd have thought older. 'Do you get many officers in here?'

'From time to time. It varies.'

He had a long swallow of champagne. 'I really enjoyed myself tonight.'

'I should hope so, winning all that money. You must be frightfully clever at roulette.'

He laughed. 'Lucky more like.'

'You're being modest now.'

He was still aroused, an arousal that had become a positive ache. He hoped it wasn't obvious.

'Are you going to become a member?' she asked.

'I hadn't thought about that. But yes, perhaps I shall.' Reflecting it would be easier that way, as he certainly intended coming again.

'I can arrange it for you before you go.'

'What's the subscription?'

She told him and he considered it reasonable.

Andrew cleared his throat. 'I, eh . . . I believe you girls go upstairs. Is that correct?'

She gave him a sweet smile and nodded.

'Can I ask how much?' He dropped his gaze. 'I'm afraid all this is rather new to me. Paying I mean.'

'There's no need to be embarrassed, Andrew. Now, which of the girls has caught your eye and I'll sort it out for you.'

'Why you, of course,' he replied hastily.

'I see.'

'How, eh . . . how much?'

'I'm not cheap, Andrew. None of us is.'

'How much?' he repeated.

'Do you wish it to be a short time or to spend the entire night?'

The ache became even more pronounced. 'All night,' he breathed, and drank more champagne. God, this was exciting. Going to bed with a tart. And such a gorgeous one at that. If he'd seen her in the street he'd never have guessed in a thousand years that's what she was.

'Again it depends on what you wish.'

He stared blankly at her. 'I don't understand?'

'Do you wish it straightforward or do you have something else in mind?'

'Like what?'

He blushed bright red as she explained. 'Straightforward,' he croaked. Sweet Jesus! Did people really get up to those sort of things? It was mind boggling to say the least.

Tina named a sum.

She was right, he thought. It was expensive. But what the hell, he was flush with funds. 'Agreed.'

'Then follow me, bring your champagne if you like.'

En route from the room Tina had a brief word with another of the girls.

In the hallway she slipped an arm round his. 'All night it is,' she said.

Andrew swallowed hard.

It had been different, Andrew reflected as he made his way through early morning mist back to the barracks. The same act of course, but different nonetheless.

Obviously her body had been younger than Jean's and she'd had far smaller breasts and a smaller bottom, the latter delectable to caress. She'd also been firmer than Jean who had an overall voluptuous softness about her.

He chuckled. Now a member of Mulligan's he'd be back there at the first opportunity.

For the roulette and Tina.

Wonky emerged from the local shop in Dalneil humming jauntily to herself. She felt it to be one of those wonderful days when it's glorious to be alive. She halted when Jack Riach rode up.

Jack dismounted and doffed his hat to her. 'Good morning, Wonky. You seem particularly happy today.'

She beamed at him; here was a piece of luck. 'I'm always happy, Jack. It's part of my nature.'

He laughed. 'I wish I could say the same.'

'And what brings you into Dalneil? The pub I'll be bound.'

' 'Fraid not, though it's a thought. No, I have to pick up a few items from the shop.'

'You should get married then you could leave that sort of thing to your wife,' she teased.

He laughed again. 'Are you trying to marry me off, Wonky Comyn?'

'Not in the least. Though I think it's high time you and my cousin Peter got round to it. You can't remain bachelors for ever you know.'

'Why not?' he replied, eyes twinkling.

'Because it would be a waste of two fine men. Besides, you want children, don't you? A son and heir for a start.'

'There is that,' he agreed.

'So what's holding you back?'

'My my, we are personal today.'

She blushed. 'Sorry, I didn't mean to be. Nonetheless, what I say is true.'

It amused him to see her discomfiture. She was a handsome young woman he thought. Now why hadn't he realised that before? Probably because he always thought of her as a child, being that much older himself, and had simply failed to notice she'd grown up. Good figure too. He wondered what her legs were like.

Wonky sensed something of what was going through his mind which thrilled her. Had she finally captured his attention at long last? She prayed she had.

Intelligent too, Jack was thinking. A quick mind, he liked that. He couldn't be doing with boring women, no matter how good looking.

'I suppose I've never married because I've never found the right person,' he said.

'Maybe the right person's been under your very nose all along,' she declared, amazed at her boldness.

'Could be,' he mused. 'There again, maybe I'm just shy.'

Now it was her turn to laugh. 'I don't believe that, Jack Riach. You shy! If you're that then I'm a blackamoor.'

He was though, but only with the fair sex. He liked them well enough, there was no doubting that. It was just . . . well he didn't know. All he could put it down to was the fact he was, beneath the outward bravado, shy.

'How's Peter?' he asked, changing the subject. 'I haven't seen him since Hogmanay.'

'He's all right. Same as usual.'

'I must go over to Drummond House and root him out one weekend. That'll be a night for the pub.'

She fervently wished Jack would take her to the pub, but that was totally out of the question. He could go there but certainly not a woman of her standing, far less the minister's daughter. The village would be scandalised.

'Well, it's been nice talking to you, Wonky. Now I'd better get on.' And having said that he tied his horse's reins to a pole situated for that purpose.

She made the first move. 'Bye bye then.'

'Bye.'

He watched her speculatively as she walked away. Wonky Comyn? Ridiculous nickname of course but it somehow suited her. It was a thought, he mused, entering the shop.

'You said what!' Nell exclaimed.

'That it was high time he and your brother Peter got married. And so it is.'

'Somewhat forward, wasn't it?' Charlotte smiled.

Wonky shrugged. 'He said I was being a bit personal. But there you are. The point is, I do believe he might be interested in me. I'm certain I detected something of that nature.'

'Are you sure you're not imagining things?' Charlotte queried.

Wonky frowned. 'I don't think so. It's so hard to explain. He was looking at me in a way he's never done before.'

Nell giggled.

'Anyway, we'll see what happens. If anything,' Wonky said, beginning to wish she hadn't confided in her cousins who'd put doubt into her mind.

'Well, I hope you're right,' Charlotte declared. 'Jack Riach is a good man and much respected.'

Wonky thought of being in Jack's arms, of him kissing her. Oh please please please . . .

'Fancy a drink in the mess tonight, old thing?' Geoffrey asked, the pair of them striding from the parade ground where they'd been putting a detachment of men through their paces.

'No, I've something else planned,' Andrew replied.

Geoffrey's gaze slid sideways to stare at Andrew. 'Do I detect a female in these proceedings?'

Andrew didn't want to tell his friend about Mulligan's and Tina, particularly the latter. He wanted to keep that to himself.

'Now why would you say that?'

'You've been so secretive lately. Always slipping off and not letting on where.'

'You're exaggerating, Geoffrey. Always indeed!' He laughed.

'There's something in the wind though. Bobby mentioned it only the other night. Not that I needed to be told.'

'Stuff and nonsense, I assure you.'

But Geoffrey knew better. Andrew was up to something, and if he wanted to keep quiet about it that was his business. He wouldn't pry any further.

'It should be a good night in the mess. It's Major Brown's birthday.'

'I'll be sorry to miss it.'

Geoffrey let the matter drop.

He sat disconsolately on a sofa in Mulligan's staring at the carpet underfoot.

'Andrew?'

He glanced up and smiled. 'Hello, Tina. How are you?'

'Fine. But you don't seem your usual cheery self.'

'I lost tonight. First time ever.'

She pulled a sympathetic face. 'I am sorry.' She sat beside him. 'Badly?'

'Twenty-odd pounds. Not a lot, but still a loss. I decided luck was running against me and got out.'

She squeezed his arm. 'You can't always win. It's gambling after all. Sometimes you win, sometimes you lose.'

'Oh well,' he sighed. 'I'm still quids up overall. That's the main thing. Where have you been anyway? I looked for you when I arrived but you were nowhere to be seen.'

Tina glanced away. 'Where do you think I was? You know what I do here. You're not the only client I have.'

He was suddenly covered with embarrassment. For some reason the obvious had never crossed his mind. He'd thought she might be ill.

'I see,' he murmured.

Tina bit her lip, having taken a genuine liking to Andrew. 'Will you play again tonight? Your luck might change.'

He shook his head.

'Well, I'm free if you have that in mind.'

Directly after another man? He wasn't too keen on that idea. There again, Tina looked gorgeous as usual. He felt a familiar stirring in his loins.

'Perhaps you haven't enough money with you?'

'Oh I have,' he replied quickly.

'Well then?'

He smiled at her, desire mounting within him. His gaze

dropped to the deep blue dress she was wearing and he thought of what lay beneath. 'All right,' he replied softly.

'That's my boy.'

Jean came onto an elbow and stared in puzzlement at Andrew lying beside her. 'Where did you learn that little refinement?' she queried.

Andrew immediately tensed, his mind racing. 'What refinement?'

'You know very well what I mean.' This time her tone was accusatory.

Andrew pretended to think. 'Oh yes that,' he answered eventually. 'I didn't learn it anywhere. It just sort of happened naturally.'

Her gaze was level, her eyes now cold. 'You wouldn't lie to me I hope?'

He laughed. 'Don't be ridiculous, Jean. Why should I do that?'

'You might if there was someone else.'

God, he thought. How stupid of him. The refinement as she'd called it was one he'd picked up from Tina, employed with Jean in the heat of the moment.

'There isn't, Jean. I swear.'

Her eyes had become gimlets, boring into him. 'If you wish to stop seeing me, Andrew, you only have to say.' That was the last thing she wanted.

Panic welled in him. 'I do want to keep seeing you, Jean. And there isn't anyone else. On my mother's grave.'

That reassured Jean. She believed him. Surely he wouldn't make an oath like that if he wasn't telling the truth. 'Come here,' she smiled, and drew him to her.

Andrew buried his face in the valley of her breasts, his heart beating wildly. That had been a near thing, too damn near. He'd have to be more careful in future.

Wonky had given Jack Riach something to think about. The lassie was right, it was time he got married. He poured himself a dram and sat, his mind roaming over the available girls in the area.

There was Winnie Urquhart, a possibility. Except for her temper that is, for which she was well known. He dismissed Winnie, he'd never get on with a woman like that.

Then there was Flora McEwan, a pretty little thing who nearly always made him laugh when they spoke. The trouble with her was her nose, a hooter if ever there was. Sweet personality though, that counted in her favour.

One by one he went through the list, leaving Wonky till last.

'Wonky Comyn,' he murmured, swilling the whisky round in his glass, seeing her again as she'd been outside the shop. He hadn't felt shy with her at all.

'Hmmh,' he mused.

The Comyns' only maid answered Jack's knock. 'Is the minister home I wonder?' he smiled.

'He is, sir.'

'Do you think I might have a word with him? The name's Mr Riach.'

'I'm certain you can, sir. If you'd care to come in.'

Jack stepped into the manse's hallway.

Chapter 9

Nell sat abruptly up in bed, her chest heaving. She'd been dreaming about the Highlander's wife, watching the woman going about her daily chores.

Such a vivid dream, everything crystal clear. Even now, awake, she could still see the woman's face with the blue eyes, the slightly aquiline nose, the full lips.

Nell frowned. In her dream the woman had reminded her of someone, someone she knew in the present. Or had it been merely her imagination?

Nell considered that. No, the woman had definitely reminded her of someone.

She laid her head back on the pillows, pulled the bedclothes up to her chin, and tried to think who.

'More tea, Mr Riach?' Moira Comyn asked politely.

'No thank you. I've already had three cups. Any more and I'd be awash.' He'd asked Tom Comyn's permission to call on his daughter and permission had been granted. This was his first visit as suitor and appallingly dreary it was proving to be.

'How about you, dear?' Moira queried of her husband.

Tom shook his head. 'But I will have another biscuit.'

Wonky rose from her chair and offered her father the large plate of assorted biscuits. Preceding those had been small, neatly cut triangular sandwiches with the crusts removed.

'Thank you, Veronica,' Tom murmured, making his choice.

Wonky returned the plate to the table and sat again. She wished her parents would leave her and Jack alone but there was no chance of that. Not on his first visit anyway.

'How are those sheep of yours coming along?' Tom inquired. 'You seem to have a fairly sizeable flock.'

'They're fine, minister, thriving. I have a little over two hundred.'

'Quite a job in the lambing season, I dare say.'

'I have two men working for me. We manage.'

'I'd love to see a lamb being born,' Wonky enthused.

Tom's eyebrows shot up. 'Hardly a sentiment to express over tea, Veronica. In fact, hardly a sentiment for a well-brought-up young lady to express in any circumstances. The very idea.'

Wonky's face fell. 'Sorry, Father.'

'I should say.'

'You like animals then?' Jack queried.

'Oh yes, very much so. I'm just an old-fashioned country girl at heart.'

Tom harumphed on hearing that.

A few seconds silence ensued. 'Those were lovely sandwiches,' Jack said to Moira, desperately trying to make conversation.

Moira inclined her head. 'Most kind of you, Mr Riach.'

'My wife is a wonderful cook and baker,' Tom commented, smiling warmly at Moira.

'I can imagine,' Jack said. She must certainly eat enough from the looks of her, he thought.

'You must come to supper one night and sample her cuisine.'

Jack groaned inwardly, he could well imagine what that would be like, tedious in the extreme. 'I shall look forward to it,' he lied. He turned his attention to Wonky. 'Are you also a good cook and baker, Veronica?' He'd realised early on that she was always referred to as Veronica by her parents and had thought it best to do the same while in their company.

'I have my moments.'

'Makes a succulent steak and kidney pudding,' Tom declared. 'And her apple crumble isn't bad either. Eh, my dear?'

Wonky gave him a thin smile.

More silence ensued, broken only by the steady ticking of the clock on the mantelpiece. Jack decided he'd have to get out of there or scream. A glance at the clock told him he'd been with the Comyns an hour; it seemed an eternity. He rose and placed his cup and plate on the table.

'Thank you for a delightful tea, Mr and Mrs Comyn, but I'm afraid I must go. I have animals to feed.' The latter a fib, the feeding would have already been done.

'So soon!' Moira exclaimed in disappointment. She wasn't half as disappointed as Wonky who knew the visit had been a total disaster. Why were her parents so formal and stuffy! For what might have been the millionth time in her life she wished she'd been born a Drummond.

Tom also rose and placed his cup and plate on the table, carefully aligning them alongside Jack's. 'I'll ring for Heather. She'll show you out.'

'I can do that, Father,' Wonky said hastily.

He frowned. That wasn't at all correct. Then he saw the pleading in his daughter's eyes and relented. 'Certainly, Veronica, if you wish.'

'I'm so sorry,' Wonky apologised quietly when she and Jack were in the hallway.

'That's all right.'

'I should have warned you but had no way of doing so.'

They reached the door which he opened.

'You will come again, Jack, won't you? Don't let my parents put you off.'

'I shall be in church Sunday morning. Perhaps I can walk you home?'

'Oh, yes please,' she smiled.

When the door was shut behind him Jack heaved a huge sigh of relief. He untied his horse and leapt into the saddle.

His next stop was the pub and a much needed drink.

'It's been so long, darling,' Geoffrey said throatily to Charlotte, who was in his arms. He had arrived at Drummond House only minutes before. A tactful Nell had left them alone when Geoffrey had joined her and Charlotte.

'I know.'

He gazed into her eyes, his own shining. 'I've missed you so much.'

'And I you.'

'You're even more beautiful than I remembered.'

She laughed. 'I think I've told you before, Geoffrey Armitage, flattery will get you everywhere. Now, how long have you got?'

'Five days only, I'm afraid. I was hoping for a week or even more but five days was all I could manage.'

'Don't worry, we'll make good use of every minute of them.'

He could contain himself no longer. His lips met hers and she melted against him.

'Oh, my angel. My wonderful, wonderful angel,' he breathed when the kiss was over.

Andrew accepted the glass of champagne he'd requested with a trembling hand. He'd just won three hundred pounds at roulette which more than made up for the few small losses he'd previously sustained. His luck had returned with a vengeance.

He caught Tina's eye, where she was sitting with a middle-aged patron, and nodded to the door. She got the message.

As soon as she could Tina excused herself and followed Andrew upstairs.

Paying beforehand, as was the custom, he delighted her by including a very large tip.

Peter placed the tray of drinks he'd fetched from the bar on the small circular table where he and Jack had decided to sit. They were in the Dalneil pub which both used frequently.

Jack lifted a pint and took a deep swallow. 'I was ready for that,' he grinned.

Peter removed the remaining three glasses then stood the tray by a leg of the table. '*Slainthe!*' he toasted, taking a sip of whisky.

Peter glanced round the pub, knowing every face there. He'd always enjoyed its warm cosy atmosphere.

'So what's new with you?' Jack inquired amiably.

'It's not what's new with me, but you. I hear you've called on Wonky.'

Jack's grin widened. 'True enough.'

Peter leant back in his chair and studied his friend. 'When did this start?'

'It was something Wonky herself said about it being high time I was married. She also said the same about you.'

'Me!'

'That's right.'

'A bit cheeky of her I'd say.'

Jack swallowed more beer. 'I got to thinking about it and decided why not her? She's pretty after all and has a pleasant temperament. I could do far worse.'

'Hardly sounds like a love match,' Peter replied drily.

Jack shrugged. 'My father once told me they don't always turn out for the best. Love can die and then where does that leave you? His advice was to marry someone you got on with, that that was far more important. It's said you can love a person and not even like them. Well, I don't want any of that.'

'I take it then that you and Wonky get on?'

'That's what I'm trying to find out and why I'm calling on her. I'll know soon enough, believe me.'

'She's very keen on you,' Peter stated quietly.

One of Jack's eyebrows slowly rose. 'How do you know that?'

'The girls told me. Apparently she's been keen for ages and upset you've never taken any notice of her. Up until now that is.'

'Well, well,' Jack murmured. That was interesting.

'And she's worried she'll lose you because of her parents. Though there's nothing she can do about them. Her father rules her with a rod of iron.'

'Never liked the man,' Jack confessed. 'Even less now that I know him better.'

'He would be your father-in-law if you married Wonky,' Peter pointed out.

Jack chuckled. 'I can handle him. Contact between us would be kept to a minimum, I'd see to that. Anyway, what about you? If Wonky was right about me she's also right about you. It is high time you were married for the old son and heir if nothing else.'

'You sound just like my father, he was on about the same thing some months back.'

'And?'

Peter employed the same argument that he had with Murdo. 'Unlike you, and your father, I think a love match is the be all and end all. I won't marry unless I'm in love, and that hasn't happened yet.'

'What if it doesn't?'

Peter gazed down into his pint pot, not wishing Jack to read his expression. Should he be honest with Jack, tell him the truth that he never intended to marry. That women left him totally cold. He decided against it. That secret was one he'd keep to himself.

'I'm sure it will one day,' he lied.

'But what if it doesn't?' Jack persisted.

'Then I'll remain a bachelor.'

Jack saw off his whisky, then had another swallow of beer. 'You're being a bit hard on yourself, aren't you? I mean, we all have needs, dear chap.'

'Mind over matter, Jack. Mind over matter.'

Jack laughed. 'You sound like a papist monk or priest. They remain celibate but it would hardly do for me.'

Peter's expression became quizzical. 'Does that mean you've . . .?'

Now it was Jack's turn to wonder if he should confess. And, like Peter, he decided not to. 'No, but as I said, we all have needs. Needs that aren't getting any easier to cope with as a single man.'

Peter nodded his understanding. 'When are you seeing Wonky again?'

'I walked her home from church last Sunday which was fine, away from Mater and Pater that is. I'm calling again for tea at the manse next Wednesday.' He pulled a face. 'God help me.'

Peter laughed. He couldn't have agreed more.

Murdo stopped just inside the malting house and drew a deep breath down into his lungs. This was his favourite part of the distillery. The odour that assailed his nostrils was one he'd known all his adult life, and one that never failed to delight him.

He watched Bill Murray and his brother Enoch, two of his maltmen, turning the germinating malt to aerate the grains, part of the whisky-making process.

Bill spotted Murdo and acknowledged him, Murdo replying with a finger wave.

Murdo stayed there for all of ten minutes, not checking up on the work but simply enjoying the experience, before moving on.

He felt quite buoyed up on leaving the malting house.

'Jesus!' Andrew exclaimed, rolling off Tina. 'That was amazing.'

She gave him a feline smile. 'I try to give money's worth.'

That irritated him for some reason. He hated the thought he was paying for it. Not that he was mean, not at all, it was just that he'd have preferred the relationship to have been a non-professional one.

'Where do you live?' he asked.

The feline smile vanished. 'Why?'

'Just curious, that's all.'

'I can't say, Andrew, it's against the rules.'

'Really?'

'Really.'

'But why?'

'You'd have to ask Mr Mulligan the owner that.'

He lay back and studied her naked form. 'Can you tell me something about yourself? I'd like to know.'

Tina sighed. 'Is this leading up to, what's a nice girl like you doing in a job like this?'

He reached across and stroked a coral-tipped breast, smiling with satisfaction when the nipple responded. She might only be nineteen, he thought, but she was all woman with a mind far older than her years. But then he supposed being a prostitute, for that's what she was, did that to a female.

'I'm one of five children, the eldest,' she stated suddenly. 'Da's a drunk and Ma's half blind with cataracts. I don't know where the family would be without me and this job.'

He took his hand away. 'I'm sorry.'

She shrugged. 'I don't come from the sort of background you obviously do. This job is a Godsend. I make far more than I would in service or a factory.'

'I can imagine,' he murmured.

'It took a bit of getting used to I can tell you, but it isn't as bad as it might be. Most of the gentlemen I entertain are exactly that, gentlemen. Not one of them has ever mistreated me or refused to pay.'

She chuckled. 'Not that there's much chance of them not paying. A shout from me and they'd be in very big trouble indeed. Mr Mulligan looks after his girls.'

'I've got two sisters,' he declared.

'Oh?'

'Charlotte and Nell. Charlotte's engaged to a fellow officer, in fact it was that engagement we were celebrating the first night I came here.'

'As I remember they all seemed decent blokes.'

'They are, Geoffrey in particular. He's the one Charlotte's going to marry.'

She stretched out beside him. 'Can I ask *you* something?'

'What?'

'There's a girlfriend, isn't there?'

He stared at her, wondering how she'd worked that out. 'What if there is?'

'It's none of my business, Andrew. What you do is your own affair.'

He laughed. 'That's exactly what the girlfriend is, an affair. She's a lot older than me.'

'So it isn't serious then?'

'I like her well enough, she's good fun. But fun is precisely what it is, she's too old for it to be anything else. She was a friend of my mother's who's now dead.'

Tina was visibly shocked. 'That's terrible.'

Andrew had the grace to look shamefaced. 'I suppose it is.'

'I mean, what would your mother think if she was still alive? And what about your father, what about him?'

'Well, he wouldn't be best pleased, that's for sure. But you see I . . .' He cleared his throat. 'I hadn't been with a woman up until Jean. It seemed an ideal opportunity.'

'Still, your mother's friend. That is rather off.'

Andrew suddenly smiled. 'She suspected something recently. I was very stupid, used a "refinement" she called it which I'd learnt from you.'

'Is she rich?' Tina asked.

'Considerably. She was left very well provided for.'

'Her husband's dead then?'

He nodded. 'She was lonely and . . . shall I say libidinous when we got together.'

Tina frowned. 'What's this libby thing?'

He gestured at his penis. 'To be blunt about it, she was missing that.'

A huge smile lit up Tina's face. 'I see.'

'Not that she's actually ever said, but I'm not daft. I can put two and two together.' He cradled his hands behind his head. 'Do you mind me talking like this?'

'It's part of the job, Andrew. Men will tell women like

me things they wouldn't to another soul. It's amazing what some of them come out with.'

'And you are discreet.'

'Completely. It would be more than my job's worth to blab. What's said between these four walls is strictly between us, you have my word on that.'

Andrew had been certain that was the case. 'Have you got a boyfriend, outside here that is?'

'No.'

'I'm surprised. You're not exactly a gargoyle you know.'

She laughed softly. 'Thank you, kind sir. I'll take that as a compliment.'

'It was meant as one. So why not?'

'A boyfriend? What decent chap would want someone like me? I'm somewhat shop soiled to say the least. But perhaps one day, who knows? I won't be here for ever after all. Mr Mulligan likes his girls to be young. After a while they're simply let go.' Tina looked wistful. 'There was a smashing woman here when I arrived, her name was Jessica and we got on like a house on fire. But she was let go on account of her age.'

'What happened to her?'

'I've no idea. She walked out the front door one day and that was that.'

'You've had a hard life,' Andrew sympathised.

'So have many. I'm not complaining. I just wish my dad was different, that's all. He drinks every penny he can get hold of. He's violent in drink too, it wouldn't be the first time he's smacked me almost senseless. Though he's stopped that since I came here, he's still got the sense to realise I can't do this job all battered and bruised.'

'Does he hit your mother?'

'Oh yes. Frequently.'

'Even though she's half blind?'

'That doesn't worry him. He's a brute. But he'll get his come-uppance some day.'

'Why don't you move out?' Andrew queried.

'My mother and brothers and sisters need me, it's as simple as that.'

He reached across and drew her into his embrace. 'I don't even know your surname. Is it permissible to ask or is that also against the rules?'

She smiled. 'It is. But I'll tell you anyway. It's Mitchell.'

'Tina Mitchell,' he mused.

'And your surname is Drummond. That's what you wrote on the membership form you filled in.'

'Correct.'

'Well, Andrew Drummond, you've paid for all night so what do you want to do next? Sleep or—'

'Or,' he interjected.

Murdo sighed as he studied the gold-rimmed invitation to the annual dinner of the Whisky Makers' Association in Edinburgh. Large amounts of their product were always consumed at the event, that was de rigueur, which meant he couldn't attend. He knew he'd succumb to temptation if he did.

'Peter?'

His elder son glanced up at him.

Murdo waved the invitation and explained what it was. 'I think you should go in my place this year,' he proposed.

Peter stared at his father in astonishment, knowing how

much Murdo enjoyed the annual dinner. 'Whatever for?'

'It'll be good for you, another step to taking over in time.'

Murdo rose from behind his desk, crossed the office and placed the invitation in front of a bemused Peter. 'You'll have a whale of a time, believe me. And you'd better put your drinking boots on, there'll be enough whisky there to sink the proverbial battleship.'

'If you're certain, Pa.'

Murdo was filled with nostalgia remembering past dinners. Yes indeed, the temptation would be too great and he didn't want another attack.

'That's settled then.'

Jack Riach took out his pocket watch and snapped it open. Hettie would just be finishing, time for the weekly assignation. He smiled in anticipation.

Hettie, Jack's dairy maid, was wiping her hands on her apron when Jack strolled into the byre.

'How are you?' he queried with a smile. She was seventeen years old and they'd been having their weekly assignation for almost eighteen months. She was a bonnie lass in a rustic way, well proportioned with generous hips and breasts.

Hettie moved away when Jack went to touch her.

He frowned. 'What's wrong with you?'

'I hear you're courting, Jack. The minister's daughter.'

'That's right,' he nodded.

She came straight to the point. 'Does this mean you're ending our arrangement?'

'Why should it mean that?' he queried.

'If you get married you won't want me no more. You'll be getting it at home.'

'I see,' he murmured. 'And that would upset you, Het?'

It damn well would, she thought. Part of their arrangement was, the most important part as far as she was concerned, that if she fell pregnant Jack would pay her off with a lump sum in return for which she wouldn't tell anyone he was the father. A sizeable sum that had been agreed on. A pregnancy Hettie was certain must happen in due course. With that lump sum behind her she wouldn't have any difficulty finding a husband, pregnant or otherwise, and would be able to afford the cottage she wanted. That was her dream which would blow away like so much chaff if Jack stopped seeing her before she fell pregnant.

'Yes,' she stated emphatically.

He laughed and chucked her under the chin. 'Not jealous, are you?'

'Might be.'

'I like that.'

'So?' she demanded.

'If I do get married to Miss Comyn, and nothing's certain, it won't be for some time yet. In the meanwhile let's just enjoy ourselves. Who knows what'll happen in the long term? I certainly don't.'

Jack was thinking he didn't want to burn any boats. He relished his weekly sessions with Hettie Campbell, she was a lustful lassie who knew how to pleasure a man.

Maybe she should try and see Jack twice a week, Hettie thought. That would double her chances. She *wanted* that cottage and hopefully a piece of land to go with it. It would be a big rise in the world for her.

Jack produced his wallet from which he extracted a pound note. 'Why don't you buy yourself a wee present, Het. That'll cheer you up,' he declared, slipping the note into her hand.

'You're good to me, Jack. Always have been,' she murmured.

The pound note vanished into her pocket.

'We're wasting time, Het. You go on to the barn and I'll follow in a minute.'

'All right, Jack.'

He watched her walk away, hips swaying provocatively. Once outside he glanced around checking that the coast was clear as it invariably was at that time on a Sunday.

In the barn he found Hettie already stretched out behind a stack of hay bales, her skirt up round her waist, her female nakedness revealed.

Standing over her he smiled as he began undoing his trousers.

Chapter 10

Andrew left the roulette table feeling sick to the very pit of his stomach. How could he have been so incredibly stupid! Of all the damn fools he was the biggest.

He sat and swallowed hard, noting that his hands were trembling. He should have got out far earlier but had kept telling himself that his bad run must end if he kept doubling up. Only it hadn't. And now . . .

'Christ!' he murmured, and closed his eyes. His senses were reeling. How could he possibly pay back that amount?

'Andrew?'

He blinked his eyes open to find Tina staring sympathetically down at him.

'How much?' she asked softly. She blanched when he told her the amount.

'Can you cover it?'

'I'll have to.'

'I have a message from Mr Mulligan. He'd like to see you in his office. I'll take you there.'

Andrew rose and teetered on the spot. What had started

as a smashing evening had somehow turned into a night-mare.

He followed Tina from the room as he'd done so many times before, only this time it was different.

A helluva lot different.

'Please take a seat, Mr Drummond,' Mulligan said from behind a fog of cigar smoke.

Andrew sat facing the small man who, despite his Irish name, was in fact Jewish. Mulligan studied Andrew from behind a huge beak of a nose.

'You signed a number of IOUs tonight, Mr Drummond. I have them here.' Mulligan tapped the pieces of paper in front of him.

'Yes,' Andrew croaked.

'The first time you've asked for credit.'

Andrew nodded.

'It's quite a sizeable amount.'

Andrew licked bone-dry lips. 'Yes,' he said again.

'I allowed the credit because of your family connections. Your family owns Drummond whisky I believe.'

Andrew nodded a second time.

'There again, perhaps you're a man of means in your own right?'

Panic was threatening to engulf Andrew. He had to get out of there, he needed to think.

'You'll get your money, Mr Mulligan,' he replied coldly, avoiding the question.

'Oh I'm sure,' Mulligan said softly.

'If you could give me a few days, a week perhaps. Surely that's reasonable?'

'Quite. As a serving officer and gentleman I know you're a man of honour and his word. A week it is.'

'Thank you,' Andrew said through gritted teeth.

'A pleasure doing business with you, Mr Drummond. You're always welcome in my establishment.'

Mulligan rose and extended a hand. 'Goodbye for now,' he declared, slightly emphasising the 'now'.

'Goodbye.'

Andrew, still in a daze, left the office and collected his coat and hat.

He stumbled out into the night.

'I was thinking,' Hettie said to Jack, having just bumped into him in the yard.

He smiled. 'What's that?'

'You know what they say about choosing a wife. Always look to the mother to see what she might one day turn into.'

The smile vanished from Jack's face. Now why hadn't he thought of that! The thing was, he hated fat women and Moira Comyn was decidedly that. It was all right to be well built like Hettie but fat women revolted him.

It pleased Hettie to see the effect her words had had on Jack, who'd once made an offhand remark, which she'd remembered, about his dislike of female corpulency.

In his mind's eye Jack was picturing Wonky the size of her mother. He shuddered.

'I'd hate you to make a mistake, Jack,' Hettie crooned.

So would he. Particularly that mistake. The thought of going to bed with a tub of lard was . . . well, just too awful to contemplate.

'It's certainly something you should give consideration,' Hettie went on.

'Yes,' Jack agreed quietly.

Hettie walked away, waiting till she rounded a corner before bursting out laughing.

Peter stared at Andrew in disbelief. 'How much?'

'Sixteen hundred pounds.'

Peter swore, then crossed to the whisky decanter and poured himself a large one. 'You're an idiot. A total idiot. That's a small fortune.'

'I know,' Andrew replied miserably.

'But how?'

'In the end it all happened so quickly. I simply kept on losing.' Andrew took a deep breath. 'I've been going to Mulligan's for months, you see, and doing terribly well on the whole. Then this.'

'Does that mean you have some cash put by?'

Andrew dropped his gaze to stare at the carpet. 'The sixteen hundred is after I've deducted what I have in the bank.'

'And now you want to ask Pa to cough up for the remainder?'

Andrew shrugged. 'Who else can I ask?'

Peter stared at Andrew over the rim of his glass. 'He'll go berserk, have a heart attack,' Peter said quietly, not realising how close to the mark his words were.

'How about you, Peter, can you lend me something?'

Peter barked out a laugh. 'I don't have any money of my own, you know that. All I have is my salary.'

Andrew went to the decanter and poured himself a dram

as hefty as Peter's. 'What a mess. What a bloody awful mess,' he muttered, before taking a long swallow.

'Of your own making, brother. No one twisted your arm encouraging you to gamble.'

'Do you think that makes it any easier? It doesn't, I assure you.'

'Sixteen hundred pounds,' Peter mused, shaking his head.

Andrew felt tears come into his eyes which he brushed away with the sleeve of his jacket. He was terrified of facing his father. Scared witless.

'When will you speak to him?' Peter asked.

'Tonight, after dinner.'

'Well, good luck, you're going to need it.'

Andrew knew that only too well.

Dinner was over and the family had retired to the drawing room. Charlotte and Nell were embroidering while Peter was reading a newspaper. Murdo was sitting in a club chair clearly in a contemplative mood.

Andrew stared at his father, willing himself to ask Murdo if he could have a private word. A dozen times during the past hour he'd opened his mouth to make the request, and a dozen times he'd closed it again.

Coward, he berated himself. And he was right. His father was a good man who'd have been the first to help in any other difficulty, but a gambling debt! That was something else entirely.

Peter glanced at the ashen-faced Andrew, partially amused to see his brother's funk, the rest of him sympathetic to what Andrew was going through. Andrew's fault mind, but nonetheless.

'Has he kissed her yet do you know?' Nell whispered to Charlotte who'd spoken with Wonky that afternoon. She was referring to Jack Riach.

'Apparently not,' came the whispered reply.

Nell giggled softly.

'She thinks he will soon. At least that's the impression she gets.'

'So it's all going well?'

'According to Wonky it is.'

Nell sighed. Lucky old Wonky, and lucky Charlotte. When was it going to be her turn?

'They have held hands. Only briefly though,' Charlotte confided.

'Is he getting on any better with Uncle Tom and Aunt Moira?'

Charlotte pulled a face. 'What do you think. But he's persevering.'

'What are you two whispering about?' Murdo suddenly demanded, causing Andrew to start.

'Nothing, Pa.'

'Well, it must be something.'

'Nothing important, Pa. Girls' talk, that's all.'

Murdo snorted and gazed enviously at the dram balanced on the arm of Peter's chair. 'Next week, Peter,' he said.

'What's that, Pa?'

'The Whisky Makers' Association dinner.'

'Oh yes, I'm looking forward to it. And Edinburgh, I always enjoy going there. A lovely city.'

'A lovely city,' Murdo agreed. His gaze focused on Andrew. 'What's wrong with you tonight? You're being very quiet, most unlike you, lad.'

'Nothing to say, Pa.'

Murdo barked out a short, sharp laugh. 'Well, that makes a welcome change.'

Ask now, Andrew thought. Ask now. He couldn't. It filled him with despair and shame.

'Ah well!' Murdo declared, rising. 'I'm off to bed. Want an early night.'

'Why's that, Pa?' Peter queried.

'Just do, that's all. No particular reason.'

'Old age I suppose,' Charlotte teased.

Murdo glowered at her. 'Less of your cheek, young lady. I'm not decrepit yet.'

Now, Andrew urged himself. Before it's too late. He said nothing.

'I'll see you all at breakfast,' Murdo declared, and strode purposefully from the room.

Peter glanced across at Andrew and shook his head.

Andrew willed himself to follow Murdo, to tell his father of his problem.

He remained sitting.

Andrew closed the bedroom door and leant back against it. Tomorrow night he promised himself, he'd speak to his father then. This had to be sorted out. But Christ, it was hard.

Sixteen hundred pounds, the figure was indelibly printed on his brain. And what if his father refused? The consequences to that were too awful to contemplate. Damn Mulligan and damn his salon. He wished with all his heart he'd never heard of the place.

It had all been so easy while he was winning, a few

hundred here, a few hundred there. And where had most of it gone? Champagne and all the other luxuries he'd so lately enjoyed. Not to mention Tina.

'God,' he groaned. If only by some miracle the whole horrible episode could be washed away, made to vanish. He'd have given anything for that to be the case.

Tomorrow night, he promised himself, taking off his jacket. He couldn't delay the inevitable longer than that. It would have to be then.

He remembered Peter's contemptuous look when he'd announced he too was off to bed. Thankfully Peter hadn't made any comment, he'd been spared that.

He was hanging his jacket in the wardrobe – they hadn't dressed for dinner that night – when he noticed the letter he'd picked up at the barracks on his way out. In his anxiety he'd forgotten all about it.

He took the letter from the jacket's inside pocket and tore it open. He frowned as he read the official contents.

It was too good to be true. Too too good. Throwing back his head he roared with laughter.

Problem solved.

'Ireland,' Murdo repeated, sitting with the family at breakfast next morning.

'My posting order came through yesterday, Pa. I'm to join the First Essex as soon as possible. They're already there, in Dublin.'

'Well,' Murdo mused. 'That's a turn up for the books. I'd have thought they'd have given you more time to get your affairs in order.'

'That's the army for you, Pa.'

Peter was staring quizzically at his brother wondering about this turn of events since the previous evening. He was pretty certain he knew how Andrew would now handle the debt situation, and totally disapproved. However, Andrew was a grown man, entirely capable of making his own decisions. Though in this case Peter was convinced it was a mistake. The expression 'lack of moral fibre' sprang to mind.

'How long will you be away for?' Nell asked.

Andrew shrugged. 'Can't say. Could be a couple of years.'

'I wonder why you've been transferred?' Nell mused.

'Search me, sis. You're rarely given a reason. The First Essex are a decent bunch from what I've heard, though I'll be sorry to leave the Watch.' Not as sorry as he might have been, he reflected.

'So we won't be seeing you for a while,' Nell said.

' 'Fraid not. Will you miss me?'

'Of course,' she replied, pretending to be sarcastic. For she would, they all would.

Charlotte suddenly clattered her knife and fork on to her plate. 'Geoffrey didn't get a similar posting order, did he?' she inquired anxiously.

'No idea. But it's doubtful he would. Not two of us at the same time. That's highly unlikely in the circumstances.'

Relief welled through Charlotte. Thank the Lord for that. Although she couldn't be absolutely certain until she heard from him.

Andrew, having already packed, left directly after breakfast, the rest of the family seeing him off.

'Well, good luck, son, and take care of yourself over in Ireland, hear?'

'Thanks, Pa. I will.'

The two men shook hands as McPhie climbed into the Rolls-Royce which would take Andrew to Pitlochry station.

Peter's eyes bored into Andrew's as they shook. 'I hope everything works out for you,' he said.

Andrew knew to what Peter was referring. 'I'd say things couldn't have worked out better,' he replied jauntily.

Fool, Peter thought.

There were more farewells from Charlotte and Nell, then Andrew was in the Rolls and waving goodbye as it purred away.

Miracles do happen, Andrew thought, sinking into the deep leather upholstery.

They really do.

'Ireland!' Jean Ritchie exclaimed.

'I'm leaving the day after tomorrow which is why I sent round the note.'

'It's so . . . sudden, isn't it?'

'The army's like that.' He was about to say he was looking forward to the adventure, then thought the better of it. To have done so would have been insensitive to say the least.

Jean put a hand to her forehead, for a moment having felt slightly dizzy. This was awful.

'There's absolutely nothing I can do about it,' Andrew declared softly.

'I appreciate that.'

'I'll be gone for quite some time. And when I do return who knows where I'll be based.'

It was over, Jean thought in despair. What had been wonderful would now only be a memory. Nor could she take him to bed for one last time. The servants were in the house. There was her reputation. But oh she was tempted, so very tempted.

'Can I see you again before you go?' she asked.

He shook his head. 'Impossible, I'm sorry. Can't be done, Jean. I have no control over it, that's just the way it is.'

'I understand,' she said huskily, and sat. Although not yet noon she wanted a drink, and something stronger than her usual sherry.

'Could you pour me a gin and "It"?' she asked Andrew. 'You know where it's kept.'

'Of course.' He decided to have one himself, to keep her company.

'How long can you stay for?' she queried.

'No more than half an hour.'

She stared at him, memorising every detail of his face, recalling the many nights of passion they'd shared together. 'I'm going to miss you dreadfully,' she stated honestly.

'And I you, Jean.'

'We didn't have long, did we?'

'No.' He hoped she wasn't going to break down, that would be embarrassing.

'Will you write?'

'I'm not much of a letter writer. But I'm sure I can manage a few lines from time to time.'

Letters she would treasure. If they came that was. 'How's everyone at Drummond House?'

'Fine. In the pink.'

'And how did they take the news?'

Andrew had a swallow of his gin. 'They were all right about it. They appreciate I'm in the army after all and that this sort of thing happens.'

'I'll miss you, Andrew,' she repeated in a cracked voice.

When he'd gone she went up to her bedroom, locked the door, laid on the bed and wept copiously.

Andrew stood at the ship's rail until the Scottish coastline vanished over the horizon. Then he smiled, for with it went Mulligan and his debt. He couldn't have been any happier.

He thought of the gold cufflinks in his suitcase, a last-minute present from Jean delivered to the barracks. That had been kind and thoughtful of her.

He then thought of Tina whom he'd also have liked to say goodbye to. But of course that had been completely out of the question.

Well, a whole new chapter in his life was opening up. What would it bring? It was going to be interesting finding out.

Putting Jean and Tina from his mind he went below.

As had become their custom Jack was walking Wonky home from church, and he was wondering how tactfully to broach the subject that had been plaguing him since his conversation with Hettie in the yard. Hettie whom he'd be seeing later on that day for the ongoing Sunday assignation. He was looking forward to that.

They strolled a little way in silence, Wonky revelling in his company, silent or otherwise.

'It was a particularly long sermon this morning,' Jack commented.

'Yes. I sometimes think Father doesn't know when to stop once he gets going.'

Jack laughed. 'It was real fire and brimstone stuff. I felt I was already roasting in hell.'

Wonky glanced sideways at him. 'Surely you haven't done anything that would put you there?'

'A few sins,' he confessed. 'Nothing major though.' He thought of Hettie, if that wasn't a major sin what was!

'Your mother seems to have lost weight,' he lied.

Wonky frowned. 'I can't say I've noticed.'

'Well, it seems to me she has.' He paused for several seconds, then asked innocently, 'Has she always been stout?'

'As long as I can remember. But I believe she had a lovely figure when young.'

Jack's heart sank.

'It started with childbirth you see. It affects some women that way, I'm told.'

Jack's heart sank even further. If that was what had happened to Moira Comyn with childbirth might it not also to Wonky, her daughter.

'Of course she eats a fair amount,' Wonky burbled on. 'But then so does Father.'

Jack had noticed that at the supper he'd had with them. And Wonky had eaten her fair share, no demure picking with her.

'I'm not surprised considering how good a cook she is. The supper I had with you was delicious.'

Wonky beamed at him. 'You'll have to come again soon.

And this time I'll make my apple crumble. *Lots* and *lots* of it.'

Those fateful words decided her fate with Jack.

He lapsed into a brooding silence for the remainder of their journey to the manse.

Jack put on his jacket, pulled out his wallet and extracted a five-pound note. 'For you,' he stated gruffly to Hettie who'd also come to her feet and was busy brushing straw from her clothes.

Her eyes snapped wide with delight. This was far more than he'd ever given her before. 'What's that for?'

'Saving me from what might have turned out to be the biggest mistake of my life.'

Hettie accepted the note, folded it and slid it safely into a pocket. 'Are you referring to Miss Comyn?'

Jack nodded.

'Have you told her yet?'

'That's still to come. It's going to be difficult, believe me. I'd rather have a tooth pulled.'

'Well, if you take my advice do it sooner rather than later. Best to get these things over as quickly as possible.'

She was right. Call at the manse or wait till next Sunday? He'd have to think about that.

Hettie turned her back to Jack so he could brush off the straw she wasn't able to reach. This was something he did every week.

Hettie smiled. Her little scheme had paid off as she'd hoped it would. Jack was still hers and hers alone.

Before leaving the barn she kissed him on the cheek. 'I'm sure you're doing the right thing, Jack, feeling as you do. It would be awful for you ending up married to a tub of lard.'

Jack shuddered at the thought.

Jack slid from his horse and tied off the reins. He'd come straight from the pub where he'd consumed a number of large drams to give him Dutch courage. At that moment he wished he'd drunk more.

He knocked and waited.

'Why hello, sir,' said Heather the maid on opening the door.

'Is Miss Comyn at home?'

'She is indeed, sir.'

'I'd like a word if I may.'

'Certainly, sir. Come in.'

In the event it proved even worse than Jack had anticipated. On leaving the manse, and a sobbing Wonky, he returned to the pub where he stayed, sat by himself in a corner, for several hours.

'Broke it off!' Charlotte exclaimed.

Wonky nodded.

'The dirty dog,' Nell said.

'But why?' Charlotte demanded.

Tears welled in Wonky's eyes. She'd been crying more or less non-stop since Jack's visit the previous day. 'He said that, in his opinion, we weren't really suited and that it was in both our interests that he stop calling on me.'

'Oh dear,' Charlotte breathed.

'It's just not true!' Wonky wailed. 'We are suited. We get on terrifically together.'

'He obviously doesn't see it that way,' Nell commented.

'Perhaps it's simply funk on his part,' Charlotte mused.

Wonky's tears rolled down her puffed-up face. 'Do you think he might change his mind?'

Charlotte sighed. 'I have absolutely no idea. But would you want him back after this?'

'Oh yes.'

'I think you should put Jack Riach right out of your mind,' Nell counselled.

Wonky gave Nell a stricken look. 'That's just it, I can't. Not now, not ever. I know that for certain.'

Charlotte squeezed her anguished cousin's shoulders, imagining what it would be like if Geoffrey were to break it off with her. It didn't bear thinking about.

'I love him,' Wonky whispered.

'This is hard to say, and will cause you pain, but it would seem he doesn't love you,' Charlotte replied in a sympathetic voice.

'Oh, Charlotte, oh, Nell, what am I to do? It's so horribly unbearable.'

Neither Charlotte or Nell had an answer to that.

Chapter 11

Murdo rose to meet this man whose letter had arrived the previous week requesting an interview. The man had written that he had delicate business to discuss with him with no clue whatsoever as to what that business was.

Mulligan extended a hand. 'I'm pleased to meet you, Mr Drummond. It's most kind of you to see me.'

Murdo had been expecting someone Irish and was momentarily thrown to discover Mulligan was Jewish. 'How do you do,' Murdo replied a trifle formally as they shook.

'Beautiful countryside, a delight to drive through. You're very fortunate to be living here, Mr Drummond.' Mulligan sighed. 'I rarely get to leave Perth myself, the city itself that is. When I do it's a treat.'

Murdo gestured to a chair. 'Would you care for a dram, Mr Mulligan?'

'Not for me thank you. But don't let that stop your good self indulging.'

There was something rather oily about Mulligan, Murdo

thought. Good-quality clothes though, well cut. Mulligan was clearly a man of standing.

'I won't bother,' Murdo said, and sat facing Mulligan. 'Now how can I help you, sir? A delicate business matter you mentioned in your letter.'

Mulligan pulled a face. 'I'm afraid so. Not only delicate but embarrassing too.'

Murdo nodded and waited for him to go on.

'I have an establishment in Perth, amongst other interests that is, a gambling salon which bears my name.'

Murdo frowned. Gambling salon? What on earth could that have to do with him.

'One of my patrons is, or was, your son Andrew.'

Murdo digested that. Andrew a patron of a gambling salon? He'd had no idea his son gambled. He was suddenly filled with foreboding, half guessing what was coming next.

Mulligan sighed again. 'This is the delicate part. Unfortunately, during your son's last visit to my salon he lost heavily, a great deal of it on IOUs which I accepted and still hold.'

Mulligan fished in an inside pocket and produced the IOUs. Rising, he crossed and handed them to Murdo, then returned to his chair from where he regarded Murdo keenly.

Murdo's face was stony as, one by one, he examined the various notes. He had no doubt that the writing and signature were Andrew's.

'I see,' he said quietly when he'd finished his perusal.

'I spoke to your son on the night of his losses and it was agreed between us that he could have a week in which to raise the money. Unfortunately, which I learned from enquiries I made, he was suddenly posted abroad during that period.'

Mulligan paused, then added with a smile, 'I'm sure that in the circumstances the matter simply slipped his mind and he had no intention whatsoever of welching on me.'

Murdo winced at the use of the word welch in connection with a member of his family.

'So I thought the best thing was to come to you,' Mulligan went on.

Murdo leafed through the IOUs again, adding the total. He paled when he arrived at it.

'A little over two thousand pounds, Mr Drummond. I'll happily round that figure off.'

If Andrew had been present in the room Murdo would have struck him. He then recalled Andrew's strange behaviour the night before he'd left, the uncharacteristic quietness of the lad. Now he knew why.

'And if I don't pay?' Murdo queried, already knowing he would. He was simply curious.

'Mr Drummond,' Mulligan replied in a sad voice. 'You must understand my position. I can't allow patrons to get away with matters of unpaid credit. There are ways and means depending on the person involved. In Andrew's case I would have to inform the army authorities which I'm certain would have unfortunate repercussions for your son.'

Cashiered, Murdo thought. Kicked out in disgrace. Officers had a code of honour to adhere to. A gentleman always paid his debts.

'I think I will have a dram after all,' Murdo declared.

Mulligan watched Murdo as he poured from the decanter and then had a large swallow. He didn't elaborate that if Murdo didn't pick up the IOUs then that would reflect on Murdo himself. He didn't have to.

Murdo finished his dram in a second large swallow. 'If you'd care to wait here, Mr Mulligan, I'll go to my study and write you out a cheque.'

Mulligan inclined his head. 'I knew you would resolve the situation, Mr Drummond. And I can assure you what has taken place will remain strictly between ourselves. You have my solemn word on that.'

'Thank you,' Murdo replied.

He paused at the door. 'Who or what shall I make the cheque out to?'

'Mulligan's will be fine.'

He was seething, raging. Two thousand pounds! How could Andrew be so irresponsible to do such a thing. It beggared belief.

Murdo poured himself a fourth dram, hardly aware that he was doing so. He continued to pace up and down the drawing room as he'd been doing since Mulligan had left ten minutes previously.

And then they hit him, the agonising pains in his chest. The glass spun from his hand as he staggered to the bell pull. He tugged it once and then sank to the floor.

Florence answered. 'Yes, sir—' She broke off and screamed when she saw a slumped, puce-faced Murdo. Turning she hared away to find Miss McQueen.

The pains lasted far longer than they ever had before, convincing Murdo he was done for. 'Get Peter and Dr McAllister,' he gasped to Miss McQueen, now kneeling beside him.

Miss McQueen rapped out an order and Florence bolted from the drawing room.

Thank God, the pains were easing. Murdo slowly drew in deep breath after deep breath.

'Can you make it to the chair, sir?' a very concerned Miss McQueen queried.

'In a minute, not yet.'

The colour in his face was beginning to fade when Peter crashed into the room. 'Get him a dram,' Peter instructed Miss McQueen, dropping down beside his father.

'No, I don't want that,' Murdo whispered.

'What is it, Pa. What's wrong?'

'I came over all funny. Some sort of turn.' Well that was true, if not the whole truth.

'Dr McAllister has been sent for,' Miss McQueen informed Peter.

He nodded his understanding and approval.

The pains were easing even further. Murdo was shaken to the very core.

Peter knew only too well what had caused this as Murdo had mentioned that a Mr Mulligan would be calling. He'd ring Andrew's bloody neck when he next saw his brother.

Peter loosened Murdo's collar and tie, then between them he and Miss McQueen managed to get Murdo to the nearest chair.

'I'll fetch some water,' Miss McQueen said and, ignoring the water by the whisky decanter, hurried off to get fresh.

'Andrew, wasn't it?' Peter said grimly.

Murdo nodded.

'Little swine.'

'Did you know about it?'

'Yes, Pa, he spoke to me the day he came back. I told him you'd . . .' He broke off in confusion.

'Well?'

'Have a fit,' Peter said hoarsely. 'I didn't think it would be a literal one though.'

Murdo managed a wan smile.

'Sixteen hundred pounds is a fortune.'

'Two thousand, Peter. That's what the IOUs amounted to.'

So Andrew hadn't even paid off what he had in the bank. That made it even worse.

Miss McQueen returned with a glass of water which Peter held to his father's lips. Murdo had a few sips and felt the better for them. 'Enough,' he croaked.

'If McAllister's out on his rounds he might be a while. I think we should get you to bed,' Peter stated.

Murdo closed his eyes. That had been a near thing, he was convinced of it. Damn Andrew.

'I didn't know Andrew gambled,' he said.

'Neither did I until he told me.'

Gambled and went to bed with Jean Ritchie. His second son was just full of surprises.

McAllister removed the stethoscope from his ears, rolled it up and replaced it in his bag. Peter looked on anxiously.

'Could you leave the doctor and me alone for a bit,' Murdo requested of Peter.

'But, Pa, I . . .'

'Please, son.'

Peter was displeased with that, and it showed. Nonetheless, he did as asked.

'He still doesn't know, I take it?' McAllister said.

Murdo shook his head.

'Is that wise?'

'It's what I wish, James. Let's just leave it at that.'

McAllister nodded. 'Now, can you tell me what happened? Was there anything specific brought this on?'

Murdo explained about Andrew, Mulligan's visit and the IOUs.

'Two thousand pounds,' McAllister mused. 'A tidy sum to say the least.'

'I was so angry, James, so bloody bloody angry. Well, you can imagine.'

McAllister could. He'd never particularly liked Andrew Drummond, there was something about the lad.

'I had a few additional drams after Mulligan left. But I've been good as gold otherwise, I swear.'

It was the combination, McAllister thought. There again, the attack might well have occurred without the whisky. He couldn't really say.

'It's bed for you for a couple of days, Murdo. You can get up and go to the bathroom, and that's it. After that complete relaxation for at least a fortnight which means no work. Understand?'

Murdo nodded.

'You're still taking the pills I hope?'

'Every morning without fail.'

'Hmmh.'

'I swear, James. Every morning without fail. I'm not a complete eejit.'

McAllister laughed. 'You're many things, Murdo Drummond, but certainly not that.'

Murdo's eyes clouded. 'How could Andrew do such a thing. It's beyond me.'

'He must have got carried away. They say that happens in gambling. Though my own opinion is that anyone who gambles in the first place is a fool.'

Murdo didn't entirely agree with that, sometimes it was necessary to gamble in business as he well knew. But to throw your money away in a gaming salon, that was something else entirely.

'What do you want me to tell Peter?' McAllister asked.

They agreed on a story.

Nell was sitting quietly by herself reading a book, Charlotte was with Miss McQueen attending to some domestic matters, when it suddenly struck her who the Highlander's wife reminded her of.

Her eyes widened in shock. It was herself!

But that was silly, she didn't look at all like the woman, not in any way. And yet, it *was* herself she'd been reminded of.

How? Why?

And then it came to her, making her go cold all over. Had she been that woman in another life? Was that the answer?

Preposterous of course. Totally ridiculous. Laughable really.

Except . . . why did she have these visions of the Highlander and his family, mainly of him? Visions so realistic she might have actually been there?

Closing her eyes she envisaged the man, the face, the smile. And it seemed to Nell something stirred deep within her, though what she couldn't have said.

Her husband all those years ago?

She shivered.

'So how does it feel to be an old married woman?' Charlotte teased Jenny who'd just returned to work, having had a week off after her wedding.

Jenny beamed. 'It's wonderful, miss. Hamish and I are ever so happy.'

Charlotte couldn't have been more pleased for the maid. 'The wedding went extremely well,' she commented. 'You looked radiant.'

'It took me Ma and me ages to sew that dress. But it was worth it in the end.' Jenny giggled. 'Hamish told me afterwards that when I walked into church he thought me an angel down from Heaven.'

The dress had been a good effort, Charlotte thought, considering it had been homemade of course. The headdress, which had fallen to Jenny's shoulders, had been bedecked with wild flowers. The dress itself had been fairly plain with few frills which had suited Jenny. The material had been mousseline de voile, the additions cream-coloured lace.

'It was ever so kind of the family to give Hamish and me that canteen of cutlery,' Jenny enthused. 'We could never have afforded anything as nice.'

'Are you using it yet?'

'Oh no, miss, it's being kept for best. I wouldn't dream of using it every day.'

There was something Charlotte was dying to ask, but found embarrassing. Nonetheless, curiosity getting the better of her, she did. 'And eh . . . you know. Is that all right between you?'

Jenny blushed bright red. 'Oh yes, miss.'

'There weren't any problems?'

Jenny's blushing deepened. 'None at all, miss.'

That was as far as Charlotte could go. 'Good, I'm pleased.'

'You'll be next I suppose, miss.'

'Probably,' Charlotte mused. She couldn't wait for that day. That day of days when she and Geoffrey, dear darling Geoffrey, would be joined.

Wonky stopped dead in her tracks on spotting a solitary figure on horseback. The horse was stationary, and the rider appeared to be staring out over the countryside.

It was Jack, she realised. A lump the size of an apple came into her throat. At least it felt that big.

'Jack,' she whispered. 'Oh Jack.'

Why oh why had he thought they were unsuited when it was so blindingly obvious to her they were a good match. What had she done to give him that impression? She couldn't for the life of her think.

Had he met someone else, was that it? Someone prettier than her, more witty. Someone rich while she was poor. If he had she hadn't heard.

How she missed him, his calling at the manse, their Sunday walks home. What joy he'd given her, joy that would have increased a thousandfold if they'd been married.

Now that would never be. Unless he came back to her that was, a hope she desperately cherished.

She stood watching Jack until he rode off.

*

Peter laid his pint and dram on the table then sat facing Jack who'd also called in for a quick one.

'So how are things, stranger?' Jack enquired amiably.

'I've been busy. Pa hasn't been well.'

'Oh? I hadn't heard.'

Peter had no intention of going into details, not even with Jack. Andrew's shame would remain a secret between him and Murdo.

'Nothing serious, but it's kept him off work which has put an extra load on my shoulders.'

'Well, I hope he's better soon. Give him my regards.'

'I will.'

Peter had a sip of whisky followed by a gulp of beer. 'I was sorry to hear about you and Wonky.'

Jack was immediately on the defence. 'How is she?'

'Still upset. As I said before, she's very keen on you.'

Jack shrugged. 'I don't consider us suited. It would have been a mistake.'

Peter studied his friend. 'Is that the real reason?'

'Of course.'

'Then why don't I believe you?'

That threw Jack into confusion which he did his best to hide. 'I've no idea.'

'The pair of you seemed very suited to me.' He paused, then added softly, 'She's broken hearted, Jack. And I mean that.'

Jack dropped his gaze to stare at the table. 'Better not to make a mistake than to make one and then have to live with it. She's a sweet lass who'll be a marvellous wife to someone, but not me.'

'The girls tell me, and this is in strictest confidence,

that she's hoping you'll change your mind . . .'

Jack felt wretched to hear that. 'I won't,' he mumbled.

'Absolutely certain?'

Jack nodded.

'Well then, there's no more to be said on the subject.'

Jack imagined Wonky like her mother, fat and gross. An appalling thought. 'She was good fun,' he admitted against his better judgement.

Peter raised an eyebrow.

'That doesn't mean to say we were suited. Merely that she was fun.'

Peter didn't reply.

Jack finished his dram and gestured to Peter's glass. 'Want another?'

'Why not.'

Jack rose and went to the bar where he thought about Wonky as he was waiting to be served. It was surprising him to find out how much he missed her. He'd only been calling on her for a short while but in that time had grown closer to her than he would have imagined possible.

He plonked himself down again at the table. 'If I give you the truth, Peter, she is your cousin after all and I suppose I owe it to you, you and I being friends, will you promise not to let on to Charlotte and Nell who'd be bound to tell Wonky?'

'I promise,' Peter nodded.

'It's her mother.'

'Aunt Moira! What's she got to do with it?'

'She's fat. Horribly so.'

'But it would be Wonky you'd be marrying, not her mother, for Christ's sake.'

'Do you know the expression, if you want to know how the girl's going to turn out look at her mother? Well I don't like fat women, Peter, never have. They repulse me. It would crucify me to be married to one.'

'I see,' Peter mused.

'I just can't take the chance.'

'But otherwise everything was fine between you?'

Jack nodded. 'We got on really well.'

'What a shame. And what happens if she doesn't turn out to get fat over the years?'

'Then it's my loss. But as I say, I can't take the chance.'

Peter could see his friend's mind was firmly made up. There would be no change of heart.

He felt dreadfully sorry for Wonky.

Murdo closed his eyes, and bent his head backwards a little, thoroughly enjoying the warm summer sun beating down on his face. This was the life, he reflected.

'Hello, Pa,' said Charlotte, joining him on the bench. 'What are you up to?'

'Precisely nothing, which is lovely.'

She laughed. 'Can't say I blame you on a day like today. I just hope this weather keeps up.'

'I should return to work you know, but somehow can't bring myself to do so. Peter's coping well enough on his own, he doesn't really need me.'

Charlotte gazed at her father, realising with shock that he'd aged considerably over the past few weeks. He'd lost weight on his face and neck and there were lines where there hadn't been any before.

'If that's how you feel I'd stay off if I was you,' she said softly. 'In fact, why don't you give up work altogether? As you say, Peter doesn't really need you.'

'It's funny you should say that, I've been considering it. Though I am young for retirement.'

'Would you be bored?'

There was a few seconds' pause while he mulled that over. 'I don't think I would, you know. I think I'd enjoy a life of idleness.' He laughed. 'My God, Murdo Drummond saying that. Me who's always thrived on hard graft.'

'Times change, Pa, and so do people.'

He wanted to live to see his grandchildren, he thought. That above all else. To dangle a bairn or two on his knee and spoil them. But with this heart thing, well you just didn't know.

'Maybe I'll speak to Peter this evening,' he declared.

'Why don't you? Hear what he has to say.'

Murdo closed his eyes again. 'If you don't mind, Charlotte, I think I'll have a wee sleep. It's so glorious.'

She pecked him on the cheek before leaving him to his nap.

'But you can manage by yourself, can't you?'

'Of course, Pa. If I have to.'

Murdo sighed. Was he doing the right thing or not?

'I just can't imagine you not involved in the distillery, that's all,' Peter stated. 'It's been part and parcel of you, and you it, since I can remember.'

'I think it's an excellent idea,' Charlotte said. 'If it's what Pa wants.'

'Me too,' Nell chipped in.

'The workforce won't like it,' Peter declared. 'You are the

distillery as far as they're concerned. They idolise you, Pa, you know that.'

Murdo allowed a small smile of satisfaction to drift across his face. He'd always prided himself on the fact he was a good boss and popular with his employees. It was his belief that what you gave you got back double.

'There is an alternative,' Charlotte declared.

Murdo focused on her. 'What?'

'You don't have to retire altogether. You could go in two mornings a week, for example. That way you'd have the best of both worlds.'

'Hmmh,' Murdo mused. 'What do you think, Peter?'

'It's entirely up to you, Pa. I'll fall in line with whatever you wish.'

Two mornings a week? The best of both worlds as Charlotte put it. The idea appealed.

He made a decision. 'That's what I'll do then, starting Monday.'

'So be it, Pa,' Peter nodded. Then, eyes twinkling, 'Just think, McPhie will be delighted now you're going to have even more time to drive the Rolls.'

They all burst out laughing.

Tina Mitchell started on spotting the back of a familiar head. Andrew, he hadn't been to the salon in ages!

'Excuse me,' she said to the client she was with, and moved across the room. The client, an elderly gentleman who only dropped in occasionally, sadly watched her go. He'd been enjoying their conversation.

He'd put on weight, Tina thought as she drew closer. Then 'Andrew' turned sideways and she saw it wasn't him at all. She'd been mistaken which filled her with disappointment.

The man had an empty glass in his hand. 'Can I get you a refill, sir?' she asked.

'That would be nice.' He flashed her a smile. 'And who are you, young lady?'

'Tina, sir.'

'Well, Tina, I'm pleased to make your acquaintance.'

'Is it your first time here, sir?'

'That's right. I'm with a chum who's toddled off for the moment.'

'Will you be playing, sir?'

'Rather. A spot of roulette I think later on.'

Andrew's game. What had happened to Andrew? she wondered, unaware he'd been posted abroad.

She took the man's glass. 'I'll get that refill for you, sir.'

Chapter 12

'I think we should set a date, don't you?' Geoffrey suggested to Charlotte. They were sitting on a riverbank tucking into a picnic that Mrs Clark, the cook, had prepared for them.

'Oh yes,' Charlotte agreed quickly.

Geoffrey topped up her wine glass, and then his own. 'Any suggestions?'

'I'll leave it all to you, darling.'

He nodded his approval. 'I'll speak to your father this evening and start the ball rolling.'

Charlotte shivered in anticipation. It was her plan to use Miss Sinclair the Glasgow dressmaker. 'Nell and Wonky will be bridesmaids, of course,' she said.

'Of course,' he echoed, thinking his intended had never looked lovelier. God, how he adored her! He was the most fortunate of men to have met Charlotte Drummond, not only to have met her but to have fallen for her and she him. Married life together would be sheer bliss.

'How is Wonky by the way?' he enquired. Charlotte had kept him informed about the Jack Riach business.

'She's slowly coming to terms with the situation. She's been hoping that Jack would change his mind but so far there's no sign of that happening.'

'Poor Wonky,' Geoffrey sympathised.

'She took it very badly. For a while she was quite inconsolable, forever bursting into tears. Thank goodness that stage is past.'

'And how about Andrew, have you heard from him?'

Charlotte, who knew nothing about the debt her brother had left behind shook her head. 'But then that's hardly surprising, it's rare for him to put pen to paper. We can only assume everything's all right.'

'I'm sure it is.' Geoffrey became thoughtful. 'I certainly miss him as do quite a few. His transfer was a loss.'

'The Watch's loss the First Essex's gain,' she laughed.

'Precisely.'

Geoffrey had a sip of wine. 'Dashed fine stuff this. Your father keeps a wonderful cellar for a whisky man.'

'Oh, he knows his wines as well, though he's never been a great wine drinker.'

Geoffrey listened to the nearby drone of bees, a soporific sound he found most pleasing.

'I wonder how he's getting on over in Ireland,' he mused. Then, with a wry grin, 'Whatever, he'll be enjoying himself. You can depend on that.'

'I'm sure,' Charlotte agreed, wishing Geoffrey would kiss her. She ached for his lips.

As though reading her mind Geoffrey laid his glass

aside and squirmed over. 'Darling,' he crooned softly into her ear.

'A July wedding it is then,' Murdo declared. 'That gives us eleven months to get everything in order.'

Charlotte sighed with satisfaction.

'Now the venue, sir, what do you suggest?'

Murdo reflected on that. 'I have of course given the matter some thought. My initial reaction was to have it in Glasgow Cathedral, or Edinburgh. But then I changed my mind as so many of the locals would be terribly disappointed at not being able to attend. So what do you say we have it here with the reception held in a marquee in our grounds. Charlotte?'

'Sounds lovely to me, Pa.'

Murdo grunted. 'Geoffrey?'

'I'm in agreement, sir.'

'Good.' Murdo rubbed his hands together. 'I'll speak to Tom after church on Sunday.'

'And hopefully, if he can arrange it which I'm sure he'll be able to, Andrew will be my best man,' Geoffrey declared.

The smile vanished from Murdo's face. 'I see.'

'We had already decided that, sir, before Andrew was posted.'

'And if he can't make it?' Peter inquired casually, thinking of the almighty row that was going to erupt when Andrew next put in an appearance at home. Murdo would have the bugger's guts for garters.

'I'm sure it'll be all right considering the advance notice he'll be able to give them. But if there is a snag for whatever reason would *you* do me the honour?'

That surprised Peter. 'Well of course, old chap. I'd be delighted.'

'That's settled then.'

'You might pour us all a dram,' Murdo instructed Peter. Setting his elder daughter's wedding date certainly called for one.

Murdo wondered how long it would be before Charlotte became pregnant. Not too long, he hoped. He smiled in anticipation of the grandchild he'd dangle on his knee. Boy or lass? He didn't mind. As long as he or she was fit and healthy, that was the main thing.

The next months flew past and for Charlotte and Murdo there were a host of arrangements to be made for the forth-coming wedding. There were the trips to Glasgow and Miss Sinclair for a start, the three girls, Charlotte, Nell and Wonky going down and coming back together, for Miss Sinclair was also making the bridesmaids' dresses. What fun those trips were, the choosing of designs, materials, initial fittings. Then there were the accessories to find which involved numerous trips round the Glasgow shops and visits to restaurants where they'd discuss what they'd seen and what were possible buys.

In the meantime Murdo had put weight back on and hadn't suffered any more attacks. His two mornings a week at the distillery were just about right, he'd long since decided, thoroughly enjoying them when he went in, and thoroughly enjoying the free time he had to himself. To McPhie's despair and chagrin he'd been doing more and more driving, not going anywhere in particular most times, just driving for the pleasure of it.

And then one day early in the new year Andrew showed up.

'Surprise!' an excited Andrew exclaimed to Murdo whom he'd found reading in the drawing room. 'I'm back.'

Murdo slowly laid the book he'd been engrossed in onto his lap and stared grimly at his younger son. 'So you are.'

Andrew put his hands on his hips. 'What kind of greeting is that? You don't look pleased to see me.'

'I can't say I particularly am.'

That shocked Andrew. 'Pa?'

'How's Ireland?'

'Some of it good, some bad.'

'Oh?'

Andrew went straight to the whisky decanter. 'I'm dying for some Drummond, you can't get it in Dublin. It's nearly all Irish muck.' He pulled a face. 'Dreadful.'

'I'd have thought you'd get plenty of Scotch whisky in the mess?'

'Oh you can, but unfortunately they don't stock Drummond either. No, I meant outside the mess.'

Have it out now or wait till later? Murdo wondered. Here and now he decided.

'Speaking of the Irish, I met a chap with an Irish name a while back who's an acquaintance of yours.'

Andrew had a deep swallow of whisky, and sighed. 'Who's that?'

'A Mr Mulligan from Perth.'

Andrew went deathly white. Now he knew the reason for the icy reception. He glanced away unable to hold Murdo's accusatory gaze.

'I can explain everything, Pa, honest.'

Murdo's lips thinned into a brittle smile. 'Well, this should be interesting.'

When Andrew left the drawing room fifteen minutes later he was literally shaking after receiving the dressing down of his life.

'Well, look what the cat dragged in,' Peter said to Andrew that evening on returning from work. He had come across his brother in an upstairs corridor.

'Now don't you start. I've already had enough from Pa.'

'Did he tell you he had an attack after this Mulligan was here and the doctor had to be called? It was a minor seizure brought on by anger and shock.'

Christ, Andrew thought. Murdo hadn't mentioned that. He shook his head.

'You could have killed him, you little swine!'

Andrew hung his head in shame.

'Did you actually think it was all going to disappear just because you'd been posted elsewhere? Of course it wasn't.'

'I honestly never thought he'd come to Pa.'

'Then you're a fool. Do you think he was just going to write it off? Those people aren't like that. And what, if instead of coming to Pa, he'd gone direct to the army? That would have been the end of your career, me lad.'

'It never crossed my mind,' Andrew mumbled. 'I was just so pleased to get out of the mess and not have to face Pa.'

Peter wasn't a particularly physical man, but what he did

next was born of extreme anger. He lashed out, cracking Andrew across the cheek with an open palm.

Andrew staggered backwards. 'There's no need for that,' he protested.

'Keep away from me as much as possible during the rest of your leave. I don't want to know. Understand?'

Andrew nodded.

'And remember, the girls know nothing about what happened and that's the way it's to stay.'

'I won't say anything,' Andrew assured him.

Peter laughed scornfully. 'Hardly in your interest to let them see you in your true colours, is it?'

He strode past his brother, knocking Andrew aside in the process.

Andrew went to his bedroom where he threw himself onto the bed. It was going to be hell facing Murdo and Peter over the dinner table. But he'd have to.

He'd cut short his leave, he decided. He'd only stay a few days and then return to Dublin.

He'd think of some excuse to explain why his leave was so brief.

'He's seeing Grizelda McPherson,' a miserable Wonky told Charlotte and Nell. 'I only heard this morning.'

Charlotte didn't know what to reply to that. Wonky had been fine of late, and now this. 'I'm sorry,' was all she could think of to say.

Nell pulled a sympathetic face. 'There's plenty more fish in the sea, Wonky. Remember that.'

'Not like Jack Riach there isn't.'

'At least now you can stop holding out hope,' Charlotte

said. 'If he's seeing Grizelda McPherson then he definitely hasn't any intention of coming back to you.'

Wonky nodded. 'I realise that.'

'Well, he's welcome to Grizelda. I've never liked her anyway,' Nell declared gallantly.

Wonky managed a small smile. 'I've never liked her either, and that's the truth.'

'She'll probably make his life a misery,' Nell went on.

'Nag him half to death,' Charlotte added.

'Drive him to distraction.'

'Up the pole.'

'Round the bend.'

'Spend all his money.'

'Put him in debt.'

'Be useless at nearly everything you can think of.'

'Soon lose her looks.'

'Develop pimples.'

'And warts.'

'And *sag*.'

Wonky threw back her head and laughed at the absurdity of all this. It was wonderful.

'Get flat feet,' Charlotte persisted, a twinkle in her eye.

'And go bald.'

That was too much for Charlotte and Nell who also burst out laughing.

'You girls are priceless. Thank you,' Wonky said, still laughing. It proved a turning point in how she felt about Jack Riach. After that her emotions truly began to mend.

'What's the verdict, James?' Murdo asked McAllister, starting to button up his shirt after the examination he'd just had.

'You're fit as a flea, Murdo, I'm happy to say.'

Murdo beamed. 'And the heart?'

'Banging away like a good one. Are you still walking?'

'Every day, hail or shine.'

'Well, it's certainly had an effect. Don't stop though, keep it up.'

'I will, James. Don't worry about that.'

'How are you off for pills?'

'I could use some more.'

McAllister sat and reached for his notebook. 'This semi-retirement business is ideal I'd say. Enough to keep your interest with lots of time to yourself.'

Murdo re-did his tie. 'I still miss my pipe I have to confess. You'd think I'd have got over that by now, but I haven't.'

McAllister gave him a mock fierce glare. 'Well I don't want any relapses there. You stay off the tobacco.'

'Will do, James. Will do.'

McAllister completed the prescription with a flourish and handed it to Murdo. 'Any news of that boy of yours?'

Murdo shook his head. 'Not since I gave him merry hell over the debts he left. He only stayed home for three days before scampering off again with the lamest of excuses about a short leave. God mend him.'

'At least there weren't any repercussions from his visit. No more attacks I mean.'

'I kept my temper, James, though it was hard. And I'll tell you, the ticking off I gave him was probably the more effective for it.' Murdo snorted. 'Two thousand pounds indeed!'

'It doesn't bear thinking about.'

'No it doesn't.'

Hettie was furious. She'd managed to get rid of that Wonky Comyn and now Jack was stepping out with Grizelda McPherson. She could have spat.

Was there anything she could do to break up that little twosome?

She'd go and visit Granny Robertson she decided, and shivered. Granny frightened her, gave her the willies, which was why she'd so far avoided visiting the old crone. But Granny had potions and mixtures that did all sorts of things. Maybe one of those would do the trick.

She'd call on Granny at the first available opportunity. She wanted that cottage.

'I'm expecting, miss,' Jenny announced to Charlotte.

Charlotte clapped her hands in glee. 'That's wonderful. Are you sure?'

'Absolutely certain, miss.'

Charlotte hugged the maid. 'I'm so happy for you, Jenny. What does Hamish say?'

'He did a wee dance when I told him, miss. Then went straight down to the pub and got drunk as a skunk.'

Charlotte laughed. 'Quite right too. I suppose he's hoping for a boy?'

'You know men, miss, a son and heir's the thing.'

'Have you thought of any names yet?'

Jenny shook her head. 'I think that's bad luck. There'll be time enough for that after the bairn's born.'

'So you'll be leaving us then?'

'I'm afraid so, miss. But I'm hoping you'll let me stay on as long as possible.'

'Of course we will. Pa will insist.'

Charlotte took several steps backwards and studied the maid. 'I swear you look pregnant,' she declared. 'There's a sort of glow about you that wasn't there before.'

Jenny blushed. 'Thank you, miss.'

'Am I the first in the household to know?'

'Yes, miss.'

'Then let's go and tell Nell. She'll be delighted for you.'

Chattering like two magpies they left the bedroom in search of Nell.

'How's it going with Grizelda?' Peter asked Jack, as the pair of them enjoyed a Saturday night drink in the pub, their favourite meeting place.

'Fine.'

'No regrets about Wonky?'

Jack considered that. 'Yes and no if you know what I mean. She was good fun and would have made a lovely wife except . . .'

'She might have become fat,' Peter interjected.

'Precisely.'

Jack had a swallow of beer. 'I was a wee bit surprised that Grizelda allowed me to call on her. It was always you she was daft on.'

'Was she?' Peter countered, pretending innocence.

'Don't try that with me, Peter. You must have been aware, she made it obvious enough.'

'Not my type, sunshine. Simply not my type.'

'And what is your type?' Jack was curious.

'Don't know really, but not redheads like Grizelda. Redheads have never appealed.'

'You're auburn.'

'That's different. Different entirely.'

Jack shook his head. 'You're a funny old stick, Peter. I've known you all my life and yet there are times when I think I don't know you at all.'

Peter smiled. 'A mystery, eh?'

'Something like that.'

'Well, maybe that's a good thing. It wouldn't do, especially for a man of business as I am, if people could read me like a book.'

Peter lifted his pint. 'Here's to you and Grizelda. I hope it works out.'

'Thank you.'

Rather Jack than him, Peter thought, his face not betraying anything of what was going through his mind.

'Well, Miss McQueen, everything going all right?' It was precisely a week to the wedding.

'Still a great deal to be done, Mr Drummond, but we'll get there in the end.'

'Good,' he nodded.

'You must be very proud.'

'Very, Miss McQueen. I only wish . . .' He broke off, having been about to say he only wished his wife Louise had been there to witness the occasion.

'I'm sure she too would have been very proud,' Miss McQueen said softly, having guessed what his thoughts were.

'Yes,' Murdo replied equally softly.

Miss McQueen smiled her understanding. 'Well, best be getting on. As I said, still lots to be done.'

She strode purposefully away leaving Murdo with his memories.

Murdo stood watching the marquee being erected. God, but it was huge. But then it had to be to accommodate all the people who'd been invited to the reception. It was all going to cost a great deal of money but well worth it as far as he was concerned.

'Hello, Pa.'

He turned to find Charlotte had come up beside him. 'How are you?'

'Fine.'

'Not nervous?'

'Not yet, Pa. But I'm sure I will be. It's such a momentous occasion after all. Frightening really.'

He frowned. 'Not having doubts, are you?'

'No, Pa, none at all. I love Geoffrey with all my heart.'

He patted her on the arm. 'You'll be all right, I promise you. Your ma was nervous as a kitten on her wedding day, her hand shaking when I slipped on the ring. But once the ceremony was over she was right as rain.'

He cleared his throat. 'There's nothing else troubling you, is there?' He averted his eyes. 'You did have that long chat with Mrs Ritchie?'

Charlotte smiled thinly. That was bothering her somewhat but she wasn't going to admit it. She only hoped she lived up to Geoffrey's expectations.

'No, Pa.'

He nodded. 'Right. Well I'm off for my walk while these chaps get on with the marquee.'

He kissed her on the cheek. 'See you later.'

Charlotte woke drowsily then, remembering that this was it, her day of days, was filled with sudden excitement.

Throwing the bedclothes back she swung out of bed.

Peter sat in the rear of the Rolls as it purred towards Pitlochry and the hotel where Geoffrey, his parents and other guests were staying.

He was to be best man after all, Andrew having written to Geoffrey a fortnight previously saying he couldn't make it as the regiment was going on manoeuvres, something he simply couldn't get out of.

Manoeuvres his backside, Peter thought grimly. He'd have bet a pound to a penny there weren't any and that Andrew had merely funked coming home. He thought it awful to have let a pal down like that, but that was Andrew for you.

Peter knocked on the bedroom door.

'Come in!'

Peter entered to find Geoffrey in his dressing gown, clearly in an agitated state. 'That bad, eh?'

'I've been awake for hours. Couldn't sleep. All manner of things kept going round and round in my head.'

Peter was suddenly alarmed. 'You're not thinking of calling it off I hope?'

'Of course not. That's the last thing I'd do or want.' He clutched his stomach. 'Wait here, Peter. Shan't be long.' And with that he bolted from the room.

Peter smiled. Nerves he thought. And that was the effect it was having on Geoffrey. Poor bugger.

He produced a hip flask when Geoffrey returned. 'Bit early I admit, but perhaps a swallow or two might settle that stomach of yours.'

Geoffrey shook his head. 'If I touched that it would be coming out both ends.'

They laughed.

'Let's get you dressed, old son.' He glanced at the uniform, Geoffrey's Number One Dress, hanging on the front of the wardrobe door. 'Though you're going to have to advise me as I help you.'

Geoffrey lifted the uniform down and placed it on the rumpled bed.

'Let's get started then.'

'Just don't worry, there's no rush. That's why I got here in plenty of time.'

'God, I hope the car doesn't break down on the way there. That would be ghastly.'

'A car looked after by McPhie break down? There's more chance of Andrew turning up than that.'

It was a private joke to himself as Geoffrey fully believed the manoeuvres excuse.

Murdo emerged from the Rolls, Geoffrey having been firmly ensconced in the church before the car returned to Drummond House for the bride, bridesmaids and himself. He helped Charlotte out, scooping up her train before it hit the ground.

Nell and Wonky were swiftly in attendance, Wonky smoothing down the dress while Nell took charge of the train.

'So how do I look, Pa?' Charlotte queried anxiously when they were ready to go in.

'Do you know how many times you've asked me that this morning? I've lost count. You look like a fairy princess and, believe me, that's the truth.'

He stared in open admiration at her dress, a confection created from the softest ivory silk, short sleeved with pleats folding to a high-waisted bodice. From there the skirt fell in folds to the ground. But the *pièce de resistance* was the three-foot train that would swirl in a soft ivory circle, echoing the embroidery of the bodice, where pearls were sewn into Buckingham lace.

The headdress had the same details, consisting of a delicate band worn across the forehead with the same ivory lace and pearls. The bandeau anchored two ostrich feathers, also ivory. Charlotte's bouquet was an elegant spray of red roses.

As for Nell and Wonky, their dresses, each with a short train, echoed the bride's in pale pink silk, falling from a high waist with short sleeves and a bodice with folded pleats over an overskirt. They carried tea roses to match their dresses. Both girls wore pearl necklaces to match the bodices of their dresses.

'Thank you, Pa,' she replied, smiling.

He gave her his arm while Nell and Wonky fell in behind them.

The organ struck up as they entered the church.

'My my, that's a massive thing between your legs,' Jack Riach, there with Grizelda, teased Geoffrey. The 'thing' was Geoffrey's sporran.

Geoffrey, already flushed from alcohol, flushed even more. 'Here, steady on, old chap.'

Jack laughed. 'It's a wonderful reception, Geoffrey. Murdo has done you and Charlotte proud.'

Geoffrey gazed about him. There were throngs of people present, among them two Dukes and a Duchess.

'All set for tonight then?' Jack further teased.

'Jack,' Grizelda admonished. 'Leave the poor man be. You're embarrassing him, not to mention me.'

'Have you had enough to eat?' Geoffrey politely enquired of Grizelda.

'More than enough, thank you. I shall be fat as a pig for weeks to come.'

Jack winced.

Charlotte joined them, slipping an arm through Geoffrey's. 'Enjoying yourselves?'

'I should say,' Jack replied.

'You looked wonderful coming down the aisle,' Grizelda said to Charlotte. 'When I saw you the breath caught in my throat.'

'Well, thank you.'

'I'm a lucky man,' Geoffrey declared.

'And I a lucky woman,' Charlotte added.

Grizelda caught sight of Peter whom she hadn't spoken to yet. Well, she thought philosophically, he'd had his chance. Now she was with Jack and that suited her fine. Peter Drummond could go fly a kite as far as she was concerned. She gave Jack her best smile.

'Quite a do,' James McAllister commented to Murdo.

'It should be, it's cost enough.'

'How many of those have you had?' McAllister asked

quietly, nodding to the glass of champagne Murdo was holding.

'Och, man, don't play the doctor today. It's my daughter's wedding for goodness' sake.'

McAllister had a sip from his own glass, hoping that Murdo just didn't overdo it too much. He wondered where his wife was, last time he'd seen her she'd been talking to that dreary Tom Comyn.

'What'll you do if Jack speaks to you?' Nell asked Wonky.

Wonky shrugged. 'I doubt he will. But if he does I shall be nothing but pleasant.' She lowered her voice. 'I say, have you noticed what big feet Grizelda McPherson has?'

Nell giggled. 'Has she really?'

'Big as boats.'

They both laughed.

Peter glanced at his watch. Time to have a word with Geoffrey. He looked around trying to pick out the bridegroom. Peter accosted Nell and Wonky. 'They should be making a move to get changed.'

'Right then,' Nell said, looking for somewhere to place her empty glass.

She suddenly giggled. 'Sorry,' she apologised, placing a hand over her mouth. 'It's all that bubbly.'

The Duke of Strathearn beamed at Murdo. 'Haven't enjoyed myself so much in ages. It's all been absolutely first class.'

'Why thank you, Duke.'

'And where are the happy couple honeymooning?'

'I don't know. Geoffrey hasn't even told Charlotte that.'

They were joined by Sir Ian Murray whose glowing

cheeks attested to the amount of alcohol he'd consumed. 'I say, there are some pretty fillies here this afternoon,' Sir Ian declared, giving Murdo a salacious wink.

That amused Murdo. Sir Ian was in his late eighties and had been married three times, losing all three wives through childbirth. It appeared there was still life in the old dog yet.

A crowd gathered to see the newlyweds off, Murdo in the forefront. He kept sniffing, telling himself not to be such an emotional ass.

'You take care of her mind,' he said sternly to Geoffrey.

'I will, sir. You can rely on it.'

Gillian Armitage, resplendent in blue, was sobbing into a handkerchief while her husband Robert gazed proudly on. He and Geoffrey shook hands and exchanged a few words, then Geoffrey kissed his mother on the cheek.

More exchanges took place and more kisses, then Charlotte and Geoffrey were climbing into the Humber T.

Before closing her door Charlotte purposely threw her bouquet to Nell who caught it with a squeal of delight.

Charlotte was waving, the majority of the crowd waving back, as the car drew away.

'That's that then,' Peter said to Murdo.

'Aye, son, that's that.'

Slowly they all trooped back to the marquee.

Geoffrey and Charlotte returned from their honeymoon on 4 August, the day Britain declared war on Germany.

Geoffrey immediately left for his regiment.

PART TWO

The Long Night

Part Twelve

Chapter 13

'Just our luck to be stranded in bloody Ireland when there's a war on,' Lieutenant Billy Roberts complained to Andrew, as the pair of them were out riding.

Andrew was a far more experienced rider than Billy who'd only taken it up eighteen months previously. He glanced sideways at his friend, not at all sure he agreed with those sentiments.

'Think of the promotions that will be going,' Billy went on. 'There are bound to be stacks.'

Only because of casualties, Andrew thought grimly. He gazed about him. It was beautiful countryside, lush in the extreme. But he wasn't too keen on the climate – it rained even more often than Scotland.

'That Captain Kennington's a right bastard,' Billy said. 'I can't tell you how much I dislike him.'

Andrew smiled. He got on with Kennington well enough, it was simply a case of how you handled the man. Toadying, some people might have called it, but it worked and, as far as he was concerned, that was all that mattered.

'You rub him up the wrong way,' Andrew commented quietly.

'It's his attitude that gets me, supercilious swine.'

Andrew reined in on spotting another horse, the rider a woman obviously in distress.

'I say, look at that,' Billy exclaimed, having also reined in. 'The beast appears to have bolted.'

'She needs help,' Andrew declared, kicking his horse forward. Billy immediately followed.

Andrew urged his horse, a powerful gelding, into a gallop. Slowly he began to narrow the gap between him and the female.

The young woman heard their approach and turned her head towards Andrew and Billy. 'Help!' she cried.

'Just hold on,' Andrew shouted back, thinking she could easily be killed or at the least badly hurt if she came off at that speed. He was well ahead of Billy whose horse wasn't nearly as fast as his.

Yard by yard, aided by some clever manoeuvring on his part, Andrew gained on the girl till at last his horse and hers were neck and neck. Leaning across he managed to grab the bridle.

For a few moments it was a fierce clash of wills between them, then the horse began to ease back and gradually slow.

When the horse finally came to a halt Andrew leapt to the ground and grabbed hold of its reins. He then assisted the young woman down.

'Thank you,' she panted. 'That was truly frightening.'

'What happened?'

She gave a wry grin. 'I was stupid and arrogant enough to think I could control Midnight, which clearly I can't.'

Midnight was an apt name, Andrew thought. The animal was velvety black from nose to tail.

'Just let me catch my breath a minute,' the young woman said, placing a hand on her chest.

Billy came charging up, reined in and also dismounted. 'Everything all right?'

'I think so,' Andrew replied.

Midnight whinnied and threw his head, but Andrew had him firmly under control.

'Dashed large beast for a girl,' Billy commented.

'He's my father's horse,' the young woman explained. 'My own is lame and I wanted a ride. A mistake with Midnight as you witnessed.'

Andrew stroked a neck that was flaked with foam. 'There there, boy. There there,' he crooned.

'I'm Alice Fortescue by the way,' the young woman said.

'Andrew Drummond, Lieutenant in the First Essex based at Dublin Castle. This is my chum Billy Roberts.'

'Delighted to meet you, Miss Fortescue,' Billy declared, giving her a small bow.

'And I the pair of you. Who knows what the outcome might have been if you hadn't been on hand.'

'How far away do you live?' Andrew enquired.

'Several miles in that direction,' Alice replied, pointing off to their left.

'Well I think it best we walk the horses for a bit,' Andrew said. 'They all need a breather after that.'

Pretty girl, Andrew was thinking. He placed her in her late teens, possibly early twenties. She was dressed in a black hunting jacket below which flowed an ankle-length grey skirt.

'I lost my hat somewhere along the line,' she explained. 'It just blew off.' She shuddered. 'I don't mind admitting that gave me quite a scare. Father will be furious if he finds out.'

'Well, we won't let on, will we, Billy?'

Billy grinned. 'Finds out what?'

Alice smiled. 'You're both very kind and gallant.' Pronouncing the latter in the French fashion.

'As every army officer should be,' Andrew retorted.

The three of them laughed at that.

Andrew could see she'd got her breath back. 'Shall we get started then?' he suggested. 'I'll lead my own horse and Midnight.'

'Fortescue isn't an Irish name,' Billy commented as they got underway.

'The family is originally English. We came over here in the seventeenth century when we were granted lands for services to the Crown. Lands succeeding generations have managed to enlarge considerably.'

'I see,' Billy nodded.

'We don't think of ourselves as English any more, but Irish through and through, albeit we're Protestants.'

That was interesting, Andrew thought. 'And what does your father do, if you'll pardon my inquisitiveness.'

'He manages our estate, which is a considerable task I can assure you. He'll be out now, doing whatever.'

Damn it, Andrew thought, when it started to rain. A light smir as the Scots call it, which nonetheless soon had them soaked. Alice seemed oblivious to it.

They made small chat as they proceeded in the direction of Alice's house till eventually Andrew decided they could remount. Alice was instructed to take Billy's horse, the smallest of the three, while Andrew took Midnight.

'Is this your land we're on now?' Andrew inquired as they proceeded onwards, keeping the horses to a walking pace.

'Oh yes. Everything round here is ours.'

Andrew wondered just how rich the Fortescues were. Considerably he reckoned, though owning land didn't always equate with having money in the bank.

Andrew reined in Midnight when the Fortescue house came into view. Dear God, he thought, it made Drummond House look like a cottage. It was vast.

'Greystones,' Alice smiled to Andrew.

'Very imposing I must say.'

'Far too big of course, costs an absolute fortune to maintain. We only live in the central part, both wings have been shut off for years.'

'You're not a large family then?'

'No, only my parents and myself. They'd hoped for more children but weren't blessed.'

'I have a brother and two sisters myself,' Andrew informed her. 'While Billy here is the youngest of five brothers. That right, old thing?'

'That's right,' Billy confirmed.

'I'd have loved to have had brothers and sisters,' Alice said wistfully. 'But it wasn't to be.'

They came onto a long drive that wound its way towards Greystones, the drive flanked by conifer trees. Then they were onto the driveway itself which, it seemed to Andrew, could have taken an entire regiment of cavalry.

They dismounted in front of terrace steps leading to a massive wooden door.

'Would you care to come in and dry out a bit?' Alice asked.

Andrew was about to accept when Billy produced his watch. 'I'm afraid that's impossible, Miss Fortescue. We really must be getting back.'

Andrew sighed. 'Duty calls I'm sad to say.' If Billy said it was time to get back then it was.

Alice's face creased with disappointment. She'd taken a shine to these two young, personable men. 'I can't thank you enough for what you did,' she said to Andrew.

'My pleasure. In every cloud, what? It gave us a chance to make your acquaintance.'

A smile replaced the look of disappointment. 'You're most kind. Perhaps you'll call another day.'

'Perhaps,' Andrew replied.

He formally shook her hand after which Billy did the same. Then he and Billy remounted.

'Goodbye, Miss Fortescue,' Billy said.

'For now,' Andrew added.

Murdo glanced up from his newspaper which he'd taken to reading at the breakfast table every morning. 'The war news is mixed again,' he said to Peter. 'Don't trust those Frenchies not to make a fist of it you know. Never did like the Frogs.'

'You said the same thing yesterday, Pa.'

Murdo snorted. 'Well, it's true. Just don't trust them.'

Charlotte looked on in concern. 'I do hope Geoffrey's all right. I haven't had a letter in over a week.'

'Oh, he'll be fine,' Peter tried to assure her. 'He'll know when to keep his head down.'

Murdo rapped his paper with a hand. 'This place Mons seems to be featuring a lot. It's been mentioned again and again.'

Charlotte wondered if that's where Geoffrey was. Closing her eyes she prayed he was safe.

John Blair was about to say something to Geoffrey when a bullet took him at the junction between nose and fore-head. There was a momentary look of surprise on his face before he slumped to the ground.

Geoffrey knelt beside him. 'John? John?'

Blood oozed from the neat little hole. Through a haze of exhaustion and fear Geoffrey dimly noted that his friend was dead, the bullet on emerging having blown away the back of John's skull.

'Dear God,' Geoffrey whispered.

'A charge!' someone shouted. 'A charge!'

Geoffrey came to his feet and hastily reloaded his pistol.

The Watch were being mauled, but far from beaten. They'd been told to stand their ground and stand it they would to the last man if necessary.

A horde of grey uniforms appeared in front of them, the Germans shrieking and shouting as they advanced.

Geoffrey took careful aim and pulled the trigger again and again and again until his pistol was empty. He then snatched up a rifle and bayonet from a fallen comrade and seconds later was in hand-to-hand combat with a snarling German infantryman.

Granny Robertson frowned when, on opening her door to a knock, she discovered Hettie standing there.

'Well?' Granny snapped.

'You said to come back if your potion didn't work, and it hasn't.'

Granny grunted.

'And I paid good money.'

'So you did, lassie, so you did.' The ancient, wrinkled leathery face regarded Hettie keenly. 'You took it exactly as I said?'

'Yes.'

'You didn't forget at any time?'

Hettie shook her head.

'Then you'd better come away in and I'll see what else I've got for you.'

Hettie's nose wrinkled in disgust as she stepped inside the hovel. The stench was unbelievable.

Geoffrey was incredibly tired, all he wanted to do was throw himself on the ground and fall asleep. But sleep was out of the question with the Germans hard on their heels.

It was a bitter pill to swallow that they were in retreat, but those were the orders. The entire British Expeditionary Force was falling back.

Geoffrey blinked and gazed about him. Christ, but the men looked more like ghosts than living soldiers. He presumed he was the same.

John gone, and so many others lying back there with a great many German corpses to keep them company. At least John's death had been instantaneous, he wouldn't have felt a thing, unlike some other poor buggers. He shuddered at the memory.

A single shot rang out and a man just ahead of him stumbled and fell.

'Sniper!' the cry went up.

Geoffrey could only wonder if he'd be next. Please God, not, he prayed. Please God.

Then another shot rang out, this one taking a soldier through the neck. The man, making terrible choking, gargling noises, fell to writhe on the ground.

A stretcher was called for but the man was dead before it reached him.

How much more of this could they take? Geoffrey asked himself. How much more?

On they went, stumbling southward towards the French frontier.

Wonky sighed and placed her knitting on her lap. 'It does get tedious after a while, doesn't it?'

Charlotte smiled her sympathy. It did. They were knitting socks and balaclavas for the men of the BEF.

'Just think how pleased the chaps will be to get these things. That's what you have to remember,' Nell said.

'I appreciate that,' Wonky replied. 'But it doesn't make it any the less tedious. I've never enjoyed knitting, though I don't mind sewing. Goodness knows why one and not the other, but there we are.'

'It's a real worry I still haven't heard from Geoffrey yet,' Charlotte said quietly a few seconds later.

'I've told you, he's probably someplace where it's difficult getting mail out,' Nell declared.

Charlotte glanced at her sister, fervently hoping she was right. That it might be other than that didn't bear thinking about.

'Why don't I ring for tea?' Wonky suggested. 'It's high time we had a break.'

'Good idea,' Charlotte responded. 'Would you?'

Wonky laid her knitting aside, rose and crossed to the bell pull.

Charlotte gazed ahead of her, visualising Geoffrey as she'd last seen him. What a strange marriage it had been to date, she reflected. A honeymoon, and that was it.

But a wonderful honeymoon full of magic moments between the pair of them. She smiled in memory at their first night together. How nervous they'd both been, how coy and embarrassed getting into bed together.

'What are you day-dreaming about?' Nell asked. Then, with a smile, 'As if I didn't know.'

Charlotte nodded.

'It's only natural,' Nell further smiled.

'I didn't tell you but I bumped into Jack Riach the other day,' Wonky declared on rejoining them.

'And?' Charlotte demanded.

Wonky shrugged. 'I was cool but polite. Naturally I didn't mention Grizelda McPherson. He seemed relieved when we went our separate ways.'

'Hardly surprising,' Nell commented.

'How did you feel about him?' Charlotte asked.

Wonky considered that. 'Not at all as I would have imagined. It was as if . . . well as though I just didn't care. I was pleased about that.'

When Florence appeared in answer to their summons Charlotte requested that tea, cake and biscuits be brought.

Andrew lay on his bed with his hands clasped behind his head. He was thinking about Alice Fortescue.

There weren't any brothers or sisters which meant that,

unlike him being a second son, she would inherit. Now that *was* interesting, very interesting indeed. It would make her an extremely wealthy woman. Had to, with all that land, not to mention the value of the house.

Did she already have a suitor? That was something else he had to find out. And if she didn't . . .

He smiled. He'd call on Alice as soon as possible.

To Geoffrey it felt as though he'd been punched very, very hard on the shoulder. I've been hit, he thought as he spun round and then collapsed to the ground.

The world went silent. And then darkness closed in.

There were thousands of Highlanders, a great army of them on the move. Some were on horseback, the majority on foot.

Was *her* Highlander there? Nell wondered. Surely he was, otherwise why would she be seeing this?

The army were in a jolly mood, many with grins and smiles on their faces. Although she couldn't hear, it seemed to her there was a lot of banter taking place.

And then there he was, looking weary but as cheerful as the rest. One of the horsemen rode up and had a brief word with him.

A city came into view where it appeared they were headed. A city different to what it was now but essentially the same. A city she correctly guessed to be Edinburgh.

And with that the vision began to fade.

Charlotte knew the moment she picked the letter up off the silver salver that it was bad news. The letter almost smelt of it. With trembling hands she ripped open the envelope and began to read its contents.

It was from Geoffrey's C.O. He'd been severely wounded in the shoulder and was being shipped home to Britain for further treatment and recuperation. The C.O. had no way of knowing which hospital Geoffrey would be going to. He went on to reassure her that Geoffrey's life wasn't in danger.

When she'd finished the letter Charlotte clasped it to her bosom and let out a huge sigh of relief.

At least Geoffrey was out of it for now. Safe and sound, apart from his wound that was, and soon to be in England.

Thank the good Lord.

Andrew dismounted and tied off his reins. He then ran up the terrace steps that led to the massive wooden door.

A maid answered his ring. 'Yes, sir?'

'Is Miss Fortescue at home?'

'She is, sir.'

He handed the maid his card. 'Would you be kind enough to ask her if she'd receive me?'

'Certainly, sir.'

The maid closed the door and left Andrew waiting. He cast an appreciative eye over the grounds stretching away on both sides. They were sumptuous.

A few minutes later the maid reopened the door. 'Miss Alice will be delighted to receive you, sir. If you'll follow me.'

Andrew removed his cap and stepped inside.

The floor of the huge hallway was tiled with marble, the walls covered in heavy embossed paper. There were various portraits on the walls who he presumed were family ancestors. His footsteps echoed hollowly as he strode after the maid.

He was ushered into a magnificent drawing room where Alice was sitting on an emerald green chaise longue. By the fireplace stood a middle-aged man in the garb of country gentleman. Partially bald he sported a very thick and heavy walrus moustache.

Andrew went straight to Alice, took her extended hand and lightly brushed his lips over it. 'Miss Fortescue.'

'Mr Drummond, what a delightful surprise.'

'I was out this way and decided to take up your invitation to call.'

'I'm pleased you did.' She turned her attention to the middle-aged man. 'Father, this is Mr Drummond whom I met when out riding recently. He's a Lieutenant with the First Essex.'

Andrew crossed and shook with Alice's father whose grip, he noted, was a particularly strong one.

'I'm Sir Henry by the way.'

A shrewd old codger, was Andrew's initial impression of Sir Henry. Nobody's fool.

'Perhaps we should ring for tea?' Alice suggested.

Sir Henry regarded Andrew keenly. 'Maybe the young man would prefer something stronger?'

Andrew guessed that's what Sir Henry himself wanted. 'Oh yes please, sir.'

'Whiskey or claret?'

'Whisky, sir.'

'Good chap. Just the ticket.'

Alice, looking on, was thinking what a fine-looking

specimen Andrew was. There was something different about him, though she couldn't have said what.

Sir Henry opened a drinks cupboard and reached inside.

'Do you have any scotch whisky, sir? I'd prefer that if you have.'

Sir Henry frowned. 'You don't care for our Irish?'

'It's not that, sir, but I suppose what you're used to.'

Sir Henry nodded his understanding. He produced a bottle and two glasses from the cupboard. 'I'll join you in that. I quite enjoy a drop of scotch myself. Though I have to admit, my own preference is Irish.'

'As I said, sir, what you're used to.'

Sir Henry poured out two stiff ones. 'Water?'

'Just a drop, please.'

He handed Andrew a glass and held his own up in a toast. 'Your very best of health, Lieutenant.'

'Thank you, sir. Isn't Miss Fortescue joining us?'

'Doesn't drink, silly girl. Doesn't know what's good for her.'

Andrew smiled at Alice.

'You seem to know your whisky, Mr Drummond,' Sir Henry said after having a swallow. He was simply making conversation.

'I should, sir, my family own a distillery.'

A hairy eyebrow shot up. 'Really? That's interesting.'

'Drummond whisky, sir. Have you heard of it?'

Sir Henry shook his head. 'Can't say that I have.'

'Then allow me to send you a case, sir. I'd value your opinion.' Masterly stroke, he thought.

Sir Henry's face lit up. 'Dashed decent of you, Mr Drummond. I'll look forward to that.'

'It may take a while, sir, but have it you shall.'

'And where exactly is this distillery located, Mr Drummond?' Alice asked.

'A small village called Dalneil in Perthshire. The distillery has been in our family for generations.'

Sir Henry saw off the rest of his drink, considered having another, then decided against it. 'Met out riding you said, Alice?'

'Mr Drummond was with a colleague. They asked me for directions.' The latter lie came out smoothly. She shot Andrew a glance warning him to support her story.

'Daft of course, two army officers getting lost. Though in truth, we weren't exactly that. Let's just say we needed confirmation of where we were going.'

Sir Henry laughed. 'I quite understand. And where are you based, Mr Drummond?'

'Dublin Castle, sir.'

'Aah, Dublin,' Sir Henry sighed. 'Wonderful city.'

'I concur, sir. I'm very happy to be there.'

'I don't get up nearly enough. Must make more effort in future.'

'Do you like Dublin, Miss Fortescue?'

'Very much so. Like Father, I think it wonderful.'

Andrew stayed for half an hour, long enough for a first visit in his estimation. He left, promising to return soon.

A good start, he thought as he rode away. A very good one. Though he still hadn't found out if Alice already had a suitor.

As for money, the answer to that seemed obvious enough.

Chapter 14

Murdo read Andrew's letter a second time then laid it down. So, the lad had written at last and appeared most contrite about the Mulligan business. And so he should be, a disgraceful episode.

According to him he was now thoroughly enjoying Ireland and his new regiment. They were nothing like the Watch apparently, but a good regiment nonetheless.

Towards the end of the letter Andrew had mentioned meeting an Alice Fortescue whose father, Sir Henry, an extremely important and prominent person in the area, he'd promised a case of Drummond whisky to and could Murdo please arrange for a case to be sent to him at Dublin Castle.

A romance? Murdo wondered. It certainly sounded like the beginnings of one. Andrew wasn't in the habit of promising cases of whisky. Done in this instance to impress the father no doubt.

Another marriage in the offing? It was a possibility, though obviously early days yet.

In his last paragraph Andrew had enquired about Geoffrey, hoping that he was well.

Murdo decided to send the whisky and a letter in reply. He wanted to let Andrew know that Geoffrey had been wounded and was currently in an English hospital.

'What do you think about Kitchener's appeal for more volunteers?' Jack Riach asked Peter, the pair of them in their usual seats in the pub.

'He must need them.'

'I presume so. Doesn't bode all that well though, I should say.'

'Hmmh,' Peter grunted.

'We couldn't lose this war, could we?' That was a truly appalling and humiliating thought.

'I don't know, my knowledge of military matters is only what I read in the newspapers. And they tell us we haven't been doing all that well so far.'

Jack nodded. 'Mons appears to have been a disaster and now the Hun are advancing on Paris. I just can't believe that'll fall. It's unthinkable.'

'From what I understand men have been volunteering in their tens of thousands to date and yet according to Kitchener he still needs more.' Peter shook his head in bewilderment.

'Everyone said it would be over by Christmas,' Jack mused. 'It would seem now that's somewhat over-optimistic.'

'Several of the chaps at the distillery joined up last week. Pa wasn't best pleased, but understood. Told them he was proud of them and wished them the very best.'

'Did they indeed.'

'Chaps our age.'

Jack thought about that.

'It means we're short handed which is a bugger. However, we'll cope somehow. Pa has the idea of asking old Ronnie Montrose who retired a few years ago to come back and help out, though he hasn't spoken to him yet.'

They sat in silence for a while, each lost in his thoughts. 'How are you getting on with Grizelda?' Peter enquired eventually.

'Fine. Things are progressing nicely.'

'I see.'

'How's eh . . . Wonky?' Jack flushed slightly on asking that.

'She's all right. She and the girls spend most of their days knitting for the troops.' He laughed. 'They're getting through mounds of wool.'

'Good for them,' Jack nodded.

'I must say I'm impressed. It makes one feel . . .' Peter broke off and reached for his pint.

'Feel what?'

'That perhaps one should be doing something oneself,' Peter stated quietly.

'I've been thinking the same thing,' Jack confessed equally quietly.

'Have you now? But how would you possibly get away?'

'Arrangements could be made. Talking of bringing people out of retirement, my parents retired to Largs as you know. I'm sure they'd come back for the duration if necessary. In fact I'm certain of it, Dad has never enjoyed retirement. What about you?'

'Same here. Pa's on hand, he could easily go full time again.'

The two men stared at one another.

'It's a thought,' Jack murmured.

'Yes,' Peter agreed. It certainly was.

Charlotte gazed eagerly into the distance, down the platform at Pitlochry station awaiting the arrival of Geoffrey. He'd spent two days in Glasgow with his parents and was now en route to Pitlochry and Drummond House.

McPhie took out his watch and peered at it. 'She's late, only minutes so far mind, but still late.'

Charlotte tried to contain her impatience. Of all the trains to be late it had to be this one. She reminded herself there was a war on, trains didn't always run to schedule during wartime.

McPhie slapped his hands together. There was a nip in the air. Winter was just around the corner and was, according to all the signs, going to be a severe one.

'There!' Charlotte exclaimed, pointing to where a thin plume of smoke had appeared. 'That'll be it.'

How would he look? she wondered. Thin probably. She'd have to feed him up, take care of him.

'Aye, that's it all right,' McPhie confirmed.

Charlotte's hand went to her hair which she was wearing in a roll at the back. Everything was in place. Her hat, a black one, brimless with a cherry-coloured bow at the front from which a similar coloured feather swept backwards. It was a favourite of Geoffrey's which was why she'd chosen to wear it.

'Hurry up,' she murmured, almost shaking with excitement. 'Hurry up.'

McPhie glanced at her in amusement. It was her man coming home from the war, he reminded himself. No wonder she was beside herself. He'd probably have been the same in her place.

For a few moments he reflected sadly that he'd never married. Not that he had anything against marriage, nothing at all, it had simply never happened for him. Anyway, he was past all that now, well past it.

What if Geoffrey had missed the train? Charlotte thought in sudden alarm. What if something had happened to make him miss it?

You're havering, she told herself. Imagining things. Geoffrey was on the train, she just knew it.

And then the train was pulling into the station and windows were being dropped so that the passengers getting out could open their doors.

The train halted in a great whoosh of steam and people began alighting. Charlotte spotted Geoffrey almost at once. 'There he is!' she exclaimed, hurrying forward.

She stopped about a foot from him and they gazed hungrily into each other's eyes.

'I'll get your case, sir,' McPhie said, and dived into the compartment from which Geoffrey had emerged.

Geoffrey broke eye contact to instruct McPhie which one was his, then he had his good arm round Charlotte and, not giving a damn what anyone thought, was kissing her.

'I'd forgotten just how truly beautiful you are,' Geoffrey said to Charlotte as the Rolls purred away from the station.

'And I how handsome you are.'

He laughed. 'We sound like a mutual admiration society.'

Reaching out he clasped her hand. 'Oh, Charlotte, my darling. I've missed you so.'

'And I you. It's been like a physical ache.'

He kissed her hand.

McPhie was studiously avoiding looking in the mirror. The sliding glass panel was shut so he couldn't hear what was being said.

Charlotte's gaze slid to the arm in a sling. 'Is it still painful?'

He nodded. 'Though nowhere as bad as it was. I was lucky in a way. It could have been far worse.'

'When . . .' She swallowed hard, 'Do you have to return?'

'When the shoulder's healed. Your Doctor McAllister will tell me when that is. A few weeks probably. Maybe more.'

A few weeks, so short a time. She vowed they'd make the best use of it.

'The hospital let me go because they need the beds. There have been an awful lot of casualties,' he said softly.

'Was it . . . really awful over there?'

His eyes clouded in memory. 'Yes,' he whispered.

'Oh, Geoffrey.'

'We lost a lot of men at Mons and during the retreat. Do you recall my friend John Blair whom I've mentioned to you in the past?'

She nodded.

'We were standing together when he was killed. It was horrible.'

'I'm so sorry,' she murmured.

'He was a good man. One of the best.' Geoffrey's voice choked on saying that.

He looked away to stare out over the passing country-side. In his mind's eye remembering . . . remembering . . .

'Well, let's hear all about it,' Murdo said, the family having just sat down to dinner. He beamed at Geoffrey.

Geoffrey dropped his gaze. 'I'd rather not, sir.'

'Rather not?'

Peter frowned. He'd been looking forward to this. 'Why, old boy?' he queried.

Geoffrey took a deep breath. 'It's certainly not the sort of thing to discuss at the dinner table.'

'I see,' Murdo mused.

'I'm sorry.'

'No need for that. I'm sure you have your reasons.'

'You're going to have to cut my meat for me when it comes,' Geoffrey said to Charlotte sitting beside him.

'Of course, darling.'

'Thank you.'

Murdo saw a great change in Geoffrey. A young man had gone away to war, a mature one had returned. A mature man with a haunted expression in his eyes.

Murdo could only imagine what it had been like. He thanked God Andrew was safe in Ireland.

'I'll help you undress,' Charlotte said later when they'd retired.

'I'd appreciate that.' He paused, then said, 'I hope I wasn't too much of a damp squib over dinner, not wanting to talk about it that is.'

'I'm sure they understood.'

'Maybe sometime, but not now.'

'Not even to me?'

He smiled lovingly at her. 'Especially not you, my darling.'

She began to assist him with his clothes and soon he was standing stark naked before her. What a pity they couldn't make love she thought, desperately wanting to do so. But that was impossible with Geoffrey's arm in a sling.

As it transpired it wasn't impossible after all, Geoffrey having already given the matter some thought.

She'd never heard of such a thing when he explained it to her, but it did the trick.

Andrew rented a carriage to take the case of whisky to Greystones having first written to Alice to tell her when he would be arriving. A return letter had invited him to luncheon on the proposed day.

The same maid as before answered his ring and again he was ushered into the drawing room.

'As promised, sir,' he smiled at Sir Henry. 'Now where shall I put this?'

'On that chair, Mr Drummond.'

Andrew placed the case on the indicated chair, then dusted his hands off. 'All the way from Bonnie Scotland compliments of my father and Drummond whisky,' he declared.

'We'll have a drop of that right away, just to ensure it hasn't "gone off" in transit,' Sir Henry said, eyes twinkling at his joke. 'But first I'd like you to meet my wife. Mr

Drummond, this is Lady Fortescue. Mr Drummond, my dear.'

Lady Fortescue was roughly the same age as her husband, dark haired like Alice and gave the impression of having a forceful personality.

'Delighted to make your acquaintance, Mr Drummond,' she said in a slightly husky voice.

'And I yours, Lady Fortescue.'

'Now that the formalities are over I'll ring and have one of the servants open this whisky,' Sir Henry said.

'No need for that, sir. I'll do it.'

Alice, who'd been sitting, rose and joined them. 'Hello, Mr Drummond,' she smiled.

He gave her a small bow. 'Hello, Miss Fortescue. It's a pleasure seeing you again.'

She continued to smile, but didn't reply to that.

It was the work of a minute, with the help of his knife, for Andrew to open the case and extract a bottle from within. 'Twelve-year-old Drummond single malt,' he declared. 'My father insists there isn't another in all of Scotland to beat it.'

'Then let's judge for ourselves, eh?' Sir Henry rounded on his wife. 'Will you join us in a drink, my dear?'

'A glass of claret would be acceptable I think.'

'Then claret it shall be.'

Andrew moved closer to Alice. 'Shall I tell you something quite shocking?'

Her eyes widened while Lady Fortescue looked on in sudden concern.

'Both my sisters drink whisky. They were brought up to it, you see. It's a family tradition.'

'Gracious,' Alice breathed.

'It raises a few eyebrows at times I can tell you.'

'I'm sure.'

Sir Henry chuckled as he poured the claret. 'Women drinking whisky, whatever next!'

'I hear French women drink absinthe which is a filthy concoction, so why not whisky,' Andrew smiled.

'Tried absinthe once, and you're right, it is filthy,' Sir Henry said, handing his wife her claret.

'When did you do that, Henry?'

'Years ago, my dear, in Dublin. We all thought it rot.'

Andrew was aware of Alice studying him and wondered what was going through her mind.

Sir Henry opened the whisky bottle and sniffed its contents. 'Doesn't seem to have "gone off",' he further joked.

Hefty measures were spilt into two glasses. 'Now what's that Scottish toast again?'

'*Slainthe*, sir.'

'Then *slainthe* it is!'

Sir Henry tasted the malt, rolling it round his mouth before swallowing. 'Capital stuff,' he declared.

'I'm glad you approve, sir.'

'Very much so, Mr Drummond. Though I have to admit . . .'

'You still prefer Irish,' Andrew finished for him.

They all laughed.

'It was most kind of you to get that whisky for my father,' Alice said later after luncheon, as she and Andrew strolled in the gardens.

'Not really. It was merely an excuse to see you again.'

She glanced sideways at him. 'You're being very forward, Mr Drummond.'

'Then I apologise. But I do believe that honesty, as they say, is the best policy.'

'Indeed.'

'And I *was* keen to see you again.'

She didn't reply to that, but her mind was whirling.

'May I ask you something?'

'That depends on what it is.'

'Do you already have a suitor, Miss Fortescue?'

She felt her heart begin to beat faster.

'It's just that I can't believe you don't.'

Alice stopped and stared out over the gardens, her emotions now mixed. On one hand she was pleased with Andrew's attentions, on the other . . .

'I did have up until last year,' she said softly. 'His name was Paul McLuskey and we were childhood sweethearts. Everyone expected us to eventually get married, which I'm sure we would have done. Except last year . . .' Her voice trembled. 'He was killed in a hunting accident.'

Jubilation filled Andrew, the coast was clear. 'I'm so sorry,' he lied.

'It was a terrible time, for all concerned. I've been something of a recluse ever since.'

Andrew thought of how they'd met. 'I'm surprised, in the circumstances, that you took out Midnight.'

She sighed. 'Stupid I agree. But there you are, we Irish love our horses and Midnight was a challenge.' She paused, then added, 'One I shan't be repeating I assure you.'

'I'm glad to hear it.'

She gave him a wan smile. 'If it hadn't been for you I might have gone the same way as Paul.'

'Which would truly have been a tragedy,' he said sincerely.

They continued walking.

'Father likes you,' she said.

'Does he indeed.'

'Oh yes.'

'And . . . what about you, Miss Fortescue?'

Again she glanced sideways at him. 'You're very pretty.'

Andrew laughed. 'I've been called many things in my time but never pretty.'

'Well you are. You also have an easy manner about you which is attractive.'

'As do you, Miss Fortescue. May I confess?'

She slightly raised an eyebrow. 'If you wish.'

'I was extremely attracted to you the first time we met.'

'I'm flattered,' she replied.

He took a deep breath. 'Were you very much in love with this Paul McLuskey?'

She considered that. 'To be honest, I don't know about love. Though I probably was. There aren't all that many Protestants in this area you see, so we do tend to interbreed somewhat.'

'I think I understand.'

'Do you?' she queried.

'It must be difficult for someone in your position. Meeting the right sort of man, I mean.'

'It is, believe me.' She stopped again. 'I think we should turn back now, don't you?'

'Only if you'll allow me to call on you again.'

'If you wish, Mr Drummond.'

'Andrew when we're alone, please.'

She smiled, a smile that lit up her face. 'And you may call me Alice.'

'As you're such a keen horsewoman perhaps we can go riding together. Or would that be in bad taste?'

'I take it you're referring to Paul. No it wouldn't be in bad taste as I ride out all the time.'

They settled a date before returning to Greystones.

Nell found Peter alone and lost in thought. 'Penny for them?' she queried.

He roused himself from his reverie. 'Oh I was just thinking.'

'About what. Work?'

'Partially.' That was true enough, work did come into it. He motioned to the settee he was sitting on. 'Come and join me.'

'Why, thank you, big brother.'

He ignored the sarcasm in her voice. 'I suppose Charlotte's with Geoffrey?'

'Of course. They've hardly been apart since he arrived.'

'He still won't talk about his experiences over in Belgium and France. I tried again to tackle him on them the other day and again he shied away.'

'They can't have been very pleasant.'

'No,' Peter nodded. 'They can't.'

'Have you noticed that look he occasionally gets in his eyes nowadays? It's scary.'

'Yes,' Peter replied softly. 'I have and it is.'

'Poor Geoffrey.'

Peter took out his handkerchief and blew his nose. He thought he had the beginnings of a cold coming on which was a nuisance. 'Pa seems in fine fettle of late,' he said.

'Yes he does. A life of leisure suits him. He never misses his daily walk you know. Not ever.'

Peter shook his head. 'I still can't get used to the idea of Pa taking up walking. It's amazing.'

'Not only taking it up but relishing it.'

Talk to Murdo before or after? Peter wondered.

Definitely after the deed was done.

'I'm going to miss that when you're gone,' Charlotte sighed, sliding off Geoffrey and snuggling up beside him.

'Just that. What about me?' he teased.

'You too, silly. You know what I mean.'

'I'll miss it and you too,' he declared.

'I'd hope so.' She ran fingers across his chest. 'When you do go back how long is it likely to be before you get a leave?'

'No way of telling, Charlotte. That's entirely in the lap of the Gods. One thing I do know, I don't want another leave because I've been shot a second time.'

She winced. 'Don't even think about that, Geoffrey.'

He wondered how the battalion was getting on. When he did return how many faces would he discover to be missing. Men dead and wounded. It was a gruesome thought.

Closing his eyes he saw John Blair being shot, and the momentary look of surprise on John's face before he slumped to the ground. Despite the warmth of the bed and Charlotte beside him he was suddenly cold all over.

'Darling?' Charlotte whispered.

He opened his eyes. 'Yes?'

'For a moment there I thought you'd dropped off.'

'No, I'm still awake. Tired though, but still awake.'

She giggled. 'Have I worn you out?'

'More or less.'

'That's good then.'

'And how about you, have I worn you out?'

'Very much so, my darling.' Her expression changed. 'I so want to please you in every way.'

'You do, Charlotte.'

'Swear?'

'I swear.'

She smiled, a smile of satisfaction. How she loved this man of hers. How she adored him. Life before Geoffrey had been comfortable but bland and colourless, now it was oh so very different. They fitted so well in every way together, like two pieces of a jigsaw.

Reaching under the bedclothes she sought and found his penis which she gently held in her hand. 'It's like a little mole,' she whispered.

He laughed. 'Really?'

'Oh yes, a little mole. My little mole.'

'It wasn't so little a few minutes ago,' he reminded her.

Her eyes sparked with amusement. 'That's true, as I'm only too well aware. And thankful for. But in this state it's a little, soft velvety mole.'

He wondered if other people said daft things like this to each other. Probably, he decided. It was perfectly natural in the circumstances.

'A little mole looking for its burrow,' he said.

She laughed softly as what she was holding began to harden. 'Not again?' she teased.

'It appears I'm not so worn out after all. What about you?'

'Funny that, but it's the same with me.'

She straddled him as his little mole continued to grow and grow.

She sighed with pleasure as the mole found its burrow.

'I think we can dispense with the sling now, Mr Armitage. You're coming along extremely well,' Doctor McAllister announced.

Geoffrey wished with all his heart that he wasn't. The sooner McAllister pronounced him fit the sooner he'd be back in France and what lay in store there.

Charlotte, he thought. Oh, my darling Charlotte, all I want is to stay here with you.

Chapter 15

'Join up?' Grizelda McPherson repeated, eyes gleaming. Jack nodded. 'So what do you think?'

'You must, if that's how you feel. I'm all for it.'

'You are?'

'Oh yes. Every able-bodied man should do his bit, as they're all saying nowadays. It's your duty.'

That was a relief, Jack thought. He'd been certain she'd be against it. Clearly he'd been wrong about that.

'You'll look wonderful in a uniform,' Grizelda enthused, voice filled with excitement. 'You have the build for it.'

'It'll mean being away for quite some time. And who knows what'll happen, there's always the possibility I won't come back.'

A tremor ran through her that was almost sexual in nature. 'You'll come back, Jack, I just know it. And come back a hero.'

He laughed. 'Here, steady on. I've no intentions of being a hero. Serving my country well, and by that I mean Scotland, is all I have in mind.'

'But a hero you'll be nonetheless. That's the sort of man you are.'

Was he? Jack wondered. Did Grizelda see something in him he didn't. He had to admit being a hero was a pleasant prospect. 'Peter Drummond and I are going to enlist together,' he confided. 'But that's something you keep to yourself for now. All right?'

She nodded.

'It rather upsets things between you and me, I'm afraid,' he said.

'Why?'

'Because I'll be away, that's why.'

She lightly caressed his cheek. 'Time spent apart won't matter. At least not to me. I'll be here waiting for you when you return.'

'Are you sure about that, Grizelda? What if you meet someone else in the meanwhile?'

She gave a scornful laugh. 'Is that what you think of me, Jack Riach, that I'd allow that to happen? Well it won't, I assure you. I'll be here waiting on your return, I swear it.'

'If you are we'll get married, after a suitable engagement of course.'

'Oh, Jack,' she breathed. 'Is that a proposal?'

'Sounds like one to me. Do you accept?'

'With all my heart, Jack. With all my heart.'

Pride swelled within him. 'Will you write?'

'Naturally I'll write, you silly man. Every single day while you're away. And I'll knit for you, and send you parcels. I understand parcels are very gratefully received over there.'

'It's settled then,' he declared. 'Enlist I shall.'

'Oh, Jack,' she breathed. Face flushed, she pressed herself closer to him and closed her eyes.

Jack, knowing what she wanted, kissed her.

'You what!' Murdo exploded.

'Enlisted, Pa. Jack Riach and I together.'

Murdo couldn't believe his ears. His face went puce as anger burst within him. 'I won't have it, Peter, I just won't! Not two sons in the army. You'll just have to unenlist, that's all.'

Peter, still tipsy from the Pitlochry pub he and Jack had repaired to after the recruiting office, shook his head. 'That's impossible, Pa, as you're well aware. Once you sign on the dotted line that's it.'

Murdo was sorely tempted to slap his son, but refrained from doing so. This was a bombshell. 'What about the distillery?' he demanded.

'You'll have to go back full time, Pa. I'm sorry about that.'

Murdo wheeled about, strode over to the whisky decanter and poured himself a huge one which he despatched in a single gulp. Christ but he was angry. He poured himself another.

'Why didn't you discuss this with me first?' he queried harshly.

'I should have thought that was obvious from your reaction.'

'I would have tried to talk you out of it. No, more than that, I would have forbidden you to go ahead.'

'I know, Pa,' Peter nodded.

Murdo's anger suddenly disappeared and he sagged like

a balloon that's had half its air let out. Peter in the army during wartime, the thought made him want to vomit.

'Kitchener's been calling for more volunteers, Pa, the country desperately needs men like me.'

'Don't you think I need you here?' Murdo snapped in reply.

Peter sighed. He'd known this wasn't going to be easy and was in fact proving even more difficult than he'd anticipated. 'You can cope on your own at the distillery, can't you, Pa?'

'I can cope all right. I'm hardly senile yet.'

'Then there isn't a problem.'

Murdo ran a hand over his face, suddenly feeling dizzy. He prayed he wasn't going to have an attack. 'When do you leave?' he asked softly.

'I don't know yet. They'll notify me by post. Probably sometime within the next few weeks.'

The next few weeks, Murdo thought bitterly. The next few weeks and then what? The casualty lists in the newspapers were lengthening all the time. How long before Peter's name appeared on one of them?

He mustn't think like that, he told himself. He should think positively. That's the only way.

The girls were subdued when Peter informed them. An anguished look sprang into Geoffrey's eyes, before he simply turned and walked silently away.

Hettie collared Jack in the yard. 'Is it true?' she queried.

'If you mean about my enlisting, then yes.'

And she still wasn't pregnant. Damn! She saw her dream of a cottage and wee bit of land fading fast.

'It'll be a glorious adventure,' Jack declared. 'I can hardly wait.'

Bloody idiot, she thought. She needed him here to make her pregnant which he could hardly do if he was over in France or whatever.

'I'll see you right before I go, Hettie, I promise.'

That meant money, she realised, hopes rising a little. But how much? Certainly not enough for the cottage.

'Will it be this Sunday as usual?' she asked.

'Oh yes. And the Sunday after if I haven't already gone.'

She put her disappointment aside, for she was genuinely fond of her boss. Tears came into her eyes. 'I hope you'll be careful, Jack. I don't want anything happening to you.'

'I'll be right as rain, don't you worry about that.'

But she did, Hettie thought. She did.

Geoffrey opened the official army communication and read its contents. He'd been promoted to Captain, missing out the rank of First Lieutenant.

In other circumstances he'd have been cock a' hoop, except he realised the full import of his promotion. He'd gone up two full ranks because of losses, what other explanation could there be?

He felt his shoulder which was almost healed. Unless he pretended otherwise to McAllister he'd be on his way after his next visit to the doctor.

A week, ten days at most. And then France again.

'Charlotte,' he whispered with a choke in his voice. 'Oh, Charlotte.'

*

Andrew gazed round the drawing room that was jam-packed with people. It was the Fortescues' anniversary party to which he'd been invited. He was having a marvellous time.

Alice joined him. 'Everything all right?' she asked.

'Fine.'

'Enjoying yourself?'

'Very much so. And you?'

'The same.'

He had a sip of champagne of which there seemed to be a never-ending supply. 'If it wasn't so cold tonight I'd ask you out onto the terrace,' he said.

'And if it wasn't so cold I'd accept.'

They both laughed.

'I haven't had the chance to say so but you look splendid,' he declared.

'Why thank you, kind sir.'

'No need for thanks, it's absolutely true.'

Her dress was a Worth in a very pale shade of mauve with a white trim. Its crossover bodice draped softly in front of a low square neckline and was high waisted. A small train fell gracefully from the skirt.

A choleric-looking man, Andrew judged him to be in his late forties or possibly early fifties, who'd clearly been imbibing heavily, came up to them.

'Why, Alice me darlin', aren't you the sight for sore eyes. 'Tis an angel I see before me.'

She smiled. 'How are you, Mr McGinty?'

' 'Tis dandy I am. And how about your good and charming self?'

'I'm dandy also.'

A pair of suddenly hostile black eyes fastened onto Andrew. 'And who might this soldier laddie be?' Andrew was in uniform.

'Mr McGinty, may I present Lieutenant Andrew Drummond of the First Essex. A friend of mine. Andrew, this is Mr McGinty, a neighbour.'

'Pleased to meet you, sir,' Andrew declared, and extended a hand which was ignored.

'A friend?' McGinty mused, glancing at Alice. 'Well well. And since when did you have friends amongst the British military?'

Alice flushed. 'Since recently, Mr McGinty.'

The hostile eyes fastened themselves back onto a now uneasy Andrew. 'One day, and it'll be sooner rather than later, you mark my words, young man, we'll have all you British out of Ireland. Now what do you think of that?' he said belligerently.

'Perhaps you're right, Mr McGinty,' Andrew replied softly.

'Right! Of course I'm right. You buggers should never have been here in the first place. Usurpers, that's what you are. Usurpers.'

'I don't think we should talk contentious politics at a party. It's rather rude.'

McGinty bristled. 'Are you calling me rude, you whipper snapper?'

'Not at all, sir. Merely that talking contentious politics is.'

Sir Henry suddenly appeared beside them. 'Are you up to your old tricks then, Seamus?'

McGinty glared at him. 'Nobody told me the British army would be here.'

'Andrew is my guest, Seamus. Just as you are. I would be most upset if there was any unpleasantness.'

McGinty snorted. 'You have a point there, Henry. Where are me manners after all. I wouldn't be shaming you in your own house.'

Sir Henry took McGinty by the arm. 'I've had enough of this champagne, a woman's drink. Why don't you and I pop into my den where I have some of the best poteen you've ever tasted.' And while saying that he gave McGinty a conspiratorial wink.

'Poteen is it!'

'I swear it's probably the best you've ever tasted. Sheer ambrosia.'

'Then lead me to it.'

McGinty and Sir Henry moved off, Sir Henry steering his companion towards the door.

'What was all that about?' Andrew queried, relieved that Sir Henry had intervened and defused what might have become a nasty incident.

'Mr McGinty is a Fenian.'

'Oh!' said Andrew. 'You mean a troublemaker.'

She regarded him curiously. 'He doesn't view it like that. He considers himself a patriot.'

'Patriot or not, he certainly doesn't like us British.'

'That's putting it mildly. He detests you. And there are many like him.'

'So I've heard.'

'Anyway, let's forget him. I don't want the evening spoiled over politics.' She hesitated, then added, 'You won't mention to anyone about the poteen?'

He smiled. 'No, Alice, I won't. You have my word.'

'Good. Now let's mingle, there are some people I want you to meet.'

'More sympathetic ones I hope,' he joked.

'To be sure to be sure,' she joked in reply, using a broad accent.

'This is it then,' Geoffrey said as his train pulled into Pitlochry station.

She wouldn't cry, Charlotte told herself. She'd promised herself she wouldn't. At least not until he'd gone.

'I'll miss you so much, Geoffrey,' she said quietly in a cracked voice.

'And I you.'

'The time seems to have flown by.'

'Yes,' he agreed.

McPhie, standing close by with Geoffrey's case, was steadfastly looking away from them.

'I love you,' she whispered.

'And I love you.'

With a great whoosh of steam the train came to a halt.

He took her into his arms, her arms encircling him tightly, and kissed her. While they were doing that McPhie was attending to the case.

'Oh, my darling,' she whispered when the kiss was finally over.

He reluctantly released her and climbed into the carriage, McPhie closing the door for him. Geoffrey released the window and leant out. God but this was hard. Excruciatingly so.

They clasped hands, each drinking in the other. 'Chin up,' he said.

'And you.'

She somehow managed a smile. 'Remember to keep your head down.'

'I will, you can rely on it.'

The tears weren't far away but she struggled to keep them back. She was thinking of the previous night, their frenetic lovemaking that had eventually left them both exhausted. And again that morning, a tender sexual farewell.

She winced when the guard blew his whistle. 'Au revoir,' she said.

They released hands as the train juddered and slowly began to move.

His last sight of Charlotte was her groping for her handkerchief.

'I wish I was a man,' Wonky announced.

Nell stared at her cousin in astonishment. 'Why?'

'So I could go and fight. It's so frustrating not being able to do anything other than knit socks and balaclavas.'

'At least you're safe doing that. I shouldn't like to be in a position where I might get shot or blown up at any moment.'

A stricken expression came onto Charlotte's face. She quickly rose and dashed from the room.

'Blast!' Nell swore. 'Me and my big mouth.'

'The fault's mine, I'm sorry,' Wonky apologised.

Nell stared after her sister who'd understandably been in a right old state since Geoffrey's departure.

'I still wish I was a man,' Wonky stated forlornly. 'If I was I'd enlist like a shot if for no other reason than to get away from home. It's stifling at the manse, Nell. There are times when I feel I could scream.'

'It must be difficult for you.'

'You've no real idea. Stifling and suffocating in the extreme. In the past I've felt as though I was buried alive.'

'Poor Wonky,' Nell sympathised.

'If it wasn't for coming here I do believe I'd have gone mad years ago.'

'Well you're always welcome. Any time, you know that.'

Wonky smiled at Nell. 'Thanks, cuz.'

A little later a now composed Charlotte rejoined them and the subject of the war wasn't mentioned again that day.

'Will you see me off, Pa?' Peter asked. He and Jack were due to leave for officer training in two days' time.

'No,' came the curt reply.

Peter's disappointment showed on his face. 'Have it your own way.'

Murdo glanced up from his desk to glare at his son. 'You'll be back soon enough anyway. It's not as though they're sending you straight to France.'

'That'll come soon enough I suppose,' Peter said quietly.

Murdo lowered his gaze to hide the apprehension and fear for his son that were evident in his eyes. If it had been possible he'd gladly have traded places, he putting himself into danger while Peter stayed safely at home.

'Pa?'

'Yes?' Murdo snapped.

'When the time comes for me to go properly I'd prefer we parted on good terms. It would be awful if . . . well something happened and we hadn't.'

Murdo blanched.

'Don't you agree, Pa?'

Peter was right, he told himself. They mustn't part with a rift between them. If anything did happen . . .

Murdo swallowed hard. 'I'll see you off then,' he stated gruffly.

'Thanks, Pa. I appreciate that.'

'Now get on with your work and stop all this chit chat. There's plenty to be done.'

McPhie heaved Jack's case onto the car rack and began belting it down. While McPhie was doing this Jack got into the Rolls.

'Today's the day,' Peter smiled.

'Nervous?'

Peter shook his head. 'Excited, but not nervous.'

'Exactly how I feel.'

'I only hope we get posted to the Watch. It would be ideal serving alongside Geoffrey.'

Jack nodded his agreement, he too was hoping to be posted to their local regiment. 'How was your father when you left?' he asked.

Peter pulled a face. 'Not exactly ecstatic. Though I have to say things have thawed somewhat between us. He'll come round, it's only a matter of time.'

McPhie climbed into the driving seat and moments later the Rolls purred into life.

'Here we go,' Peter declared as the car moved off.

Jack didn't realise it but their departure was watched by a heavy-hearted Hettie.

*

Murdo sighed and laid his pen aside. A glance at the wall clock informed him Peter would be on his way, providing the train had arrived on time.

What would be the outcome of all this? God alone knew. All he could do was hope and pray the war would end soon, though there seemed little likelihood of that.

There was Geoffrey too to worry about. Charlotte would be devastated if anything happened to him. He wondered if Geoffrey was back in France, Charlotte hadn't heard anything for over a week.

There was a tap on the door and Isobel entered with coffee and biscuits.

'He's away then, eh, sir,' she said brightly.

Murdo nodded.

'You'll have your work cut out for you while he's gone I'm afraid.'

'I will that, Isobel.'

'Och you'll manage, sir. You did in the past before Mister Peter joined you.'

He gave her a wry smile. 'I was a lot younger then don't forget. Time takes its toll you know.'

'You, sir! You've got lots of life in you yet.'

He drank his coffee and ate his biscuits in brooding solitude after she'd departed.

He missed Peter dreadfully already.

Geoffrey discovered the war had taken a different turn on his arrival back at the regiment. Both sides had dug in, the fighting now conducted from trenches.

'Well well well,' Bobby Baxter smiled at him as he entered the dugout. 'Stopped skiving then?'

Geoffrey laughed. 'It was hardly that.'

'Reported to the C.O. yet?'

Geoffrey nodded. 'It was he who told me to join you here.'

Geoffrey glanced round the dugout which contained four cots plus a rickety table and four chairs. There were also rudimentary cooking facilities over in a corner. 'I take it this is to be home from home,' he said, slightly sarcastically.

'Don't complain, it's a palace compared to what the men have to put up with. And it's a haven when the shelling, not to mention the whizz bangs and "Jack Johnsons" start flying about.'

Geoffrey sat at the table beside his friend. 'So how have we been doing?'

'Holding our own just about. Remember Bob Reid?'

Geoffrey nodded.

'Gone west. Charlie McFarlane?'

Geoffrey nodded a second time.

'The same. Direct hit by a shell and blown to smithereens.'

Geoffrey listened to a list of dead and wounded that seemed interminable. 'Christ,' he muttered when Bobby finally stopped.

'And it's going to get worse,' Bobby added, a note of hysteria in his voice.

A soldier appeared at the entrance of the dugout. 'Ah, McMillan!' Bobby exclaimed. 'What's the news?'

'Bacon and tinned peaches for tea, sir.'

'Excellent, excellent.'

'Is this the new officer, sir?'

'Captain Armitage, McMillan.' To Geoffrey he said, 'I'd

heard of your promotion. As you can see I'm a captain now myself.'

'Pleased to meet you, sir,' McMillan declared, coming to attention.

'McMillan's our batman, and a splendid chap he is too. Has a knack of "acquiring" things which is most useful.'

'Like peaches for tea, sir.'

'Like peaches for tea,' Bobby agreed.

There was a rattle of rifle fire, followed by silence.

'Cut along then, McMillan,' Bobby said.

'Certainly, sir. All four gentlemen for tea, sir?'

'As far as I know. But that could easily change as has happened so many times.'

'I understand, sir. Thank you, sir.'

And with that McMillan left them.

Geoffrey pulled out his cigarettes, offered Bobby one and they both lit up. 'How's old Blighty then?' Bobby asked wistfully.

'The same, yet different. Half the people in my experience don't seem to really appreciate what's going on out here. They think we're having some sort of party.'

Bobby laughed. 'Some party! I can tell you, it's one to which I wish I'd never had an invitation.'

Geoffrey felt exactly the same.

'How's the wife?'

Geoffrey thought of Charlotte as he'd last seen her at the station and a lump came into his throat. 'Fine. Bearing up under the circumstances.'

'There's going to be a big push soon,' Bobby said softly. 'That'll be fun and games.'

'When?'

Bobby shrugged. 'Your guess is as good as mine. But soon. We'll know when the continuous shelling starts. That can go on for days you know and then at an appointed time it suddenly stops. That's when we go over the top.'

Geoffrey glanced away. 'Will it be bad?'

'In theory no. In practice yes. A lot of chaps will be going west.'

'We're being supported on our left flank by the Indians, top hole fellows. On the right by Australians and New Zealanders, cracking troops as well. No respect mind you, a difficult lot. But damned good men to have alongside you in a fight.'

'Who else is billetted here?' Geoffrey asked, gesturing round the dugout.

'Ronnie Bell, remember him?'

'Of course.'

'And Jim Massie. He's new, only joined us a fortnight ago. He replaced Danny Black whom I mentioned.' Danny had lost both legs and been shipped home to Britain.

'Poor Danny,' Geoffrey murmured.

'At least he's still alive,' Bobby said, eyes glittering strangely. 'At least he's that.'

Geoffrey felt sick.

Chapter 16

'I think I'm pregnant,' Charlotte announced to Nell.

Nell's face lit up. 'That's wonderful!'

'Only think, mind you, I'm not absolutely certain yet.'

'How many have you missed?'

'Only one, but I never miss. I'm regular as clockwork which is why I think I have to be.'

'Oh, Charlotte,' Nell breathed. 'I'm so deliriously happy for you. What do you want, a boy or girl?'

'A boy really, a little Geoffrey. But I won't complain if it's a girl. Just as long as whatever I'm blessed with is healthy.'

'That's the main thing,' Nell nodded.

A child, Charlotte thought with delight. Geoffrey if a boy and, providing her Geoffrey agreed, Louise if a girl, named after her mother.

She knew Murdo would be ecstatic if the latter.

'I can't wait to see Jack in his uniform,' Grizelda McPherson gushed to the others who'd come to tea.

'He'll be ever so dashing I'm sure,' Harriet Henderson

smiled. 'Uniforms really do something for a man. Even my brother Leo whom you both know hasn't exactly got the best of builds.' Leo Henderson was serving with the Seaforth Highlanders.

Antonia Phillips, who had neither boyfriend or brother to talk about, popped a piece of chocolate cake into her mouth. 'Hmmh,' she murmured appreciatively.

'Good, isn't it?' Grizelda beamed.

Antonia nodded. 'Scrumptious.'

'It's a new recipe of cook's,' Grizelda informed them. Her eyes took on a faraway look. 'I wonder what Jack's doing now? What he's up to at his officer training.'

'Goodness knows,' Harriet said.

Grizelda shivered. 'Only another week now till he's home. I can't wait to see him.'

'Will you go to the station?' Antonia asked.

'I'd like to. It depends on whether or not I know exactly when he's arriving back.'

Antonia helped herself to more chocolate cake, meanwhile eyeing the other cakes on offer. She would definitely have some of the Dundee she decided.

'I know he's going to be a hero when he sees action,' Grizelda stated. 'I told him that.'

'I think they're all heroes,' Harriet declared.

Grizelda gave her friend a withering look. 'They can hardly *all* be that.'

Harriet shrugged. 'In my opinion they are by just being over there in the first place. It must be ghastly. I mean . . .' She giggled. 'Frightfully awful thing to say, but can you *imagine* what the sanitary arrangements are?'

'They are soldiers after all,' Grizelda reminded her. 'And

I hardly think you should be mentioning sanitary arrangements. It's so unladylike.'

'Sorry,' Harriet apologised.

'How long will Jack be home for?' Antonia enquired.

'He's not sure about that, but is hoping for a fortnight. We'll have a spiffing time together.'

'Lucky you,' Antonia said, jealous of her friend. A jealousy not lost on Grizelda who positively preened with smugness and self satisfaction.

'How's Peter Drummond doing?' Harriet queried.

Grizelda's face hardened at the mention of Peter's name. Now there was someone who'd never be a hero, not in a million years. How fortunate she was to have landed Jack. She could not imagine what had once possessed her to have been so keen on Peter.

'Jack has never mentioned him in his letters,' she replied rather tartly, a lie for Jack had written about Peter.

'I wonder when someone will catch *his* eye,' Antonia said, pretending innocence but knowing full well that Grizelda had previously set her cap at him.

Grizelda changed the subject.

A Very light sailed into the night sky and burst directly overhead. Seconds later a German machine gun opened up.

Oh my God, Geoffrey thought, they'd been spotted. He swiftly pulled himself towards a shell crater and dropped inside, swearing involuntarily when another body dropped on top of him.

'Sorry, sir,' Private McMillan apologised.

'That's all right.'

Someone screamed, the scream tailing off and then ceasing altogether.

One of them had bought it; Geoffrey wondered who. He and McMillan remained cowering at the bottom of the crater as the machine-gun fire continued.

An ashen-faced Geoffrey lurched into the dugout to find Bobby writing a letter by the light of a hurricane lamp. Ronnie Bell and Jim Massie were both asleep, Ronnie snoring loudly.

'How did it go?' Bobby queried, glancing up.

Geoffrey slumped onto a chair. 'We were spotted,' he croaked.

'And?'

'I lost three men. I was damned lucky to get back alive myself. There was one point where . . .' He broke off and shuddered.

Bobby rose and crossed to his kit from which he produced a bottle of whisky. 'You'd better have some of this, old chap,' he declared, splashing a hefty measure into a tin cup.

Geoffrey's hands were shaking as he accepted the cup. 'I really thought my number was up that time,' he said, voice trembling.

'I know the feeling,' Bobby stated quietly. 'Who were the men?'

Geoffrey named them.

'No wounded?'

Geoffrey shook his head. 'Only dead.'

'Are you certain about that?'

'Yes,' Geoffrey breathed.

'Were you spotted on the way out or back?'

'Out.'

Bobby swore. 'Which means one of us will have to try again tomorrow night. That wire has to be reinforced.'

'I'm sorry,' Geoffrey mumbled.

'Not your fault, old bean. Hardly that.'

Geoffrey swallowed the whisky which immediately warmed the coldness of his stomach.

'You'd better get some shut eye,' Bobby advised.

Sleep! How could he do that feeling as he did. And yet he'd have to. 'Right,' he sighed, placing the cup on the table.

'Another two days and we're in reserve again. It'll go quickly enough,' Bobby said.

Two days, an eternity where they were, Geoffrey thought. He touched the pocket containing Charlotte's last letter. Would he ever see her again, ever again hold her in his arms?

'Thanks for the whisky,' he said, getting up.

'My pleasure.'

He did fall asleep, to dream, as he so often did, of Charlotte.

Peter stepped from the Rolls and gazed at Drummond House, a lump coming into his throat.

The door flew open and Charlotte, Nell and Wonky came tumbling out to stare at him while he stared back. McPhie began unloading his case from the car rack.

Peter had rather hoped Murdo would also be there to welcome him, but of course his father would be working. He'd stroll over to the distillery shortly.

He went to his sisters and cousin and hugged and kissed them each in turn.

'They posted you to the Watch I see,' Charlotte said, having noted the tartan of his kilt.

'They did indeed. And Jack. We'll be serving together.'

'How long?' Nell asked.

'Ten days. We were hoping for a fortnight but ten days is all we've got. Then it's straight to France.'

'You've lost weight, cuz,' Wonky smiled.

'So would you if you'd been through what I have.' He laughed. 'I enjoyed it though. In parts it was quite fun.'

'Are you hungry?' Charlotte queried.

'I am, but couldn't eat anything right away. I'm too excited at being home.'

He put an arm round Charlotte's shoulders and the other round Nell's. 'So how have you two been?'

Nell caught Charlotte's eye. Would she tell Peter or not? The possible pregnancy was a closely guarded secret between the pair of them that hadn't even been confided to Murdo yet. Charlotte, correctly guessing what was in her sister's mind, imperceptibly shook her head.

'In the pink,' Charlotte replied.

'Knitting mainly,' Wonky said, pulling a long face.

'I'll take this inside for you,' McPhie declared, passing them with Peter's case.

Peter hugged his sisters again. Oh, but it was grand being home! It had surprised him how much he'd missed it.

'Let's go on in,' he said.

Murdo glanced up as the office door opened and there was Peter resplendent in his uniform.

'You're back then,' Murdo commented dourly.

'You might look just a little bit pleased to see me, Pa.'

Murdo was, but wasn't going to show it. 'How did you get on?' he queried.

'Fine.'

'You've lost weight.'

'That's what Wonky said, and it's true. I feel the better for it.'

Murdo grunted. 'So now you've come to pester me during working hours.'

Peter glanced around, all sorts of memories of the office flooding his mind. 'I could sit down and help out if you like?' he offered.

Murdo waved a dismissive hand. 'Don't be daft. I wouldn't dream of it.'

'It's good to see you, Pa,' Peter declared softly.

'And you, son. And you. Now bugger off and we'll talk over dinner.'

When Peter had gone Murdo produced a handkerchief and wiped his eyes.

Sentimental eejit, he thought.

It was a full minute before he could concentrate again on the invoices in front of him.

'It's not fair!' Grizelda wailed. 'I'm streaming with cold.'

Jack grinned, she was indeed a sorry sight. 'You look gorgeous to me,' he declared gallantly.

'How can I possibly look gorgeous with a runny nose and puffy eyes. I wanted to come to the station but how could I in this state?'

'Well I'm here now,' he said, and going to her took her into his arms. 'You certainly smell gorgeous.'

She sniffed. 'Do I?'

'Wondrously so.'

That consoled her a little. 'I had all kinds of plans which will now have to be abandoned.'

'Don't worry. You'll probably be better in a couple of days and then we can carry out those plans of yours. You'll see.'

'I only hope so.'

He pressed her tightly to him and began stroking her hair. He hastily disentangled himself when he felt a distinct reaction between his loins.

'I'd love a cup of tea,' he declared.

She nodded, wiping her nose with a scrap of lace hanky. 'I'll ring for some.'

The shelling had gone on for forty-eight hours nonstop and now, precisely on the stroke of noon, it was about to stop. Geoffrey held his watch in one hand, revolver in the other. The men on either side of him had tense, expectant faces.

This was it, he thought. Any second now and . . .

The shelling stopped, leaving a strange, eerie silence that hurt the ears almost as much as the noise of the artillery barrage.

Next moment a whistle blew followed by many others up and down the line.

'Right, lads, here we go,' Geoffrey shouted. 'Over the top!'

Somewhere the pipes struck up, Hielan Laddie, the regimental tune.

Then, with thousands of others, he was advancing over No Man's Land towards the German trenches.

Halfway there the German machine guns began to chatter.

Bobby was shaking all over as he rummaged in his kit for the whisky. A shocked Geoffrey stood watching him.

'What a fucking disaster,' Geoffrey eventually choked.

Bobby didn't bother with the niceties of a tin cup, he simply took the cork from the bottle and upended the latter into his mouth.

'So many hanging on the wire,' Geoffrey whispered, his voice seeming to come from a long way off.

'Here,' said Bobby, thrusting the bottle at Geoffrey who followed Bobby's example of upending it into his mouth.

'I saw Jim Massie get it,' Bobby said. 'He was almost cut in half.'

'Ronnie bought it as well. His head just sort of exploded.'

'At least we won't have to put up with Ronnie's snoring any more,' Bobby said, and laughed hysterically.

'Hanging on the wire,' Geoffrey repeated. 'All those men hanging on the wire.'

Bobby threw up.

Charlotte had left Nell and Wonky knitting while she attended to some household duties with Miss McQueen. She was returning to the pair of them when she came across Peter standing at a window gazing out. He was clearly lost in thought.

'Peter?'

He blinked himself out of his reverie and turned to smile at her.

'You were miles away,' she stated.

'Yes.'

'Are you worried about France?'

He ran a hand over his face, and sighed. 'I suppose so, but that wasn't what I was thinking about. Or not exactly anyway.'

'Oh?'

'I can't say, Charlotte. It would sound so . . . morbid.'

She went to him and hooked an arm round his. 'Can I help?'

'Not really.'

'It's sometimes best to talk things over, Peter. A problem shared and all that.'

He smiled again. 'You're a poppet at times. Geoffrey's a lucky man.'

'Well?' she persisted.

His expression became serious. 'You won't mention the following conversation to anyone. Promise?'

'You have my word.'

He gazed around him. 'I was just wondering if I'll ever see Drummond House and the family again.'

Her face reflected her concern.

'It's possible I won't you know. Anything could happen over there.'

She kissed him tenderly on the cheek. 'You're right, that is morbid. You'll be back, Peter, I'm certain of it.'

'And how can you be that?'

She touched her heart. 'I can feel it here. So I'd stop worrying if I was you.'

He laughed softly. 'A woman's intuition, eh?'

'That's right, Peter. A woman's intuition.'

'Well if that's the case then I'm bound to be back. There can't be any doubts about it.' He took a deep breath. 'Thanks for cheering me up, sis. I feel a lot better now.'

'No more dark brooding?'

'Now you have *my* promise.'

'Good.'

She kissed him again before continuing on her way.

'Having a baby!' Murdo repeated, eyes shining.

Charlotte nodded.

He swept her into his arms. 'I couldn't be more pleased, darling. I'm delighted.'

'I thought you would be,' she smiled.

He released her. 'A grandchild. The first of many I hope.'

'In the summer, Pa.'

He nodded. 'Are you feeling all right? Your mother used to get terrible morning sickness I remember.'

Charlotte held up crossed fingers. 'So far none of that. A couple of queasy moments, but no sickness.'

'This calls for a dram,' he declared, and strode to the decanter. 'You?' He realised what he'd said. 'No, I think that's unadvisable in the circumstances.'

'Quite.'

He chuckled as he poured his dram. 'A grandchild, well well well.'

'If it's a girl I thought I might call her – with Geoffrey's consent of course, which I'm sure he'll give – Louise.'

The glass stopped halfway to Murdo's mouth and he swallowed hard. A hint of tears came into his eyes. 'That would make me very happy, Charlotte. You've no idea how much. Thank you.'

'It might be a boy, mind.'

Murdo nodded. 'Of course. But there's bound to be a wee lassie along the way. I doubt you'll be stopping at one.'

Charlotte doubted that as well.

'Tell you what,' he said. 'We'll have a party tonight. Just us, the family, to celebrate. What do you say?'

'That would be lovely, Pa.'

'Then a party it is.'

He didn't add that it would double up as a party for Peter who'd be leaving for France in two days' time.

Murdo was drunk and didn't give a damn. It wasn't every day you were told you were going to be a grandfather. He beamed across the room at Charlotte who was eating a slice of cream sponge Cook had made especially for the occasion.

'Another dram, Pa?' Peter asked, he none too sober either.

Murdo held out his glass which Peter topped up, before doing the same to his own glass.

'The day after tomorrow,' Murdo said.

'That's right, Pa.'

'I'll be coming to the station with you. Can Jack Riach make his own arrangements? I'd prefer if it was just the pair of us.'

Peter nodded. 'I'll speak to Jack in the morning. Probably best he makes his own arrangements as Grizelda's going with him.'

'How are those two getting on?'

'Extremely well according to Jack. A right couple of love birds.'

'You'll be seeing Geoffrey I presume. Give him my regards, won't you.'

'I will, Pa.'

Murdo cleared his throat. 'This isn't easy for a man like me. But I was angry at you joining up because . . . well because you're my son and all that entails.'

'I understood that, Pa,' Peter replied softly.

'A parent tries to keep his children out of danger. It's only natural, as you'll find out for yourself one day.'

Peter glanced away. That was something that wouldn't happen. 'Of course, Pa.'

Murdo suddenly reached out and gripped Peter's arm. 'You will watch out for yourself, lad. No stupid heroics and any of that nonsense.'

'No stupid heroics, Pa. You can rest assured.'

Murdo squeezed Peter's arm, then released it. 'That's good then.'

'I have always loved you, Pa, remember that,' Peter said very softly.

This time there was more than a hint of tears in Murdo's eyes. He raised his glass in a toast. 'Here's to you, son. Here's to you.'

'And you, Pa.'

It was a golden moment to be treasured.

McPhie knew Murdo better than Murdo realised. He opened the car door when Murdo, having escorted Grizelda to her vehicle, came striding towards the Rolls. Murdo's face told its own story.

'I took the liberty of putting something inside for you, sir,' McPhie said when Murdo reached him.

Murdo glanced into the car where there was a bottle of whisky and a glass lying on the back seat.

'Thank you, McPhie,' he replied gruffly. 'And by the way, take your time driving home. I'm not in any rush.'

'I fully understand, sir. We'll go the scenic route.'

Murdo waited till they'd left the station well behind them before opening the bottle.

They were almost halfway to Drummond House when McPhie looked in his rear-view mirror to see tears streaming down Murdo's anguished face.

He thanked God he didn't have a son who'd just gone off to war.

Alice reined in her horse and waited for Andrew to catch up with her. 'You let me beat you on purpose,' she laughed when he drew alongside.

'I did not,' he protested.

'Liar!'

He pretended indignation. 'I am nothing of the sort. You outrode me fair and square.' She was right of course, he had allowed her to win.

'Let's walk for a bit,' she proposed, dismounting.

Andrew dismounted also, patted his horse, then fell into step beside her. 'I was just thinking earlier,' he said. 'I'd love to take you home to meet Pa and the girls. They'd adore you.'

She glanced sideways at him. 'I believe I'd rather enjoy that. I've never been to Scotland.'

'I have a decent leave coming up and might go myself. But taking you is out of the question.'

'Why?'

'U-boats, Alice, they're proving quite a menace. I doubt

your father would allow you to take the risk. And even if he did I wouldn't.'

Something fluttered inside her. 'You're very protective.'

'Naturally, I don't wish you to come to harm.'

'That's kind of you.'

'Kind? I think it's more than that, Alice. I've told you before I'm very attracted to you. An attraction that keeps on increasing.'

The fluttering grew.

'And we have been seeing rather a lot of one another,' he went on.

'Yes, we've become good friends.'

'I was hoping it was leading to more than friendship,' he said.

So had she, very much so. 'Is there any likelihood of your regiment being posted elsewhere?' she asked, changing the subject.

He shrugged. 'Of course, eventually. Why?'

'I was thinking of France.'

Andrew sighed. 'There's always that possibility. They might well take troops out of Ireland and send them over there.'

'Would you wish to go?'

He laughed. 'No thank you. I'm perfectly happy with my billet here where there aren't bullets flying round my ears. Besides . . .' His tone changed. 'That would mean being parted from you.'

She didn't want to be parted from him either, he had come to mean a great deal to her. 'Will you always stay in the army?' she queried.

'I am a career officer.'

'I appreciate that, but it doesn't mean you have to remain in the army until retirement.'

He guessed what she was getting at. 'I certainly couldn't resign my commission before the end of the war. But afterwards? Who knows. It all depends.'

'On what?'

'Whether or not I had a reason to resign. I'm not entirely against it. I'm well aware there is life outside the army. Though what I'd do I couldn't say. I'm not trained for anything else.'

'That might not be a problem,' she said.

'Oh?'

She smiled enigmatically and didn't reply.

The fish was taking the hook, Andrew thought jubilantly. What she was presumably hinting at was that he could work for her father in some capacity or even, and the prospect thrilled him, be a man of leisure. But, on reflection, he doubted it was the latter.

'I wish you wouldn't go to Scotland. I don't want you taking any risks either.'

'I'm a soldier, Alice. It's our job to take risks.'

'But not unnecessary ones,' she argued.

He stopped and stared at her, she stopping also. 'All right,' he replied softly. 'I shan't go.'

Her face lit up. 'You could spend your leave with us.'

'Meaning you,' he smiled.

She didn't reply to that either.

He took her into his arms, noting there wasn't any hesitation on her part, and the next moment his lips were hungrily on hers.

It was their first kiss.

Chapter 17

Peter took in Geoffrey's dreadfully drawn and haggard face. Christ, he thought, his brother-in-law had aged a good ten years if not more.

'Hello, old bean,' he smiled.

The two men shook hands.

'You look fit,' Geoffrey commented.

Peter could hardly say the same. He gave Geoffrey the parcel he carried tucked under one arm. 'That's from Charlotte and crammed with goodies including a couple of bottles of best Drummond.'

'Is it by Jove!' Geoffrey exclaimed, placing the parcel on the table. 'We'd best have some of that straight off.'

Peter frowned. It was nine o'clock in the morning. 'This early?' he queried as Geoffrey began ripping the paper.

Geoffrey gave a dry, cynical laugh. 'We don't worry about things like that out here. Any time, night or day, is right for a drink. We do a lot of that in the trenches, drink, I mean. When we can get hold of it. Stiffens the sinews you know.'

Dear me, Peter thought. Was it really as bad as that. There again, the sights he'd seen so far were pretty grim.

'When did you arrive?' Geoffrey asked.

'Yesterday afternoon. I'm billetted further down the line towards Machelle.'

Geoffrey removed the lid from the cardboard box inside the wrapping paper and grunted. 'Charlotte's done me proud. I'll thank her in my next letter.'

He removed a bottle of Drummond and quickly uncorked it. There was still some tea left in the tin mugs which he threw onto the ground. He then poured two enormous drams and handed Peter one. 'Chin chin!' he toasted, and had a deep swallow.

Geoffrey closed his eyes and sighed with satisfaction. 'God that's good,' he whispered.

Peter wasn't so sure on sampling his dram, almost immediately feeling his head swim. He wasn't used to drinking at that hour.

Geoffrey had another swallow. 'Charlotte wrote they'd posted you to the Watch.'

'It's what I was hoping for.'

'Well, it's great having you here. Sit down.'

'I can't stay long,' Peter explained. 'I'm on duty in an hour.'

'What have they got you doing?'

'Observation work to start with.'

Geoffrey nodded. 'There's a great deal worse than that, I can assure you.'

He finished his whisky and poured himself another enormous one. 'You've joined us at a difficult time, the battalion's considerably under strength which means we're having to do all sorts of extra duties.'

'Why's that?'

Geoffrey regarded his brother-in-law with amusement. 'Why the hell do you think? Dead and wounded, old chap, dead and wounded. We lost two officers alone out of this dugout only a few weeks back who haven't been replaced yet. I hope to God they are soon.'

Geoffrey scratched himself. 'I'd love a bath but won't manage that till we're in the reserve line again. Roll on, roll on.'

McMillan appeared at the entrance to the dugout and saluted. 'Shall I clear and wash the breakfast things, sir?' he asked, addressing Geoffrey.

'Not now, McMillan. I've got a guest, my brother-in-law, who's just joined us.'

McMillan saluted Peter. 'Welcome to hell, sir.'

'Cut along then, McMillan.'

'Yes, sir.' And with that McMillan disappeared.

'How is Charlotte?' Geoffrey queried softly, the hint of a catch in his voice.

'Doing well.'

'She hasn't said, so I presume there isn't any trouble with the pregnancy so far.'

'None that I'm aware of.'

Geoffrey nodded. 'If it's a girl she wants to call her Louise after your mother.'

'So I believe.'

'Your father must have been pleased about that.'

'Tremendously.'

Geoffrey chuckled. 'Liked him right from the off. Fine man.'

Bobby Baxter entered. 'I say, what's all this then. A flaming booze up?'

Geoffrey introduced Peter and explained about the parcel. He then waved a hand at the opened bottle. 'Help yourself, Bobby. Don't stand on ceremony.'

Bobby poured himself a dram as large as those Geoffrey had. 'Here's how,' he toasted, and drank his dram straight off.

'Well,' commented Bobby, gazing into the box. 'How absolutely spiffing.'

Peter started when a single shell screamed overhead, followed shortly by an explosion.

'You'll get used to it,' Geoffrey smiled, knowing that to be a lie as far as he was concerned.

He never had.

It was a grand gathering, Nell observed, a ball perhaps or something similar, many of those present bewigged. She focused on one female in particular, a youngish lass wearing a hooped purple gown, silk by the looks of it, woven through with scarlet flowers.

The men were a colourful lot, some in best Highland garb, others in Lowland attire. Everyone appeared to be having a wonderful time.

Edinburgh? Nell wondered. That would tie in with her last vision. Was this taking place in Edinburgh?

And then there he was, her Highlander, a glass of wine in hand talking to a knot of people.

A woman in the group threw back her head and laughed uproariously while another Highland gentleman clapped her Highlander on the shoulder. Obviously he'd just told a joke or funny story.

All conversation and merriment abruptly ceased when a young man, most handsomely dressed, entered the room, everyone bowing to him.

Bonnie Prince Charlie? Nell speculated, a thrill running through her. It could well be.

The prince, she presumed it to be he, progressed through the throng. A word here, a word there. His hand kissed by this one, then that, the ladies curtsying as he passed.

She watched as her Highlander took the prince's hand and kissed it. How radiant he looked afterwards, almost glowing with pride. She guessed he was thinking how he would describe the occasion when he got back home.

And then the vision began to fade.

Charlotte caressed her abdomen which had started to expand, mentally counting off the months that were left to her. Her pregnancy was going better than she'd dared to have hoped. It couldn't have been more smooth.

A long way yet, she warned herself. Still time for lots of trials and tribulations.

'What's wrong with you?' Wonky queried. Nell took a deep breath, having just come out of her vision. Had it ended because of Wonky's approach? She didn't know. All she did know was that she never had them when others were present.

'Sorry, I was day dreaming,' she replied.

'You seemed transfixed.'

'Did I?' she answered innocently.

'Quite.'

'I suppose I was.'

'Day dreaming about what?'

Nell smiled at her cousin. 'You wouldn't believe me if I told you.'

'Go on, try me,' a curious Wonky urged.

'Well, for some reason I was thinking about Bonnie Prince Charlie.'

Wonky stared at Nell in astonishment. 'You're pulling my leg.'

'No I'm not, honestly. I was thinking about the Bonnie Prince.'

Wonky shook her head in bewilderment. 'But why?'

'I've no idea, he just came into my mind. I was trying to imagine what it must have been like in those days. The clothes they wore, that sort of thing.'

Wonky smiled. 'It must have been ever so romantic. Until Culloden that is. It wouldn't have been very romantic after that.'

Culloden, Nell thought. The great battle the Scots and their prince had lost to the English after which the prince had eventually fled to France where he'd died in exile.

What about her Highlander, the man she now believed had once been her husband. Had he also survived?

She prayed with all her heart that he had.

Andrew snapped awake as his bedroom door creaked open. What on earth was going on?

The door closed again. 'Andrew?' Alice whispered.

He sat up in bed. 'What are you doing here?' he queried, also in a whisper when she perched beside him.

'Don't think badly of me. I'm not fast and don't want you to make love to me. I simply couldn't sleep and wanted to be with you.'

He immediately thought of Jean Ritchie and how he'd slipped into her bedroom at Drummond House. There had been no protestations of not making love then.

Reaching out he grasped Alice by the hand. 'This is madness, what if someone saw you? There are other house guests not to mention staff don't forget. That would be the end of your reputation.'

'I was extremely careful, I promise.'

He'd never have believed Alice capable of such a thing. It was so out of character. Unless he'd misjudged her that is.

'Come into bed, you'll catch your death out there,' he said.

There was a sigh of material falling to the floor and then she was snuggling up to him.

'Oh, Andrew,' she breathed.

Her scent was strong in his nostrils, her body a temptation alongside his.

'Why couldn't you sleep?' he asked.

'Because of you. I just couldn't get you out of my mind.'

The fish was well and truly hooked, he thought, smiling in the darkness. Hooked but not yet landed.

Dare he? She shuddered when his hand brushed her breast.

'Kiss me, Andrew.'

He did, a passionate kiss with an interplay of tongues. He could feel the fire of desire mounting within him.

His hand now touched the same breast and cupped it.

The kiss continued, Alice writhing against him, he not knowing if he could stop from going further. He was hard as rock.

'Sorry,' she apologised, breaking the kiss. 'I'm not being fair.'

'That's all right.'

'I'm a virgin, Andrew.'

'I presumed that to be the case.'

'Can I be honest?'

'Of course.'

She took a deep breath. 'No man has ever affected me the way you do. I go dizzy sometimes just being in your company.'

He undid the top buttons of her nightdress and dipped his hand inside, she giving a small gasp as he slid fingers over her nipple.

'Please don't think less of me for being here, Andrew. I couldn't bear that.'

'I don't. I swear to you.'

'I . . .' She broke off in confusion. 'No, I can't say.'

'Yes you can.'

'I can't. It wouldn't be right. The declaration has to come from you first.'

'Are you telling me you love me, Alice?' he queried softly.

She didn't reply.

'Because I love you.'

There was a sharp intake of breath. 'Do you, Andrew?'

'With my entire being. I don't know when it happened but it did. Perhaps it was that day I stopped Midnight and

I just didn't realise until later.' He was almost bursting inside with jubilation.

'And I love you, Andrew,' she said with a tremor in her voice.

'Oh, my darling. My sweet sweet darling.'

His lips again fastened onto hers while the hand inside her nightdress gently kneaded and massaged. He knew, despite the protestation on her arrival about not wanting to make love, that she was his for the taking. Should he or shouldn't he? The decision, considering the state of arousal he was in, was an agonising one. Reluctantly he decided against it. Everything should, and would, be done properly. Oh, but the temptation!

'Will you marry me?' he asked.

'Yes.'

He removed his hand from her breast and smoothed it over a silken cheek. Greystones and all that went with it was as good as his.

'I'll speak to your father before I return to Dublin,' he promised.

Dawn was breaking before a still-intact Alice left him to go back to her own bed.

Andrew stood at a downstairs window watching Sir Henry clearly remonstrating with Seamus McGinty. Now what was that all about? He'd been hoping to catch Sir Henry on his own to ask for Alice's hand in marriage, but now obviously wasn't the time.

McGinty stamped off a few paces, stopped and turned to yell something at Sir Henry. Sir Henry's reply was vehemently to shake his head.

He'd try again later, Andrew decided, moving away from the window.

Peter knelt in the forward post he was manning staring through binoculars at the German line. Nothing was moving.

He sighed. God, but this was tedious. Hour in, hour out, waiting for something to happen. He'd have welcomed any diversion, no matter what.

A little later he glanced round when he heard the approach of his relief whom he smiled thankfully at. He couldn't wait to get back to his dugout for a bite to eat and a rest.

The relief was a Second Lieutenant whom he'd trained with. A chap called Matheson.

'What's happening?' Matheson asked on reaching him.

'Nothing.' He was about to add it was quiet as the grave out there then thought the better of it. That would have been in extremely bad taste.

Matheson yawned.

'Been asleep?'

'Sound. I was only wakened about ten minutes ago.'

Peter handed over the binoculars. 'Have fun.'

'Oh very droll!' Matheson grinned in reply.

Peter slid down the trench wall allowing Matheson to take his place, which Matheson did.

Peter undid his flies to urinate, having needed to go for some time. He was in midstream when a single shot rang out.

Finished, he did himself up again and turned to Matheson. The shot had obviously come from a sniper.

'Did you manage to spot him?'

Matheson didn't reply.

'Well?'

Then Peter noticed that Matheson was in a curiously slumped position.

'Matheson?'

When he touched Matheson the man slid down the trench wall to fall onto his back.

Matheson was dead.

The steady tick tock of the clock was driving Wonky out of her mind. Another evening in, another evening of crashing boredom.

She stared at her father engrossed in his Bible which he read every night. Then at her mother dozing in a chair.

Tick tock, tick tock, tick tock . . .

Wonky ground her teeth to stop herself jumping up and screaming out her frustration.

'Engaged?' Sir Henry mused, stroking his moustache.

'Yes, sir. If you'll give us your permission.'

'I see.'

Sir Henry produced a leather case of cigars, took one out, clipped it and lit up. 'I presume Alice knows you've asked for her hand?' he queried eventually.

'Oh yes, sir.'

'Hmmh.'

Sir Henry regarded Andrew through a haze of smoke. 'I've nothing against you personally, Andrew, you're a decent chap from a good family by all accounts, but I can't say I'd be happy Alice marrying an army officer.'

'We've discussed that, sir. As you'll appreciate I can't resign my commission while there's a war on, but most certainly could when it was over.'

'And would you?'

'If that's what Alice wished, sir.'

'And then what?'

'Well I'm not trained for anything other than army life. There's always the distillery of course, I'm sure my father would find me something there.'

Sir Henry considered that. It would mean Alice living in Scotland which didn't please him one bit. He wanted his only child at hand, as would her mother.

'I won't give you an answer right away, Andrew, I'd like to discuss the matter with my wife first.'

'Naturally, sir. I fully understand.'

Sir Henry eased himself forward in his chair a fraction. 'I take it you love my daughter?' His eyes bored into Andrew's.

'Very much, sir.'

Sir Henry was only too well aware of how good a catch Alice was and how unscrupulous certain men could be where a fortune was concerned.

'You mentioned once that your brother inherits when your father dies,' he said.

'That's perfectly correct, sir.'

'And what about you?'

'I'm bound to come into some money, sir, though how much I couldn't say. Pa has never mentioned.'

'Uh-huh,' Sir Henry nodded.

'We're not exactly a poor family, sir. We are of some substance.'

'I appreciate that,' Sir Henry murmured. Nonetheless, he'd find out what he could about the Drummonds. Always best to be on the safe side.

'Thank you for your time, sir,' Andrew said. 'Now if you'll excuse me, Alice and I are going out riding.'

Sir Henry gazed speculatively at the door through which Andrew had left.

'Well?' Alice demanded eagerly.

'He says he wants to speak to your mother first. But I have the definite feeling it'll be all right.'

Alice, face aglow, hugged Andrew. 'I'm certain so too.'

As they rode off Andrew twisted in his saddle to gaze back at Greystones.

He smiled at the thought of it one day being his.

'Are you convinced you love him?' Sir Henry asked softly.

'Yes, Father, I am.'

'And that *he* loves you?'

'Yes again.'

Sir Henry grunted. His daughter wasn't a fool, surely if Andrew was pretending love she'd see through him. On the other hand she might not considering how she felt.

'He said he'd resign his commission after the war,' Sir Henry stated.

'We've discussed that. I thought . . . well maybe you could find him a position.'

'There is that possibility.' It would be more than that, he told himself. He'd do his damnedest to keep Alice close by.

'So what's the verdict, Father?'

'Your mother isn't against the match, I've already spoken to her. Therefore it's all down to me.'

'You wouldn't refuse us, Father, surely? As I said, I love him dearly.'

He'd never been able to refuse Alice anything which she was well aware of. Still, this was a momentous step and his instincts were to be cautious.

'Tell you what, Alice. Give me a few weeks and you'll have my answer. Let's say the next time Andrew visits. Now how's that?'

Her disappointment clearly showed. 'If you wish, Father.'

'I think that's wise. There's no hurry anyway, is there?'

She smiled. 'Not really. Except . . .' She trailed off.

'Except what?'

'I'd rather have liked a decision to have been made today.'

'On his next visit,' Sir Henry repeated. That would give him time to make a few enquiries.

Jack Riach lay back in the tin bath, luxuriating in the warmth of the water it contained. He was in a deserted farmhouse that had somehow remained intact. He and the rest of the Watch were in deep reserve miles from the front line.

Closing his eyes he started to sing a song currently popular with the British troops:

'I don't want to die,
I want to go home.
I don't want to go to the trenches no more,
Where the whizz bangs and shells do whistle and
  roar.

'I don't want to go over the sea,
To where the alleymen will shoot at me,
I want to go home
I don't want to die.'

Peter breezed in. 'What a bloody caterwauling. Whatever else you can do, Jack, you certainly can't sing. You've got a voice like a foghorn.'

Jack grinned at his friend. 'What's for lunch? I'm starving.'

'Bully beef.'

Jack pulled a face. 'Is that the best that can be done?'

'We can always call in on Geoffrey. That McMillan of his seems to do wonders where food is concerned.'

'Then call we shall, old bean. Call we shall.'

Peter sat on an upturned box. 'Was that letter I saw you reading earlier from Grizelda?'

Jack nodded. 'She's in the pink and wondering when I'm going to win the Victoria Cross.'

Both men laughed.

'She'll be lucky,' Jack commented wryly.

Peter's expression changed to one of introspection.

'What are you thinking about?' Jack queried softly.

'Home, Jack. Drummond House, Pa, the girls, the distillery. I miss them all dreadfully. I wish . . .' He trailed off.

'What?'

'I could just transport myself back there for a few hours. That would be wonderful.'

'Yes,' Jack smiled in agreement.

'But no chance of that I'm afraid. Such magic doesn't exist.'

'Oh I don't know.'

Peter stared in puzzlement. 'What does that mean?'

'You can't do it in actuality of course, but the mind and imagination are marvellous things. You can always think yourself back.'

Peter sighed. 'There is that.'

Jack closed his eyes again and conjured up a picture of Grizelda. Silly female at times, but he adored her. They'd be a splendid couple together when married. When all this . . . awfulness was over.

'Right!' exclaimed Jack, suddenly standing upright in the bath revealing himself in all his naked glory. 'Dried, dressed and a trip to your brother-in-law.'

They both laughed.

'You're right as rain as far as I can ascertain,' McAllister declared to Charlotte.

'I must say if this is being pregnant then it's far easier than I'd ever imagined.'

McAllister smiled. 'You've been very fortunate, lassie. There are many who have a considerably hard time of it.'

'So I believe.'

'Aye.'

'Is there anything else I can do, doctor?'

McAllister shook his head. 'Just keep on the way you are, and come and see me again in a month's time.'

'I'm, eh . . .' She blushed. 'A bit scared of the birth itself doctor. I've heard tales.'

McAllister snorted. 'It's painful, I'll grant you that. But every mother has to go through it. And in your case, from the way things have gone to date, you'll probably pop the bairn as easily as a pea from a pod.'

She grinned at him. 'You're very reassuring, doctor.'

'And I'll be there don't forget.' His eyes twinkled. 'I wish I had a pound for every baby I'd delivered. Why, I'd almost be as rich as your father.'

Murdo roared when Charlotte recounted that to him.

Chapter 18

'So how are you, Murdo?' McAllister enquired, accepting the dram he was handed.

'Oh, so so.'

'If I was honest I'd say you were looking tired.'

Murdo sighed. 'I am, James, I am. I suppose it's simply that I'm not the man I once was. Work you know.'

McAllister thought of Peter. Damn the lad for going off as he had. That must be a terrible strain on Murdo. There again, it was partially Murdo's fault for not confiding in his son.

'Any more attacks?'

Murdo shook his head. 'You'd have known if there had been, believe me.'

McAllister tasted his whisky, pleased to note that Murdo hadn't joined him. 'Are you keeping up your walking?'

'By the time I get home at night I'm buggered,' Murdo explained. 'All I seem able to do is eat and fall asleep in a chair afterwards. And sometimes I'm not too keen to eat either.'

'You must Murdo. You could be in real trouble if you let that slide.'

Murdo ran a hand over his face. 'I drag myself out of bed in the morning and it's a real effort to walk up the road, far less anything else.'

McAllister tried not to let his concern show. 'Can you get some help?'

'You mean at the distillery? There isn't anyone. It's all on my shoulders.'

McAllister swirled the whisky round his glass. 'Heard from Peter recently?'

'The other day. He's as well as can be expected being out there in that hell. He tries not to be too pessimistic but I can detect his real mood underneath the things he says. And it isn't good.'

'Aye,' McAllister murmured sympathetically. He reflected on the list of dead in the previous day's newspaper and inwardly shuddered. Thank the Lord he was too old to fight.

'What about Charlotte?' Murdo asked. 'She came to see you the other day I understand.'

'Och, she's fine. Apprehensive about the birth, mind, but that's only natural. I'll get her through it, don't you worry.'

'You're a true friend, James. And that's a fact,' Murdo said softly.

McAllister smiled. 'It cuts both ways as you're well aware. You've always been a good friend to me. There are things you've done in the past for me and mine I'll never forget.'

Murdo waved a dismissive hand. 'Stop your havering, man. If the positions had been reversed you'd have done the same.'

McAllister knew that to be true. 'Can I say something?'

'What's that?'

'I sincerely hope it is a lassie that Charlotte has. I know that would give you more pleasure than anything else.'

'Another Louise,' Murdo muttered. 'Aye, it would.'

McAllister toasted Murdo, and drank. 'I'd better be moving. I've other calls to make.'

Murdo saw him to the door.

Charlotte gave a sudden gasp and bent over in her chair.

'What's wrong?' Wonky queried in alarm.

Nell jumped up and went to comfort her sister. 'Are you all right?'

Charlotte took a deep breath. 'Indigestion I think.'

'Is it bad?'

Charlotte took another deep breath. 'Dinner was extremely rich last night. Perhaps that's the cause.'

It had been rich, Nell thought. Charlotte could well be right. 'Why don't you go and lie down for a while?' she suggested.

Charlotte considered that. It seemed a good idea. 'Maybe I will.'

'Do you want some help upstairs?' an anxious Wonky offered.

Charlotte shook her head. 'I can manage.'

She winced as another griping pain grabbed her insides. 'Do we have anything?'

'I'll speak to Miss McQueen,' Wonky replied and hurried from the room.

'I'll have to be more careful about what I eat in future,' Charlotte said. 'At least until the baby's born.'

Nell nodded her agreement.

Charlotte laid her knitting aside and came to her feet. It was so unlike her to suffer from indigestion, but then she'd never been pregnant before. She gave Nell a weak smile. 'If this is all I have to contend with then I'll have no complaints.'

'Do you want me to send for Dr McAllister?'

'Don't be daft. I'm not calling the doctor out because of indigestion. Heaven knows what he'd think.'

'Are you certain of that?'

'Absolutely. Now I'm off to bed.'

Within the hour Charlotte had rejoined Nell and Wonky with the declaration that her indigestion had gone.

Sir Henry laid down the letter he'd received from the lawyer he'd contacted in Scotland, which confirmed that the Drummonds were an honourable and much respected family, highly thought of in Perthshire. Also that their business was a successful one.

He took out a cigar, clipped it and lit up. That seemed to be that then. There weren't any reasons he shouldn't give his blessing to Alice and Andrew's engagement.

And yet, why did a niggle of doubt remain in his mind? He couldn't for the life of him think why.

He thought again of Andrew, picturing him, going over conversations they'd had together. A totally personable young man in all respects, whom his daughter loved.

Perhaps it was the fact that Andrew was so smooth which disturbed him. He would have liked to have seen a bit more grit there, more solidness of character. A man he could have had a damn good argument with which he could never envisage being the case with Andrew.

He sighed. Children! You did everything you could for them but in the end you had to let them go.

Was it jealousy on his part? he wondered. Alice was their only child after all, and a girl at that. He knew that fathers often over-zealously protected their daughters, that fathers were often somewhat in love with them themselves.

Was that it? Was he simply digging in his heels not wishing to give Alice up, not wanting her to escape the family fold.

The truth was, he just didn't know.

Sir Henry leant back in his chair and blew smoke at the ceiling. The last thing he wanted was to hurt Alice which he would if he refused her and Andrew permission to get engaged. Permission he had no logical reason to deny.

No logical reason, he repeated to himself. Surely the real nub of the matter.

So be it, he decided.

So be it.

Andrew flushed on hearing Sir Henry's words, while Alice gave a small exhalation of relief.

'Congratulations, darling,' Lady Fortescue smiled.

'And congratulations to you, my boy,' Sir Henry said, striding to Andrew and warmly shaking him by the hand.

Andrew was exultant. Not that he'd been worried, but still, you never knew. He glanced at Alice, his wife to be.

'I think this calls for a celebration,' Sir Henry declared with a chuckle.

Alice went to Andrew and they stared into one another's

eyes. Then he took her into his arms and held her tight. Kiss her in front of her parents? Why not!

Sir Henry tugged on the bell pull. 'Champagne I think. Don't you?' he beamed at his wife who nodded her agreement.

'One thing though,' Sir Henry said, addressing Andrew. 'You won't be wed until the war's over and you've resigned your commission. That's the way I want it to be.'

'Certainly, sir. I understand.' Sir Henry was worried about him being posted to France and killed, Andrew correctly guessed, which was fair enough. He prayed the First Essex wouldn't be sent to the front line. That would be a nightmare.

A servant entered the room and Sir Henry ordered champagne to be brought. After which he lit up a cigar.

'Happy?' Andrew queried quietly of Alice.

'You know I am. And you?'

'The same.'

What a lovely couple they were, Lady Fortescue was thinking. They might have been made for each other.

Andrew wrote to his father that night telling him the news.

'Engaged!' Charlotte exclaimed across the breakfast table.

'So it would seem,' Murdo replied. 'To an Alice Fortescue of an old Irish Protestant family. The father's a knight of the realm.'

'Good for Andrew,' Nell declared. 'I wonder what she looks like?'

'They're not getting married till the conflict's over apparently,' Murdo went on.

'Are you going to reply to his letter, Pa?' Charlotte asked.

'Of course.'

'Then perhaps you'll suggest he sends us a photograph of his Alice. I'm sure we'd all love to see one.'

'Good idea,' Murdo nodded, he too curious about Alice Fortescue.

'And we'll have to send them an engagement present,' Nell declared, eyes gleaming at the prospect. 'Something decent, can't let the side down.'

'The three of us can go to Glasgow and shop there,' Charlotte said. 'You, me and Wonky. It'll be ever such fun.'

Nell laughed and clapped her hands together. It would indeed.

Murdo regarded his daughters with wry amusement. Women, how delightful they could be. Then he had another thought. 'Will you be up to such a trip?' he queried of Charlotte.

'Oh, Pa, stop being an old fusspot. I'm pregnant, not terminally ill.'

He'd still consult McAllister on the matter Murdo decided. You couldn't be too careful after all.

Charlotte was with Mrs Clark, the cook, when it happened. They were discussing culinary matters when the pain hit her. She staggered and clutched the nearest level surface.

'Miss Charlotte?'

Charlotte felt the blood drain from her face as pain tore at her insides. This certainly wasn't indigestion.

For a moment Mrs Clark watched in horror as Charlotte slowly began to sink to the floor, then grabbed her.

'Get Miss McQueen!' she screamed to Florence standing transfixed nearby.

'Well?' Murdo demanded when McAllister entered the small sitting room where he'd been anxiously pacing up and down.

McAllister sighed. 'These things happen, Murdo. I'm so sorry.'

Murdo stared at him aghast. 'Are you saying what I think you are?'

'Aye, that's right. She's lost the baby.'

Murdo reeled on the spot. This was calamitous. 'How. . . . how is Charlotte?'

'Sedated for now.'

'Does she know?'

McAllister nodded. 'Yes. She became quite hysterical which is why I sedated her. And a strong sedation too. The best thing for her is sleep and lots of it.'

Murdo stumbled to a chair and sat. 'What happened?' he croaked.

McAllister shrugged. 'I honestly don't know. The lassie hasn't done anything untoward as far as I can make out. It's simply, for whatever reason, Nature intervening.'

Murdo gestured towards the whisky decanter. 'Will you pour us out a couple, James. And no lectures please.

'Geoffrey is going to be devastated,' Murdo remarked quietly as McAllister did as requested.

As he himself was, McAllister thought, making the measures generous ones.

'Was it a . . .?' Murdo trailed off as McAllister handed him his dram.

'I don't know,' McAllister lied. 'The foetus was too young for me to be able to tell.'

Murdo stared into his whisky, then wafted the lot straight down. 'Poor Charlotte,' he whispered.

'Nell's with her.'

'Aye. Is she asleep?'

'Sound.'

'I'll go to her myself in a few minutes.'

Murdo lurched to his feet. 'I need another,' he declared, glaring at the doctor.

'Just don't overdo it, man, that's all,' McAllister cautioned.

'You're a friend, James, but away to hell.'

Murdo stood over the decanter and closed his eyes. What a rotten thing to happen. What bloody awful luck.

'I take it Charlotte will be all right?' he said after a while.

'As far as I can make out. There certainly doesn't appear to be any physical damage. If you're wondering if she'll conceive again I can't see why not.'

Murdo nodded. 'Thank you, James.'

'She's going to be extremely upset for some time to come, you do appreciate that? It's no small thing losing a baby.'

'I understand, James.'

'Lots of cosseting and spoiling is my advice.'

'She'll have it, I assure you.'

McAllister went to Murdo and put an arm round his shoulders. 'I really am sorry, Murdo. From the bottom of my heart.'

'I know,' came the whispered reply.

*

Peter and Jack both stood when the Colonel entered their dugout. 'Afternoon, sir,' they said in unison.

The Colonel sat and ran a weary hand over his face; he hadn't slept for more than twenty-four hours. He was dead beat. 'We need the information, it's as simple as that,' he stated.

Peter and Jack joined him round the table. 'We appreciate that, sir,' Jack replied.

'Someone has to go. It's only a pity it's you two.'

'Can't we make a surprise raid further up the line after dark?' Peter asked softly.

The Colonel shook his head. 'I've already spoken to the Brigadier about that and the answer's no.'

'The Boche are sitting over there with a dozen machine guns trained on that hole we broke in their wire,' Jack said. 'They're just waiting for us.'

The Colonel didn't reply. Personally, he didn't give their chances of survival a snowball in hell's chance. But orders were orders. If he'd been in their shoes he'd also have to have gone.

'I was a headmaster in civilian life,' he said hollowly.

'Oh?' That was Peter.

'So many of the fine young men I looked after are now in this war. I often wonder . . .' He trailed off.

'If only the trench mortars could have blown more holes in their wire,' Jack said.

'It took three hours to blow the one you're going through. You see the problem, don't you?'

Jack nodded. He did, only too well. It was like being handed a loaded revolver and told to put it to your head and pull the trigger.

'Chosen the ten men going with you yet?' the Colonel asked.

'Yes, sir,' Peter replied. 'They're hand picked.'

'It's a sod, isn't it?' the Colonel said softly.

'Yes, sir.'

'A sod and a half,' Jack added.

The Colonel laughed and rose from his chair. 'Report to me personally when you return.'

Peter and Jack both thought how funny that was. Return! Fat bloody chance.

Charlotte woke into a hazy world, her head seemingly filled with cotton wool. And then she remembered.

Murdo, who'd been dozing, came awake at the sound of her whimper. 'Charlotte?'

She turned a grief-stricken face to him. 'Pa?'

'I'm here, girl, I'm here.'

'The baby's dead, Pa.'

'Yes I know.'

'Oh, Pa!' she wailed, tears springing into her eyes. 'I so wanted that baby. I so wanted it.'

He sat on the edge of her bed and took her into his arms. 'There will be others in time. Doctor McAllister says so.'

'But this one. What about this one?'

He gently rocked her the way he'd done so often as a child. There were now tears in his eyes also.

'I feel so empty, Pa.'

'Yes.'

'As though my insides had been ripped out.'

He stroked her cheek, wiping away the streaming tears, thinking it was one of those occasions as a parent when you felt completely inadequate. Why had God done this to his lassie? Why? It was a question for which he hadn't an answer. Didn't even have the beginnings of one.

'There there,' he murmured.

She sobbed, a harsh choking sound from the back of her throat. 'I should never have named the baby in advance,' she said. 'That was bad luck.'

'I don't believe that,' he replied softly, trying to console her.

'I do. I really do.'

'Hush, ma wee. Hush,' he crooned.

Charlotte continued sobbing, totally and utterly bereft. In the space of a few short hours her world had collapsed. If only Geoffrey had been there to share her grief, to hold her as her father was. Just to be with her.

Peter glanced at his watch. 'It's time,' he said. 'The smoke bombs will have been laid down.'

An ashen-faced Jack nodded in reply having just finished writing two letters, one to his parents, the other to Grizelda.

'How do you feel?' Peter asked hoarsely. He knew how he felt, scared half to death.

'How do you think?'

Peter laughed. 'Same here.'

'I wish we weren't out of whisky,' Jack reflected. A large tot would have done him the world of good.

Peter rose. 'We'd best be getting on with it then.'

Jack also rose and extended his hand. 'Good luck, old boy.'

'And you.'

'It'll all be over before we know it.'

Yes, but how? Peter thought.

Outside they found the ten selected men waiting. More good lucks were given then Peter and Jack together led the party into a swirling smoke-filled No Man's Land.

How had all this happened? Murdo wondered, sitting in his study staring vacantly ahead. Charlotte's baby, Peter at the front, his damn heart. How had it all happened?

He sighed in despair. Another couple of hours and he'd have to go to work, but at least Charlotte was sleeping again. What a night, he never wanted to go through another like it. It had been his worst since Louise died.

He sucked in a deep breath, rose and crossed to the cabinet where he kept his pipe. The tin of tobacco was old and fairly dried out, but that didn't matter. All he wanted was a smoke. Camel dung would have sufficed.

He shouldn't be doing this he reflected as he packed the bowl. It was stupidity in the extreme. But there again, what the hell!

Moments later sheer bliss descended on him.

Suicide, Peter thought. Sheer bloody suicide and madness. It was exactly as they'd expected.

'These cream cakes are delicious,' Alice smiled to Andrew. She'd come to Dublin so the pair of them could choose the engagement ring – a single diamond surrounded by a cluster of smaller ones.

Andrew smiled in return. 'You look radiant, my darling. I must be the envy of every man in this tearoom.'

She tinkled a laugh. 'Flatterer.'

Crossing his heart he said, 'I swear I'm telling the truth.'

She lightly placed her hand over his. 'We're going to be so happy together, Andrew. I just know it.'

'I couldn't agree more.'

'I love you,' she whispered.

'And I you,' he whispered in reply.

She sighed with pleasure and happiness, thinking how lucky she was to have met Andrew. He was a dream come true.

'Are you going to flash it again?' he asked innocently.

'Flash what?'

'That ring. You've done nothing but since we arrived here.'

'Have I?' she queried, equally innocently.

'You know you have. Come on, own up.'

She laughed again. 'It's not every day a girl puts on an engagement ring. Let me enjoy myself.'

How pretty she was he thought. Was he actually falling in love with her? That was possible.

'Father has asked me to pick up a few things from a shop before I return home. You don't mind, do you?'

'Not in the least.'

'It won't take long.'

'The length of time doesn't matter, just as long as I'm with you.'

He wondered what she'd be like in bed. Whatever, he'd soon train her up the way Jean Ritchie and Tina had trained him. Once wed she'd find out what it was all about. He only hoped she liked 'it', he knew there were women who didn't. He was certain she would, there was a passionate side to Alice quite contrary to outward appearances.

'I think I'll be piggy and have another,' she declared.

He watched in fascination as she ate an éclair.

A trench mortar exploded throwing Peter sideways. He landed on all fours, his head reeling. A quick fumbling examination told him he hadn't been hurt.

The German machine guns were chattering incessantly sending streams of death in all directions. A man close to Peter gave a cry and threw his hands in the air, his rifle spiralling off, his chest a sudden flood of blood. The man pitched forward to lie half in, half out of a shell crater.

How long had it been? One minute, two, five? It seemed like eternity.

They'd never get those prisoners for interrogation, Peter thought. It was an impossibility. What had Command been thinking of sending them into this? But then, what were Command ever thinking of.

The smoke was thinning now, wisps of it floating past his face. He had to go on, he told himself. They had to at least try to get to the hole in the wire.

A soldier called McGillvary staggered up to Peter, smiled grotesquely, and died. Peter watched mesmerised as McGillvary slumped to the ground. He knew McGillvary to be eighteen years of age. A lad from Perthshire like himself.

Suddenly Jack was by his side. 'It's fucking murder,' Jack swore.

Peter realised he'd dropped his revolver and picked it up again. A useless action he vaguely thought. He'd never get close enough to the Boche bastards to fire the damn thing.

'Let's go,' Peter said, and started forward again, bullets whizzing round his ears like angry wasps. He was wondering how much longer he had to live.

Jack was numb all over, petrified from fright. But not funk; he was doing, and continuing to do, his duty. They'd never say he turned and ran.

And then a huge orange flame blossomed in front of him and the world went quiet. That was it, he thought before the blackness descended.

Peter saw Jack go down and immediately dashed to his friend. Jack's face was a mess but he was still breathing.

Peter pulled Jack onto his side then lifted him in a fireman's carry.

'Retreat!' he yelled. 'Retreat!'

The machine-gun bullets continued to hum and whizz as Peter stumbled back to their own line.

He and Jack were the only ones who returned.

Chapter 19

A ndrew jumped up and began pacing. God but he was randy, incredibly so. All he could think of was Alice and imagine what it would be like being with her.

He flicked sweat from his brow, and swallowed hard. He was in a lather of sexual excitement.

He stopped by his room's window and stared out over Dublin. In his mind's eye . . .

He swung away again. That wasn't doing him any good, only making matters worse. Damn, but the woman was getting to him. He wanted her so badly it literally hurt.

He thought of Jean Ritchie, and groaned. He'd have given anything for Jean to have been there, to have stripped her naked, laid her on his bed and . . .

'Christ Almighty!' he swore. This was intolerable.

Or Tina. He recalled vividly what it had been like with her. The sweetness of her, the wildness. Her total lack of inhibition.

Taking a deep breath he made a decision. There was a place he knew by repute only, never having visited it before. He'd go there now and indulge himself. Find release.

He had to.

'Charlotte?'

Charlotte didn't respond, continuing to stare vacantly ahead.

Nell sat on the edge of her sister's bed. 'Charlotte, this isn't doing any good. You must know that.'

Charlotte's eyes drifted sideways and what might have been something of a smile came onto her face. 'Hello, Nell.'

'Why don't you get up? You can't stay in bed for ever. It's been days now.'

'Has it? Time seems to . . . have no meaning any more.'

Nell's heart was breaking for her sister. 'The doctor said you weren't to blame. That you didn't do anything wrong.'

'But I must have. Somewhere along the line I must have. That's why God punished me.'

Nell shook her head. 'You're talking tosh, Charlotte. You had a miscarriage, pure and simple. There was no punishment involved.'

The hint of a smile became wry. 'No?'

'No,' Nell stated emphatically. 'It just wasn't to be, that's all.'

'Easy for you to say, sis.'

'Because it's the truth.'

Charlotte sighed. 'I keep thinking . . . I keep . . .' She trailed off and turned her head away.

Nell caressed her cheek. 'I know it's difficult but you've got to pull yourself together.'

'*Know?*' Charlotte replied scornfully. 'How would you know anything about this? You've never been pregnant and lost the baby.'

'We're all on your side,' Nell declared softly. 'There's not one of us wouldn't do anything for you.'

'Does that include you?'

'Of course.'

'Then write to Geoffrey for me. I can't.'

Nell was appalled. 'Write to Geoffrey?' she repeated, a catch in her voice.

'I'm not able to, Nell. And he should be told.'

Nell dropped her head and thought about that. What a letter to write. What a burden to set on her shoulders. 'Are you sure?'

'I simply can't, Nell.'

Nell, against her better judgement, nodded. 'I'll do it this evening. Any messages?'

'Only that I love and miss him.' She hesitated, then went on, 'Say that when he gets back we'll have another baby together.'

'I will,' Nell whispered.

Charlotte felt that was the hardest thing she'd ever had to say in her life.

Make another baby together. One to replace . . .

Geoffrey ducked into Peter's dugout, pleased to find his brother-in-law alone. 'How's Jack?' he queried.

Peter glanced up to stare at Geoffrey through red-rimmed eyes, 'Alive when he was stretchered off. His face was badly burnt.'

'I brought this,' said Geoffrey, holding up a nearly full bottle of whisky. 'Want some?'

'Please.'

Geoffrey slopped generous measures into a brace of tin mugs and handed Peter one. 'How bad was it?'

'That's a bloody silly question.'

It was too, Geoffrey thought. He'd only been trying to make conversation

They sat in silence for a bit, each preoccupied with his own thoughts.

'I miss Dalneil so much,' Peter said eventually in a small voice. 'I dream about it almost every night.'

'And I miss Charlotte.'

'I imagine you do.'

'I keep seeing her. It's uncanny, like some sort of ghost. I look up and there she is, smiling, laughing, sometimes waving. And when I'm in my cot I . . .' He trailed off. 'This war's a bastard.'

'Yes,' Peter agreed hollowly.

'I hope Jack's going to be all right.'

'I'm not sure. It was a pretty awful burn. His face was all . . .' Peter also trailed off.

Geoffrey slopped more whisky into their mugs. 'Whisky, best thing ever invented. Especially in a situation like we're in.'

Peter nodded his agreement.

'I hear you've been put up for a medal, old boy.'

Peter laughed, a terrible strangulated sound. 'What do I

want with a bloody medal. Chunk of metal that's all it is. I wouldn't trade Jack's face for a dozen VCs.'

Geoffrey didn't have an answer to that.

'How are things at your part of the line?'

'The same basically.' Geoffrey paused, then said, 'I believe there's to be another push shortly. That's on the QT for now.'

'A big one?'

'So I understand. That's one of the reasons they wanted those prisoners so badly. Find out exactly which units are facing us.'

That was some consolation, Peter thought. At least there had been a viable reason behind the raid. One he could understand.

'Jesus, I'm tired,' Peter said.

'Aren't we all. Still, there's only two days left till we're pulled back into reserves.'

'I never thought it would be like this,' Peter said morosely, staring into his mug.

'All honour and glory, eh?'

Peter smiled cynically. 'Not really. But I never thought it would be like this.' He hesitated, then went on. 'I don't think any of us will ever leave here you know. For each and every one of us it's only a matter of time. Hours, days, perhaps months. But only a matter of time.'

Captain Kennington came striding into the mess where Andrew, Billy Roberts and a few others were taking their ease.

'All right you lot, get kitted up straight away. There's some sort of disturbance this side of Halfpenny Bridge and the police have requested assistance.'

Andrew glanced at Billy. What was this all about?

'Snap to it!' Kennington barked, and left the mess as quickly as he'd entered it.

Everyone present leapt to his feet and hurried after him.

There were dozens of them, maybe a hundred, all milling about, their mood an ugly one. A howl went up as the various detachments from the First Essex took positions.

This could turn nasty, Andrew thought, unloosening the snap to his revolver holster. He noted that behind the mob several shop windows had been broken.

'Go home, you English bastards. You're not wanted here!' a rough Irish voice called out.

Next moment a brick flew through the air to land harmlessly in front of Andrew's platoon.

'Fix bayonets!' Captain Kennington yelled.

The mob quietened at that, though continuing to stare malevolently at the soldiers.

'Take your man's advice and go home. Leave Ireland to the Irish,' another voice shouted.

Scouring the crowd Andrew recognised Seamus McGinty.

'Disperse quietly and all will be well,' Kennington bellowed.

'Away to fuck, you English jackal,' came a stentorian reply. That raised a few laughs amongst the mob.

Kennington went puce with rage.

'Ireland for the Ireland. Up the Fenian cause!' yet another voice shouted.

Andrew slowly took his revolver from its holster, wondering what Kennington would do next. This needed delicate handling and he wasn't known for it.

Kennington seemed to regain control of himself. Taking several paces forward he put his hands on his hips. 'I warn you, if necessary we'll shoot. Make no mistake about that. Now disperse I say or take the consequences.'

The angry mood of the crowd suddenly subsided into muttering truculence and the danger was over.

Thank God, Andrew thought, who'd hardly been relishing the idea, no matter how in the wrong they were, of firing upon these people.

He made a mental note to mention McGinty to Sir Henry next time they met.

Peter was directed to Jack's bed by a nurse who then went off about her duties. Jack's head was swathed in bandages.

'Is that you, Peter?' Jack queried, having recognised his friend's voice.

'It is. We're in reserve and I managed to get away to come and visit.'

Peter sat on the chair beside Jack's bed. 'I'd have brought you some grapes but they're in short supply at the moment,' he joked.

Jack chuckled.

'So how are you, old thing?'

Jack eased himself slightly further up the bed. 'Have they told you?'

Peter's expression became grim in the extreme. 'Yes,' he replied quietly. 'I'm sorry.'

'You saved my life, Peter. To be honest I don't know whether to thank you or not.'

'You're still here. That's the main thing.'

Jack laughed bitterly, a sound that tore at Peter. 'Alive,

but blind.' His voice cracked. 'They had to remove what little was left of my eyes. Fried in my head they were.'

Peter couldn't think what to reply to that.

'And my face . . . God alone knows what that'll look like when it heals. A gargoyle's no doubt.'

Peter took a deep breath. 'It's what's inside a man, Jack, not the outside that counts.'

'Is it really?' Jack replied dully. 'I wonder if Grizelda will agree.'

'I'm sure . . .' Peter broke off. How could he say he was sure when he wasn't at all.

'Anyway, for what it's worth, thanks for pulling me out, Peter.'

'You'd have done the same for me.'

There was a hiatus between them, then Jack said, 'I understand you and I were the only survivors.'

'That's right.'

Jack swore. 'Suicide mission, that's all it was. They knew we never had a chance.'

'It was an important raid, Jack. I've since found out the reason behind it.'

'Oh?'

He glanced around to ensure they weren't being over-heard then repeated what Geoffrey had confided to him. 'And keep that strictly to yourself. This next big push is strictly hush hush.'

'I see,' Jack murmured.

'Geoffrey's had some bad news I'm afraid. Charlotte's lost the baby.'

'That is rotten luck. How's he taking it?'

'Better than might be expected. But there again, being

out here does alter one's perspective. He's upset for Charlotte of course.'

There was another pause between them. 'So it's Blighty for you,' Peter said.

'In time.'

'Then home to Dalneil.'

Blind men without tear ducts don't cry. At least not outwardly.

Murdo joined Charlotte who was sitting on a bench outside the house, staring far into the distance.

'It's a beautiful summer's day,' Murdo commented.

'Yes,' she murmured in reply without looking at him.

'I wish you'd gone to church this morning.'

Her lips thinned into a cynical smile. 'I'm not in the mood for churches at present, Pa. They seem a rather sick joke really.'

'I understand.'

'Do you?'

'Don't forget I lost your mother. Someone I loved and lived with, who bore my children. Her loss was awful.'

Charlotte snapped out of her reverie. 'I apologise, Pa, I shouldn't have said that. Of course you understand.'

He placed a hand over hers. 'These things are just something you have to come to terms with. Life goes on regardless. And at least, small comfort though it might be, you can always have other children. That must be some consolation.'

If Geoffrey came back, she thought. *If* he came back. The casualty lists were horrendous.

'You're right of course, Pa. As you usually are.'

'Now let me make a suggestion. Why don't you and I, just the two of us, go for a nice walk. Stretch the legs a bit.'

She put a cheek on his chest and encircled him with her arms. 'That would be lovely.'

'It isn't easy, girl. I know only too well.'

At that moment he felt closer to Charlotte than he'd ever done. Her pain was his, as was her loss.

They sat there in silence for a few minutes, then Charlotte roused herself.

'Where shall we go?'

'Who cares. As the mood takes us.'

'Then come on.'

After a few minutes he actually got her to laugh.

There had been a battle of some sort and the Highlanders had clearly won. Laden with booty they were in obvious high spirits as they marched.

There was her Highlander astride a spirited horse, laughing as he cantered past men who waved and appeared to make ribald remarks to him.

Nell shivered, and didn't know why. It didn't fit with the mood of the scene she was watching. It was as though . . . She felt tragedy, death, destruction. Her own mood was one of terrible foreboding.

The Highlander reined in his horse and swung from the saddle, laughing as he led the horse forward.

The countryside she could see was different somehow. Certainly not Scotland, it simply didn't have that 'feel' to it. England she surmised. The army was somewhere in England.

Her Highlander leapt back into the saddle and galloped

off, waving his bonnet to the men he'd been talking to as he went.

Be safe, she thought. Oh, be safe, my bonnie laddie.

'I'm sorry, sir, but that's the way of it,' Enoch Murray, the maltman, said to Murdo.

Another one gone, Murdo thought in despair. How in God's name was he supposed to keep the distillery turning over when he was becoming more and more short staffed. He stared morosely at Enoch whom he'd known all his life.

'What about your brother?'

'Och he's married as you know, sir. He'll hang on for a while.'

'And you haven't actually signed up yet?'

Enoch shook his head. 'Out of respect I considered it only polite to speak to you first, Mr Drummond.'

Murdo sighed. 'I don't suppose I can talk you out of this?'

'No, sir, my mind's made up. They need men and I'm not one to shirk my duty.'

Murdo sighed again. Damn and blast this war! It was turning into a total nightmare. Suddenly he felt incredibly tired, not the tiredness that comes from lack of sleep but the sort that comes from the very heart and soul.

'Have I your good wishes, sir?'

Murdo rose and came from behind his desk. He'd manage somehow, he'd have to. Extending a hand he said, 'You have my very best wishes, Enoch, though I can't say I'm happy to lose you. You're a good chap, one of the best. I hope and pray nothing happens to you and that one day you'll be back here at the distillery.'

'Thank you, sir.'

'Now you'd better be off, I've work to be getting on with.'

'I'll stay with you until the moment I have to leave, Mr Drummond. I owe you that.'

'Fine then.'

Murdo sat again after Enoch had gone feeling as though he had the weight of the world on his shoulders.

Closing his eyes he prayed for the umpteenth time that Peter was all right and would come through unscathed.

Hettie came up short in the hallway when she heard the sound of sobbing. Now what was that all about? She was in the Riach house on an errand.

She tapped the door from behind which the sobbing was coming. 'Hello?'

The sobbing continued unabated. What to do? She was only a servant after all, but someone was in distress. She tapped again.

The door opened to reveal Mrs Riach. 'Yes, Hettie?' she choked.

'Sorry to bother you but . . . can I help at all?'

Mrs Riach waved her into the room, crossing to a settee onto which she slumped. 'I've had some awful news, lass, and I don't know how I'm going to tell my husband.'

Fear clutched at Hettie. 'Is it about Mr Jack?'

Mrs Riach nodded. 'He's been wounded.'

Hettie took a deep breath, at least he hadn't been killed.

'I've had a letter from the hospital, written by a nurse. He was unable to write it himself.'

'How bad is it?' Hettie asked softly, picturing Jack in her

mind. Remembering the times they'd had together. The lovemaking.

'He's been . . . he's been . . .' Mrs Riach dropped her head and cried.

It didn't matter their difference in stations. It was one woman comforting another. Hettie sat beside Mrs Riach and put her arm round the older woman's shoulders.

'He's been blinded,' Mrs Riach whispered.

The breath caught in Hettie's throat. 'Permanently?'

'Aye, lass, permanently.'

Oh Christ! Hettie inwardly swore. For that to happen to Jack Riach. A chap like him.

She hugged the older woman whose shoulders were heaving, her own tears not far away. 'Is there anything I can get you?'

Mrs Riach didn't reply, too overcome by grief.

Hettie thought of Grizelda McPherson and wondered how she'd react to this news.

'Is he coming home?' Hettie asked.

Mrs Riach nodded. 'When he's fit to travel which won't be for some while yet. He's still in France though expecting to be shipped to England before long.'

'It could be worse, Mrs Riach,' Hettie said. 'He could have been killed.'

'Aye, there is that.'

'At least he's coming back. There's that to be thankful for.'

'But blind,' Mrs Riach choked. 'My boy blind.'

Hettie stayed with Mrs Riach until the older woman had recovered enough to go in search of her husband.

*

At midnight precisely the guns started. Geoffrey lay on his cot listening to the sound of shells screaming overhead. It was to be the longest barrage of the war so far, and when it stopped he and everyone else would be going over the top.

They'd all be going, but how many would be coming back?

Closing his eyes he thought of Charlotte, wishing . . . wishing . . .

'I'll stand by him of course,' Grizelda declared to Harriet Henderson and Antonia Phillips who both nodded their approval.

'Good for you,' Harriet replied.

'Well, I mean, what else can I do. I love him after all.'

They were interrupted by a servant girl bringing in coffee and cakes, Antonia noting with pleasure there were chocolate ones among the latter.

'My hero,' Grizelda breathed, eyes shining.

'It will be difficult for you, mind,' Harriet said.

Grizelda snorted. 'Nothing I can't cope with I'm sure. It's not as though he has to work for money, he has plenty of that. More than enough for the pair of us to live in style.'

'How brave of you,' Antonia murmured, itching to get at the cakes.

'Shall I be mother?' she offered after the servant girl had left them.

'Please,' Grizelda beamed.

'I must say I admire your fortitude,' Harriet declared as Antonia busied herself with the coffee pot. 'If Jack's a hero then you're a heroine and no mistake.'

'How kind of you to say so, Harriet.'

'Kindness has nothing to do with it, it's true. I admire you tremendously.'

'Cream?' Antonia asked Grizelda.

'Please, but no sugar. I always watch my figure, as you know.'

Grizelda accepted the cup given her as did Harriet. Antonia helped herself to a chocolate cake before passing the plate round.

'I can't wait to see him again,' Grizelda went on. 'I shall welcome him with open arms and have already written telling him so.'

'You'll be wanting to start a family as soon as possible,' Antonia commented.

Grizelda blushed. 'Of course.'

Harriet sighed. 'You know, it's ever so romantic when you think about it. In a tragic way that is.'

Which was precisely what Grizelda thought, though she refrained from saying so.

Antonia reached for another chocolate cake.

Murdo noted his hands were shaking from fatigue as he poured himself a large dram. God but he was tired.

Charlotte entered the room and stared at her father. 'You look exhausted,' she commented.

'I am.'

'This is getting ridiculous, Pa. You can't keep working the hours you have.'

He leant against the sideboard for support. 'I have to, there's nothing else for it. I'm not only running the business but helping out with the men as well. It's necessary because we're so short staffed.'

'Come and sit down before you fall down.'

He sank into a comfy chair and closed his eyes, thinking he could happily have gone to sleep there and then.

'Mrs Clark has put something by for you as you missed dinner yet again.'

He considered that. 'I couldn't eat. I honestly couldn't.'

'Pa, you must! You'll make yourself ill.'

He drained his glass. 'Could you get me a refill, lass?'

She took his glass and crossed to the decanter. 'At least try and have a few mouthfuls of food. That'll be better than nothing.'

'But I'm not hungry.'

'Pa!'

'All right, all right,' he sighed wearily. 'If it'll stop you nagging.'

She handed him his refill. 'There must be some answer to the problem.'

He shook his head. 'If there is I can't come up with it. There simply aren't any suitable men available to take on. If there were I'd snap them up.'

'Oh, Pa,' she whispered sympathetically.

'I'll get by, Charlotte. You'll see, I'll get by.'

Not for long he wouldn't, she thought. Not at this rate. He was on the verge of collapse.

'I'll get that food,' she said, and strode from the room.

When she returned it was to find Murdo snoring.

Chapter 20

Murdo looked up in surprise when Charlotte breezed into the office. 'What are you doing here?' he queried.

She glanced about her. Typical untidy male room she thought, and it smelt.

'I've come to help.'

'Help?'

'That's right. Anything Peter can do I can do as well, given some guidance and experience that is.'

Murdo leant back in his chair and studied his elder daughter. 'But you're a lassie.'

'So? I can read, count and I've got a brain in my head. What else is required?'

He tried to digest that.

'There are all sorts of women going out to work who never have before,' she went on. 'And doing pretty hard work at that. The munitions factories for instance are full of them.'

Murdo was flabbergasted. 'But they're working class, not like you,' he protested.

Charlotte crossed to his desk and stared him straight in the eye. 'Are you saying because I've had a privileged upbringing I can't do my bit? For that's how I see replacing Peter.'

'No, I, eh . . .'

'Because I fully intend to,' she interrupted. 'I have no intention seeing you come home night after night the way you have of late when I could be here easing the burden.'

How like Louise she could be at times, he thought. But working in the distillery!

'You're my daughter,' he stated.

'That's correct.'

'It's not right or proper.'

Charlotte gave a scornful laugh. 'The world's gone topsy turvy, Pa. The old rules don't apply any more. As far as I'm concerned, given the circumstances, it's quite right and proper for me to lend a hand where it's needed. And needed it most certainly is.'

He shook his head. 'I won't have it, lass. I thank you for the offer, but the answer is no.'

She'd always been able to twist him round her little finger, and would do so now. For his own good. 'If I help you, Pa, you'll be helping me.'

He frowned. 'How so?'

'It would take my mind off things. Stop me brooding.'

'Oh!' he exclaimed softly, all resistance to her idea completely melting away. 'I understand.'

She went to a window and opened it. 'A little fresh air would be a good thing for a start. Now where and how do I begin?'

*

'Cognac I'm afraid, no whisky,' Peter apologised to Geoffrey who'd come to visit. The other officer present was fast asleep.

'Better than nothing, eh?'

'It is that.'

They both had a sip from their tin mugs. 'Any news of Jack?' Geoffrey asked.

'None.'

'At least he's out of it, lucky sod.'

Peter laughed. 'I'd hardly call him lucky, but there we are. As you say, he's out of it.'

'Two days from now,' Geoffrey stated softly.

'Yes I know.'

'It'll be a bastard.'

They sat in silence for a few minutes listening to the sound of shells screaming overhead. A barrage that was into its third week.

'I don't know how I sleep through this bloody noise but I somehow do,' Peter commented.

'It'll be strange when it stops, that's for sure.'

Peter drank some more of his cognac which he didn't really like, thinking of the French further down the line who'd be attacking with them. Funny blokes the French, he didn't particularly like them either. Their officers could be exceptionally arrogant, brimming over with self importance. Thankfully his contact with them had been minimal.

'My father's unwell,' Geoffrey suddenly said.

'Oh?'

'Pleurisy according to Mother. But he'll come through it all right, he's a tough old nut.'

'I watched an aeroplane come down yesterday,' Peter said. 'All I could think of was the poor bugger trapped inside. That must be an awful way to go.'

Geoffrey nodded his agreement.

'The ones that do survive are usually terribly burnt. Hideously so in some cases.'

They both thought of Jack.

Geoffrey finished his cognac and rose. 'I'd better be getting along. Duty calls and all that.'

Peter also rose and extended his hand. 'Best of luck for the day after tomorrow.'

'And you.'

They stared at one another, wondering if they'd ever see each other again.

Geoffrey patted his brother-in-law on the shoulder, smiled and left.

'Pa, I don't understand this. Can you explain?' Charlotte said.

She really was doing extremely well, Murdo thought. Picking things up very quickly.

He came round from behind his desk and crossed to hers. 'Now what's the problem?'

'Lucky old Charlotte working at the distillery,' Wonky said, setting her knitting aside for a few moments.

Nell also laid hers aside, it was time for a breather. 'I'd offer to help there myself but I'm a dunderhead when it comes to facts and figures. I'd be a hindrance more than anything else.'

'If I suggested it to Father he'd have a fit,' Wonky

declared with a sigh. 'You know what he's like. His precious daughter over there with all those rough men. He'd have the vapours.'

Nell laughed. 'I don't think men have the vapours, do they?'

'Well, you know what I mean.'

'Charlotte's certainly the better for it,' Nell went on. 'She said it would take her mind off things and it has. She's enjoying it too apparently. Told me only the other evening it can quite fascinating.'

'I saw Grizelda McPherson in the village,' Wonky stated. 'From what I hear she's all of a burble awaiting Jack's return.'

'Poor Jack,' Nell said, pulling a face.

'Yes.' Wonky thought of the past. It might have been her in Grizelda's shoes. If things had been different that is. If Jack hadn't preferred Grizelda to her.

'When will it all end?' Nell mused aloud. 'When will it all end?'

'When we've won,' Wonky stated emphatically. 'That's when.' There was no doubt in her mind that they would.

Geoffrey slid into the trench unable to believe he was still alive. How had he possibly come through that hell? That armageddon?

He'd seen 'Pop' Smith go down, and Charlie Abercrombie. Major Allan also, like a puppet whose strings had suddenly been cut.

As for the men, hundreds of them, thousands, all dying like heroes if you could possibly call it that.

Geoffrey dropped his head and put his hands to his face,

desperately wanting to vomit and willing himself not to.

A private he didn't know collapsed into the trench beside him. 'Dear God!' the soldier breathed.

The German machine guns were still chattering which meant there were still men out there. Geoffrey shuddered.

More chaps tumbled into the trench, one of whom started to howl like a banshee. The lad had gone mad, Geoffrey thought. Stark staring mad. And who could blame him? Certainly not he.

Another great push that had ended in massacre, Geoffrey thought bitterly. How much more of this sense-lessness before it was his turn to die out there in No Man's Land? For die he would, he was convinced of it.

'Water, sir?'

Geoffrey focused on the speaker, a plain-faced boy with red hair and freckles. The boy had a deep gash on his left cheek but otherwise appeared unhurt.

'Thank you.'

He accepted the already open canteen and drank. Tepid water that was still welcome beyond belief. He hadn't realised how parched he was.

'It was a disaster, sir. A sheer bloody disaster.'

Geoffrey returned the canteen. 'Yes,' he agreed softly. That's exactly what it had been.

He wondered if Peter had made it.

'McGinty, you're sure it was him?' Sir Henry Fortescue queried.

'Oh yes, sir. I saw him plain as the nose on your face.' It had been some weeks, due to duties and manoeuvres, since Andrew had last been to Greystones.

'Hmmh,' Sir Henry mused thoughtfully.

'I thought you should know, being a friend of his, that is.'

Sir Henry smiled. 'I wouldn't exactly call him a friend. No, that's going too far. Neighbour and acquaintance is more like it. Someone it's best to humour rather than alienate.'

'Well, he was there, sir, take my word for it.'

Sir Henry stroked his moustache. 'It doesn't surprise me really. McGinty's a Fenian and that cult have become stronger of late.'

'So I understand, sir.'

'Nationalists, Andrew, they want a free Ireland. In fact, are determined to have one. To their way of thinking it's only a matter of time.'

Andrew frowned. 'But surely that's impossible. They could hardly take on Britain and its Empire.'

'Under normal circumstances I'd agree, but don't forget Britain is at war. Britain *and* her Empire. Which means she's weak at the moment, weak in places like Ireland that is. And don't think the Nationalists don't know that. If there should be an uprising . . .' He broke off and shook his head.

'Uprising, sir?'

'It's possible, entirely so. The Irish are a proud race, very proud indeed, and they're under the British yoke. What better time than now to try and throw off that yoke?'

Andrew tried to digest that. He knew something of Irish history, but not a great deal. To him Ireland was part and parcel of the homeland and that was that.

'A free Ireland,' Andrew mused. It would take fighting

for that to happen, fighting he'd be in the thick of. He didn't relish the prospect.

'And what about yourself, sir. How do you feel?'

Sir Henry laughed. 'Good question. I consider myself Irish through and through, but I'm Protestant Irish, an import no matter how long my family has been here. Me and mine aren't native Irish stock. So I suppose I'm rather ambivalent on the nationalist question. With one exception that is. I wholeheartedly believe it would be financially ruinous for this country to break free and go it alone. It's basically a poor country, Andrew, and I don't see how that can possibly change. So in my opinion it's in Ireland's best interests to stay shackled to the mainland. Though I have to say that's not an opinion held by many. Pride again, Andrew, pride of which the Irish come stuffed full of, God bless and keep them all.'

'But Irishmen are fighting with our troops in France and Belgium,' Andrew said.

'Young blood,' Sir Henry replied. 'Young blood, hot blood and a sense of duty. But where does their first duty lie? Put it to the test and the answer will be Ireland. Put it to the test and those selfsame Irishmen will always come down on the side of Ireland before anything and anyone else.'

'I see,' Andrew murmured.

'So be careful, lad. Who knows what might happen in the near future. Who knows? And you'd be at the sharp end. I'd hate to lose a potential son-in-law whom my daughter loves.'

'So you think there might be insurrection, sir?'

Sir Henry thought of recent conversations he'd had, of the mood of the people. If McGinty and his like had their way . . .

At which point they were interrupted by a tap on the door and the appearance of Alice.

'Now what are you two talking about closeted away here?' she demanded.

They both rose. 'Politics I suppose,' Andrew answered.

She made a face. 'How boring!'

Sir Henry smiled. 'Not really. We've been having a very interesting conversation.'

'Which I'm now halting. Andrew's only here for three days and I want more of him to myself.'

Sir Henry shrugged. 'I can hardly argue with that.'

'Shall we go for a walk, Andrew?' Alice proposed.

He knew what that meant. An invitation for kissing and cuddling. 'Of course.'

'Good.'

'Enjoy yourselves,' Sir Henry declared, eyes twinkling, remembering only too well the joys of courtship. Sighing inwardly with nostalgia. Which made him think of his wife Sybil and the fact he had the rest of the afternoon free. Now that would be lovely, if she was of a like mind that was. Sybil wasn't always. But then they had been married a long time.

'Run along the pair of you. We'll all meet up again at dinner.'

When the youngsters had gone Sir Henry went in search of his wife whom he found in a most amiable mood.

'It's agreed then?' Wonky said.

Nell nodded.

Wonky took a deep breath. 'I'm so excited. We should have thought of this before.'

'How about your father?'

'That's going to be the hard part,' Wonky nodded. 'But I'll tackle him about it tonight.'

'And what if he forbids you?'

A determined expression came onto Wonky's face. 'This is my big chance to get away from the manse and Dalneil. At least for a while. He'll see it my way if I have to argue till the cows come home.'

Nell thought of her own father. He wasn't going to be best pleased either. There again, Murdo was a far more reasonable man than Tom Comyn.

At least he always had been in the past.

Geoffrey took Peter's hand and they silently shook.

'It's good to see you all in one piece,' Geoffrey said.

'And you.'

'I said it was going to be a bastard and that it most certainly was.'

Both men sat. They were in Peter's dugout, Peter now the sole survivor of the four officers who'd been billetted there.

'I've nothing to drink I'm afraid,' Peter apologised. 'We drank it all before . . .' He broke off and looked away.

'It was the same in my dugout,' Geoffrey said softly.

They fell silent.

'Christ,' Peter muttered after a while. 'Christ!'

Geoffrey knew exactly what he meant.

Tom Comyn stared at his daughter, aghast. 'You can't be serious, girl.'

'But I am, Father.'

'It's preposterous, I won't allow it. You hear? I won't allow it.'

Moira Comyn stared at Wonky in consternation. This was terrible. A complete bolt out of the blue.

'A nurse!' Tom exclaimed, and barked out a harsh laugh.

'Not quite a nurse, Father, a Voluntary Aid Detachment. VADs they're called. You must have read about them in the newspapers.'

'Naturally I have.'

'And that's what I intend becoming. The country is crying out for them. They're desperately needed to help the proper nurses.'

'Have you any idea what it would entail? The sort of men you'd have to come into contact with. Ruffians, scum.'

Wonky's temper flared. 'I hardly think that's quite fair, Father. You're talking about men fighting for their country. Prepared to lay down their lives if necessary. And again, according to the newspapers, only too many of them have.'

Tom waved a dismissive hand. 'It's out of the question, Veronica, and that's an end of it.'

'No it isn't, Father,' she replied hotly. 'This is a terrible war we're fighting and I propose to do my bit. And don't forget Nell's joining up also.'

'Veronica,' Moira said.

'Yes, Mother?'

'Why don't you think on this further. There's no rush after all.'

'There's no more thinking to be done,' Tom declared. 'I have said no and will be obeyed.'

'I'm going, Father, with your blessing or not.'

He swung on her, eyes blazing with fury. 'You will do nothing of the sort even if I have to resort to locking you in your room.'

Wonky laughed which infuriated her father even more. 'Who knows how long the war will last. Are you going to keep me locked up for the duration? That's absurd and you know it.'

He snorted, unwilling to admit to himself she was right.

'You have your knitting,' Moira said. 'Surely that's enough?'

'No it isn't. It's far from enough. The country needs me and those like me and I intend to respond.'

Tom fought back the urge to slap his daughter. 'And what if you're sent to France, eh. Answer me that?'

'If I'm sent I'm sent. There will be no hesitation on my part.'

'But you could be injured, girl, killed even.'

'Aren't we all in God's hands, Father?'

That made him halt and think, for he was a truly religious man. 'Maybe so,' he admitted reluctantly. 'But that doesn't mean you have to put yourself at unnecessary risk.'

'I'm joining, with or without your blessing, Father,' Wonky repeated emphatically.

'I . . .' He suddenly stopped and sagged, knowing he was beaten.

'You won't have my blessing,' he croaked.

Moira Comyn began to cry.

Murdo let himself into his study, closed the door behind him, and sat to stare vacantly into space.

That had been a bombshell. Nell joining the VADs

which would mean her leaving home as well. Now only Charlotte would be left.

How empty the house would seem, he thought. When Andrew had gone it hadn't been noticed all that much with three children still remaining.

Then it had been Peter, and now Nell.

Leaning back in his chair he closed his eyes, remembering them all as children, how it had once been. The laughter, the fun. And the difficult times too. The childhood illnesses, the problems of growing up, the sibling rivalry.

The time . . .

His memories rolled on and on.

Peter stared up into a leaden grey sky from which rain was lashing down. Rain meant the return of the terrible mud which would make their lives even more of a misery.

He shivered with cold, thinking of the awful months that lay ahead until spring. At least there wouldn't be any more big pushes for the foreseeable future. The fighting would continue of course, the unremitting patrols and the like, but no more big pushes for now. Thank the Lord.

Faces swam before him, friends, acquaintances, men under his command. Faces now gone for ever.

Damn the Kaiser for starting this carnage, damn him to everlasting perdition. He hoped the bastard roasted for all eternity.

Peter trudged on his way, stooping as always to avoid sniper fire.

You never knew when . . . You just never knew.

*

After months in hospital Jack Riach was returning to Pitlochry. It was something he was in two minds about, nervous as a kitten at the prospect.

'It's your station, young man,' the kindly female voice said, a middle-aged woman he'd chatted to off and on since leaving Glasgow.

'Thank you.'

'Shall I help you with the door?'

'No, I can manage.'

He came to his feet and groped on the overhead rack for his suitcase. He didn't have to ask which side to get off knowing that from past journeys.

'I want to wish you all the very best,' the lady said.

'I appreciate that. And the same to you.'

The train came to a halt and Jack fumbled with the window, eventually getting it down allowing him to open the door. Suitcase in hand he carefully descended onto the platform from where he swung the door shut again.

'Jack!'

He placed his case on the platform and turned to the sound of his father's voice.

Bob Riach swallowed hard as he came nearer, the sight of Jack's dark glasses like a punch in the stomach. He stopped in front of his son, tears involuntarily springing into his eyes at the close-up view of Jack's badly scarred face.

'Hello, son.'

'Hello, Dad.'

'You're home at last.'

'Aye, at last.'

Bob Riach wasn't a particularly demonstrative man but

he now put his arms round Jack and hugged him tight. 'It's so good to have you back, Jack. Your mother's been on tenterhooks.'

'Is she here?'

'No, she's at the house preparing the fatted calf.'

Bob released his son and picked up the case. 'If you take my arm we'll be on our way. There's the taxi waiting.'

Jack's white stick tap tap tapped as they made their way up the platform.

Nell sank onto a chair beside Wonky, the pair of them enjoying a tea break. They'd been assigned to the Southern General Hospital in Glasgow.

'I'm exhausted,' Nell sighed. 'All I want to do is go to bed and sleep.' They both lived in the nurses' quarters where they shared a room.

'I never realised the work would be so hard or the hours so long,' Wonky stated.

'Me neither. It just goes on and on.'

'It's the bed pans I hate most. I'll never get used to those. They're disgusting.'

'How about the back rubs?' Nell teased.

Wonky gave a small laugh. 'That was a bit of a shock to start with. I'd never seen a man's bare bottom before, far less touched one.'

Nell grinned ruefully. That had been a shock for her also.

'There's another batch of war casualties arriving tomorrow,' Wonky said. 'Staff told me.'

'Many?'

'She had no idea but thought there probably would be.'

Nell thought of the never-ending stream of wounded men who'd passed through their hands so far, and the deaths. Hardly a day went by when there wasn't a death on the ward.

Another VAD came into the room carrying a huge teapot. 'It was a case of help yourself, everyone else is busy,' she declared.

Nell lurched wearily to her feet. 'I'll get yours as well,' she said to Wonky. The tea was foul, as it always was. But at least it was hot and wet which was something.

Ten minutes later they were both back on duty.

Grizelda was waiting with Mrs Riach, her presence a surprise for Jack who wouldn't be expecting her. She was atwitter with excitement.

'They're here!' she exclaimed on hearing a car draw up.

Bob paid off the driver and led Jack inside. He hadn't warned Jack about Grizelda, having been told not to. He hoped he'd done the right thing.

'Well here he is,' he declared when the pair of them entered the front room where his wife and Grizelda were.

The huge smile Grizelda was wearing vanished when she saw Jack's face.

'Oh my God!' she breathed in horror.

Chapter 21

'Hello, Jack.'

He recalled the voice only too well. 'Hello, Hettie. How are you?'

'Never better. What are you doing standing out here all by yourself?'

'I've been cooped up in the house for four days. I wanted a breath of fresh air.'

She nodded her understanding. 'I heard you were back of course, I've been looking forward to seeing you.'

He smiled thinly. 'Seeing?'

'That's right.'

'Not a pretty picture I'm afraid.'

He could smell her acutely, a fresh country odour that brought back memories.

'It's not that bad,' she said.

He barked out a laugh. 'Come off it, Hettie. Grizelda keeled over in a dead faint when she saw my face.'

'Did she indeed!' That angered Hettie. 'And then what?'

'She came round, stayed for a short while and fled.'

'Grizelda McPherson is a silly, vain woman, I've always thought so. What a dreadful thing to do.'

'She said she'd return in a few days when I've had a chance to settle in. But so far hasn't. I can only presume it's all over between us.'

'And good riddance in my opinion,' Hettie snorted.

'I half expected as much, mind. I should have been more explicit in the letters I had written about the extent of the scarring, but somehow couldn't bring myself to do so.'

He paused, then said softly, 'It's like a nightmare that you keep hoping you'll wake up from. Only of course you won't. It's all too horrid reality.'

Hettie gently touched his face. 'Well you're not the good-looking young buck you once were and that's a fact, but you're still Jack Riach to me and anyone else with sense.'

'Thank you, Hettie,' he said with a small choke in his voice.

'Now why four days indoors?'

'Why do you think?'

'You can't stay hidden away for the rest of your life, Jack. That's nonsense.'

'I had thought of going to the pub with my father, but when it came down to it I couldn't. I didn't have the courage.'

'*You* lacking in courage, Jack? I can't believe that.'

'Well it's true.'

She sighed. 'You're going to have to come to terms with that reality you spoke of and the sooner the better in my opinion. Now, will you buy a girl a drink? If you're not ashamed to be seen out with someone of my station that is.'

'How do you mean?'

'Have you got money on you?'

He tapped his wallet. 'Yes.'

'Then we'll go to the pub together and you can have a pint.'

'You mean now?'

'That's right.'

He hesitated. 'I don't know, Hettie.'

'Is it me?'

'No, of course not.'

'Then let's go. The walk will do you good.'

Still he hesitated.

'Sooner or later, Jack. Sooner or later.'

He suddenly made up his mind. 'All right then. The pub it is.'

She hooked an arm round his and they set off.

'That wasn't so bad now, was it?' she said later when they emerged from the pub.

'They were very kind.'

'Kind my arse, Jack. You're a local whom they all know and respect. Certainly they were sympathetic but that's as it should be. And they're only too well aware how you came by your injuries, fighting for your country and freedom. If anything they respect you even more than before.'

'I don't want to be a figure of pity,' he said softly.

'You'll only be that if you keep on pitying yourself. If folk see you don't then they won't either. At least not for long they won't.'

'You're a good woman, Hettie,' he said. Unlike some he thought to himself.

'Want to hear a joke?'

He nodded. She then proceeded to tell him the filthiest joke he'd ever heard which caused him to roar with laughter.

'Come in!' Sister McAuliffe called out when Nell tapped on her door. Nell and Wonky went into the office.

Sister looked up from the paperwork she was dealing with and smiled. 'I've got good news for the pair of you,' she stated.

Nell and Wonky glanced at one another, then back at Sister.

'You're being sent to France to work over there. A group of VADs from here and the other Glasgow hospitals will be leaving on the fifteenth of next month. You're to be included in that group. Unless you decline that is. You do have the option.'

France! Nell swallowed hard.

'Well? Or do you wish time to think about it.'

'I'll go, Sister,' Wonky declared.

'And me,' Nell added.

'Good, that's settled then. You'll have a week off before then to see your families, then back here and France.'

'Thank you, Sister,' Wonky said.

A somewhat stunned Nell and Wonky returned to their duties, this new development in their lives having not quite sunk in yet. There had always been the possibility of course, but now it had actually happened.

It took Grizelda three weeks to reappear at the Riach house where she was ushered into the room where Jack was and the two of them left tactfully alone.

'This is difficult, Jack,' she said, voice trembling.

He knew what was coming next. 'You want to break it off between us.'

'I'm sorry. Truly I am.'

'That's all right, I understand.'

'I thought I could, but I can't.'

'The face is pretty horrendous I'm told.'

She winced.

There was no need to prolong this, he thought. He may as well put her out of her misery. 'Goodbye, Grizelda.'

'I really am sorry . . .'

'Goodbye,' he interjected.

'Bitch!' was Hettie's sole comment when she heard.

The Post Office was blazing uncontrollably, the sky an enormous mass of flame. To the observer it seemed the entire Dublin city centre was on fire, though it wasn't. Somewhere off to Andrew's left the British artillery was booming.

Andrew leant against a wall and wiped his sweat-streaked face. Christ, but he was tired, and scared. The insurrection he and Sir Henry had discussed had finally taken place and he was at the sharp end of quelling it.

A bullet hissed, knocking a chunk out of the wall about a foot away. Andrew was galvanised into action, ducking into a doorway which offered temporary cover. He was joined there by a private called Stockton.

'Fun and games, sir, eh?' Stockton grinned.

Idiot! Andrew thought.

'Rebels!' someone shouted. 'Coming this way.'

Andrew peered round the corner of the doorway and

quickly spotted them. About a dozen in all, heading directly for his platoon's current position.

He yelled out an order and the platoon opened up. One rebel clutched his side and then pitched over. Others were also hit.

The first wounded rebel turned on his side, clearly in great pain, crossed himself and started to crawl away. He'd only gone a few yards when he collapsed and could go no further. Unknown to Andrew and his platoon the man was a leader of the rising, and now dead. His name was O'Rahilly.

The artillery, 18-pounders, continued to boom inflicting terrible carnage.

Sergeant Mills joined Andrew as bullets flew in both directions. 'What shall we do, sir?'

'Keep firing and let's see if we can get them on the run.'

Andrew glanced up at a window opposite and saw a frightened female face staring down at him. His orders were to make for Jacob's Biscuit Factory but he was having a devil of a time getting there. There were rebels everywhere.

It was Easter 1916.

'I've made a decision, Dad,' Jack Riach announced to his father.

'Aye, what's that, son?'

'I'm going to sell this place and move into a cottage where I'll be able to cope.'

'You mean the house and land. The whole kit and caboodle?'

'That's right, Dad. It makes sense when you think about it. You're doing a splendid job, but I've got to think in the long term.'

Bob considered that. The house, land and everything else were Jack's to sell, having been signed over to him years previously. But it had all been in the family for so long.

'I can keep on till the end of the war, Jack, and then you can get a manager. Selling's not necessary.'

'I want to sell,' Jack stated softly. 'It just wouldn't be the same with a manager. It would . . . hurt too much. Can you understand that?'

Bob wasn't sure he could.

'I've decided, Dad, and that's how it's going to be.'

'What about if you have a family?'

Jack laughed. 'I'll never have one of those. What woman is going to have me now? No, I'm afraid I'm the last of the Riachs of Dalneil. I'll never have a son and heir.'

'You can't be certain . . .'

'Look at me, Dad! For Christ's sake, no woman in her right mind is going to take me on. Not unless she was blind like myself and there are damned few of those of marrying age around here.'

'You could come and stay with us,' Bob suggested. 'Your mother and I would be delighted to have you.'

Jack shook his head. 'It's best I'm on my own.'

'But what about cooking and cleaning? You can't do that.'

'I'll employ someone, a housekeeper. In fact I already have someone in mind, if she'll agree.'

'Who's that?'

'Hettie Campbell. I'm certain she'll jump at the chance

as it's a step up from dairy maid. She'll take good care of me.'

Bob thought of Hettie whom he'd always found a personable lassie, conscientious in her work too. She'd be ideal.

'It's up to you, Jack. It's entirely up to you.'

'I'll get things started then,' Jack replied.

'Housekeeper?'

'With better pay than you're getting now. So what do you say?'

Hettie was thrilled. 'Of course I'll do it for you, Jack. But are you absolutely certain about selling?'

His expression became serious and wistful at the same time. 'There are too many memories here, Hettie, of which I don't wish to be constantly reminded. The old Jack Riach lived here, not the one who came back from the war.'

A lump came into her throat. 'Oh, Jack!' she whispered.

'My father proposed a manager but that wouldn't be the same at all. I don't want to be stumbling round the house while someone else takes care of things. I'd hate that.'

'But you'd be there to consult and advise.'

'To begin with yes, but I'd soon become redundant. No, Hettie, that's how it's going to be. A little cottage somewhere, a new start. I had thought of moving right away from Dalneil, but that would be too big a wrench. As you said, I'm known here, a local. I'd rather remain amongst "my ain folk".'

She wanted to take him to her bosom and hold him tight, treat him like a child, comfort and console him, but refrained, knowing that wouldn't be appreciated. As Jack had told her, he didn't want to be a figure of pity and that's how such an action would be construed.

'Are there any cottages available around Dalneil?' she queried.

'I'll have to make enquiries. I'm sure I'll come up with something given time.'

'And when will you go on the market?'

'Right away, though how long it will take to sell is hard to say. In normal circumstances there wouldn't be any bother, but with a war on who knows? I'll just have to wait and see.'

He laughed. 'Wait and *see*. That's a good one.'

'Don't be too hard on yourself, Jack,' she whispered.

Jack thought of Grizelda keeling over at the sight of him. How could he not be hard on himself. To spend the rest of his life not only blind but hideously scarred. Not for the first time he wished Peter Drummond had left him to die, for in death there was peace which he certainly didn't have now. Despair welled within him. Terrible, terrible despair.

Wonky found Nell and Charlotte in the drawing room. It was the evening of the day she and Nell had arrived home from Glasgow.

'I've left my case in the hall,' Wonky announced. 'Can I stay here during my week off?'

'Well of course you can,' Charlotte answered, face registering her surprise. 'What happened?'

Wonky took a deep breath. 'What do you think? *Father*. He went through the roof when I told him I was going to France.'

'As bad as that,' Nell commiserated.

'Worse, I can assure you. He actually swore. Can you imagine? Father swearing, I believe it's the first time I've ever heard him do so.'

Nell hid a smile. Wonky was right. For Tom Comyn to swear was almost beyond belief.

'He wants me to remain in Glasgow,' Wonky went on. 'Or better still give up the VADs and come home. I naturally refused to do either.'

'Good for you,' Charlotte said.

'Does he know where you've gone?' Nell asked.

Wonky shook her head. 'No doubt he'll guess when he's calmed down so I can expect a visit tomorrow. I expect support from you two!'

'Which you'll have,' Nell assured her. 'And I'm glad you've stood your ground. The man, albeit he's my uncle, is a tyrant.'

Charlotte rose from where she was sitting. 'It's not long till dinner so I'd better inform Cook there'll be four instead of three.'

'Now tell me all about it,' Nell requested when Charlotte had left the room. 'Word for word.'

Nell groaned – was she going to vomit again? She'd already done so twice.

'I can see land!' Wonky exclaimed excitedly. 'It won't be long now.'

Thank God, Nell thought. She couldn't wait for the boat journey to France to be over and to be on dry land again. This was awful.

Wonky turned a sympathetic gaze on her cousin, wishing

there was something she could do other than just be there. She felt fine, the rough crossing hadn't bothered her in the least.

'I feel so . . . ridiculous,' Nell gasped.

'Well, you're not the only one being sick. There are a number from what I've seen.'

Nell groaned again as the boat pitched.

'Listen!' said Wonky.

The wind had suddenly changed direction and now they could distinctly hear the sound of heavy guns. Wonky shivered in apprehension.

Nell closed her eyes, wishing the boat to go faster.

'I was worried half to death for you when I heard what had happened,' Alice crooned to Andrew. 'You must have been right in the thick of it.'

Was he falling in love with her? he wondered. It seemed so, which delighted him. He certainly missed her when they were apart and thought of her constantly. Was that love?

'I was,' he acknowledged, pretending to be humble. 'The Post Office, Jacob's Biscuit Factory, I was there.'

'Oh, my darling,' she whispered.

'At one point a rebel bullet missed me by . . . oh! that much.' He held two fingers about an inch apart. An exaggeration of course.

Her eyes widened.

'I was lucky.'

She touched his cheek, lightly running her fingers over it. If that bullet had been any closer . . . she shuddered at the thought.

'And then Pearse saw sense and surrendered. That was an enormous relief I can tell you. I was amongst those who escorted the prisoners down O'Connell Street to Richmond Barracks. They gave a great cheer when they saw the tricolour still flying over the portico of the Post Office, but that was soon hauled down.'

Andrew became introspective. 'Some of those chaps seemed quite reasonable really. It was hard to imagine we'd been trying to kill each other only a short while previously.'

'Well, you're here now, safe and sound,' Alice declared. 'And with you, my pet, which is the best thing of all.'

She gave him a radiant smile which quite melted him inside. His lips met hers, and then she was in his arms.

It would be a good marriage he thought. Especially considering all that came with it.

Lucky! He was that and no mistake.

'It's strange there just being the two of us again,' Murdo said to Charlotte sitting beside him at the dinner table.

'Yes, Nell and Wonky certainly livened things up a bit.'

Murdo gazed about him. 'It's like living in a mausoleum.'

'It's hardly that grim, Pa!'

Murdo grunted.

Charlotte laid down her soup spoon. 'Why don't you go for a walk tomorrow afternoon? I'll be all right on my own for a while.'

He frowned. 'That's out of the question.'

'No it isn't,' she insisted. 'And you came to enjoy your walks so much. I know you miss them.'

He did, he thought. He most certainly did. He didn't feel nearly as well as he had when taking them.

'Well?' she demanded.

'I'll think about it.'

Charlotte smiled, knowing she'd won and that he would. 'I wonder how the girls are getting on in France?' she mused.

'Probably up to their eyes in it. God help them.'

'Amen,' Charlotte murmured.

'Gas!' a lookout shouted. '*GAS!*'

Peter grabbed for his respirator which he quickly had in place. These gas attacks were increasing in frequency and a constant nightmare.

A young soldier who'd only arrived in the trenches for the first time that day froze with fear. Then he was fumbling with his respirator which, in his terror, he dropped.

He stared at the fallen respirator in horror as gas enveloped him and the others.

His first day in the trenches was his last.

Alice was laughing as she reined in her horse. 'You're letting me win again. That's not fair,' she called out.

Andrew reined in alongside her. 'No I'm not. I swear. It's simply that you're a far better rider than I.'

She gazed adoringly at him. 'Fibber.'

'Not so!' he protested.

Her face fell. 'I've just remembered you're returning to Dublin tomorrow.'

'Duty calls, Alice.'

'I wish you didn't have to go.'

'So do I, I assure you. I'd much rather be here with you.' He meant that most sincerely.

'Can I come to you tonight, be with you for a while? We could snuggle up.'

'No!' he replied sternly, the truth being he simply didn't trust himself.

'Please?'

'No, Alice. You know my feelings on that subject.'

She pouted. 'Spoilsport.'

'Indeed I am.'

As they rode on he thought of the brothel he'd been using and wondered if it would be safe to return there so soon after the rising.

'I don't think I'll ever get used to living in a tent,' Nell said to Wonky as she and the others present got dressed. There were six of them in the bell-tent to which she and Wonky had been assigned. This was the accommodation provided for the VADs by the 22 General Hospital, Camiers.

'It could be worse,' Wonky replied, thinking but not much.

Hope Langton, another of the six, laughed. 'Consider yourself fortunate, girls. You should have seen where I was before this. Now *that* was something to complain about.'

'I'm not complaining,' Nell retorted. 'Only remarking that I don't think I'll ever get used to it.'

'Can anyone lend me some hairpins?' Georgina Fletcher asked. 'I appear to have mislaid mine.'

'You're always mislaying things. I wouldn't be surprised if you mislaid yourself one day,' Rebecca Levi commented.

Georgina pulled a face. 'I can't help the way I am. I've always been the same.'

Rebecca sighed. 'Here, have some of mine.'

Georgina accepted the pins with a word of thanks and used them to secure the white cap which tailed down to her shoulders. Their white aprons were ankle length, full in cut, and held in place by a belt. Each apron sported a red cross on the bosom.

'Well I'm ready. I wonder what's for breakfast?' Wonky declared jauntily.

A few minutes later all six of them left together for the mess after which they started their shift.

'Yes!' Murdo called out when there was a rap on the office door, expecting it to be Isobel with their coffee and biscuits. He stared in astonishment when it was Miss McQueen who entered.

Miss McQueen's face was stone hard as she crossed to his desk. 'This came and I thought you'd better have it right away, sir,' she said, laying down an official telegram in front of him.

A mesmerised Murdo stared at the telegram. It might have been a hissing snake that had been put on his desk.

'Pa?'

Murdo didn't reply but instead continued to stare at the telegram. He'd heard of telegrams like these, who hadn't. And now one had been sent to him.

It took all his willpower to reach out and pick up the envelope. Slowly, unwillingly, he slit it open and took out the single sheet it contained.

Charlotte was on her feet now, the atmosphere in the office having changed to one of deep foreboding.

Murdo read the sheet and went white.

'Pa?' Charlotte repeated.

He looked at her through eyes filled with tears. 'Peter's been killed,' he stated simply.

'Oh, my God.'

Miss McQueen glanced away.

'Killed,' Murdo said again.

The pain that erupted in his chest was more intense than any he'd previously experienced. He gasped and clutched himself.

'Pa!' Charlotte screamed, rushing round from behind her desk. 'Pa!'

Miss McQueen got to Murdo first, cradling him in her arms. Then Charlotte was there also.

Murdo's colour changed from white to puce as he struggled for breath.

'Peter,' he murmured. 'Peter.'

'Get Doctor McAllister!' Charlotte ordered Miss McQueen. 'And hurry.'

Miss McQueen fled the room.

'It was a massive heart attack brought on by the news,' McAllister said to a distraught Charlotte. 'There was nothing you could have done. I'm truly sorry.'

Her brother and father in one day. Dear God.

'It's best Miss McQueen takes you home and I'll attend to what has to be done here. I'll be over later with a sedative.'

Before leaving Charlotte knelt and kissed her father on the lips. 'Goodbye, Pa. Say hello to Peter for me.'

Somewhere in her mind she heard his voice reply:

'I will, lass. I will.'

Chapter 22

Charlotte sat alone in the drawing room staring vacantly ahead, her mind in turmoil. She was racked with grief.

The funeral was in three days' time, she had to hold herself together for that. Andrew had been notified and was on his way home, as was Nell.

But what happened after the funeral, what then? She simply did not know.

'Hello, sis.'

Charlotte turned from the window through which she'd been staring to give her brother a wan smile. 'Hello, Andrew.'

He went to her and kissed her on the cheek. 'How are you?'

'Dreadful. And you?'

'Still in shock.'

She nodded her understanding.

'How was the trip over?' she enquired.

'Uneventful, thank goodness. There wasn't a moment went by when I didn't expect to be blown sky high. The U-boats are causing terrible carnage out there.'

'So I read in the newspapers.'

He went to the decanter and poured himself a dram. 'You?'

'No thanks.'

Andrew stared at her thoughtfully over the rim of his glass. 'Peter *and* Pa, it's hardly credible,' he said.

'Yes.'

'Right there in the office.'

'In my arms.'

'Christ,' Andrew muttered.

He gazed about him, thinking this was now all his. Who would have believed but he'd inherited after all. Not that that changed his plans for Alice, not a whit of it.

'Everyone has been so wonderful,' Charlotte declared. 'They couldn't have been kinder. The workforce in the distillery are soldiering on in the meantime. They're all coming to the funeral. Each and every one of them. Pa was so well liked.'

'When's Nell arriving?'

'Sometime today I believe. I just hope she isn't held up in any way.'

'I hope so too. It would be awful if she missed the funeral tomorrow. She'd never forgive herself.'

'Yes,' Charlotte agreed.

She shivered, she just couldn't seem to get warm since Murdo's death. Even in bed with a heavy quilt on top she was still cold. Reaction of course, she knew that.

'Have we heard yet what actually happened to Peter?'

Charlotte shook her head. 'There should be a letter from his C.O. I understand that's the procedure. But it hasn't come yet.'

'I hope this isn't tactless, but when's the will being read?'

'Monday of next week. You'll still be here I take it?'

'Oh yes. I've got a full fortnight's compassionate leave. By the way, Alice, my fiancée sends her condolences and hopes you're bearing up. So also do her father and mother, Sir Henry and Lady Fortescue.'

'You must tell me all about her before you leave.'

'I shall, sis. I shall.'

'Uncle Tom's taking the service. He and Aunt Moira are very upset.'

Andrew poured himself another dram.

'Jack Riach will be coming to the funeral. Did you hear about him?'

Andrew shook his head.

Charlotte told him.

'Poor bugger,' Andrew whispered, profoundly thankful he was in Ireland and not at the Western Front.

'He was supposed to marry Grizelda McPherson you know, but she broke it off when he got back. That caused a few comments I can tell you.'

'Is his face that bad?'

'Pretty ghastly. It was Peter who saved his life. Now Peter's gone.'

Two hours later Nell arrived home.

A huge turnout filled the church to capacity. There were people standing against the walls and a large number at the rear. Andrew spoke, doing justice to both his father and brother.

After Murdo had been interred those who'd been invited went to Drummond House where a buffet meal and drinks had been provided.

It was hours before the last mourner left.

'Sell the distillery!' Charlotte exploded, aghast.

Andrew shrugged. 'What else can I do? With Pa and Peter gone there's no one left to run the damn thing.'

'But it's been in the family for generations,' an equally aghast Nell objected.

'Nothing's for ever, Nell. And even if I could get out the army, which I can't for the present, I couldn't run it. I wouldn't even know where to start.'

'What about the house?' Charlotte queried.

'That'll remain the family home, for now anyway. I'd hardly toss you out onto the street.'

The will had been read that morning. As expected, with Peter's death, the main part of the estate had gone to Andrew. Both Charlotte and Nell had been well provided for.

'You can't sell the distillery. You simply can't,' Charlotte stated emphatically.

'Then come up with an alternative,' Andrew challenged.

She stared at her brother, eyes blazing. 'I'll run it.'

'You!' he scoffed. 'That's ridiculous.'

'Not as ridiculous as it might seem. I've been working with Pa there for some time now during which he taught me a lot. I believe I'm quite capable of taking over.'

Andrew leant back in the sofa and regarded Charlotte

with amusement. 'Women don't run businesses, sis. It just isn't done.'

'There are lots of things women didn't do before the war which they're doing now, so why not this?'

'Hear hear,' Nell agreed.

'You're serious then?'

'I most certainly am. If you sell the distillery, Andrew, I'll never forgive you or speak to you again. You have my word on that.'

'And mine,' Nell added.

He frowned. He'd never considered this option. And the distillery might be difficult to sell during wartime. There was that.

'You've been working with Pa and he taught you a lot?' Andrew repeated.

'That's right. Pa took over again after Peter left, which you know, and was running himself into the ground because we're so short staffed. I offered to help to get my mind off losing the baby.'

Andrew dropped his gaze. 'Yes, Pa penned me a note about that. I'm sorry.'

'Not half as much as me. Anyway, those are the reasons I offered to help Pa and a great success my help has been, if I say so myself. Pa was coming to rely on me more and more.'

'I see,' Andrew mused.

'She's quite capable,' Nell said. 'I'd have every faith in her if I was you.'

This was going to take some considering, Andrew thought. He wasn't about to rush into any decisions. Certainly not ones as important as this.

'Let me sleep on it,' he said with a smile.

Charlotte, after a few moments hesitation, nodded her agreement.

'I'm drunk as a lord,' Bobby Baxter declared to Geoffrey. The pair of them were in an Amiens nightclub, a husky-voiced female singer, on what passed for a stage, singing in French.

'Me too,' Geoffrey grinned back.

Bobby glanced about him. 'We could easily get fixed up you know, old bean. There are lots of ladies present who, for a price, would be most accommodating.'

Geoffrey shook his head. 'Not interested, Bobby. I'd never betray my Charlotte. She's the one and only for me.'

Bobby sighed. 'I envy you that. It must be an inspiration for you.'

'It is.'

'Someday . . .' Bobby murmured. 'Someday.'

A waiter approached and spoke to them. 'Yes, another bottle of champers,' Bobby nodded. Then to Geoffrey, 'We may as well make a real night of it. Who knows when we'll get a decent one out again.'

The smell of cheap perfume, female flesh and sweat was almost overpowering, Geoffrey thought. It had a strange intoxicating effect that wasn't entirely unpleasant.

'Two more days and we're back in the front line,' Bobby stated.

Geoffrey didn't reply to that. Two days could be a life-time in their situation. You simply lived each day at a time and tried not to think of tomorrow.

The singer finished her song and was given a rapturous applause which she acknowledged flamboyantly.

'Lovely pair of tits,' Bobby commented.

Geoffrey roared, for Bobby was right. They were lovely.

'I've decided to let you go ahead,' Andrew declared to Charlotte.

Relief surged through her. 'So you won't be selling?'

He turned away, not wanting her to see the expression on his face. 'Let's wait a bit and see how it all goes.'

She knew that was the best she could hope for. 'Thank you, Andrew.'

He shrugged.

'I won't let you down. I swear.'

'I'm sure you won't,' he replied. The only reason he'd agreed to her proposal was because it suited his purposes. For the time being.

'I'll be back to work tomorrow,' she stated.

The workforce had assembled as Charlotte had instructed. She now stepped forward to address them.

'As I'm sure you're all aware my brother Andrew has inherited the distillery. Unfortunately he can't leave the army with the war on to take charge, so in the meantime I'm going to run things.'

A muttering went up.

She raised an eyebrow. 'Any questions?'

Don McLeod, a stillman in his late fifties, held up a hand. 'That's ridiculous, lassie. Who's ever heard of a female boss?'

He laughed, as did many of the others present. 'You don't approve of the idea then?' she replied caustically.

'No offence, Miss Charlotte, but the notion's a load of nonsense.'

'Really?'

'Oh aye,' he grinned.

'I see.' She paused. 'Well that's that then. I'll have to close the distillery down. There's nothing else for it.'

Don's grin vanished. 'Close down?'

'What else can I do? Nothing.'

She stared defiantly at him, then the others.

'Aye, well . . .' Don muttered.

'And if I close down that means you're all out of work,' she pointed out unnecessarily. 'Is that what you want?'

Their faces reflected it was the last thing they wanted.

She softened her tone. 'I know I'm a woman and that might cause difficulties, not only with you but wholesalers and the like. Nor do I pretend to understand whisky making, I don't. But I am prepared to try to run the administration side of things if I can rely on your wholehearted cooperation. Without that we close and a For Sale sign goes up.'

The men glanced from one to the other.

'I'll tell you this,' she went on. 'My father would have hated the idea of the distillery being closed down and ultimately sold. You all know how much he loved this place. And how loyal he was to you and yours. Is it too much to expect a little of that loyalty back now that he's dead?'

Sandy McTavish raised his hand. 'May we speak amongst ourselves, Miss Charlotte?'

'Of course, Sandy.'

'Thank you, miss.'

The men conferred together, the women in the work-force excluded though the decision affected them also.

After a few minutes' consultation the men broke apart from the huddle they'd formed into.

'We're with you, Miss Charlotte,' Sandy declared. 'You'll get our full cooperation.'

'Does that go for everyone?'

'Everyone,' Don McLeod nodded.

She hesitated, then said, 'There are bound to be times when I have to come to some of you for advice. That seems inevitable. I hope you'll be patient with my lack of practical knowledge.'

'We'll be patient,' Sandy replied.

Jamie, the gaffer from bottling, raised his cap aloft. 'Three cheers for Miss Charlotte. Hip hip . . .!'

'Now let's get on with it, myself included,' she smiled when the cheering had died away.

Wonky, having heard Nell was back, had sneaked away for a few minutes from the hospital. She found Nell sitting morosely in their tent.

'So how was it?' Wonky asked.

'Pretty awful.'

'I can imagine.'

'I still can't believe that Pa and Peter have gone. It's . . .' She broke off and shook her head.

'Is there anything I can do?'

Nell took a deep breath. 'No. But thanks for asking. Your father did an excellent service by the way. It couldn't have been better if that's the right word to use for that sort of thing.'

Wonky placed a comforting hand on Nell's shoulder. 'They were both good men who'll be sorely missed.'

'Pa seemed . . . well indestructible somehow. A rock.'

'I know,' Wonky whispered.

'I could smell him everywhere in the house. And half the time expected him to come breezing in through the door. Charlotte said she felt the same.'

'How's Charlotte taking it?'

'As you'd expect. Andrew better than the two of us, but then he's a man.'

'Andrew was there?'

'Oh yes. He got compassionate leave. He's agreed to let Charlotte run the distillery for now. I'm sure she'll make a success of it.'

'I agree, Charlotte's a very resourceful woman. Anyway, I'd better get back on the ward before Sister realises I'm missing. I'll get a rocket if she does.'

Nell smiled at her cousin. 'Thanks for popping over.'

Wonky bent and kissed Nell on the cheek. 'Cheer up. We'll have a proper natter later.'

'All right.'

Wonky swished from the tent.

Wonky hadn't long gone when the familiar tingling took hold of Nell, followed by the trembling of her hands. It had been ages since she'd last had a vision.

The Highland army appeared to be in retreat, their mood one of utter dejection. They looked as though they hadn't eaten or slept in days.

Her Highlander was at the rear and seemed to be having trouble walking. His face was gaunt and unshaven, his shoulders drooping, and there was a blood-stained rag tied round his left arm.

Oh my poor darling, Nell found herself thinking. Her impulse was to rush to him and take care of him.

A horse stumbled and dropped to the ground where it writhed for a few moments. Its rider, who'd jumped clear, wearily examined the animal, then took a pistol from his waistband, cocked it and shot the beast. Others, completely uninterested in the situation, continued to trudge by.

Her Highlander glanced up at the sky as though wondering if it was going to rain, then continued on his way.

It was still England, Nell thought.

The Highland army was still south of the border.

Andrew was sitting alone in the mess when he was joined by Billy Roberts. 'You'll never guess what happened when I was out on patrol?' Billy said.

'What?'

'Somebody took a potshot at us. Luckily he missed.'

'A potshot?' Andrew mused.

'A Fenian of course. At least I presume it was.' Billy tasted his beer. 'I think we made a bad mistake executing all those rebels. We went overboard in my opinion.'

'I disagree. They were rebels as you say. They deserved what they got.'

'Maybe. But to execute so many? I'm certain that was wrong.'

Andrew leant back in his chair and closed his eyes.

'Something up?'

'I've been tired ever since I returned from Scotland.

Perhaps I'm coming down with a cold or the flu.'

'It could simply be reaction. Losing a father and brother at the same time must knock the stuffing out of you. I know it would me.'

'It certainly wasn't easy,' Andrew said. 'Nor was the trip over there and back. Rotten weather in both instances plus the worry about U-boats. There was a ship sunk on the day I made the return journey. It could easily have been the one I was on.'

'Still, you had to go. And take the risk involved I suppose.'

Andrew sighed. 'Anyway, it's all over and done with now, thank God.'

'And you've become a man of property and means,' Billy grinned.

Andrew's mood lightened. 'There is that. I only wish it wasn't at Peter's expense though. We were never the closest of brothers, but . . .' He broke off. 'Well, you understand.'

'Of course,' Billy muttered.

'A potshot?' Andrew mused again thoughtfully. 'Well well well.'

He made a mental note to be extra vigilant while he was on patrol.

'How are you today, Jack?' Hettie enquired.

'So so. And yourself?'

'All right, bearing up. Any news of that cottage?'

He shook his head. 'There's absolutely nothing going at the moment but something's bound to come up in time. It's simply a case of waiting.'

'I'm looking forward to being a housekeeper. It should be fun.'

'Fun,' he chuckled.

'Well, different anyhow.'

He sighed, a melancholy sound. 'I feel so useless, Hettie. I just wish I could do something. But what?'

She had no reply to that.

'You know what I miss most?'

'What, Jack?'

'Riding. I used to enjoy that so much. Now I'll never ride again.'

She bit her lip in consternation. 'Now don't take offence but you could always mount up and have someone lead you.'

That amused him. 'Not exactly the same, Hettie. Not by a long chalk.' He laughed bitterly. 'What would I look like? Ridiculous that's what. Completely ridiculous.'

'No you wouldn't!' she replied hotly.

'Well, that's how I feel.' He reached out and groped till he found her arm. 'I appreciate you're only trying to be helpful so thank you for that.'

'Been to the pub recently?'

'As a matter of fact I went last night with my dad. We had a smashing time. All sorts came over and joined us for a chat.'

'And what else have you been doing?'

'Nothing, Hettie, nothing at all. Thinking mainly, remembering how it used to be. I think of Peter Drummond quite a bit. We were great pals he and I.'

'I know,' she said softly.

'I miss the old bugger. At least . . .' He trailed off.

'What?'

Jack spoke in almost a whisper. 'At least he didn't end up crippled or disfigured.'

'You're not crippled, Jack.'

'Then what do you call being blind? I'm a cripple as much as if I'd lost my arms or legs. Crippled,' he repeated.

Hettie swallowed hard, her heart going out to him. She was wise enough to know the last thing he needed was self pity, but how could she tell him that. It was something he had to learn for himself.

'I'd best be getting on my way, Jack. I still have lots to do.'

'Crippled,' he further repeated after she'd gone.

Isobel placed Charlotte's coffee and biscuits in front of her. 'Excuse me remarking, miss, but you look fair wabbit.'

Charlotte gave the girl a wan smile. 'I am, Isobel. Believe me.'

Isobel stared at her employer in concern. 'You're working too hard, miss. That's what folk are saying.'

Charlotte took a deep breath thinking how welcome the coffee was. 'There's a great deal to be done, Isobel, and I'm still learning the ropes. It isn't easy.'

'No, miss,' Isobel agreed.

Charlotte spooned sugar into her coffee, then added milk.

'Can I say something, miss?'

'Certainly, go ahead.'

'The workers all admire you, miss. They weren't sure

about this to begin with but now they've come to respect and admire all you're doing. They're right behind you. Especially the women, they all think it's grand.'

That warmed Charlotte, as did the coffee when she sipped it.

'Is there anything else, miss?'

'No, Isobel. And thank you for your support.'

Isobel gave Charlotte a huge beaming smile. 'Not at all, miss. Not at all.'

Charlotte forced herself to take her time over the coffee and biscuits, before getting back to work.

'It's gorgeous!' Alice exclaimed, staring at the sparkling emerald necklace nestling on black velvet. She threw an arm round Andrew's neck. 'Thank you.'

'It'll maybe make up for the engagement ring I bought you. Money was tight then which it isn't now.'

'My ring is beautiful, Andrew. It's what it represents that matters, not the value of the ring itself.'

He *was* in love with her, he thought. He damned well was. He'd thought of her constantly, even through the traumas of Scotland, since their last meeting. Touching her, smelling her, gave him a thrill.

'Why don't you try it on,' he suggested.

She took the necklace from its box and he helped fasten it round her neck.

'There,' he declared. 'Perfect.'

Her eyes shone. 'Thank you again,' she whispered.

'Do I get a kiss?'

The kiss was long, deep and wonderful.

*

Sir Henry Fortescue was a worried man. He was pleased with Andrew's good fortune, albeit out of tragedy, but as Andrew now owned the Drummond distillery surely that meant Andrew, and Alice, would be residing in Scotland after the war. That was the last thing he wanted. What he did want was for Alice to stay nearby.

Sir Henry surveyed Andrew across the dinner table. 'And what are your plans for the future now, me lad?' he queried, trying to keep the anxiety out of his voice.

'How do you mean, sir?'

'The distillery of course. I presume you'll be taking over as soon as you can?'

Andrew glanced at Alice who smiled back at him. She was wearing the necklace which Lady Fortescue had cooed over.

'I'm not sure, sir.'

'Not sure?'

'I have a mind to sell it, sir. Though I haven't made a final decision yet.'

Sir Henry immediately brightened. 'And why would you do that?'

Andrew's reason was that it would give him enough money, if properly handled that was, to live a life of ease and luxury. After all, why work if you didn't have to? And then there was Greystones and the Fortescue inheritance. When they came Alice's way it would really be a life of luxury at the highest level.

'I've never really been interested in the distillery, sir,' Andrew said honestly. 'Perhaps things might have been different if I'd been the firstborn and trained into the business as my brother Peter was. But I wasn't and that's why I went into the army which appealed.'

'I see,' Sir Henry murmured, much relieved. 'I understand your sister is currently running it.'

Andrew smiled. 'A conceit on her part, sir. The idea of a woman in charge is absurd of course. But if she can keep things ticking over, till the end of the war that is, and perhaps somewhat beyond, then that suits me.'

'You're thinking of the price you'll get when you finally do sell?' Sir Henry asked shrewdly.

'Precisely, sir. To my way of thinking I should get a lot more after the war than I would now. So if I can hang on, thanks to Charlotte, then why not.'

Sir Henry chuckled. 'Good for you.'

Lady Fortescue frowned. 'Isn't that rather devious of you, Andrew? And what of your poor sister if she does make a go of it?'

'Devious perhaps, but then isn't that what business is all about? As for Charlotte, she'll lose interest when her husband Geoffrey gets back from the war and they start a family.'

'And what if he doesn't come back?' Alice queried.

Andrew had a sip of wine, a rather good Bordeaux. 'That'll alter things of course. In the short term, that is, for I'm certain after a suitable period Charlotte would marry again. She's a fine-looking woman and would not be one to remain a widow in my opinion.

'Anyway,' he shrugged. 'The decision of when to sell, regardless of the circumstances, is mine and mine alone. She has no say whatever in the matter.'

'So your plans are still to remain in Ireland?' Sir Henry asked, twiddling his moustache.

'Most assuredly, sir.'

'Aahhh!' Sir Henry breathed, and shot his wife a jubilant glance. That was excellent.

'There would naturally be trips to Scotland, but my home would be here.'

Sir Henry nodded his approval.

'Isn't he clever,' Alice beamed at her parents.

Sir Henry wasn't going to dispute that. 'Changing the subject. What have you heard about this torching in West Cork?' he asked Andrew.

'Torching? Nothing at all, sir.'

'Dreadful affair,' Lady Fortescue muttered.

Andrew was intrigued and waited for Sir Henry to explain.

'Two Protestant families were burnt out of their houses,' Sir Henry said. 'Luckily no one was injured.'

'Disgraceful,' Alice declared.

Sir Henry frowned. 'It's a worrying development for the likes of us who've managed to rub along with the Catholics all this while.' He shook his head. 'The majority of the populace weren't with the Fenians before the rising, but now . . . Well let's just say I detect a new mood in the land. One I don't like one little bit.'

Andrew recalled his conversation with Billy Roberts. 'Do you think we were too harsh with the rebel leaders, sir?'

'It's not what I think but the populace itself. And yes, I believe they do, that the British government went too far.'

He sighed. 'Who knows what the outcome will be.'

'Who knows?'

Andrew woke with a start when a body slipped into bed beside him.

'Ssshh!' Alice whispered.

'What are you doing here?'

'Don't be angry, darling, please? I just wanted to snuggle up for a while.'

'But you know . . .' He was silenced by her hand being placed across his mouth.

'Instead of talking, kiss me.'

What else could he do? He couldn't exactly chuck her out of bed. That would have been a terrible insult. Besides, now she was here, why not make the best of it. Within limits that was.

Their lips met and his hand moved to her breast. She jerked slightly when he cupped it.

'You really are a hussy,' he whispered when the kiss was over.

'Only where you're concerned, Andrew. I'd do anything for you. Anything at all.'

His ego swelled. By Jove! he thought. Talk about a conquest. 'And I you. But this isn't right, Alice. You don't realise what a temptation you are.'

'Or what a temptation you are for me.'

Her hand wormed its way into his pyjama jacket and began roving over his chest. 'Stop it!' he hissed.

She didn't. Instead her other hand suddenly delved to encompass his bottom.

Andrew groaned. This was too much. He exposed the breast he'd been fondling and dropped his mouth to it.

All previous resolution he'd had evaporated. He lifted up her nightdress and squirmed out of his pyjama bottoms. He had to have her. He simply had to.

He must pull out in time he told himself. He must.

Alice gave a small grunt as he broke into her. And from then on it was sheer bliss for both of them.

'It's Charlotte Drummond to see you,' Bob Riach announced to Jack, sitting in a chair by the fire.

Jack immediately rose. 'Charlotte?'

She went to him and kissed him on the cheek. 'Hello, Jack.'

'You're brave to do that.'

'Am I indeed. I don't think so.'

He ignored her reply. 'Would you care for a dram. Or perhaps something else?'

'A dram would be lovely. It's been a long, hard day.'

'I'll get you one then.'

'Can I do it?'

He gave her a crooked smile. 'I can manage, thank you.'

She watched him go to a cupboard, open it and fumble inside. 'I'll sit down if you don't mind.'

'Please do.'

She further watched as he poured the whiskies then tentatively made his way back. 'Which seat are you in?' he queried.

She told him.

He came to her and handed her a glass. 'If you want water I'll have to shout for my mother or father.'

'Neat's fine.'

'Right then.'

He made his way over to the chair he'd been sitting in and sat again. '*Slainthe!*' he toasted.

'*Slainthe.*'

They both drank.

'Drummond,' she commented.

'Of course. What else?' He had another sip. 'Now why the visit, Charlotte. What can I do for you?'

'It's more what I can do for you.'

'Oh?'

'You know old Mrs Murchie?'

'Of course.'

She went on to explain to a delighted Jack the reason she'd called.

Chapter 23

Wonky found the driver leaning against his ambulance smoking a cigarette. 'I'm the VAD for the CCS,' she smiled. The latter was short for Casualty Clearing Station where the wounded were taken from the frontline.

He had an open, intelligent face with deep blue eyes. 'Hi!' he replied. 'I'm Dale Kutchinsky.'

She frowned. 'Are you American?'

'Sure am. All the way from Albany, New York State. Hop aboard and we'll get underway.'

'An American,' she thought, going round to the other side of the ambulance. She'd heard there were some around, albeit America wasn't in the war, but this was the first she'd encountered.

She climbed into the passenger seat and closed the door. Moments later they moved off.

'New to this duty, eh?' he said.

'That's right.'

'Knew I hadn't driven you before. What's your name?'

'Wonky Comyn.'

He laughed. 'Wonky! What sort of name is that?'

'A nickname. My real name is Veronica.' She then went on to explain why she was called Wonky.

'Like it,' he declared. 'Never known a Wonky before.'

'Nor I a Dale.'

'That makes us even then.'

There was an easiness of manner about him which she liked, she decided. Not bad looking either, in a different sort of way. Now that she'd had something of a chance to study him he certainly didn't look British. Perhaps it was something to do with the relaxed way he carried himself.

'Been out here long?' she asked.

'Couple of months. You?'

'A little longer.'

He grunted, took a last draw on his cigarette then tossed it away.

'Are you a professional ambulance driver?' she enquired politely.

He laughed again. 'Hell no! I'm a lawyer, graduate of Harvard Law School. I haven't practised yet though, came straight over after graduation. Much to my folks' dismay. They sure were angry as can be when I told them my intention. Said I was stupid to put myself in danger when I didn't have to.'

She immediately warmed to him. 'It was the same with me. My father was beside himself when I told him I was joining the VADs, which was nothing to what he was like when I broke the news that I was coming to France.'

'Sometimes parents don't realise you've grown up and are capable of your own decisions,' he grinned amiably. 'They still think we're babies in diapers who have to be looked after.'

She frowned. 'Diapers?'

'You know. Those things you put round a baby's a—' He suddenly checked himself. 'Rear.'

'You mean nappies?'

'Whatever.'

Wonky flushed slightly. What a subject! 'Kutchinsky did you say?'

'Correct, maam. We're of Polish extraction. My grandfather and grandmother went to the States on an immigrant ship and made good. He was a tailor by trade.'

Wonky found that fascinating. 'And your other set of grandparents?'

'Oh, they stayed on in Poland. We lost touch with that side of the family long ago.

'Sorry,' Dale apologised as the ambulance bounced. 'These roads are a bitch.'

'So why did you decide to be in a war when your own country isn't fighting?' she asked, curious.

'Conscience, pure and simple. I'm also quite a Francophile, sure love those frogs. Their literature, art, cuisine.'

He took out a packet of cigarettes. 'You don't object I hope?'

'No I don't.'

'Do you?'

She shook her head.

He lit up.

'How long will it take to get there?' she inquired.

'Varies, maam. Depends on the roads and other things. In other words we get there when we get there.'

He gave her a sideways glance. 'You English?'

'Scots.'

'I thought it wasn't an English accent. Leastways none of the ones I've heard.'

'What's Albany like? Sounds nice.'

He then proceeded to enthuse about his home town for the remainder of the bumpy ride.

'Wonky!'

She was supervising stretcher cases being loaded aboard the ambulance, and turned round in surprise at the sound of her name. She couldn't believe her eyes when she saw Geoffrey hurrying towards her.

He took her into his arms, a bemused Dale looking on, and kissed her on the cheek. 'Well isn't this a turn up for the books!'

'What are you doing here. You're not injured, are you?'

Geoffrey shook his head. 'Seeing a fellow officer who's been wounded. And you?'

She explained her new duty.

'You look wonderful!' he declared.

Which was more than she could say about him. How aged he was. There was even grey in his hair which hadn't been there before.

'How are you?' she asked with a smile.

'All right. Well, as right as can be, considering.'

'It was terrible about Peter.'

Geoffrey's face fell. 'Yes,' he agreed softly. 'It, eh . . .well, best not speak about it.'

'I'll write and tell Charlotte I bumped into you. She'll be thrilled.'

'Quite a coincidence.'

'Quite.'

'Charlotte's doing awfully well in the distillery, I understand. I'm proud of her.'

She touched him on the sleeve. 'It was rotten about the baby, Geoffrey. Really rotten.'

He glanced away. 'So much death and destruction nowadays. It's all about us. A day doesn't go by but . . .' He broke off and shrugged. 'Enough of that, have to look on the bright side, what?'

'That's the ticket.'

'Nurse, we need you,' Dale called out.

'I have to go,' Wonky apologised.

'Of course. You take care now.'

'And you, Geoffrey.' He kissed her again on the cheek, a misty look in his eyes. 'Ta ra for now.'

'Ta ra.'

He left her and strode away.

'Friend?' Dale enquired as she joined him.

'My cousin's husband.'

'Ah!'

Geoffrey turned and waved to Wonky but by then she was far too busy to notice.

'What's it like?' Jack asked.

Hettie glanced about her. They were in old Mrs Murchie's rented cottage which she'd given up to go and live with her daughter and family. The cottage belonged to Charlotte who'd inherited it when Murdo died, being in that part of the estate which had come to her. She now intended selling it to Jack.

'Just as you'd expect of an old woman who's lived alone. It's going to need a lot doing to it.'

Jack nodded. 'I thought as much.'

'It appears solid enough, though no doubt you'll have that checked over.'

'I shall have everything ripped out and we'll start from scratch,' Jack declared. 'You'll do the choosing of carpets and curtains, those sort of things.'

That delighted Hettie.

'We'll go to Pitlochry when it's time and tour the shops there. How about that?'

'Sounds a real treat, Jack.'

If he could pluck up the courage to go to Pitlochry that was, he wasn't at all sure he could. 'How big is this sitting room we're in?'

Hettie gave him a rough estimate.

'Now take me to the kitchen.'

That was in an even worse state than the sitting room, and filthy in the extreme.

Hettie began the very next day to scrub out the cottage.

Charlotte coldly eyed Mr Strachan, her Glasgow and surrounding area's distributor, across his desk. The meeting was at her request.

'How pleasant of you to call, Miss Drummond,' he beamed. 'Can I offer you sherry?'

'No thank you.'

He made a pyramid with his hands. 'And to what do I owe the honour?'

'You've put up your prices.'

'That's correct.'

'I've been in touch with other distilleries you handle and you haven't done the same with them.'

His smile faded.

Charlotte arched an eyebrow and waited for an explanation.

'We will in time, Miss Drummond.' She could read in his face and from the fact he'd coloured that was a lie.

'Could it be you thought I was a soft touch being a woman?' she asked.

'Of course not!' he protested.

'No?'

'It is somewhat unusual I admit. I've never done business with a woman before.'

'There are other distributors in Glasgow, Mr Strachan, most of whom would jump at the chance of acting on my behalf. Perhaps I should get in touch with several of them.'

He stared grimly at her.

'Distributors whose prices would be more acceptable,' she added, driving the point home.

He rocked back in his chair. Lose the Drummond account! That was unthinkable. It may only be a small distillery but its account was prestigious.

'I'm sure we can come to some agreement, Miss Drummond,' he said.

'The only agreement I'm interested in is the one we had before.'

He slowly nodded. 'Then that's what'll happen.'

'Good.'

She rose. 'Good-day to you, Mr Strachan.'

He also rose. 'Good-day to you, Miss Drummond. I'll see you out.'

'I'm perfectly capable of seeing myself out thank you very much.'

And with that she swept from the room.

Wonky had decided to go for a stroll after dinner, Nell declining to accompany her, and it was while out walking she came across Dale Kutchinsky sitting on a bale of supplies having a smoke.

'Hello,' she smiled.

'Come and join me,' he said, patting the bale. 'There's room enough for two.'

She sat. 'You looked as though you were deep in thought.'

'I was. Reminiscing you could say. Memories.'

'A girl perhaps?'

He shook his head. 'Oh sure there've been girls along the way, but no one in particular. There isn't anyone at home pining for me if that's what you mean. What about you?'

'Me neither.'

He studied her. 'I find that hard to believe, a gorgeous creature like yourself.'

Wonky blushed. 'Flatterer.'

'No, it's true. Honest!' he protested.

Her blushing deepened. 'There was someone once, but that didn't last.'

'What happened. Or am I being rude in asking?'

Wonky gazed up as a plane with French markings flew overhead. She could clearly see the pilot in the cockpit. From the direction he was taking he was heading straight for the German lines. She silently wished the pilot luck and a safe return.

She turned her attention again to Dale. 'I really don't know what happened. I thought it was good between us but apparently he took a different view.'

'I see. Do you still miss him?'

'No, I got over Jack long ago. He's home again after fighting with the Black Watch, a Scottish Regiment. He was blinded and left with a badly scarred face.'

'I'm sorry,' Dale sympathised.

'He was an extremely active man. The blindness must be terrible for him.'

'There are going to be a lot more like him when this war's finally over,' Dale murmured. 'Men with all sorts of horrible injuries.'

'Yes,' Wonky agreed, thinking of the many who'd already passed through her hands.

'Will you practise in Albany when you return?' she asked.

'That's the plan. What about yourself?'

Wonky thought about that. 'One thing for certain, I can't go back to the humdrum life I had. Not after all this.'

'Did you work?'

'I only wish I had but my father would never allow it. No, I stayed at home with my parents and that was about it really. Too, too boring for words.'

'And what does your father do?'

'He's a minister in the Church of Scotland.'

'Really!'

'A very domineering man who likes to get his own way in everything, which he usually does.'

'I see.'

'And your father?'

'He's a lawyer too. He and I have always got on great, until I told him I was coming here that was. But even then he was only upset for my safety which is understandable. He writes all the time.'

Wonky thought of Tom and Moira and wondered what they were doing. Tom might be writing his next sermon, or there again he could be out on his rounds visiting people. As for Moira, who knew. Cooking or baking perhaps. Her mother always seemed to spend an awful lot of time doing that.

Wonky sighed, and stood up. 'I'd better get back. I'm on early shift tomorrow.'

'But you'll still be coming with me to the CCS?'

She nodded. 'I will that.'

He smiled. 'I shall look forward to it.'

What a nice chap, she thought as she walked away. She'd really enjoyed their conversation.

Sir Henry was fuming as he burst into the room and strode straight for the decanter.

'Something wrong, Henry?' Lady Fortescue queried in concern.

Andrew and Alice were also present in the drawing room, Andrew having managed to wangle a day away from Dublin.

'It's that damned McGinty,' Sir Henry retorted. 'Asked me again for a contribution, blast his eyes!'

'Oh dear,' his wife murmured.

Andrew looked to Alice for an explanation, which she wasn't about to give. In the event Sir Henry did.

He glared at Andrew. 'Wants me to give money to his Fenians, and me a Protestant. I ask you!'

'Was there a row?' Lady Fortescue asked.

'Of course there was. McGinty isn't a man to take refusal easily. He started shouting at me, the fool.'

'Was he involved in the rising?' Andrew asked quietly.

Sir Henry had a large gulp of whiskey. 'I can't say for certain, but I'm sure he was. All I do know is that he wasn't one of those arrested.'

Lady Fortescue went to her husband and put an arm round his shoulders. 'You shouldn't let him upset you so much. You look quite distraught.'

'That's because I am, Sybil. McGinty's put me in a dreadful position, and not for the first time either. He doesn't appreciate I have divided loyalties.'

Andrew felt sorry for Alice's father. As Sir Henry said, it was a dreadful position to be in. 'Would you like me to have him picked up, sir? It can be easily arranged.'

Sir Henry considered that. 'No, despite everything I rather like the idiot. Or eejit as we say here. His intentions are honourable, as he sees them that is. There isn't any real harm in the man.'

'There are a number of dead British soldiers killed in the rising who, if they were here, might not agree with that,' Andrew commented.

'I know, I know,' Sir Henry sighed, shaking his head. 'But I still don't want him arrested. At least not at my instigation. It would lie too heavily on my conscience.'

'So be it,' Andrew declared.

Sir Henry's eyes flashed fire. 'Had the impertinence to threaten me, the bounder.'

'Threaten?' Lady Fortescue queried in alarm.

'Oh don't worry, it was said in the heat of the moment. Not to be taken seriously. All bluster and wind in my opinion.'

A worried Andrew sincerely hoped that was all it was.

'You don't keep having to ask my permission to smoke, I've told you often enough I don't mind.'

Dale grinned at Wonky. 'I'm just trying to be polite the way the British always seem to be. Those guys sure have manners.'

She grinned back. 'You mean Americans don't?'

'Not like you British. I think we cause offence at times without realising it. I guess we just do things a different way that's all.'

'I guess,' Wonky repeated, which made Dale laugh.

'Are you taking the mickey, Nurse Comyn?'

'Who me?' she replied, pretending innocence.

'It seems to me like you might be.'

She could see how amused he was. 'It's simply that you speak so strangely, to my ear that is. It's almost as though it's a different language.'

He thought about that. 'I suppose it is, or is becoming so. We may both speak English but American English is very different to English English.'

'Or Scottish English,' she smiled.

Next moment Wonky screamed as there was a huge explosion and their ambulance was thrown onto its side.

'Holy shit,' Dale swore, finding himself sprawled on top of her. They had to get out of there, he thought. 'You hurt, Wonky?'

She gulped in air, the breath having been knocked out of her. She was terrified and wondering if she was about to die.

There was a second explosion nearby followed by a third.

'We're being shelled goddamnit!' Dale exclaimed.

'I don't think I'm hurt,' Wonky said in a small voice.

Dale prised himself off her and reached for his door which was now above them. It took an effort but he managed to get the door open.

'Come on,' he urged.

He clambered onto the side of the ambulance and reached down for Wonky who grasped his hand. She could feel a trickle of blood on her face as he pulled her clear.

Dale glanced about them wondering where to take refuge. Another hit that close could send up the gas tank.

He spotted a deepish crater about ten yards away, the result of previous shelling. There wasn't any other cover he could see.

He dropped off the ambulance and beckoned her to follow suit, catching her when she did. Hand in hand they raced for the crater which they thankfully jumped into. All the while other shells had been exploding around them.

Wonky sobbed, her heart beating erratically.

'I don't know why these crazy Krauts are shelling here, it shouldn't be a target,' Dale said, wincing at another close explosion.

'Perhaps they're targeting the wrong area?'

That had to be it, he thought.

He threw himself on top of Wonky when there was the scream of an incoming shell that sounded as though it might be a direct hit. To their relief it landed far enough away not to be of concern, though the ground beneath them literally shook on impact.

How nice his body was, Wonky found herself thinking. Hard and taut, and she could feel his manhood pressing into her, the danger of the situation having aroused him. She didn't find the latter an unpleasant experience.

And then as suddenly as it had started the shelling stopped.

Dale waited for a bit to confirm it actually had stopped before getting off Wonky and dusting himself down.

'That seems to be it,' he declared. 'They must have realised their mistake.'

She touched the now dried blood on her face and he immediately bent to her in concern. 'Let me see,' he said.

His hands were warm and firm, his probing making her shiver slightly.

'You're OK,' he pronounced. 'It's only a small scratch.'

He helped her to her feet. 'Any other problems?'

She felt herself all over. 'No, I'm only shaken. How about you?'

'I'm OK as well. And shaken like yourself. That came out of nowhere.'

He lit a cigarette, inhaled deeply and then blew out a long stream of smoke. 'This butt sure tastes good,' he smiled at her.

'Butt?'

'Cigarette.'

'Oh!'

Her cap had come adrift and her apron was filthy beneath her cape. She would have to change when she got back to the hospital.

They climbed out of the crater, Dale helping Wonky, and stared at the ambulance.

'It's a long walk home,' Dale declared. 'You up to it?'

'I'll have to be I suppose.'

'That's the spirit.'

She smiled at him. 'Thanks for saving my life, Dale.'

'Hell, I did no such thing!' he protested. 'Certainly nothing that any other guy wouldn't have done.'

'That may be so, but I'm still thanking you for saving my life.'

There were a few seconds during which their eyes locked, then he glanced away.

'Shall we start hoofing it?'

'May as well.'

They started back down the road.

'Are you all right?'

Charlotte snapped out of her reverie and turned to Miss McQueen. 'I'm fine thank you. Just day dreaming, that's all.'

Miss McQueen moved closer. 'You looked like a lost soul there, if you don't mind me saying.'

A lost soul? How appropriate Charlotte thought. 'I suppose I am in a way,' she admitted. 'Outside work that is. It's so lonely living here all by myself. I miss everyone dreadfully. Pa, Nell, even Andrew albeit he hasn't lived at home for years. I just seem to rattle around.'

Miss McQueen nodded her sympathy. 'It must be difficult for you.'

'It is. There's you and the rest of the staff of course, which means I'm not entirely alone. Still . . .' She trailed off.

'The war can't go on for ever, miss, and then Master Geoffrey and Miss Nell will be back. What a grand day that'll be.'

How she missed Geoffrey, desperately so. And worried about him. The lists of missing and killed in action printed daily in the newspapers seemed endless. Surely the war would stop soon, surely!

'Is there anything I can get you, a cup of tea or coffee perhaps?'

Charlotte shook her head. 'Some cocoa later would be nice. But not now.'

'And a bite of late supper?'

'No thank you, Miss McQueen. Cook's lovely dinner will see me through to breakfast.' She gave a low laugh. 'I do believe Mrs Clark is trying to fatten me up. The portion's she's serving are enormous.'

'We are all somewhat worried about you, Miss Charlotte. You've lost a deal of weight.'

Charlotte smoothed down her dress, a dress that had fitted perfectly a few months previously and now hung on her. She had lost weight, possibly more than she'd realised.

'Running the distillery takes it out of you,' she confessed.

'And thinking of Master Geoffrey no doubt.'

Charlotte glanced away. That most of all. The work she could cope with. But it was the constant worry about Geoffrey that was affecting her most of all.

Poor Jenny who'd worked for them as a maid had lost her husband Hamish only a fortnight ago. She'd gone and seen Jenny to offer her condolences – how distressing that had been! What could you possibly say to a young mother who'd lost her husband. Platitudes, that was all, mere platitudes.

'I think I'll try and read,' she said to Miss McQueen.

'Very good. I'll return later with that cocoa.'

'Thank you.'

When Miss McQueen had left her Charlotte did try and read, but it was useless.

She fell again into a reverie. Thinking, remembering, worrying.

Chapter 24

'You appear to have taken a shine to that driver of yours,' Nell commented to Wonky, as the pair of them came off duty one night.

'Why do you say that?'

'You just do, that's all. I spotted the pair of you chatting earlier like the oldest of friends.'

Wonky coloured slightly. 'Dale's nice, very pleasant to be with. And yes we do get on.'

'Do I detect a budding romance?'

'Don't be silly, Nell. He's an American.'

Nell laughed. 'What on earth has that got to do with it? You can fall for an American as well as a Scotsman or Englishman you know. Perhaps more easily as they're so different and colourful.'

Was she falling for Dale? Wonky wondered. Or were they simply friends, pals? She wasn't sure. He certainly seemed very keen on her. There again, maybe he just enjoyed female company.

'Well?' Nell demanded.

'Of course not.'

Nell arched an eyebrow. 'No?'

Wonky thought of Jack Riach, the last thing she wanted was to be let down again. That experience had hurt her a lot more than she'd actually let on.

'He's a lawyer you know,' Wonky said. 'From Albany, New York State.'

'America,' Nell mused. 'I'd love to go there. It must be such an exciting place.'

She'd love to go as well, Wonky thought. What a thrill that would be. So utterly different to Dalneil.

'Are you encouraging him?' Nell asked.

'I beg your pardon?'

'You know, giving off those little signals that tell him you're interested.'

'I'm doing no such thing.'

'I'll bet you are!' Nell teased.

'Can we change the conversation please. You're embarrassing me.'

She was, Nell thought, delighted for her cousin. 'He's certainly good looking, I'll grant him that. But what a peculiar surname.'

'I've told you before, he's of Polish extraction. It's like that in America, everyone, apart from the Red Indians that is, originally came from somewhere else, or at least their forefathers did.'

'There are a lot of Scots over there I understand, more so in Canada,' Nell declared. 'So no doubt you would feel right at home.'

'Will you stop it!' Wonky chided.

Nell grinned.

'I mean it. This nonsense has gone far enough.'

'OK,' Nell replied, purposely using the American expression.

Wonky glared at her. 'Very funny.'

Nell laughed.

That night Nell dreamed of her Highlander. She was in his arms, his hot breath on her cheek, her body pressed against him.

Their lips met in a kiss while his arms tightened even further around her.

Then he was leading her by the hand to a large bed which he stopped beside. Slowly, carefully, he began unbuttoning her dress.

The dress fell away to her hips and he started on her underthings. When her breasts were exposed his hands closed over them.

She was moaning at his touch, knowing what was to follow. He muttered love words as he fondled her, she eagerly responding.

And suddenly she knew his name. Rory.

The dress dropped to the floor, followed by her underclothes. Now she was standing naked in front of him, shivering in anticipation.

Rory.

Nell woke with a gasp to find herself covered in sweat, the dream vivid in her memory.

Good God, she thought. That had been so real. Better than a vision because she could hear, smell and touch him.

As for her, how brazen she'd been. How shameless. To stand before a man naked like that. She who was a virgin.

Nell gulped in a deep breath, trying to compose herself.

Rory, she thought. A lovely name and so familiar, albeit she didn't know anyone of that name.

But she had once she reminded herself. For back in time the Highlander had been her husband, she his wife.

'Rory,' she murmured aloud.

She could only wonder what it would have been like if the dream had continued.

The whole thing had been so real. So very very real.

'I don't believe it,' Billy Roberts exclaimed softly. 'I just don't believe it.' He and Andrew were sitting by themselves in the mess having a drink, and Billy had just glanced at the front page of that evening's newspaper.

'Don't believe what, old boy?' Andrew smiled.

'Wait a moment, let me read this through.'

Andrew sipped his whisky, wondering what had perturbed his friend.

Billy looked at Andrew, his expression grim. 'It's the Fortescues,' he said, voice tight.

'What about them?'

'They're dead!'

It was a joke, Andrew thought. Billy was pulling his leg. 'Oh yes? All three I suppose?'

'All three,' Billy nodded. 'Here, read for yourself.' And with that he passed the newspaper to Andrew.

The headline hit Andrew like a hammer blow. Greystones had been gutted by fire. He went white as he read through the report.

'I am sorry,' Billy murmured when Andrew, ashen faced, finally looked up from the paper.

Andrew was in shock, his mind reeling. This couldn't be

true. It had to be a lie. It had to be. Alice, his Alice, dead?

'Let me get you a refill,' Billy said, and picking up Andrew's glass he hurried to the bar.

Andrew started re-reading the article. The tragedy had occurred the previous evening according to the paper, the entire family perishing in the blaze as had some of the servants. Other servants had escaped to raise the alarm, to no avail. Arson was suspected.

Alice! Dear sweet Alice to whom he was engaged and was now in love with. Alice dead.

Billy was still at the bar as Andrew rose and stumbled from the mess. All he wanted was to be alone.

Alice dead. It was impossible. Impossible.

He managed to hold back the tears until his door was shut and locked behind him.

'Major Armitage, sir?'

Geoffrey glanced up at the officer who'd entered his dugout. He was in the middle of writing a report. 'That's correct.'

The officer snapped to attention and saluted. 'Second Lieutenant McKie reporting for duty, sir.'

How young he was, Geoffrey thought. No more than a boy really. Probably straight from school. They were getting younger and younger with every passing month, fresh faced and pimply, lambs to the slaughter. How long would this one survive? he wondered. For the last it had been a week before being blown to smithereens.

How old he felt himself, he thought. How dreadfully old. Methuselah had nothing on him. Old, drained and tired beyond belief.

Geoffrey returned the lad's salute. 'Nice to meet you, Lieutenant.'

'Thank you, sir.'

'Where are you from?'

'Perth, sir.'

Geoffrey nodded. 'I'm from Glasgow myself. Dirty place, but there you are. I like it.'

McKie beamed which depressed Geoffrey even further. 'First time in the front line I take it?'

'Yes, sir.'

'You'll soon pick things up. Got your gas mask I see.'

McKie patted it. 'Yes, sir.'

'Well don't go anywhere without it. Take it to bed with you. You can need it at a second's notice.'

'I understand that, sir.'

'Straight from school, are you?'

'Yes, sir. How did you know?'

Geoffrey laughed inwardly. How did he know! 'Which school was that?'

McKie named a prestigious one.

'Age?'

Geoffrey winced when McKie told him. Dear God above! A year younger than his predecessor.

'What would you have me do, sir?'

'Find Captain McLennan and ask him to show you the ropes.' There was a recce party going out that night he thought. Put McKie on it, give him a taste of what it was all about? He decided against that. He'd give the lad a day before putting him into danger. Not that just being there wasn't danger enough.

'Remember to keep your head down when in the

shallower trenches and saps,' he advised. 'That's important.'

'I understand, sir.'

'Don't and you'll get your head blown off. Now toddle along and find McLennan.'

McKie saluted again. 'Yes, sir. Thank you, sir.'

A weary Geoffrey returned to his report.

It was a combined funeral for Sir Henry, Lady Fortescue and Alice and the church was packed. Andrew was present with Billy Roberts there for support.

The hymn finished and they all sat. 'Now we will pray,' the minister announced.

Andrew didn't hear a word of the prayer. All he could think of was Alice and how desperately he missed her. He still couldn't really accept that he'd never see her again, that she was gone.

At the end of the prayer he looked up and the first person he saw was Seamus McGinty.

Was that the hint of a smile on McGinty's face? Surely not. It couldn't be. And yet . . . and yet . . .

Then Andrew remembered the conversation with Sir Henry when Sir Henry had mentioned the two Protestant houses in West Cork being torched by Fenians. And the row Sir Henry had had with McGinty and the fact McGinty had threatened him, a threat Sir Henry had dismissed.

Suddenly, and with absolute certainty, Andrew knew it was McGinty who'd torched Greystones. Or if he hadn't done it personally had been behind it.

Arson had been suspected but so far the police hadn't made an arrest. Their investigations hadn't come up with anything.

But Andrew knew who the culprit was.

Sitting there in church, consumed by grief and hatred, Andrew swore an oath to himself.

McGinty, the bastard, would pay.

An eye for an eye.

So it would be.

'I was wondering, would you like to go into town tonight for a drink?' Dale asked casually, as he and Wonky were en route yet again to the CCS.

She wasn't surprised, she'd been expecting as much. That or some other invitation.

'A drink?'

'Yeah, that stuff which comes in glasses and makes you feel good.'

She laughed. 'I don't know.'

'What do you mean, you don't know. You either will or won't.'

She didn't wish to appear too eager. 'How about transport?'

He snorted. 'Leave that to me. I'm a driver, aren't I? Transport won't be a problem.'

'I'm on duty till eight.'

'So?'

'I'd have to get washed and changed.'

'That doesn't bother me.'

'Would this be what you Americans call a date?'

'Damn right it would.'

'Dale, I . . .' She trailed off.

'What, Wonky?'

What indeed. It was wartime and anything could

happen. All she knew above all else was that she didn't want to be hurt again.

'I'd love to go for a drink,' she said in a small voice.

'Good. That's settled then.'

She wondered what she'd let herself in for.

Andrew had bided his time, now the score would be settled. He was standing in front of the McGinty farmhouse in the early hours of the morning, three full jerrycans of petrol at his feet.

The house was dark, the McGintys, he presumed, fast asleep. It was an overcast night with no stars or moon showing. Perfect for his purpose.

He thought again of all that he'd lost. Alice, Greystones and the fortune that would have come to her, and him eventually. All lost because of the Fenian bastard inside.

He picked up two of the jerrycans and walked softly towards the house. Stopping at the door he opened both cans. Then, using a knee to assist, he began pouring petrol through the letter box.

When the two cans were empty he took them back to the third with which he returned to the door and letter box. When that can was empty he took a deep breath, struck a match, dropped it through the letter box, picked up the can and ran like mad.

There was an enormous whoof! behind him which brought a smile of grim satisfaction to his face. He placed the can beside the others and turned to watch.

It didn't take long. Seconds later he could see flames licking behind the front downstairs windows and then wisps of smoke began to appear.

Would the smoke get them or the fire? Andrew wondered. If neither he had an alternative.

There was the sound of a small explosion. Now what was that? Could have been any of a dozen things.

Then he heard a female scream. Mrs McGinty or the daughter? He couldn't tell. Whoever, someone was now awake.

A young woman appeared at an upstairs window and threw it open, staring out in blind terror. She clearly considered jumping, then changed her mind and vanished from view.

Andrew took out his service revolver just in case it was needed. Using his thumb he slipped off the safety catch.

He wondered if they'd try the rear door. Well if they did they wouldn't have any luck there, he'd jammed it. If they did come out it would have to be at the front.

The daughter, her name was Roisin and she was twenty-two years old – Andrew knew that from discreet enquiries he'd made, and the McGinty's only child, just as Alice had been the Fortescues' – opened the front door and rushed out, her long hair ablaze.

Andrew took careful aim and shot her through the head. She tumbled to the ground, hair still ablaze, where she lay still.

The entire house was now an inferno. Through the open door Andrew could see banks of flames leaping and dancing.

Mrs McGinty was the next to emerge, coughing and spluttering, her nightdress burning at the hem.

'For Lady Fortescue, you bitch,' Andrew muttered as he pulled the trigger a second time.

And then McGinty was there, stark naked which Andrew considered for some reason or other, an added bonus. McGinty stopped to stare at the bodies of his wife and daughter.

Andrew pulled the trigger a third time, only there was to be no quick bullet in the brain for McGinty. Andrew shot him in the stomach.

McGinty grunted and slumped to the ground beside his wife where he writhed in agony, blood dribbling from his mouth.

Andrew went and stood over him, smiling at the knowledge of how excruciatingly painful that particular death could be. McGinty stared up at him through bulging eyes.

'It's for my Alice and her parents, the Fortescues,' Andrew explained, wanting McGinty to know why he'd done all this.

'Protestant cunt,' McGinty croaked through a froth of pink-tinged bubbles.

'You're going straight to hell, and that's exactly where you belong. You're going to roast,' Andrew crooned in reply.

McGinty continued to writhe, all the while clutching at where he'd been shot.

Then Andrew had an idea. He put his revolver away and grasped McGinty by the shoulders. McGinty, too weak to resist, groaned as Andrew dragged him towards the doorway.

The heat was almost too much for Andrew but he was determined to do what he intended. Sweat rolled down his face as he hoisted McGinty to his feet and pointed him at the door.

'No . . . no!' McGinty choked.

'And the roasting starts here,' Andrew declared, pitching McGinty inside.

McGinty screamed and continued to scream until it was all over.

Andrew collected the three jerrycans and tossed them through the door as well, then beat a hasty retreat.

He walked away, not looking back. Alice, and his thwarted aspirations, had been revenged.

And sweet revenge it was.

'Shall we dance?'

Wonky giggled. 'I'm feeling tipsy from so much wine.'

'So am I,' Dale replied earnestly. 'Only in my case the wine is only part of it.'

What a lovely man, she thought. A lovely lovely man. She glanced at the three-piece band playing smoochy French music. It was all so terribly romantic.

She rose. 'Let's.'

He took her hand as they walked the few short yards to the tiny dance floor. 'I'm not much of a dancer I'm afraid. So I apologise in advance,' he said as she melted into his arms.

'I'm not so hot myself.'

'Anyway, with this sort of music all you have to do is shuffle.'

How warm he was, she thought. And how nice he smelt. Like . . . She didn't know what. And then she had it. Like an American. Though why they should smell differently to the British was beyond her.

'Enjoying yourself?' he asked softly.

'You know I am. And you?'

'I'm in seventh heaven, kid. And that's no lie.'

She laughed. How strangely he put things at times. American English again. It never ceased to fascinate her.

Wonky started when he licked her ear. No one had ever done that before.

'You can see why I'm such a Francophile,' he said. 'You wouldn't find a place like this in the States. Maybe down south, but not where I come from.'

Nor Dalneil, she reflected. Certainly not Dalneil. Dalneil was as far removed from this place as the moon was from earth.

The band finished the number and they stopped dancing. 'Will you stay up?' he queried.

'If you wish.'

'I wish.'

'Then I'll stay up.'

Dale pulled the car off the road. 'Before we get back I want to thank you for a wonderful evening.'

His eyes were glowing in the dark. Sensual, wonderful eyes. She shivered. 'It was wonderful for me as well.'

In the distance guns were booming but at that moment the war seemed a million miles away. All that existed was the pair of them.

'Shall we do it again sometime?'

'That would be nice.'

He grinned. 'Don't be too enthusiastic. Talk about British reserve.'

'Or American lack of it,' she countered.

He touched her cheek. 'You've come to mean a lot to me, Wonky Comyn.'

'Have I?'

'Darned tootin' you have.'

He was going to kiss her, she thought. And couldn't wait for it to happen. She wanted to kiss him too. In fact ached for it.

'Wonky?'

'Yes?'

'Nothing,' he whispered.

And then his lips were gloriously on hers.

Did he have any regrets? Andrew asked himself. And the answer was none at all. McGinty and family had deserved what they'd got. Those who live by the sword . . .

He pictured Alice the last time they'd been together and felt his throat clog with emotion. He'd come to love her, and she him. Now she was gone like so much smoke in the wind. And with her Greystones and the family fortune.

He understood there was a relative somewhere who'd now inherit, money and property that would one day have been his. At least he had the distillery, that was something. A great deal when you considered it. Not that it rivalled what would have come from the Fortescues, but he'd be comfortable for the rest of his days.

Good old Charlotte, doing a grand job. He'd been fortunate there.

He wondered how Geoffrey was doing? A major now, he understood. Poor sod out there on the Western Front. It must be a nightmare.

He shifted on his bed, smiling at the memory of McGinty's bulging eyes and how he had writhed in agony.

'And the roasting starts here.' He'd enjoyed saying that. Positively revelled in it.

His smile widened recalling McGinty's screams as the fire had consumed him. He could almost imagine . . .

Andrew sighed in the darkness, his mind turning to the one and only time he'd made love to Alice. How enjoyable that had been, for her as well as him.

'Alice,' he murmured. 'Alice.'

'Finished at last,' Hettie declared as she and Jack emerged from the sixth shop they'd visited that day.

'Well thank goodness for that is all I can say. It was beginning to get tedious.'

She laughed. 'Shopping is never tedious for women, we adore it. I could shop all day.'

'Not with me in tow you wouldn't.'

'Now what, the train back?'

He stopped, which forced her to stop also, her arm hooked round his, and considered that. 'What time is it?'

'A little before one.'

'Then it's lunch. I'm starving.'

'I am too, but didn't want to say.'

'And while we're eating you can describe everything we bought to me again in detail.'

Hettie suddenly frowned and Jack, who'd now become used to picking up her moods, said, 'What is it?'

Hettie slipped her arm out of Jack's. 'Grizelda McPherson is coming this way.'

'Is she indeed,' Jack said softly. 'Is she alone?'

'No, she's with Harriet Henderson.'

'Ah!' Jack exclaimed.

Grizelda came up short when she spied Jack, her first impulse being to cross the road. But she realised she couldn't do so as that Hettie female had seen her. Imagine Jack consorting with someone as common as muck. What was he thinking of!

'I know just the place for lunch,' Jack declared to Hettie. 'We'll have a slap-up meal. We deserve it.' Not least for his venturing into Pitlochry he thought.

'Hello, Jack.'

'Hello, Grizelda. And you, Harriet. You both know Hettie my housekeeper of course.'

'Of course,' Grizelda replied disapprovingly, which neither Jack or Hettie failed to pick up.

What a bitch, Jack thought. She'd done him a huge favour in dropping him. The woman was shallow as a puddle.

They exchanged a few polite words and then Grizelda and Harriet moved on.

'The Lord truly moves in mysterious ways,' Jack commented.

'How do you mean?'

'If I hadn't been blinded and scarred I'd have ended up married to her. What a lucky escape.'

'Amen,' Hettie said.

Geoffrey was instructing Sergeant Smith about leading a probing party up one of the saps when the frantic cry went up that an attack was underway.

It was a foggy day, ideal for an attack which the Canadians had mounted that morning. Now the Germans were counter-attacking at their part of the line.

A fusillade of shots rang out, Geoffrey turning to the trench wall to assist when a potato-masher grenade landed on the far side of Sergeant Smith.

Geoffrey spotted it a moment before it exploded.

PART THREE

A New Day Dawning

Chapter 25

'It's Miss Drummond,' Hettie announced.

Jack immediately rose from his chair. 'How are you, Charlotte?'

She went to him and kissed him on the cheek. 'Well, to be truthful I could be better which is why I've come to see you.' She glanced about her. The room was cosy in the extreme with a fine log fire burning in the grate. 'But first of all let me say how nicely you've done this place up. It has a lovely feel to it.'

Jack smiled. 'I've Hettie to thank for that. She chose and organised everything.'

Charlotte turned to Hettie hovering by the door. 'You've done a wonderful job. You must be proud.'

Hettie blushed. 'Did my best, miss.'

'Very tasteful. Congratulations.'

'Would you like some tea or coffee, Charlotte?' Jack asked.

'Coffee would be nice.'

'Hettie, would you?'

'Of course, Mr Riach.'

Hettie vanished from the room.

'Will you sit down,' Jack said, gesturing to a chair facing his.

'Thank you.'

'How are you getting on?' Charlotte queried when she'd sat.

'I have a buyer for the house and property which is going through. As you probably know my mother and father have already returned to Largs.'

'Yes, I heard.'

Jack sighed. 'I miss them. I got used to having them around. But there you are. They have their lives to lead and I have mine.'

'And how are you coping?'

'You mean with blindness?'

Charlotte hadn't meant that at all. She'd meant being in the cottage. 'That as well,' she replied.

He shrugged. 'It's one of those things. To quote the Bard, "What's done is done and cannot be undone".'

How bitter he sounded she thought. But then that was only natural. She couldn't even conceive being blind herself. 'Hettie looking after you all right?'

'She's the proverbial treasure. I certainly couldn't manage without her. It was a wise choice on my part. There again, I knew her work from before. She's always been a grafter.'

Charlotte nodded her approval. 'How about meals?'

'Well I have to admit Hettie isn't up to Ma's standards, but then that would be asking something. She's very good nonetheless. I certainly don't have any complaints in that department.'

'You're looking fit.'

'I go for a walk every day, weather permitting, with Hettie of course. She guides me and we chatter along the way. She tells me what she sees and what's going on around us. It's the highlight of my day.'

Going for a walk reminded Charlotte of Murdo whom she missed terribly. She knew now why he'd started walking; Doctor McAllister had told her.

'And what else do you get up to?' she queried.

Jack ran a hand over his badly scarred face. 'Not a lot, there isn't much I can do. I sit and think a great deal I suppose, remembering.'

'The war?'

Jack's face clouded. 'Yes,' he whispered.

She studied him intently. 'Was I being insensitive in asking that question?'

'No, Charlotte. It's the past and we all have to live with that.'

Again she thought of Murdo, and her brother Peter.

'Have you heard from Nell and Wonky?'

'I had a letter the other day. They're both fine. Wonky's met a chap apparently, an American.'

'An American!' Jack exclaimed.

'He drives ambulances which is how they came to meet. According to Nell he's a lawyer in civilian life.'

'Well well well,' Jack mused. 'How about that.'

'As for Nell, she's happy enough, though no romance in her life yet. She says the work is hard and . . . not very pleasant. The casualties according to her simply mount and mount.'

A scene flashed into Jack's mind which made him

shudder. He knew all about casualties. The dead, dying and wounded. So many men he'd known, good men for the best part, who'd never be coming home again. And those who did . . . well he was testament to what they could be like. The whole thing was horrendous. No, worse than that.

Hettie reappeared with a tray. 'That was quick,' Charlotte commented.

'The kettle was almost on the boil anyway. I've put a few wee biscuits on a plate in case either of you is peckish.'

How nice, Charlotte thought. She wasn't peckish in the least but would have one just to be polite.

'Would you care to join us?' Jack asked Hettie.

That startled Charlotte. Ask the housekeeper to join them? How odd. Was there something going on here that she hadn't realised. She looked at Hettie through new eyes. A comely lass if ever there was, and certainly not unintelligent. Were they . . .?

'I've got a pile of ironing still to do,' Hettie replied quickly. 'I'd best get on with that.'

'Fine,' Jack answered with warmth in his voice.

Hettie disappeared again.

'Will you play mother, as the English say,' Jack suggested.

'My pleasure.'

Charlotte did the necessary. 'Biscuit?'

'Not for me thanks. They are home made by the way, by Hettie.'

Charlotte leant back in her chair with one of the biscuits on her saucer. 'You and Hettie seem to be very close,' she ventured.

Jack laughed. 'Of course we are. I rely on her for nearly everything.'

'Yes, I can understand that.'

'You don't really. She's been a Godsend, Charlotte. I don't know what I'd have done without her. She makes my day-to-day existence, and I mean existence, somehow tolerable. She's a most compassionate woman to whom I shall be eternally in debt.'

Jack had a sip of coffee. 'Now enough about me, why the visit? Is there a reason?'

Charlotte glanced down into her own cup. 'I had a letter from Geoffrey yesterday,' she said in a small voice.

'Oh?'

'He's been wounded again.'

'Badly?'

'I'm not quite sure exactly. He said it's to his groin and that I'm not to worry. He's in hospital in France though shortly to be moved to England.'

Jack didn't reply, waiting for Charlotte to continue.

She sighed. 'I wanted to speak to you because you know what it's like over there. I can only imagine. And pretty horrible imagining it makes I can tell you.'

'It sounds like he's been lucky to me,' Jack replied. 'Anything that takes you out of the front line for a while is good fortune. A groin injury isn't so bad, not bad at all.'

'It's just . . .' Charlotte trailed off. 'I don't know, I really don't. There was a tone to his letter that worried me. It's hard to explain.'

'A tone?' Jack mused in concern.

'As though he wasn't telling me everything. It wasn't like

any other letter I've ever had from him. It was cold, distant somehow.'

Jack had a chilling thought. 'Did Geoffrey describe the wound?' he queried softly.

'Not at all. Only that it was to his groin.'

'He'll be fine,' Jack reassured her. 'He probably wrote while still in a state of shock. Besides, being out there does funny things to people. The sights they witness, what they themselves go through. You certainly can't expect the same Geoffrey to come home who went away.'

Charlotte nodded. 'That's probably it.'

'Don't forget the poor chap's been wounded, he'd hardly be in the mood to write you a love letter.'

Charlotte laughed. 'You're right of course. I'm just being silly.'

'No you're not. You love Geoffrey, so naturally you worry. It would be a poor show if you didn't.'

'I wish . . . oh how I wish he was home again and this entire ghastly business was over. It's a living nightmare.'

Too true, Jack thought. How true that was.

'Anyway, you've bucked me up as I knew you would.'

'I'm glad to be of some use,' Jack commented drily, something that was lost on Charlotte.

'So how's the biscuit?' he asked, changing the subject.

She had a bite and pronounced it to be delicious.

Wonky felt as though she'd just had a bucketful of ice-cold water poured over her. 'Transferred?'

'To number twenty-seven U.S. Base Hospital, Angers, I'm afraid. I leave the day after tomorrow,' Dale replied.

It had never crossed her mind that either of them might

be transferred. She'd stupidly thought the pair of them would be together for the duration. 'I see.'

'There's nothing I can do about it, Wonky. If there was I would. You know what it's like.'

She did, only too well. 'It's a shock, that's all.'

Dale took her in his arms and gazed deeply into her eyes. 'I'll miss you, Wonky. You wouldn't believe how much.'

She'd miss him too, far more than she cared to admit even to herself. What rotten luck she had with men. First of all Jack, and now Dale. Her eyes welled with tears.

'Don't cry, honey, please don't cry.'

'I can't help it.'

'It isn't over, I swear. We'll meet up again. You'll see.'

Would they? Perhaps.

'I have a photograph I want you to have. Taken in the States.' He pulled out a wallet from his hip pocket and extracted a small photo which he handed her. It was one of him taken when graduating from Law School. He looked a lot younger.

'Thank you,' she whispered.

'I don't suppose you have one of yourself?'

She shook her head.

'No matter. I'll hardly forget what you look like.' He was trying to be jocular but for some reason it wasn't working.

'Day after tomorrow,' she said.

'That's right. Early.'

She mustn't blub too much, she thought. That would be awful. Let the side down and all that.

'I'll write as soon as I get there,' he promised.

'Will you?'

'On my word of honor. Will you write back?'

She forced a smile onto her face. 'You know I will, Dale.'

'I'm sorry, sweetheart, really I am. But I should have been with my own people all along. My being here with you British was purely by chance.'

She stared into his face, desperately memorising every line, every feature.

'Kiss me,' she whispered.

It was the sweetest, longest kiss she'd ever experienced.

'What's wrong?' Nell queried, Wonky having requested she leave the tent with her. Inside Rebecca Levi and Hope Langton were chattering away nineteen to the dozen.

'Oh dear,' Nell replied when Wonky explained.

'I just can't believe it,' Wonky said, shaking her head.

They both paused to glance skywards as a flight of British planes flew overhead. They didn't get many pilots at the hospital, most of those shot down never survived as parachutes were forbidden them.

'Angers,' Nell said. 'Where's that?'

'A long way from here. Certainly too far for either of us to travel to see the other.'

Nell put her arms round her cousin and hugged her tight. 'You must feel pretty bloody.'

'I do, Nell,' Wonky whispered. 'I certainly do.'

'Was it that serious between you?'

'It was getting that way, Nell. If things had been different who knows?'

Nell released Wonky. 'Is there anything I can do?'

'Not really. Just being able to talk helps a little. Though not much I have to confess.'

A single artillery gun opened up, booming in the distance. Then another.

'I dream of home almost every night,' Nell said. 'Dalneil and our life there seems a world away.'

Wonky nodded. 'I know what you mean. I'll never be able to go back there, not permanently anyway. How stifling it all was, how very very insular.'

Nell thought of Drummond House and the days, weeks, months they'd spent knitting for the troops. They'd been like children playing a game. What they were in now was deadly reality. Day after day of horrors. How it changed one. How precious every day now seemed.

How was the Highlander, Rory, faring? Nell wondered. Her husband in a different time. And the wife herself, how was she? It would only be a matter of time before she found out. The trouble was she was so rarely on her own nowadays and the visions only came when she was alone.

Rory, even to think of the name brought an excitement to her, made her pulse race. What a love that must have been to have survived over the centuries, to make her recall what she did. Was there a purpose to it all? She had no idea.

'Angers,' Wonky whispered. It might have been on the moon as far as she was concerned.

'Will you see him off?'

'If I can.'

In the event that proved impossible, for Wonky was on duty at the time.

Billy Roberts knocked on Andrew's door.

'Come in!'

'Lazy sod.' Billy smiled at Andrew, stretched out on bed reading the latest copy of *The Bystander*.

'To hell with you. I'm off duty and relaxing. Nothing wrong with that, old boy.'

Billy leant against a chest of drawers. 'The word's just out. We've been posted.'

Alarm flared in Andrew. Not the Western Front! Anything but that. 'Where to?'

'County Cork. They're having a lot of trouble down there apparently and we're being sent to sort it out.'

'Fenians, I take it?'

'What else.'

Andrew laid *The Bystander* aside and thought about that. 'The back of beyond, I should imagine, populated by pig-trotter-eating Irish boggers.'

Billy raised an eyebrow, only too well aware how Andrew's attitude to the Irish had changed since the Fortescue fire. Not that he blamed him. 'I suppose so,' he replied.

'When do we leave?'

'A week this Saturday.'

Andrew grunted. That suited him just fine.

'I shall miss old Dublin town,' Billy commented.

So would Andrew, a certain house and lady in particular. He suddenly wondered how Jean Ritchie was doing, and Tina who'd worked at Mulligan's. Still, there were bound to be available women in County Cork, there always were no matter where you went. That was something he'd learned. Available for a price, and money was something he no longer had to be concerned about.

Andrew swung his feet off the bed. 'I think this merits a visit to the mess, what do you say?'

Billy nodded. 'My sentiments exactly.'

'And it's your round. You were one short the last time we were there.'

'Bloody Scotsmen, you never forget anything when it comes to money.'

Andrew laughed.

'Do you know what I miss most, colours,' Jack said to Hettie who was sitting across from him doing a bit of darning.

'Colours?'

'That's right. I can picture them in my mind of course, but that's not the same.'

'I can understand that,' she replied.

'Can you?'

She smiled. 'Now don't be patronising to me, Jack Riach. I won't stand for it.'

'Patronising,' he mused. 'A big word for an ex-dairy maid.'

'I may be an ex-dairy maid but I had a good Scots education until I left school. And I've been reading ever since to improve my mind.'

Reading, Jack thought. That was something else he missed. Not that he'd been a great reader but from time to time he'd enjoyed a book. Another thing denied him.

'What are you reading now?' he asked.

Hettie told him.

'Interesting?'

'Very. Well I find it so.'

Jack nodded. 'I've just had an idea. Why don't you read to me sometimes in the evenings? I'd enjoy that.'

'There's no reason why not. Any suggestions?'

'I've always liked the Waverley novels. Why don't we start with those?'

Hettie pulled a face. 'Not exactly my cup of tea.'

'Then what would you favour?'

She decided to tease him. 'How about Shakespeare?'

'Good grief,' he muttered. 'Surely you don't like that turgid stuff?'

'It's very good, I'll have you know. Especially his comedies.'

Jack laughed. 'I'd never have imagined in a thousand years that you'd read Shakespeare.'

'And Burns. Filthy bugger.'

He laughed again. 'Yes, Rabbie could be that. Have you ever come across "Nine Inches Becomes A Lady"?'

Hettie blushed slightly. 'No I haven't. Though I've certainly experienced it.'

This time he roared. 'May I inquire from whom?'

Her eyes glittered with memory. 'You, Jack, you fool. Who else?'

He'd never thought of himself being that large. 'Really?'

'Oh yes,' she said softly.

'Well well. I'm a bigger boy than I realised.'

And probably a better lover, she thought. Jack had never failed to satisfy her. Either in size or anything else.

Jack's mood abruptly changed and he fell into a morose silence. He was remembering the times with Hettie, times that would never come again with her or any other woman. For who would look twice at a blind chap with a face as scarred as his.

'Penny for them?'

He shook his head.

'Oh come on, don't be a spoilsport.'

He reached for his stick and rose. 'I'm off to bed, Hettie. Will you do what has to be done? I'll see you in the morning.' See you! Only an expression of course. His days of seeing anything were over.

'Are you all right, Jack?'

He could smell her across the distance between them, and how it made him itch inside. 'Fine, thank you. It's just that I feel a headache coming on and that it's best I go to bed.'

Hettie didn't believe a word of that. And furthermore had a fair idea of what was troubling Jack.

It was one subject never broached between them.

'Miss Charlotte?'

Charlotte was sitting gazing into the fire, lost in thought. She roused herself. 'Yes, Miss McQueen?'

Miss McQueen stared at her in concern. 'You seem so troubled. You were miles away.'

Charlotte gave her a thin smile. 'I was. I was thinking about Geoffrey.'

Miss McQueen considered that. 'It's hardly my place, but with your sister in France and your cousin there also you don't have anyone to talk things over with. If I can be of help . . .' She paused, then added. 'I'm most discreet as I'm sure you're well aware.'

Charlotte gestured to a chair. 'That's kind of you.'

Miss McQueen sat. 'Is it your husband, is that it?'

Charlotte nodded. 'I haven't heard from him in over three weeks now. I'm worried sick.'

'I take it you've written yourself?'

'Every other day. But no reply.'

Charlotte put a finger to her mouth and chewed it. What was wrong with Geoffrey? This was so unlike him. Had there been developments of some sort that she wasn't aware of? That could be the answer. There again, and this terrified her, had he met someone else? A nurse perhaps?

'Where's the hospital, miss?'

'Berkshire, in England.'

'Maybe you should take time off and pay him a visit.'

Charlotte shook her head. 'In one of his letters he asked me specifically not to do that. He said I was to concentrate on the business and that he would be fine.'

'I see,' Miss McQueen murmured.

Charlotte wrung her hands. 'I just don't know what to do.'

Nor did Miss McQueen. If Geoffrey had specifically asked Charlotte not to visit then she shouldn't. He was a man, her husband after all. His wishes should be obeyed.

'Have you any idea when he's expected home?' Miss McQueen queried, presuming he'd be given leave after being wounded.

'No.' That came out as a whisper.

'Then I suppose you'll just have to wait until you find out. There's nothing else you can do.'

'No,' Charlotte whispered again.

'Now how about a nice cup of cocoa. Would that help?'

'Please, and thank you, Miss McQueen. I appreciate your concern.'

Miss McQueen left to make the cocoa.

*

It was a terrible battle. Nell stared on in horror as the English redcoats massacred the Scots. Nor was it only English against Scots, but Scot against Scot.

Men's faces contorted in agony as they died. Muskets flashed, bayonets lunged, broadswords and claymores whirled. Everywhere was death and destruction.

Nell knew with absolute certainty that she was witnessing the battle of Culloden, the last stand of Bonnie Prince Charlie before he took to the heather and exile.

Where was her Rory? She couldn't see him anywhere. Was he already amongst the fallen? Cold fear gripped her heart to think that might be so.

Blood spurted, fountains of it on both sides, but the English were clearly winning. They and the turncoats on their side. She grimaced as a head was cleanly lopped off to go spinning away.

And then there he was, targe in his left hand, broadsword in his right, fighting for his life against three English soldiers. She could almost hear him screaming at his adversaries.

One of the soldiers went down, and another, leaving it man to man.

Live, Rory, she pleaded inside her head. Dear God, live.

The third Englishman's eyes started as he was sliced neatly across the belly, then he was on his knees and Rory's broadsword was raised for the *coup de grâce*. The Englishman died from a thrust into his back.

Rory jerked his sword free and turned to face another onslaught, this from turncoat clansmen.

The battle continued to rage as it slowly faded from Nell's vision.

When it had blinked out of view she collapsed forwards in the chair with her head in her hands.

Had he lived?

Nell found tears streaming down her face.

'Well, it certainly isn't Dublin Castle,' Andrew pronounced, staring round the room he'd be sharing with Billy Roberts. 'The place stinks and it's filthy.'

'We'll soon get that sorted,' Billy replied, gazing about him in distaste. The house they were in had been commandeered.

Andrew went to the window and looked out. The countryside, in his opinion, was most uninspiring.

'Bloody Irish,' Andrew muttered.

'They're not all bad. You should know that.'

Andrew turned to his friend and smiled, a strange metallic glint in his eyes.

'I wonder what's for dinner,' he said.

Charlotte laid down her pen, deciding to take a few minutes' break. She had awful stomach cramp due to her period coming on which didn't help matters. If she could she'd have stayed home, but that was impossible with a business to run. As always when this time came round she felt dreadfully depressed.

She thought of Geoffrey, picturing him as she'd last seen him. How she missed him, how she craved his company.

The nights were so interminably lonely, her sleep almost always disturbed by dreams and half-waking memories. How many times had she reached out to touch him and he hadn't been there? Without number.

To snuggle up to him, smell him, hear him murmur to her. For him to caress her, put an arm round her neck and pull her close.

An why, oh why were the letters so infrequent. Why couldn't he write more often?

'Geoffrey,' she whispered. 'Darling, dear beloved Geoffrey. I so want you here with me.'

She closed her eyes, recalling their lovemaking, the sheer gloriousness of it. Sensations she'd never previously dreamt about. She missed those, but most of all she missed him. It was as though she'd lost an arm or leg.

At least he'd be coming back soon, and for good. Discharged on medical grounds, he'd said in his last letter, though unable at that point to give her a date for his arrival. He'd be staying in Glasgow first for a couple of days then travelling on. Only right he saw his parents of course, they being on the way. Only right . . .

The groin injury must have been worse than he'd said, otherwise why the discharge?

Charlotte smiled. Just like Geoffrey not to cause her too much concern, to minimise what had happened. At least it was over for him now, no more the horrors of the Western Front. That was history as far as he was concerned.

'Geoffrey,' she whispered again.

Her loving husband.

'We've got them cold,' Sergeant Plackett said with a smile to Andrew.

Andrew smiled also. Six of the Fenian bastards were in a gulley into which they'd scuttled after their truck had careered off the country road with its tyres shot out.

'So what do we do?' Plackett asked.

Andrew didn't reply straight away, thinking about that. The Fenians were armed and dangerous so all care had to be taken.

'I have twenty men under my command so it's best you show yourselves and surrender,' he called out.

There was no reply.

'I'll give you two minutes and then we move in!'

Again there wasn't a reply.

'Do you think they will surrender, sir?' Plackett queried.

'Oh yes,' Andrew replied softly. 'They're not eejits after all. Why die for nothing.'

He closed his eyes for a brief second, recalling Sir Henry using the word *eejit*. Sir Henry, Lady Fortescue and his Alice. Now all gone because of Fenians like those trapped in the gulley. Well, McGinty had paid the price of that episode, him and his family. But that wasn't enough, not by a long chalk. These murdering Fenians would also pay. That was only right.

A white handkerchief tied to a rifle was suddenly raised in the air. 'We're coming out, all peaceful like,' a thick-brogued Irish voice shouted.

'Drop your weapons then and proceed with your hands up. You've nothing to worry about,' Andrew yelled back.

The Fenians appeared one by one, a range of ages from an old man to a young boy who couldn't have been more than sixteen.

Andrew studied them as they came forward, hate aching in his heart. He slowly stood up revealing himself.

The rest of his detachment also rose, their rifles trained

on the Irishmen, the only weapon carried by the latter being the rifle with the white handkerchief attached.

Andrew waited till they were halfway to him then raised his revolver.

'Fire!' he screamed, and pulled his trigger again and again till the weapon was empty.

All about him was the crash of rifles.

Sergeant Plackett stared aghast at the six dead bodies then up at a smiling Andrew. 'They were unarmed,' he whispered.

'Were they? That's not what'll go in the report.'

'But, sir . . .'

Andrew silenced him with a dismissive wave of the hand. 'We've been too soft for too long with these people, sergeant. Not any more.'

Plackett's expression became grim in the extreme. He didn't agree with that one little bit but would never have dreamt of voicing his opinion to a superior officer.

'We were attacked and defended ourselves, understand?' Andrew went on.

Plackett nodded.

'And make sure the men do as well. If any word of the truth gets out then we're all for the high jump. Not just me but them as well.'

Sergeant Plackett came to attention. 'Yes, sir.'

'Good. Carry on.'

'Yes, sir.' That with a salute.

Greystones, Andrew thought. Greystones and Alice lost to him because of vermin like these now lying sprawled around him.

*

'Morning, miss,' McPhie said to Charlotte, opening the door of the Rolls. 'A big day for you.'

'It is indeed. Not every day your husband comes back from the war.'

'Indeed not, miss.'

Charlotte settled herself and McPhie closed the door behind her. She hadn't thought she'd be nervous, but was. It had been so long, so very long. She couldn't wait for Geoffrey to take her in his arms, for his lips to be on hers.

McPhie glanced in the rearview mirror as the Rolls purred away. The job wasn't the same any more, not since the old man died. Miss Charlotte didn't use the car nearly as much.

Charlotte stared out at the passing countryside, lost in thought.

Charlotte waved the moment she spotted Geoffrey stepping from the train. At last!

She flew along the platform and into his arms. 'Welcome home, darling,' she whispered.

She stared into his face, shocked at how he'd aged. She'd expected some of that but not as much. What he must have been through.

'Hello, Charlotte. It's good to see you.'

'And you, Geoffrey.'

He turned and instructed McPhie about his case, after which Charlotte linked an arm through his.

'Let's go home,' she said, wishing he'd kissed her.

'Let's go home,' he agreed.

Chapter 26

'Mrs Clark excelled herself, that really was the most excellent dinner,' Geoffrey declared as he and Charlotte entered the drawing room.

Charlotte beamed. 'I'd have had something to say if she hadn't. It was quite an occasion after all.'

'Would you like something, a Drummond or brandy perhaps?'

Charlotte sat, puzzled by his behaviour. He seemed so distant somehow, as though there was a barrier between them. There again, perhaps he was simply finding it difficult being back.

'A Drummond I think,' she replied.

She watched him as he crossed the room, noting a slight stiffness in his walk. 'You said in your letters that you were treated very well in the hospital.'

'In Berkshire, yes. The one in France was rather more hectic. An awful lot of . . .' He broke off, having been about to say deaths.

'Pretty nurses?'

He laughed. 'All sorts really. Pretty, plain and a few that were downright gruesome.'

'You must have become friendly with them.'

He turned and stared quizzically at her. 'To an extent. You can't help but get to know them and they you.'

'Of course.'

He poured them each a stiff one, remembering the vast amounts of alcohol he'd consumed in France. Alcohol that temporarily took away the fear and gave you some courage. Alcohol without which there had been many things he could never have got through.

He handed her the drink, but disappointed her when he didn't join her on the sofa but instead chose a facing chair.

'So how are you really, Geoffrey?' she asked.

He dropped his gaze to stare into his glass. 'Not bad, considering.'

'And the wound?'

The hand holding his glass tightened. 'Healed sufficiently to let me come home.'

'Are you badly scarred?'

'Yes,' he whispered, wanting to jump to his feet and rush from the room. How was he going to tell her? It was something he'd agonised over for months.

She smiled. 'At least you're back in one piece.'

He blanched. Why couldn't she just shut up! He swallowed his whisky in a single gulp. 'It was dreadful about your father,' he said, changing the subject.

Now it was her turn to stare into her glass. 'It was,' she agreed softly.

'I liked him very much. He was a decent man. You must miss him a great deal.'

She nodded.

'Not easy for you either having to take over the business. That must have caused a few raised eyebrows.'

'More than a few. But what else could I do with Andrew in the army. I was capable and that was the end of it. Drummond survives with a Drummond at its helm.'

Geoffrey rose and returned to the decanter. 'Do you want me to try and help? I know nothing at all about that kind of thing but am willing to learn.'

She flashed him a grateful smile. 'I was hoping you'd suggest that.'

He shrugged. 'It seems the obvious thing to do. Just as long as you remember army life is all I know. It's going to be quite a change for me.'

'You'll cope, Geoffrey. I have no doubts about that.'

He hoped he would. A desk job was always something he'd tried to avoid.

'There's one other matter,' he said, keeping his back to her.

'What's that?'

'I have to sleep on my own for a bit. Separate bedrooms and all that. For a while anyway.'

She bit back her disappointment. 'The wound obviously.'

'That's right.'

'Of course if it's necessary, Geoffrey. Of course.'

Well, at least that was over he thought. The first hurdle. But the second, the truth? God alone knew how he'd summon up the courage to tell her that.

He saw off his second large whisky and poured himself another.

*

It wasn't at all how she'd imagined his first night home, Charlotte thought, staring up at the bedroom ceiling. She'd imagined a night of passion, or if not that, she wasn't daft, it had been a groin injury after all which might still be troubling him, his presence in bed and cuddles, caresses, lovetalk, kisses.

He hadn't kissed her since arriving back. Not once, not even on saying goodnight.

The latter had shocked her, though she'd tried not to show it. When offering herself for a kiss he'd pulled away with a muttered excuse about how dreadfully tired he was.

Was he involved with another woman, one of his nurses? That wasn't what had come across when she'd quizzed him about the hospital. So what was wrong?

It was the long separation, she decided. That and all he'd been through. She'd been expecting too much for him to arrive home and them to immediately take up where they'd left off. Not that they'd had much of married life, they'd only been wed five minutes before he'd been off to war.

And how he'd aged. There was a heaviness about him where there had been lightness before. Again understandable.

She wondered what Peter would have been like if he'd survived. No doubt he would have aged dramatically also.

Dear Peter, her big brother. The last person she would ever have seen as being a soldier. But wasn't that the case with so many others. They'd been needed and gone off to do their duty, men no more suited to soldiering than she was to what . . .? Being a navvy she thought, and inwardly laughed, picturing the absurd sight of herself with a pick in her hands. How ridiculous.

Oh, Geoffrey, if only you were here in bed with me, snuggled up close, instead of in another bedroom.

Somehow it was worse with him being in the same house as herself and she still alone.

Much, much worse.

Hettie closed the book she'd been reading. 'So how was that?'

'Absolutely splendid. Thank you.'

'We'll have the next instalment tomorrow night.'

He ran a hand over his face, feeling the scarring, loathing it. Vanity, he told himself. Sheer vanity. 'You read extremely well.'

'You mean for an ex-dairy maid?' she commented drily.

He laughed. 'Not at all. You simply read well, ex-dairy maid or no.'

'Why thank you, kind sir. Now would you like a cup of tea or anything else before I trot off?'

He shook his head.

Hettie studied Jack, thinking how much nicer he was since returning from the war. Not that he hadn't been nice, and certainly kind, before, but now he was even nicer and somehow more mellow. Vulnerability she suddenly realised. That was the key, he was now far more vulnerable than he'd ever been previously.

'Will you do what has to be done before you leave?' he said.

'Don't I always?'

He smiled. 'You're a good woman, Hettie. Never think I don't appreciate that.'

'You'll manage as usual.'

'As usual. Darkness is the norm for a blind man.'

That brought a lump to her throat. 'I thought cottage pie for tomorrow. How does that appeal?'

'Very much so.'

'And a crumble afterwards.'

'I can hardly wait.'

She laughed, knowing he was making fun of her. Setting the book aside she rose and went about extinguishing the lights, coming back to him with her coat on and a single lamp in her hand.

'Goodnight, Jack.'

'Goodnight, Hettie.'

'Sleep tight and don't let the bugs bite.'

'If there are any bugs in my bed you're for the sack.'

She laughed again. 'Tyrant!'

'On you go then. I'll sit here a while longer before going up.'

'See you in the morning.'

'I'll be here,' he replied, a trace of bitterness in his voice.

She left him to the darkness and his thoughts.

'Do you understand?'

It was Geoffrey's first day at the distillery and Charlotte had begun to teach him what was what.

He stared at the ledger. 'I think so.'

'It's easy really.'

Bookwork, he thought, and inwardly groaned. How

could he face bookwork for the rest of his life. He, a man who'd led such an active life. The prospect was appalling. He was sitting at the desk Peter had once occupied.

'Just say if you have any problems,' Charlotte smiled.

He looked at her, thinking how gorgeous she was. How he ached to take her into his arms and smother her with affection. This woman he'd dreamt about so often, whom he desperately loved.

He bowed his head and got on with the task he'd been given which proved every bit as tedious as he'd expected it to be.

Charlotte entered the bathroom to find an aghast Geoffrey staring at her from the bathtub. All he could think was he'd stupidly forgotten to lock the door.

'I'm sorry, I—'

'Get out!' he screamed. 'Get out!'

A thoroughly shaken Charlotte fled, banging the door shut behind her.

'I sincerely apologise for earlier,' Geoffrey said to her over dinner, when they were alone.

'It *was* rather unnecessary, don't you think? You are my husband after all.'

He coloured slightly. 'It's my nerves, Charlotte. Shot to hell. And you did catch me by surprise.'

She was instantly sympathetic. 'I understand.'

Oh no you don't, he thought. You don't even begin to. 'You live on a knife edge for so long when anything can happen any second of the day or night. It has its effects, I'm afraid.'

'I said I understand, Geoffrey.'

'I'm only trying to explain.'

'And you have. Let's forget it now.'

But, despite her smile, she was still shaken nonetheless. She'd never forget his face as he'd screamed at her. It was the face of a man in torment.

'Cheer up,' Nell said to Wonky, the pair of them in the still room. 'You're so melancholic of late.'

'Am I?' Wonky rinsed a kidney dish. 'It's just not the same since Dale left. I miss him dreadfully.'

Nell put an arm round her cousin. 'He writes regularly. That's the best you can do in the circumstances.'

'I know that. And I write to him too, all the time. I just wish he was still here that's all. Letters aren't the same as being with someone.'

'I know.'

Wonky shook her head. 'He's lost to me, Nell, I'm sure of it. Lost to me for ever.'

'You mustn't say that.'

'But it's what I believe. He and I are as much casualties of this rotten war as those poor souls lying out there on the ward.'

Nell didn't know what to reply to that for Wonky was probably right. So many relationships had been uprooted and torn apart because of the conflict, it was a common enough story. One you almost heard daily.

'We'd better get on with this or Sister will give us a flea in our ear,' she smiled.

Wonky rinsed another kidney dish.

*

'I never realised before how much I really enjoyed stories,' Jack declared to Hettie who'd just finished her evening reading.

'They certainly fill the time.'

His face clouded. 'And that's something I have plenty of. I get so bored with nothing to do, Hettie. There are times when I'm almost suicidal from it.'

'We walk.'

'And lovely that is too.'

'We go to the pub where you have a good chaff with people.'

'But it's not enough, Hettie, can't you understand that? I want to be doing things, a job. Keeping my mind occupied.' He smashed a fist into his opposite palm. 'Only I can't work and never will be able to do so again. It's so damned frustrating. I feel like . . . well a bomb that's on the point of explosion.'

He hadn't had to tell Hettie that, she'd been aware of it for ages. If only she could come up with some sort of solution. But Jack was right, what could a blind man do? Nothing. At least nothing she could think of. How her heart went out to him.

'You'd better go,' he said.

'We could have a trip to the pub if you wish?'

He shook his head. 'I'm not in the mood for company. At least not that sort anyway.'

'Would you like me to stay a while longer?'

There was a long pause, then he said very quietly, 'Please.'

She read him more of the book after which they had a drink together.

*

'A letter from Dale?' Nell queried. Rebecca Levi, the only other one present in the tent, was combing her hair of which she was extremely proud. She'd said more than once it was her best feature.

Wonky looked up at Nell, the beginnings of tears in her eyes. 'From my mother.'

'Oh?'

'It's Dad, he's had a stroke.'

Rebecca stopped combing to stare at Wonky in concern.

'That's awful,' Nell said.

'It's worse than that. Ma wants me home. Says she needs me there.'

Nell sat on the cot beside Wonky, took her hand and squeezed it. 'Will you go?'

'I'll have to. If Ma says she needs me then she does.'

'I'm sorry, Wonky,' Rebecca said.

The tears came, floods of them. 'You know what this means, don't you?' she wailed to Nell.

'It won't be so dreadful.'

'Yes it will. There's been some purpose in my life since arriving in France. There's been Dale. Now I'll be going back to total humdrum and boredom. Probably for the rest of my life.'

Nell bit her lip.

'I'll leave you two alone for a while,' Rebecca said tactfully and, setting down her comb, walked from the tent.

'Humdrum and boredom,' Wonky repeated, remembering how she'd hated living at the manse. Now she'd not only be living there again but would have the responsibility of looking after her father. A complete tie.

'How bad is the stroke?' Nell asked softly.

'Fairly bad according to Ma. He'll probably be bedridden until . . .' She trailed off. 'Whenever.'

'Sweet Jesus,' Nell whispered, thinking of her Uncle Tom whom neither she nor Charlotte had ever really liked. But how awful.

Wonky shook her head. 'I'll make arrangements as soon as I can. Matron isn't going to be best pleased, but what can I do?'

It was the one question Nell didn't want to ask, but did, 'What about Dale?'

Wonky covered her face with her hands, picturing Dale in her mind. How different things might have been, if only . . .

'I won't answer any more of his letters.'

'Oh, Wonky!'

'For a short while I thought we might have a future together, but how can we now? He's in Angers and I'm here. We don't even see one another any more. And now I'll be returning to Dalneil and at the end of the war he'll be going home to Albany to take up practice there. It's best it's ended now, for both our sakes.'

'You'll write to explain of course?'

'No, I couldn't do that, it would simply be too painful. Let him think I just lost interest.'

It certainly wasn't what Nell would have done had she been in Wonky's position. 'I think he's owed an explanation, don't you?'

'He'll forget me soon enough. Though I'll never forget him. It just wasn't to be, that's all. As Jack Riach and I weren't to be. I'm ill fated, Nell, I tell you that. I'll end up an old maid, I know I will.'

'Nonsense.'

'It isn't nonsense. Let Dale find himself someone else in time, an Albany girl probably. He and I come from two different worlds and if it wasn't for the war would never have met. A short time, that's all we had. All we were ever destined to have. Better a quick severance and happy memories than a long one and regrets.'

'It's your decision,' Nell said disapprovingly.

'Oh, Nell,' Wonky whispered, eyes awash. 'Oh, Nell!'

Wonky left for Scotland exactly one week later with instructions to Nell that Dale's letters were to be torn up unread.

Andrew stared at the burnt-out skeleton of Greystones. He was on leave and had decided to spend it in Dublin. The memories of the house and Alice were thick in his head.

It could all have been his, now everything was gone, literally, up in smoke.

Alice, whom he'd loved and who'd loved him.

Greystones.

He remounted his horse and rode away, vowing never to return.

Charlotte stared at Geoffrey across the office. She didn't recognise this man, he certainly wasn't the Geoffrey she'd married. And why wouldn't he sleep with her? It had been months now.

He was putting on weight, she thought. And thinning on top. His face had become quite podgy.

'Geoffrey?'

He looked up from his work and smiled at her.

'What is it? What's really wrong?'

The smile abruptly vanished.

'You're going to have to tell me sometime. Was there someone else, is that it?'

He shook his head.

'Then what? We can't go on as we are. You've become a stranger to me.'

An icy feeling crept into his belly. He wasn't ready yet. He needed more time. The last thing he wanted to do was hurt her, and yet what was he now doing? Better by far he'd died out there in France than come home to this.

'The wound is still painful. It'll take more time,' he mumbled.

'Are you sure that's all it is?'

'There hasn't been anyone else, Charlotte, I swear. I love you as I've always done.'

'Then why!' she cried.

He glanced away. 'The war does funny things to people. It's hard to explain to someone who's never experienced it. But there has never been anyone else, on my word of honour as an officer and a gentleman.'

'I want you back in my bed,' she declared simply.

'No, not yet.'

'We don't have to make love if that's a problem. You just being there would be enough.'

He laughed inwardly. How that tune would change if she knew the truth.

'Is there something I don't know about?'

He swallowed hard. 'The nerves, Charlotte, the nerves. As I said I need more time.'

'Then let me help instead of keeping me at arm's length the way you do. Do you know you've kissed me only three times since coming back and all three on the cheek.'

He paled.

'Well?'

'Excuse me,' he said and, rising, strode from the office.

He didn't return until that afternoon when the matter wasn't referred to again.

'Can I leave promptly at six tonight, Jack?'

'Oh?'

She hadn't thought she'd be embarrassed, but was. 'You see I've been asked out.'

Jack readjusted his dark glasses which didn't need re-adjusting. 'Of course, Hettie. Am I allowed to enquire who the chap is?'

'Jimmy Carruthers. You must remember him.'

'Oh yes.' A spotty-faced lad, he was about to comment but decided that wouldn't be tactful. 'So why isn't he in the army?'

'Reserved occupation, Jack.'

'Is this . . .' He coughed. 'The first time you've been out together?'

Hettie could see the hurt on Jack's face. 'Yes.'

'Then I hope you have a good time together.'

'It's only a drink in the pub. There's nothing else to do in Dalneil.'

'No,' he agreed.

'So that's fine then.'

'Naturally.'

'Then if you'll excuse me I want to go through to the

kitchen and get on with the ironing. I've let it pile up a bit.'

She left him in a brooding silence.

'Hello, Ma.'

Moira Comyn started having been lost in thought. 'Veronica! I didn't hear the door.'

'I let myself in.'

Wonky gazed about her, dismayed by the dreariness of the room and her general surroundings. She felt like a prisoner who'd escaped and now been recaptured and returned to jail. There was a tremendous sinking feeling inside her.

'How's Father?'

Moira went to her daughter and hugged her tightly. 'It's good to have you home again. I can't say how much. As for your father, I'll take you up in a moment and you can judge for yourself.'

Moira disentangled herself and gazed adoringly at Wonky. 'I must say you're looking well.'

Her mother had put on weight Wonky noted. She was even fatter than before. Tom's stroke hadn't affected her appetite.

'And feeling it.'

'Are you hungry?'

Wonky shook her head. 'Not in the least.'

'How about a wee scone? I baked some earlier.'

'No thanks, Ma.'

'Are you sure?'

'Certain, Ma,' Wonky sighed.

'Then would you like to see your father?'

'Of course.'

Moira gripped Wonky by the arm. 'Try not to appear too shocked. There's an awfully big change in him as you can imagine.'

'I've been dealing with front line casualties, Ma, there's not much would shock me any more.'

How grown up she was, Moira was thinking. There wasn't any real change physically, but certainly in the eyes. There was maturity there which there hadn't been before.

'Let's go on up then. He's expecting you.'

Wonky felt her shoulders slump as she followed her mother out the room.

'Can I have a word with you, Miss Charlotte?' Miss McQueen requested.

'Go ahead.'

Miss McQueen had bided her time, waiting till Geoffrey was absent. Now she'd got Charlotte on her own.

'What is it, Miss McQueen?'

'I hope you don't think this presumptuous of me, or impertinent, but it's Mr Geoffrey.'

'Oh?'

'He's not sleeping very well. I've heard him.'

Charlotte frowned. 'Heard him?'

'Prowling. He prowls round the house at night for hours on end. And in his room, walking up and down, up and down into the small hours. I thought . . . Well I just thought it was something you should be aware of if you weren't already.'

'No, I wasn't.'

'Have I done wrong? It is personal, after all.'

'No, Miss McQueen, I'm glad you've told me.'

'Then I'll be getting on.'

'Thank you, Miss McQueen,' Charlotte said as the housekeeper was about to leave.

Well, Charlotte thought, frowning.

Well.

Chapter 27

Charlotte woke with a start to find someone staring down at her. She gasped in fright and clutched the bedclothes.

'I'm sorry, love,' Geoffrey's voice said. 'I shouldn't have ... I ...'

Turning, he fled.

Charlotte knocked on the door. 'Geoffrey, can I come in?'

There was no reply.

'Geoffrey?'

The door slowly opened. 'I'm sorry,' he repeated, shamefaced.

'We have to talk, Geoffrey.'

'Not now, I ...'

She brushed past him into the bedroom. '*Now*,' she stated emphatically.

He groaned. It had been madness going to her, sheer utter madness. But the longing was still there, the terrible longing that tormented him day and night.

'I'll put a light on,' she declared.

'No please, don't.'

She hesitated, then decided to comply. She sat on his bed and patted a spot alongside. 'It's high time you told me what this is all about. I have to know, I'm your wife after all.'

He sat beside her. 'This is difficult, Charlotte. You've no idea how difficult.'

'I'm listening.'

He thought of the hospital in France and the doctor who'd broken the awful news. Probably the worst day of his entire life.

'I'm not a man, any more,' he muttered huskily.

That rocked her. 'How do you mean?'

'There was a grenade. It killed a sergeant and wounded me. In the groin.'

It was beginning to dawn on her what he was getting at. 'Go on.'

'I have . . . I still have . . .' He fell silent for a few moments, struggling with himself to utter what finally had to be said.

'I still have a penis, Charlotte, or most of one anyway. But not the other bits.'

She was stunned. How stupid of her, how incredibly stupid not to have realised. 'I see,' she breathed.

He leant forward and put his head in his hands, feeling absolutely ghastly. He was in a living, waking nightmare. Better he'd died in France. Oh how he wished he had.

He started to cry. 'You've no idea what it's like to be with you day after day, to want you, and not be able to do anything about it. And know that I never will again.'

She put an arm round him. 'You should have explained sooner.'

'I meant to, I wanted to, but just couldn't.'

Children, she thought. There would never be any now. Nor any more of the lovemaking she'd so enjoyed. What a brief interlude that had been.

'Come on, pull yourself together,' she said sympathetically, squeezing him.

'Oh, Charlotte,' he moaned. 'I love you so.'

'It isn't the end of the world, Geoffrey. We'll manage.'

'Will we?'

'Of course we will. It's simply something that has to be lived with, that's all.'

'And how do you live with it? Knowing your manhood's been taken from you.'

She blanched.

'It's just hanging there, useless.'

'There's more to a marriage, Geoffrey. How little you must think of me to believe that was all I was interested in. I married you for what you are, not simply because of that.'

'But we're both so young. There's a whole lifetime ahead without . . .' He trailed off.

'I want you to come back to bed with me, Geoffrey. For us to cuddle up. That'll be enough, I promise you.'

'How can it be!' he cried out, wrenching himself from her embrace and throwing himself backwards.

She mustn't show pity, she thought. Not now, not ever. That would surely destroy him.

'You're alive, Geoffrey, that's all I ever prayed for. It's enough, I swear.'

'No it isn't. Better I was dead leaving you the chance to meet someone else who could . . .'

'No it isn't!' she interjected sternly. 'I meant what I said. You are my love, the only one there will ever be. All right, it isn't an easy burden to carry, but one we will. I love you and you love me, that's all that matters.'

He turned a tearstained face to her. 'Do you really mean that?'

'With all my heart. Now let's go to my bed, *our* bed, where you should be. Where I insist you are.'

Later, he fell asleep in her arms. But there wasn't any sleep for her that night.

All she could do was think, remember what had been.

'Right, the book,' Hettie declared to Jack, picking up the novel she was currently reading, her other chores for the day finished.

'I don't think we'll bother tonight,' he replied stiffly.

She stared at him. 'But you enjoy it so much.'

He shrugged.

She replaced the book. He'd been in a strange mood all day, irritable. Not snapping at her exactly but not far off it.

'Are you ill?'

'No. I'm right as rain.'

'Then what's the matter, Jack?'

'There's nothing the matter.'

'Yes there is.'

'Don't contradict me. There isn't.'

She knew then what it was all about. Jimmy Carruthers whom she'd been out with several times now. Jack was jealous.

'I'll go then,' she said.

He nodded. 'See you tomorrow morning.'

'I'll do the usual first of course.'

'Fine.'

He harumphed when she said goodbye.

God but it was awful, cleaning your own father's bottom. And if it was awful for her what was it like for him?

'I won't be long, Father,' Wonky smiled to Tom whose eyes were shut as they always were when she did this particular job.

His legs were paralysed, as was one arm, his face grotesquely misshapen. It had been a massive stroke.

When she'd finished with his bottom, she began on his blanket bath.

Tom's eyes remained firmly closed.

Rory was alone on the heather, a gaunt emaciated figure stumbling forward. He paused for breath and stared about him through eyes filled with pain and defeat.

At least he'd survived the battle, Nell thought. Thank God for that. But what a state he was in.

Rory gulped in several more deep breaths and then, chest heaving, continued on his way.

Oh my love, Nell thought. Oh my dearest love.

'I've stopped seeing Jimmy Carruthers,' Hettie announced.

'Oh?'

'He wasn't for me. Nice enough chap really, but boring! I can't tell you how boring. Being with him was one long yawn.'

Jack chuckled. 'I don't remember him as being particularly bright or entertaining. A simple country clod is my recollection.'

Hettie smiled to herself, that had certainly perked Jack up as she'd supposed it would. His entire body had suddenly become more animated.

'I've had an idea,' she said.

'And what's that?'

'I'll only tell you if you take it seriously. I won't have you laughing at me, Jack Riach.'

'As if I would,' he replied drily.

'I may be an ex-dairy maid and your housekeeper but I do have a brain in my head. One I can use when required.'

He folded his hands in front of him. 'Come out with it then.'

'You enjoy stories, right?'

'Very much so. We've already discussed that.'

'And you've nothing to do most of the day except sit on your arse.'

He laughed at that. 'How delicately put.'

'Well, it's true. Apart from our walks and visits to the pub you spend most of your time in that chair. You've also complained to me many times that you wished you had something to do. In other words, a job.'

His interest quickened. 'Go on, my dear Hettie.'

'Why don't you try and write some stories yourself?'

This time his laugh was a roar. 'How can I possibly do that when I'm blind? It's preposterous.'

'No it isn't. Hear me out. You dictate and I'll write it down for you.'

His laugh subsided as he considered that. 'It's a thought,' he conceded eventually. 'Though what sort of thing would I attempt? I mean, I've never written anything other than a composition at school.'

'You'll have to think about it of course. Work it out in your mind. That's still totally functional after all. There's nothing wrong with that, which is your problem.'

Could he? Was it possible? The notion certainly appealed.

'There's the war for a start,' she said. 'You could do a story about that.'

Excitement gripped him. A story about the war.

'Anyway, I'll leave you with it, I have to get on,' she declared and swept from the room.

A bemused Jack started thinking.

Nell stared at the letter, the sixth one that had arrived now from Dale to Wonky, his name clearly written on the back.

With a sigh she tore it up.

He was whimpering again in his sleep, waking Charlotte who turned to him in concern. Night after night it was the same. The whimpering, the talking, the shaking, the reliving of terror.

'Geoffrey?' she said, tugging his shoulder.

'The wire, all hanging on the wire,' he mumbled.

'Geoffrey?'

He whimpered again, then came awake.

'Geoffrey?'

His chest heaved. 'Was I . . .?'

'Yes, my darling.'

'I'm sorry.'

'There's no need to apologise. I understand.'

He wished he could have a cigarette but had left his case downstairs. 'Are you certain you want me in bed with you? I disturb you so much, and there's the business to consider.'

She took him in her arms. 'Of course I want you here, even if you do disturb me.'

'It was too . . . unspeakable, Charlotte,' he said in a low, hollow voice. 'I know I'll have nightmares about it for the rest of my life.'

Charlotte cradled him against her breasts which she instantly realised was a mistake when she felt his body stiffen.

'Is there anything I can get you?' she asked, releasing him. 'A cup of tea perhaps?'

'No thank you.'

'Do you want to talk?'

'Not really.'

She smoothed his hair which was wet with sweat. 'My poor darling.'

'So many men . . . so many incidents,' he muttered, and shuddered.

She thought of her brother Peter and others from the village who'd gone off to war and never returned. The whole thing had been catastrophic and was far from over yet. At least the Americans were now in the war, that must hasten its end.

'I think the gas was the worst,' Geoffrey said. 'The effects of that were horrendous.'

'We've a long day tomorrow. Try and get some sleep,' she counselled.

'All right.'

They lay side by side, a couple who weren't really one any more. Fate, war and a grenade had brought that about.

Charlotte wept silently.

Wonky stared out of the window at the driving rain lashing the ground. The new minister was due to arrive sometime that day, a bachelor from Glasgow who'd be taking her father's place. Luckily for them they'd been allowed to stay on at the manse which wouldn't have been the case had the new minister been married with a family.

She thought of Dale and wondered what he was doing and how he was. Nell had recently been in touch to report that Dale's letters had finally stopped.

'Dale,' she whispered to herself, picturing him in her mind. How she longed to be with him in person. To touch him, kiss . . .

Enough of that, she rebuked herself sharply. Dale was out of her life for ever. She'd never see him again, or he her. Dale was in the past, a lovely memory. One she'd treasure always, no matter what.

'Dale,' she whispered a second time.

'You're hurting me,' the girl complained.

An amused glint came into Andrew's eyes. 'Am I? Sorry.'

'There's no need to be so . . . vigorous.'

Andrew laughed inwardly. Of course there wasn't, but he enjoyed hurting her. And a fine-looking Dublin whore she was too, the prettiest in the house.

He withdrew and started to turn her over. This was extra, a great deal extra. But he knew that, although she did it, she hated the experience.

Another way of getting back at them, he thought glee-fully as he thrust himself into her again.

The girl's face contorted.

He was an excellent preacher this John McLean, Charlotte thought, as she and Geoffrey sat in church. The service was the first conducted by the new minister. He had a way with words, an eloquence. And was certainly less 'fire and brimstone' than her Uncle Tom. She approved.

Quite handsome too. How old? she wondered. Late twenties, possibly early thirties. And what beautiful expressive hands. She liked men with nice hands.

Geoffrey glanced sideways at her, bored rigid with the proceedings. He couldn't wait for the service to be over so they could get home again.

McLean concluded his sermon, and departed the pulpit.

The next hymn was one of Charlotte's favourites, 'By Cool Siloam's Shady Rill'.

She sang it with gusto.

Geoffrey was already in his pyjamas when Charlotte joined him in the bedroom. 'Another Monday tomorrow, another week,' she sighed.

He wasn't looking forward to work either; like the service it bored him. Far more than he'd ever truly admitted to his wife.

His eyes fastened on Charlotte as she started to undress, the ache of longing heavy within him.

He winced when, for a few brief seconds, she stood naked before slipping into her nightdress. A few brief seconds that made him want to vomit.

He groaned inwardly and closed his eyes. 'You all right?' she asked, having turned round to catch him like that.

'Fine,' he smiled. 'I was just thinking.'

'About what?'

'Nothing important.'

She gazed at him in concern. 'The war?'

He shook his head.

Charlotte sat at her vanity table and began brushing her hair as she did every night, Geoffrey meanwhile getting into bed.

Another night of her lying beside him, available and yet unavailable. Another night of torture.

Better by far . . . Better by far . . .

'How kind of you to call, Mr McLean,' Charlotte smiled at the new minister.

Geoffrey gazed on disconsolately having taken, for no reason he could put his finger on, an instant dislike to the man.

'Will you please order tea, Geoffrey,' Charlotte requested, sitting.

Geoffrey went to the bell pull. How long would McLean stay? he wondered. He certainly couldn't make his excuses and leave, that would be extremely rude and make Charlotte furious.

He mustn't indulge in too many of the scones, teacakes or crumpets, Geoffrey told himself for he was piling on the weight. He'd become quite rotund which distressed him.

His hair was also thinning rapidly which was another cause of distress. If he went on at the current rate he'd be bald before he knew where he was, a hateful prospect.

McLean settled himself in a chair facing Charlotte. What a striking female, he was thinking, just as he'd thought it when thanking them for attending the service the previous Sunday. He had stood outside the church having a quiet word with members of the congregation as they left.

'It's my pleasure entirely to call, Mrs Armitage, I assure you,' McLean smiled in return.

'And how are you settling in at the manse?'

'Admirably thank you. I've been made to feel most at home.'

'Good.'

He glanced about him. 'What a lovely room.'

'How sweet of you to say so.'

'Indeed, I've heard a great deal about you and this house from your cousin. She says it's a house she adores.'

Geoffrey slumped into another chair.

'I believe you were invalided out of the war, Mr Armitage?'

Geoffrey went cold, for a horrible moment thinking the minister might know why. But that was impossible, only Charlotte knew the true extent of his injuries. 'That's correct.'

Christine, a new maid, appeared in the room. 'You rang, ma'am?'

That she'd presumed it had been Charlotte who'd rung irritated Geoffrey. 'No I did. Can we have tea for three?'

'Of course, sir,' Christine replied, and left them.

Charlotte thought Geoffrey's tone had been somewhat harsh. Why shouldn't the girl presume it had been her after all. There again, irritability was fast becoming a common feature with Geoffrey, so unlike his manner of old.

'The war's a terrible business,' McLean declared, shaking his head.

Idiot, Geoffrey thought. What the hell would you know about it, you pious, sanctimonious clown. You've never been in the trenches, seen, experienced what I have.

Geoffrey, not caring what the minister thought, pulled out his cigarette case and lit up.

'I've been considering your idea,' Jack said to Hettie. 'And come to the conclusion I'd like to write a play.'

She stared at him in astonishment. 'A play!'

He chuckled. 'It is a bit strange I admit. And I have to confess I know little about plays, though I have seen a few in my time. But that's what I'd like to attempt.'

'Why?'

He folded his hands in front of him. 'I'm not sure I could adequately describe what I went through in the war. Whereas with a play it would be more or less reproducing what I heard. Does that make any sense at all?'

Hettie thought about it. 'Possibly.'

'We could send off to London for some published plays to find out how they're put together, and then go on from there. What do you think?'

Hettie hadn't seen him so animated or enthusiastic since his return home. 'It's worth a try.'

'Good,' he nodded.

*

Geoffrey swore and threw down his pen. 'I find this so damned difficult, I really do,' he fumed.

Charlotte frowned. 'It's only adding up figures.'

'Mathematics was never one of my strong points.'

She laid her own pen aside. He was quite apoplectic. 'I'll do it if you wish.'

'No, it's my job. My responsibility. I'll get it right even if I'm here all night.'

Oh dear, she thought.

'Four times I've added up this column and four times I've come up with different answers.'

Geoffrey lurched to his feet and crossed to a cupboard from which he took a bottle of Drummond. 'A dram might help. God help me, but I need one.'

'In working hours, Geoffrey?' she gently admonished.

He glared at her. 'In working hours if I so *choose*. I may be deficient in other departments but I'm still capable of making my own decisions and knowing how they'll affect me.'

'That's not fair,' she said softly.

He swore again. Took a glass from the same cupboard and poured a huge measure which he despatched in a single gulp, after which he shuddered.

'Geoffrey?'

He glared at her again, then poured another hefty measure. He then returned the bottle to the cupboard and slammed the door shut.

She didn't know what to do or say.

He returned to his desk and threw himself into his chair, whisky slopping onto the sheet of figures he'd been trying to add up.

'Buggeration,' he said.

Charlotte bit her lip. 'Would you like me to join you?'

'In what?'

'A dram.'

He laughed cruelly. 'You just said it wasn't right in working hours and now you propose to do the same. Isn't that called hypocrisy?'

'I'm only trying to help.'

'I don't need your bloody help,' he snarled.

She sat back in her chair, concern written all over her face. Everything she seemed to do nowadays was wrong. She just couldn't please him. How she yearned for the Geoffrey she'd fallen in love with. Of course she knew the reason for his changing, but that didn't make it any easier to put up with. She'd have done anything to have been able to wave a magic wand and make things as they'd once been. But of course that was impossible.

Geoffrey ran a hand through what was left of his hair, thinking the prospect of a life in this office was completely stultifying. Maybe he should leave, go away somewhere, be on his own for a while. Though how could he possibly suggest that to Charlotte?

'Why don't you take a walk,' she suggested.

He considered that. Anything to get out of the damned office and away from these figures.

'All right.'

'Then off you go.'

His temper flared again. 'Don't talk to me as if I'm a child.' He mimicked her. 'Off you go!' Followed by, 'Yes, mummy dear.'

'I didn't mean it that way, Geoffrey.'

'Well, that's how it sounded.'

'I'm sorry.'

'And so you should be, you patronising bi—' He stopped himself in time.

He drank the remainder of his whisky. 'I'll be back when I arrive.'

'Fine.'

He gave her a look of utter contempt before leaving, slamming the door as he'd slammed the cupboard.

Charlotte was bereft, as though her insides had been gouged out and only an empty shell remained. It was a full fifteen minutes before she was able to pick up her pen again.

Geoffrey's walk took him straight to the pub.

Hettie eagerly opened the packet, knowing what was inside. The six plays that she'd ordered for Jack from London. Three were comedies, three tragedies.

He was delighted when she told him and instructed her to sit down there and then and read one to him.

She began with the description of the set.

Chapter 28

Jack came to his feet the moment he heard Hettie arrive. 'I'm here!' he called out.

'It's a lovely day,' she smiled on entering the room.

'Yes, I could feel that.'

'I'll get started . . .'

He waved a dismissive hand. 'Forget the housework for the moment. Get pen and paper, I want to make some notes on a few ideas I've had.'

'About the play I take it.'

'That's right. I'm considering setting it in the trenches, in a dugout more specifically. A group of four officers coming and going, mainly talking about what they're going through, how they miss home, loved ones, that sort of thing. That's just how it was. On the surface anyway, but there was a lot more going on underneath.'

'I understand,' she nodded.

'Now get that pen and paper and we'll crack on.'

He spoke for almost an hour while perched on the arm

of a chair, Hettie assiduously writing down every word he uttered.

When he'd finished he made her repeat it back to him, at the conclusion of which he grunted.

'Reaction?'

'So far so good, I'd say.'

He beamed.

'You're drunk,' Charlotte accused when Geoffrey staggered into the drawing room. He'd disappeared after work without an explanation of where he was off to.

'Drunk! I should hope so after the amount I've put away,' he slurred in reply.

She stared at him disapprovingly. His tie was askew, his cheeks flushed. His eyes were glazed.

'You missed dinner,' she said. 'We held it for ages and then I ate on my own. Mrs Clark wasn't best pleased.'

'Sod Mrs Clark, she's only a servant after all. Not paid to approve or disapprove.'

Charlotte was shocked. 'The staff may be servants but should be treated with respect, as well they deserve. Pa always said that.'

'Pa!' Geoffrey sneered. 'Well he's dead and gone and won't be saying anything any more.'

Charlotte's eyes blazed. 'You won't speak ill of my father, that's one thing I simply won't allow.'

'Or what?' Geoffrey taunted, swaying on the spot. 'Or what?'

'I simply won't allow it, that's all.'

He threw back his head and laughed uproariously, knowing there was nothing she could do. She certainly wouldn't chuck him out for that would be scandalous in her position. As for divorce, quite out of the question for that would be even more scandalous.

He staggered over and leered into her face. 'I'll say what I like and that's an end of it.'

'But you liked my father.'

'Hardly the point.'

'Then what is the point? That you're trying to assert your masculinity?'

She realised the instant she'd said it that it was a mistake. His hand flashed cracking her hard across the cheek. With a cry she jerked backwards on the sofa.

'That wasn't very nice,' he declared.

'I'm sorry.'

'Being sorry doesn't help matters, Charlotte. For it tells me what you truly think, that I'm only half a man.'

She clutched his arm. 'Geoffrey, I . . .'

He tore himself away. 'Don't touch me. And don't look at me with such pity in your eyes. Have you any idea what it does to me?'

He lurched over to the whisky decanter and poured himself a large dram, spilling some on the floor in the process. How he hated himself, loathed himself. Peter had been lucky, so damned lucky. If there was a hell then he was now living in it, every moment of consciousness sheer torment. He could almost see grinning devils prodding tridents into him.

'Surely you've had enough,' Charlotte forced herself to say.

'Enough! I haven't even started yet, Mrs Armitage. I'll be the judge of when I've had enough.'

She rose. 'I'm going to bed.'

'Yes go. Get out of my sight. And never ever mention my masculinity, or lack of it, again.'

'I won't,' she promised in a quiet voice.

'Good. For your sake, believe me.'

Upstairs she started to shake and it was a long time before it finally subsided.

When Geoffrey eventually joined her in bed she pretended to be asleep.

He soon was, snoring in a drunken stupor.

Nell fell onto her cot, totally and utterly exhausted having just come off an eighteen-hour shift. She was due back on duty in six hours' time.

'I don't know how much of this I can take,' she said to Hope Langton.

'Me neither.'

'It's become a nightmare. I'm so tired I hardly know what I'm doing half the time.'

'And the Sisters never let up,' Rebecca Levi chipped in. 'You'd think they'd show a little compassion, but not them. They're all slave drivers.'

Georgina Fletcher sighed. 'I could sleep for a fortnight. No, a month more like.'

'It isn't a hospital any more,' Nell commented. 'A butcher's shop is more apt.'

Hope nodded her agreement. 'It certainly wouldn't do to be squeamish.'

'And that's a fact,' Rebecca added, shuddering at the memory of a particularly grisly amputation she'd witnessed earlier that day.

In the distance a battery of guns opened up.

Nell hardly heard them as her eyes began to droop.

Next thing she knew it was morning with another gruelling day stretching ahead of her.

Charlotte woke to find herself alone in bed. Where was Geoffrey? She thought about the situation for a few moments then got up and slipped on her dressing gown. She found him sitting in the drawing room, a single light on, staring into space.

'Geoffrey?'

He blinked, then focused on her. 'What are you doing up?'

'I came looking for you. What's wrong?'

He laughed hollowly. 'The same thing as always.'

She crossed and sat beside him. 'It doesn't do you any good brooding like this.'

'I'd rather brood down here than up there. It's . . .' He broke off.

'It's what?'

He took a deep breath, and slightly turned away from her. 'It's even worse being in bed with you than it was being in the other bed thinking about you. It's agony, Charlotte, sheer agony.'

She didn't know what to reply to that.

'You're there beside me, driving me to distraction. It's like standing outside a sweetie shop without any money in your pockets staring in. It's all there in front of you but you can't have it.'

'Oh, Geoffrey,' she murmured.

'I want to move back to the other room,' he stated. 'At least that way I may keep my sanity.'

'If you wish.'

'I do.'

'I've told you before, Geoffrey, you mustn't worry on my account. A cuddle and kiss is good enough for me.'

He barked out a laugh. 'So you say. But for how long? You're a normal woman, for God's sake. You won't be content to put up with a cuddle and kiss for the rest of your life. And then what?'

'I will, Geoffrey. Because they'll be coming from you whom I love. I suppose women are different to men in that respect. It's not a subject I know a great deal about, but I think it must be true.'

He shook his head. 'Even if you're right, and I doubt it, there's me to consider. What's on offer isn't enough. I'd rather have nothing than a reminder of what's been taken away from me. It's still all there, Charlotte, the urge. An urge I can't satisfy.'

She sighed. 'You'll come to terms with it in time, Geoffrey. I'm sure of it.'

'How long?' he replied sarcastically. 'Five years. Ten. Twenty? Oh, wonderful!'

She wanted to hold him, comfort him, but refrained from doing so knowing it wouldn't be appreciated. 'I'll instruct Miss McQueen that you're moving back to the other room tomorrow. Though she and the others are going to think it strange.'

'I don't care what they think,' he groaned. 'Tell them I'm impossible to sleep with any more, that I'm restless in the extreme because of my wound. Tell them any damn thing you please as long as I move.'

Charlotte got up. 'I'm going back to bed, are you coming?'

He shook his head.

'You'll be tired in the morning and there's work.'

Work! he thought. Revolting, horrible, boring boring work. 'I'll come soon,' he said.

'All right.'

She left him to it, wishing there was something she could do to help.

But what? That was the question she'd asked herself a hundred times.

'Is that really her husband?' Charlotte queried of Mrs Ogilvie as they emerged from church. Geoffrey had stayed behind at Drummond House not wishing to attend the service.

'It is indeed,' Mrs Ogilvie giggled. 'He's old enough to be her father.'

He was that, Charlotte thought, glancing back to where the Grahams were talking to John McLean. They'd moved into the area a few weeks previously and this was their first time at church.

'Pretty thing,' Charlotte commented, referring to Mrs Graham.

'Well one thing's for sure, it can't be a love match. She must have married him for his money. He's substantially well off I understand. Well he'd have to be to buy the old Sneddon place.'

Charlotte was intrigued. 'Are you sure we haven't got the wrong end of the stick and that's not his daughter?'

'His *wife*,' Mrs Ogilvie stated emphatically. 'Take my word for it.'

She'd invite them over some time, Charlotte decided. Welcome them to Dalneil. It would be an excuse to entertain which she hadn't done in a long time. It would be fun to have the house alive again and hopefully Geoffrey would enjoy it.

Charlotte glanced again at Mr Graham. Late fifties, she thought, even early sixties while his wife – well early twenties at the most.

'What does he do?' Charlotte asked.

'Had a firm in Perth I believe which he sold and has retired early. I couldn't tell you what sort of firm though. No doubt we'll hear on the grapevine soon enough.'

No doubt, Charlotte thought.

'It's bliss getting out of that house and away from Mother and Father, sheer bliss,' Wonky declared.

Charlotte made a sympathetic face. 'It must be awful for you.'

'And how. You've no idea. Imagine having to look after your father the way I do. He's mortified every time I have to wash his bottom.'

'I can imagine. Not very pleasant for either of you.'

'If only Ma would help, but she refuses point blank to do so. Oh, she'll sit with him for hours on end chattering away, but when it comes to the dirty work that's strictly my province. Says she couldn't possibly do those things.'

'But you can, eh?'

Wonky smiled. 'So it would seem. Anyway, how are you and how's Geoffrey?'

Charlotte desperately wanted to unburden herself about Geoffrey but wouldn't. His secret had to remain strictly between the pair of them. 'He's fine,' she lied.

'And you?'

'Never better.' Another lie.

'That's good then,' Wonky sighed. 'I'm glad somebody's happy for I'm certainly not.'

'It won't last for ever,' Charlotte replied. 'Your father . . . well, without being unkind, there must be an end in sight in the foreseeable future. What does Dr McAllister say?'

'More or less the same. But Father could still last for years and in the meantime I'm hardly getting any younger. I know I'll end up one of those horrible prune-like spinsters, I just know it.'

'It was a pity about Dale,' Charlotte murmured.

Wonky's face clouded. 'There isn't a day goes by but I don't think of him. I miss him terribly.'

'And what about the new minister? He seems personable enough.'

'John's smashing, I like him a lot.'

'Any . . . eh, interest on his part there?'

Wonky laughed. 'None whatsoever. We're just good friends and that's it.'

'Pity.'

Wonky shrugged. 'Maybe. It would be difficult after Dale. He was very special to me.'

Her eyes narrowed in memory. Dale Kutchinsky, whom she'd never see again. How cruel life could be.

Charlotte patted her cousin's hand. 'Cheer up. Things can only get better.'

Wonky smiled in agreement.

'Hello, Jack, it's Geoffrey Armitage.'

'Geoffrey, old boy! Have a seat.' Jack patted the space beside him. 'How are you?'

'Oh, fit to middling. And yourself?'

Jack gave a hollow laugh. 'Coping, I suppose. What else can you do.'

Geoffrey wished he was. 'I've been meaning to cut along and see you but between one thing and another . . .' He trailed off and shrugged.

'I understand,' Jack nodded.

'Can I get you another drink?' They were in the Dalneil pub.

'Sounds like a good idea.'

'Right then. Dram and pint?'

'Please.'

Geoffrey went up to the bar where he gazed around waiting to be served. A group of women whom he recognised from the distillery were at the table next to his and Jack's, the tables separated by a wooden and glass partition. From the looks of them they were far from sober.

Geoffrey returned with a tray. 'Just in front of you,' he said, placing Jack's pint and dram on the table.

'Thank you.'

Geoffrey stood the tray against a table leg. 'They seem to be having a fine old time next door,' he commented quietly to Jack.

'It's a twenty-first. They were here when I arrived and are intent on making a night of it. I've had a few chuckles to myself listening to the conversation. Whoever said women are the fairer sex?'

Geoffrey smiled. 'At least they don't have work in the morning.' For it was a Saturday night.

Jack took off his dark glasses and rubbed empty eye sockets. 'Sorry about that,' he apologised, replacing the glasses. 'They get itchy from time to time.'

'It must be difficult for you,' Geoffrey said softly.

'Well, it certainly isn't easy. At least you came out of it more or less unscathed.'

Geoffrey blanched. If only Jack knew. 'Yes,' he lied.

'Groin, wasn't it?'

'Damage to the thighs. Bad enough for them to discharge me.'

'Can you walk all right?'

'A slight limp on occasions, that's all.'

'Lucky you,' Jack sighed, and tasted his pint.

A raucous shriek went up from the next table. They *were* enjoying themselves, Jack thought.

'And then the swine . . .'

The woman who was speaking dropped her voice to confide in her companions which concluded in a concerted bellow of laughter.

Something dirty, Geoffrey thought correctly.

'I think of Peter a lot,' Jack stated quietly. 'I miss him.'

'You were good pals.'

'Even closer when we were over there. You share so much in a situation like that, as you well know.'

'Yes,' Geoffrey agreed softly.

Jack considered telling Geoffrey about his intended play, then decided against it. That was something best kept between himself and Hettie for the time being.

'Do you manage to get around by yourself?' Geoffrey queried.

'I'm learning. The pub I've got down pat, and the shop, which gives me some freedom. It's so demeaning having to be totally reliant on someone else.'

'You've got a housekeeper, I understand. Charlotte mentioned.'

'A lass who used to work for me before. She's wonderful, looks after me a treat.'

'It was this size, I swear,' a female at the next table declared, that followed by more laughter.

Jack laughed also. 'It's amazing how alcohol loosens the tongue. They're having a whale of a time.'

Something he could do with himself, Geoffrey reflected. He hadn't had that since . . .

He picked up his whisky and saw it off, shuddering from that and the many memories suddenly crowding his mind.

'It was hysterical on our wedding night. The damn bampot was so pissed he couldn't get it up. Talk about a let down! I could happily have slaughtered him. There was me all eager and champing at the bit and he was absolutely useless.'

Those overheard words were like a knife plunged into Geoffrey's heart. He went rigid, eyes staring fixedly ahead. He jerked slightly when another roar of feminine laughter rang out.

'Working lasses,' Jack mused, shaking his head. 'The salt of the earth.'

'I've got to go, Jack. I was only in for the one.'

'Oh, come on, stay and have another. Keep me company.'

'I'm sorry, I have to be on my way. Another time.'

'Another time then,' Jack agreed with a smile and small salute.

Couldn't get it up! The words screamed in Geoffrey's mind as he hurriedly left the pub.

Couldn't get it up. Followed by a roar of derisory female laughter. He hadn't gone more than a couple of yards when he stopped and vomited.

Wonky dropped into the armchair and sighed heavily. Over at the desk where her father had written his sermon for years John McLean was now writing his for that coming Sunday.

He glanced up at her and smiled. 'Tired?'

She nodded.

'It's a hard task you've been set by the good Lord.'

Didn't she know it, she thought.

He laid down his pen and studied her. 'Is there something on your mind? Anything you'd care to talk about?'

'Not really, John, but thank you for your concern.'

'Simply tiredness, is that it?' He regarded her shrewdly, for John was no fool. He had insight into people which was why he was such a good minister. He knew Wonky was a troubled soul, had recognised that shortly after his arrival.

'You're extremely peaceful to be with,' she said. 'I like that.'

'Oh?'

'There's a sort of calmness about you which you exhude. It washes over one.'

'Why thank you, Veronica.'

'Call me Wonky, please. At least when Ma isn't around.'

He smiled again. 'I'm a good listener. And can occasionally offer a decent piece of advice when required.'

She closed her eyes for a moment, then opened them again.

'Is it all getting too much for you?'

'It's not just that,' she heard herself saying.

'Then what is it?'

Ma was with her father and would be there for ages which meant she was able to speak freely if she so chose.

'I met someone in France,' she stated simply.

'I see.'

'Someone I fell in love with.'

'Was he killed?'

'No, at least not to my knowledge. Although who knows what's happened since I last saw him.'

He didn't reply, waiting for her to go on.

She did, telling him all about Dale Kutchinsky.

John hadn't lied, he was a good listener.

Geoffrey stared at the papers in front of him, seeing nothing. All he could think about was that ghastly overheard conversation in the pub.

Couldn't get it up! Those words had reverberated round and round in his mind ever since. How they'd laughed those distillery women. Cruel laughter that had cut him to the bone. Thank God no one other than Charlotte knew his secret. That would have been too much to bear.

'Geoffrey?'

He glanced up at his wife, suddenly hating her. 'Yes?'

'You've been staring at those invoices for ages.'

'Are you complaining, is that it?' he snapped in reply.

Oh dear, she thought. It was another of those days. 'No, I just wondered if there was anything wrong. Perhaps something you didn't understand?'

He wanted to cross the office and slap her. What satisfaction that would give.

'I understand what I'm doing perfectly,' he replied, managing to control his voice.

'Fine then,' she smiled.

He recalled how it had once been between them, how wonderful those nights. How she'd trembled to his touch, sighed with pleasure as he'd moved within her.

Stop torturing yourself, he thought. That was over, gone. Would never come again, couldn't.

For the umpteenth time he wondered how she really felt about the situation. He didn't believe a word of it when she said a kiss and cuddle were all she needed. Not one bloody word of it.

Not one bloody word.

Charlotte had considered having a large dinner party, then decided she wouldn't. There would be just the four of them, she, Geoffrey and the Grahams. That way they'd get to know the Grahams better.

Geoffrey was in a filthy mood, she thought. But then that was nothing unusual nowadays. As for the Grahams, Sandy and Christina, they were perfectly charming.

'I do adore your house,' Christina declared across the table. 'If you don't mind I think I'll steal a few ideas for our place which as you're no doubt aware is being done up.'

'Please feel free,' Charlotte smiled back.

'This lamb is delicious,' Sandy commented. 'Your own?'

'No, bought from a neighbour. I'll give you his name and address before you leave.'

Sandy beamed.

Geoffrey glanced again at Christina, thinking how pretty she was. Ridiculous her married to that old buffoon. There again, Sandy Graham could still no doubt do what he couldn't. The thought of that was depressing in the extreme.

'Terrible trouble getting workmen with the war on,' Sandy said. 'It's quite a job I can tell you.'

Charlotte nodded her understanding.

'You were in the war I believe, Geoffrey,' Christina smiled.

He grunted.

'Invalided out.'

'I don't like to talk about it if you don't mind,' he replied gruffly.

'I understand.'

'Too old myself of course,' Sandy stated. 'Otherwise I'd have been over there as well.'

Geoffrey stared sourly at him. 'I doubt you'd have been so keen if you knew what it's really like.'

Charlotte shot him a warning look.

'Well, it's true.'

Christina changed the subject.

Charlotte was getting out of bed when a distraught Miss McQueen burst unannounced into her bedroom. Charlotte stared at her in astonishment.

'You'd better come, miss, right away. It's Mister Geoffrey. McPhie found him in the garage. He's . . .' She broke off and took a deep breath.

'Oh, Miss Charlotte, he's hanged himself!'

Chapter 29

Rory's wife, standing at a window, suddenly became extremely agitated. Turning to the children who were in the room with her she seemed to snap out an order. Next moment they'd turned and fled leaving her alone.

What was going on? Nell wondered. And where was Rory? Why wasn't he present?

The wife stood stock still, as though waiting for something to happen, eyes wide with fear and anxiety.

And then that something did happen. The door was thrown open and five redcoats came rushing in. Four had muskets with bayonets attached.

The wife was questioned, that was clear, the questioner being some sort of officer. The wife kept shaking her head as she replied.

They were asking about Rory, Nell guessed. And she was right.

The officer's hand flashed, striking the wife on the cheek, spinning her away. The officer then appeared to bark out an order.

His men disappeared into the house, undoubtedly

searching it. Nell's heart came into her mouth, fearing for the children.

The wife picked up a kitchen knife and came at the officer like a tiger, her face contorted. The officer quickly disarmed her and threw her contemptuously onto the floor where she lay stunned.

The officer was laughing as he began undoing his britches. When they'd dropped to the floor he squatted over the wife.

Oh dear God no, Nell thought, mesmerised by what she was witnessing. He was going to rape her.

The wife came round as her skirts were thrown up over her waist exposing the lower part of her body. Her mouth opened in a silent scream as the officer plunged into her.

Nell was transfixed with horror. She wasn't only witnessing a rape, but she herself being raped. It made her go icy cold all over.

One by one the other redcoats returned, all laughing at what was going on. When he was finished the officer stood up and gestured to the nearest soldier.

The man began unbuttoning his britches while the wife started trying to crawl away. She was soon stopped and turned onto her back, her skirts once more pulled up to her waist.

A third was enjoying himself when the vision began to fade.

'Read that scene to me again,' Jack instructed Hettie.

She did, while he listened intently. 'I think we'll change a couple of lines. The ones . . .'

When that had been done he sat back in his chair, going

through the scene in his mind. The two men involved were himself and Peter, though under different names. He could recall the original conversation with crystal clarity, though he had altered a few of the lines for what he considered better dramatic effect and to tighten it up a bit.

'What do you think?' he asked eventually.

'It seems good to me, Jack.'

'You wouldn't fib, would you?'

'No.'

He believed her.

Jack sighed. 'So many memories. It seems a lifetime away, yet on the other hand as if it was only yesterday.'

'It must have been terrible,' she murmured.

Jack removed his glasses and rubbed his eye sockets. 'Terrible isn't the word for it. It was more than that. Far more.'

Hettie glanced again over the words she'd written to his recent dictation and shuddered. Thank God she wasn't a man. Thank God she hadn't had to go through what they had in France and Belgium.

'It's finished,' Jack announced. 'That's the end.'

Hettie digested that. 'Now what?'

'We'll get the manuscript typed up. We'll have to go to Pitlochry for that – we can't have it done in Dalneil.'

'And then?'

He smiled wryly.

'We send it away and wait to see what happens.'

'You'll want a number of copies done.'

'Several I should think.' He suddenly laughed. 'You know, it must be a bit like having a baby. At least that's how I feel about it.'

'You still haven't given it a title,' she said.

'Oh I have. I just haven't mentioned it that's all. It's to be called "The Long Night".'

'"The Long Night",' she mused.

'For that's what it was. Seeming darkness without end.'

'Oh, Jack,' she whispered.

'"The Long Night",' he repeated.

'It's Mrs Graham,' Florence the maid announced to Charlotte, sitting by herself in the drawing room.

'Show her in.'

A few moments later Christina Graham entered the drawing room to smile sympathetically at Charlotte who'd risen to greet her.

'How kind of you to call.'

The two women shook hands.

'Please have a seat.'

She looked dreadful, Christina thought. But then what would you expect. 'I would have called before, but . . . well we hardly know one another and you probably wanted to be alone or with close friends.'

Charlotte closed her eyes for a second. 'It's been a difficult time.'

'I can well imagine. What a tragedy.'

'It was the war you know. He never recovered from it.' She paused, then said in a small voice, 'The man who came back wasn't the man who went away. He was entirely different.'

'Sandy and I just wanted you to know how much we feel for you in your grief, and of course if there's anything we can do just say.'

Charlotte smiled. 'That's kind of you.'

'Are you, eh . . . managing at the distillery?'

Charlotte considered that. 'I suppose so. Though most of the time my mind's in a fog. I seem to somehow muddle through the days. The workforce has been magnificent, they've rallied round wondrously.'

'That's excellent.'

'I've been very lucky in that respect. The minister too, the Reverend McLean, he's been to see me on a number of occasions. I've found great solace in his company. He has a soothing presence.'

'We like him also.'

'And my cousin Wonky's been a brick. A tower of strength.'

Christina nodded.

'It's just . . .' Charlotte hesitated. 'So lonely with Geoffrey gone. It was like that when he was away, but now it's worse. Now I know for certain he won't be coming back. That he's gone for ever. In this lifetime anyway.'

'I'm so sorry,' Christina murmured.

Charlotte thought of Geoffrey and how it had been with him. Perhaps what had happened was all for the best. He'd been a tortured soul since coming back from France. Anguished in the extreme. But how she missed him. She still couldn't really believe he was dead.

'Will you take some tea or coffee?' she smiled.

'No thank you, I must be getting on.'

Pleasant woman, Charlotte thought. Someone who could become a good friend.

'Perhaps you'll come over to us one evening?' Christina

suggested. 'We're still in a muddle but it would be lovely to have you if you could put up with that.'

'I'd be delighted,' Charlotte responded.

'Then let's set a date.'

'They've arrived, Jack,' Hettie stated, beaming broadly.

'Let me have them.'

She gave him the packet which he carefully opened. He dropped the wrapping paper by his side and clutched the six copies of his play. Slowly, and lovingly, he ran his fingers over the crisp paper of the title page of the top copy.

'Are you proud?'

'Of course I am, Hettie. Even if it isn't put on I feel I've achieved something. And that's thanks to you.'

She blushed.

'The next step is to send them to the managements we've agreed on. Will you do that today?'

'Of course.'

'Just let me keep holding them for a while though. I know it's daft but . . .'

'I fully understand, Jack,' she interjected softly.

It was the Jack of old, she thought. She didn't see his scars any more, or his blindness. It was just Jack Riach. A lump came into her throat.

He continued to run his fingers over the top copy, recalling the scenes the manuscript contained, remembering the dialogue, reliving the reality.

He started when he was suddenly kissed on the cheek.

'Hettie?'

'Well, it wasn't a bloody fairy.'

He laughed, then frowned. 'How can you bring yourself

to do that? I mean, considering how I now look.'

'You look fine to me, Jack,' she replied, a choke in her voice, and abruptly left the room.

He went on stroking the top copy while he thought about that.

Charlotte stood staring at the spot where Geoffrey had been buried, her heart heavy with memories. Kneeling, she placed a bunch of flowers on the grave.

'Sleep easily, my darling, sleep easily,' she murmured.

'Am I interrupting?' a male voice queried.

She rose and turned to find John McLean standing behind her. 'Not really.'

'One never knows in these situations. Just say and I'll leave you alone.'

She shook her head. 'I'm pleased to see you.'

John gazed sorrowfully down at the grave. 'Pretty flowers.'

'From our own garden.'

John sighed. 'This war has an awful lot to answer for. I've often wondered what God's intention and purpose is. So many millions . . . why?'

'You tell me.'

He smiled. 'I may be a minister, Charlotte, but that doesn't mean I have all the answers. What I do have is faith, faith that there must be a reason behind it all. Not only this war but all wars. And life, the trials and tribulations we all have to go through.'

'How's Wonky?' she asked.

He pulled a face. 'Bearing up, though not finding it easy. We talk at times, she seems to enjoy that.'

Again he was struck by what a handsome, good-looking

woman Charlotte was. Not presently at her best, but there again she'd only recently lost her husband.

'I wish you'd known Geoffrey before,' she said. 'You'd hardly have recognised him as the man we buried.'

'The war again,' John murmured.

'If I tell you something will it be in confidence? And I mean exactly that. Strictly between the two of us?'

John nodded.

'Geoffrey's wound was more than he ever let on to people. He . . . well he couldn't make love any more. That was something he could never come to terms with.'

'I see,' John breathed.

'He found it very difficult, as I'm sure you can well imagine.'

John thought of the situation. Being married to Charlotte and not being able to . . . Yes, that must have been excruciating.

'I could cope with the situation, but he never believed me. He simply felt he wasn't a man any longer and in the end couldn't live with that.'

She paused. 'You're the only person I've told this to. Not even Wonky. It was our secret, Geoffrey's and mine.'

Charlotte glanced down at the grave, remembering the first occasion she'd met Geoffrey. Who would have thought then that in such a few short years he and so many others would be dead. Her brother Peter for one, her father for another.

'Are you all right, Charlotte?'

She nodded.

'Perhaps I should walk you home? For company's sake if nothing else.'

How kind he was, she thought. A real gem.

'Let's go,' she said, and moved away from the graveside. He fell into step beside her.

'Are you Scots, lassie? You sound it.'

Nell paused in her rebandaging. The soldier was a Glasgow Highlander who'd been severely wounded.

'I am,' she replied.

He sighed. 'Where frae?'

'A little place called Dalneil in Perthshire.'

'Perthshire,' he breathed. 'I've never been there. Heard of it mind, but never been there. In fact I'd never been out of Glesca until I joined up. I'm Glesca through and through.'

'I like Glasgow, it has some fine shops.'

'Aye, and pubs too. Best pubs in the world I always thought.'

She laughed. 'Well I'm not an expert on pubs, though I am somewhat on whisky.'

He stared at her in amazement. 'Whisky! Get away, you're pulling my leg.'

'No, it's true. My family own a distillery. Ever heard of Drummond whisky?'

'Oh aye, I've drunk a few drams of that in my time. Good stuff.'

'Well I'm Nell Drummond.'

'Would you credit that!' Then, half joking, half serious, 'I don't suppose you'd have a few wee samples tucked away somewhere?'

'I'm afraid not.'

'Ah well,' he sighed. 'No harm in asking.'

He went on to tell her about his life in Glasgow where he'd worked as a coalman before the war. She found some of his anecdotes, the native Glasgow wit shining through, excruciatingly funny.

Hettie opened the large buff-coloured envelope to find a copy of Jack's play inside with an accompanying letter.

'Well?' he queried.

She perused the letter. 'It's from the Curzon Management, they've turned down the play.'

'Damn!' Jack muttered.

'Oh come on, you mustn't be downhearted, it's only your first reply after all. Your first refusal.'

'I know but . . .' He trailed off.

'We've still the others to hear from. And even if they all turn it down there are other managements to approach.'

He smiled thinly. 'You're right of course.'

'It might be a case of try, try and try again until you eventually succeed. And succeed you will, I'm sure of it.'

'Oh, are you?' he replied drily.

'Yes I am. Call it female intuition if you like, but I'm certain in my heart of hearts it'll be put on.'

'Come here.'

She approached to stand beside him.

'Give me your hand.'

She did.

'You're priceless, Hettie Campbell. Absolutely priceless. Whatever man lands you is going to be very lucky indeed.'

'Is that a fact?'

'It is. Take it from me.'

She hesitated in saying what she did next, but said it nonetheless. 'And what about you, Jack? What about the woman who gets you?'

He laughed scornfully. 'Me! The state I'm in? No right-minded female would ever take me on now.'

'Maybe you'd be surprised.'

Jack shook his head. 'I doubt it. Very much so. In fact I know so.'

'Do you now?'

'Oh yes,' he replied softly.

'I'll make your morning coffee,' she said, and left him.

Charlotte stared out of the window, listening to the repeated cracks of thunder and watching the lightning that was zig-zagging across the sky in spectacular fashion. Torrential rain was sheeting down.

It was as though God was making a statement, she reflected. But on what? The war perhaps, humankind in general. Who knew?

How tired she was, absolutely drained. There was so much work at the distillery it was wearing her out. If only she could take a break, go on holiday. But of course that was impossible. There was no one to take her place if she went away.

She started when a particularly loud peal of thunder boomed, or so it seemed anyway, almost directly overhead.

'Oh, Pa,' she whispered. 'I wish you were here to help me.'

Charlotte had been surprised to find John McLean at the Grahams when she'd arrived, then realised he'd been invited to make up the numbers. There were only to be the four of them.

'As I said to you before we're still in a bit of a muddle,' Christina apologised to Charlotte across the dinner table. 'There's still a great deal to be done.'

Charlotte was enjoying herself, the company excellent. 'And decent workmen hard to come by at present,' Charlotte smiled back.

'*Any* workmen,' Sandy chipped in.

John was trying not to stare too often or too directly at Charlotte. She quite fascinated him. And how elegant she looked in her pale green silk gown with a deep cut, V neckline, this line enhanced by loose, short sleeves.

'You owned a factory I understand, Sandy,' John said.

Sandy nodded. 'Sold it due to ill health. That's why we came to the country, for the quiet life. Suits me down to the ground. I'm not so sure about Christina though. Eh, my dear?'

'Oh I enjoy it well enough. I must admit it takes a little getting used to after Perth, but I feel I'm settling in all right.'

'You mean the country's boring?' Charlotte teased.

'I wouldn't say that, just different. I'm sure I'll find lots to do when I'm settled completely in.'

'There's always the church,' John said. 'We're forever needing people to help out.'

'I'll remember that,' Christina replied, thinking the church was the last thing she wanted to get involved with. They'd go to Sunday service of course, but that was it as far as she was concerned.

Christina glanced sideways at her husband. A sweet man

if ever there was, but hardly the most exciting. Still, she'd known what she was getting into. And he'd been well aware of what he was getting in return.

'Tell me about your family, Charlotte,' Sandy requested. 'I believe you lost your father and brother some while back.'

'That's right.' She then recounted the story of Peter's death and how her father had suffered a massive heart attack on learning about it.

Sandy shook his head. 'Very sad indeed.'

'I miss them both dreadfully. We were a lively house before the war, now I'm all on my own until my sister returns from France where she's serving as a VAD.'

'Don't you have a brother left?' John enquired.

'That's correct. Andrew, he's over in Ireland with the army.'

Christina went very still. It couldn't be. Surely not! But the name Andrew Drummond, and he in the army. Just a coincidence, surely?

'Army?' she smiled.

'In Ireland.'

Christina frantically trawled through her memory. 'Which regiment is he with?'

Charlotte told her.

Christina breathed an inward sigh of relief. It wasn't the same man.

'But he used to be with the Black Watch.'

Christina couldn't believe it. 'The Black Watch,' she repeated dully.

'The same regiment my elder brother Peter was in when killed. They're normally based in Perth as you probably well know.'

'Yes,' Christina whispered huskily.

'I say, are you all right?' John queried anxiously. 'You've gone very pale.'

Christina gave him a thin smile. 'I came over all strange there for a moment.' She laughed. 'Probably someone walking over my grave.'

She suddenly realised what she'd said and focused on Charlotte. 'Oh I am sorry. That was tactless when we've just been talking about your father and brother.'

'No offence taken, I assure you. It's a common enough expression. I use it myself.'

It had been a splendid evening, Charlotte reflected later when she was home again. It had bucked her up no end.

Sandy Graham came awake to find Christina sitting up in bed worrying at a nail.

'Christina?'

'Go back to sleep, Sandy.'

He rolled onto an elbow. 'Can't you sleep yourself?'

'A bit of indigestion, that's all,' she lied. 'The pudding was rather rich.'

He grunted in acknowledgement; the pudding had been rich. 'No more funny turns?'

'None. It's simply indigestion. Now go back to sleep.'

'If you insist, my dear.'

'I do.'

He yawned.

Christina continued worrying at her nail.

'It's another rejection I'm afraid,' Hettie said to Jack.

'Bugger!' he swore.

She smiled in sympathy.

'So much for your female intuition,' he declared.

'It's only the third. You must be patient.'

'I suppose so,' he replied.

'And in the meantime, why not start something else? Another play perhaps?'

He considered that. 'It's an idea.'

'It'll keep your mind occupied, stop you moping.'

'Oh, I mope do I!' he retorted sarcastically.

'You know you do.'

'I know nothing of the sort.'

She sighed. 'Jack Riach, you're a bloody liar. And if you want to sack me for saying that then go ahead.'

Alarm filled him. 'I don't want to sack you, Hettie. Not now, not ever.'

She stared at him. Remembering how it had once been between them, and how it was now all so terribly changed. A softness and warmth engulfed her.

'Would you like to go to bed?' she queried.

He drew in a sharp breath. 'I beg your pardon?'

'You heard me.'

'Bed,' he repeated, a catch in his voice.

'That's what I said.'

He shook his head. 'I won't have your pity, Hettie. Anything but that.'

She went to him and gently stroked his cheek. 'I didn't offer through pity, Jack. You have my word on that.'

'Then why?'

'Because I'd like to.'

'But look at me!' he cried. 'My face is awful and I'm blind.'

'They don't matter to me, Jack. I swear.'

He swallowed hard. 'No?'

'No,' she repeated emphatically.

He took her hand in his and squeezed it. 'I never thought I'd be with a woman ever again, Hettie. I believed that was all over for me.'

'Then you were wrong.'

'Oh, Hettie,' he breathed. 'Are you sure?'

'Yes. I still fancy you, Jack, as I've always done. You still excite me.'

He tried to digest that, finding it amazing. 'We had some good times you and I.'

'And there's nothing to stop us having more. You talk about pity, well you should stop pitying yourself. Now what about it?'

He rose. 'It's been so long.'

'Don't worry. I'll go easy on you.'

He laughed. 'Will you indeed?'

'Unless that's unnecessary.'

In the event, it was.

Charlotte was at her desk when the church bells suddenly started ringing. She frowned. It was a Monday, not Sunday. So why on earth was it ringing?

And then the office door crashed open and a wild-eyed Isobel flew in.

'Oh, miss!' she gasped. 'Oh, miss. The war's over!'

Chapter 30

Wonky was in the kitchen helping her mother prepare lunch when their maid Heather appeared. 'Miss Comyn, there's someone at the door to see you.'

'Oh!' Wonky picked up a teatowel and began drying her hands, having been peeling potatoes.

'A Mister . . .' Heather struggled, trying to correctly remember the strange sounding name. 'Kuzinsky?'

For Wonky it was as though the world had suddenly stopped turning. She came over all faint. 'Kutchinsky?'

'That's it, miss. He has a foreign accent.'

Moira Comyn glanced at her daughter. 'Who on earth is that?'

Wonky had to hold onto the edge of the sink to stop herself from falling over. 'Someone I met in France.'

'Then don't keep him waiting, dear. Manners.'

Moira wondered why someone from France should be calling on Veronica. Another place for lunch she thought. Luckily they had enough in.

Wonky laid the teatowel aside and slowly took off her

pinny. She couldn't believe this was happening. Dale in Dalneil!

He smiled wryly at her as she approached him down the hall. 'Hello, Wonky,' he said.

'Hello, Dale. This is a surprise.'

'Not a nasty one I hope?'

She shook her head. 'You'd better come in.'

'Thank you.'

He removed his hat which she took from him and placed on the hallstand. Then his coat when he removed that.

'It sure is beautiful countryside,' he declared.

'We like to think so.'

'Unlike anything I've ever seen before.'

She was so filled with emotion she thought she might burst. Dale, here! It was incredible.

'Come on through,' she said, and led the way.

'This is a bit of a shock,' she declared when they'd both sat facing one another.

'I considered writing, and then . . .' He broke off and shrugged. 'To be truthful I wasn't sure I'd have the nerve to knock when I arrived here. Or even if I'd have the guts to arrive at all.'

She nodded. 'I understand.'

'Do you?'

She glanced away. 'So, how have you been?'

'Fine. As you can see I survived the war intact. Though I must admit there were a few times when it was touch and go. I got blown up once but walked away. That sure was my lucky day.'

How good it was to see him, she thought. She suddenly

felt alive for the first time in a long while. It was like . . . well being reborn. Or walking out of a dark room into the light.

'And how are you?' he asked.

She shrugged. 'Managing I suppose.'

'Just that?'

'I have duties at home which keep me occupied.'

'Oh?'

'My father had a stroke which is why I had to come home. He needs constant care and attention.'

'I see.'

No you don't! a voice screamed inside her head. You don't at all.

'Where are you staying?' she heard herself ask.

'At the local tavern. They've fixed me up with a room as long as I want one.'

'And how long will that be for?'

He regarded her steadily, his expression quizzical. 'That depends entirely.'

'On what?'

He didn't reply.

Wonky rose. 'I'm being rude. I haven't offered you anything. Would you care for coffee or tea? We also have whisky in the house if you'd like.'

'Whisky would be just great,' he smiled, hoping his nervousness wasn't showing. He wondered what she'd think if she knew he'd stood a full five minutes outside before summoning up the courage to knock.

'Right,' she declared, and hurried from the room.

He glanced about him. He'd often wondered about where she lived. Now he knew, and wasn't all that impressed. Dreary was the word that came to mind. Dreary and dull.

Wonky returned with the dram and a small jug of water. 'No soda I'm afraid,' she apologised.

'That's just dandy,' he replied, accepting both dram and jug.

Wonky sat again, gazing at him as though he was a genie who'd just popped out of a bottle.

'Your father had a stroke?' he said.

'That's right. And a bad one.'

'I'm sorry to hear that.'

He sipped his whisky and water. Things between them were suddenly difficult, strained.

'You'll stay for lunch of course?'

He waved a hand. 'I wouldn't impose.'

'But you must.'

He had another sip of whisky. 'I came to ask a question,' he stated.

She glanced away again, waiting.

'Why?'

'Why what?'

'I thought you and I had something together. I thought . . .' He broke off. 'Well no matter. The question is still why?'

'I didn't answer your letters?'

He nodded.

Wonky closed her eyes, remembering their journeys together in the ambulance travelling to and from the CCS. How intimate it had become between them. Of course he was due an explanation. Especially now as he'd come all the way to Dalneil to see her.

'I thought it best,' she stated simply.

'Best?'

She was about to reply when her mother breezed into the room.

'Hello,' Moira smiled at Dale.

Wonky could have killed her.

Hours had gone by. Lunch had been taken after which Wonky had dealt with her father. Now she had a little time to herself again.

'Shall we go for a walk?' she asked Dale.

'That would be pleasant.'

'You won't be long I hope?' Moira queried, frowning at the clock.

'No,' Wonky replied with a forced smile.

'In case . . . Well you know.'

Wonky sighed. She knew only too well. 'We won't be long,' she repeated, and ushered Dale from the house.

'Do I get the correct impression you ain't exactly the happiest of bunnies?' he queried when they were outside and alone.

She thought his phraseology amusing, though hardly the content. 'No,' she replied softly.

'When you broke off contact I imagined you must have met someone else.'

She rounded on him. 'There wasn't, and isn't, anyone else, Dale. I swear.'

'Then why the silence?'

They walked a good ten yards before she replied. 'You're an American, I'm Scots. We met under unusual circumstances. We were forced to part, so why continue the pain by writing. You'll go back to Albany and start practising while I'm stuck here nursing my father. You'll no doubt meet an Albany girl and marry. It all seemed very clear to me when I thought it through.'

'So there isn't anyone else?'

'I just said so, didn't I?'

He sighed. 'You're a fool, Wonky Comyn.'

'I'm nothing of the sort.'

He suddenly stopped and took her into his arms. 'It wasn't until after we parted that I realised just how much I'd come to love you and by then it was too late.'

She gulped. Love!

'Wonky?'

'Do you still?'

'No,' he replied drily. 'I only came to Dalneil for the experience.'

She laughed.

'I was a prize fool too. I should have cottoned on earlier.'

'Oh, Dale!' she whispered.

'So what about it?'

Wonky frowned. 'So what about what?'

'Marrying me.'

Tears misted her eyes. 'If only I could, Dale. If only I could.'

'Marry you!' Nell exclaimed. 'How wonderful.'

Wonky shook her head in misery. 'How can I marry him? I have my duties at home, my responsibilities. There's Ma and Father to consider.'

'But surely they'd understand?'

'Marrying Dale means going to America, Nell. Who

would look after Father if I wasn't there. Ma isn't capable, or refuses to be. So it's down to me.'

'Oh, Wonky,' Nell breathed in sympathy, wishing Charlotte was there to give advice, but her sister was at work.

'I've told him I need time to think about it. Which is a lie, I suppose. My answer is a foregone conclusion.'

'Do you love him?'

Wonky nodded.

'And he loves you obviously.'

'So he said.'

They stared at one another in grim silence.

'I never had any luck with men,' Wonky said tremulously. 'But this takes the biscuit.'

'It's certainly a poser and that's a fact,' Nell declared.

Wonky nodded her agreement.

'Have you spoken to the minister about this?'

Wonky stared blankly at Nell. 'You mean John?'

'Of course. Charlotte says he's very wise for his age and might give you good counsel. If I was you I'd have a word with him.'

Wonky considered that. It was a thought.

She rose. 'I'd better get back and see to Father. He can't be left unattended for too long.'

'I wish I'd been more help,' Nell stated at the door.

Wonky kissed her cousin on the cheek and hurried off.

What to do? Dale wondered, sitting on the chair his room at the pub provided. It sure was a problem. And a problem he couldn't, for the time being anyway, see any way round.

Wonky was committed to her parents, that was obvious. And he admired her for that. But it sure as hell made things difficult for the pair of them.

Was it possible for him to stay on in Dalneil, make a living there? He couldn't see how. He was trained as a lawyer and wanted to practise as one. Nor could he practise law in Scotland, that was a whole different system. No, it had to be the States.

Wonky. His heart beat faster just thinking about her. She was the woman he wanted in life, to be his wife, the mother of his children. And yet it seemed, even though she was willing, that was to be denied him.

He swore.

John McLean exhaled slowly. 'You are in a bind, aren't you.'

Wonky nodded.

He thought about what she'd told him. 'Time,' he said.

'I beg your pardon?'

'Your father, time. Will Dale wait for you?'

She considered that. 'You mean . . .?'

John nodded.

'I don't know.'

'I don't see any other way round it. Unless of course you just shrug off your responsibilities and go to America.'

'I couldn't do that,' Wonky replied in a small voice. 'I simply wouldn't be able to live with myself. It would ruin the relationship between Dale and myself.'

John nodded his approval. 'You're a good woman, Wonky. And often that, as being a good man, is hard to be.'

'I want to sleep at nights,' she said. 'At ease with myself and conscience.'

She was far more intelligent than he'd first given her credit for, he decided. 'Then perhaps you must take a chance,' he declared.

'Take a chance?'

'That your Dale might not find someone else in the meantime.'

Would he? she wondered. He was an attractive man after all, and wealthy she knew from certain things he'd let drop. In other words a catch. No doubt when he returned to Albany the available ladies would swarm round him like bees round a honeypot.

'I'm sorry, but I can't think of anything else to say,' John smiled.

What a risk, she thought. But how could she possibly leave her mother alone to look after her father. That, no matter how hard, was out of the question. She was her father's child, brought up in the faith, and it went deep. Deeper than she'd ever previously realised.

They both glanced round when Moira entered the room. 'Your father needs you,' Moira stated to Wonky.

Wonky dutifully rose and went upstairs.

Rory stood staring aghast at the smoking ruins of what had once been his home. He unleashed his broadsword and broke into a loping run.

Nell's heart was in her mouth as she watched, his expression terrible to see.

Rory found his wife first, butchered worse than any animal in an abattoir. He dropped his broadsword and sank onto his knees beside the blackened corpse. Face awash with tears he lifted the body and held it tight against his chest. He then began rocking to and fro. Although she couldn't hear, Nell was certain he was keening his grief.

That was her there, she thought, filled with cold horror. Raped and then brutally, savagely murdered. She felt sick inside.

After a while Rory laid his wife down again, then went in search of his children. He eventually discovered them in what remained of a byre, also dead, burnt beyond recognition.

Nell felt vomit crowding her throat as she continued to witness the vision. Those were her children, the flesh of her own flesh and Rory's. Young lives wiped out.

Rory collapsed, prostrate over the girl, shoulders heaving.

Thank God, thank merciful God, the vision began to fade.

When it had finally gone Nell wept for hours.

'Well?' Dale demanded softly.

Wonky considered them the hardest words she'd ever had to utter. 'I can't,' she whispered.

'You'd have a wonderful life, want for nothing. I promise you that.'

'I know, Dale.'

'And you still won't come with me?'

She wanted to, oh how she wanted to. To be Mrs Dale Kutchinsky. 'It's just not to be,' she replied.

'Surely your mother can make some accommodation. Realise the situation you're in?'

Wonky took a deep breath. 'Ma flatly refuses to deal with Father. She'll talk to him all right, be with him. But when it comes to the nursing side she swears she can't. How can I possibly leave her in a situation like that?'

He knew then it was useless. 'I understand,' he sighed.

'I spoke to the minister about us,' she said.

'And?'

'He said time.'

'Time?'

'Father won't last forever, then I'd be free. It would then be a case of whether or not you were still free and wanted me.'

'I see,' he murmured.

'What do you think?'

He wasn't at all certain. He loved Wonky, there was no doubt about that. But how long did love last? Her father could linger for years and who was to say what would happen in the meantime.

'I honestly don't know,' he replied.

Her heart sank. But hadn't that been the answer she'd been expecting?

'When will you leave?' she asked.

He couldn't look her straight in the face, his insides churning. 'As soon as possible I guess. A few days in London and then passage home.'

'Oh, Dale!' she choked.

He turned and abruptly left the room, collecting his coat from the hallway.

Outside he stood and stared at the manse, believing he'd never see it or Wonky again.

Charlotte and Nell stared at their cousin in consternation. 'He's gone then,' Nell said.

Wonky nodded. 'The only man I'll ever love.'

'You can't be certain of that,' Charlotte declared.

'I am. Totally and utterly.'

Charlotte went to Wonky and took her into her arms. 'There there,' she murmured.

Wonky began to shake with grief. 'I love him so, Charlotte. With all my heart and soul.'

'Would you like me to have a word with Aunt Moira? See if I can't talk some sense into her?'

'It's no use. Both she and Father think it's my duty to be doing what I am. And so do I. The dutiful daughter and what have you.'

How unfair life was, Charlotte reflected, thinking of Geoffrey. Now this and Wonky. When would it ever end? Never was the answer. That was simply the way it was.

'I'm going to miss him so much,' Wonky sobbed.

Nell wrung her hands, wishing there was something she could say which would help. But nothing came to mind.

'How about a nice cup of tea?' Charlotte suggested. 'And possibly cake if Mrs Clark has been baking.'

'Please,' Wonky murmured in reply.

Nell hurried off.

Hettie's good mood vanished the moment she saw Jack's face. 'What's wrong?' she queried.

He shrugged.

'Come on, what is it?'

'It just seems all . . . so pointless.'

Hettie sighed, and sat facing him. 'You're having trouble with the new play, I appreciate that. But it isn't the end of the world.'

He laughed softly. How true that was. The end of the world was in Ypres, or the Somme, or going back to the Marne. '"The Long Night" has been rejected by everybody,' he stated.

'That's true enough.'

'So why go on with this pretence that maybe I can write? Obviously I can't.'

She wasn't sure what to reply to that. 'So are you just going to give up? That doesn't sound like the Jack Riach I used to know.'

'I'm not the Jack Riach you used to know. I'm a different man entirely.'

'Are you now?' she replied caustically.

'You know damned well I am.'

'I know nothing of the sort. Of course you've changed, you've been through a war which is something I can only try and imagine. You've been blinded and had your pretty face damaged. But does that really make you all that different?'

He stared hard in the direction of her voice.

She smiled. 'And apart from anything else you're still wonderful in bed. That hasn't been taken away from you, so be thankful.'

He shook his head. 'What is it about you, Hettie? You always know when to say the right thing to cheer a chap up.'

Her smile widened. 'I suppose you're now going to suggest we go upstairs?'

'It's a thought.'

'Well not before you've earned it. The new play needs working on which is precisely what you're going to do.'

'Bully,' he retorted good humouredly.

*

Wonky ran the sponge over her father's back, then his buttocks. How she hated doing this, positively loathed it. It had been different in France where the men had been strangers, but to be so intimate with her own father.

Tom's eyes were shut as usual while Wonky did these ministrations, he reflecting, for the umpteenth time, that life had indeed come to a sorry pass when your own daughter had to wash your backside.

He began thinking of his courting days. What a happy, glorious time that had been.

Moira had been a tremendous catch, a Drummond and all that went with the name. Not that there had been all that much money, though there had been some. It was the prestige of marrying into a family so well placed in the area.

He hadn't married her just for that of course. Oh no, he'd been genuinely in love with her, and she with him. A match made in Heaven for which he'd be eternally grateful.

Moira, he recalled her as she'd been on their wedding day. A fine figure of a lass. She'd put on weight since then, a lot of it actually. But that had never mattered to him. She was still his Moira, his beloved.

'I'm going to move you over now, Father,' Wonky declared.

He continued keeping his eyes shut and day dreaming of times past.

Dale stood on a deck of the S.S. *Paul Jones* watching the English shoreline gradually diminish in the distance. London had been fun, but how much better it would have been if Wonky had been with him.

Wonky.

He shook his head in despair. What a waste for the pair of them. She shackled to her bedridden father, he . . . Well he with a life to get on with. A life he'd wanted Wonky to share and which she never would.

It was best to try and put her out of his mind, he thought. Forget her. There would only be ongoing pain if he didn't.

Wonky.

England finally slipped from view and all that could be seen was green rolling sea.

Turning from the rail he headed for the nearest bar, of which there were four on the liner.

All four of which he came to know well before eventually disembarking in New York.

Charlotte was dozing in a chair after another long, hard day at the distillery, when John McLean was ushered in.

'Oh, I'm sorry, am I disturbing you?' he queried.

She buried a yawn behind a hand and sat up straight. 'Not at all, John. I must have dropped off.'

'I can come again if you wish?'

She shook her head. 'I'm delighted to see you. Some company will be most pleasurable.'

'Well, if you're sure.'

She waved a hand at the nearest chair. 'Go and sit down. Now what can I do for you?'

She looked pale and drawn he thought. And there were black smudges under her eyes. Perhaps he shouldn't make his request. It would appear she already had enough on her plate.

'I don't know about you,' she declared, standing. 'But I could use a drink.'

'Wonderful idea,' he smiled.

'How is everyone at the Comyns?'

'The same as usual,' he sighed. 'I've done my best to jolly up Wonky to no avail.'

'Yes, that was very sad. Has she heard from Dale?'

'Not that I know of. Nor if she's written to him. She hasn't said.'

'A dram?'

'Please.'

Charlotte handed him his drink and sat down again, thinking how much she always enjoyed John's company. He was very relaxing to be with.

'I was wondering . . .' He paused and took a deep breath. 'You mustn't feel obliged about this. But I was wondering if you'd consider reading the lesson from time to time.'

'A woman?'

He laughed at her incredulity. 'I know it's always been the province of a man, but why not?'

Why not indeed, she thought.

'Please don't feel the necessity to give me an answer now. Take a while to think about it if you wish.'

She was about to reply when another male figure strode into the room.

'Hello, sis,' smiled Andrew. 'I'm home for good. Resigned my commission and all that. Back to take over the reins.'

Chapter 31

'We haven't had much luck of late you and I,' Andrew said later when John had left. The pair of them were now alone, Nell having earlier gone visiting before his arrival. 'I lost my Alice, you Geoffrey.'

'No,' Charlotte agreed softly.

'Well I'm going to make a go of it. If you don't mind that is. I mean, after all, you've been running the show for a while now. You'll have to teach me of course. I know sod all about the business. But I will be an eager pupil.'

She regarded him steadily. 'I take it you've given up the idea of selling then?'

He nodded. 'That's right.' He thought of Alice, it would all have been so terribly different if she was still alive and they'd married. But she was dead, her inheritance lost to him, so getting involved in the distillery, and eventually taking it over himself when he'd learnt the ropes, seemed the obvious thing to do.

Relief welled through Charlotte. It had been an ongoing anxiety that Andrew, as was his right after all, might sell.

'I'm pleased,' she stated.

'The army was fine and well in the circumstances, second son and all that, but now Peter and Pa have gone it changes things entirely. Also I would have had to wait years for promotion, so many chaps having been promoted over my head because of the war, that it was senseless to stay on.'

She nodded her understanding.

'So here I am. Raring and eager to go.'

'You can start Monday,' she declared quietly. 'At Peter's old desk, the one where . . .' She broke off.

'Geoffrey sat?'

'Yes.'

'Then Monday it is.'

'What do you think?' Jack demanded, Hettie having just read aloud the latest version of his new play.

She stared at him in consternation. 'It lacks something in my opinion, Jack. Don't ask me what, I don't know. But I do feel it lacks something.'

Which bore out his own doubts. His shoulders sagged. It had been a lovely dream, a wonderful idea, but it seemed he just wasn't cut out to be a writer.

'You mustn't give up, Jack. That would be awful.'

'I don't believe in wasting time, Hettie,' he replied sharply. 'My own or anyone else's. I'm just going to forget it. The whole damn thing.'

'Oh, Jack!' she whispered.

'And don't try to argue me out of it. I can't write worth tuppence and you know it.'

'I know nothing of the sort!' she retorted. 'I thought "The Long Night" was a smashing play. It really gripped me.'

'Well it didn't grip any of the managements we sent it to. They were most unimpressed.'

'More fool them!' she riposted.

Jack suddenly smiled. 'What an ego booster you are, Hettie. A veritable light in the darkness. God knows what I'd do without you.'

That touched her deeply. 'I'm only telling the truth as I see it, Jack.'

He crooked a finger. 'Come here.'

He reached out a hand when she stood beside him. 'Give me a kiss, wench. I want to taste you.'

'Taste me, is it? What are you, a cannibal?'

Jack laughed. 'I could be where you're concerned. Eat you up each and every day.'

'Indeed.'

'Indeed,' he repeated.

She bent and kissed him lightly on the lips. 'There.'

'That's no good!' he protested.

'Well, it's all you're going to get for now.' And with that she removed her hand and moved away.

'You're becoming more of a tyrant with every passing month, Hettie Campbell.'

And he more adorable, she thought. Their lives had become so intertwined. They might have been a plaited piece of string.

'What are you thinking?' he asked.

'About lunch.'

'Liar!'

'I am not.'

'Whatever, you weren't thinking about lunch. And don't ask me how I know. I just do.'

'Shall we go through the play again?' she queried softly. 'See if you can somehow improve it.'

He shook his head. 'It's a dead duck, Hettie. Chuck it on the fire.'

'I will not.'

'You'll do as you're told,' he replied, pretending anger. A pretence she saw straight through.

There was a few seconds silence between them, then, simultaneously they both broke out laughing.

'I'd like to invite a couple to dinner this Saturday,' Charlotte announced to Andrew across the office.

He glanced up. 'Who?'

'You don't know them. They're called the Grahams and are new hereabouts. He's a lot older than she is which has caused some comment, believe me. I like them both.'

Andrew shrugged. 'Suit yourself.'

'Good. I'll have McPhie deliver an invitation.'

Andrew went back to the work in hand, thinking how much easier this all was than he'd expected. He had a tremendous amount to learn about the actual whisky making of course, but the men were being most helpful in tutoring him.

He was also enjoying himself which was a surprise.

Sandy Graham read the handwritten note. 'It's an invitation from Charlotte Drummond to dinner this Saturday. How kind. We'll naturally accept.'

Christina went cold all over.

'As you know, her brother Andrew is back from Ireland. It'll be interesting meeting him.'

A true gentleman or not? Christina wondered. She was about to find out.

Pray God he was.

'Christina, how are you!' Charlotte exclaimed as the Grahams were shown in. Crossing to Christina she kissed her on the cheek while Sandy beamed on.

Andrew, who'd come to his feet the moment the Grahams appeared, was frowning. This Christina Graham was familiar, but from where if she was new in Dalneil? Certainly far younger than her husband, no wonder it had caused so much comment.

Charlotte made the introductions. 'Delighted to meet you,' Andrew declared, shaking her by the hand.

'And I you, Mr Drummond.'

He gazed into her eyes and in that moment it clicked. Tina from Mulligan's, by all that was holy!

'So what did you think of them?' Charlotte asked Andrew after the Grahams had gone.

'Charming.'

'I'm pleased you like them. I believe Christina and I could become extremely good friends in time. We have an empathy together.'

Andrew smiled inwardly. If only you knew, sis.

If only you knew.

'I'm so nervous,' Charlotte stated. She, Andrew and Nell were on the way to church in the Rolls.

'You'll be fine,' Andrew assured her, patting her hand.

'A woman has never read in our church before.'

'Well, it's high time one did!' Nell retorted fiercely. 'It doesn't say anywhere in the Bible that only men should read the lesson after all.'

Andrew gave a soft laugh. 'The war certainly changed you, Nell. And I approve.'

'Do you?'

'Oh yes. You have my word on that.'

Charlotte wrung her hands, noting they were sweating. This was turning out to be far more of an ordeal than she'd anticipated. She could just imagine some of those old Presbyterian eyes gazing disapprovingly at her while she stood at the lectern.

Well, she wouldn't let them put her off, she decided. She was a Drummond after all. A pillar of the community even if she was a woman.

She swallowed hard as the Rolls drew up outside the church.

Charlotte was in the middle of her reading, and an excellent job she was doing of it too, when Andrew caught Tina's eye. Still as good looking as ever, he thought. More so. The years, and a more expensive, tasteful, grooming had improved her.

He began reminiscing, remembering how it had been between them. How good she'd been in bed. The tricks she'd taught him.

As though realising what was going through Andrew's mind Tina, or Christina as she now called herself, blushed bright red and stared fixedly at her clenched hands.

'I came round to repeat how splendidly you read today,' John McLean declared to Charlotte.

'Why thank you. You're very kind.'

'There's nothing kind about it. I mean what I say.'

'And the reaction from the congregation?'

He chuckled. 'There were a few mutterings I must admit. But mutterings to be disregarded as far as I'm concerned. The world moves on, and we must move with it.'

She agreed with that. 'Can I get you something?'

He shook his head. 'Not for the present, thank you. I have other calls to make and certainly mustn't make them smelling of alcohol. As for tea and coffee, I get plied with them all the time to the point where I sometimes wish I'd never see either again.'

She laughed. 'I never thought of that.'

'It's quite a hazard I can tell you. There are occasions when I'm so full of liquid I think I must explode.'

Charlotte waved him to a seat. 'I was very nervous. I hope it didn't show.'

'Not in the least. In fact you came across as most composed.'

What a relief. Despite Nell and Andrew's assurances she hadn't been totally convinced. Now she was.

'May I ask you a personal question? In my capacity as minister that is.'

'Of course.'

'Have you come to terms with your husband's death? Or let me rephrase that, are you coming to terms with it? These things take time you know.'

Charlotte considered that. 'I believe I am. It was a tremendous shock and loss you understand. And a certain sense of guilt.'

'Guilt?'

She looked down into her lap. 'That perhaps I could have done more than I did. Been more understanding in some way. Prevented from happening what did.'

'That's a perfectly normal reaction, Charlotte, I promise you. The bereaved often feel guilty, it's very common.'

She glanced up at him, her expression tortured. 'But he committed suicide, John, that's the difference between me and others. My husband killed himself.'

John sighed. 'I didn't know Geoffrey all that well, but he struck me as someone who knew his own mind. Although I heartily disapprove, though cast no judgement, I'm sure he decided to die because the burden he was carrying was simply too hard to bear. It can't have been easy after all, in fact it must have been intolerable. You're a beautiful woman, Charlotte, and Geoffrey was very much in love with you. Not being able to fulfil his natural desires, and I understand the desires remain even though the body is incapable, must have been terrible for him.'

'Yes,' Charlotte agreed softly.

'You weren't harsh in any way, I take it?'

'No, John, not in the least. I was quite prepared to . . . put up with things as they'd become.'

'Then there shouldn't be any guilt on your part. None at all.'

She found great solace in those words. 'Thank you, John. I appreciate that.'

'If I may give some advice?'

'Naturally.'

'You should try and get out and about more. That would surely help.'

She smiled thinly. 'I might if I had the energy. My work

at the distillery takes it out of me. I get so tired nowadays that all I want to do is sleep when I get home.'

'But now you have Andrew to assist that must remove some of the burden from your shoulders?'

'That's true. He's impressing me no end by how fast he's learning. He hasn't been with me that long and already I feel the difference.'

'There then,' John beamed.

He paused, then said slowly, 'Talking of getting out and about. We're having a whist drive in the church hall next Friday evening. The usual light refreshments afterwards. Would you care to attend as my guest?'

Why not, she thought. Why ever not. 'Yes, I'd like that.'

'It'll be a change if nothing else,' he smiled.

'What's wrong with you lately?' Sandy Graham queried of Christina. 'You're all of atwitter. Not your usual self.'

Oh dear, she thought. Had it been that obvious? She hadn't been aware.

'Well, darling?'

'I suppose it's just the worry of getting the house finished,' she lied. 'That and . . . well, ladies' things.'

'Oh, I see!'

She went to him and kissed him on the cheek. 'Sorry if I've been a bore or difficult.'

'You could never be either, Christina. If anyone's going to be a bore it's bound to be me.'

'That you're not, Sandy, nor ever will be. You're the most wonderful and entertaining of husbands.'

'Perhaps a holiday?' he suggested. 'We could go away for a few weeks.'

She was tempted, but decided against it. She wouldn't rest easy until she'd spoken to Andrew Drummond. The question was, how did she get to speak alone with him?

'Wait till later when everything's completed here. That'll be the time for us to go away.'

She was right of course, he thought. 'Then that's what we'll do.'

He was such a dear man, she reflected. If it became common knowledge that she'd been what she had, it would hurt him dreadfully. That was why they'd chosen Dalneil, thinking there couldn't possibly be anyone here who'd know of her past. And then Andrew Drummond had turned up.

It was excruciatingly bad luck.

How alone she felt nowadays, Nell mused, gazing out over the garden from the bench on which she was sitting. She had Charlotte and Andrew to keep her company, but most of the time they were at the distillery.

She smiled, remembering France. She'd never been alone there. There had always been something to do, someone to chat to. Coming home was like walking out of a whirlwind into a dead calm.

France, how exciting that had been, though terrible at the same time. How she missed it.

She must write to some of the others she decided. Rebecca Levi for one, Hope Langton for another. Find out how they were doing.

Were they finding readjusting as difficult as she, she wondered, rising and going back into the house.

*

'OK, kiddo, tell me all about it?'

Dale focused on his mom, having been lost in thought. 'About what?'

'Whatever's troubling you. And something certainly is. I'm your mother don't forget. I know you inside out.'

Dale gave a small smile. 'I'd forgotten that.'

'Is it the war?'

Dale sighed. 'Partly, Mom.'

'Something happened, didn't it?'

'Lots of things happened, Mom. Things I never wish to speak about.'

She nodded her understanding. 'But I take it there was something in particular?'

'Someone,' he replied slowly.

'Ah!'

'A girl.'

She'd guessed as much, Nancy Kutchinsky reflected. 'Want to talk about it?'

'Her name is . . .'

Nancy sat back in her chair when Dale finally finished his story. 'That's very sad,' she stated.

'I can't get her out of my mind, Mom. I try to but she just keeps popping back in again.'

'Do you want to return to England and see her again?'

'Scotland, Mom, she lives in Scotland. The Scots get very upset if you refer to the whole country as England.' He paused. 'I've considered it, but what's the point? There isn't one.'

How hurt he looked, Nancy thought. And that hurt her. He might be a grown-up man but he was still her little boy, and always would be. His hurt was hers.

Dale lapsed into a moody silence.

'Have you run into Marybeth Schneider since you got back?'

'No.'

Nancy smiled. 'Maybe I'll invite her and her folks round for supper one night.'

'Mom!' Dale protested. 'Are you trying to matchmake?'

'Not me,' Nancy lied. 'But you should see Marybeth nowadays. She quite transformed while you were away.'

'Transformed?'

'She was always a bit of a dumpy little thing, and then suddenly, wow! She ain't half something I can tell you.'

Dale was curious. 'Really?'

'Knock your eyes out. And lovely personality to go with it. She's a piece of cake all right.'

Dale recalled the kid he'd known, finding it hard to believe that what his mother said was true.

'No matchmaking, son, I promise you. But this Wonky . . . crazy name that . . . is in the past. You got to think of the future, make a new start. If having Marybeth to supper is that start then why not? It doesn't have to go any further after all. Where's the harm in supper, for Pete's sake?'

'OK, Mom,' Dale capitulated. 'You arrange it.'

Wait till he saw Marybeth, Nancy thought with glee. Just wait!

John excused himself from the group surrounding him and hurried over to Charlotte who was preparing to leave.

'Did you enjoy yourself?'

'Very much so. Thank you for asking me.'

'How are you getting home?'

'It's McPhie's night off so I'll walk, which won't be a hardship as it's a lovely night. At least it was when I arrived.'

'May I escort you?'

She stared at him, her expression curious.

'To ensure you're all right. We don't want anything happening to you after all.'

She laughed. 'In Dalneil! It's hardly Glasgow.'

'Nonetheless, I'd feel better seeing you to your door. Ravening wolves and all that.'

She laughed again. 'There hasn't been a wolf, ravening or otherwise, in Scotland for hundreds of years.'

He winked conspiratorially. 'Who said all wolves have four legs. There are quite a few of the other sort in this parish, believe me.'

She found that funny. 'What a cynic you are, John.'

'Not so. Merely a realist.'

She considered his suggestion. 'I'd be delighted if you'd accompany me.'

'Good. Because I have a proposal to make.'

An eyebrow rose. 'Oh?'

'Regarding the church,' he qualified hastily.

'Then shall we?'

He glanced about, knowing he really should hang on a while longer. 'Let's,' he said.

A number of disappointed females watched them depart.

Dale couldn't believe this was the same Marybeth Schneider. His mom hadn't been exaggerating when she'd used the word transformed.

'Hello, Dale. How are you?'

She was gorgeous, he thought. Talk about the ugly duckling. 'Just fine. And you?'

'Fine also.'

'It's been a while.'

'Well, you were off in France enjoying yourself.'

That chilled him slightly. 'I'd hardly call it enjoying myself. It was a war after all.'

'I used the wrong word then. I simply meant you've been away while I've been stuck here in ole Albany.'

Her figure was stupendous he reflected. Where before she'd been dumpy she was now all curves. And what spectacular curves, enough to make a man . . . Well enough of that.

'You've matured,' she stated.

'You've changed somewhat yourself.'

She laughed. 'So I'm told.'

He stopped himself adding, and *how*. He gazed into her dark liquid brown eyes and felt he was drowning in them.

'Are you cold, Dale?'

He shook his head.

'I swear you're trembling.'

With a shock he realised he was. 'I do that from time to time,' he lied. 'Aftermath of France. It soon stops.'

Her expression became one of concern. 'You poor thing.'

He basked in her sympathy. 'Can I get you a drink, Marybeth? A martini perhaps. Or how about a Tom Collins?'

'A juice would be lovely.'

'Then a juice it is.'

He needed a drink himself, he reflected. And it wasn't a juice he had in mind.

Hettie tore open the bulky letter and read the top page, the rest being documents of some kind. A smile lit up her face. This was wonderful. Absolutely marvellous.

'Why don't you forget the housework and all that malarkey for a while,' Jack said when he heard her enter the room. 'And read to me.'

'What would you like me to read?'

'I don't know. What's available.'

A little teasing, she thought. Then she was going to take him up to bed and give him the time of his life. He deserved it. God knows he did.

She reeled off the titles of a few books she'd acquired in the past week.

'Hmmh,' Jack mused. 'Difficult there.'

'Or I could read you a contract.'

He frowned. 'A what?'

'You've heard of a contract, haven't you?'

'Of course.'

'Well I could read you one of those, Jack Riach.'

He leant back in his chair and stared in the direction of her voice. 'What are you up to, Hettie?'

'Me?' she replied, pretending astonishment. 'Why nothing.'

'Then what's all this about a contract?'

'Remember Curzon Management?'

He nodded.

'It seems they've changed their minds and decided to stage "The Long Night".'

His jaw literally dropped. 'You're joking!'

'They intend doing a short pre-London tour and then putting it on at the Savoy Theatre. They say they have a brilliant new young actor who they intend casting in the lead.' She glanced again at the accompanying letter.

'Someone called Noel Coward.'

Chapter 32

'Hello, Tina.'

She started, and turned away from the coconut shy where she'd been watching a youth trying his luck. 'Why, hello, Mister Drummond.'

He smiled in amusement. 'Enjoying the fête?'

'Very much so.'

'They suspended them during the war you know. Not a time for frivolity and games. This is the first one since.'

'So I understand.'

He closed his eyes for a brief second, drinking in the scent of her, remembering . . .

'I thought we'd got to first-name terms,' he said.

She glanced quickly about her. 'I've been wanting a word. It's important.'

'I thought you might. Shall we stroll?'

They fell into step beside each other.

'Does Sandy know?' he queried quietly.

'Oh yes. He was a client. That's how we met.'

'Well, well,' Andrew muttered. Sandy Graham didn't at all look the type to be frequenting Mulligan's, far less going upstairs. It just went to show how you could misjudge someone.

'Please promise me you'll never blab about our secret, Andrew. It would devastate Sandy.'

'I can imagine,' Andrew replied drolly.

'He's such a nice, kind man. I owe him a great deal.'

Andrew smiled again. 'Quite a change in lifestyle, what?'

Her heart sank. She'd always known Andrew could be a bit of a bastard. It had been a side of him that had rather attracted her.

'Quite,' she agreed, spotting Sandy about a hundred yards off chatting to some people.

'Tart to lady,' Andrew chuckled. 'Still, I suppose it's not the first time that's happened.'

'I'm a different person, Andrew, I swear. Sandy has given me respectability for which I'll be eternally grateful.'

'And what do I get in return?'

She stopped and stared at him blankly. 'How do you mean?'

'For keeping your secret. What do I get in return?'

Her heart sank even further. 'Are you trying to blackmail me?'

He pretended astonishment. 'Me?'

'Yes you,' she snapped crossly.

'A bargain goes both ways, Tina. You don't get something for nothing, at least not in my experience.'

She was appalled, this was the last thing she'd expected. 'I thought you were a gentleman,' she said.

'How wrong of you.'

'But I'm a married woman now. You can't ask that.'

'Ask what?' Oh but he was enjoying this. Her discomfiture was delicious.

She swallowed hard. '*That*,' she replied in a small voice.

He felt himself becoming aroused and knew he could have taken her there and then if they'd been alone. 'What Sandy doesn't know won't bother him.'

'But it would be wrong, Andrew, a betrayal on my part. Can't you understand that?'

He shrugged.

She felt she was going to burst into tears and fought not to. All the good fortune that had come her way was about to be put in jeopardy because of Andrew Drummond. A bit of a bastard? She'd been wrong, a *total* one. And yet, strangely, the idea of sleeping with Andrew again excited her. Damn his eyes! Truth was, Sandy wasn't very good in bed, hardly adequate. Whereas, she recalled, Andrew had been excellent with great staying power. A far younger man of course.

'It's impossible,' she stated.

'Nothing's that, Tina.'

'Christina, please.'

'Christina then.'

Sandy noticed her and waved. She waved back and was infuriated when Andrew did too.

'Well?' Andrew queried.

'Please don't insist on this. I beg you.'

'How's the house coming along?'

The sudden change of subject startled her. 'Fine, why?'

'Almost finished?'

'More or less.'

'And I believe Sandy enjoys it here. Feels you're both

settling in well. It would be a shame if he had to move again. Especially after all the work you've had done on that house of yours. All that inconvenience.'

She knew Sandy would hate moving again, positively loathe it. But would feel they had to if their secret got out.

'You're a swine,' she hissed.

'Oh, through and through.'

'You wouldn't really blab, would you?'

He felt like an angler with a fish wriggling on the end of his hook. He had her, and knew it. He couldn't wait to again enjoy that body he remembered so well.

'You can bet your life on it,' he stated.

She'd have given anything to have been able to slap him with all the strength she could muster. But that, in the circumstances, was out of the question. Her excitement was increasing, much to her disgust.

'When?' he queried softly.

She thought about that. 'Sandy and I are supposed to be going away for a few days next month, back to Perth to visit some friends. I can always feign illness at the last moment, though whether or not he'll go without me I don't know.'

'Insist,' Andrew said.

'And then what?'

'I'll no doubt bump into you before then. We'll arrange something.'

The damnable thing was, she reflected, she was looking forward to it.

'It's going well, don't you think?' John smiled to Charlotte, who was also at the fête.

'Extremely.'

He beamed about him. 'I always think these are such jolly occasions, especially if you get the weather.'

'Yes,' she agreed.

'May I say you're looking splendid. Quite the belle of the fête, to coin an expression.'

Charlotte laughed. 'You are an old flatterer.'

'Less of the old please.' His expression softened. 'And it isn't flattery, I assure you. I mean every word.'

She turned away in embarrassment.

John coloured slightly. 'Sorry.'

'For what?'

'Being forward. I shouldn't have been.'

Charlotte found herself thinking of Geoffrey, and what a tragic end he'd come to. As much a casualty of the war as her brother Peter. How halcyon those early days had been, and how short in duration before the conflagration.

'Excuse me,' John said. 'I'm being summoned.'

She watched him as he strode away, a picture of Geoffrey in her mind. Geoffrey as he'd once been, not as he'd become.

God, did she never stop talking, Dale thought as Marybeth babbled on. The woman was all mouth.

'And so I said . . .'

Dale glanced down at the remainder of his meal in distaste, having completely lost his appetite. They were in the best restaurant Albany had to offer, and how he wished he hadn't invited her. She might be stunning to look at, but was irritating in the extreme.

He started thinking of Wonky and how much he missed her.

'Dale?'

He glanced up. 'Sorry?'

'I just asked you a question.'

He hoped his smile wasn't as artificial looking as it actually was. 'My mind strayed for a moment,' he apologised.

'I said . . .'

He groaned inwardly, wondering how soon before he could take her home.

Nell was dumbfounded. 'Is that so?'

'Well, that's how it appears,' Charlotte replied.

'I see.'

Charlotte sank into a chair. 'He's a pleasant enough man, I can't deny that. Good fun, and . . . soothing to be with. In fact more than that.'

'Ah!' Nell smiled. 'Do I detect the beginnings of interest?'

Charlotte considered that. 'Much as I loved Geoffrey I don't, and God forgive me, wish to remain a widow for ever. That prospect is just too ghastly.'

Nell thought of herself. Not a beau in sight, not even the glimmerings of one. Was she destined to be an old maid? As Charlotte said, the prospect was just too ghastly, not to mention downright frightening. She shuddered inwardly.

'It's too soon after Geoffrey though,' Charlotte declared. 'Far too soon.'

'I'm sure John appreciates that and is biding his time, if what you assume is correct. He hasn't actually said anything, has he?'

Charlotte shook her head. 'He doesn't have to. It's becoming more and more obvious.'

'You could do a lot worse,' Nell stated.

'I suppose.'

'How do you feel about him?'

Charlotte sighed. Good question, she thought. 'I don't love John, there was no instant attraction the way there was with Geoffrey. And yet . . .' She trailed off.

'And yet what?' Nell prompted.

'I suppose I'm realist enough to know you can't fall head over heels every time. He'd certainly be a good husband, of that I've no doubt.'

'And father?'

Charlotte coloured slightly. 'Yes.'

'And you want children.'

Charlotte thought back to the one she'd lost and how empty she'd been afterwards. 'If possible,' she breathed.

'I certainly think you should give it some consideration. In other words don't give him the cold shoulder but a little encouragement. That seems the intelligent thing to me to do.'

Nell paused, then added, quietly, 'I'm sure Geoffrey would have approved. He wouldn't want you to remain on your own either. He loved you too much.'

True, Charlotte reflected.

The new minister and Charlotte, Nell mused. Now there was a turn up for the books.

Wonky was sitting alone in her room, in darkness, tears streaming down her face. How she'd come to hate her father. If it wasn't for him her life would be completely different. She'd never have lost Dale and would now be Dale's wife living in America.

She sobbed into her hands. There wasn't a day went by when she didn't think of Dale, when he wasn't with her in imagination. Oh how it might have been.

If only . . . if only.

The ship was a three-master flying the French flag. A forlorn Rory stood on deck staring into the distance.

He'd escaped, Nell thought with relief. He'd lost his family but he himself had got away. Clearly going off into exile, as so many Jacobites who'd survived Culloden had done.

His face was wretched, contorted with pain and grief. He was no doubt thinking of his wife, children and lost homeland. Nell's heart went out to him.

Suddenly she knew this was the last vision she'd ever have, knew it with absolute certainty. This was her goodbye to the man who, in another life, had been her husband.

He turned, and for a moment their eyes met, though there wasn't any recognition of seeing her in his.

'Goodbye, my darling,' she whispered. 'Stay safe.'

And then the vision began to fade.

Andrew watched in admiration as Christina started to undress. How he'd been looking forward to this. Fairly champing at the bit.

'We must keep quiet,' Christina said. 'The servants . . .'

'I understand.'

She was furious with herself for being so excited at the prospect of going to bed with Andrew again. It was all so wrong. So very very wrong.

Andrew also began to undress, meanwhile never taking

his eyes off Christina. It had been so long since he'd had a woman, he positively ached for one. And Christina . . . Tina . . . well he knew what he was in for with her.

He smiled at the memory of creeping in through the back door, of she anxiously waiting for him. Her reassurances that Sandy had gone to Perth and the servants were fast asleep. It had all, so far anyway, gone exactly as planned.

He sucked in a breath when she was finally naked, having forgotten just how magnificent she was. His arousal was instantaneous.

'Come here,' he commanded huskily.

She came into his arms, he closing his eyes as he drank in the scent of her. What memories were invoked, memories of the sweetest and most erotic kind.

He undid the comb holding up her hair which now tumbled over her shoulders. It took all his willpower not to thrust into her there and then.

His hand caressed a breast, her nipple immediately responding. She felt her legs turn to jelly as his hardness pressed into her.

'Oh, Tina,' he whispered. Then they were on the bed, his mouth covering hers, a hand roaming freely.

How she wanted him, Christina thought, despising herself at the same time. She couldn't help moaning when the roving hand slipped between her thighs.

Andrew bided his time, tuning her up as one would a fine instrument.

Christina stifled a scream as he entered her. And that was only the beginning.

*

'Christ,' Christina muttered afterwards. 'I'd almost forgotten what it was like.'

Andrew grinned at her. 'Good, was it?'

'Don't be stupid. You know it was.'

He inwardly preened.

Christina closed her eyes, revelling in the aftermath of their lovemaking. She felt as replete as any woman could. How tame Sandy now was by comparison.

'I often thought about you after you left so mysteriously,' she said, eyes still closed.

'Oh?'

'You just stopped coming.'

'Hardly,' he smiled.

She biffed him on the arm. 'You know what I mean.'

'I was posted. It all happened very quickly.'

She rolled onto her side. 'I thought you might have said goodbye.'

Tell her the truth or not? For she obviously didn't know. Not, he decided. 'As I said, it was sudden. There simply wasn't time to pay my farewells.' He paused, then queried softly, 'Why, did you miss me?'

'You were slightly special, Andrew. Don't ask me why, but you were. I was hurt when you just vanished without a word.'

'Sorry. Couldn't be helped.'

'So what happened to you?'

'I went to Ireland, you know that. And there . . .' He trailed off.

'What?'

'I met someone,' he confessed.

She could see the distress on his face. 'And?'

'The Fenians killed her. They torched her house and she was killed.'

'Oh, Andrew,' Christina breathed. 'That's awful.'

He took a deep breath, the pain of memory strong within him. 'They paid though. I saw to that. They paid all right.'

'How?'

He shook his head. 'That I won't tell you. But take my word, they paid for it.'

Christina felt a sudden chill creep over her. 'And you were directly responsible for the reprisal or reprisals?'

He came out of his reverie. 'I never said that. Only that those responsible paid.'

'What was her name?'

'Alice.'

'Pretty?'

'As a picture. And worth a bloody fortune. Though in the end the money was secondary. It was Alice herself. We could have been so happy together.'

'I am sorry,' Christina said.

'Not half as much as I was. It was like having the whole world in your hands and then somehow letting it slip through. I was . . . well distraught to say the least.'

'Are you over it yet?'

Andrew thought about that. 'It's hard to say. I don't think you ever get over something like that. It stays with you for ever.'

Sympathy welled within her. 'You were obviously very much in love with your Alice.'

'Very. Strange, it didn't start out that way, but that's how it became. When she died it was as if I'd lost part of myself.'

'I'm so sorry,' Christina repeated.

He turned to her and smiled. 'Anyway, that's in the past. It's the here and now which is important.'

She watched in fascination as he twitched in renewed arousal. With Sandy . . . She put that from her mind.

'This is going to be a regular thing,' he declared quietly.

She wanted to protest, to argue against that, but couldn't. For in her heart of hearts it was what she too wanted. Though God help the repercussions if Sandy ever found out.

Andrew reached for her.

'When are you taking Marybeth out again?' Nancy Kutchinsky enquired casually. 'It's been a week now since your date.'

Dale stared dejectedly at his mother. 'I'm not.'

Nancy was genuinely shocked. 'But why?'

'Because she bores the pants off me.'

'But Marybeth's so beautiful.'

Dale sighed. 'That's as may be. She still bores the pants off me. The date I had with her was excruciating in the extreme. I couldn't wait to offload her.'

Nancy bit back her disappointment. 'Is it still this Wonky?'

Dale nodded. 'I don't say I won't take up with someone else, but it certainly won't be Marybeth.'

Nancy sat facing her son. 'Don't you think it's time you went to work? I appreciate you've been through a war and all, but you have had a good rest and recuperation. Dad's just waiting for you to say the word to welcome you into the practice.'

Dale had been resisting going to work because somehow he felt it would for ever sever his ties with Wonky. Why he should think that he didn't know, but think it he did.

'I suppose,' he replied sourly.

'Then speak to your dad.'

Dale thought for a moment. 'I feel . . . I feel . . .' He trailed off.

'Yes?'

He shook his head. 'Nothing. I'll have that word with Dad tonight.'

'Good, son. It's all for the best.'

Was it? he wondered. He wasn't at all sure.

Andrew capped his fountain pen and stood up. 'I'm going for a wander round the distillery, sis,' he declared.

She stared at him in mild astonishment. 'For a reason? Is there something wrong I don't know about?'

He came from behind his desk and perched on the front of it. 'I don't think I really ever understood Pa until I came here, concerning the distillery that is.'

Charlotte frowned. 'Could you explain that?'

'His love for the place and what we do. If I was married I'd say it's almost like having another wife.'

Charlotte couldn't believe she was hearing this from Andrew of all people, the original Philistine. 'Graphically put,' she smiled.

'Well it is.'

She knew then the distillery was safe, for their generation at least. And her shoulders sagged with relief.

She closed her eyes for a brief second. How pleased Pa

would have been. How very pleased. She could almost see Murdo shaking Andrew by the hand and clapping him on the back.

'Sis?'

'Go and have your wander,' she said quietly.

'Won't be long,' he declared, striding to the door.

'Take as long as you like, Andrew,' she further smiled.

'Is something wrong, dear?'

Christina glanced across at her husband, her mind having been filled with thoughts of Andrew. 'No.'

'You seem so . . . preoccupied.'

'Am I?' she queried innocently.

'And not for the first time of late either.'

He came over and sat on the sofa beside her, taking her hand in his. 'You're not ill are you?'

'Not in the least, Sandy.'

'Then is something bothering you? A domestic matter perhaps?'

She gazed into his face, remembering what had passed for lovemaking the night before, and how different it was with Andrew. God how she ached to be with Andrew again, to experience all those wonderful sensations which Sandy was simply incapable of arousing in her.

She flushed slightly from embarrassment, the sense of betrayal great within her.

'Darling?' he queried with a frown.

She removed her hand and ran it over his cheek. 'You're a lovely man, Sandy Graham. I owe you so much.'

Now it was his turn to colour. 'We'll have less of that. I always consider I got the best of the bargain. What other young thing would have taken on an old fuddy duddy like me. I'm the lucky one and no mistake.'

'You're still a lovely man. Kind, generous, all that a girl could wish for. And if you are that bit older, what of it. It doesn't matter.'

An enormous warmth welled within him. 'Thank you, my dear,' he replied softly.

She kissed him tenderly on the lips.

Hettie appreciated the irony of the situation. All those years she'd so desperately wanted it to happen, and now that it had she didn't. It upset everything.

'Jack, I have to speak to you.'

'Speak away,' he beamed.

'I'm, eh . . .' She took a deep breath. Damn but this was difficult. 'I'm afraid I'm going to have to leave your service.'

His beam abruptly vanished. 'What!'

'Leave your service,' she repeated.

He stared in the direction of her voice, thunderstruck. 'But why? Aren't I paying you enough, is that it?'

'The pay's fine, Jack.'

'Then why, for God's sake?'

'Because I'm pregnant.'

'You're . . .' He broke off and swallowed hard.

'There's no doubt about it. I'm three months gone.'

'Well, bugger me,' he swore, trying to digest her news.

'I'm hoping . . . Well I'm hoping you'll keep to the bargain we once had and see me right. Moneywise that is.'

'Of course, of course.'

She hadn't thought for a moment that he'd renege on her, still it was a relief to have it confirmed. But now . . .

well, once it had all seemed so important, but not any more. Although she didn't stay overnight she'd come to think of Jack's cottage as her own. The cottage and garden she'd always wanted.

How would he manage without Hettie? Jack was wondering. He'd come to rely on her so much. That he could easily replace her he had no doubt, but it wouldn't be the same. Never could be.

'When?' he asked despondently.

'Sometime after we've been to London for your first night. I think that would be about right.'

'Surely you can continue on longer than that?' he protested.

'Well . . . if you insist.'

'I do.'

He had a thought. 'Is there someone else?'

That angered her. 'No, Jack bloody Riach. You're the father. Believe me.'

He heard her blunder from the room and when he went in search of her couldn't find her anywhere.

Chapter 33

Wonky glanced at the clock. Time to administer to her father again. With a heavy heart, she climbed the stairs to his room. She forced a cheery smile onto her face before entering.

Tom was lying on his back, staring at the ceiling. There was something different about him, Wonky thought, crossing to the bed. Though she couldn't think what.

'Hello, Father, ready for . . .'

She broke off to stare at Tom in consternation. Then gasped. A quick feel of his neck pulse confirmed he was dead.

She hurried from the room in search of John.

Moira had hysterics when John broke the news to her. 'Dear God, dear God!' she screamed, and covered her face with her hands.

'Surely it's a welcome release for him, Moira. You must think of it that way.'

Moira's whole body was shaking, her ample bosoms jiggling from side to side.

'The doctor's been sent for. Heather's gone for him.'

A shaken Wonky came into the kitchen where her mother and John were. John grimaced at her over Moira's head.

Wonky went to Moira and put a comforting arm round her shoulders. 'There there, Ma,' she crooned.

The hysterics suddenly subsided, leaving Moira gulping in deep breaths of air. 'It's such a shock,' she choked.

Wonky had already entertained the selfish thought that her father's death let her off the hook. What a relief that was.

'Come and sit down,' John proposed. Together he and Wonky led Moira to a chair.

Moira sat, then abruptly stood up again. 'I want to see him. I want to see my Tom.'

'Is that wise right now? Perhaps a little later,' John counselled.

'No, now!' Moira stated emphatically.

Wonky and John took her up.

'He suffered a second massive stroke,' Doctor McAllister informed Moira and Wonky.

'Would he have suffered, doctor?'

'I doubt it,' McAllister replied. 'The end would have been quick.'

'Praise the Lord,' Moira declared.

'I'll arrange the death certificate and then we can go from there,' McAllister stated. 'Now I'd better be on my way.'

'I'll see you to the door,' Wonky said.

Moira began to weep.

*

Jack couldn't sleep. He'd been tossing and turning for hours thinking about Hettie and her child. *Their* child.

She hadn't gone to bed with him since announcing her pregnancy, or suggested it. He'd already decided if that was what she wanted then he wouldn't suggest it either.

He was so confused. He didn't want to lose her, she'd become such an integral part of his life. And yet . . . what?

That was the question. Bloody what?

'You will write to Dale of course and tell him the news,' Nell said to Wonky a week after the funeral.

Wonky shook her head.

'Why ever not?'

'Who knows what his situation is now, Nell. It's been long enough for him to find someone else. And he'll have his work.' She shook her head again. 'No, our time is gone.'

'I think you're being extremely foolish if you don't mind me saying so.'

Wonky gave her cousin a weak smile. 'I don't. Dale's gone out of my life for ever and that's that. A situation I accepted quite some time ago.'

Her expression became wistful. 'I do miss him though. He and I . . . we just got on so well together.'

'And loved one another.'

'I beg you, reconsider, Wonky. What have you got to lose?'

Wonky considered that. 'It would break my heart if he wrote back saying there was another woman. That he was engaged or something, or even married.'

'It's hardly been that long!' Nell protested.

'But you never know, do you. No, I simply can't risk that humiliation.'

Nell sighed. 'I still think you're being foolish.'

'And I still don't. Now, can we change the subject please?'

'Will you take charge of a stall at the bring and buy sale, Charlotte? It would be wonderful if you could.'

The more she saw of John McLean the more she liked him.

'Let me consider it, John. I've never done that sort of thing before.'

'Perhaps you think you're too grand?' he teased.

She smiled, not taking the slightest offence, realising it was a tease. 'Maybe I do.'

'Then you're not the woman I think you to be.'

'And what sort of woman is that?'

He glanced away. 'A rather lovely one actually.'

'Indeed.'

He wondered how far he could go. 'And intelligent. I admire that in you. As I admire the way you took over your father's business. That was splendid. Showed enormous character and grit. You also have a big heart.'

Initially she'd thought John McLean something of a weakling, but as she'd come to know him better had found out there was a steely side to his nature. John was certainly no namby pamby man of the cloth.

'I thought you might do cakes,' he said.

'Do I have to supply any?'

'It would be helpful.'

'Well, actually we've always supplied things to the bring and buy. I'd have thought you'd have known that.'

'I did.'

She burst out laughing.

'I'd take it as a . . . personal favour, Charlotte.'

She knew then she would help out, but wouldn't say so there and then. She'd keep him dangling for a few days at least.

A British stamp, Dale mused. He then opened the letter that had just arrived. He frowned as he started to read.

The letter was from Nell, Wonky's cousin.

'I don't see that it's a problem, Moira. You'll still be getting Tom's pension so there's no reason whatever that things can't continue on as they are.'

Relief flooded her face. 'Thank you, John. You're a most Christian man.'

He laughed. 'I should hope so. I am a minister after all.'

'I've been so worried that you might wish Veronica and me to leave now that Tom's gone.'

'Then you've been worrying yourself unnecessarily. Now I must get on, I have a call to make.'

He sighed. 'More tea and scones I suppose.'

They both laughed.

'Why don't you take a couple of days off, sis. You're looking peaky.'

'Do you think so?'

Andrew nodded. 'I do.'

A couple of days off, Charlotte reflected. That would

be lovely. 'Are you sure you can manage by yourself.'

He gave her a pained look.

'All right,' she said. 'I shall.'

'Good.'

'Tomorrow and the next day then.'

She'd start with a long lie-in, she decided. Sheer luxury. And breakfast in bed.

'Charlotte!'

She'd decided to go for a long walk to blow the cobwebs out of her head and put some colour back into her cheeks. Andrew had been right, she was peaky.

She stopped and turned to find John McLean hurrying towards her.

'Why, hello,' he smiled when he reached her.

'What are you doing out here?'

'I've been to visit the Hendersons who live a few miles back the way. Not an easy place to get to.'

She knew the Hendersons and their house. 'No,' she agreed.

'And you. Shouldn't you be at the distillery?'

She explained about taking a few days off.

'Quite right too. I did think you were looking a touch pale at the bring and buy last week. I said to you afterwards, but thank you again for your help. It was most appreciated.'

'My pleasure.'

They strolled on together.

John took a deep breath. 'Charlotte, I've been waiting for an opportunity to speak to you. And this seems perfect.'

'Oh?'

'It's difficult.'

She didn't reply to that.

'You must be aware by now that I'm . . . well, attracted to you.'

Again she didn't reply.

'And I get the impression you like me well enough.'

She remained silent.

'You're not making this easy for me.'

She smiled inwardly. 'Go on, John.'

'Is it too soon after Geoffrey for me to call on you? Not as the minister, you understand, but as a gentleman calling on a lady.'

Too soon? she wondered. She wasn't sure. Certainly an appropriate amount of time had passed for comment not to be made in the village. As for herself, would she feel any different about the situation this time next year, or the year after that?

'Of course, perhaps I've misinterpreted things. If I've caused offence I do apologise.'

'John, stop wittering.'

'Sorry.'

They walked a short way in silence. 'Why don't you come to tea this Saturday,' she suggested.

His face lit up.

Charlotte suddenly felt lighter inside, somehow buoyed up.

It was a good sign.

The stage curtains closed to deafening silence. Jack's heart sank. They didn't like his play. It was a disaster. He of course hadn't seen it but had listened intently to every word. He felt Hettie's hand squeeze his.

And then the audience erupted and a huge wave of applause filled the theatre.

Robert De la Noy of Curzon Management who was sitting on Jack's other side, clapped him on the shoulder. 'Well done, old boy. Well done.'

Hettie couldn't have been more pleased or delighted for Jack.

And then the curtains parted again and the cast began taking their bows.

The applause rose to a crescendo.

'We've a sure-fire hit on our hands,' Robert De la Noy declared to Jack a little later over drinks. 'There's no doubt about it. "The Long Night" is in for an extensive run.'

That was music to Jack's ears.

'Young Coward was quite outstanding. That chap has a big future ahead of him.'

'He sounded excellent to me,' Jack replied.

Robert hesitated for a moment, having forgotten Jack wouldn't have been able to see the play. 'Quite.'

The cast were milling about, chattering away like so many demented parrots. The atmosphere in the crush bar, which had stayed open for them, was adrenaline charged.

Robert glanced at his watch, then called out, 'Drink up, everybody. We're due in The Grill in a few minutes.'

What a night, Jack thought. What an amazing, incredible night.

They all proceeded to The Grill where they remained wining and dining until the early hours.

'This is your room, Jack,' Hettie declared with a yawn. 'Do you want me to come in and see you're all right?'

'Please. I wanted you to come in anyway. I wish to speak to you.'

'Oh? Something wrong?'

'Hardly.'

They entered the room and she guided him to the bed where he sat.

'Now what's bothering you, Jack? Surely nothing after a night such as this?'

He smiled. 'It was stupendous, wasn't it?'

'Very.'

His smile turned to a frown. 'Hettie, I've something to ask you.'

The tone of his voice told her this was important. 'Yes, Jack?'

He patted the bed. 'Sit beside me.'

She did, wondering what this was all about.

'Would you consider marrying me, Hettie?'

Her jaw dropped open. 'Marry you?' she croaked a few seconds later.

'That's what I said.'

'But, Jack, I can't possibly.'

'Why not? You told me my blindness and face didn't matter. Was that a lie?'

'No it wasn't. They don't. And they have nothing at all to do with my refusal.'

'You just don't care for me enough then.'

She ran a hand tenderly over a scarred cheek. 'Now you know that's nonsense. I think the world of you, Jack Riach. You've always been very special to me.'

'Then why won't you marry me?'

'Jack, you're a rich man and come from a different class

to me. Somebody like you doesn't marry an ex-dairy maid or even a housekeeper. It simply isn't done. Think what folk would say.'

'I don't give a damn what folk would say!' he retorted angrily. 'If they didn't like it they could lump it.'

Marry Jack? Her mind was reeling with shock. His proposal was the last thing she'd ever expected.

'It's just not on, Jack. If you marry it's got to be with someone from your own situation in life.'

Jack took the hand still on his cheek and held it. 'First of all, Hettie, I'm my own man. Always have been. I don't wish to offend others but they're certainly not going to influence how I run my life. You and I are good together. And you're carrying my child. A child I'd like to be a proper father to.'

'You really are serious about this, aren't you?'

'I wouldn't joke about marriage, Hettie. Not on your Nellie Duff.'

'Or your Grizelda McPherson,' she teased.

Jack tensed. 'She was a terrible mistake. God alone knows what I was thinking about. A weak, shallow lassie not worth tuppence. You're ten times the woman she is. No, a hundred.'

'Am I really?'

'Yes you are. The Grizeldas of this world are pale shadows compared to the real thing. And believe me, you're the real thing.'

Hettie thought about marrying Jack. It was tempting, so very tempting. A dream come true. She'd be living in his cottage which she'd already come to think of as almost hers, looking after the garden she'd come to adore. It all seemed so right somehow. If it wasn't for the gossip and rumour-mongering that would inevitably take place. There again, the latter and former would eventually die down, they always did. Die down perhaps, but never quite go away.

'So where would we tie the knot?'

Elation leapt in him. 'There's a place in London called Caxton Hall, a Register office. We could make the arrangements and get married there so that when we arrived back in Dalneil you would already be my wife. It would be what's known as a *fait accompli.*'

Dare she? she wondered. Dare she?

'Well?' he demanded.

Hettie took a deep breath. 'All right, we'll do it.'

A huge smile lit up Jack's face. 'We'll go out first thing in the morning and start making the arrangements.'

He took her in his arms and kissed her deeply, savouring the scent of her.

When the kiss was over he said, 'I swear I've never been happier in my life than I am at this moment.'

'Me neither. And that's the truth.'

Sandy Graham switched off the engine of his car and sighed from exhaustion. It had been a damnably long drive, the weather conditions not the best, and he was exhausted. He glanced up at the house which was in darkness. As it should be at that late hour. He promised himself a large dram before going up.

The dram became two during which he almost fell asleep in the chair. This won't do, he thought, rousing himself and finishing off his whisky.

He stopped outside their bedroom door, the bedroom at the rear of the house, and frowned for there was light showing underneath. Christina must still be awake.

He opened the door and went in, stopping dead in his tracks at the sight which greeted him. In that instant his heart was broken.

'Get dressed and come downstairs, you two,' he said quietly, barely able to control his voice.

Turning, he left the appalled lovers.

'How long has this been going on for?' Sandy demanded when Andrew and Christina joined him a short while later.

'Not too long, Sandy,' Andrew replied.

'*Mr* Graham to you from now on. *Mr* Graham. Understand?'

Andrew nodded.

'You weren't supposed to be back until tomorrow,' Christina said in a quiet voice.

'I managed to conclude my business and get home early. I was missing you.'

Christina blushed bright red.

'Once a tart always a tart, I suppose. I should have known better,' Sandy declared, knowing that would hurt. From the look on Christina's face it had.

'We've known each other a long time, since before she met you,' Andrew explained. 'I was also a client of hers at Mulligan's.'

'Indeed.'

'So as someone who's used tarts as well I shouldn't take such a high moral tone.'

Sandy drank more whisky, having no intention whatsoever

of offering Andrew any. 'The difference between you and me though is, I not only paid for her services, I married her and gave her respectability. The only thing you gave her is money and what's between your legs.'

Andrew swallowed hard.

'I thought that by coming here we'd be safe from her past, that no one would ever know. How wrong I was. It's ironic really if you think about it. I must have been mad to marry her in the first place.'

'Oh, Sandy, I'm so sorry.'

'I'll bet you are. Sorry for having an affair and betraying me or sorry for being found out?'

Christina didn't reply to that.

Sandy pointed a finger at Andrew. 'Now, you, get out of my house.'

Andrew glanced at Christina who didn't meet his gaze, continuing to stare at the floor. He proceeded to do as he'd been told.

When Andrew had gone Sandy placed his glass aside and crossed to Christina. Taking her by the chin he raised her face till it was looking into his.

His other hand suddenly flashed to crack against her cheek. With a cry Christina went tumbling backwards to end up on her bottom.

Sandy picked up his glass again and the whisky decanter. He left Christina where she'd fallen and headed for a spare room.

Robert De la Noy and his wife Tatiana acted as witnesses at Jack and Hettie's wedding. When it was over they all went to a restaurant for a celebratory lunch.

'So how does it feel being an old married man?' Robert teased Jack as the car got under way.

'Just fine.' He groped for Hettie's hand, found and squeezed it. 'You all right?'

She'd transferred the posy she was carrying to her other hand. 'I couldn't be better, Jack.'

Tatiana beamed on, thinking again how splendid Hettie looked in the stylish charcoal grey jacket and matching ankle-length skirt. The lapels of the jacket were edged in black piping. Initially she'd thought it rather severe for a wedding but somehow it worked.

Robert rubbed his hands together. 'Can't wait to get to the champagne and toast the happy couple.'

The meal was a rip-roaring success at the conclusion of which Jack and Hettie returned to the suite they'd reserved at the Savoy, where they'd be spending the next week on honeymoon.

Sandy hadn't spoken to Christina for three days now. The atmosphere was chill in the extreme.

Sandy finished his breakfast, this the morning of the fourth day, and carefully laid his knife and fork together on his plate. After which he wiped his mouth with a napkin.

'I've made a decision,' he announced.

She went very still. Here it was, what she'd been dreading.

He stared steadily at her. 'I'm leaving you and returning to Perth where I shall initiate divorce proceedings.'

He waited for comment on that, but there wasn't one.

'As you no doubt know, divorce in Scotland can be lengthy so until it actually comes through I shall allow you to stay on here in this house. Until that date I shall continue to maintain the house, you and the staff.'

'That's very kind of you, Sandy,' she murmured.

For a moment his expression softened. 'The act of an old fool no doubt, but I was fond of you, Christina. Very much so.'

'Can't we . . . patch things up?'

'Don't be ridiculous. With that man living just up the road? I'd be reminded of what happened every time I saw him.' Sandy shook his head. 'No, I can't live with that.'

He paused, then asked, 'Why, Christina. The age difference?'

How could she hurt him further by telling him that Andrew was a far better lover than he. That would be sticking another knife in his back.

'Andrew and I were quite close when I knew him. I don't know, it just happened,' she prevaricated.

'I see.'

Christina laid down her own knife and fork having lost what little appetite she'd had.

'Within a week of the divorce coming through I shall expect you to move out, taking whatever of your belongings you wish. And the house will be put up for sale.'

She nodded.

'Where you go is of course entirely up to you.' He couldn't resist the jibe, 'Probably back to that hovel I rescued you from.'

She blanched.

'Further, I shall settle a small amount of money on you. And I mean small. I don't want you to leave penniless.'

'Thank you, Sandy.'

He closed his eyes for a brief moment. How good it had been between them he thought. At least he'd believed so. Her deception had been the cruellest thing that had ever happened to him.

'Any questions?'

She shook her head.

'I shall be leaving here as soon as I can get organised.' He paused, then said, 'When I do leave I never want to see or hear from you again.'

'I understand,' she croaked.

Sandy rang the small bell that would summon his coffee.

'There's a gentleman here to see you, miss,' Heather declared.

Wonky wondered who this could be. 'Show him in.' She was darning John's socks, a job she loathed. But you could hardly expect a man to darn his own socks when there were two able-bodied women available. Besides, John had been so good to her and Moira he deserved a lot more in return than merely having his socks darned.

She was laying her darning aside when the gentleman strode into the room. When she saw who it was her expression became one of sheer incredulity.

'Hello, Wonky, I told Heather not to let on who it was. I wanted to surprise you.' Dale Kutchinsky smiled.

Chapter 34

The stars were bright in the sky, the moon full, as Wonky and Dale gazed up at them. It was a perfect evening.

'So how did you find out?' Wonky queried.

'Your cousin Nell. She wrote to me about your father's death. As that changed everything I immediately hot-footed it back here.'

Nell, Wonky thought. Trust her to do something like that.

'She explained why you hadn't written yourself.'

'I take it there isn't anyone else then?'

'Oh sure, I got married on my return and we now have four kids with another on the way.'

'You're a fast worker,' she grinned.

'Aren't all of us Yanks? At least that's the rep we've got.'

'Rep?'

'Reputation.'

He took her into his arms. 'I've been looking forward to this all the way across the Atlantic. So brace yourself, kid, you're gonna be kissed like you've never been kissed before.'

He was right. The kiss was spectacular.

'Oooh!' she murmured when their lips finally parted.

'As sweet as I remembered. Sweeter even.'

A thrill ran through her to hear that.

He gazed into her eyes, sparkling in the moonlight. 'I'm gonna ask you a second time, Wonky, and I hope you won't let me down. I didn't come all this way for another refusal. Will you marry me?'

The breath caught in her throat. 'Oh, Dale.'

'Well?'

'What about Ma? She'd be left all alone.'

'That isn't a problem. She can come with us. We'll find her a nice little place and see she's taken care of.'

Wonky doubted Moira would agree to that.

'There's sacrifice and stupidity, Wonky. I could understand the business with your father. If she stays she's perfectly capable of looking after herself.'

Moira was, Wonky thought. Moira would be upset at losing her of course, perfectly natural. She'd let Dale slip through her fingers once, she'd be the fool Nell had called her if she allowed it to happen again.

'What is it you Americans say? OK.'

Dale threw back his head and roared with laughter. 'Goddamn! Yahoo!'

Now Wonky laughed. How did she feel? Incredibly excited. A door had just opened, a door she was going to walk through into an entirely new life. Walk through with the man of her dreams. She shivered at the prospect.

'Get married?' Moira gasped.

'That's right, Mrs Comyn.'

'I had no idea that . . .' Moira stumbled to a chair and sat. This was a bolt out the blue.

'Veronica will be returning to the States with me and we'll get married there. We're hoping you'll accompany us and stay on if you care.'

Moira was having trouble focusing on Dale. 'Oh, I couldn't do that. It's impossible.'

'You mean come for the wedding or stay on?'

'Both. I, eh . . . Well I've never been outside Scotland.'

'Then it would be a big adventure for you, think of it that way.'

Wonky went and knelt beside her mother. 'I appreciate this must be a shock for you.'

'Shock isn't the word. I'm . . . I don't know what I am.'

'I sure could use a Scotch if you have any in the house,' a still jubilant Dale declared.

Wonky told him where he could find some.

'Your father not long gone, and now you. I'll be all alone,' Moira sobbed in self pity.

'You won't be, Ma. You've all your friends. You know everyone.'

'But that's not the same.'

'Ma, if Dale could remain here he would, but he can't make a living in this country. He has to be in the States and I'm going back with him.'

'You selfish girl,' Moira spat.

Dale stared on appalled on hearing that.

'No, Ma, it's not me who's being selfish, but you. I'm not giving up Dale merely to sit around and keep you company of an evening. I'm sorry, but that's how it is.'

Moira sagged, reluctantly accepting the inevitable. 'When will you leave?'

Wonky glanced at Dale.

'A couple of weeks,' he informed them.

'So soon?'

'I have my work to get back to, Mrs Comyn. The trip here was unplanned as you'll appreciate.'

'Unplanned?'

Wonky explained about Dale proposing when he'd been there previously and how she'd turned him down because of her father and that responsibility.

'I didn't know.'

'Because I never told you, Ma.'

Moira took a deep breath. 'This is going to take a while to get used to. In the meantime can I have some of that whisky, young man. All us Drummonds are brought up on the stuff.'

Wonky knew then it was going to be all right.

'Time,' John beamed when Wonky told him the next day. 'That's what I said, time.'

'And you were right, as it's turned out.'

He held her at arm's length. 'I'm so happy for you. The only regret is I won't be marrying you myself.'

'Dale and his family want it in America and that's how it'll have to be.'

John pecked her on the cheek. 'Congratulations from the very bottom of my heart.'

Andrew was sitting in the pub lost in thought, thinking about Christina and her new situation. Rather than calling on him personally she'd written to him at Drummond House explaining what had happened between her and Sandy, and that Sandy had now left. A letter to which he hadn't yet replied.

What was he to do about her, if anything? The road was

now open for him to pay as many secret visits to her as he liked, if she agreed that was. He wasn't at all sure she would.

What a farce that had been. He and she right in the middle of. . . . And then Sandy walking in. A farce in hindsight, there had been nothing funny about it at the time.

He had a swallow from his pint and was putting the glass down again when he heard a familiar name mentioned at the bar. He began listening.

'Imagine Jack Riach marrying an ex-dairy maid! Who would believe it. What a come down for him.'

There was a murmur of agreement.

The speaker winked. 'She went for his money I shouldn't wonder. What other reason could there be?'

That was greeted with various sniggers.

Andrew's eyes narrowed. 'Archie Douglas!' he called out.

Archie, the speaker, turned to face Andrew who'd been so quiet in the corner they'd forgotten he was there.

'You find Jack Riach marrying Hettie Campbell funny I take it.'

Archie became wary. 'Yes, sir. Who wouldn't.'

Andrew leant forward fractionally, his now hard gaze boring into Archie's. 'I would remind you that Jack went "over there" to fight for Dalneil and Scotland. Coming back with appalling injuries as we all know. Do you think it's right to make fun of a man like that?'

Archie swallowed.

'A man who's not only been blinded but horribly scarred into the bargain.'

Archie swallowed again.

'If Jack's found happiness with Hettie, and she with him, then he's earned it. More than earned it in my book. As for the money – nonsense! Jack's far too astute to be taken in by a gold digger, believe me.

'Regarding a "come down" as you call it, Hettie may be a working-class girl but there's nothing wrong with that. It isn't the first time the gentry have married into the working class and it won't be the last.'

'Yes, sir,' Archie mumbled, and shuffled his feet.

Andrew's gaze swept over the small knot of men. 'You work for me, Tod Gemmill.'

'That's correct, Mr Drummond.'

'Well, let me remind you now that the war's over there isn't the shortage of labour there was. You and any other member of the workforce at the distillery can be replaced.'

Tod went pale.

'And you, Archie Douglas, you work for James Semple. Isn't that so?'

Archie nodded.

'A word from me to James, who incidentally is a good friend of Jack's, and you too could find yourself suddenly unemployed.'

Archie dropped his gaze to stare at the floor.

'There will be no more gossiping about Jack and Hettie, you pass that on to your wives and friends and neighbours. Because if there is, and I get to hear about it, then the gossiper and his or her family will pay the consequences. Do I make myself clear?'

The group nodded in unison.

'Jack's a bloody brave man who doesn't deserve to be laughed at. And I shall personally see that he isn't.'

'We understand, Mr Drummond,' Archie croaked.

'I only hope you do for I don't make idle threats. Not

only will you lose your jobs but won't find another in the area. You have my word on that.'

Andrew rose and strode from the pub leaving a stunned silence behind him.

'Andrew!' Charlotte burst out the moment he entered the room. 'Wonderful news. Wonky and Dale are to be married.'

Andrew smiled, then crossed to Dale and shook him by the hand. He'd taken a liking to the American during their previous meetings. 'Congratulations! When did you get back?'

'Today.'

'I see.'

Andrew kissed Wonky on the cheek. 'Congratulations, cuz.'

'We're to be married in America. Isn't it exciting?'

'I'll say.'

Andrew rounded on Charlotte. 'Where are your manners? We should be toasting the happy couple.'

'I was getting round to that.'

'Leave it to me.' And with that he headed for the whisky decanter.

'It's all thanks to Nell,' Wonky said as he poured. 'She wrote and told him about Father's death.'

'She was always an interfering lassie,' Andrew replied drily.

'Andrew! I am not. Quite the contrary.'

Andrew began distributing drams. 'That's all right, Nell. I was only joking.'

When they all had a glass Andrew raised his in a toast. 'Here's to Wonky and Dale. May their marriage be a long and joyous one. And may there never be a single day when they regret the dirty deed.'

Everyone laughed.

When Dale and Wonky had gone Andrew took himself off to the study, now his, where he continued the ruminations that had been disturbed in the pub.

It was hours before he re-emerged.

'Sit down,' Christina said to Andrew, indicating a chair. She sat opposite him.

She was far from looking her best, Andrew observed. She was pale and drawn with the hint of dark smudges under her eyes. He doubted she'd been sleeping very well, understandable in the circumstances.

'I was beginning to think I wasn't going to hear from you again,' she stated matter-of-factly.

He smiled. 'Well, here I am.'

'What did you think of my letter?'

He shrugged. 'Sandy clearly took it very badly indeed. Poor chap.'

'Wouldn't you have done?'

'I'd hope I'd never find myself in that situation.'

'Would you care for some tea?'

He shook his head. 'So, what are your plans?'

'To stay on here until the divorce comes through and then return to Perth. What else can I do?'

'You mentioned that Sandy was going to settle some money on you.'

'A small amount, he was quite specific about that. But hopefully it'll be enough to tide me over in Perth until I get myself sorted out.'

'Hmmh,' Andrew mused. 'What sort of work do you have in mind?'

'Certainly not the sort I had at Mulligan's. Those days are over. Perhaps I can find a position as a shop assistant, that sort of thing.'

He closed his eyes for a brief second, again tempted. But only for that brief second. 'I feel guilty about all this, Tina. Please believe that.'

'I was as much to blame as you, Andrew. What I did was foolish in the extreme.'

'And has cost you everything.'

She turned her head, unwilling to meet his gaze.

'I had thought . . . considered . . .' He broke off and took a deep breath.

'Yes?' she queried softly.

He shook his head. 'It would be impossible, Tina. If your background ever got out . . . well, I'm a Drummond after all. Head of the family now. A position of responsibility, of respect.'

'I understand, Andrew,' she replied, a small cynical smile drifting onto her face. 'You've no need to explain.'

He thought of their times in bed together and how wonderful they'd been. 'I don't suppose you'd . . .'

'No,' she stated emphatically, interrupting him, having correctly guessed what he'd been about to say. 'That's over. I simply couldn't, not after what's happened.'

He nodded. That was the answer he'd expected. What a pity. He'd miss the delightful Tina and her lovely body. Still, he reflected philosophically, everything had to come to an end sometime. And there were other fish in the sea. Others more acceptable to one day be the wife of Andrew Drummond.

'Let me know what Sandy settles on you and I'll match it,' he declared.

That surprised her. 'Thank you.'

'It's the least I can do.'

Christina suddenly felt very tired, lost and alone. She'd lie down after he'd gone she decided.

Andrew rose. 'I'd better be getting on my way.'

She rose also. 'I'll see you out.'

At the door they paused, each uncomfortable, unsure what to say next.

'Good luck, Tina,' Andrew said, forcing a smile onto his face. 'And don't forget to let me know about the money.'

'I won't. And thank you again.'

He hesitated, then pecked her on the cheek.

There was a huge lump in her throat as she shut the door behind him.

It was a highly charged emotional farewell as they'd all expected. Wonky and Dale were to travel to Pitlochry station in the Rolls-Royce. Their luggage was already on board and carefully strapped down by McPhie.

She wasn't going to cry, Moira told herself. She'd save that for after they'd gone. Oh, but this was hard, so very very hard. To see her only child off to a foreign country far away across the ocean. Would she ever see Veronica again? She had no idea. Her heart was swollen almost to bursting.

Andrew and Charlotte had come over from the distillery, Nell from Drummond House.

'Well, this is it,' Wonky declared to Charlotte and Nell, a huge lump in her throat.

'Have a safe journey,' Charlotte replied.

'Write to us when you get there,' Nell added.

Then Wonky was in Charlotte's arms with Nell hugging the two of them. A few more words were quietly exchanged after which the girls broke apart.

'Goodbye, old sport, take care,' Andrew said to Dale, solemnly shaking hands.

Wonky glanced about her, imprinting what she saw in her memory. Despite all the years of wanting to be away from Dalneil she would miss it dreadfully.

Andrew kissed Wonky on the cheek. 'You look after yourself now, cuz.'

'I don't need to, Andrew. Dale will do that for me.'

Andrew smiled. 'Of course he will. And a fine job he'll do of it too.'

Dale spoke to Moira, again reassuring her that all would be well.

Now it was the moment both women had dreaded, the farewell. 'Goodbye, Ma.'

'Goodbye, Wonky.'

Wonky started. It was the first time her mother had ever called her that. She laughed, and Moira did too.

'Now get on with you, you've a train to catch.'

They kissed, had a final hug, and then Wonky fled to the refuge of the Rolls. Dale joined her and moments later the Rolls purred into life.

Moira was proud of herself. The car was almost out of sight before she burst into tears to be helped inside by a consoling Charlotte and Nell.

It was now a year since John had started to pay court to Charlotte. A year during which they'd grown closer and closer.

They were out for their weekly stroll together, which had become, weather permitting, a highlight in both their lives.

'Charlotte?'

She smiled at him.

'How would you feel about . . .' He sucked in a deep breath. 'Getting engaged?'

She stopped and turned to face him, having known for quite some time this would eventually be coming.

'Are you proposing, John?' she teased.

He coloured. 'Yes.'

He was such a dear man, she thought, having already made up her mind months before. It would mean leaving her work at the distillery, a minister's wife having a great deal to do in the parish if the job was done properly. Something she'd always considered Aunt Moira to be somewhat lax about. As for Andrew, he was entirely capable now and she'd always be on hand to give advice if required. She thought of Andrew who, to her amazement, was becoming more and more like their father every day. That was a turn up for the books. Andrew who'd become quite settled back in Dalneil.

'I don't know,' she further teased. 'I don't know.'

John's face fell. 'Please, Charlotte. I love you so.'

Love was a strange animal, she reflected. It came in many forms. She didn't love John the way she had Geoffrey, but love him she did in another way. A gentler, less intense way. John had become an integral part of her life, someone she'd be content to spend the rest of her days with.

'Charlotte?'

She gazed into his eyes and saw happiness there. 'Yes, I'll marry you.'

The face that had fallen now lit up. 'Oh, Charlotte!'

Children, she thought. She wanted many of those.

Nell was excited, having been looking forward to this day for weeks, ever since receiving a letter from Hope Langton whom she had known in France. Hope had written saying she and her brother Philip would be in the area and could they come and visit. It would be wonderful talking over old times.

Nell had immediately replied saying she'd be delighted to see them and why didn't they stay a few days. Hope had written accepting Nell's invitation.

Nell picked up a book, then laid it down again when she found she couldn't concentrate. She sighed, wishing Hope would hurry up and arrive.

It was a pity that Wonky wasn't there for the reunion, she'd have adored it.

Nell started when she heard voices out in the hall. They'd arrived at last! She hastily rose and smoothed down her dress.

Christine the maid entered the room. 'A Mister and Miss Langton,' she announced.

Hope breezed in. 'Nell!' she squealed, and the two women flew into each other's arms.

'You're looking so well,' Hope gushed.

'And you.'

'We've lots to talk about.'

'Lots,' Nell agreed, and they both laughed.

The laugh died in Nell's throat the moment she caught sight of the man accompanying Hope. She'd heard of the expression poleaxed; well, that was exactly how she felt.

'Nell, I'd like you to meet my brother Philip. Philip, this is Nell Drummond.'

Philip came forward and formally shook Nell's hand. 'How do you do, Miss Drummond. I trust we're not inconveniencing you in any way.'

She tried to speak and couldn't.

Hope frowned. 'Nell?'

'I, eh . . . I'm pleased to meet you, Mister Langton.'

He was staring at her quizzically. 'I don't mean to be rude, but have we met before? You seem strangely familiar.'

Oh yes, she thought. They had indeed met before. For Philip Langton was the spitting image of Rory, her Highlander husband in another life.

'I doubt it,' she lied in reply.

A feeling of calmness and peace descended on her. Rory had been returned to her. The outcome of this meeting was inevitable.

The circle was complete.